"In every way Dickensian: huge, unflinching in its description of the grubby Victorian world, and melodramatic in the very best way." —Paul Constant, *The Stranger*

"The plot of *Drood* is so tantalizing that it's tempting to speed through, but that would be to miss the wonderful writing that infuses each page with the aura of an era. One would think that Dickens himself would have devoured *Drood,* recognizing in Simmons a truly masterful storyteller." —Sherryl Connelly, *New York Daily News*

"An engaging historical thriller....*Drood* delivers a romp beyond your wildest drug-induced dreams." —Ellen Kanner, *Miami Herald*

"If Collins is untruthful as a storyteller he is compelling as a character. His paranoid yet learned voice moves carefully through the last five years of Dickens's life, ever intertwining fact with fantasy until it is impossible to determine whether it is Simmons or Collins who is most in control of the story....The equivalent of a splendidly caloric Victorian bonbon." —Marjorie Kehe, *Christian Science Monitor*

"Richly imagined....Having an opium-addicted, gout-afflicted novelist on the trail of a dark conspiracy is extravagant, even exhilarating." —Nick Owchar, *Los Angeles Times*

"*Drood* is a stunning exercise in misdirection, one that keeps the reader perpetually off balance until the last sentence." —Michael Berry, *San Francisco Chronicle*

"This is a rich and strange book, and the pages fly by.... Simmons has taken great pains to make his backdrop of everyday Victorian life convincing." —Jake Kerridge, *Telegraph*

Drood

A NOVEL

DAN SIMMONS

LITTLE, BROWN AND COMPANY
NEW YORK   BOSTON   LONDON

Copyright © 2009 by Dan Simmons
Excerpt from *Flashback* copyright © 2010 by Dan Simmons
All rights reserved. Except as permitted under the U.S. Copyright Act of 1976, no part of this publication may be reproduced, distributed, or transmitted in any form or by any means, or stored in a database or retrieval system, without the prior written permission of the publisher.

Little, Brown and Company
Hachette Book Group
237 Park Avenue
New York, NY 10017
Visit our website at www.HachetteBookGroup.com

Printed in the United States of America

The publisher is not responsible for websites (or their content) that are not owned by the publisher.

Originally published in hardcover by Little, Brown and Company, February 2009
First Back Bay trade paperback edition, February 2010
First Back Bay international mass market edition, February 2010
First Little, Brown and Company mass market edition, January 2011

10 9 8 7 6 5 4 3 2 1

"What brought good Wilkie's genius nigh perdition?
Some demon whispered—'Wilkie! Have a mission.'"

—A. C. Swinburne
Fortnightly Review, Nov., 1889

Drood

CHAPTER ONE

*M*y name is Wilkie Collins, and my guess, since I plan to delay the publication of this document for at least a century and a quarter beyond the date of my demise, is that you do not recognise my name. Some say that I am a gambling man and those that say so are correct, so my wager with you, Dear Reader, would be that you have neither read nor heard of any of my books or plays. Perhaps you British or American peoples a hundred and twenty-five or so years in my future do not speak English at all. Perhaps you dress like Hottentots, live in gas-lighted caves, travel around in balloons, and communicate by tele-graphed thoughts unhindered by any spoken or written language.

Even so, I would wager my current fortune, such as it is, and all future royalties from my plays and novels, such as they may be, on the fact that you *do* remember the name and books and plays and invented characters of my friend and former collaborator, a certain Charles Dickens.

So this true story shall be about my friend (or at least about the man who was once my friend) Charles Dick-ens and about the Staplehurst accident that took away his peace of mind, his health, and, some might whisper, his sanity. This true story will be about Charles Dick-ens's final five years and about his growing obsession during that time with a man—if man he was—named Drood, as well as with murder, death, corpses, crypts, mesmerism, opium, ghosts, and the streets and alleys of that black-biled lower bowel of London that the writer always called "my Babylon" or "the Great Oven." In this manuscript (which, as I have explained—for legal reasons as well as for reasons of honour—I intend to seal away from all eyes for more than one hundred years after his death and my own), I shall answer the question which perhaps no one else alive in our time knew to ask—"Did the famous and loveable and honourable Charles Dickens plot to murder an innocent person and dissolve away his flesh in a pit of caustic lime and secretly inter what was left of him, mere bones and a skull, in the crypt of an ancient cathedral that was an important part of Dickens's own childhood? And did Dickens then scheme to scatter the poor victim's spectacles, rings, stickpins, shirt studs, and pocket watch in the River Thames? And if so, or even if Dickens only dreamed he did these things, what part did a very real phantom named Drood have in the onset of such madness?"

THE DATE OF DICKENS'S DISASTER was 9 June, 1865. The locomotive carrying his success, peace of mind, sanity, manuscript, and mistress was—quite literally—heading for a breach in the rails and a terrible fall.

I do not know if you Dear Readers living so many years hence still record or remember history (perhaps you have renounced Herodotus and Thucydides and dwell perpetually in the Year Zero), but if any sense of history remains in your time, you must know well the important events of the year we called Anno Domini 1865. Some events, such as the end of the fraternal conflagration in the United States, were considered of some drama and considerable interest by many in England, although not by Charles Dickens. Despite his great interest in America—having travelled there already and written books about it, not altogether flattering books one must add, and after having struggled so fiercely to receive some recompense for the piracy of his works in that copyright-flaunting chaos of former colonies—Dickens had little interest in a war between some distant North and more-distant South. But in 1865, the year of his Staplehurst disaster, Charles Dickens had reason to be very satisfied indeed with his own personal history.

He was the most popular novelist in England, perhaps in the world. Many people in England and America considered my friend to be—outside of Shakespeare and perhaps Chaucer and Keats—the greatest writer who had ever lived.

Of course, I knew this to be nonsense, but popularity, as they say (or as I have said), breeds more popularity. I had seen Charles Dickens stuck in a rural, doorless privy with his trousers down around his ankles, bleating like a lost sheep for some paper to wipe his arse, and you will have to forgive me if that image remains more true to me than "the greatest writer who ever lived."

But on this June day in 1865, Dickens had many reasons to be smug.

Seven years earlier, the writer had separated from his wife, Catherine, who obviously had offended him in their twenty-two years of marriage by uncomplainingly bearing him ten children and suffering several miscarriages, all the while generally putting up with his every complaint and catering to his every whim. This endeared his wife to him to the point that in 1857, during a walking trip we were taking in the countryside during which we had sampled several bottles of local wine, Dickens chose to describe his beloved Catherine to me as "Very dear to me, Wilkie, very dear. But, on the whole, more bovine than entrancing, more ponderous than feminine…an alchemist's dull brew of vague-mindedness, constant incompetence, shuffling sluggishness, and self-indulgent idleness, a thick gruel stirred only by the paddle of her frequent self-pity."

I doubt if my friend remembered telling me this, but I have not forgotten.

Actually, it was a complaint that did Catherine in, domestically speaking. It seems (actually, it does not "seem" at all—I was there when he purchased the blasted thing) that Dickens had bought the actress Ellen Ternan an expensive bracelet after our production of *The Frozen Deep,* and the idiot jeweller had delivered the thing to the Dickenses' home in London, Tavistock House, not to Miss Ternan's flat. As a result of this misdelivery, Catherine had given forth several weeks' worth of bovine mewlings, refusing to believe that it was merely her husband's token offering of innocent esteem to the actress who had done such a wonderful (actually, I would say barely competent) job as the hero's beloved, Clara Burnham, in our…no, *my*…play about unrequited love in the Arctic.

It is true, as Dickens continued to explain to his deeply hurt wife in 1858, that the author had the habit of showering generous gifts on his fellow players and participants in his various amateur theatricals. After *The Frozen Deep* he had already distributed bracelets and pendants, a watch, and one set of three shirt studs in blue enamel to others in the production.

But, then, he wasn't in love with these others. And he was in love with young Ellen Ternan. I knew that. Catherine Dickens knew that. No one can be sure if Charles Dickens knew that. The man was such a convincing fictionalist, not to mention one of the most self-righteous fellows ever to have trod the Earth, that I doubt if he ever confronted and acknowledged his own deeper motivations, except when they were as pure as springwater.

In this case, it was Dickens who flew into a rage, shouting and roaring at the soon-cowed Catherine—I apologise for any inadvertent bovine connotation there— that his wife's accusations were a slur on the pure and luminously perfect person of Ellen Ternan. Dickens's emotional, romantic, and, dare I say it, *erotic* fantasies always revolved around sanctified, chivalric devotion to some hypothetical young and innocent goddess whose purity was eternally beyond reproach. But Dickens may have forgotten that the hapless and now domestically doomed Catherine had watched *Uncle John,* the farce that we had put on (it was the tradition in our century, you see, always to present a farce along with a serious drama) after *The Frozen Deep.* In *Uncle John,* Dickens (age forty-six) played the elderly gentleman and Ellen Ternan (eighteen) played his ward. Naturally, Uncle John falls madly in love with the girl less than half his age. Catherine must have also known that while I had written the bulk of the drama, *The Frozen Deep,* about the search for the lost Franklin Expedition, it was her husband who had written and cast the romantic farce, *after he had met Ellen Ternan.*

Not only does Uncle John fall in love with the young girl he should be protecting, but he showers her with, and I quote from the play's stage directions, "wonderful presents—a pearl necklace, diamond ear-rings."

So it is little wonder that when the expensive bracelet, meant for Ellen, showed up at Tavistock House, Catherine, between pregnancies, roused herself from her vague-minded shuffling sluggishness and bellowed like a milk cow with a Welsh dairyman's prod between her withers.

Dickens responded as any guilty husband would.

But only if that husband happened to be the most popular writer in all of England and the English-speaking world and perhaps the greatest writer who ever lived.

First, he insisted that Catherine make a social call on Ellen Ternan and Ellen's mother, showing everyone that there could be no hint of suspicion or jealousy on his wife's part. In essence, Dickens was demanding that his wife publicly apologise to his mistress—or at least to the woman he would soon choose to *be* his mistress when he worked up the courage to make the arrangements. Weeping, miserable, Catherine did as she was bid. She humiliated herself by making a social call on Ellen and Mrs Ternan.

It was not enough to assuage Dickens's fury. He cast the mother of his ten children out.

He sent Charley, his eldest son, to live with Catherine. He kept the rest of the children to live with him at Tavistock House and eventually at Gad's Hill Place. (It was always my observation that Dickens enjoyed his children until they began to think and act for themselves in any way...in other words, when they ceased behaving like Little Nell or Paul Dombey or one of his other fictional constructs...and then he quickly grew very bored with them.)

There was more to this scandal, of course—protests by Catherine's parents, public retractions of those protests forced by Dickens and his solicitors, bullying and misleading public statements by the author, legal manoeuvrings, much terrible publicity, and a final and irrevocable legal separation forced on his wife. He eventually refused to communicate with her at all, even about the well-being of their children.

All this from the man who epitomised, not just for England but for the world, the image of "the happy home."

Of course Dickens still needed a woman in his house. He had many servants. He had nine children at home with whom he did not wish to be bothered except when he was in the mood to play with them or dangle them on his knee for photographs. He had social obligations. There were menus and shopping lists and florists' orders to prepare. There was much cleaning and organising to oversee. Charles Dickens needed to be freed from all these details. He was, you must understand, the world's greatest writer.

Dickens did the obvious thing, although it might not have seemed so obvious to you or to me. (Perhaps in this distant twentieth or twenty-first century to which I consign this memoir, it *is* the obvious thing. Or perhaps you have, if you are smart, abandoned the quaint and idiotic institution of marriage altogether. As you will see, I avoided matrimony in my time, choosing to live with one woman while having children with another, and some in my time, to my great pleasure, called me a scoundrel and a cad. But I digress.)

So Dickens did the obvious thing. He elevated Catherine's spinster sister Georgina to the role of surrogate wife, mistress of his household, and discipline-mistress of his children, hostess at his many parties and dinners, not to mention Sergeant Major to the cook and servants.

When the inevitable rumours began—centred on Georgina rather than on Ellen Ternan, who had receded, one might say, from the gaslights to the shadows—Dickens ordered a doctor to Tavistock House. The doctor was told to examine Georgina and then was ordered to publish a statement, which he did, declaring to all and sundry that Miss Georgina Hogarth was *virgo intacta*.

And that, Charles Dickens assumed, would be that.

His younger daughter would later say to me, or at least say within my hearing, "My father was like a madman. This affair brought out all that was the worst—and all that was the weakest—in him. He did not care a damn what happened to any of us. Nothing could surpass the misery and unhappiness of our home."

If Dickens was aware of their unhappiness, or if it mattered to him if he was indeed aware, he did not show it. Not to me, nor to his newer and ultimately closer friends.

And he was correct in his assumption that the crisis would pass without his readers' abandoning him. If they knew of his domestic irregularities at all, they had obviously forgiven him. He was, after all, the English prophet of the happy home and the world's greatest writer. Allowances must be made.

Our male literary peers and friends also forgave and forgot—with the exception of Thackeray, but that is another story—and I must admit that some of them, some of us, tacitly or privately, applauded Charles's freeing himself of his domestic obligations to such an unattractive and perpetually dragging sea anchor. The break gave a glimmer of hope to the bleakest of married men and amused us bachelors with the thought that perhaps one *could* come back from that undiscovered matrimonial country from which it was said that no man could ever return.

But, I pray you, Dear Reader, remember that we are speaking of the man who, sometime earlier, shortly before his acquaintance with Ellen Ternan, as he and I cruised the theatres for what we called "the special little periwinkles"—those very young and very pretty actresses we found to our mutual aesthetic satisfaction—had said to me, "Wilkie, if you can think of any tremendous way of passing the night, in the meantime, do. I don't care what it is. I give, for this night only, restraint to the Winds! If the mind can devise anything sufficiently in the style of Sybarite Rome in the days of its culminating voluptuousness, I am your man."

And for such sport, I was his.

I HAVE NOT FORGOTTEN 9 June, 1865, the true beginning of this cascade of incredible events.

Dickens, explaining to friends that he was suffering from overwork and what he had been calling his "frost-bitten foot" since mid-winter, had taken a week off from his work of finishing *Our Mutual Friend* to enjoy a holiday in Paris. I do not know if Ellen Ternan and her mother went with him. I do know they returned with him.

A lady whom I have never met nor much wish to, a certain Mrs William Clara Pitt Byrne (a friend, I am told, of Charles Waterton—the naturalist and explorer who reported his bold adventures all over the world but who had died from a silly fall at his estate of Walton Hall just eleven days before the Staplehurst accident, his ghost later reported to be haunting the place in the form of a great grey heron), loved to send little bits of malicious gossip to the *Times*. This malevolent morsel, reporting the sighting of our friend on the ferry from Boulogne to Folkestone that day of the ninth of June, appeared some months after Dickens's accident:

> *Travelling with him was a lady not his wife, nor his sister-in-law, yet he strutted about the deck with the air of a man bristling with self-importance, every line of his face and every gesture of his limbs seemed haughtily to say—"Look at me; make the most of your chance. I am the great, I am the only Charles Dickens; whatever I may choose to do is justified by that fact."*

I am told that Mrs Byrne is known primarily for a book she published some years ago titled *Flemish Interiors*. In my modest opinion, she should have reserved her vitriolic pen for scribbling about divans and wallpaper. Human beings are clearly beyond her narrow scope.

After disembarking at Folkestone, Dickens, Ellen, and Mrs Ternan took the 2.38 tidal train to London.

As they approached Staplehurst, they were the only passengers in their coach, one of seven first-class carriages in the tidal train that day.

The engineer was going full speed—about fifty miles per hour—as they passed Headcorn at eleven minutes after three in the afternoon. They were now approaching the railroad viaduct near Staplehurst, although "viaduct"—the name given the structure in the official railways guide—may be too fancy a word for the web of girders supporting the heavy wood beams spanning the shallow river Beult.

Labourers were carrying out a routine replacement of old timbers on that span. Later investigation—and I have read the reports—showed that the foreman had consulted the wrong timetable and did not expect the tidal train for another two hours. (It seems that we travellers are not the only ones to be confounded by British railway timetables with their infinite holiday and weekend and high-tide-time asterisks and confounding parentheses.)

A flagman was required by railway policy and English law to be stationed 1,000 yards up the rails from such work—two of the rails had already been lifted off at the bridge and set alongside the track—but for some reason this man with his red flag was only 550 yards from the gap. This did not give a train travelling at the speed of the Folkestone–London tidal express any chance of stopping in time.

The engineer, upon seeing the red flag so tardily waved and—a much more soul-riveting sight, I am sure—upon seeing the gap in rails and beams in the bridge ahead, did his best. Perhaps in your day, Dear Reader, all trains have brakes that can be applied by the engineer. Not so in our day of 1865. Each carriage must be braked individually and then only upon instructions from the engineer. He madly whistled for the guards along the length of the train to apply their brakes. It did little good.

According to the report, the train was still doing almost thirty miles per hour when it reached the broken line. Incredibly, the engine *jumped* the forty-two-foot gap and leaped off the track on the other side of the chasm. Of the seven first-class carriages, all but one flew free and plummeted to their destruction in the swampy riverbed below.

The surviving coach was the one carrying Dickens, his mistress, and her mother.

The guards' van immediately behind the engine was flung to the other track, dragging the next coach—a second-class carriage—with it. Immediately behind this second-class carriage was Dickens's coach and it jolted partially over the bridge as the other six first-class carriages flew by and crashed below. Dickens's carriage finally ended up dangling over the side of the bridge, now being kept from falling only by its single coupling to another second-class carriage. Only the very rear of the train remained on the rails. The other first-class carriages had plummeted and crashed and rolled and buckled and generally been smashed to matchwood and splinters on the marshy ground below.

Dickens later wrote about these moments, in letters to friends, but always with discretion, taking care never to mention, except to a few intimates, the names or identities of his two fellow travellers. I am certain that I am the only person to whom he ever told the complete story.

"Suddenly," he wrote in his more widely disseminated epistolary version of events, *"we were off the rail, and beating the ground as the car of a half-emptied balloon might do. The old lady…"* [We must read "Mrs Ternan" here] *"…cried out, 'My God!' The young lady travelling with her* [this is Ellen Ternan, of course] *screamed.*

"I caught hold of them both…and said: 'We can't help ourselves, but we can be quiet and composed. Pray don't cry out!'

"The old lady immediately answered: 'Thank you. Rely on me. Upon my soul I will be quiet.' We were then all tilted down together in a corner of the carriage, and stopped."

The carriage was indeed tilted steeply down and to the left. All baggage and loose objects had fallen down and to the left. For the rest of his life, Charles Dickens would suffer repeated spells of feeling as if "everything, all of my body, is tilted and falling down and to the left."

Dickens continues his narrative:

"I said to the two women, 'You may be sure that nothing worse can happen. Our danger must be over. Will you remain here, without stirring, while I get out the window?'"

Dickens, still lithe enough then at the age of fifty-three, despite his "frost-bitten foot" (as a long-time sufferer of gout, which has required me to partake of laudanum for many years, I know gout when I hear its symptoms, and Dickens's "frostbite" was almost certainly gout), then clambered out, made the tricky jump from the carriage step to the railbed above the bridge, and reported seeing two guards running up and down in apparent confusion.

Dickens writes that he grabbed and stopped one of them, demanding of the man, "Look at me! Do stop an instant and look at me, and tell me whether you don't know me."

"We know you very well, Mr Dickens," he reports the guard replied at once.

"Then, my good fellow," cried Dickens, almost cheerily (at being recognised at such a time, a petty soul such as Clara Pitt Byrne might have interjected), "for God's *sake give me your key, and send one of those labourers here, and I'll empty this carriage."*

And then, in Dickens's letters to his friends, the guards did as they were bid, labourers laying down planks to the carriage, and then the author clambered back into the tilted coach and crawled down its length to retrieve his top hat and his flask of brandy.

I should interrupt our mutual friend's description here just long enough to say that, using the names listed in the official railway report as my guide, I later tracked down the very guard that Dickens reports stopping and galvanising into such useful action. The guard—a certain Lester Smyth—had a somewhat different recollection of those moments.

"We were trying to get down to 'elp the injured and dying when this toff who'd climbed out of the teetering first-class coach runs up to Paddy Beale and me, all wild-eyed and pale, and keeps shouting at us, 'Do you know me, man!? Do you know me!? Do you know who I *am*??'

"I admit that I replied, 'I don't care if you're Prince Albert, mate. Get out of my bleedin' way.' It was not the usual way I'd speak to a gentleman, but that wasn't no usual day."

At any rate, Dickens did commandeer the work of some labourers to help extricate Ellen and Mrs Ternan, he did crawl back into the carriage to retrieve his flask and top hat, he did fill his top hat with water before clambering down the steep bank, and all witnesses agree that Dickens went immediately to work down among the dying and the dead.

IN HIS FIVE REMAINING YEARS after Staplehurst, Dickens would only say about what he saw in that riverbed—"It was unimaginable"—and of what he heard there—"Unintelligible." This from the man generally agreed to have the greatest imagination, after Sir Walter Scott, of any English writer. And from a man whose stories were, if nothing else, always eminently intelligible.

Perhaps the unimaginable began when he was clambering down the steep embankment. Suddenly appearing next to him was a tall, thin man wearing a heavy black cape far more appropriate for a night at the opera than an afternoon's voyage to London on the tidal train. Both men were carrying their top hats in one hand while grabbing at the embankment for balance with their free hands. This figure, as Dickens later described to me in a throaty whisper during the days after the accident when his voice "was no longer my own," was cadaverously thin, almost shockingly pale, and stared at the writer from dark-shadowed eyes set deep under a pale, high brow that melded into a pale, bald scalp. A few strands of greying hair leapt out from the sides of this skull-like visage. Dickens's impression of a skull was reinforced, he said later, by the man's foreshortened nose—"mere black slits opening into the grub-white face than a proper proboscis" was how Dickens described it—and by small, sharp, irregular teeth, spaced too far apart, set into gums so pale that they were whiter than the teeth themselves.

The author also noticed that the man had two fingers missing—or almost missing—on his right hand, the little finger and the ring finger next to it, as well as a missing middle finger on his left hand. What especially caught Dickens's attention was the fact that the fingers had *not* been cut off at the joint, as is so often the case in an accident to the hand or subsequent surgery, but appeared to have been severed halfway through the bone between the joints. "Like tapers of white wax that had been partially melted," he told me later.

Dickens was nonplussed as he and this strange black-caped figure slowly worked their way down the steep embankment, both using shrubs and rocks as handholds.

"I am Charles Dickens," gasped my friend.

"Yesss," said the pale face, the sibilants sliding out through the tiny teeth. "I know."

This nonplussed Dickens all the more. "Your name, sir?" he asked as they slid down the embankment of loose stones together.

"Drood," said the man. At least Dickens thought this is what the man said. The pale figure's voice was slurred and tinged with what may have been a foreign accent. The word came out sounding most like "Dread."

"You were on the train going to London?" asked Dickens as they approached the bottom of the steep hill.

"To Limehoussse," hissed the ungainly form in the dark cape. "Whitechapel. Ratcliff Crossss. Gin Alley. Three Foxesss Court. Butcher Row and Commercial Road. The Mint and other rookeriessss."

Dickens glanced up sharply at this strange recital, since their train had been going to the station in central London, not to these dark alleys in East London. "Rookeries" was a slang term for the worst of the tenement slums in the city. But now they had reached the bottom of the hill, and without another word, this "Drood" turned away and seemed to glide into the shadows under the railway bridge. In a few seconds the man's black cape blended with the darkness there.

"You must understand," Dickens was to whisper to me later, "I never for a second thought that this strange apparition was Death come to claim his own. Nor any other personification of the tragedy that was even then unfolding. This would have been too trite even for far lesser fiction than that which I create. But I do admit,

Wilkie," he said, "that I wondered at the time if Drood might have been an undertaker come from Staplehurst or some other nearby hamlet."

Alone now, Dickens turned his attention to the carnage.

The train carriages in the riverbed and adjoining swampy banks were no longer recognisable as railway coaches. Except for iron axles and wheels protruding here and there at impossible angles from the water, it was as if a series of wooden bungalows had been flung out of the sky, perhaps dropped from some American cyclone and smashed to bits. And then the bits looked to have been dropped and smashed yet again.

It seemed to Dickens as if no one could have survived such impact, such destruction, but screams of living sufferers—for in truth the injured far outnumbered the dead—began to fill the river valley. These were not, he thought at the time, human sounds. They were somehow infinitely worse than the moans and cries he had heard when touring overcrowded hospitals, such as the East London Children's Hospital at Ratcliff Cross—which Drood had just mentioned—where the indigent and unclaimed went to die. No, these screams seemed more as if someone had opened a portal to the pit of Hell itself and allowed the damned there to cry out one last time to the mortal world.

Dickens watched a man stagger towards him, arms outstretched as if for a welcoming hug. The top of the man's skull had been torn off rather the way one would crack an eggshell with a spoon in preparation for breakfast. Dickens could clearly see the grey-and-pink pulp glistening within the concave bowl of splintered skull. The fellow's face was covered with blood, his eyes white orbs staring out through crimson rivulets.

Dickens could think of nothing to do but offer the man some brandy from his flask. The mouth of the flask came away red from the man's lips. Dickens helped him lie on the grass and then used the water in his top hat to clean the man's face. "What is your name, sir?" asked Dickens.

The man said only, "I am gone," and died, the white eyes continuing to stare up at the sky from their bloody pools.

A shadow passed over them. Dickens whirled, sure—he told me later—that it would be Drood, the apparition's black cape widening like a raven's wings. But it was only a cloud passing between the sun and the river valley.

Dickens refilled his top hat from the river and came upon a lady, who also had blood streaming down over her lead-coloured face. She was almost naked, her clothes reduced to a few token strips of bloody cloth dangling like old bandages from her torn flesh. Her left breast was missing. She refused to pause for the writer's ministrations and did not seem to hear his urgings that she sit down and wait for help. She walked past Dickens in a brisk manner and disappeared into the few trees that grew along the bank.

He helped two stunned guards extricate the crushed body of another woman from a flattened carriage and lay the body gently on the bank. A man was wading downstream, screaming, "My wife! My wife!" Dickens led him to the corpse. The man screamed, threw his arms above his head, and ran wildly into the swampy field near the river, crashing and thrashing about, all the while emitting sounds that Dickens later said "were like the hisses and death grunts of a boar pierced through the lungs by several large calibre bullets." Then the man fainted, dropping into the marsh more like someone shot through the heart than through the lungs.

Dickens went back towards the carriages and found

a woman propped against a tree. Except for a little blood on her face, perhaps from a slight scalp wound, she seemed uninjured.

"I shall bring you some water, madam," he said.

"That would be very kind of you, sir," she replied. She smiled and Dickens flinched. She had lost all of her teeth.

He went to the stream and looked back to see a figure he took to be Drood—presumably no one else was foolishly dressed in a heavy opera cape on that warm June day—solicitously bent over the woman. When Dickens returned a few seconds later with his top hat filled with river water, the man in black was gone and the woman was dead but still showing her ragged, bloodied gums in a parody of a final smile.

He went back to the smashed carriages. Amidst the rubble of one coach, a young man moaned feebly. More rescuers were sliding down the slope. Dickens ran to get several strong guards to help extricate the fellow from the broken glass, torn red velvet, heavy iron, and collapsed wooden floor of the compartment. While the guards grunted and lifted the heavy window frames and shattered flooring that had now become a fallen roof, Dickens squeezed the young man's hand and said, "I shall see you to safety, my son."

"Thank you," gasped the injured young gentleman, obviously an occupant of one of the first-class carriages. "You are most kind."

"What is your name?" asked our novelist as they carried the young man to the bank.

"Dickenson," said the young fellow.

Charles Dickens made sure that Master Dickenson was carried up to the railway line where more rescuers had arrived, then he turned back to the carnage. He rushed from injured person to injured person, lifting, consoling, assuaging thirst, reassuring, sometimes covering their nakedness with any rag he could find, all while checking other scattered forms to confirm that they were no longer amongst the living.

A few rescuers and fellow passengers seemed as focused as our author, but many—Dickens told me later—could only stand there in shock and stare. The two figures doing the most that terrible afternoon amidst the wreckage and groans were Dickens and the bizarre form who called himself Drood, although the black-caped man seemed always to be just out of ear-shot, always on the verge of vanishing from sight again, and always appearing to glide rather than walk from wrecked carriage to wrecked carriage.

Dickens came upon a large woman, the peasant cloth and design of her dress showing that she had come from one of the lower-class carriages. She was face-down in the swamp, her arms under her body. He rolled her over to be certain that she was no longer among the living, when suddenly her eyes popped open in her mud-covered face.

"I saved her!" she gasped. "I saved her from *him!*"

It took a moment before Dickens noticed the infant clasped fiercely between the fat woman's heavy arms, the small white face pressed deep against the woman's pendulous bosoms. The baby was dead—either drowned in the shallow swamp or asphyxiated by its mother's weight.

Dickens heard a hissing call, saw Drood's pale form waving to him from the web of shadows under the broken bridge and walked towards him, but came first to a collapsed, upside-down carriage where a young woman's bare but shapely arm protruded from what was left of a window. Her fingers moved, seeming to beckon Dickens closer.

Dickens crouched and took the soft fingers in his own two hands. "I am here, my dear," he said to the darkness inside the small aperture that had been a window only fifteen minutes earlier. He squeezed her hand and she squeezed his back, as if in gratitude for her deliverance.

Dickens crouched but could see nothing but torn upholstery, dark shapes, and deep shadows within the tiny, triangular cave of wreckage. There was not enough room for him to squeeze in even his shoulders. The top frame of the window was pressing down almost to the marshy ground. He could only just hear the rapid, terrified breathing of the injured woman above the gurgle of the river running by. Without thinking of the possible impropriety of it, he stroked her bare arm as far as he could reach it in the collapsed wreckage. There were very fine reddish hairs along her pale forearm and they glowed coppery in the afternoon light.

"I see the guards and possibly a doctor coming," Dickens said into the tiny aperture, squeezing her arm and hand all the while. He did not know for sure if the approaching gentleman in the brown suit who carried a leather bag was indeed a doctor, but he fervently hoped so. The four guards, carrying axes and iron pry rods, were jogging ahead, the gentleman in the formal suit puffing to keep up.

"Over here!" Dickens cried to them. He squeezed the woman's hand. Her pale fingers squeezed back, the first finger closing, opening, and then curling and closing again around his first fingers much as a newborn baby would instinctively but tentatively grasp its father's hand. She said nothing, but Dickens heard her sigh from the shadows. It seemed almost a contented sound. He held her hand in both of his and prayed that she was not seriously injured.

"Here, for God's sake, hurry!" cried Dickens. The men gathered around. The heavy, suited man introduced himself—he was a physician by the name of

Morris—and Dickens refused to relinquish either his place by the wrecked window or the young lady's hand as the four guards began levering the window frame and smashed wood and iron upward and to the side, enlarging the tiny space that had somehow been the woman's shelter and salvation.

"Careful now!" shouted Dickens to the guards. "With great care, by all means! Allow nothing to fall. Careful with the bars there!" Crouching lower to speak into the dark space, Dickens fiercely gripped her hand and whispered, "We almost have you, my dear. Another minute. Be brave!"

There came a last, answering squeeze. Dickens could feel the gratitude in it.

"You'll have to get back a minute, sir," said Dr Morris. "Back just a moment while the boys heave and lift here and I lean in to see if she is too injured to move yet or not. Just for a moment, sir. That's a good gentleman."

Dickens patted the young lady's palm, his fingers reluctant to release her, feeling the final, parting pressure from her thin, pale, perfectly manicured fingers in return. His mind pushed away the very real but totally inappropriate sense of there being something physically exciting in such intimate contact with a woman whose acquaintance he had not yet made and whose face he had not yet seen. He said, "You'll be out of all of this and safe with us in a moment, my dear" and surrendered her hand. Then he crawled backwards on all fours, clearing the way for the workmen and feeling the marsh moistness seeping up through the knees of his trousers.

"Now!" cried the doctor, kneeling where Dickens had been a moment before. "Put your backs into it, boys!"

The four burly guards literally put their backs into it,

first lifting with their pry bars and then setting their backs against the ragged wall of collapsed flooring that now became a heavy pyramid of wood. The cone of darkness widened a bit beneath them. Sunlight illuminated the wreckage. They gasped as they strained to hold the debris up and then one of the men gasped again.

"Oh, Christ!" cried someone.

The doctor seemed to leap back as if he had touched an electrified wire. Dickens crawled forward to offer his help and finally saw into the space.

There was no woman, no girl. Only a bare arm severed just below the shoulder lay in the tiny open circle amidst the debris. The knob of bone looked very white in the filtered afternoon light.

Everyone shouted. More men arrived. Instructions were repeated. The guards used their axes and iron bars to pry open the wreckage, carefully at first and then with a terrible, almost wilfully destructive abandon. The rest of the young woman's body simply was not there. There were no complete bodies anywhere in this pile of wreckage, only mismatched tatters of torn clothing and random bits of flesh and gouged bone. There was not so much as an identifiable scrap of her dress left behind. There was only the pale arm ending in the bloodless and tightly curled and now motionless fingers.

Without another word, Dr Morris turned and walked away, joining other rescuers milling around other victims.

Dickens got to his feet, blinked, licked his lips, and reached for his flask of brandy. It tasted of copper. He realised that it was empty and that he was tasting only the blood left on it from some of the victims to whom he had offered it. He looked around and around for his top hat and then saw that he was wearing it. River water from it had soaked his hair and dripped down his collar.

More rescuers and onlookers were arriving. Dickens judged that he could be of little further help there. Slowly, awkwardly, he climbed the steep riverbank up to the railbed where the intact carriages now sat empty.

Ellen and Mrs Ternan were sitting in the shade on some stacked rail ties, calmly drinking water from teacups someone had brought them.

Dickens started to reach for Ellen's gloved hand and then did not complete the motion. Instead, he said, "How are you, my dear?"

Ellen smiled, but there were tears in her eyes. She touched her left arm and an area just below her shoulder and above her left breast. "A bit bruised, I believe, but otherwise well. Thank you, Mr Dickens."

The novelist nodded almost absently, his eyes focused elsewhere. Then he turned, walked to the edge of the broken bridge, jumped with the easy agility of the distracted to the step of the dangling first-class carriage, crawled through a shattered window as easily as if it were a doorway, and clambered down through rows of seats that had become rungs on the now-vertical wall of the coach floor. The entire carriage, still dangling precariously high above the valley floor and connected by only one coupling to the second-class carriage on the rails above, swayed slightly like a vibrating pendulum in a broken hallway clock.

Earlier, even before rescuing Ellen and Mrs Ternan, he had carried out his leather bag carrying most of the manuscript of the sixteenth number of *Our Mutual Friend*, which he had been working on in France, but now he had remembered that the last two chapters were in his overcoat, which still lay folded in the overhead above their former seats. Standing on the backs of this last row of seats in the swaying, creaking coach, the river thirty feet below reflecting darts of dancing light through the shattered windows, he retrieved the overcoat, pulled the manuscript out to make sure that all the pages were there—it had been slightly soiled but was otherwise intact—and then, still balancing on the seats, he tucked the papers back into his overcoat.

Dickens then happened to look straight down, down through the shattered glass of the door at the end of the carriage. Far below, directly beneath the train car, some trick of the light making him appear to be standing *on* the river rather than *in* it, apparently totally unconcerned by so many tons of wood and iron swaying above him, the person who called himself Drood was tilting his head far back to stare straight up at Dickens. The man's pale eyes in their sunken sockets seemed to have no eyelids.

The figure's lips parted, its mouth opened and moved, the fleshy tongue flickered out from behind and between the tiny teeth, and hissing sounds emerged, but Dickens could make out no distinct words over the metallic groaning of the dangling carriage and the continuous cries of the injured in the valley below. "Unintelligible," murmured Dickens. "Unintelligible."

The first-class carriage suddenly swayed and sagged as if preparing to drop. Dickens casually caught the overhead with one hand to keep his balance. When the swaying ceased and he looked down again, Drood was gone. The writer tossed the coat with his manuscript in it over his shoulder and clambered up and out into the light.

CHAPTER TWO

$\mathscr{I}$ was out of town on the day of my friend's disaster at Staplehurst, so it was a full three days after the accident that I received a message from my younger brother, Charles, who had married Dickens's oldest daughter, Kate, telling me of the novelist's brush with death. I immediately hurried down to Gad's Hill Place.

I would presume, my Dear Reader who resides in my impossibly distant and posthumous future, that you remember Gad's Hill from Shakespeare's *Henry IV*. You do remember Shakespeare even if all the rest of us scribblers have been lost to the fogs of history, do you not? Gad's Hill is where Falstaff plans a robbery but is foiled by Prince Hal and a friend who disguise themselves as robbers wishing to rob the robber; after the fat Sir John flees in terror, his retelling of the story has Hal and his accomplice become four brigands, then eight, then sixteen, and so forth. There is a Falstaff Inn very close to Dickens's home, and I believe that the author enjoyed his home's connection to Shakespeare as much as he enjoyed the ale that the inn served him at the end of his long walks.

As I approached the home in a carriage, I was reminded that Gad's Hill Place had yet another claim on Charles Dickens's emotions, one that long predated his purchase of the place a decade earlier in 1855. Gad's Hill was in Chatham, a village that blended into the cathedral town of Rochester about twenty-five miles from London, an area where the writer had spent the happiest years of his childhood and one to which he returned constantly as an adult, roaming there rather like some restless ghost searching for his final haunting ground. The house itself—Gad's Hill Place—had been pointed out to the seven- or eight-year-old Charles Dickens by his father on one of their countless walks; John Dickens had said something to the effect that "If you work hard enough, my boy, and apply yourself, such a mansion might one day be yours." Then, on that boy's forty-third birthday in February of 1855, Dickens had taken some friends to Chatham on one of his regular sentimental hauntings and discovered, to his real shock, that the unobtainable mansion of his youth was for sale.

Dickens was the first to admit that Gad's Hill Place was not so much a mansion as it was a moderately comfortable country house—in truth, the author's former home Tavistock House had been more imposing—although after purchasing Gad's Hill Place, the writer did pour a small fortune into renovating, modernising, decorating, landscaping, and expanding it. At first he had planned to use his late father's dream of opulence as a rental property, then began to think of it as a sometime country home, but after the bitter unpleasantness of his separation from Catherine, he first leased out Tavistock House and then put that city house up for sale, making Gad's Hill Place his primary residence. (His habit, though, was to keep several places in London for occasional—and sometimes secret—residence, including quarters above his office at our magazine *All the Year Round*.)

Dickens had told his friend Wills upon purchasing the place—"I used to look at it as a wonderful mansion (which God knows it is not) when I was a very odd little child with the first shadows of all my books in my head."

As my carriage turned off the Gravesend Road and rolled up the curved drive towards the three-storey red-brick home, I thought of how those shadows had taken on substance for hundreds of thousands of readers and how Dickens, in turn, now lived within those very substantial walls that his incorrigible father, a failure in the arenas of both family and finances, had once held up to his son as the highest possible reward of domestic and professional ambition.

A MAID-SERVANT ADMITTED ME and Georgina Hogarth, Dickens's sister-in-law and now the mistress of the home, greeted me.

"How is the Inimitable?" I asked, using the author's favourite sobriquet for himself.

"Very shaken, Mr Collins, very shaken," whispered Georgina and held one finger to her lips. Dickens's study was off the entryway to the right. The doors were closed but I knew from my many visits and stays at Gad's Hill that the master's study doors were *always* closed, whether he was there working or not. "The accident upset him so much that he had to spend the first night at his apartment in London with Mr Wills sleeping outside the door," she continued in her stage whisper. "In case Mr Wills might be needed, you know."

I nodded. First hired as an assistant for Dickens's magazine *Household Words*, the eminently practical and unimaginative William Henry Wills—in so many ways the opposite of the mercurial Dickens—had become one of the famous author's closest friends and confidants, moving aside such older friends as John Forster.

"He's not working today," whispered Georgina. "I'll see if he wants to be disturbed." She approached the study doors with some obvious trepidation.

"Who is it?" came a voice from within the study when Georgina knocked lightly.

I say "a voice" because it was not Charles Dickens's voice. The novelist's voice, as all who knew him long remembered, was low, quick, and burdened with a slight thickness which many mistook for a lisp and which had caused the writer, in recompense, to over-enunciate his vowels and consonants so that the rapid but very careful and rolling elocution sometimes sounded pompous to those who did not know him.

This voice was nothing like that. It was the reed-thin quaver of an old man.

"It's Mr Collins," said Georgina to the oak of the doorway.

"Tell him to go back to his sickroom," rasped the old man's voice from within.

I blinked at this. Since my younger brother, Charles, had married Kate Dickens five years earlier, he had suffered bouts of serious indigestion and occasional ill health, but—I was certain at the time—it was nothing serious. Dickens thought otherwise. The writer had opposed the marriage, had felt that his favourite daughter had married Charles—a sometimes illustrator of Dickens's books—just to spite him, and obviously had convinced himself that my brother was dying. I'd recently heard on good authority that Dickens had said to Wills that my dear brother's health rendered him "totally unfit for any function of this life," and even had it been true—which it absolutely was not—it was a remarkably callous thing to say.

"No, Mr *Wilkie*," Georgina said through the doors, glancing apprehensively over her shoulder as if in hopes that I had not heard.

"Oh," came some oldster's quavering syllable. "Why the deuce didn't you say so?"

We heard vague scrambling and scrabbling sounds and then the turning of a key in the lock—which was extraordinary in itself, as Dickens had the odd habit of locking his study when he was *not* in it but never when he *was*—and then the doors were thrown open.

"My dear Wilkie, my dear Wilkie," said Dickens in that odd rasp, throwing his arms open wide, then clasping my right shoulder with his left hand briefly before removing it to join the other hand that was enthusiastically shaking mine. I noticed that he was glancing at his watch on its chain. "Thank you, Georgina," he added absently as he closed the doors behind us, not locking them this time. He led the way into his dark study.

Which was another oddity. As many times as I had visited Dickens in his sanctum sanctorum over the years, I had never seen the drapes drawn across the bow windows in the daytime. They were now. The only light came from the lamp on the table in the centre of the room; there was no lamp on the writing desk that faced those three windows and which was set into the small bay they created. Only a few of us had been privileged to see Dickens actually in the act of creation in this study, but all of us who had must have noted the mild irony that Dickens invariably faced the windows looking out into his garden and towards Gravesend Road but never *saw* anything of the scene before him when he looked up from his quill and paper. The writer was lost in the worlds of his own imaginings and effectively blind while working, except when glancing into a nearby mirror to see his own expressions while acting out the grimaces, grins, frowns, expressions of shock, and other caricature-like responses of his characters.

Dickens pulled me deeper into the dark room and

waved me to a chair near his desk and sat in his cushioned work chair. Except for the closed drapes, the room looked as it always had—everything neat and orderly in an almost compulsive manner (and without a hint of dust, even though Dickens never allowed the servants to dust or clean in his study). There was the desk with its tilted writing surface, the little array of his carefully arranged tools, never out of order, arrayed like talismans on the flat part of the desk—a date calendar, ink-bottle, quills, a pencil with a nearby India rubber eraser that looked to have never been used, a pincushion, a small bronze statuette of two toads duelling, a paper-knife aligned *just so*, a gilded leaf with a stylised rabbit on it. These were his good-luck symbols—his "appurtenances," Dickens called them, something, he once said to me, "for my eye to rest on during the intervals between writing"—and he could no more write at Gad's Hill without them than he could without his goose quills.

Much of the study was lined with books, including shelves of false books—most with ironic titles of Dickens's own invention—that he'd had made for Tavistock House and which now were set into the back of the door, and the real built-in bookcases that circled the room were broken up only by the windows and a handsome blue-and-white fireplace decorated with twenty Delft tiles.

Dickens himself looked almost shockingly aged this June-day afternoon, his encroaching baldness, deep-set eyes, and the wrinkles and lines in his face emphasised by the harsh light from the gas lamp on the table behind us. He kept glancing at his unopened watch.

"So good of you to come, my dear Wilkie," rasped Dickens.

"Nonsense, nonsense," I said. "I would have been here sooner had I not been out of town, as I trust my brother informed you. Your voice sounds strained, Charles."

"Strange?" said Dickens with a flash of a smile.

"Strained."

He barked a laugh. Very few conversations with Charles Dickens did not include a laugh from him. I had never met a man so given to laughter. Almost no moment or context was too serious for this author not to find some levity in it, as some of us had discovered to our embarrassment at funerals.

"*Strange* is more appropriate, I would venture," said Dickens in that odd old-man's rasp. "I most unaccountably brought someone else's voice out of the terrible scene of the Staplehurst disaster. I do wish that person would return my voice and take back his own....I find this ageing-Micawber tone not at all to my liking. It feels rather as if one is applying sandpaper simultaneously to vocal cords and vowels."

"Are you otherwise uninjured, my friend?" I asked, leaning forward into the circle of lamplight.

Dickens waved away the question and returned his attention to the gold watch now in his hands. "My dear Wilkie, I had the most astonishing dream last night."

"Oh?" I said sympathetically. I assumed I would be hearing his nightmares about the accident at Staplehurst.

"It seemed almost as though I were reading a book that I had written in the future," he said softly, still turning the watch over and over in his hands. The gold caught the light from the single lamp. "It was a terrible thing...all about a man who mesmerised himself so that he, or his other self created by these mesmeric suggestions, could carry out terrible deeds, unspeakable actions. Selfish, lustful, destructive things that the man—for some reason in the dream I wanted to call him Jasper—would never consciously do. And there was another...creature...involved somehow."

"Mesmerise himself," I murmured. "That is not possible, is it? I defer to your longer involvement and training in the art of magnetic influence, my dear Charles."

"I have no idea. I have never *heard* of it being done, but that does not necessarily mean it is impossible." He looked up. "Have you ever been mesmerised, Wilkie?"

"No," I said with a soft laugh. "Although a few have tried." I did not feel it necessary to add that Professor John Elliotson, formerly of the University College Hospital and Dickens's very own mentor and instructor in the art of mesmerism, had himself found it impossible to make me submit to the mesmeric influence. My will was simply too strong.

"Let us try," said Dickens, dangling the watch by its chain and beginning to swing it in a pendulum motion.

"Charles," I said, chuckling but not amused, "whatever on earth for? I came to hear the details of your terrible accident, not to play parlour games with a watch and…"

"Humour me, my dear Wilkie," Dickens said softly. "You know that I have had some success with mesmerising others—I have told you, I believe, of my long and rather successful mesmeric therapy with poor Madame de la Rue on the Continent."

I could only grunt noncommittally. Dickens had told *all* of his friends and acquaintances about his long and obsessive series of treatments with "poor" Madame de la Rue. What he did not share with us, but which was common knowledge among his intimates, was that his sessions with the married and obviously insane lady, which occurred at odd times of the night as well as day, had made Dickens's wife, Catherine, so jealous that—for perhaps the first time in her married life—she had demanded Dickens stop them.

"Please keep your eyes on the watch," said Dickens

as he swung the gold disk back and forth in the dim light.

"This won't work, my dear Charles."

"You are getting very drowsy, Wilkie… *very* drowsy.… It is difficult for you to keep your eyes open. You are as sleepy as if you had just taken several drops of laudanum."

I almost laughed aloud at this. I had taken several *dozen* drops of laudanum before coming to Gad's Hill, as I did every morning. And I was overdue in sipping more from my silver flask.

"You are getting… very… sleepy…" droned Dickens.

For a few seconds I tried to comply, just to humour the Inimitable. It was obvious that he was seeking distraction from the terrors of his recent accident. I focused on the swinging watch. I listened to Dickens's droning voice. In truth, the heavy warmth of the closed room, the lowered lights, the single gleam of gold swinging back and forth, but mostly the amount of laudanum I had taken that morning, lured me—for the briefest of instants—into the briefest state of fuzzyheadedness.

If I would have allowed myself to, I might have fallen asleep then, if not into the mesmeric trance that Dickens would have so loved to induce in me.

Instead, I shook the fuzziness away before it took hold and said brusquely, "I am sorry, Charles. It simply does not work with me. My will is too strong."

Dickens sighed and put away the watch. Then he walked over and opened the drapes a bit. The sunlight made both of us blink. "It's true," said Dickens. "The wills of real writers are too strong to be subdued by the mesmeric arts."

I laughed. "Then make your character Jasper—if you ever write this novel based on your dream— something other than a writer."

Dickens smiled wanly. "So I shall, my dear Wilkie." He returned to his chair.

"How are Miss Ternan and her mother?" I asked.

Dickens did not hide a frown. Even with me, any discussion of that most personal and secret aspect of his life, however properly circumscribed it was in conversation and however much he *needed* to speak of her to someone, made him uncomfortable. "Miss Ternan's mother escaped any real injury other than the shock to the system of someone her age," rasped Dickens, "but Miss Ternan herself did suffer some rather serious bruises and what her doctor suggests was a slight cervical fracture or dislocation in her lower neck. She finds it very difficult to turn her head without serious pain."

"I am very sorry to hear that," I said.

Dickens did not say more about this. He asked softly, "Do you wish to hear the details of the accident and its aftermath, my dear Wilkie?"

"By all means, my dear Charles. By all means."

"You understand that you shall be the *only* person to whom I shall reveal all of the details of this event?"

"I will be honoured to hear it," I said. "And you can trust in my discretion until the grave and beyond."

Now Dickens *did* smile—that sudden, sure, mischievous, and somehow boyish show of stained teeth from within the cumulus of beard he'd grown for my play *The Frozen Deep* eight years earlier and never shaven off. "Your grave or mine, Wilkie?" he asked.

I blinked in a second's confusion or embarrassment. "Both, I assure you," I said at last.

Dickens nodded and began rasping out the story of the Staplehurst accident.

DEAR GOD," I whispered when Dickens was done some forty minutes later. And then again, "Dear God."

"Exactly," said the novelist.

"Those poor people," I said, my voice almost as strained as Dickens's. "Those poor people."

"Unimaginable," repeated Dickens. I had never heard him use this word before, but in this account he must have used it a dozen times. "Did I remember to tell you that the poor man whom we extricated from that truly extraordinary heap of dark ruins—he was jammed in upside down, you see—was bleeding from the eyes, ears, nose, and mouth as we searched frantically for his wife? It seems that a few minutes before the crash, this man had changed places with a Frenchman who disliked having the window down. We found the Frenchman dead. The bleeding man's wife also dead."

"Dear God," I said yet again.

Dickens ran his hand over his eyes as if shielding them from the light. When he looked up again there was that intensity in his eyes that I confess I have never seen in another human being. As we shall see in this true tale I share with you, Dear Reader, the will of Charles Dickens was not to be denied.

"What did you think of my description of the figure that called itself Drood?" Dickens's rasping query was soft but very intense.

"Quite incredible," I said.

"Does that mean that you do *not* credit his existence or my description of him, my dear Wilkie?"

"Not at all, not at all," I said hurriedly. "I am sure his appearance and behaviour were exactly as you described, Charles.... There is no more talented observer of individual human features and foibles either living or interred with all literary honours in Westminster Abbey than you, my friend...but Mr Drood is... incredible."

"Precisely," said Dickens. "And it is our duty now, my dear Wilkie—yours and mine—to find him."

"Find him?" I repeated stupidly. "Why in heaven's name should we do that?"

"There is a story in Mr Drood that must be unearthed," whispered Dickens. "If you will pardon the grave overtones of that phrase. What was the man—if man he was—doing on the tidal train at this time? Why, when questioned by me, did he say that he was going to Whitechapel and the rookeries of the East End? What was his purpose among the dead and dying?"

I did not understand. "What *could* his purpose have been, Charles?" I asked. "Other than the same as yours—to help and console the living and to locate the dead?"

Dickens smiled again, but there was no warmth or boyishness in that smile. "There was something sinister afoot there, my dear Wilkie. I am sure of it. Several times, as I described to you, I saw this Drood...if that is the creature's name...hovering near injured people, and when I later went to attend to those individuals, they were dead."

"But you described how several of the people to whom *you* attended, Charles, also died when you returned to help them."

"Yes," rasped Dickens in that stranger's voice, lowering his chin into his collars. "But I did not *help* them over to the other side."

I sat back in shock. "Dear God. You're suggesting that this opera-caped, leprous-looking figure actually... *murdered*...some of the poor victims at Staplehurst?"

"I'm suggesting that some sort of cannibalism went on there, my dear Wilkie."

"Cannibalism!" For the first time I wondered if the accident had mentally unhinged my famous friend. It was true that during his narration of the accident, I'd held serious doubts about the description and even the actual existence of this "Drood"—the man seemed

more a character out of a sensationalist novel than any human reality that could be encountered on the tidal train from Folkestone—but I had ascribed that possibility of hallucination to the same sense of shock and disorientation that had robbed Dickens of his voice. But if Dickens were imagining *cannibalism*, it was quite possible that the accident had robbed him of his reason as well as his voice.

He was smiling at me again and the intensity of his gaze was precisely the kind that made so many first-time interlocutors believe that Charles Dickens could read their minds. "No, my dear Wilkie, I am *not* deranged," he said softly. "Mr Drood was as corporeal as you or I and even stranger—in some indefinable way—than I have described. Had I conceived of him as a character for one of my novels, I would not have described him as I met him in reality—too strange, too threatening, too physically grotesque for fiction, my dear Wilkie. But in reality, as you well know, such phantom figures *do* exist. One passes them on the street. One finds them during nocturnal walks through Whitechapel or other parts of London. And often their stories are stranger than anything a mere novelist could devise."

It was my turn to smile. Few had ever heard the Inimitable refer to himself as "a mere novelist" and I was quite sure that he had not done so now. He was speaking of *other* "mere novelists." Myself, perhaps. I asked, "So what do you propose we do to find this Mr Drood, Charles? And what do we do with the gentleman once we've located him?"

"Do you remember when we investigated that haunted house?" asked the writer.

I did. Several years ago, Dickens—as head of his new magazine, *All the Year Round*, that had supplanted his former *Household Words* after a spat with his publishers—had become embroiled in debates with various spiritualists. The 1850s had been a mad time for table rapping, seances, mesmerism—some of which Dickens not only *did* believe in but in which he was an eager practitioner—and other such fascination with invisible energies. As much as Dickens believed in and relied upon mesmerism, sometimes called animal magnetism, and as superstitious as I knew him to be at heart (he truly believed that Friday was his lucky day, for instance), he had chosen (as editor of his new journal) to pick a quarrel with various spiritualists. When one of his adversaries in the debate, a spiritualist named William Howitt, was giving details of a haunted house in Cheshunt, near London, to prop up his arguments, Dickens immediately decided that we—the editors and managers of *All the Year Round*—should set up an expedition to investigate the hauntings.

W. H. Wills and I had gone ahead in a brougham, but Dickens and one of our contributors, John Hollingshead, walked the sixteen miles to the village. After some trouble finding the house in question (luckily Dickens had sent along a repast of fresh fish with Wills and me, since he would not trust the local fare), we finally found a villa that was said to be on the property of the so-called haunted house and spent the rest of our afternoon and evening questioning neighbours, nearby tradesmen, and even passers-by, but in the end we decided that Howitt's "ghosts" consisted of rats and a servant named Frank who enjoyed poaching rabbits in odd hours of the night.

Dickens had been brave enough on that outing, in the daylight and in the company of three other men, but I'd heard that on another ghost expedition, this one at night and investigating a reputedly haunted monument near Gad's Hill Place, the writer had brought his male servants and a loaded shotgun along. According to the author's youngest son, called Plorn by the family, his father had been quite nervous and had announced, "...if anybody is playing tricks and has got a head, I'll blow it off." And they *did* hear an unearthly wailing, moaning, "terrific noise—human noise—and yet superhuman noise."

It turned out to be an asthmatic sheep. Dickens restrained himself from blowing its head off. He treated everyone—servants and children all—to rum-and-water when they returned to the house.

"We knew where the haunted house was," I pointed out to Dickens this June day in his dark study. "How do we find Mr Drood? Where do we look, Charles?"

Suddenly Dickens's expression and physical stance changed. His face seemed to lengthen and crease and grow even paler. His eyes widened until it seemed he had no eyelids and the whites of those eyes glowed in the lamplight. His posture became that of a crooked old man, or a lurking gravedigger, or a buzzard. His voice, still raspy, became high and reedy and afflicted with a hiss as his long, pale fingers stabbed at the air like a dark magician's.

"To Limehoussse," he hissed, acting out the Drood in his former tale. "Whitechapel. Ratcliff Crossss. Gin Alley. Three Foxesss Court. Butcher Row and Commercial Road. The Mint and other rookeriessss."

I admit that the hair stood on the back of my neck. Charles Dickens was first, as a lad, even before he began to write, such a mimic that his father would take him to public houses to imitate locals they had encountered on their walks. At this moment I began to believe that there was such a creature as Drood.

"When?" I asked.

"Sssooooon," hissed Dickens, but smiling now, himself again. "We've taken such excursions into Babylon before, my dear Wilkie. We have seen the Great Oven at night."

We had. He had always been fascinated with this underbelly of our city. And "Babylon" and "the Great Oven" were the author's pet expressions for the worst slums in London. Some of my nocturnal ventures with Dickens into these dark lanes and tenement hovels in earlier years still bothered my dreams.

"I am your man, my dear Dickens," I said with enthusiasm. "I will report for duty tomorrow night, if that is your pleasure."

He shook his head. "I have to recover my voice, my dear Wilkie. I am behind schedule on the last numbers of *Our Mutual Friend*. There are other things to be seen to in the coming days, including the recovery of the Patient. Are you spending the night, sir? Your room is ready, as always."

"Alas, I cannot," I said. "I have to get back to the city this afternoon. There are business affairs there that must be attended." I did not tell Dickens that those "business affairs" consisted primarily of buying more laudanum, a substance which I could not do without, even then in 1865, for so long as a day.

"Very good," he said, rising. "Could you do me a great favour, my dear Wilkie?"

"Anything in the world, my dear Dickens," I said. "Command me, my friend."

Dickens glanced at his watch. "It's too late for you to catch the next train in from Gravesend, but if Charley gets the pony cart out, we can get you to Higham in time for the express to Charing Cross Station."

"I am going to Charing Cross?"

"You are, my dear Wilkie," he said, clasping me firmly on the shoulder as we came out of the gloom of his study into the brighter light of the entry hall. "I shall tell you why as I accompany you to the station."

. . .

GEORGINA DID NOT COME out of the house with us, but the Inimitable's oldest son, Charley, had come down to spend a few days with his father and was sent round to hitch up the basket cart. The front yard at Gad's Hill was as tidy as everything else under the man's control: Dickens's favourite flower, scarlet geraniums, planted in precise rows; the two large cedars of Lebanon just beyond the neatly trimmed lawn and now throwing their shadows to the east along the road.

Something about the rows of geraniums we were walking between as we approached Charley and the basket cart bothered me. In fact, they made my heart pound faster and my skin go cold. I became aware that Dickens had been talking to me.

"...I took him on the emergency train straight to Charing Cross Hotel immediately after the crash," he was saying. "I have paid two nurses to be with him so that he is not alone night or day. I would very much appreciate if you could look in on him this evening, my dear Wilkie, to give him my compliments and let him know that as soon as I am able to come into town again—most probably tomorrow—I will look in on him myself. If the nurses tell you that his injuries have worsened in any way, I would take it as a personal favour if you would send a messenger out to Gad's Hill with the information as soon as possible."

"Of course, Charles," I said. I dimly realised that he must have been talking about the young man he had helped extricate from the wreckage at Staplehurst and then had personally put up in the hotel at Charing Cross. A young man named Dickenson. Edmond or Edward Dickenson, I seemed to recall. A rather extraordinary coincidence when one thinks about it.

As we came down the drive and away from the scarlet geraniums, the sense of panic left me as quickly and curiously as it had arrived.

The cart was small but Dickens insisted on squeezing into it with Charley and me as the young man urged the pony out to Gravesend and then on to the Rochester Road towards Higham Station. We had enough time.

At first Dickens was at ease, chatting with me about small publishing details at *All the Year Round*, but as the pony and cart picked up speed, moving along with carriages on the road—the Higham Station almost within sight—I saw the writer's face, still sun darkened from his time in France, grow first paler and then the colour of lead. Beads of perspiration stood out on his temples and cheeks.

"Please slow down a bit, Charley. And cease swaying the cart from side to side. It is very distracting."

"Yes, Father." Charley pulled on the reins until the pony was no longer trotting.

I saw Dickens's lips become thinner and thinner until they were little more than a bloodless slash. "Slower, Charley. For heaven's sake, less speed."

"Yes, Father." Charley, in his twenties, looked as apprehensive as a boy when he glanced towards his father, who was now clutching the side of the basket cart with both hands and leaning unnecessarily to his right.

"Slower, please!" cried Dickens. The cart was now moving at a slow walking pace, certainly not at the steady four-miles-per-hour stride that Dickens could—and did—keep up for twelve and sixteen and twenty miles per day.

"We shall miss the train…" began Charley, glancing forward at the distant steeples and depot tower, then back to his watch.

"Stop! Let me out," commanded Dickens. His face was now as grey as the pony's tail. He staggered out of the cart and quickly shook my hand. "I shall walk back.

It is a nice day for walking. Have a safe trip and please do send a communication to me this evening if young Mr Dickenson needs anything at all."

"I shall, Charles. And I shall see you again soon."

My last sight of Dickens from the back seemed to be of a much older man, not striding with his usual confident and extraordinary pace at all, but almost feeling his way along the side of the road, leaning heavily on his walking cane as he headed back towards Gad's Hill.

CHAPTER THREE

*C*annibalism.

As I rode the train to Charing Cross Station I thought about that odd, barbaric word and reality—cannibalism—and how it had already affected Charles Dickens's life. (I had no idea at that time how terribly—and soon—it would affect mine.)

There had always been something in Charles Dickens's make-up that reacted especially strongly to the idea of cannibalism and of being consumed in any manner. During the time of his public separation from Catherine and the scandal that he had done the most to publicise and bring about—although he would never recognise that fact—the writer had said to me more than once, "They're eating me alive, Wilkie. My enemies, the Hogarths, and the misinformed public who wish to believe the worst are devouring me a limb at a time."

Many had been the time in the past decade when Dickens would invite me to join him on a trip to London's Zoological Gardens—a place in which he always took great delight—but as much as he loved the hippopotamus family and aviaries and lions' den, it was the reptile house feeding time that was the central purpose and destination for his visit. Dickens would not miss it and hurried me so that we would never be late. They fed the reptiles, most specifically the snakes, a diet of mice and larger rats and the spectacle seemed to mesmerise Dickens (who, a mesmerist himself, absolutely refused to allow anyone to mesmerise him). He would stand transfixed. Several times—riding somewhere together, waiting for a play to begin, even when sitting in his parlour at home—Dickens would remind me of how, frequently, two snakes would begin devouring the same rat at exactly the same time until the head and tail and hindquarters of the rodent were invisible in the snakes' gullets, while the struggling rat was still alive, hind and forelegs scrabbling in the air even as the powerful jaws advanced on them.

Only a few months before the Staplehurst accident, Dickens had confided in me that he was seeing the legs of furniture in his house—his bathtub, the serpentine table and chair legs in various rooms, even the heavy cords for the drapes—as snakes slowly consuming the tabletops and draperies and tub. "When I am not looking, the house is devouring itself, my dear Wilkie," he'd said to me over rum punch. He also told me that often at a banquet—most frequently a banquet in his honour—he would look down the long table and see his peers and friends and colleagues filling their faces with veal or mutton or chicken, and for a moment, just for a single, terrible second, he would imagine that the utensils lifted to those mouths were wriggling appendages. But not of mice or rats, he said—of men. He said that he found the frequent illusion . . . unsettling. •

But it was actual cannibalism—or at least the rumour of it—that had changed the course of Charles Dickens's life eleven years ago.

In October of 1854, all of England was shocked to read Dr John Rae's report on what he had discovered during his search for the missing Franklin Expedition.

If you have never heard of the Franklin Expedition, Dear Reader from my future century, I need to tell you only that it was an attempt by Sir John Franklin and 129 men in 1845 to explore the northern Arctic in two ships provided by the Royal Navy's Discovery Service—HMS *Erebus* and HMS *Terror*. They set sail in May of 1845. Their primary orders were to force the North-West Passage connecting the Atlantic and Pacific north of our colony in Canada—England was always dreaming of new and shorter trade routes to the Far East—and Franklin, an older man, was a seasoned explorer. There was every possible expectation of success. The two ships were last seen in Baffin Bay in the late summer of 1845. After three or four years of no word from the expedition, even the Royal Navy became concerned and various rescue expeditions were organised. But the two ships, to this day, have not been found.

Both Parliament and Lady Franklin offered huge rewards. Search parties, not just British but from America and other nations, crisscrossed the Arctic searching for Franklin and his men. Or at the very least for some sign of their fate. Lady Franklin was outspoken in her belief that her husband and the crews were still alive, and few in government or in the Navy wished to contradict her, even when so many Englishmen had given up all hope.

Dr John Rae was an officer in the Hudson Bay Company who had gone north by land and spent several seasons exploring remote northern islands (consisting, it is said, of little more than frozen gravel and endless blowing snow) and the vast stretches of ocean ice into which *Erebus* and *Terror* had disappeared. Unlike the Royal Navy or the majority of searchers, Rae had lived with the various Esquimaux savages in the region, learned their crude languages, and—in his report—quoted testimony from many of them. He had also returned to England with various artefacts—brass buttons, caps, ships' dishes bearing the crest of Sir John, writing instruments—that had belonged to Franklin or his men. Finally, Rae had discovered human remains, both in shallow graves and above ground, including two skeletons actually still seated in one of the ship's boats tied to a sledge.

What shocked England, beyond this terrible proof of Franklin's probable fate, was that according to the Esquimaux that Rae had interviewed, Franklin and his men had not only died but had resorted to cannibalism in their final days. The savages told Rae of coming across white men's camps where there were chewed bones, stacks of hacked-off limbs, and even tall boots with feet and leg bones still within.

This horrified Lady Franklin, of course, and she rejected the report in its entirety (even going so far as to hire another ship, out of her own dwindling fortune, to resume the search for her husband). Dickens also was appalled—and fascinated—by the idea.

He began publishing articles on the reported tragedy then in his journal, *Household Words,* as well as in other magazines. At first he was simply doubtful, stating that the report was *"hasty…in the statement that they had eaten the dead bodies of their companions."* Dickens told us that he had consulted "a wilderness of books"—although he cited no specific sources—to prove that *"the probabilities are all against poor Franklin's people having dreamed of eating the bodies of their companions."*

As the rest of the nation either began to believe in Rae's report (he did claim the government's reward for conclusive proof of Franklin's fate) or to forget, Dickens's denial turned to serious anger. In *Household Words* he launched a scathing attack on "the savage"—his phrase for all non-whites, but in this case the scheming, lying, untrustworthy Esquimaux whom John Rae had lived with and interviewed. Dickens in our time was, of course, considered a radical liberal, but those credentials were not impeached when he spoke for the majority of Englishmen and wrote—"...*we believe every savage to be in his heart covetous, treacherous, and cruel.*" It was simply impossible, he argued, that any of Sir John Franklin's men had *"prolonged their existence by the dreadful expedient of eating the bodies of their dead companions."*

Then our friend did a very strange thing. From the "wilderness of books" he had consulted to support his opinion, he chose *1001 Arabian Nights*—one of the most important books from his childhood, as he had told me several times—to prove his point. He wrote in summary—*"In the whole wide circle of the* Arabian Nights, *it is reserved for ghoules, gigantic blacks with one eye, monsters like towers of enormous bulk and dreadful aspect, and unclean animals lurking on the sea shore..."* to resort to eating human flesh, or cannibalism.

So there you have it. *Quod erat demonstrandum.*

IT WAS IN 1856 that Dickens took his campaign against the possibility of cannibalism amongst Sir John Franklin's noble men to a new level...and one which would intimately involve me.

While we were sojourning together in France—Dickens called me his "vicious friend" on such voyages and the time in Paris "our dangerous expeditions" (although while he enjoyed the night life and occasional conversations with young actresses, the writer never availed himself of the women of the night as I did there)—he came up with the idea that I write a play, to be performed at Dickens's home at Tavistock House. Specifically it was to be a play about a lost Arctic expedition such as Franklin's in which the Englishmen showed courage and valour. It also, he explained, had to be a story about love and sacrifice.

"Why don't you write it, Charles?" was my obvious response.

Well, he simply could not. He was beginning work on *Little Dorrit,* giving readings, putting out his magazine . . . I was to write it. He suggested the title *The Frozen Deep,* since the play would not only be about the northern wilderness, but about the secret depths of the human heart and soul. Dickens said that he would aid me with the scenario and "do the odd editorial chore," which I immediately understood to mean that the play would be his and I would just be the mechanism to put words on paper.

I agreed to do it.

We began work on it in Paris—or rather *I* began work on it while Dickens flitted in and out between dinners with friends, banquets, and other social occasions—and by the end of that hot summer of 1856 we were both at his home in London. Our habits, writerly and otherwise, did not always mesh. In France, I enjoyed the Casino until the early morning hours and Dickens insisted on breakfast between eight and nine. There were more than a few occasions where I had to breakfast alone on pâté de foi gras around noontime. Also, in both Tavistock House and later at Gad's Hill, Dickens's work hours were between nine AM and either two or three PM, and *everyone* in the house, family and guests alike, was expected to stay equally busy during that time. I have seen Dickens's daughters or Georgina pretend to read proof sheets while Dickens was locked away in his study. At that time—it was before the second Wilkie Collins had begun to fight me for my writing desk and instruments—I preferred working late at night, so I often would have to find a nook in the library in Dickens's home where I could smoke a cigar and nap in privacy during the day. And more than a few times Dickens would emerge unexpectedly from his study to roust me out of my hiding place and order me back to work.

My work—our work—on the play continued through the autumn of that year. I had conceived of a main character (to be played by Dickens, of course) named Richard Wardour—a sort of combination of what was known about the indomitable Sir John Franklin and his second-in-command, a rather common Irish fellow named Francis Crozier—and my idea was that the Wardour character would be older, perhaps not very competent (after all, the men on Franklin's Expedition had, apparently, all died), and a bit demented. Perhaps even somewhat of a villain.

Dickens completely rewrote this idea, changing Richard Wardour into a young, intelligent, complex, angry, but—in the end—totally self-sacrificing character. *"Perpetually seeking and never finding true affection"* was the phrasing in Dickens's voluminous notes on the re-creation of his character. He wrote many of the character's monologues by himself and actually kept them to himself until our final rehearsals (yes, I was one of the primary actors in the amateur production). When visiting or staying at his home, I would see Dickens starting out or ending his twenty-mile walks through the country fields of Finchley and Neasden, rehearsing his Wardour monologues in a booming voice—*"Young, with a fair sad face, with kind tender eyes, with a soft clear voice. Young and loving and merciful. I keep her face in my mind, though I can keep nothing else. I must wander, wander, wander—restless, sleepless, and homeless—till I find her!"*

With hindsight, it is easy to see the truth and depth of these sentiments in Charles Dickens that year when his marriage was ending (and ending by his own choice). The writer had spent his entire life waiting for and searching for that fair sad face with the kind tender eyes and soft clear voice. For Dickens, his imagination was always more real than the reality of daily life, and he had imagined this true, virginal, attentive, young, beautiful (and merciful) woman since his own youth.

My play premiered at Dickens's Tavistock House on 6 January, 1857—Twelfth Night, which Dickens always celebrated with some special programme, and his son Charley's twentieth birthday. The author had gone to great lengths to make the experience as professional as possible: having carpenters turn the schoolroom at his home into a theatre that could hold more than fifty people comfortably, ripping out a small stage that was already there and replacing it with a full-size one in the bay windows; having a musical score composed for the play and hiring an orchestra to perform it; hiring professionals to design and paint the elaborate scenic backdrops; spending a small fortune on costumes—he later bragged that we "polar explorers" in the production could walk straight from London to the North Pole in the authentic polar gear we were wearing; and, finally, supervising the theatrical gas lighting himself even while devising elaborate lighting effects that could simulate every hour of the odd polar day, evening, and sunlit Arctic night.

Dickens himself brought a strange, intense, underplayed yet incredibly powerful realism to his essentially melodramatic role. In one scene, in which several of us attempt to restrain "Wardour" from running in anguish from the stage, the author warned us that he meant to "fight in earnest" and that we would have to use all our resources to stop him. This, as it turned out, was an understatement. Several of us were bruised and battered even before we had finished with rehearsals. His son Charley later wrote to my brother—*"He went at it after a while with such a will that we really did have to fight, like prize-fighters, and as for me, being the leader of the attacking party and bearing the brunt of the fray, I was tossed in all directions and have been black and blue two or three times before the first night of the performance arrived."*

On opening night, our mutual friend John Forster read the prologue that Dickens had written at the last moment, attempting, as he so often did in his books, to be understood by all as he compared the hidden depths of the human heart to the terrible and frozen depths of the Arctic North—

> *that the secrets of the vast Profound*
> *Within us, an exploring hand may sound,*
> *Testing the region of the ice-bound soul,*
> *Seeking the passage at its northern pole,*
> *Soft'ning the horrors of its wintry deep,*
> *Melting the surface of that "Frozen Deep"*

THE TRAIN HAD COME into London, but I did not go on to Charing Cross. Not yet.

The bane of my life was—is, ever shall be—rheumatical gout. Sometimes it is in my leg. More often it moves to my head, frequently lodging like a hot iron spike behind my right eye. I deal with this constant pain (and it *is* constant) through strength of personality. And opium taken in the form of laudanum.

This day, before continuing with the errand on which Dickens had sent me, I took a cab from the station—I was too uncomfortable to walk farther—to a small chemist's shop around the corner from my home. The chemist there (as with certain others within the city and elsewhere) knew of my battle with this pain and sold me ameliorative medicine in quantities generally reserved for physicians, or—to be specific—laudanum by the jug.

I would venture the guess, Dear Reader, that laudanum is still used in your future day (unless medical science has come up with a common remedy even more efficacious), but in case it is not, let me describe the drug to you.

Laudanum is simply tincture of opium distilled in alcohol. Before I began buying it in large quantities, I would—following my physician and friend Frank Beard's advice—simply apply four drops of opium into a half- or full glass of red wine. Then it became eight drops. Then eight or ten drops twice a day with wine. Finally, I discovered that pre-mixed laudanum, as much opium as alcohol, it seems, was more effective on such unrelenting pain. In the past months I had begun what would become a lifelong habit of ingesting pure laudanum from a glass or from the jug itself. I confess that when I once drank such a full glass at home in front of the famous surgeon Sir William Fergusson—a person whom I certainly thought would understand the necessity for it—the doctor exclaimed that such an amount taken at once should have and could have killed everyone at the table. (I had eight male guests and one woman there that night.) After that incident, I have kept the amount of medicine of which I partake a secret, but not the fact of my general use of the blessed drug.

Please understand, Dear Reader of my posthumous future, that everyone in my day uses laudanum. Or almost everyone. My father, who distrusted all medicines, in his last days consumed huge quantities of Battley's Drops, a powerful form of opium. (And I am certain that the pain from my rheumatoid gout has been at least the equal, if not worse, than his deathbed pains.) I remember the poet Coleridge, a close friend of my parents, weeping at our home because of his dependency upon opium and I remember my mother's warnings to him. But also, as I have reminded the few friends who had the bad manners to become censorious about my own dependency on this important medicine, Sir Walter Scott used great quantities of laudanum while writing *The Bride of Lammermoor,* while such contemporaries of Dickens's and mine as our close friend Bulwer-Lytton and De Quincey used far greater quantities than I.

That afternoon I returned to my home—one of my two homes—at 9 Melcombe Place, off Dorset Square, knowing that Caroline and her daughter, Harriet, would be out, and secreted the new jug of laudanum, but not before drinking two full glasses of it.

Within minutes I was my real self again . . . or as close to my real self as I could be while such pain from rheumatoid gout still battered at the windows and scratched at the door of my corporeal self. At least the background noise of pain was diminished enough by the opiate so that I could concentrate again.

I took a carriage to Charing Cross.

THE FROZEN DEEP had been a great success.

The first act was set in Devon, where beautiful Clara Burnham—played by Dickens's more attractive daughter, Mary (known as Mamie)—is haunted by fears for her dashing fiancé, Frank Aldersley (played by me, in the earliest days of my current beard). Aldersley has been away on a polar expedition, sent, as Sir John Franklin's real-life expedition had been, to force the North-West Passage, and both ships—the HMS *Wanderer* and HMS *Sea-mew*—have not been sighted for more than two years. Clara knows that Frank's commander on the expedition is Captain Richard Wardour, whose proposal Clara has rejected. Wardour does not know the identity of the rival who succeeded him in Clara's love, but has sworn to kill the man on sight. My character, Frank Aldersley, is, in turn, totally ignorant of Richard Wardour's love for his fiancée.

Knowing that the two ships are almost certainly frozen in together somewhere in the Arctic ice, Clara is agonised at the thought that some accident will reveal her two lovers' identities to one another. So poor Clara is not only in terror of what the Arctic, its weather, beasts, and savages, may do to her beloved, but is in even greater terror of what Richard Wardour might do to her darling Frank should he discover the truth.

Clara's anxieties are not allayed when her nurse, Esther, who has the Second Sight, shares her bloody vision in the crimson Devon sunset. (As I mentioned earlier, Dickens went to great pains to create lighting effects in his little schoolroom theatre at Tavistock House that realistically depicted sunlight at all hours of the day.)

"I see the lamb in the grasp of the Lion..." gasps Nurse Esther in the trance of her Second Sight. "Your bonnie bird alone with the hawk—I see you and all around you crying...Bluid! The stain is on you—Oh, my bairn, my bairn—the stain of that bluid is on you!"

THE YOUNG MAN'S NAME was *Edmond* Dickenson.

Dickens had said that he'd provided a room at Charing Cross Hotel for the injured man, but in truth it was a large suite. An older and not-very-attractive nurse had set up her station in the outer sitting room and showed me in to the invalid.

From Dickens's description of the difficult extrication of young Dickenson from the wreckage, not to mention the author's melodramatic narration of blood, clothes torn away, and the young fellow's need for medical assistance, I expected to find a near-corpse swathed in bandages and rigidified with splints and casts elevated by cables and counterweights. But young Dickenson, although in pyjamas and a dressing-gown, was sitting up and reading in bed when I was shown in. The room's dresser and bedside tables were bedecked with flowers, including a vase of crimson geraniums that brought back some of the sense of panic I had felt in the yard at Gad's Hill Place.

Dickenson was a soft young man, perhaps twenty or twenty-one, with a round face, pink cheeks, sparse sandy hair that was already receding from his pink forehead, blue eyes, and ears as delicate as tiny seashells. His pyjamas looked to be made of silk.

I introduced myself, explained that I was Mr Dickens's envoy sent to enquire into the young gentleman's state of health, and was quite surprised when Dickenson blurted out, "Oh, Mr Collins! I am deeply honoured to have such a famous writer visit me! I so greatly enjoyed your *The Woman in White* that was serialised in *All the Year Round* immediately after Mr Dickens's *A Tale of Two Cities* ended."

"I thank you, sir," I said, almost colouring at the compliment. It is true that *The Woman in White* had been a huge success, selling more copies of the magazine than most of Dickens's serialised tales. "I am very pleased that you enjoyed my modest efforts," I added.

"Oh, yes, it was wonderful," said young Dickenson. "You are *so fortunate* to have someone like Mr Dickens as your mentor and editor."

I stared at the young man for a long moment, but my stony silence went unnoticed as Dickenson babbled on about the Staplehurst crash, the awfulness of it all, and then about Charles Dickens's incredible courage and generosity. "I would not, I am sure, be alive today if it had not been for Mr Dickens finding me in the wreckage—I was quite hanging upside down and found it all but impossible to breathe, Mr Collins!— and he never left me until he'd summoned guards to help pull me from the terrible wreckage and super-vised their carrying me up to the railbed where the injured were being prepared for evacuation. Mr Dickens stayed by my side during the ride to London on the emergency train that afternoon and—as you see!—insisted on putting me up in this wonderful room and providing nursing until I shall be fully recovered."

"You are not seriously injured?" I enquired in a per-fectly flat tone.

"Oh, no, not at all! Merely bruised all black and blue around the legs and hips and left arm and chest and back. I could not walk three days ago after the accident, but today the nurse helped me to the toilet and back and it was a completely successful expedition!"

"I am so glad," I said.

"I expect to go home tomorrow," burbled the young man. "I shall never be able to repay Mr Dickens for his generosity. He truly saved my life! And he has invited me to his home at Gad's Hill for Christmas and New Year's!"

It was 12 June. "How wonderful," I said. "I am sure that Charles appreciates the value of the life he helped save. You say you go home tomorrow, Mr Dickenson... may I enquire as to where that home is?"

Dickenson babbled on. It seemed he was an orphan— Charles Dickens's favourite sort of human being, if one is to believe *Oliver Twist* or *David Copperfield* or *Bleak House* or any of a dozen other of his tales—but had been left money in a Jarndyce-and-Jarndyce manner of labyrinthine inheritance, and had been appointed an elderly Guardian who lived in a Northamptonshire estate that might well have been the model for Chesney Wold. Young Dickenson, however, preferred to live in modest rented rooms in London, where he lived alone, had few (if any) friends, and studied the occasional instrument and apprenticed for the occasional profession, with no real intention of mastering or practising in any of them. The interest on his inheritance allowed him to purchase food and books and theatre tickets and the occasional holiday to the seashore—his time was his own.

We discussed theatre and literature. It turned out that young Mr Dickenson, a subscriber to Dickens's previous journal *Household Words* as well as to the current *All the Year Round,* had read and admired my story "A Terribly Strange Bed" that had appeared in the former magazine.

"Good heavens, man," I exclaimed. "That was published almost fifteen years ago! You must have been all of five years old!"

Young Dickenson's blush began in his shell-like ears, migrated quickly to his cheeks, and rose like pink climbing ivy through the vault of his temples to the long curve of his pale forehead. I could see the blush spreading even under his thinning, straw-coloured hair. "Seven years old, actually, sir," said the orphan. "But my Guardian, Mr Watson—a very liberal M.P.—had leather-bound copies of both *Punch* and such journals as *Household Words* in his library. My current devotion to the written word was formed and confirmed in that room."

"Really," I said. "How interesting."

My joining the staff of *Household Words* years earlier had meant another five pounds a week to me. It seems to have meant the world to this orphan. He could almost recite my book *After Dark* from memory and was dutifully amazed when I told him that the separate tales which formed the volume had been based in large part upon my mother's diaries and a more formal manuscript in which she had reminisced about being the wife of a famous painter.

It turned out that the eleven-year-old Edmond Dickenson had travelled up to Manchester with his Guardian to see *The Frozen Deep* in the huge New Free Trade Hall there on 21 August, 1857.

ACT II OF *THE FROZEN DEEP* is set in the Arctic regions where Dickens-Wardour and Wardour's second-in-command, Lieutenant Commander Crayford, are discussing their slim chances of survival in the face of cold and starvation.

"Never give in to your stomach, and your stomach will end in giving in to you," the veteran explorer advises Crayford. Such determination—a will that would accept no master—came not only from the pen of Charles Dickens, but from his very soul.

Wardour goes on to explain that he loves the Arctic wastes precisely "because there are no women here." In the same act he exclaims—"I would have accepted anything that set work and hardship and danger, like Ramparts, between my misery and me…Hard work, Crayford, that is the true Elixir of our life!" And finally, "…the hopeless wretchedness in this world, is the wretchedness that women cause."

It was, nominally, my play. My name was listed on the playbill as author (as well as my listing there as an actor), but almost all of Richard Wardour's lines had been written or rewritten by Charles Dickens.

These were not the words of a man happy in his marriage.

At the end of Act II, two men are sent out across the

ice as the trapped crews' last chance for rescue. These men must cross a thousand miles of the frozen deep. The two men, of course, are Richard Wardour and his successful rival for Clara Burnham's hand, Frank Aldersley. (Perhaps I have already mentioned that Dickens and I both grew beards for our roles.) The second act ends with Wardour discovering that the injured, starved, weakened Aldersley is his worst enemy, the man he swore to murder on sight.

DID YOU HAPPEN TO SEE the gentleman named Drood at the accident site?" I asked Edmond Dickenson when the young fool finally stopped talking and the nurse was out of the room.

"A gentleman named Drood, sir? In faith, I am not sure. There were so many gentlemen there helping me, and—other than our wonderful Mr Dickens—I learned so few of their names."

"It seems this gentleman has a rather memorable appearance," I said and listed some specifics of Dickens's description of our Phantom: the black silk cape and top hat, the missing fingers and eyelids and attenuated nose, the pallor and baldness and brittle fringe of hair, the terrible stare, his odd way of seeming to glide rather than walk, the sibilant hiss and foreign accent in his speech.

"Oh, good heavens, no," cried young Dickenson. "I surely would have remembered seeing or hearing such a man." Then his gaze seemed to turn inward, much as Dickens's had several times in his darkened study. "Even in spite of the incredibly terrible sights and sounds everywhere around me that day," he added.

"Yes, I am sure," I said, resisting the impulse to tap the bedclothes above his bruised leg in a minor show of sympathy. "So you've never heard the name Drood or heard others talking about him...on the train that day, perhaps?"

"Not to my knowledge, Mr Collins," said the young man. "Is it of some importance to Mr Dickens to find the man? I would do *anything* for Mr Dickens, if it were in my power."

"Yes, I am sure you would, Mr Dickenson," I said. This time I did tap at his knee under the blankets. "Mr Dickens specifically charged me with asking you if there were any additional service that he might offer," I said and checked my watch. "Any want or lack or pain that the nurses or our mutual friend might remedy?"

"Nothing at all," said Dickenson. "Tomorrow I should be able to walk well enough to leave this hotel and begin living on my own again. I do have a cat, you know." He laughed softly. "Or rather, she has me. Although, as is the nature of so many of her species, she comes and goes at will, hunts for her own meals, and certainly will not be inconvenienced by my absence." Again there came that sense of his gaze turning inward, staring at the death and dying at Staplehurst just three days earlier. "Actually, Pussy would not be unduly inconvenienced had I died. No one would have missed me."

"Your guardian?" I prompted, not wishing to bring on a torrent of self-pity.

Dickenson laughed easily. "My current Guardian, a gentleman of the law who had known my grandfather, would have mourned my passing, Mr Collins, but our...relationship...is more of a *business* nature. Pussy is about the only friend I have in London. Or elsewhere."

I nodded briskly. "I shall check on you again in the morning, Mr Dickenson."

"Oh, but there is no need..."

"Our mutual friend Charles Dickens feels otherwise," I said quickly. "And, his health permitting, he may come tomorrow to see you and enquire in person about your recovery."

The boy blushed again. It was not unbecoming, although it did make him somehow appear all the softer and sillier in the late-afternoon June sunlight filtering in through the hotel drapes and curtains.

Nodding and fetching my walking stick, I left young Edmond Dickenson and went out through the sitting room past the silent nurse.

ACT III OF *THE FROZEN DEEP* opens with Clara Burnham travelling to Newfoundland to search for news (much as the real Lady Franklin had hired her own ships and gone to the Far North with her niece Sophia Cracroft in search of her husband, Sir John). Into a remote ice cavern along that coast staggers a starved, exhausted man just escaped from the frozen sea. Clara sees that it is Wardour, and there are hysterical accusations that he has murdered—and perhaps eaten? the audience wonders—her fiancé, Frank Aldersley. Wardour—Dickens—rushes out and returns with Aldersley—me, in ragged clothes that left me more naked than not—in his arms and alive. *"Often,"* gasps Wardour, *"in supporting Aldersley through snow-drifts and ice-floes, have I been tempted to leave him sleeping."*

Delivering that line, Dickens...Richard Wardour... collapses, his exertions, starvation, and exhaustion from keeping his rival alive on the ice for so long finally catching up to him. Wardour manages to say, *"My sister, Clara!—Kiss me, sister, kiss me before I die!"* He then dies in Clara's arms with Clara's kiss upon his cheek and Clara's tears streaming down his face.

At our dress rehearsal, I was tempted to vomit on stage. But during all four performances at Tavistock House, I found myself weeping and heard myself whispering, "This is an awful thing." You may, Dear Reader, interpret that in any way you wish.

Dickens's performances were powerful and ... strange. William Makepeace Thackeray, one of our attendees the night of the first performance, later remarked of Dickens—"If that man would now go upon the stage, he would make his £20,000 a year."

This was wild hyperbole in 1857, but by the time of the Staplehurst accident, Dickens was making almost that much through his "acting" in his reading tours in the United States and throughout England.

The audiences blubbered like children during the four performances of *The Frozen Deep* at Tavistock House. Professional reviewers whom Dickens had invited to the opening nights professed to be deeply impressed by Dickens's performance and his strange immersion in the role of Richard Wardour. Indeed, it was the author's terrible intensity—a sort of dark energy which filled the room and swept all viewers and listeners into its vortex— that *everyone* remarked upon.

Dickens was depressed after the last performance of *The Frozen Deep*. He wrote to me of the "sad sounds" of the workmen "battering and smashing down" his schoolroom theatre.

There was a clamour for Dickens to stage more performances of my play; many urged him to do so for profit. It was rumoured, correctly it turned out, that the Queen herself wanted to attend a performance. But Dickens resisted all such suggestions. None of us in the amateur production wished to be mere performers for money. But in June of that year, 1857, that fateful year in which Dickens's domestic life would change forever, the writer was shocked to hear of the death of our mutual friend Douglas Jerrold.

Dickens told me that just a few nights before the other author's death, the Inimitable had dreamt that

Jerrold had given him copy to edit but Dickens could not make sense of the words. This is every writer's nightmare—the sudden breakdown of meaning in the language that sustains and supports us—but Dickens found it interesting that he had dreamt it just as Jerrold was, unbeknownst to any of us, on his deathbed.

Knowing that Jerrold's family would be left in dire financial circumstances (Douglas was much more the reformer radical than Dickens, despite his posturing, would ever be), Dickens came up with the idea for a series of benefit performances: T. P. Cooke in revivals of Jerrold's two plays, *Black Eyed Susan* and *Rent Day;* Thackeray and the war correspondent William Howard Russell giving lectures; and Dickens himself doing afternoon and night readings.

And, of course, a return of *The Frozen Deep.*

Dickens's goal was to raise £2,000 for Jerrold's family.

The Gallery of Illustration on Regent Street was rented for the series of performances. The Queen—always careful not to appear at a benefit for a single charity—not only gave her name in support of this effort, but sent word that she was intensely eager to see *The Frozen Deep* and suggested that Mr Dickens select a room in Buckingham Palace in which he could provide a private performance for Her Majesty and her guests.

Dickens refused. His reasons were clear enough: his daughters, who appeared in the play, had never been introduced at Court and he did not want their first appearance before the Queen at the palace to be as actresses. He proposed that Her Majesty should come to a private performance at the Gallery of Illustration a week before subscription night and that she should bring her own gallery of guests. Faced with the iron will of the Indomitable, the Queen agreed.

We performed before her on 4 July, 1857. Her Majesty's guests included Prince Albert, the king of Belgium, and the prince of Prussia. It was especially in honour of Prince Albert that Dickens had directed the entrance and stairs to be decked with flowers. Some of us, I confess, were apprehensive that such a royal audience might not react with the passions of those who had been our audience at Tavistock House the previous winter, but Dickens assured us that the Queen and her guests would laugh at the funny parts, weep at the sad parts, blow their noses exactly when our more common audiences had, and that—during the farce called *Uncle John* presented after *The Frozen Deep*—some of the royalty would bray like donkeys. He was, as usual, correct on all counts.

After our performance, the delighted Queen invited Dickens to come forth to accept her thanks.

He refused.

The reason he sent this time—"I could not appear before Her Majesty tired and hot, with the paint still upon my face."

Actually, of course, it was more than the actors' paint that kept Dickens from allowing himself to be presented to Her Majesty and her guests. You see, our romantic farce of *Uncle John* had left Dickens in his Uncle John costume of a floppy dressing gown, a silly wig, and a red nose. There was no way on earth that Charles Dickens, one of the proudest and most self-conscious men who ever lived, was going to allow himself to be introduced to Queen Victoria in that regalia.

Once again, the Queen politely gave way.

We offered two more performances of *The Frozen Deep* at the Gallery of Illustration, but though the play once again met with wild enthusiasm and ecstatic reviews from everyone who attended and its receipts accounted for the vast majority of the money raised for the Jerrold family fund, we still fell short of the £2,000 goal.

John Dean, manager of the Great Manchester Art Exhibition, had been pressing Dickens to perform *The Frozen Deep* at that city's New Free Trade Hall, and—unwilling to end up with anything less than the full £2,000 he had promised the Jerrolds—Dickens immediately went up to Manchester to do a reading of *A Christmas Carol* there and to inspect the hall, which could easily hold two thousand people.

He decided at once that it would be a perfect venue for the play but that it was simply too large for the meagre acting skills of his daughters and sister-in-law Georgina, all of whom had central roles. (It never occurred to Charles Dickens that *he* might not be up to the professional requirements of such a huge hall and such large audiences. Dickens knew from experience that he could master crowds of three thousand and more with his magnetic influence.)

He would need to hire and rehearse some professional actresses. (Mark Lemon, Dickens's son Charley, and I were allowed to stay in the troupe, but the Inimitable began rehearsing us all as if we had never performed the play before.)

Alfred Wigan, manager of the Olympic Theatre, suggested to Dickens two promising young actresses whom he had recently hired for his theatre—Fanny and Maria Ternan—and with Dickens's rapid approval (he and I had already seen both of these Ternan girls, their younger sister, and veteran-actress mother perform in other plays), Wigan approached them to see if they would be interested in appearing in *The Frozen Deep*. They were eager to do so.

Wigan then suggested to Dickens that he might also consider the young women's mother, Frances Eleanor Ternan, as well as the youngest and least impressive member of the acting family—just eighteen—a certain Ellen Lawless Ternan.

And thus Charles Dickens's life changed forever.

AFTER LEAVING THE CHARING CROSS HOTEL I took a hackney cab part of the way home and decided to walk the rest of the way, stopping for supper at a club to which I did not then belong but at which I had guest privileges.

I was angry. That impertinent young Dickenson whelp with his "You are *so fortunate* to have someone like Mr Dickens as your mentor and editor . . ." had put me in a foul mood.

When, five years earlier in late summer of 1860, my novel *The Woman in White* had begun appearing in *All the Year Round* the week that Dickens's *A Tale of Two Cities* concluded (and I should note to you, Dear Reader, that Dickens's character of Sydney Carton had been taken most liberally from *my* selfless and self-sacrificing character of Richard Wardour in *The Frozen Deep*—why, Dickens even said as much, allowing that the Carton character and idea of *Tale of Two Cities* had come to him during the last performance of *The Frozen Deep* while he lay on the floorboards with Maria Ternan's—the new Clara Burnham—real tears soaking his face and beard and ragged clothes, to the point that he had to whisper to her—"My dear child, it will be over in two minutes. Pray compose yourself!") . . .

Where was I?

Oh, yes, when *The Woman in White* appeared in eight-months' serialisation in Dickens's new weekly magazine—and appearing to tremendous interest and acclaim, I might modestly add—there was much idle chatter and some small written comment to the effect that I, Wilkie Collins, had learned my craft from Charles

Dickens and honed my skills under the tutelage of Charles Dickens and had even borrowed my narrative styles from Charles Dickens. It was said that I lacked Dickens's depths and whispered in certain quarters that I was "incapable of character-painting."

This, of course, was pure nonsense.

Dickens himself had written me a note after first reading my manuscript in which he said that it was *"a great advance on all your former writing, and most especially in respect of tenderness…in character it is excellent.… No one else could have done it half so well. I have stopped in every chapter to notice some instance of ingenuity, or some happy turn of writing."*

But then, of course, Dickens…being Dickens… ruined the effect by adding that he must *"always contest your disposition to give an audience credit for nothing, which necessarily involves the forcing of points on their attention."*

One might have responded that Charles Dickens invariably gave his audiences credit for too much and, through his self-indulgent flights of impenetrable fantasy and unnecessary subtlety, left far too many ordinary readers lost in the thick forest of Dickensian prose.

To be honest with you, Dear Reader who lives and breathes in such a remote branch of my future that no hint of my candour could possibly get back to anyone who loved Charles Dickens, I am…was…almost certainly always shall be…ten times the architect of plot that Charles Dickens ever was. For Dickens, plot was something that might incidentally grow from his marionette-machinations of bizarre characters; should his weekly sales begin slipping in one of his innumerable serialised tales, he would just march in more silly characters and have them strut and perform for the gullible reader, as easily as he banished poor Martin

Chuzzlewit to the United States to pump up his (Dickens's) readership.

My plots are subtle in ways that Charles Dickens could never fully perceive, much less manage in his own obvious (to any discerning reader) meandering machinations of haphazard plotting and self-indulgent asides.

Impudent and ignorant people, such as this orphanwhelp Edmond Dickenson, were always saying that I was constantly "learning from Charles Dickens," but the truth is quite the opposite. Dickens himself admitted, as I have mentioned earlier, that his idea for self-sacrificing Sydney Carton in *A Tale of Two Cities* had come from my character of Richard Wardour in *The Frozen Deep*. And what was his "old woman in white" in *Great Expectations,* the much-ballyhooed Miss Haversham, if not a direct steal from my central character in *The Woman in White*?

I SETTLED DOWN to my solitary meal. I enjoyed coming to this club because of how the chef here prepared lark pudding, which I considered one of the four great works produced by my present age. Tonight I decided to dine relatively lightly and ordered two types of pâté, soup, some sweet lobsters, a bottle of dry champagne, a leg of mutton stuffed with oysters and minced onions, two orders of asparagus, some braised beef, a bit of dressed crab, and a side of eggs.

While enjoying this modest repast at my leisure, I recalled that one of the few things I had ever liked about Dickens's wife was her cooking—or at least the cooking she oversaw at Tavistock House, since I had never seen the woman actually don an apron or lift a ladle. Years ago Catherine Dickens had (under the name Lady Maria Clutterbuck) brought out a volume of recipes, based on what she served regularly at their home at

Devonshire Terrace, in a book called *What Shall We Have for Dinner?* Most of her choices were to my liking—and many were visible on my table here this evening, although not in such plentitude or with an equal glory of gravies (I consider most cooking as simply a prelude to gravies)—as her tastes had also run towards lobsters, large legs of mutton, heavy beefs, and elaborate desserts. There were so many variations of toasted cheese in Catherine's volume of recipes that one reviewer commented—*"No man could possibly survive the consumption of such frequent toasted cheese."*

But Dickens had. And had never put on a pound over the years. Of course, it is possible that his habit of briskly walking twelve to twenty miles a day might have something to do with that. I am, myself, of a more sedentary nature. My inclinations, as well as my chronic illness, keep me close to my desk and couch and bed. I walk when I must but recline when I can. (It was a ritual of mine, when spending time at Tavistock House or Gad's Hill Place, to hide in the library or some empty guest room until two PM or three PM—whenever Dickens finished his writing labours and came hunting for someone to go on one of his confounded forced marches with him. Of course, it was a ritual of Dickens's to seek me out—often tracking me by the smell of my cigar smoke, I realise now—so I was often good for a mile or two of Dickens's long walks, which would be less than twenty minutes or so at his impossible pace.)

This night, I could not decide between two desserts, so—Solomon-like—I chose both the lark pudding and the well-cooked apple pudding. And a bottle of port. And coffees.

While finishing my pudding I noticed a tall, aristocratic, but very old man rising from a chair across the room and for an instant thought it was Thackeray. Then

I remembered that Thackeray had died on Christmas Eve of 1863, almost a year and a half ago.

I had been in this very club, a guest of Dickens, when the older writer and the Inimitable had reconciled after several years of cold silence. That breach had begun during the height of the madness surrounding Dickens's separation from Catherine, when he was most vulnerable. Someone at the Garrick Club had mentioned that Dickens was having an affair with his sister-in-law, and Thackeray, evidently without thinking, had said something to the effect—"No, it is with an actress."

Word got back to Dickens, of course. It always did. Then a young journalist friend of Dickens's, part of his "squad" as it was said then, a certain Edmund Yates (who, like Iago, always had a lean and hungry look, I thought), had written a truly unpleasant and dismissive profile of Thackeray in *Town Talk*. Deeply stung, the old gentleman-writer noted that both he and Yates were members of the Garrick and asked the club to expel the younger man on the grounds that his conduct in writing such a piece had been "intolerable in the society of gentlemen."

In an astounding act of insensitivity towards his old friend Thackeray, Dickens had taken the young man's part in the dispute and then resigned from the Garrick himself when the membership committee had agreed with Thackeray and expelled the journalist.

So it was here in the Athenaeum Club, years later, that the breach was finally healed. I had heard Dickens describe the reconciliation to Wills. "There I was hanging up my hat in the Athenaeum," he said, "when I looked up and saw Thackeray's haggard face. The man looked like a ghost, Wills. He looked as dead as Marley and lacked only the chains. So I said to him, 'Thackeray, have you been ill?' And we struck up a conversation after the years of silence and shook hands and all now is as it was before."

This is very touching. It is also very false.

I happened to have been in the Athenaeum that night, and both Dickens and I saw Thackeray trying to struggle into his coat. The old gentleman was speaking to two other members. Dickens, coming in, passed close by the old writer without giving him a glance. I was putting away my stick and hat and Dickens had already passed Thackeray and had his foot on the stair when the older author chased after Dickens, catching him on the stairway. I heard Thackeray speak first and then hold out his hand to Dickens. They shook hands. Then Dickens went into the dining room and I watched Thackeray return to his interlocutor—I believe it was Sir Theodore Martin—and I heard him say, "I am glad I have done this."

Charles Dickens was a kind and frequently sentimental man, but he was never the first to mend a quarrel. A fact that I would be reminded of soon enough.

As I TOOK A CAB HOME, I thought about Dickens's queer plan to seek out this phantom named Drood.

As I was listening to Dickens tell his story of the Staplehurst disaster that morning, I had gone through shifting opinions on the veracity of the "Mr Drood" commentary. Charles Dickens was not a liar. But Charles Dickens was also always convinced of the veracity and truth of whatever position he took on any subject and—through his telling, but especially through his own writing—he would always convince *himself* that something was true, simply because he said it was, even when it was not. His various public letters blaming his wife, *Catherine,* for the separation eight years earlier, a separation that was obviously *his* idea, *his* need, and *his* instigation, is a perfect example of this phenomenon.

But why invent this Drood character?

Then again, why tell everyone that *he*, Dickens, had taken the initiative to settle his long breach with Thackeray when it had been the older writer's move to do so?

The difference is that Charles Dickens's lies and exaggerations, while perhaps not told deliberately—speaking as a novelist myself, I know that members of our profession live in our imaginations as much or more as we inhabit what people call "the real world"—were almost always promulgated in order to make *Charles Dickens* look better.

By all objective accounts, including that of the pudgy little homunculus Edmond Dickenson—may his bruises fester and rot and turn to cankers—Dickens had been *the* hero of the Staplehurst railway disaster. Adding a phantasm such as Drood to the telling did nothing to increase the Inimitable's heroism in the telling. Indeed, Dickens's obvious anxiety in describing the odd, almost inhuman man detracted from the Dickensian aura of heroism.

So what was all this about?

I had to assume that there *had* been a very strange personage named Drood at the wreck site and that something very close to their brief conversation and bizarre interactions as Dickens had described them *had* occurred.

But why try to find the man? Agreed, there was a certain mystery in such an odd figure, but London and England and even our railways were full of odd figures. (Even that impertinent mayfly young Mr Dickenson seemed a character out of a Dickens novel—orphaned, with his rich Guardian and Chancery-endowed fortune, listless, aimless, given only to reading and lazing about. What extra stretch was there to believe in a "Mr Drood" with his leprous appearance, missing fingers and eyelids, and lisping utterances?)

But again, I wondered as I approached my street, why try to find this Drood?

Charles Dickens was a man given to much planning and careful premeditation, but he was also a creature of impulses. During his first tour of the United States, he had alienated the majority of his audiences and almost *all* of the American newspapers and journals with his insistence on the creation of an International Copyright. The fact that Dickens's fiction—and most English authors' fiction—was being blatantly stolen and published in America with no recompense whatsoever to its author evidently seemed only right and fair to the upstart Americans, so Dickens's anger was justified. But, shortly after the tour—after the damage was done between Dickens and his original adoring audiences there—Dickens simply lost interest in the Copyright. He was, in other words, a careful man with careless impulses.

At Gad's Hill Place or his earlier homes, or on any voyage or outing, it was invariably Charles Dickens who decided on the destinations for outings, who decided on the location of picnics, and who decided on the games to be played, who decided who the captains would be, and—most frequently—it was Dickens who kept score, announced the winners, and awarded the prizes. The occupants of the village nearest to Gad's Hill Place even treated him rather like a squire, obviously honoured to have the famous author hand out awards at fairs and competitions.

Dickens had always been the boy who led the other boys in play. He never doubted that this was his role in life and he never relinquished that role as an adult.

But what game would we be pursuing if Dickens and I actually sought out this Mr Drood figure? What purpose would it serve other than to gratify yet another boyish impulse of Charles Dickens's? And what dangers would be involved? The neighbourhoods that Drood had allegedly mentioned to Dickens as they descended the railway grade to the carnage below were anything but safe areas of London. They were indeed, as Dickens called them—the Great Oven.

I WAS IN GREAT PAIN from the rheumatical gout as I arrived home.

The light from the street gas lamps hurt my eyes. My own footfalls struck my brain like chisel blows. The rumble of a passing waggon made my entire body twitch with pain. I was trembling. A sudden, bitter taste of coffee filled my mouth—not an echo of the coffee I had enjoyed with dessert, but something far more vile. There was a confusion in my mind and a nauseating sickness permeating my body.

Our new home was at Melcombe Place; we had moved from Harley Street a year earlier, partly because of the greater income and literary position that *The Woman in White* had afforded me. (For my next novel, *No Name,* I received more than £3,000 for book publication and a guaranteed £4,500 if British or American serialisation was included.)

When I say "our" or "we" I refer to the woman I had been living with for some years, a certain Caroline G—— and her then fourteen-year-old daughter, Harriet, whom we often called Carrie. (There was a rumour that Caroline was my model for *The Woman in White*— and it is true that I had encountered her running away from a blackguard in the night outside a villa in Regents Park and, running after her, later rescued her from the streets much as was the case with the character in my novel—but I had conceived the idea for *The Woman in White* long before I met Caroline.)

But Caroline and Harriet were away this week, visiting

a cousin in Dover, and—with our two real servants also gone this night (I admit to listing Caroline's daughter as a "maid-servant" on our annual tax role census at this time)—I had the house to myself. It was true that not too many miles from this home was another house with another woman in it—a certain Martha R——, a former hotel servant in Yarmouth, now visiting London for the first time and with whom I also hoped to live in a comfortable domestic circumstance in the future, but I had no intention of visiting Martha tonight or any time soon. I hurt too much.

The house was dark. I found the jar of laudanum where I kept it in a locked cupboard and drank two glasses, then sat at the servants' table in the kitchen for several minutes, waiting for the worst of the pain to pass.

The physik soon did its work. I felt renewed, re-energised, and deciding that I would go up to my study on the first floor and write for an hour or two before turning in, I went up the closest stairway.

The back stairway, the servants' stairway, was very steep and the flickering gaslight at the first-storey landing worked poorly, casting but the smallest circle of doubtful light, leaving the rest of the stairs in deepest darkness.

Something moved in that darkness above me.

"Caroline?" I called, knowing that it would not be she. Nor would it be one of the servants. Our maid-servant's father had come down with pneumonia and they were in Wales.

"Caroline?" I called again, expecting—and receiving—no answer.

The noise, obvious now as a silk dress rustling, descended the dark stairway from the attic above. I could hear the careful placement of small bare feet in the darkness there.

I fumbled with the light on the wall, but the uncertain jet only flared and faded again, returning to its low flickering.

She stepped into the distant perimeter of ebbing and flowing light then, a mere three steps above me. She looked as she always did—wearing an aged green silk dress with a high bodice. On the dark green silk were tiny gold *fleurs-de-lis* that descended in constellations to her black-banded waist.

Her hair was drawn up in a bun from a previous era. Her skin was green—the green of very old cheese or of a moderately decomposed corpse. Her eyes were solid pools of black ink that glistened moistly in the lamplight. Her teeth—when her mouth opened as it did now as if to greet me—were long and yellow and curved like tusks.

I had no illusions as to her purpose on the stairs. She wished to grab me and fling me down the long flight of steps. She preferred this back stairway to the wider, brighter, less dangerous front steps. She took two more steps down towards me, her yellow smile widening.

Moving quickly but not in fear or great haste, I flung open the servants' door to the first-storey landing, stepped through, and closed and locked the door behind me. I heard no breathing through the door—she did not breathe—but there was the faintest of scramblings at the wood, and the porcelain knob turned slightly and then shifted back.

I lighted all the lamps on the first storey. There was no one else here.

Breathing deeply, I undid my pin and collar and went into my study to write.

CHAPTER FOUR

*T*hree weeks passed and according to my brother, Charley (who, with his wife, Kate, Dickens's daughter, was staying at Gad's Hill Place), the author was slowly recovering from his terrible ordeal. He was working every day on *Our Mutual Friend*, meeting people for dinner, frequently disappearing—almost certainly to call on Ellen Ternan—and even performing readings for select groups. A reading by Charles Dickens was the most exhausting performance I have ever witnessed, and the fact that he was up to it, even if he collapsed afterwards, as Charley reported he frequently did, suggested the reservoirs of energy remaining in the man. It still bothered him to ride in a train but, Dickens being Dickens, he forced himself to travel into town by rail almost daily for precisely that reason. Charley reported that when there was the slightest vibration in the carriage, Dickens's face would turn grey as flannel and great beads of sweat would pop out on the writer's forehead and furrowed cheeks and he would fiercely grip the seat ahead of him, but with a sip of brandy he soldiered on, refusing to show any other sign of his inner turmoil. I was sure that the Inimitable had forgotten all about Drood.

But then, in July, the hunt for the phantom began in earnest.

This was the hottest, most feverish time of the hot,

feverish summer. The excrement of three million Londoners stank in open sewers, including that greatest of our open sewers (despite this year's engineering attempt to open an elaborate system of underground sewers)—the Thames. Tens of thousands of Londoners slept on their porches or balconies just waiting for rain. But when the rain fell, it was like a hot shower bath, simply adding a layer of wetness to the heat. July lay over London this summer like a heavy, wet layer of decomposing flesh.

Twenty thousand tons of horse manure *per day* were gathered from the reeking streets and dumped in what we politely and euphemistically called "dust heaps"—huge piles of feces that rose near the mouth of the Thames like an English Himalaya.

The overcrowded cemeteries around London also stank to high heaven. Grave diggers had to leap up and down on new corpses, often sinking to their hips in rotting flesh, just to force the reluctant new residents down into their shallow graves, these new corpses joining the solid humus of festering and overcrowded layers of rotting bodies below. In July, one knew immediately when one was within six city blocks of a cemetery—the reeking miasma drove people out of surrounding homes and tenements—and there was *always* a cemetery nearby. The dead were always beneath our feet and in our nostrils.

Many dead bodies lay uncollected in the poorest streets of this Great Oven, decomposing next to the rotting garbage that also was never picked up. Not just trickles and rivulets but actual rivers of raw sewage flowed down these streets past and through the garbage and dead bodies, sometimes finding a sewer opening but more often simply accumulating in puddles and ponds that mottled the cobblestones. This brown water flowed into basements, accumulated in cellars, contaminated wells, and always ended up—sooner or later—in the Thames.

Shops and industry shovelled out tons of hides, flesh,

boiled bones, horse meat, catgut, cow hooves and heads and guts, and other organic detritus every day. It all went to the Thames or was stacked up in giant piles along the banks of the Thames, *waiting* to go into the water. Shops and homes along the river sealed their windows and soaked their blinds with chloride, and the city officials dumped ton after ton of lime into the Thames. Pedestrians walked with perfume-soaked handkerchiefs covering their mouths and noses. It did not help. Even carriage horses—many of which would soon die from the heat and add to the problem—vomited from the smell.

The air this steaming July night was almost green with the heated effusions of three million human beings' excrement and the effluvia of the urban and industrial slaughter that was the hallmark of our era. Dear Reader, perhaps it is worse in your day, but I confess I do not see how.

Dickens had sent a note for me to meet him at eight PM at the Blue Posts tavern on Cork Street, where he would host me to a meal. The note also told me to wear serious boots for a "late-night excursion related to our friend Mr D."

Even though I had been feeling indisposed earlier in the day—the gout often is aggravated by such heat—I arrived on time at the Blue Posts. Dickens threw his arms around me in the entrance to the tavern and cried out, "My dear Wilkie, I am so happy to see you! I have been terribly busy at Gad's Hill these past weeks and have missed your company!" The meal itself was extensive, slow, and excellent, as were the ale and wine we enjoyed with it. The conversation was mostly from Dickens, of course, but was as animated and higgledy-piggledy as most conversations with the Inimitable. He said that he hoped to finish *Our Mutual Friend* by early September and that he had every confidence that the last numbers would boost sales of our *All the Year Round*.

After dinner we took a cab to a police station house in Leman Street.

"Do you remember Police Inspector Charles Frederick Field?" Dickens asked as our cab rumbled towards the police station.

"Of course," I said. "Field was in the Detective Department at Scotland Yard. You spent time with him when you were obtaining background material for *Household Words* years ago, and he escorted us that time we toured the...ah...less appealing areas of Whitechapel." I did not mention that I'd always felt sure that Dickens had used Inspector Field as his template for "Inspector Bucket" in *Bleak House*. The overly assured voice, the sense of easy dominance over obvious criminals and brigands and women of the street who had crossed our path that long night in Whitechapel, not to mention the big man's ability to take one's elbow in an iron grip one could not escape and which would then move one in directions one had not planned on going...all of Inspector Bucket's rough skills had described the real Inspector Field to a "T," as they say.

I said, "Inspector Field was our protective angel during our descent into Hades."

"Precisely, my dear Wilkie," said Dickens as we exited the cab in front of the Leman Street police station. "And while Inspector Field has gone on to retirement and new endeavours, it is my sincerest pleasure to introduce you to our *new* protective angel."

The man waiting for us there under the gas lamp outside the police station seemed more wall than man. Despite the heat, he wore a full coat—rather like the loose, long sort that Australian or American cowboys are so often shown wearing in illustrations for penny-dreadful novels—and his massive head was topped with a bowler hat set firmly on a mop of tight, curly hair. The man's body was absurdly wide and stolidly

square—a sort of granite pedestal to the square block
of stone that was his head and face. His eyes were small,
his nose a blunt rectangle seemingly carved out of the
same stone as his face, and his mouth appeared to be
little more than a thin sculpted line. His neck was as
wide as the brim of his bowler. His hands were at least
thrice the size of mine.

Charles Dickens stood five foot nine inches tall. I
was several inches shorter than Dickens. This square
hulk of a man in the grey cowboy duster looked to be at
least eight inches taller than Dickens.

"Wilkie, please meet former sergeant Hibbert Aloysius Hatchery," said Dickens, grinning through his
beard. "Detective Hatchery, I am pleased to introduce
my most valued associate and talented fellow writer and
fellow seeker of Mr Drood this night, Mr Wilkie Collins, Esquire."

"Pleasure, sir, indeed," said the wall looming above
us. "You may call me Hib if it pleases you, Mr Collins."

"Hib," I repeated stupidly. Luckily, the giant had
merely tipped his bowler hat in greeting. The thought of
that huge hand enveloping my own and crushing all the
bones of my hand made me feel weak about the knees.

"My father, a wise man but not a learned one, if you
follow my meaning, sir," said Detective Hatchery, "was
sure that the name Hibbert was in the Bible. But, alas,
it weren't. Not even as a resting place for the Hebrews
in the wilderness."

"Detective Hatchery was a sergeant in the Metropolitan Police Force for several years but is currently
on...ah...leave and is *privately* employed as an investigative detective," said Dickens. "He may decide to
rejoin Scotland Yard's Detective Bureau in a year or so,
but it appears that being privately employed pays more."

"A privately employed detective," I muttered. The
idea had wonderful possibilities. I filed it away at that

moment and the result—as perhaps you know, Dear Reader from my future, if I might be so immodest— would later become my novel *The Moonstone*. I said, "Are you on holiday, Detective Hatchery? Some form of police sabbatical?"

"In a way as you might say, sir," rumbled the giant. "I was asked to take a year off because of irregularities in my treatment of a blackguard felonious sort in the pursuance of my duties, sir. The press made a row. My captain thought it might be better for the Bureau and myself if I went into private practice, a leave of absence as you might say, for a few months."

"Irregularities," I said.

Dickens patted me on the back. "Detective Hatchery, in arresting the aforementioned blackguard—a presumptuous daytime burglar who specialised in preying upon elderly ladies right here in Whitechapel— accidentally snapped the worthless thief's neck. Strangely, the thief lived, but now has to be carried around in a basket by his family. No loss to the community and all a proper part of the job, as Inspector Field and others in the profession have assured me, but some of the over-sensitive *Punch* group, not to mention the lesser news-papers, decided to make a fuss. So it is our great fortune that Detective Hatchery is free to escort us into the Great Oven tonight!"

Hatchery removed a bullseye lantern from beneath his coat. The lantern seemed like a pocket watch in his huge hand. "I shall follow you, gentlemen, but will endeavour to remain silent and invisible unless called upon or needed."

It had rained while Dickens and I were dining, but it only served to make the hot night air around us thicker. The Inimitable led the way, setting his usual absurd walking pace—never less than four miles per hour, which he could maintain hour after hour, I knew from painful experience—and once again I struggled to keep up. Detective Hatchery flowed along ten paces behind us like a silent wall of solidified fog.

We left the wider highways and streets, and with Dickens leading, we entered into a maze of increasingly dark and narrow byways and alleyways. Charles Dickens never hesitated; he knew these terrible streets by heart from his many midnight rambles. I knew only that we were somewhere east of Falcon Square. I retained vague memories of this area from my previous expeditions into the underbelly of London with Dickens—Whitechapel, Shadwell, Wapping, all parts of the city a gentleman would avoid unless looking for the lowest sort of woman—and we seemed to be headed towards the docks. The stench of the Thames grew worse for every gloomy, narrow block we advanced into this rats' maze. The buildings here looked as if they went back to the medieval period, when London lay fat and dark and diseased within its high walls, and, indeed, the ancient structures on either side of the sidewalk-free streets here overhung us so as almost to shut out the night sky.

"Do we have a destination?" I whispered to Dickens. This particular street was empty of people, but I could feel the eyes watching us from the shuttered windows and filthy alleys on either side. I did not want to be overheard, although I knew that even my whisper would carry like a shout through this thick, silent air.

"Bluegate Fields," said Dickens. The brass-shod tip of his heavy walking cane—one he carried only on such nocturnal descents into his Babylon, I had noticed—clacked on the broken pavement stones at every third step of his.

"We sometimes calls it Tiger Bay, sir," came a voice from the darkness behind us.

I admit that I was startled. I had all but forgotten that Detective Hatchery was with us.

We crossed a wider thoroughfare—Brunswick Street, I believe—but it was no cleaner or more illuminated than the rotting slums on either side. Then we were back in the narrow, overhanging labyrinth again. The tenements here crowded high and close except for the few that were total ruins, merely collapsed heaps of masonry and wood. Even there, in those tumbled or charred absences, I could sense dark shadows moving and stirring and watching us. Dickens led us over a narrow, rotted footbridge that crossed a reeking tributary to the Thames. (This was the year, I should point out to you, Dear Reader, that the Prince of Wales officially turned the wheel that opened the Main Drainage Works at Crossness, the first great step in chief engineer Joseph Bazalgette's attempt to bring a modern sewage system to London. The cream of England's nobility and high clergy attended that ceremony. But, setting all delicacy aside, I should also remind you that the Main Drainage Works—and all future sewer systems as well as the myriad of old tributaries and ancient sewers—still drained unfiltered shit into the Thames.)

The more terrible the streets and neighbourhoods became, the more crowded they became. Groups of men—clusters of shadows, actually—were now visible on street corners, in doorways, in empty lots. Dickens strode on, keeping to the centre of the broken streets so that he could better see and avoid the holes and reeking pools of filthy water, his gentleman's cane clicking on cobblestones. He seemed indifferent to the murmurings and angry imprecations from the men we were passing.

Finally a group of such ragged shadows detached itself from the darkness of an unlighted building and moved to block our way. Dickens did not hesitate but continued striding towards them as if they were children come to ask for his autograph. But I could see him change his grip upon his walking stick so that the heavy brass head of it—a bird's beak, I believe—was aimed outwards.

My heart was pounding and I almost faltered as Dickens led me towards that black wall of angry ruffians. Then another wall—a grey one with a bowler hat atop it—moved briskly past me, catching up to Dickens, and Hatchery's voice said softly, "Move along now, boyos. Go back to your 'oles. Let these gentlemen pass without so much as another glance from you. *Now.*"

There was just enough light from the private detective's shaded bullseye lantern for me to be able to see that his right hand had disappeared within his loose coat. What did he carry there? A pistol? I thought not. Almost certainly a leaded club though. Perhaps handcuffs. The ruffians ahead of us and behind us and to the sides of us would know.

The circle of men shuffled away as quickly as it had coalesced. I expected heavy stones or at least gobs of refuse to be thrown at us as we passed, but when we moved on, nothing stronger than a muffled curse was flung in our direction. Detective Hatchery faded into the darkness behind us and Dickens continued his rapid cane-tapping march to what I believed to be the south.

Then we entered the area ruled by prostitutes and their owners.

I seemed to remember having come here in my student days. The street was actually more respectable in appearance than most of those we had traversed in the past half hour or so. Dim lights shone through closed blinds on the upper windows. If one did not know better, it would be easy to think that these dwellings belonged to hard-working factory hands or mechanics. But the stillness was too oppressive. On the steps and balconies and on the cracked slabs of what passed for sidewalks gathered groups of young women—we could see them by the lamplight escaping from the unshuttered lower windows—most of them appearing no older than eighteen. Some looked to be fourteen or younger.

Rather than scatter at the sight of Detective Hatchery, they called out to him in soft, mocking girl-voices—"Hey, 'Ibbert, bringing us some business, eh?" or "Come in and relax a bit, Hib old cock." Or "No, no, the door's not shut, Inspector H, no neither are our room doors neither."

Hatchery laughed easily. "Your doors are never shut, Mary, although well they should be. Watch your manners now, girls. These gentlemen don't want none of your wares this 'ot evening."

That was not necessarily true. Dickens and I paused near one young woman, perhaps seventeen years of age, as she leaned over a railing and studied us in the dim light. I could see that her figure was full, her dark skirt high, and her bodice low.

She noticed Dickens's interest and gave him a wide smile that showed too many missing teeth. "Are you searching for bacca, dearie?" she asked the writer.

"Bacca?" said Dickens and gave me a sideways glance filled with mirth. "Why no, my dear. What makes you think I have come in search of tobacco?"

"'Cause if you want it, I've got it," said the girl. "Screws and arf ounces of it, an' cigars and all other sorts what you may want and you may well have it of me if you wish. You only 'ave to come inside."

Dickens's smile faded slightly. He set both his gloved hands on his cane. "Miss," he said softly, "have you given thought to the very real possibility of changing your life? Of giving up..." His white glove was visible in the dark as he gestured to the silent buildings, silent gatherings of girls, shattered street, and even the distant line of rough men waiting like a pack of forest wolves beyond the circle of pale light. "Of giving up this life?"

The girl laughed through her broken or rotted teeth, but it was not a girl's laugh. It was a bitter presage of a diseased crone's dry rattle. "Give up my life, sweetie? Why not give up yours then, eh? All you 'ave to do is walk back up there where Ronnie and the boys is waitin'."

"Yours has no future, no hope," said Dickens. "There are homes for fallen women. Why, I myself have helped commission and administrate one in Broadstairs where..."

"I ain't about to fall," she said. "Unless it's on my back for the right bit o' payment." The girl turned to stare at me. "What about you, little man? You look like you 'ave some life left in you. You want to come inside for a screw of bacca before ol' 'Atchery 'ere turns sour on us?"

I cleared my throat. To be honest with you, Dear Reader, I found some allure hovering about the wench, despite the heat and stench of the night, my male companions' gazes, and even her ruined smile and ignorant language.

"Come," said Dickens, turning and striding off into the night. "We are wasting our time here, Wilkie."

DICKENS," I said as we crossed yet another creaking, narrow bridge over yet another reeking, foetid stream, the lanes ahead of us mere alleys, the dark buildings there more medieval than any we'd yet seen, "I have to ask, does this...excursion...really have anything to do with your mysterious Mr Drood?"

He stopped and leaned on his stick. "Absolutely, my dear Wilkie. I should have told you at dinner. Mr Hatchery has done more for us in this regard than merely escort us through this...unseemly...neighbourhood. He has been in my employ for some time now and has put his detective abilities to good use." He turned to the large shape that had come up behind us. "Detective Hatchery, would you be so kind as to inform Mr Collins of your discoveries to date?"

"Certainly, sir," said the huge detective. He took off his bowler, rubbed his scalp under the explosion of tight curls, and squeezed the hat into place again. "Sir," he said, addressing me now, "in the past ten days I 'ave made enquiries of the various railway ticket takers at Folkestone and other possible stops along the way—although the tidal express did not make no stops along the way—as well as discreet enquiries of other passengers, the guards on the train that afternoon, the conductors, and others. And the fact is, Mr Collins, that nobody named Drood or resembling the very odd description Mr Dickens gave me of this Mr Drood had a ticket to ride or was in one of the passenger carriages at the time of the accident."

I looked at Dickens in the dim light. "So either your Drood was a local there at Staplehurst," I said, "or he didn't exist."

Dickens only shook his head and gestured for Hatchery to continue.

"But in the second mail carriage," said the detective, "there was three coffins being transported to London. Two of them had been loaded at Folkestone and the third had come over on the same ferry what brought Mr Dickens and...his party. The railway papers showed that this third coffin, the one what had come from France that day—no record of from where in France—was to be released to a Mr Drood, no Christian name listed, upon arrival in London."

I had to think about this for a minute. There came muted shouts from the direction of the "dress lodgers'" houses far behind us. Finally, I said, "You think Drood was *in* one of those coffins?" I looked at Dickens as I posed the question.

The author laughed, almost delightedly, I thought.

"Of *course,* my dear Wilkie. As it turns out, that second mail carriage derailed, displacing all of the parcels and bags and…yes…coffins, but it was not thrown into the ravine below. That explains why Drood was descending the hillside with me a few minutes later."

I shook my head. "Why would he choose to travel by…my God…by coffin? It would cost more than a first-class ticket."

"A little less, sir, a little less," interposed Hatchery. "I checked into that. Cargo rates for transporting the deceased is a little less than first class, sir. Not much, but a few shillings lighter."

I still could make no sense of it. "But certainly, Charles," I said softly, "you're not suggesting that your bizarre-looking Mr Drood was a…what? A ghost? A ghoul of some sort? The walking dead?"

Dickens laughed again, even more boyishly this time. "My dear Wilkie. *Really.* If you were a criminal, Wilkie—known to the port police as well as to London police—what would be the easiest and most effective way that *you* could get from France back to London?"

It was my turn to laugh, but not with any delight, I can assure you. "Not by *coffin,*" I said. "All the way from France? It's…unthinkable."

"Hardly, my dear boy," said Dickens. "Merely a few hours of discomfort. Hardly more uncomfortable than normal ferry and rail travel today, if one must be perfectly candid. And who bothers to inspect a coffin with a week-old corpse rotting in it?"

"*Was* his corpse a week old?" I asked.

Dickens only flicked the white fingers of his glove at me, as if I had made a jest.

"So why are we going towards the docks tonight?" I asked. "Does Detective Hatchery have some information on where Mr Drood's coffin has floated?"

"Actually, sir," said Hatchery, "my enquiries in this

part of town has led us to some folks who say they know Drood. Or knew him. Or have done business with 'im, as it were. That's where we're 'eaded now."

"Then let's press on," said Dickens.

Hatchery held up a huge hand as if he were stopping carriage traffic on the Strand. "I feel it my duty to point out, gentlemen, that we are now entering Bluegate Fields proper, although there is precious little proper about it. It ain't even on most city maps, officially speaking, nor New Court, where we're 'eaded, neither. It's a dangerous place for gentlemen, gentlemen. There's men where we're going as will kill you in a minute."

Dickens laughed. "As would those ruffians we encountered a while ago, I presume," he said. "What is the difference with Bluegate Fields, my dear Hatchery?"

"The difference is, gov'ner, that them what we met a while ago, they'd take you for your purse and leave you beat senseless by the road, p'hraps even to the point of death, aye. But them what's up ahead...they'll slit your throat, sir, just to see if their blade still 'as an edge."

I looked at Dickens.

"Lascars and Hindoos and Bengalees particular and Chinamen by the gross," continued Hatchery. "Also Irishmen and Germans and other such flotsam, not to mention the scum o' the earth sailors ashore a'hunting for women and opium, but it's the Englishmen 'ere in Bluegate Fields you have to fear most, gentlemen. The Chinee and other foreigners, they don't eat, don't sleep, don't talk mostly, just live for their opium...but the Englishmen 'ereabouts, they are an uncommonly rough crew, Mr Dickens. Uncommonly rough."

Dickens laughed again. He sounded as if he had been drinking heavily, but I know he only had some wine and port with dinner. It was more the carefree laugh of a child. "Then we will just have to entrust our safety to you once again, Inspector Hatchery."

I'd noticed that Dickens had just given the private detective a promotion in rank, and from the way the huge man shuffled modestly from foot to foot, it appeared that Hatchery had interpreted it that way as well.

"Aye, sir," said the detective. "With your pardon, I'll take the lead now, sir. And it might be'oove you gentlemen to stay close for a while now."

MOST OF THE STREETS we had already passed through were not marked and the maze of Bluegate Fields was even less delineated, but Hatchery seemed to know exactly where he was going. Even Dickens, striding next to the huge detective, seemed to have a sense of his destination, but the detective answered my whispered question by listing, in his normal tone of voice, some of the places we had been or were soon to see: the church of St Georges-in-the-east (I had no memory of passing it), George Street, Rosemary Lane, Cable Street, Knock Fergus. Black Lane, New Road, and Royal Mint Street. I had noticed none of these names posted on signs.

At New Court, we left the stinking street, passed into a dark courtyard—Hatchery's bullseye lantern was our only illumination—and proceeded on through a gap that was more hole in the wall than formal gateway into a series of other dark courtyards. The buildings seemed abandoned, but my guess was that the windows were merely heavily shuttered. When we stepped off pavement, the ooze of the river or seeping sewage squelched underfoot.

Dickens paused by what had once been a broad window but which now, with all the glass gone, was merely a ledge and black hole in the blinded side of a black building.

"Hatchery," he cried, "your lamp."

The cone of light from the bullseye lantern illuminated three pale, whitish, indistinct lumps on the broken stone sill. For a moment I was sure that three skinned rabbits had been left there. I stepped closer and then stepped quickly back, raising my handkerchief to my nose and mouth.

"Newborns," said Hatchery. "The one in the middle was stillborn, is my guess. The two others died shortly after birth. Not triplets. Born and died different times from the look of the maggots and rat nibblings and other signs."

"Dear God," I said through my handkerchief. Bile rose high in my throat. "But why...leave them here?"

"'Ere's as good a place as any," said the detective. "Some of the mothers try to bury 'em. Dress 'em up in what rags they may have. Put little caps on 'em before dropping the wee things into the Thames or burying 'em in the courtyards 'ere. Most don't bother. They 'ave to get back to work."

Dickens turned towards me. "Still tempted by the wench who wanted to take you inside for 'bacca,' Wilkie?"

I did not answer. I took another step back and concentrated on not vomiting.

"I've seen this before, Hatchery," said Dickens, his voice strangely flat, calm, and conversational. "Not just here in the Great Oven during my walks, but as a young child."

"Have you indeed, sir?" said the detective.

"Yes, many times. When I was very young, before we moved from Rochester to London, we had a servant girl named Mary Weller who would take me with her, my tiny hand trembling in her large calloused one, to countless lyings-in. So many that I have often wondered if my true profession should not have been that of midwife. More often than not, the babies died, Hatchery.

I remember one terrible multiple birth—the mother did not survive either—where there were five dead infants—I believe it was five, as astounding as that sounds, although I was very young, it might have been four—all laid out side by side, on a clean cloth on a chest of drawers. You know what I thought of at my tender age of four or five, Hatchery?"

"What, sir?"

"I thought of pigs' feet the way they are usually displayed at a neat tripe-shop," said Charles Dickens. "It's hard not to think of Thyestes' feast when encountering such an image."

"Indeed, sir," agreed Hatchery. I was sure the detective had no idea of the classical reference to which Dickens was referring. But I did. Again the bile and vomit rose in my throat and threatened to explode.

"Wilkie," Dickens said sharply. "Your handkerchief, if you please."

After a pause, I handed it over.

Taking out his own larger, more expensive silk handkerchief, Dickens carefully laid both cloths over the three rotting and partially eaten infant bodies, weighting down the ends with loose bricks from the broken sill.

"Detective Hatchery," he said, already turning away, his walking cane clicking on stone, "you shall see to the disposition?"

"Before daybreak, sir. You may count on it."

"I am sure we can," said Dickens, lowering his head and holding his top hat as we stepped through another aperture into yet an even darker, smaller, more pestilential courtyard. "Come, come, Wilkie. Keep up to the light."

The open doorway, when we finally reached it, was no more distinguished than the last three dozen shadowy doorways we had passed. Just inside, shielded from view from without, set into its own deep niche, was a small blue lantern. Detective Hatchery grunted and led the way up the narrow black stairs.

The first-storey landing was dark. The next flight of stairs was narrower than the first, though not quite as dark, since there was the dim glow of a single fluttering candle above us on the next landing. The air was so thick here, the heat so intense, and the stench so over-powering that I wondered how the candle managed to continue burning.

Hatchery opened a door without knocking and we all filed in.

We were in the first and largest of several rooms, all visible through open doorways. In this room two Las-cars and an old woman sprawled over a sprung bed that seemed heaped with discoloured rags. Some of the rags stirred and I realised that there were more people on the bed. The whole scene was lit by a few burned-down candles and one red-glassed lantern that cast a bloody hue over everything. Eyes peeped furtively at us from beneath rags in the adjoining rooms even as I realised that there were more bodies—Chinese, Occidental, Lascar—sprawled on the floors and in corners. Some tried to crawl away like roaches exposed to a sudden light. The ancient crone on the bed immediately before us, its four posts carved with years of idle knives, its draperies hanging down like rotted funeral cloths, was blowing at a kind of pipe made of an old penny ink-bottle. The thickness of smoke and harsh, aromatic stink in the room, blended with the sewer-Thames stench wafting in through the close-slatted blinds, caused my gout-hounded stomach to lurch again. I wished then that I had imbibed a second glass of my medicinal laudanum before joining Dickens this evening.

Hatchery prodded the old woman with a wooden

police club he had smoothly retrieved from his belt. "'Ere, 'ere, old Sal," he said harshly. "Wake up and talk to us. These gentlemen have questions for you, and by my oath, you're going to answer them to my satisfaction."

"Sal" was a wrinkled ancient, missing teeth, lacking colour in her cheeks and lips, and showing no light of character other than the debauchery visible in her weak, watery eyes. She squinted at Hatchery and then at us. "'Ib," she said, recognising the giant through her daze, "are you back on the force? Do I need to pay thee?"

"I'm here to 'ave some answers," said Hatchery, prodding her again on the rags above her sunken chest. "And we'll 'ave them before we leave."

"Ask away," said the woman. "But give me leave first to refill old Yahee's pipe, that's a good copper."

For the first time I noticed what appeared to be an ancient mummy reclining on pillows in the corner of the room behind the large bed.

Old Sal reached to a tumbler in the centre of the room, on a japan tray, that appeared to be half-filled with something like treacle. Lifting some of the thick treacle with a pin, she carried it to the mummy in the corner. As he turned towards the light, I saw that old Yahee was attached to an opium pipe and had been since we had entered. Without fully opening his eyes, he took the bit of treacle in his yellowed, long-nailed fingers, rolled it and rolled it until it was a little ball hardly larger than a pea, and then set it into the bowl of his already smoking pipe. The old mummy's eyes closed and he turned away from the light, his bare feet tucked under him.

"There's four pennies more to my own modest coffers," said Sal as she returned to our small circle of red light near the lantern. "Yahee, you should well know, 'Ib, is more nor eighty years old and been a'smoking the opium through sixty nor more of those years. It's true 'e don't sleep, but 'e's wonderfully 'ealthy and clean. In the morning, after a night o' smoking, 'e buys his own rice and fish and vegetables, but only after a'scrubbin' and a'cleanin' 'is house out and own person off. Sixty years o' opium, and never a sick day. Ol' Yahee 'as smoked his way 'ealthy through the last four London Fevers while those arounst 'im were fallin' like flies, and..."

"Enough," commanded Hatchery, silencing the crone. "The gentleman's going to ask you a few questions now, Sal...and if you value this rat hole you call a 'ome and business and don't want to see it shut down around your poxy ears, then by God you had better answer quick and honest."

She squinted at us.

"Madam," said Dickens, his tone as easy and cordial as if he were addressing a lady visitor to his parlour, "we are seeking out an individual named Drood. We know that he used to patronise your...ah...establishment. Could you tell us, please, where we might find him now?"

I saw the shock and sobriety hit the opiated woman as surely as if Dickens had thrown a bucket of freezing water on her. Her eyes widened for a few seconds, then closed in an even more narrow and suspicious squint. "Drood? I don't know no Drood..."

Hatchery smiled and prodded her harder with his stick. "That won't wash, Sal. We know he was a customer 'ere."

"Who says?" hissed the crone. A dying candle on the floor extended her hiss.

Hatchery smiled again but also prodded her again. The club pressed against her skeletal arm, harder this time.

"Mother Abdallah and Booboo both told me that

they've seen someone you called Drood 'ere in years past...a white man, missing fingers, strange accent. Said he used to be a regular of yours. He smells of rotting meat, Mother Abdallah told me," said the detective.

Sal attempted a laugh but it came out only as a wheezing rattle. "Mother Abdallah's a crazy bitch. Booboo's a lying Chinaman."

"It may be." Hatchery smiled. "But no more crazy nor lyin' than you, my Puffer Princess. Somebody named Drood has been 'ere and you know it and you'll *tell* us." Still smiling, he brought the end of the weighted baton down on her long but arthritis-gnarled fingers.

Sal howled. Two heaps of rags in a corner began dragging themselves and their opium pipes into another room where the noise, should someone be murdered, would not disturb their dreams.

Dickens removed several shillings from his purse and jingled them in his palm. "Telling us everything you know about Mr Drood shall be to your advantage, madam."

"And you'll spend a few nights—maybe weeks—not just in my station cell but in the dankest pit in Newgate if you *don't* tell us," added Hatchery.

The impact of that struck me on a level that could not affect Dickens. I tried to imagine a few nights, much less *weeks*, without my laudanum. This woman obviously ingested much more of the pure opium than I ever had. My own bones ached at the mere idea of being deprived of my medicine.

There were real tears in the Puffer Princess's watery eyes now. "All right, all right, leave off wi' the bludgeonings and threatenings, 'Ib. I've always done right by you, ain't I? I've always paid up when pay-up was due, ain't I? 'Aven't I always..."

"Tell the gentlemen about this Drood and shut your gob about anything else," Hatchery said in his most quiet and threatening voice. He laid the length of his club along her quivering forearm.

"When did you know this Drood?" asked Dickens.

"Up to about a year ago," breathed the Puffer Princess. "'E don't come around no more."

"Where does he live, madam?"

"I don't knows. I swears I don't knows. Chow Chee John Potter brought this Drood bird in for the first time about eight...maybe nine years ago. They smoked prodigious amounts of the product, they did. Drood always paid in gold sovereigns, so 'is credit was pure gold and all paid up for the sweet future, as it were. He never sung or shouted like the others...there, you 'ear one now in t'other room...'e just smoked and sat there and looked at me. And looked at the others. Sometimes 'e'd leave first, long before t'others, sometimes 'e'd be the last t'leave."

"Who is this Chow Chee John Potter?" asked Dickens.

"Jack's dead," she said. "He *was* an ol' Chinee ship's cook who had the Christian name 'cause he'd been christened, but he was never right in 'is head, sir. 'E was like a sweet child, 'e was...only a mean, vicious child if he drank rum. But never mean just from smokin'. No."

"This Chow Chee was a friend of Drood's?" asked Dickens.

Old Sal rattled another laugh. It sounded as if her lungs were almost gone from the smoke or consumption or both.

"Drood—if that was 'is name—didn't have no friends, sir. Everyone was afraid of 'im. Even Chow Chee."

"But the first time you saw him here—Drood—he came in with Chow Chee?"

"Aye, sir, he come with 'im, but I suspect that 'e'd

just run into old Jack and had the old pleasant idiot show 'im the way to the nearest opium house. Jack would've done that for a kind word, much less for a shillin'."

"Does Drood live around here?" asked Dickens.

Sal started to laugh again but then started coughing. The terrible noise went on for what seemed like an endless amount of time. Finally she gasped and said, "Live 'round 'ere? 'Round New Court or Bluegate Fields or the docks or Whitechapel? Nossir. No chance of that, sir."

"Why not?" asked Dickens.

"We would've known, gov'ner," rasped the woman. "Someone like Drood would've scared every man, woman, and child in Whitechapel and London and Shadwell. We all would've left town."

"Why?" asked Dickens.

"Because of his Story," hissed the crone. "His *true* and awful Story."

"Tell us his story," said Dickens.

She hesitated.

Hatchery ran the edge of his club up the outside of her arm and lightly rapped her on her bony elbow.

After her howling stopped, she told the story as she had heard it from the late Chow Chee John Potter, another opium dealer named Yahee, and yet another user named Lascar Emma.

"Drood's not new to these 'ere parts; them what knows says 'e's been a'haunting these neighbourhoods for forty years and more...."

I interrupted with "What is this Mr Drood's Christian name, woman?"

Hatchery and Dickens both scowled at me. I blinked and stepped back. It was the only question I was to ask the Puffer Princess that night.

Sal scowled at me as well. "Christian name? Drood ain't got no Christian name. He ain't no Christian and never was. It's just *Drood*. That's part of his Story. Do you want me to tell it or don't you?"

I nodded, feeling the blush heat the skin between the lower rim of my spectacles and the beginnings of my beard.

"Drood's just Drood," repeated Old Sal. "Word from Lascar Emma was that Drood was a sailor once. Yahee, who's older than Mother Abdallah and dirt combined, says he wasn't no sailor, just a passenger on a sailing ship that come here long ago. Maybe sixty years ago—maybe a hundred. But them all agreed that Drood come from Egypt...."

I saw Dickens and the huge detective exchange glances, as if the crone's words were confirming something they already knew or suspected.

"'E was an Egyptian, and dark-skinned as all of 'is damned-to-hell Mohammadan race," continued Sal. "Word was that 'e had 'air then, too, black as pitch. Some says 'e was handsome. But 'e was always an opium man. As soon's 'e set foot on English soil, they says, 'e was puffing at the blue bottle pipe.

"First 'e spent all the money 'e had on it—thousands of pounds, if the story is true. He must've come from royalty there in Mohammadan Egypt. At the very least, 'e come from money. Or come *by* it some'ow shady. Chin Chin the Chinaman, the old Chinee dealer in the West End, stole Drood blind, charging him ten, twenty, fifty times what 'e charged 'is reg'lar customers. Then, when 'is own money runned out, Drood tried to work for the money—sweepin' at crossin's and doin' magic tricks for the gents and ladies up at Falcon Square— but 'onest-come-by money didn't buy 'im enough. It never does. So the 'gyptian became a cut-purse and then a cut-throat, robbin' and a'killin' sailors near the docks. That kept 'im in Chin Chin's good graces and guaranteed the 'ighest-quality smoke, bought by the

Chinaman from Johnny Chang's establishment up at the London and Saint Katharine Coffee-'ouse on Ratcliff 'ighway.

"Drood gathered 'round him some others—most 'gyptians, some Malays, some Lascars, some free niggers off the ships, some dirty Irish, some mean Germans—but mostly, as I say, other 'gyptians. They've themselves sort of a religion and they live and worship in the old Undertown...."

Not understanding but afraid of interrupting again, I looked first at Dickens and then at Hatchery. Both men shook their heads and shrugged.

"One day, or night it were, maybe twenty year ago," continued Sal, "Drood went to waylay and sap a sailor; some say 'is name was Finn, but this Finn waren't as drunk as 'e seemed nor as easy a target as Drood thought. The 'gyptian Drood used a skinning knife for 'is dark work—or maybe it was one of them curvy bonin' knives you see up at them Whitechapel butchers, what with their cry of *'prime and nobby jintes for to-morrer's dinner at nine-a-half, and no bone to speak of'*...and it was true, gentlemen and Constable 'Ib, that when Drood was a'finished with 'em on the docks, there was money for smoke in 'is purse and no bone to speak of for the sailor whose 'ollowed-out corpse was then dumped like so many fish guts into the Thames...."

There came a low moaning from one of the adjoining rooms. I felt the hair on my neck rise, but this other-worldly moaning was no response to Old Sal's story. Just a customer with a pipe in need of a refill. The crone ignored the moaning and so did her rapt audience of three.

"Not this night twenty years ago," she said. "Finn— if Finn was 'is name—wasn't no regular customer for Drood's blade; 'e got Drood's arm before it done 'im harm and then he got the bonin' knife, or skinnin'

knife, whichever, and cut off the 'gyptian's nose. Then
'e cut 'is would-be murderer open from crotch to col-
larbone, 'e did. Oh, Finn knew 'ow to wield a knife
from his years 'afore the mast, is how ol' Lascar Emma
tells it. Drood, all slashed but still alive, yells no, no,
mercy, no, and Finn cuts the blackguard's tongue out
of his mouth. Then 'e cuts off the heathen's privy parts
and offers to place 'em where the missin' tongue had
been. And then 'e done what 'e offered."

I realised that I was blinking rapidly and breathing
shallowly. I had never heard a woman talk this way. One
glance towards Dickens told me that the Inimitable was
equally enthralled by the tale and the teller.

"So finally," continued Sal, "this Finn—this sailor
by any other name who knew 'is knife-work—cuts
Drood's 'eart out of 'is chest and dumps the 'gyptian's
dead body into the river from a dock not a mile from
this 'ouse. So 'elp me God, gentlemen."

"But wait," interrupted Dickens. "This occurred
more than twenty years ago? You said earlier that
Drood was your customer here for seven or eight years,
up until about a year ago. Are you so dazed with the
drug that you are forgetting your own lies?"

The Puffer Princess squinted evilly at Dickens and
showed her clawed fingers and arched her bowed back
while her wild hair seemed to stick out farther from her
head and for a minute I was certain that she was trans-
mogrifying into a cat and would begin spitting and
clawing within another second or two.

Instead, she hissed—"Drood's dead is what I been
tellin' you. Been dead since 'e was carved and tossed
into the Thames by the sailor nigh onto twenty year ago.
But 'is band, 'is group, 'is followers, 'is co-religionists—
them other 'gyptians, Malays, Lascars, Irishmen, Germans, Hindoos—they fished 'is rotting, bloated corpse
out of the river some days after 'is murder and did their

heathen ritules and brought Drood back to life again. Lascar Emma says it was down in Undertown, where 'e dwells to this day. Old Yahee, who knew Drood when 'e was alive, 'e says the restorrection was over across the river in the mountains o' 'orse and 'uman shit what you gentlemen so politely call 'dust 'eaps.' But wherever they done it, 'owever they done it, they brought Drood back."

I glanced at Dickens. There was something both thrilled and mischievous in the author's eye. I may have mentioned earlier that Charles Dickens was not the man one wants to stand next to at a funeral service—the boy in the man could not resist a smile at the least appropriate time, a meaningful glance, a wink. Sometimes I thought that Charles Dickens would laugh at anything, sacred or profane. I was afraid that he would start laughing now. I say I was *afraid* that he would start laughing, not just because of the embarrassment of the situation, but because I had the most uncanny certainty at that moment that the entire opium den around us, all the poor wretches buried in rags and secreted in corners and hidden under blankets and draped on pillows, in all three filthy, dark rooms there, were listening with all of the attention that their drug-addled minds could command.

I was afraid that if Dickens started laughing, these creatures—Old Sal first among them, fully changed into a huge cat—would leap upon us and rend us limb from limb. Even huge Hatchery, I was sure in that instant of my fear, could not save us if it came to that.

Instead of laughing, Dickens handed the crone three gold sovereigns, setting the coins gently in her filthy yellow palm and closing her curled and twisted fingers around them. He said softly, "Where can we find Drood now, my good woman?"

"In the Undertown," she whispered, clutching the

coins with both hands. "Down in the deepest parts of Undertown. Down where the Chinee named King Lazaree provides Drood and t'others the purest pure opium in the world. Down in Undertown with the other dead things."

Dickens gestured and we followed him out of the smoke-filled room and onto the narrow, dark landing.

"Detective Hatchery," said the writer, "have you heard of this subterranean Chinese opium dealer named King Lazaree?"

"Yes, sir."

"And you know of this Undertown that Sal talks about with such trepidation?"

"Yes, sir."

"Is it within walking distance?"

"The entrance is, yes, sir."

"Will you take us there?"

"To the entrance, yes, sir."

"Will you go with us into this . . . Undertown . . . and continue being Virgil to our questing Dantes?"

"Are you asking if I'll take you down *into* Undertown, Mr Dickens?"

"That I am, Inspector," Dickens said almost gleefully. "That I am. For *twice* the rate we agreed upon, of course, since this is *twice* the adventure."

"No, sir, I won't."

I could see Dickens blinking in amazement. He raised his stick and tapped the giant gently on the chest with the brass bird's beak. "Come, come now, Detective Hatchery. All joking aside. For *three* times our agreed-upon sum, will you show Mr Collins and me to this and into this tantalising Undertown? Lead us to Lazaree and Drood?"

"No, sir, I won't," Hatchery said. His voice sounded ragged, as if the opium smoke had affected it. "I won't go into Undertown under any circumstances. That's my final word on that, sir. And I would beg you, if you value your souls and sanity, not to go down there yourselves."

Dickens nodded as if considering this advice. "But you will show us the...what did you call it?...the *entrance* to Undertown."

"Yes, sir," said Hatchery. His low words came out like someone tearing thick paper. "I will show you... regretfully."

"That's good enough, Detective," said Dickens, taking the lead down the dark stairway. "That's fair and more than good enough. It is past midnight, but the night is young. Wilkie and I will press on—and down—by ourselves."

The huge detective lumbered down the steps behind Dickens. It took me a minute to follow. The dense opium smoke in the closed room must have affected my nerves or muscles below the waist, because my legs felt heavy, leaden, unresponsive. In quite literal terms, I could not force my legs and feet to take the first step on the stairs.

Then, tingling and hurting all over as a limb does after falling asleep unbeknownst to its owner, I was able to take that first clumsy step down. I had to rely on my walking stick to keep my balance.

"Are you coming, Wilkie?" came Dickens's accursedly excited voice up the black stairwell.

"Yes!" I called down, adding a silent *God d——n your eyes.* "I'm coming, Dickens."

CHAPTER FIVE

I must pause in my narrative here for a moment, Dear Reader, to explain how and why I had chosen to follow Charles Dickens into absurd and dangerous situations before this. There was the time, for instance, when I followed him up Mount Vesuvius. And the more serious incident in Cumberland, where he almost got me killed on Carrick Fell.

Vesuvius was just one of the minor adventures of the 1853 trip around Europe which Dickens and I shared with Augustus Egg. Strictly speaking, there were only two bachelors in that three-man travelling party, and both were younger than the Inimitable, but Dickens certainly acted as carefree and boyish as any young bachelor with the majority of his life and career ahead of him as we gambolled about Europe that autumn and winter. Visiting most of Dickens's old haunts on the Continent, we eventually headed for Lausanne, where the author's eccentric old friend Reverend Chauncey Hare Townshend lectured us on ghosts, jewelry, and— one of Dickens's favourite topics—mesmerism, and then we were off to Chamonix and climbing the Mer de Glace, where we looked down into glacial crevasses a thousand feet deep. In Naples, which I had hoped would be a respite from all the adventure, Dickens immediately insisted that we climb Vesuvius.

He was disappointed, deeply disappointed I would

say, that there was no fire belching and blazing from the volcano. Evidently a major eruption in 1850 had taken some of the energy out of the mountain; there was much smoke while we were there, but no flames. To say that Dickens was crestfallen would be an understatement. Nonetheless, Dickens quickly put a climbing party together, including the archaeologist and diplomat Austen Henry Layard, and we promptly threw ourselves at the smoking mountain.

Eight years before our climb, on the night of 21 January, 1845, Dickens had found all the Vesuvian fire and sulphur that someone as indifferent to danger as he might ask for.

It was the Inimitable's first trip to Naples and the volcano was very active indeed. With his wife, Catherine, and sister-in-law Georgina in tow, Dickens set off with six saddle horses, an armed soldier for a guard, and—because the weather was harsh and the volcano very treacherous then—no fewer than twenty-two guides. They began their ascent around four PM with the women being carried in litters while Dickens and the guides led the way. The walking stick that the author used that evening was taller and thicker than the bird-beaked cane he was clacking against cobblestones this night in the slums of Shadwell. I am sure that his pace that first time on Vesuvius was no slower than it was tonight on such flat ground at sea level. Charles Dickens's response to an intimidating slope—as I have witnessed to my chagrin and fatigue many times—was to double his already too-quick pace.

Near the top of the cinder cone that is Vesuvius's summit, no one would go on save for Dickens and a single guide. The mountain was in eruption. Flames shot hundreds of feet into the sky above them and sulphur, cinders, and smoke belched from every crevice in the snowfields and rockfields. The author's friend Roche, who had climbed to within a few hundred feet of the crater but who could not go farther towards the fiery maelstrom, screamed that Dickens and his guide would be killed if they ventured closer.

Dickens insisted on climbing right to the brink of this crater, on the windy and most dangerous side—the fumes alone have been known to kill people miles below this level—and looking, as he wrote his friends later, *"down into the crater itself...into the flaming bowels of the mountain.... It was the finest sight conceivable, more terrible than Niagara...."* The American waterfalls had been his previous exemplar of transcendence and awe in Nature on this world. Equal, he wrote *"...as fire and water are."*

All the other members of the party that night, including the horrified and exhausted Catherine and Georgina (who had ridden up the mountainside), attested that Dickens came down the cinder cone "alight in half a dozen places and burnt from head to foot." The author's remaining rags of clothing smouldered during the long night's descent—and the descent was also harrowing. On an endless and exposed ice slope where some of the party had to rope up for safety and guides had to chip footsteps in the ice, one guide slipped and fell screaming down into the darkness, followed a minute later by one of the Englishmen who had joined the party. Dickens and the others descended through the night without learning the fates of these men. The writer later told me that the Englishman had survived; he never learned the status of the guide.

Twelve years before this Drood-quest in London, Dickens had dragged Egg and me up Vesuvius, but, thank God and the volcano's relative quiet, it was a far less taxing and dangerous outing. Dickens and Layard pressed ahead at high speed, which allowed Egg and me to rest, discreetly, whenever we felt the need. In truth, it was beautiful as we watched the sun setting towards Sorrento and Capri from our vantage point near the mouth of the crater, the sphere of the sun growing huge and blood red through the pall of smoke and vapour from Vesuvius. We descended easily by torchlight with a new moon rising above us and all of us singing English and Italian songs.

This was as to nothing compared to our near-fatal—to me—adventure on Carrick Fell shortly after our last performance of *The Frozen Deep* in Manchester in 1857.

Dickens was filled then, as he was this night in the Shadwell slums, with a terrible and unquenchable energy, arising, it seemed, from a soul-deep dissatisfaction. He told me some weeks after the play closed that he was going mad, that—if I remember his words correctly—"the scaling of all the mountains in Switzerland, or the doing of any wild thing until I dropped, would be but a slight relief." In a note he sent me one morning after we had been dining, drinking, and discussing things both solemnly and with wild humour the night before, Dickens said, "I want to escape from myself. For when I do start up and stare myself seedily in the face, as happens to be my case at present, my blankness is inconceivable—indescribable—my misery amazing." And I could tell that besides being amazing, his misery was very real and very deep. I thought at the time that it had only to do with his failing marriage to Catherine; I know now that it had even more to do with his new love for the eighteen-year-old child-woman named Ellen Ternan.

In 1857, Dickens announced to me suddenly that we were leaving immediately for Cumberland to get inspiration for some jointly penned articles about the North of England for our magazine *Household Words*. He was to call the piece *The Lazy Tour of Two Idle Apprentices*.

Even as co-author—in truth primary author, I may tell you, Dear Reader—I have to say that what resulted was an unoriginal and uninspired series of travel essays. It was only later that I realised that Dickens had little interest in Cumberland, other than climbing that damned Carrick Fell, and almost no interest at all in writing travel articles.

Ellen Ternan and her sisters and mother were appearing on stage in Doncaster, and that, I know now, was the real purpose for our wild travels north.

How ironic it would have been if I had died on Carrick Fell because of Charles Dickens's covert passion for an eighteen-year-old actress who had absolutely no awareness of his feelings for her.

We took the train from London to Carlisle and the next day we rode to the village of Heske, at the base of this "Carrock or Carrick Mountain or Carrock or Carrick Fell I have read about, my dear Wilkie. The spellings are unreliable."

So it was at Carrick Fell that I fell.

Dickens's burning frustration and energy demanded a mountain, and for some reason known to no one—not even to himself, I am sure—Carrick or Carrock Fell was to be the mountain we were to throw ourselves against.

There were no guides in tiny Heske to lead us to or up this hill. The weather was terrible: cold, windy, rainy. Dickens finally convinced the landlord of the rather sad little inn where we were staying to be our guide, even though the older man confessed to "havin' never bin oop or doon that partic'lar hill, sirrr."

We managed to find Carrick Fell, its summit disappearing in the lowering evening clouds. We began to climb. The innkeeper hesitated frequently but Dickens usually pushed on, guessing at our course. A bone-chilling wind rose up around nightfall—more a mere dimming of the twilight into deeper darkness as mist and fog rolled in—yet still we climbed. We soon were lost. The landlord confessed to having no idea even of which side of the mountain we were on. As dramatically as when he played the wandering Richard Wardour on stage, Dickens produced a compass from his pocket, pointed the way, and we pressed on into the gloom.

Within thirty minutes, Dickens's city-bought compass was broken. The rain poured harder and we were soon soaked through and shivering. Darker and darker came on the northern night while we wound our way round and round the rocky fell. We found what could have been its summit—a slippery, rocky ridge set amidst a plethora of identical slippery, rocky ridges all disappearing into the fog and night—and we started down, having not the slightest sense of which way lay our village, our inn, our dinner, our fire, or our beds.

For two hours we wandered so with the rain terrific, the fog thick, and the darkness now approaching some Stygian absolute. When we came to a roaring stream that blocked our path, Dickens greeted it as if it were a long-lost friend. "We follow it down to the river at the base of the peak," Dickens explained to the shivering, miserable wretch of a landlord and to his equally miserable co-author. "The perfect guide!"

This guide may have been perfect, but it was treacherous. The sides of the gully became steeper and steeper, the rocks along the sides ever more treacherous with rain and incipient ice, the torrent beneath us wilder. I fell behind. My foot slipped, I fell heavily, and I felt something twist terribly in my ankle. Lying half in the stream, hurting and shivering, starving and weak, I had to call into the darkness for help, hoping that Dickens and the trembling innkeeper had not descended beyond earshot. If they had, I knew I was a dead man. I could not even put weight on the ankle while using my walking stick. I would have had to crawl down the streambed itself some miles to the river, then—if I somehow guessed the proper direction to the village—crawl miles more along the river's bank that night. I am a city man, Dear Reader. Such exertions are not in my physical vocabulary.

Luckily, Dickens heard my calls. He came back and found me lying in the stream, my ankle already swollen to more than twice its normal size.

At first he merely assisted me as I hopped down the treacherous slope with him, but eventually he actually carried me. I knew without any doubt that Dickens was imagining himself as the hero Richard Wardour carrying his rival, Frank Aldersley, across the Arctic wastes to safety. As long as he did not drop me, I did not care what fantasies he indulged in.

Eventually, we found the inn. The landlord—shaking and muttering and cursing under his breath—woke his wife to cook us some late-night supper or early-morning breakfast. Servants stoked the fires in the public room and in our rooms. There was no doctor in Heske—there really was no *Heske* in Heske—so Dickens iced and bound my swollen ankle as best he could until we reached civilisation.

We went on to Wigton and then to Allonby and then to Lancaster and then to Leeds—continuing the charade that we were gathering material for a travel tale, even though I could not walk without the aid of two sticks and spent all my time in the hotels—and then finally went on to Doncaster, which had been our true and secret (or rather, Charles Dickens's secret) destination all along.

There we saw several plays, including the one in which Ellen Ternan had a brief appearance. The next day, Dickens went on a picnic with the family and—I am certain now—also on a long, private walk with Ellen Ternan. Whatever transpired on that walk, whatever thoughts or feelings were expressed and rejected, remains a mystery to this day, but I know for a fact that the Inimitable returned from Doncaster in a foul and murderous mood. When I tried to arrange times at the *Household Words* office for us to finish our writing and editing of the weak *Lazy Tour of Two Idle Apprentices* essays, Dickens sent me an unusually personal reply in which he said, *"...the Doncaster unhappiness remains so strong upon me that I can't write and (waking) can't rest, one minute."*

As I said, I did not then know and do not now know the precise nature of that Doncaster unhappiness, but it was soon to change all of our lives.

I share this, Dear Reader, because I suspected that night in July of 1865, and I suspect more firmly now as I write this some years later, that our search for the mysterious Drood that hot, reeking night was not so much for the resurrected phantom Drood as it was for whatever Charles Dickens sought out in Ellen Ternan in Doncaster in 1857—and in the eight mystery-filled years since then up until Staplehurst.

But as was true of Carrick or Carrock Fell, such obsessions can have their terrible price for other people through no planning of the obsessor: other people can end up just as injured or dead as if it had all been premeditated.

WE WALKED for about twenty minutes through even darker and more reeking slums. At times there were signs of crowded human habitation in the sagging tenements, whispers and catcalls rising out of the thick darkness on both sides of the narrow lanes, and at other times the only sound was that of our boots and Dickens's cane tapping on the cobblestones of those few lanes that had cobblestones. I was reminded that night of a passage in Dickens's most recent—and still uncompleted—book, *Our Mutual Friend*, one of the first numbers to be serialised in the past year, in which our author has two young men riding in a carriage down to the Thames to identify a body found drowned and dragged out of the river by a father and daughter who do that daily for a living—

> *The wheels rolled on, and rolled down by the Monument, and by the Tower, and by the Docks; down by Ratcliffe, and by Rotherhithe; down by where accumulated scum of humanity seemed to be washed from higher grounds, like so much moral sewage, and to be pausing until its own weight forced it over the bank and sunk it in the river.*

In truth, like the dissolute young characters in the coach in Dickens's tale, I had been paying little attention to the direction we were going; I merely followed the large shadow of Detective Hatchery and the lithe shadow of Dickens. I was later to regret my inattention.

Suddenly the constant background stench changed its flavour and grew in intensity. "Pfah!" I cried to my shadowy companions ahead. "Are we nearing the river again?"

"Worse, sir," said Hatchery over his wide shoulder. "It's burial grounds, sir."

I looked around. For some time I had been under the general but contradictory impression that we were approaching either Church Street or the London Hospital area, but this dark avenue had opened instead on our right onto a sort of field encircled by walls and an iron fence and a gate. I saw no church nearby, so this was no churchyard cemetery, but rather a municipal cemetery of the kind that had become so common in the past fifteen years.

You see, Dear Reader, in our time, the almost-three-million of us in London lived and walked above the corpses of at least that many of our common dead, and almost certainly more. As London grew and devoured its surrounding suburbs and villages, those graveyards were also subsumed, and it was to them that the hundreds of thousands upon hundreds of thousands of rotting bodies of our beloved dead were consigned. St Martin-in-the-Fields churchyard, for instance, was only about two hundred feet square, but by 1840, some twenty-five years before this eventful night, it was estimated to contain the remains of between 60,000 and 70,000 of our London departed. There are many more there now.

In the 1850s, about the time of the Great Stink and the worst of the terrible cholera epidemics, it was becoming apparent to all of us that these overcrowded churchyards were creating a health risk to those unlucky enough to live nearby. Every burial place in the city was—and remains—overcrowded to the point of overflow. Thousands of bodies were buried in shallow pits beneath chapels and schools and workplaces and in empty lots and even behind and beneath private homes. So the Burial Act of 1852—a piece of legislation which Dickens had spoken for—demanded that the General Board of Health establish some cemeteries open to all the dead regardless of their religion.

Perhaps you also know, Dear Reader, that until recently in my lifetime, all those to be buried in England had to receive Christian burial in parish churchyards. There were few exceptions. It was as late as 1832 that an act of Parliament put an end to the common practice of my fellow Englishmen burying suicides in public highways with a stake driven through the dead sinner's heart. The Act—a paragon of modern thought and philanthropy—allowed the corpses of suicides to be buried in churchyards with Christians, but only if the dead one was interred between the hours of nine PM and midnight, and always then without the rites of the Church. And I should mention that the compulsory dissection of murderers' corpses was also abolished in 1832—that enlightened year!—and even murderers may be found in Christian cemeteries in this liberal era.

Many—I should say *most*—of those graves remain unmarked. But not necessarily undiscovered. Those men digging new graves each day or night here in London invariably sink their spades into rotting flesh—layers of it, I am told—and then into unnamed skeletons beneath. Some churchyards hire men to check the grounds each morning for chunks of decaying parishioners that have risen to the surface—especially after heavy rains—in too-eager anticipation of the Final Trumpet Call. I have seen these workers carrying arms and hands and other, less distinguishable parts, in wheelbarrows while in the pursuit of their rounds, rather like a diligent gardener on an estate will carry off fallen limbs and branches after a storm.

These new interment areas were called "burial grounds" as distinct from parish "churchyards" and they had been very popular. The first burial grounds were commercial ventures (and as was still the custom in so many places on the Continent, if the family fell behind on payment on their loved ones' graves, the bodies were dug up and tossed aside, the beautiful headstones used to pave retaining walls or walkways, and the earth sold to a more reliable customer), but since the 1850s Acts enforcing the closure of many overflowing London churchyards, most of our new cemeteries were of the municipal variety, with separate seating, as it were, for religious Conformists (complete with chapels and consecrated ground) and a different area for Dissenters. One wonders if they were uncomfortable spending Eternity within a cricket pitch's distance of one another.

The burial ground we were approaching now in the dark looked to have been an ancient churchyard at some point—until the church was abandoned as the neighbourhoods here got too dangerous for decent people, then its structure burned down in order to raise more tenements so that landlords could squeeze more money out of immigrants with nowhere else to light—but the churchyard itself had remained and been used...and used...and used...perhaps taken over by Dissenters a century or two ago, then converted to a bury-for-profit graveyard some time in the last twenty years.

As we approached the sweating walls and black iron fence of the place, I wondered who would pay even a penny to be buried here. There had once been large trees within the churchyard, but these were only calcified skeletons now, dead for generations, with their amputated arms rising towards the black buildings leaning over the site on every side. The stench from within this walled and fenced space was so terrible that I reached for my handkerchief before remembering that Dickens had taken it earlier in the night to drape across the dead babies. I half expected to see an actual green cloud of miasma hanging over this place and—in truth—there was a sick glow to the mist that had arrived to serve as harbinger for the next warm-blanket of rain.

Dickens reached the high, closed, black iron gate first and tried to open it, but it was locked with a massive padlock.

Thank God, I thought.

But Detective Hatchery reached under his coat and

brought a heavy ring of keys from his impossibly burdened belt. He had Dickens hold the bullseye lantern
while he fumbled through the clanking keys before
finding the one he wanted. It fit in the lock. The huge
gate, all black arches and scallops, opened slowly with
such a creaking that it seemed as if it had been decades
since anyone had paid to open it to rid themselves of a
loved one's corpse.

We walked between the dark headstones and sagging sepulchres, passing under the dead trees and down
uneven paving stones on narrow lanes between ancient
vaults. I could tell by the spring in his step and the clack
of his cane that Dickens was enjoying every second of
this. I was concentrating on not retching from the stink
and not stepping, in the darkness, on anything soft and
yielding.

"I know this place," Dickens said suddenly. His voice
in the darkness was loud enough to make me leap a
small distance into the air. "I have seen it in daylight. I
have written about it in *The Uncommercial Traveller*.
But I was not within its gates before tonight. I called it
the 'City of the Absent' and this particular place 'Saint
Ghastly Grim's.'"

"Aye, sir," said Hatchery. "It once were exactly
that."

"I did not see the skulls and crossbones decorating
the iron spikes on the gate," said Dickens, his voice still
far too loud for the circumstances.

"They are still there, Mr Dickens," attested Hatchery. "I did not feel it politick to shine my light up on
'em. 'Ere we are, sirs. Our entrance to Undertown."

We had stopped before a narrow, sealed crypt.

"Is this a joke?" I asked. My voice may have sounded
a bit brittle to my companions. I was overdue for an
application of my medicinal laudanum; the gout was
causing many parts of my body to hurt and I could feel

a terrible headache tightening like a metal band around my temples.

"No, Mr Collins, no joke, sir," said Hatchery. He was fumbling at his key ring again and now he set yet another massive key into an ancient lock on the metal door of the crypt. The tall door groaned inward when he leaned his weight against it. The detective shone the light inside and waited for Dickens or me to enter.

"This is absurd," I said. "There can be no Undertown or underground anything here. Our boots have been squelching in the reeking muck of the Thames for hours. The water table here must be shallower than these graves around us."

"That does not prove to be the case, sir," whispered Hatchery.

"This part of the East End lies over rock, my dear Wilkie," said Dickens. "Ten feet down and it is solid rock. Certainly you know the geology of your city! That is why they chose to build them here."

"Build what?" I asked, attempting, without total success, to keep the asperity I felt out of my voice.

"The catacombs," said Dickens. "The ancient underground spaces of a monastery crypt. The Roman *loculi* before that, even deeper here, almost certainly beneath the Christian catacombs."

I did not choose to ask what *"loculi"* meant. I had the sense that I would learn its dark etymology soon enough.

Dickens entered the crypt, then did the detective, then I. The cone of light from the bullseye moved over and around the tiny interior. The pedestal bier in the centre of the small mausoleum, just long enough to hold a coffin or sarcophagus or shrouded body, was empty. There were no obvious niches or other places for bodies.

"It's empty," I said. "Someone's pilfered the corpse."

Hatchery laughed softly. "Bless me, sir. There was never a corpse 'ere. This partic'lar house o' the dead is—'as always been—just an entrance to the *land* o' the dead. If you'll move aside, Mr Collins."

I stepped back against the sweating stone wall at the rear of the crypt as the detective bent low, set his shoulder to the cracked marble bier, and shoved. The sound of stone scraping across solid stone was extremely unpleasant.

"I noticed the arcs gouged into the old pavers as we came in," Dickens commented to the still-labouring detective. "As clear a clue as the grooves the post of a sagging gate makes in the mud."

"Aye, sir," panted Hatchery, still shoving. "But usually leaves and dirt an' such in 'ere hide that, even in direct lantern light. You're very observant, Mr Dickens."

"Yes," said Dickens.

I was sure that the screech and moans of the slowly shifting bier were loud enough to bring mobs of curious ruffians into the graveyard. Then I remembered that Hatchery had locked the cemetery gate behind us. We were locked in. And since the door of the crypt itself had taken much of Hatchery's considerable bulk and strength to open—he had shouldered it shut after we entered—we might as well have been locked into this tomb as well. As steep stone stairs became visible in the black wedge beneath the floor now growing wider as the bier was moved, the sense of *that* weight being set back in place, essentially entombing us below the stone beneath the locked tomb within the locked cemetery, I felt cold shivers running down my back despite the thick heat of the night.

Finally Hatchery stopped pushing and stood upright. The triangular wedge of the dark opening was not large, little more than two feet wide, but when Dickens shone the bullseye down into it, I could see very steep stone steps descending.

Dickens's face was lighted from below by the lantern as he looked at the detective and said, "You're sure you will not come down with us, Hatchery?"

"No, sir, thank you, sir," said the big man. "I have agreed not to."

"*Agreed* not to?" Dickens's tone was one of mild curiosity.

"Aye, sir. An old arrangement that many of us former and current constables and inspectors 'ave with those in Undertown. We don't go down to complicate their lives, sir; they don't come up to complicate ours."

"Rather like the arrangement most of the living attempt to make with the dead," Dickens said softly, his gaze returning to the dark hole and steep steps.

"Exactly, sir," said the detective. "I knew you would understand."

"Well, we should be going down," said Dickens. "Will you be able to find your way home without a lantern, Detective? We'll obviously need this one below."

"Oh, yes, sir," said Hatchery. "I 'ave another one on my belt should I need it. But I won't be going 'ome yet. I'll wait here until dawn. If you're not back by then, I'll go straight to Leman Street Station and report two gentlemen missing."

"That's very kind of you, Detective Hatchery," said Dickens. He smiled. "But as you said, the constables and inspectors won't go below to look for us."

"Oh, I don't know, sir," said the detective, shrugging. "What with you both being famous authors an' fine gentlemen, perhaps they'd see fit to make an exception in this case. I just 'ope we don't have to find out, sir."

Dickens laughed at this. "Come along, Wilkie."

"Mr Dickens," said Hatchery, reaching under his

coat and coming out with a huge pistol of the revolver variety. "Perhaps you should take this with you, sir. Even if just for the rats."

"Oh, posh," said Dickens, waving the weapon away with his white gloves. (You need to remember, Dear Reader, that in our era—I have no idea of the custom in yours—none of our police carried firearms of any sort. Nor did our criminals, for the most part. Hatchery's talk of "agreements" between the underworld and law enforcement was true in many unspoken ways.)

"I will take it," I said. "And gladly. I hate rats."

The pistol was as heavy as it looked and it filled my right jacket pocket. I felt strangely off balance with the massive thing pulling me down on one side. I told myself that I might soon feel far more off balance should I need such a weapon and not have one.

"Do you know how to fire a pistol, sir?" asked Hatchery.

I shrugged. "I assume that the general idea is to aim the end with the opening at one's target and to pull the trigger," I said. I was hurting all over now. In my mind's eye, I could see the jug of laudanum on my locked kitchen's cupboard shelf.

"Yes, sir," said Hatchery. His bowler was pulled down so tight that it seemed to be compressing his skull. "That *is* the general idea. You may have noticed it 'as two barrels, Mr Collins. An upper one and a larger lower one."

I had not taken notice of this. I tried to pull the absurdly heavy weapon from my pocket, but it snagged on the lining, ripping the cloth of my expensive jacket. Cursing softly, I managed to extricate it and study it in the lamplight.

"Ignore the lower one, sir," said Hatchery. "It's made for grapeshot. A form of shotgun. Nasty thing. You won't be needin' that, I 'ope, sir, and I have no ammunition for it anyway. My brother, who was in the army until recently, bought the gun from an American chap, although it was made in France...but not to worry, there are good English proof marks on it, sir, from our very own Birmingham Proof 'ouse. The cylinder for the smoothbore barrel *is* loaded, sir. There are nine shots in the cylinder."

"Nine?" I said, putting the huge, heavy thing back in my pocket while taking care not to rip the lining any worse than it had been. "Very good."

"Would you like more bullets, sir? I 'ave a bag of them an' caps in my pocket. I'd 'ave to show you 'ow to use the ramrod, sir. But it's fairly simple, as such skills go."

I almost laughed then, thinking of all the things that might be in Detective Hatchery's pockets and on his belt. "No, thank you," I said. "Nine balls should suffice."

"They're forty-two calibre, sir," continued the detective. "Nine should be more than sufficient for your average rat...four-legged or two-legged, as the case may be."

I shuddered at that.

"We'll see you before dawn, Hatchery," said Dickens, tucking his watch into his waistcoat and leading the way down the very steep steps, the bullseye lantern held low. "Come, Wilkie. We have less than four hours before the sun rises."

Wilkie, do you know Edgar Allan Poe?"

"No," I said. We were ten steps down with no end of the steep shaft in sight. The "steps" were more like pyramid blocks, at least three feet from one level down to the next, each step and slab slick with trickles of underground moisture; the shadows thrown by the small lantern ink black and deceptive, and if either of us stumbled here, it would certainly result in broken bones and most probably a broken neck. I half-stepped, half-jumped to the next step down, panting as I tried to keep up with the tiny cone of bobbing light emanating from Dickens's hand. "A friend of yours, Charles?" I asked. "An expert on crypts and catacombs, perhaps?"

Dickens laughed. The echo was wonderfully awful in the steep stone shaft. I hoped with all my heart that he would not do it again.

"A definitive 'no' to your first question, my dear Wilkie," he said. "Quite possibly a 'yes' to the second surmise."

Dickens had stopped on a level area and now he turned the lantern to illuminate steep walls, a low ceiling ahead, and a corridor stretching off into the dark. Black rectangles on both sides of the corridor suggested open doorways. I jumped down onto the last step to join him. He turned to me and rested both hands and the bullseye on the brass beak of his stick.

"I met Poe in Baltimore during the last weeks of my 1842 tour in America," he said. "I must say that the fellow forced first his book, *Tales of the Grotesque and Arabesque,* on me, and then his attention. Freely conversing as if we were equals or old friends, Poe kept us talking—or kept himself talking, I should say—for hours, about literature and his work and my work and again about his work. I never did get around to reading his stories while I was in America, but Catherine did. She was quite enthralled. Evidently this Poe loved to write about crypts, corpses, premature burials, and hearts ripped out of living breasts."

I kept peering into the darkness beyond the tiny circle of light from the bullseye. Straining so hard—my eyes are not strong—made the shadows everywhere coalesce and shift, like tall forms stirring. My headache grew worse.

"I presume that all this has some relevance, Dickens," I said sharply.

"Only in the sense that I am receiving the distinct impression that Mr Edgar Allan Poe would be enjoying this outing more than you are at the moment, my dear Wilkie."

"Well then," I said a bit sharply, "I wish your friend Poe *were* here now."

Dickens laughed again, the echo not so intense this time but even more unnerving as it bounced off unseen walls and niches in the dark. "Perhaps he is. Perhaps he is. I remember reading that Mr Poe died only six or seven years after I met him, quite young and under odd and perhaps unseemly circumstances. From our brief but intense acquaintanceship, this place seems to be *exactly* the kind of stone barrow his ghost would enjoy haunting."

"What *is* this place?" I asked.

As if in answer, Dickens raised the lantern and led the way down the corridor. The doorways I had sensed on both sides were actually open niches. Dickens aimed the bullseye into the first niche on our right as we reached it.

About six feet into this space, an elaborate iron grille rose from the stone floor to stone ceiling; the grille was massive, its cross-members solid, but had openings in the shape of florettes. The blood-red-and-orange iron looked so ancient and rusted that I felt that it would crumble away if I stepped in and struck it with my fist. But I had no intention of stepping into the niche. Behind the iron grille were rows and columns of stacked coffins so solid that I guessed them to be lined with lead. I counted about a dozen in the shifting light and shadows.

"Can you read that plate, Wilkie?"

Dickens was referring to a white stone plaque set

high on the iron grille. Another plaque had fallen into the accumulated dirt and heaps of rust on the floor of the niche and a third was lying on its side at the base of the grille.

I adjusted my glasses and squinted. The stone was streaked and stained white by the rising damp and was pockmarked with dark red from the rusted grille beneath and around it. The letters appeared to be—

E. I.
THE CAYA[obscured]**OMB**
OF
[missing]**HE REV**[obscured]**D**
L.L. B [stain obscured]

I read this to Dickens, who had stepped inside for a closer look, and then I said, "Not Roman, then."

"These catacombs?" said Dickens in his distracted manner as he crouched to try to read the plate that had fallen into the dirt like a tumbled headstone. "No. They were built in the essential Roman manner—deep corridors lined on both sides with burial niches—but original Roman catacombs would be labyrinthine in layout. These were Christian, but very old, Wilkie, very old, and therefore designed, as some of our city is above, on the grid. In this case, it is laid out as a central cross surrounded by these burial niches and smaller passages. You notice the arched brick rather than stone above me here..." He aimed the lantern higher.

I did notice the arched brick vault then. And for the first time I realised that the reddish "dirt" on the floor, several inches deep in places, was detritus from the crumbling bricks and mortar falling from that vaulted ceiling.

"This was a Christian catacombs," repeated Dickens. "Installed directly under the chapel above."

"But there is no chapel above," I whispered.

"Not for many years," agreed Dickens, rising and trying to flick the dirt from his gloves while still holding the lantern and his stick. "But there was long ago. A monastery chapel would be my guess. Part of the Monastery of the Church of Saint Ghastly Grim's."

"You made that up," I said accusingly.

Dickens looked at me oddly. "Of course I did," he said. "Shall we move on?"

I hadn't liked standing in the dark corridor with no light behind me, so I was grateful when Dickens emerged from the niche and prepared to press on. But first he shone the light back into the vault again, passing its beam over the rows and columns of coffins stacked behind the rusting grille.

"I neglected to mention," he said softly, "that as with their Roman originals, these burial niches are called *loculi*. Each *loculus* is reserved for a family or perhaps for members of a specific order of monks over many decades. The Romans tended to excavate their catacombs logically, all at one time, but these later Christian tunnels were dug out over a much longer period of time and tend to stray and wander. Do you know Garraway's Coffee House?"

"On Exchange Alley?" I said. "Cornhill? But of course. I've had coffee there many a time while waiting for a sale to begin in the adjoining auction house."

"There is a similar old monastery crypt under Garraway's," said Dickens, whispering now as if he were afraid some spectral form had joined us. "I have been in it, down there among the port wine. I have often wondered if Garraway's is taking pity on the mouldy men who wait in its public-room all their lives by giving them that cool crypt down below to hold the rest of those gone missing from what fools call 'real life' up there on the surface." He glanced at me. "Of course, my dear Wilkie, the catacombs of Paris—and you have been there, I know, since I took you there—the catacombs of Paris would not be large enough to hold the rest of the truly missing souls of London if we were all forced to go below, out of the light, down into the mouldy dark where we belong when we forget how to live well among upright men."

"Dickens, what in the deuce are you going on about…" I stopped. There had been a stirring or footstep down the dark corridor, out of the weak glow of our single small lamp.

Dickens turned the bullseye but there was nothing in the cone of light but stone and shadows. The roof of the main passageway was flat stone, not arched brick. It went on for at least fifty yards. Dickens led the way down this corridor, pausing only to shine his beam in some of the niches that opened to the left and right of the passage. They were all *loculi,* niches holding stacks of massive coffins behind identical rusted-iron grilles. At the end of the passage Dickens passed his beam of light over the wall and even ran his free hand over the stone, pressing here and there as if searching for some spring-lever and secret passage. None opened to us.

"So…" I began. What was I going to say? *You see? There's no Undertown after all. No Mr Drood down here. Are you satisfied? Let us go home, please, Dickens, I need to take my laudanum.* I said, "This seems to be all there is."

"Not at all," said Dickens. "Did you see that candle on the wall?"

I had not. We walked back to the next-to-last *loculus* and Dickens aimed the bullseye higher. It was there in a niche, a thick tallow candle burned to a stub.

"Left by the ancient Christians, perhaps?" I said.

"I believe not," Dickens said drily. "Light it, please, my dear Wilkie. And walk ahead of me back towards the entrance."

"Why?" I asked, but when he did not answer, I reached for the candle, fumbled matches out of my left pocket—the absurdly heavy pistol still weighed down my jacket on the right—and lit the thing. Dickens nodded, rather brusquely I thought, and I held the stub of candle in front of me as I walked slowly back the way we had come.

"There!" cried Dickens when we had covered about half the distance.

"What?"

"Didn't you see the candle flame flicker, Wilkie?"

If I had, it hadn't registered, but I said, "Just a draught from the entrance stairs, no doubt."

"I think not," said Dickens. His emphasis on the negative every time I spoke was beginning to annoy me.

Using his lantern, Dickens peered into the *loculus* on our left and then into the one on our right. "Ahhh!" he said.

Still holding the slightly flickering candle, I peered into the niche but saw nothing to evoke such an ejaculation of surprise and satisfaction.

"On the floor," said Dickens.

I realised that the red dust there had been trod down into a sort of path that led to the iron grille and the coffins. "Some recent interment?" I said.

"I seriously doubt it," said Dickens, continuing his string of negative assessments of my contributions. He led the way into the arched vault, handed me the lantern, and shook the iron grille with both gloved hands.

A section of the grille—its joints and edges and hinges invisible from even a few feet away—swung inward towards the stacks of coffins.

Dickens went through without a pause. In a second his lantern seemed to sink into the red dust beneath him. It took me a minute to realise that there were steps back there and that Dickens was descending them.

"Come along, Wilkie," echoed the writer's voice.

I hesitated. I had the candle. I had the pistol. I could be back at the base of the steps in thirty seconds and up them and out into the crypt above—under Detective Hatchery's protection again—thirty seconds after that.

"Wilkie!" The lantern and the author were both out of sight now. I could see the brick ceiling still illuminated above the place where he had disappeared. I looked back towards the dark entrance to the *loculus*, then at the heavy coffins stacked atop their biers on either side of the path in the red dust, and then back towards the opening again.

"Wilkie, please hurry now. And snuff the candle but do bring it along. This bullseye does not have unlimited fuel."

I walked through the open grille door and past the coffins and towards the still-not-visible stairs.

CHAPTER SIX

*T*he stairway was of unsteady stone, the narrow vault ceiling of brick, and within a few minutes we had come out into another level of corridor and *loculi*.

"More crypts," I said.

"Older here," Dickens whispered. "Notice that this corridor curves, Wilkie. And the ceiling is much lower here. And the entrances to these *loculi* have been bricked up, which reminds me of a story by the late Mr Poe of whom I was speaking somewhat earlier."

I did not ask Dickens to share the story. I was about to ask him why he was whispering when he whispered over his shoulder, "Do you see the glow ahead?"

At first I did not because of the bullseye lantern's glare, but then I did. It was very dim and appeared to originate somewhere around the bend in the stone corridor.

Dickens lowered the shield over most of the bullseye's lens and gestured for me to follow him. The paving stones on this lower, older level of the catacombs were uneven, and several times I had to use my stick to brace myself from falling. Just around the bend in the corridor, more main passageways branched to the right and left.

"Is this a Roman catacomb?" I whispered.

Dickens shook his top-hatted head, but I felt it was more to quiet me than to answer me. He pointed to the passage on the right from which the glow seemed to be coming.

It was the only *loculus* not bricked up. A dark and ragged curtain covered most of the arched opening, but not so completely as to hide the glow from within. I touched the pistol in my pocket as Dickens walked brazenly through the rotted gauze.

This *loculus* was long and narrow and opened into other niches and vaults and *loculi*. And the corpses here were not in coffins.

The bodies lay along wooden benches that ran from floor to ceiling for the entire length of the narrow passage. They were all corpses of men—and not Englishmen or Christians or Romans from the looks of them. They were skeletal, but not mere skeletons; the tanned skin and stringy flesh and glass marble–looking eyes appeared to have been mummified. Indeed, these might be Egyptian mummies we were walking past, lying there in their rotted robes and tatters, except for the Oriental cast to the mummified features and unblinking eyes. When Dickens paused for a moment, I leaned closer to inspect one of the mummies' faces.

It blinked.

I let out a cry and leaped back, dropping the candle. Dickens picked it up and came closer, holding the bullseye high to illuminate the shelf and the corpse on it.

"Did you think them dead, Wilkie?" the author whispered.

"Are they not?"

"Did you not see the opium pipes?" he asked softly.

I had not. I did now. These pipes—largely lost to sight where they were clutched against the mummies' bodies, the bowls and mouthpieces in the mummies' hands—were much more elaborately carved than the cheap pipes in Sal's emporium in Shadwell above.

"Did you not smell the opium?" whispered Dickens.

I had not but I did now. It was a softer, sweeter, infinitely more subtle smell than the drug stench in Sal's. I looked back the way we had come and realised that the dozens of dead men on these rotted shelves in this crypt were all ancient but still-breathing Asiatics lying there with their pipes.

"Come," said Dickens and led me into a side room from whence came the glow.

There were more shelves and bunks there, some with cushions visible, and a heavier cloud of opium, but in the middle—sitting cross-legged in a Buddha posture atop a backless wooden couch set on a stone bier so that his Oriental eyes were at the same height as ours—was a Chinaman who looked as ancient and mummified as those forms on the shelves behind us and ahead of us. But his gown or robe or whatever it should be called, as well as his headpiece, were made of bright, clean silk, all reds and greens with gold and blue patterns sewn throughout, and his white moustache drooped down ten inches beneath his chin. Behind this figure were two huge men, also Chinamen but much younger, shirtless, standing against the empty stone wall with their hands folded over their crotches. Their muscles gleamed in the light from the two red candles that rose on either side of the thin Buddha-figure.

"Mr Lazaree?" said Dickens, stepping closer to the cross-legged man. "Or should I say King Lazaree?"

"Welcome, Mr Dickens," said the figure. "And welcome to Mr Collins as well."

I took a step back at hearing my name spoken in such perfect and unaccented English from this pure stereotype of Yellow Peril. In truth, I realised later, his English *had* been lightly accented... but it was a Cambridge accent.

Dickens laughed softly. "You knew we were coming."

"Of course," said King Lazaree the Chinee. "Very little occurs in Bluegate Fields or Shadwell or Whitechapel or London itself, for that matter, that I do not hear about. News of a visit from someone of your fame and eminence...and I include both of you literary gentlemen, of course, in that phrase...is conveyed to me almost instantly."

Dickens made a slight but graceful bow. I could only stare. I realised that I was still holding the unlighted candle in my left hand.

"Then you know why we have come down here," said Dickens.

King Lazaree nodded.

"Will you help us find him?" continued Dickens. "Drood, I mean."

Lazaree held up one open hand. I was shocked to see that the fingernails on that hand must have been six inches long. And curved. The nail on the little finger of that hand was at least twice that long.

"The benefit of Undertown," said King Lazaree, "is that those who wish not to be disturbed here are *not* disturbed. It is the one understanding that we share with the dead who surround us here."

Dickens nodded as if this made eminent sense. "Is *this* Undertown?" he asked.

It was King Lazaree's turn to laugh. Unlike Opium Sal's dry rattle, the Chinaman's laughter was easy and liquid and rich. "Mr Dickens, this is a simple opium den in a simple catacomb. Our customers once came from—and returned to—the world above, but now most prefer to stay here through the years and decades. But Undertown? No, this is not Undertown. One might say that this is the foyer to the antechamber of the porch of the vestibule of Undertown."

"Will you help us find it...and *him*?" asked Dickens. "I know you do not wish to disturb the other... ah...inhabitants of this world, but Drood let me know that he *wanted* me to find him."

"And how did he do that?" asked King Lazaree. I admit to being curious on that point myself.

"By going out of his way to introduce himself to me," said Dickens. "By telling me where in London he was going. By creating such a mystery around himself that he knew I would try to find him."

The Chinaman on the wooden couch did not nod or blink. I realised then that I could not remember seeing him blink during this entire interview. His dark eyes seemed as glassy and lifeless as those belonging to the mummified figures on the benches all around us. When Lazaree did finally speak, it was in a lower tone, as if he were debating with himself.

"It would be very unfortunate if either of you gentlemen were to write and publish anything about our subterranean world here. You see how fragile it is . . . and how easily accessible."

I thought of Hatchery's having to put his heavy shoulder so energetically to the crypt bier that hid the upper doorway, about the barely visible path in the red dust to the invisible door in the iron grate, about the narrowness and eeriness of the stairway descending to this level, and the labyrinth we had traversed just to find this second opium den. . . . All in all, I was not so sure I agreed with the Chinaman king about the accessibility of this place.

Dickens appeared to, however. He nodded and said, "My interest is in finding Drood. Not in writing about this place." He turned to me. "You feel the same, do you not, Mr Collins?"

I was able to grunt and let the King of the Opium Living Dead take that as he wished. I was a novelist. Everything and everyone in my life was material. Certainly this writer whom I stood next to in the candle-light here had already proven that maxim more than had any other writer of our or any other age. How could he speak for me and say that I would never write about such an extraordinary place? How could he speak honestly for *himself* and say such a thing…this man who had turned his father, mother, sad figure of a wife, former friends, and former lovers into mere grist for his fictional-character wheel?

King Lazaree lowered his head and silken cap ever so slowly. "It would be *very* unfortunate if some harm were to come to you, Mr Dickens, or you, Mr Collins, while you were our guests here or explorers of Undertown beyond here."

"We feel precisely the same way!" said Dickens. He sounded almost merry.

"Yet no guarantees for your safety can be made beyond this point," continued the Chinaman. "You will understand when…*if*…you proceed."

"We ask for no guarantees," said Dickens. "Only for advice on how and *where* to proceed."

"You do not fully understand," said King Lazaree, his voice sounding harsh and Asiatic for the first time. "*If* something were to happen to one of you gentlemen, the other would not be allowed to return to the world above to write, tell, and testify about it."

Dickens looked at me again. He turned back to Lazaree. "We understand," he said.

"Not completely," said the thin Buddha-figure. "If something *were* to happen to both of you down here— and if it were to happen to one, as you now understand, it *must* happen to both—your bodies will be found elsewhere. In the Thames, to be precise. Along with Detective Hatchery's. The detective already understands this. It is imperative that you also do before you decide to proceed."

Dickens looked at me again but did not ask a question. To be honest, I would have preferred at that instant that we retire for a moment to discuss the matter and to take a vote. To be *completely* honest, I would have preferred at that moment that we simply bid the Opium Chinaman King a pleasant evening and have retired altogether—up out of that underground charnel house and back into the fresh night air, even if that fresh air carried the stinking miasma of the overcrowded burial ground that Dickens called St Ghastly Grim's.

"We understand," Dickens was saying earnestly to the Chinaman. "We agree to the conditions. But we still wish to go on, down into Undertown, and to find Mr Drood. How do we do that, King Lazaree?"

I was in such shock at Dickens having made this life-and-death decision for me without so much as a consultation or by-your-leave that I heard Lazaree's response as if from a great, muffled distance.

"*Je suis un grand partisan de l'ordre,*" the Chinaman was saying or reciting.

> "*Mais je n'aime pas celui-ci.*
> *Il peint un éternel désordre,*
> *Et, quand il vous consigne ici,*
> *Dieu jamais n'en révoque l'ordre.*"

"Very good," replied Dickens, although, in my shock at Dickens's speaking for me, at Dickens's having gambled *my* life along with his in such cavalier fashion, I had not understood a word of the French.

"And how and where do we find this eternal disorder and order?" continued Dickens.

"Understanding that even eternal disorder has a perfect order such as Wells, find the apse and the altar and descend behind the rude screen," said King Lazaree.

"Yes," said Dickens, nodding as if he understood and even glancing at me as if telling me to take notes.

"All that they boast of Styx, of Acheron," recited
Lazaree,
"Cocytus, Phlegethon, our have proved in one:
The filth, stench, noise; save only what was there
Subtly distinguishèd, was confusèd here.
Their wherry had no sail, too; ours had none;
And in it two more horrid knaves than Charon.
Arses were heard to croak instead of frogs,
And for one Cerberus, the whole coast was dogs.
Furies there wanted not; each scold was ten;
And for the cries of ghosts, women, and men
Laden with plague-sores and their sins were heard,
Lashed by their consciences; to die, afeard."

I tried to catch Dickens's eye then, to tell him
through sheer glare and intensity that it was time to
leave, past time to leave, that our opium-lord host was
insane, as were we for coming down here in the first
place, but the Inimitable—d——n his eyes!—was nodding again as if all this made sense and saying, "Very
good, very good. Is there anything else we need to
know to get us to Drood?"

"Only to remember to pay the horrid knaves," whispered King Lazaree.

"Of course, of course," said Dickens, sounding absolutely delighted with himself and the Chinaman. "We
shall be going, then. Ah...I presume that the corridor
we entered through and your...ah...establishment
here are, in terms of, well, wells, part of the eternal dis-
ordered order?"

Lazaree actually smiled. I saw the gleam of very
small, very sharp teeth. They looked to have been filed
to points. "Of course," he said softly. "Consider the
former the south aisle of the nave and the latter the
Cloister Garth."

"Thank you very much indeed," said Dickens. "Come,

Wilkie," he said to me as he led us back out of the opium den of mummies.

"One last thing," said King Lazaree as we were ready to go out through the doorway into the main hall of the mummies.

Dickens paused and leaned on his stick.

"Watch out for the boys," said the Chinaman. "Some are cannibals."

WE HEADED BACK into and down the outer corridor the way we had come. The bullseye lantern seemed dimmer than before.

"Are we leaving?" I asked hopefully.

"Leaving? Of course not. You heard what King Lazaree said. We're close to the entrance of the actual Undertown. With any luck at all, we shall meet with Drood and be back to take Detective Hatchery out to breakfast before the sun rises over Saint Ghastly Grim's."

"I heard that obscene Chinaman say that our bodies— and Hatchery's—would be found floating in the Thames if we continued with this insane quest," I said. My voice echoed from stone. It was not a completely steady sound.

Dickens laughed softly. I believe I began hating him at that moment.

"Nonsense, Wilkie, nonsense. You understand his point of view. Should something happen to us down here—and we are, after all, men of some public notice, my dear Wilkie—then the ensuing attention on their little sanctuary here would be devastating."

"So they will dump us in the Thames together," I muttered. "What was all that French about?"

"You did not understand?" asked Dickens as he led us back towards the first corridor. "I thought you spoke some French."

"I was distracted," I said sulkily. I was tempted to add, *And I have not been crossing the Channel to the little village of Condette to visit an actress in secret for the past five years, so I have had less opportunity to practise my French,* but I restrained myself.

"It was some small poem," said the author. He paused in the darkness, cleared his throat, and recited...

> *"I am a great partisan of order,*
> *But I do not like the one here.*
> *It depicts an eternal disorder,*
> *And, when he consigns you here,*
> *God never revokes the order."*

I looked left and right at the walled-up entrances to the ancient *loculi*. The poem almost—not quite—made sense.

"That and his mention of Wells made it all clear," continued Dickens.

"Mention of wells?" I said stupidly.

"Wells Cathedral, certainly," said Dickens, lifting the lamp and leading us on again. "You've been there, I assume."

"Well, yes, but..."

"This lower level of the catacombs obviously is laid out in the design of a great cathedral...Wells, to be precise. What seems random is quite determined. Nave, chapter house, north and south transepts, altar, and apse. King Lazaree's opium den, for instance, as he was kind enough to explain, would be where the Cloister Garth is in Wells Cathedral. Our entrance point from above would be at the western towers. We have just returned to the south aisle of the nave, you see, and have turned right towards the south transept. Notice how this corridor is wider than the one to the cloister?"

I nodded but Dickens did not look back to see the

motion as we pressed on. "I heard some mention of an altar and a rude curtain," I said.

"Ah, yes. But perhaps you did not follow that the word is 'rood'—r-o-o-d—my dear Wilkie. As you must know, and certainly I must, since I grew up quite literally in the shadow of the great cathedral at Rochester, about which I hope to write someday, the apse is the semicircular recess at the altar end of the chancel. On one side of the high altar, to hide the work of the priests from the common eyes, is the altar screen. On the other side, the transept side, the opposing screen is called the rood screen. Fascinating, is it not, how that word ... 'rood' ... rhymes so charmingly with 'Drood.'"

"Fascinating," I said drily. "And what was all that rot about Styx, of Acheron, more horrid knaves than Charon, and arses croaking instead of frogs?"

"You did not recognise that?" cried Dickens. He actually stopped in his surprise and swung the lamp in my direction. "That was our own dear Ben Jonson and his 'On the Famous Voyage,' written somewhere around the Year of Our Lord 1610, if I am not mistaken."

"You rarely are," I muttered.

"Thank you," said Dickens, completely missing my sarcasm.

"But what did all that verse about Cocytus, Phlegethon, filth, stench, noise, and Charon and Cerebus have to do with Mr Drood?"

"It tells me that a river voyage lies before one or both of us, my dear Wilkie." The lantern showed the corridor—the "nave" as it were—narrowing ahead towards multiple openings. Transept and apse? Altar screen and rood screen? Shelves of opium-smoking Asian mummies? Or just more foul, bone-filled crypts?

"A river voyage?" I repeated stupidly. I wanted very

much to have my laudanum then. And I wished very much that I were at home to have it.

THE "APSE" WAS a circular area of the catacomb set under a dome of stone rising about fifteen feet above the floor. We came to it from the side, as if stepping in from the choir aisle, should this be the layout of an actual cathedral. The "altar" was a massive stone bier much like the one that Hatchery had shifted so far above us now.

"If we are meant to move that," I said, pointing to the bier, "then our voyage ends here."

Dickens nodded. "We're not" was all he said. There was a rotted curtain to the left—perhaps once a tapestry, although all patterns had faded to black and brown in the subterranean darkness over the centuries— partially shielding the bier-altar from the apse-area under the dome. Another, plainer, even more rotted curtain hung against the stone wall to the right of this rude presbytery.

"The rood screen," said Dickens, pointing with his stick at this second curtain. Still using his cane, he moved the rotted fabric aside to reveal a narrow gap in the wall.

The descent here was much steeper and narrower than anything we had yet seen. The steps were of wood; the tunnel appeared to have been gouged out of soil and stone; there were crude wooden pilings shoring up the sides and ceiling.

"Do you think this is older than the catacombs?" I whispered ahead to Dickens as we carefully descended the steep and winding staircase. "Earlier Christian? Roman? Some sort of Saxon Druidic passage?"

"Hardly. I think this is quite recent, Wilkie. No more than a few years old. Notice that the steps appear to be made from railway timbers. They still show signs of pitch. It is my guess that whoever tunnelled this staircase out, tunnelled *up* to the catacombs above."

"Up?" I repeated. "Up from what?"

A second later the stench hit me as surely as if I'd stepped into a rural privy and answered my question. I reached for my handkerchief, only to be reminded once again that Dickens had taken it and used it for other purposes so many dark hours ago.

We emerged into the sewer proper a few minutes later. It was a low, vaulted channel only seven or eight feet across and less than six feet high, the floor of it more oozing mud than flowing liquid, the walls and vaulted ceilings of brick. The stench brought so many tears to my eyes that I had to wipe them in order to be able to see what Dickens's pale cone of bullseye light illuminated.

I saw that Dickens held another silk handkerchief to his nose and mouth. *He had brought two!* Rather than use both of his, he had commandeered mine for the corpses of the babies, fully knowing, I was sure, that I would need it later. The anger in me deepened.

"This is as far as I go," I told him.

Dickens's large eyes seemed puzzled as he turned to me. "Why, for heaven's sake, Wilkie? We have come so far."

"I'm not wading in that," I said, gesturing angrily at the deep and putrid ooze of the channel.

"Oh, we shan't have to," said Dickens. "Do you notice the brick walkway along each side? It's several inches higher than the foul matter."

"Foul matter" is what we writers call the manuscripts and written-upon galley pages that the publishers return to us. I wondered if Dickens was making some weak joke.

But the "walkways" were there on each side just as he said, curving out of sight in both directions along the narrow sewer tunnel. But they were hardly side-walks; the one on our side could not have been more than ten inches wide.

I shook my head, unsure.

Handkerchief still held firmly over his lower face and walking stick now tucked under his arm, Dickens had retrieved a clasp knife from his pocket and quickly made three parallel marks on the crumbling brick where our crude staircase opened into the sewer.

"What is that for?" I asked, knowing the answer as soon as I asked the question. Perhaps the vapours were affecting my higher ratiocinative abilities.

"To find our way back," he said. Folding the knife, he held it in the lamplight and said irrelevantly, "A gift from my American hosts in Massachusetts during my tour. I've found it very useful over the years. Come along; it's getting late."

"Why do you think our goal lies in this direction?" I asked as I shuffled behind him to the right along the narrow strip of brick, lowering my head to keep the low arching wall there from knocking my top hat into the muck.

"A guess," said Dickens. Within minutes we had come to a three-tunnel branching of the sewer. Luckily the channel was narrower there and Dickens hopped across, using his stick to keep his balance. He cut three marks on the corner of the centre channel and made room for me to hop after him.

"Why this channel?" I asked when we were twenty or thirty yards in.

"It seemed wider," said Dickens. We came to another parting of tunnels. He chose the one to the right and marked his three stripes on the brick.

A hundred yards into this lesser channel and he stopped. I saw on the wall opposite—there was no walkway on that side—a metal candle reflector held up on a spade, its handle buried in the muck, with some sort of round wood-and-wire screen propped against the wall beneath it. A quarter of an inch of tallow candle remained in the reflector.

"What on earth could that be?" I whispered. "To what purpose here?"

"The property of a sewer-hunter," Dickens replied in conversational tones. "Haven't you read your Mayhew?"

I had not. Staring at the filth-rimmed pan obviously made for screening, I said, "What in Christ's name could they be sifting and hunting for in this muck?"

"All those things that we lose into the sewers sooner or later," said Dickens. "Rings. Coins. Even bones can have their value to those who own nothing." He poked at the spade and circular sieve with his stick. "Richard Beard illustrated just such an apparatus in Mayhew's *London Labour and the London Poor*," he said. "You really must read it, my dear Wilkie."

"As soon as we get out of here," I whispered. It was a promise I planned to honour in the breach.

We moved on, sometimes having to scuttle forward in an almost crouching position as the vaulted ceiling grew lower. For a moment I felt panic when I thought of Hatchery's little bullseye running out of fuel, but then I remembered the heavy stub of catacomb candle in my left pocket.

"Do you think these are part of Bazalgette's new sewer system?" I asked sometime later. The only good news in our progress was that the overwhelming power of the stench had all but numbed my sense of smell. I realised that I would have to burn my clothes; a misfortune, since I particularly prized the jacket and waistcoat.

I may have mentioned earlier that Joseph Bazalgette, chief engineer of the Board of Works, had proposed a complex system of new sewers to drain off sewage from the Thames and to embank the mudflats along its shores. The passage of the plan had been expedited by the Great Stink of June 1858, when the work of the House of Commons had been disrupted as the members fled the city. The Main Drainage Works at Crossness had been opened just the previous year, but dozens of miles of main and ancillary sewer projects were proceeding across and beneath the city. The Embankment part of the works was scheduled to be opened just five years hence.

"New?" said Dickens. "I doubt it very much. There are hundreds of ancient attempts at sewers under our city, Wilkie...some going back to the Romans...many of the passages all but forgotten by the Board of Works."

"But remembered by the sewer-hunters," I said.

"Precisely."

Suddenly we emerged into a taller, wider, drier space. Dickens stood still and shone the bullseye in all directions. The walls were stone here and the vaulted brick roof was supported by multiple pillars. Along the drier sides of this bowl lay sleeping mats of every description, some of rough rope, others of expensive wool. Heavy lamps hung by chains and the ceiling was darkened by smoke. A square cast-iron stove stood at the highest point on an island in the middle of this concavity and I could see a sort of stovepipe which—rather than rising through the stone ceiling—extended downward into one of four adjacent sewers that radiated from this place. Rough planks on boxes served as a table and I could see dishes and dirty utensils stowed in the boxes themselves, alongside smaller boxes that might hold provisions.

"I don't believe it," gasped Dickens. He turned to me with eyes alight and a huge grin on his face. "Do you know what this reminds one of, Wilkie?"

"The Wild Boys!" I cried. "I cannot believe that

you are reading those particular advanced editions, Dickens!"

"Of course," laughed the most famous author of our day. "*Everyone* literary I know is reading it, Wilkie! And none of us admitting such to the others for fear of censure and ridicule."

He was talking about advanced copies of *The Wild Boys of London; or, The Children of the Night—A Story of the Present Day*. It was a dreadful series currently circulating in galley form but soon to be published for the general public, if the authorities did not suppress it completely on grounds of obscenity.

I have to admit that there was little obscene about the turgid tale of wild boys living like pitiable animals in the sewers beneath the city, although I do remember a particularly gruesome and suggestive illustration of several of the boys finding a mostly nude body of a woman in their sewer searches. In another scene, mercifully not illustrated, a boy new to the Wild Boys group comes across the corpse of a man being consumed by rats. So perhaps it was obscene after all.

But who was to imagine that such a fantastical tale, indifferently told, was based on the truth?

Dickens laughed—the sound echoing down different dark channels—and said, "This place is not so different from my favourite London club, Wilkie."

"Except that King Lazaree warned us that some of these diners are cannibals," I said.

As if in response to our witticisms, there came the squeak and scuttle of rats from one of the openings, although it was impossible to tell which. Perhaps from all.

"Do we turn back now?" I asked, perhaps a shade plaintively. "Now that we have discovered the heart of the mystery of Undertown?"

Dickens looked sharply at me. "Oh, I doubt very

much that this is the heart of the mystery. Nor even the liver or lights of same. Come, this channel looks the widest."

Fifteen minutes and five turnings and scratchings on the wall later, we emerged into a space that made the Wild Boys' living area look like a minor *loculus.*

This tunnel was a major thoroughfare compared to the low and mean sewers through which we had already passed: at least twenty-five feet across, fifteen feet high, the centre a river of quickly moving water—albeit a sludge-thick sorry excuse for water—rather than the mere oozes of mud and filth we had been scuttling past. The walls and brick path before us now, as well as the high vaulted arches, were built of gleaming new brick.

"This must be part of Bazalgette's new works," said Dickens, his voice sounding awed for the first time, the weakening beam of his bullseye playing across the wide thoroughfare and ceilings. "Although perhaps not officially opened yet."

I could only shake my head, as much in weariness as in astonishment. "Which way now, Dickens?"

"No way from here, I believe," he said softly. "Unless we swim."

I blinked and realised what he meant. This brick walkway was wide—five feet wide at least, as clean and spotless as a new city sidewalk above—but it only extended fifteen feet or so in each direction from our tunnel opening.

"Do we retrace our steps?" I asked. The idea of entering one of those tiny pipes again made my skin crawl.

Dickens turned his light on a post two yards or so to our left. It was made of wood and held a small ship's bell on it. "I think not," he said. Before I could protest, he had rung the bell four times. The brash sound echoed up and down the broad bricked thoroughfare above the quickly flowing waters.

Dickens found an abandoned pole at the end of this strange brick dock we were on and he thrust it down into the current. "Seven feet deep at least," he said. "Perhaps deeper. Did you know, Wilkie, that the French are preparing boat tours of their sewers? They are to be spotlit—women in the boats, men walking alongside for parts of the tour. A sort of bicycle apparatus will propel the flat-bottomed vessels while searchlights within the boat and others carried by *égoutiers* alongside will illuminate features of interest along the way."

"No," I said dully. "I didn't know that."

"There is talk of high society in Paris arranging rat-hunting tours."

I had had enough of this. I turned back towards the tunnel from which we had emerged. "Come along, Dickens. It's almost dawn. If Detective Hatchery goes to Leman Street Station and announces that we are lost, half the constables in London will be down here searching for the most famous writer alive today. King Lazaree and his friends would not want that."

Before Dickens could reply, there was a sudden flurry and several clusters of rags floating around white, rodent-like faces exploded from the tunnel.

I fumbled out the pistol. At the moment, I was convinced that we were being attacked by gigantic grub-faced rats.

Dickens stepped between me and the surging, feinting forms. "They're boys, Wilkie," he cried. "Boys!"

"Cannibal boys!" I cried back, raising the pistol.

As if to confirm my statement, one of the pale faces—all tiny eyes and long nose and sharp teeth in the bulls-eye light—lunged at Dickens and snapped, as if he were attempting to bite off the author's nose.

Dickens swatted away the face with his stick and

made to seize the child, but his hand came away with a wad of rags and the naked boy was gone along with his two or three cohorts, skittering down the low, dark passage from which they—and we before them—had emerged.

"Dear God," I gasped, still holding the heavy pistol high. I heard a sound behind me, from the water, and turned slowly, the pistol still raised. "Dear God," I whispered again.

A long, narrow boat of no design I had ever seen before had glided up to our brick esplanade. There was a tall figure holding a pole in the bow and another at a sweep in the stern, although except for the high stern and bow and oarsmen and lanterns hanging fore and aft, the craft bore only a vague resemblance to an Italian gondola.

The male figures were not quite men—the faces were absolutely pale and not yet shaped into manhood—but neither did they look still to be boys. They were very thin and dressed in tights and tunics that almost seemed to be uniforms. Their hands and glimpses of their chests and midriffs between the ill-fitting costumes showed flesh as ghastly pale as their faces. Most strangely in the dimness of the wide sewer, each boy-man was wearing a pair of square smoked glasses over domino masks, as if they had ventured out of a midnight masked ball into brilliant sunlight.

"I believe that our ride has arrived, Wilkie," whispered Dickens.

Glancing apprehensively over my shoulder at the black opening from whence I expected the wild boys to emerge again at any second, I crowded close to Dickens as he prepared to board the little boat. He paid the silent form in the bow two sovereigns, then paid the man at the sweep in the stern the same amount.

The two shook their heads and each handed one of the

sovereigns back. They pointed at Dickens and nodded. Then they pointed at me and shook their heads again.

Clearly I was not invited.

"My friend must accompany me," said Dickens to the silent pair. "I will not leave him." He fumbled out more coins. The shadowy shape at the sweep and the one in the bow shook their heads almost in unison.

"Are you from Mr Drood?" asked the author. He repeated the question in French. The silent pair did not respond to either language. Finally the one at the stern pointed to Dickens again and motioned for him to board. The one in the bow pointed to me and then to the brick walkway I was on, telling me to stay. I felt that they were commanding me as if I were a dog.

"The blazes with this," I said loudly. "Come back with me, Dickens. *Now.*"

The author looked at me, looked at the tunnel behind me—from which there were renewed scuttling sounds—looked at the boat, and craned to see up and down the underground river. "Wilkie..." he said at last. "After coming so far...after learning so much...I can't...just...turn back."

I could only stare. "Come back another night," I said. "For now we must be away."

He shook his head and handed me the bullseye lantern. "You have the pistol and...how many shots did Hatchery say?"

"Nine," I said. Disbelief rose in me rather as one's gorge might in a rough trailing sea. He *was* going to leave me behind.

"Nine shots and the lantern and the way back is clearly marked with three stripes the whole distance," said Dickens. I noticed the lisp in his voice that others often had commented upon. I thought that perhaps it became more noticeable when he was carrying out an act of treachery.

"And if there are more than nine wild cannibal boys?" I said softly. I was amazed to hear how reasonable my voice sounded, although the echo in the large bricked space distorted it some. "Or legions of rats that come to dine after you are gone?"

"That boy was no cannibal," said Dickens. "Only a lost child in rags so loose that they wouldn't stay on his back. But if it comes to that, Wilkie…shoot one of them. The others will scatter."

I laughed then. I really had no choice.

Dickens stepped aboard the little boat, bade the oarsman to wait a second, and consulted his watch by the lamp at the stern. "In another ninety minutes it will be too late to get back to Hatchery before the sun rises," he said. "Wait for me here on this clean dock, Wilkie. Light the candle to give more light alongside the bullseye and wait for me. I shall insist that my interview with Mr Drood not exceed an hour. We shall go back up into the light together."

I started to speak or laugh again, but no sound emerged. I realised that I was still holding the huge, heavy, idiotic pistol…and that it was aimed in the general direction of Dickens and his two boatmen. I did not need the grapeshot-shotgun barrel to send all three of them falling lifeless into the surging current of London's sewage. All I had to do was pull the trigger thrice. That would leave six cartridges and balls for the Wild Boys.

As if reading my thoughts, Dickens said, "I would take you along if I could, Wilkie. But obviously Mr Drood has a private interview in mind. If you are here when I return—in less than ninety minutes, I assure you—we will go up and out together."

I lowered the pistol. "And if I leave before you return—if you return," I said hoarsely, "you will have a hard time of it finding your way to the surface without the bullseye."

Dickens said nothing.

I lit the candle and sat between it and the lantern, my face to the tunnel opening, my back to Charles Dickens. I set the cocked pistol on my lap. I did not turn as the flat-bottomed boat slipped away from my tiny dock. The sweep and bow pole made such little noise that the sound of them was lost under the echoing rush of the underground river. To this day, I do not know if Dickens was carried upstream or down.

CHAPTER SEVEN

*T*he rest of that summer of 1865 remained hot. By early September the unusually warm and frequently stormy weather receded and London enjoyed clear skies, pleasant days, and cool nights.

I rarely saw Dickens during those intervening two months. His children, during the summer and school holidays, put out their own little paper—the *Gad's Hill Gazette*—and my brother, Charles, dropped off a packet of these in August. There were articles about picnics, outings to Rochester, cricket matches, and note of the first correspondence from Alfred, Dickens's son who had left for Australia in May to become a sheep farmer. Mentions of the Inimitable, other than the expected observations that he had presided over the picnics, Rochester outings, and cricket matches, merely confirmed that he was working hard on *Our Mutual Friend*.

From our common friend Percy Fitzgerald I learned that Dickens had taken a relatively large party of friends and family up to Bulwer-Lytton's estate, Knebworth, in order to celebrate the opening of the first homes for indigent artists and writers established by the Guild of Literature and Art. Dickens was in charge of the gathering and—according to Fitzgerald—"seemed to be his old, merry self." The Inimitable had made an energetic and upbeat speech, at one point in conversation privately compared his too-pompous friend John Forster to

Malvolio (in the company of several writers, knowing therefore that the comparison would get back to Forster), led a large group to drop in on a nearby tavern named Our Mutual Friend, and even took part in the open-air dancing before decamping back to London with his friends and family.

I was not invited.

It was also from my brother that I learned that Dickens was still suffering the after-effects of the Staplehurst disaster, including having to take the slow train whenever possible because rapid rail travel—and occasionally even travel by coach—would bring on the "shakes." And Charles also informed me of the postscript that Dickens had added to *Our Mutual Friend* when he finished it in the first week of September—it was the first postscript that Dickens had ever added to one of his books—in which the author defended his rather unusual method of narration in the novel, then briefly described his experience at Staplehurst, expurgating the presence of the Ternans and Drood, of course, and ended with the mildly disturbing peroration—*"I remember with devout thankfulness that I can never be much nearer parting company with my readers for ever, than I was then, until there shall be written against my life, the two words with which I have this day closed this book—THE END."*

It is perhaps not telling you too much, Dear Reader, since you do reside in our future, that Charles Dickens would not live to ever again pen those two words— THE END—at the close of another novel.

IT WAS ON A PLEASANT DAY in early September that Caroline came up to my study where I was working and presented me with the card of a gentleman waiting on the landing. The card read in its entirety—

INSPECTOR
CHARLES FREDERICK FIELD
Private Enquiry Bureau

Caroline must have seen my reaction in my expression, for she said, "Is there anything wrong? Shall I tell him to go away?"

"No, no...show him in. Be sure to close the door behind you after you do show him in, my dear."

A minute later and Field was in the study, bowing slightly, pumping my hand, and chatting away before I could say a word. As he spoke, I remembered an early description in one of Dickens's essays in *Household Words* about the inspector—"...*a middle-aged man of a portly presence, with a large, moist, knowing eye, a husky voice, and a habit of emphasising his conversation by the air of a corpulent forefinger, which is constantly in juxtaposition with his eyes or nose.*"

Field was beyond middle age now—I realised he must be about sixty years old—and only a fringe of grey hair remained where I remembered a lion's mane of darker curls over his ears, but the husky voice, knowing eye, and corpulent forefinger remained accurate and operative.

"Mr Collins, Mr Collins, it's a pleasure to see you again, sir. And to see you prospering so obviously and delightfully, sir. What a lovely room this is, sir. So many books. And I believe that is a copy of your own *The Woman in White* there by the ivory tusk—yes, upon my soul, it is. A wonderful book, so I hear, although I've not yet found the time to read it, but my wife has. You may remember me, sir..."

"Yes, of course, you accompanied Charles Dickens and me..."

"On one of your expeditions into the darker parts of our fair city, indeed I did, Mr Collins. Indeed, I did. And perhaps you remember that I was present the first time you met Mr Dickens."

"I am not sure that I . . ."

"No, no, sir, no reason for you to recall my presence there. It was 1851, sir. Mr Dickens had hired me, on a private basis you might say, to provide security for his performance of Lord Lytton's play *Not So Bad as We Seem* at a benefit by the Duke of Devonshire. You were an aspiring actor then, I believe, sir, and Mr Dickens—on the advice of Mr Egg, I do seem to recall—invited you to play the part of Smart. 'A small part,' I remember Mr Dickens saying to you during that first rehearsal, 'but what there is of it, decidedly good!' As were you, Mr Collins. As were you. Decidedly good. And I saw several performances, sir."

"Why, thank you, Inspector. I . . ."

"Yes—oh, may I be seated? Thank you very much. Beautiful stone egg here on your desk, Mr Collins. Is it onyx? Yes, I believe it is. Fascinating."

"Thank you, Inspector. To what do I owe . . ."

"You remember, I am sure, Mr Collins, that the Duke of Devonshire provided Devonshire House for that first performance of Lord Lytton's play. It was all for the good of the Guild of Literature and Art, as I recall. Sir Edward was president of the Guild at that time. Mr Dickens was vice-president. You may recall that I—and a few carefully chosen associates of mine—were hired to be present in what we call plain clothes because Lord Lytton's estranged wife, Rosina was her name, I believe, had threatened to disrupt the play. I saw the first note she sent Lord Lytton. She promised to pose as an orange-seller and to pelt the stage with fruit, as I recall." Inspector Field chuckled and I worked to return a smile.

"In another note," he continued, "she promised to throw rotten eggs at the Queen, who did attend despite the threats, I am sure you recall, sir, you having the memory of a writer after all. Her Majesty the Queen was there with Prince Albert that evening of the first performance and witnessed your first public appearance anywhere with Mr Dickens. Sixteen May, 1851, that was—seems like just last week, does it not, sir?—and you had your own special guests that night, Mr Collins. Your brother Charles, I do believe, and your mother...Harriet, I believe her name is, and I hope her health is good, Mr Collins, I surely do, and I seem to remember that she lives with your brother Charles and his wife, Kate, Dickens's eldest daughter, I do believe, when your mother is staying in town. At Clarence Terrace, I think the address is. A lovely neighbourhood. And a wonderful lady, she is. Oh, and you had other guests that night of the Command Performance fifteen years ago, I seem to recall. Edward and Henrietta Ward...a cigar? Why yes, sir. I don't mind if I do."

The offer of a fine cigar had served to stem the verbal flow, and the silence continued as we each trimmed our cigars, lit them, and savoured the first minute of smoking them. Before the detective could get his second wind, I said, "Your memory does your profession and yourself credit, Inspector Field. But I should ask—to what do I owe the pleasure of your visit?"

He removed the cigar from his mouth with his left hand and allowed the corpulent forefinger on his right hand to touch first the side of his nose, as if he were sniffing something out, and then to tap his lips, as if the finger were helping to form his next words. "Mr Collins, you should know that the 'Inspector' before my name now is a pure honourific, as I am no longer employed by the Scotland Yard Bureau of Detectives. Haven't been since the year after I protected the integrity of *Not So Bad as We Seem,* to be one-hundred-percent accurate."

"Well, I am sure the honourific is well deserved and should be and will be maintained by all who know you," I said, not bothering to point out that the "Inspector" title was plainly there on his card.

"Thank you, Mr Collins," said the florid detective, exhaling a great cloud of smoke. With the doors to my study closed and the window open only a small bit, as was my habit due to the noise from the streets outside, the little room was quickly filling up with blue smoke.

"Tell me, Inspector," I said, "how can I be of assistance today? Are you writing your memoirs? Is there some small gap in your otherwise voluminous and incredible memory which I could help fill in some way?"

"Memoirs?" chuckled Inspector Field. "Now *that* is an idea...but bless you, no, sir. Others, such as your friend Mr Dickens, have written about my...well, exploits would not be too bold a word for them, would it, sir?...about my exploits before, and I suspect that more will write about them in the future, but no memoirs on my docket for now, sir."

"How *can* I help you, then, Inspector?"

Cigar firmly clamped between his teeth, Field leaned forward, planted his elbows on my desk, and freed his corpulent forefinger to point first up, then down, then to prod the desk, and finally to point it at me. "It came to my attention, Mr Collins—came to my attention too late, I regret—that you and Mr Dickens were in Tiger Bay and the Undertown searching for a certain personage named Drood."

"Who told you that, Inspector?" My voice was cool. This former Scotland Yard detective had already exhibited too much curiosity and intrusion to suit me.

"Oh, Hib Hatchery, of course. He works for me.

Hatchery is an operative of my Private Enquiry Bureau.
Did not Mr Dickens tell you that?"

I remembered Dickens saying something about
Inspector Field having moved on from police work and
not being available for our outing, and of Field having
recommended Hatchery, but I had not paid much
attention to the comment.

"No," I said. "I don't believe he did."

Field nodded and his finger seemed to move of its
own volition to a place alongside his beak of a nose even
as his other hand removed the cigar from his mouth.
"He is, sir. Hatchery is a good man. Not imaginative,
perhaps, as the great inspectors and detectives must be,
but a good man. A dependable man. But when Dickens
contacted me about finding someone to escort him into
the…ah…difficult parts of the city again, I assumed
that it was another little slum-jaunt of his, of the sort I
escorted him and you on and him and the American
visitors on, sir. I was out of London for a while, on Private Enquiry Bureau business, and did not hear until I
returned recently that Drood was the object of Mr
Dickens's pursuit."

"I would hardly call it pursuit," I said.

"Search, then," said Inspector Field, breathing blue
smoke out. "Enquiry. Investigation."

"Is there something about Charles Dickens's interests that concerns *you*?" I asked. My tone was not sharp,
but it was meant to put a former policeman in his place
when it came to the interests and actions of gentlemen.

"Oh, yes, sir. Yes, Mr Collins. Indeed there is," said
the inspector, sitting back in the chair until it creaked.
He was inspecting his still-burning cigar and frowning
slightly. "Everything about this Drood person concerns
and interests me, Mr Collins. *Everything*."

"Why is that, Inspector?"

He leaned forward. "Drood—or the monster that

calls itself Drood—appeared and began its depradations upon my watch, Mr Collins. Quite literally upon my watch. I had just become Chief of the Detective Branch of Scotland Yard, taking over from Inspector Shackell…it was 1846, sir…when Drood's reign of terror began."

"Reign of terror?" I repeated. "I do not remember reading in the newspapers about any such reign of terror."

"Oh, there's lots of horrors that happen in those dark parts of town you and Mr Dickens went voyaging into in July that don't end up in the newspapers, Mr Collins. You can be assured of that."

"I'm sure you're right, Inspector," I said softly. The cigars were close to being smoked in their entirety. When they were, I would claim the press of creative business and show the retired old policeman to the door.

He leaned forward again and this time his active finger was pointed at me. "I need to know what you and Mr Dickens discovered about Drood that night, Mr Collins. I need to know *everything*."

"I do not see how that is your concern, Inspector."

Field smiled then and it was a broad enough smile to rearrange his ageing face into an entire new complexity of wrinkles, folds, and planes. It was not a warm smile. "It *is* my concern, Mr Collins, in ways that you cannot and could not ever comprehend. And I *will* have this information in all its details."

I sat straight in my chair, feeling the pain from my rheumatical gout fuel my displeasure and impatience. "That sounds like a threat, Inspector."

The smile grew wider. "Inspector Charles Frederick Field, either of the police Detective Bureau or of his own Private Enquiry Bureau, does not make threats, Mr Collins. But he *will* have the information he requires to carry on his battle with an old and implacable foe."

"If this...Drood...has been your foe, as you put it, for almost two decades, Inspector, you hardly need our help. You must know much more about...your foe... than Dickens or I ever will."

"Oh, yes, sir," agreed Field. "I do. I would blush to say that I know more about the creature you call Drood than does any man now living. But Hatchery informs me that Mr Dickens has had *recent* contact with the entity. And out of Undertown. At the Staplehurst accident, to be precise. I need more information about that and about what the two of you saw in Undertown in July."

"I thought the arrangement, or at least Detective Hatchery explained it as such, was for you police and private detectives to leave the denizens of Undertown alone as long as they continue to leave us surface dwellers to our own devices," I said drily.

Field shook his head. "Drood don't leave us alone," he said softly. "I know for a fact that the creature has been responsible for more than three hundred murders in London alone since I first crossed his trail twenty years ago."

"Good God," I said. The shock was real. I felt it coursing through me like a full glass of laudanum.

The inspector nodded. "I need to have the information from your amateur search, Mr Collins."

"You will have to ask Mr Dickens for any information," I said stiffly. "It was *his* outing. Drood was of *his* interest. I assumed from the beginning that our 'outing'—as you put it—with Detective Hatchery was part of some research that Dickens is doing for a future novel or story. I still assume that to be the case. But you will have to speak to him, Inspector."

"I went to speak to him as soon as I returned to London after my long absence and heard from Hatchery the reason for Dickens having hired him," said

Field. He rose and began pacing, walking back and forth in front of my desk. His corpulent finger was first at his mouth, then to his ear, then alongside his nose, then touching the stone egg on my desk or the ivory tusk on my bookshelf or the Persian dagger on the mantel. "Mr Dickens was in France and unavailable. He has just returned and I interviewed him yesterday. He gave me no information of any use."

"Well, Inspector..." I said, opening my hands. I set my cigar on the edge of the brass tray on my desk and rose. "You see then that there could be nothing I could add to help you. It was Mr Dickens's research. It is Mr Dickens's..."

He pointed at me. "Did you see Drood? Were you in his presence?"

I blinked. I remembered being awakened from my slumber on the subterranean brick wharf—my watch showed that it was twenty minutes after the sunrise above, after the time at which Hatchery had said he must leave—when Dickens returned in the flat-bottomed boat with the two tall and silent oarsmen. He had been gone for more than three hours. Despite the real danger, despite the real risk of being attacked and eaten by the wild boys, I had dozed off while sitting cross-legged there on the damp bricks, the loaded and cocked revolver still on my lap.

"I saw no one of Mr Drood's alleged description," I said stiffly. "And that is all the information I intend to impart on this subject, Inspector Field. As I said and shall repeat to you for the last time, it was Mr Dickens's outing, his research, and if he chooses not to share the details of the evening, then I am, as a gentleman, bound to a corresponding silence. I wish you good day, Inspector, and also wish you good luck on your..."

I had come around the desk and opened the door for the ageing inspector, but Field had not budged from his place standing by my desk. He smoked the cigar, looked at it, and said quietly, "Do you know why Dickens was in France?"

"What?" I was sure that I had heard wrong.

"I said, Mr Collins, do you know *why* Charles Dickens was in France this week past?"

"I have no idea," I said, voice almost brittle with irritation. "Gentlemen do not pry into other gentlemen's travel or business arrangements."

"No, indeed, they do not," said Inspector Field and smiled again. "Dickens was in Boulogne for a few days. More specifically, he divided his time between Boulogne and the tiny village a few miles south of Boulogne, a place called Condette, where for some years, since 1860 to be precise, Mr Dickens has leased the former modest chalet and gardens of a certain Monsieur Beaucourt-Mutuel. This chalet in Condette has been the frequent residence of a certain actress, now twenty-five years of age, named Ellen Ternan, along with her mother. Charles Dickens has enjoyed their company at Condette—some of the visits have been up to a week in length—more than fifty times since he purportedly leased, although in truth purchased, the chalet in 1860. You may want to close the door, Mr Collins."

I did so but remained standing by the closed door, thunderstruck. Counting Ellen Ternan, her mother, Dickens, and myself, there were no more than eight people in the world who had any hint of the chalet in Condette or the reason for Dickens's many visits there. And were it not for my brother Charles's being married into the Dickens household, I would never have learned about it myself.

Inspector Field resumed his pacing, his finger by his ear as though he were hearing facts whispered to him from the digit. "Miss Ternan and her mother live full-time in England, now, of course, since the Staplehurst accident in June. We can assume that Mr Dickens was winding up their affairs—and his own—at the chalet in Condette during his recent four days in Boulogne. To do this, Mr Dickens had to retrace—precisely—the same route that he took when the Staple-hurst accident occurred. We both know, Mr Collins, that this could not have been easy on Mr Dickens's nerves...which have not been strong since the accident."

"No," I said. What in the blazes did the man want?

"After his time in Boulogne," continued the apparently indefatigable old man, "Dickens went on to Paris for a day or two. A more suspicious mind than mine might suggest that the Paris trip was to cover his tracks, as some detectives like to say."

"Inspector Field, I do not believe that any of this is..."

"Not to interrupt, sir, but you should know—for future reference as you talk to your friend in the immediate days to come—that it was while in Paris that Mr Dickens suffered a brain haemorrhage of some apparent severity."

"Dear God," I said. "A brain haemorrhage. I've heard nothing about this. You are sure?"

"One cannot be certain of such things, as you know, sir. But Mr Dickens was struck down in Paris, was carried to his hotel room, and for some hours was quite insensible—incapable of either responding to his interlocutors or of speaking any words that made sense. The French doctors wished to have him in hospital, but Mr Dickens put it down to 'sunstroke'—his phrase, sir—and merely rested one day in his Paris hotel and another two in Boulogne before returning home."

I went back around the desk and collapsed into my chair. "What do you want, Inspector Field?"

He looked at me and his eyes widened with innocence. "I told you what I not only want, but require, Mr Collins.

Any and all information that you and Charles Dickens have on this personage called Drood."

I shook my head wearily. "You've come to the wrong man, Inspector. You shall have to return to Dickens to learn anything new about this phantom Drood. I know nothing at all that can help you."

Field was nodding slowly. "I will indeed return to talk to Mr Dickens again, Mr Collins. But I have not come to the wrong man. I look forward to great cooperation from you in my Droodian enquiries. I fully expect *you* to get the information I need from Charles Dickens."

I laughed a trifle bitterly. "And why would I betray a friend and his trust to funnel information to you, Inspector—by honourific only—Charles Frederick Field?"

He smiled at the thinly veiled insult. "The maid-servant who answered the door and showed me in, Mr Collins. She is very attractive, despite her age. Also a former actress, perhaps?"

Still smiling myself, I shook my head. "As far as I know, Inspector, Mrs G—— has no history whatsoever upon the stage. If she had, it would be none of my business, sir. Just as it is none of yours now."

Field nodded and resumed his pacing, smoke trailing above and behind him, his finger back alongside his beak of a nose. "Absolutely true, sir. Absolutely true. But we can assume, nonetheless, that this is the same Mrs Caroline G—— whom you first started recording in your bank account as of 23 August, 1864—just a little more than a year ago, sir—as having received twenty pounds from you. Payments that you have made every month since then through your bank?"

I was weary of this. If this despicable little man was truly attempting to blackmail me, he had chosen the wrong writer. "What of it, Inspector? Employers pay their servants."

"Indeed, sir. So I am told. And besides Mrs Caroline G——, her daughter, Harriet, I believe her name is— same name as your mother's, sir, which is a pleasant coincidence—also receives payments from you through your bank, although in young Harriet's case, and I believe you sometimes call her Carrie, and I believe she only recently turned fourteen years of age, sir, in young Harriet's case the expenditures go towards her private education and music lessons."

"Is there a point to this, Inspector?"

"Only that Mrs Caroline G—— and her daughter, Harriet G——, have been listed in city census and household tax records as having been both lodgers in your home and maid-servants in your employ for some years now."

I said nothing.

Inspector Field quit pacing and looked at me. "All I am pointing out here, Mr Collins, is that few employers are so generous as to, first, employ former lodgers when times go hard for them and then to put one's young maid-servant through a fine school, much less hire rather high-priced musicians to give them music lessons."

I shook my head wearily. "You may abandon this sad attempt at ungentlemanly leverage, *Mr* Field. My domestic arrangements are known to all of my friends, as is my resistance to marriage and towards the more unimaginative versions of middle-class life and morals. Mrs G—— and her daughter have been my guests here for some years, as you well know, and my friends accept it. Caroline has been at my table helping me entertain for years now. There is no hypocrisy here, nor anything to hide."

Field nodded, frowned, stubbed out what was left of

his cigar, and said, "Your *male* friends, some of them, certainly do accept it, Mr Collins. Although you would agree that they do not bring their wives along when they dine at your table. And although there may not be any hypocrisy other than in your public records—in which you told city census officials that Mrs G—— was your servant and a certain 'Harriet Montague' was your maid-servant, age sixteen (even though Mrs G——'s daughter, Harriet G——, here in your home, was only ten at the time)—and other sworn statements relating to these two worthy ladies, it does explain why Mr Dickens has referred to the child Harriet as 'the Butler' and to her mother as 'the Landlord' for several years now."

This startled me. How could this man have known of Dickens's small drolleries unless the retired inspector had men going through my most private correspondence?

"Harriet is not my daughter, Inspector," I said through gritted teeth.

"Oh, no, of course not, Mr Collins," said the old man, waving his finger and smiling. "I never meant to suggest such. Even the poorest detective would know that a certain Caroline Compton, daughter of the carpenter John Compton and his wife, Sarah, met and married a certain George Robert G——, an accountant's clerk from Clerkenwell, and married him on . . . I do believe it was 30 March, 1850, sir. The young Caroline was just twenty years of age that year, George Robert G—— only a year older. Their daughter, Elizabeth Harriet, whom you prefer to call Harriet, sir, perhaps to honour your own mother, or Carrie, for reasons known only to yourself, was born in Somerset, on the outskirts of Bath, on 3 February, 1851. It's sad that her father, George G——, came down with consumption the following year and died of it at the Moravian Cottages in Weston, near Bath, on 30 January, 1852, leaving his widow, Caroline, and twelve-month-old baby daughter, Elizabeth Harriet. Poor Mrs G—— came to the attention of authorities a few years later, when she was running a junk shop in Charlton Street—near Fitzroy Square, I'm sure you know, sir—and ran into difficulties paying her debts. It could have been a tragic tale, possibly including a debtors prison, Mr Collins, had it not been for the intervention of a gentleman. Probably in May of 1856."

"Inspector Field," I said, rising again, "our conversation here is over." I moved towards the door again.

"Not quite over, sir," he said softly.

I rounded on him, the fury obvious in my shaking voice and clenched fists. "I say to you, sir, *do your worst*. I challenge you. Your petty and dishonourable attempts to blackmail me into betraying the confidence and trust of one of my dearest friends will earn you nothing but the ridicule and disapprobation you so obviously deserve. I am a free man, sir. *I have nothing to hide*."

Field nodded. His forefinger, which I had already learned to despise, was tapping at his lower lip. "I am sure that is true, Mr Collins. Honest men have nothing to hide from others."

I opened the door. My hand was shaking on the brass of the handle.

"Tell me before I go, sir," said Field, picking up his top hat and moving closer, "just for my own edification…have you ever heard of a girl by the name of Martha R——?"

"What?" I managed to say through a constricted throat.

"Miss Martha R——," he repeated.

I closed the door so quickly that it slammed audibly. I had not seen Caroline lurking in the hallway, but she often stayed within earshot. I opened my mouth again but found no words.

That problem did not afflict the despicable Inspector Charles Frederick Field. "There's no reason you *should* know Miss R——," he said. "She's a poor serving girl— domestic service and hostelry, to hear her poor parents tell of it, sir, and they *are* poor, both in finances and emotion these days. Both parents are illiterate. They're from Winterton, sir. Her father's male ancestors had served in the herring fleet out of Yarmouth for a century or more, but it seems that Martha's father made do with other odd jobs around Winterton while Martha, who left home two years ago at the age of sixteen, worked in local hotels."

I could only stare at Field and force down nausea.

"Do you know Winterton, sir?" asked the despicable man.

"No," I managed. "I don't believe I do."

"Yet you took an extended holiday up Yarmouth's way just a year ago this summer, is that not true, Mr Collins?"

"Not a holiday," I said.

"What was that, sir? I could not quite understand you. The cigar smoke affecting your voice, perhaps?"

"It was not a holiday, as such," I said and walked back to my desk but did not sit. Using all ten splayed and quavering fingers, I leaned forward and supported my weight against the top of that ink-splattered desk. "It was research," I added.

"Research, sir? Oh...for one of your novels."

"Yes," I said. "For my current novel, *Armadale,* I needed to research some coastal waters and landscapes and such."

"Ah, yes...to be certain." The despised man's finger patted his own chest and then pointed towards mine. Patted, pointed. "I have read some of your book, this *Armadale,* which is currently being serialised in *The Cornhill Magazine,* if I am not mistaken. There is a fictional Hurle Mere in your tale that sounds very much like the real Horsey Mere, which can be reached by sea from Yarmouth or by taking a road north from Winterton, can it not, sir?"

I said nothing for a minute. Then I said, "I enjoy sailing, Inspector. My research was part holiday, after all, to tell the full truth. I went north with two good friends of my brother, Charles.... They also enjoy sailing."

"I see." The inspector nodded, his eyes moist and unreadable. "Telling the full truth is always a good idea, is my opinion. It avoids so many later problems if one starts with the full truth. Could those friends have been a Mr Edward Piggot and a Mr Charles Ward, sir?"

I was beyond surprise. This creature with the moist eyes and corpulent forefinger appeared to be more omniscient than any narrator in any tale written by me, by Dickens, by Chaucer, by Shakespeare, or by any other mortal writer. And more evil than any villain created by any of us, Iago included. I continued to lean on my desk as my splayed fingers turned white with pressure and I continued to listen.

"Miss Martha R—— turned eighteen last summer, Mr Collins. Her family believes that she met a man last year, last July to be precise, either at the Fisherman's Return in Winterton itself or in the hotel in Yarmouth where she was then working as a maid." He stopped. His forefinger tapped at the dead cigar in the brass tray as if his finger alone could breathe its embers back to life. I was almost surprised that it did not succeed.

I took a breath. "Are you telling me that this...this Miss R——...is missing, Inspector? Or murdered? Presumed dead by her family and the authorities in Winterton or Yarmouth?"

The man laughed. "Oh, bless me, no, sir. Not at all. Nothing like that. They've all seen young Martha, on and off, since she reported meeting this 'nice gentle-man' last summer. But she has gone missing in a way, sir."

"Oh?"

"Yes. This summer, this June to be precise, when the 'nice gentleman' appears by all accounts to have made yet another short trip to Yarmouth, perhaps as part of his work, Martha R—— seems to have disappeared for a while from Winterton and Yarmouth but, if such unofficial reports are to be believed, to have made an appearance here in London."

"Really?" I said. I had never fired the huge two-barrelled pistol that Detective Hatchery had given me. After uncocking the massive thing, I had carried it up and out of the levels of sewers and catacombs with me and—in our tremendous relief in finding Hatchery waiting for us despite the late hour and obvious sun-shine outside the crypt—given it back to the hulking detective. I wished now that I had kept the weapon.

"Yes," said Inspector Field. "Rumour has it that the nineteen-year-old domestic servant from Winter-ton is currently staying in a rented room on Bolsover Street—the elderly landlady lives there as well, although I am told that lodgers have a separate entrance to their rooms. I think I am not mistaken in saying that Bols-over Street is not so great a walk from where we stand now, in Melcombe Place near Dorset Square."

"You are not mistaken," I said. If voices could be said to have colours, mine was absolutely colourless.

"And I believe I am not mistaken if I say that Mrs Caroline G——, with whom you have lived in a condi-tion very similar to man and wife, if I may say so, although without society's and God's blessings as such, for a period of almost ten years now, nor her daughter, Miss Harriet G——, whom you treat very honourably and generously, as if she were your own child, know of the existence of Miss Martha R——, formerly a hotel maid-servant in Yarmouth and currently a lodger on Bolsover Street, much less the role Miss R—— currently plays in your life."

"Yes," I said. "I mean, no."

"And I also believe I am not mistaken, Mr Collins, if I were to say that it would not be in your interest or in the interest of the two ladies who live under this roof with you were this knowledge to become known...to them or to anyone else."

"You are not mistaken."

"Good, good," said Inspector Field. He picked up his top hat but made no move to leave. "I dislike being mistaken about things, Mr Collins."

I nodded. My legs suddenly felt too weak to support me.

"Would you by any chance be planning to go see Mr Dickens soon, sir?" asked the detective, spinning his top hat while tapping its brim with his accursed forefinger. "And, in the course of your visit, have an opportunity to speak with him about his possible meeting with the personage called Drood in the Undertown tunnels some two months ago?"

"Yes," I said and sat down.

"And do we have an understanding, sir, that such information as you elicit from Mr Dickens will be shared with me as soon as is humanly possible?"

I nodded again.

"Very good, sir. There will be a boy waiting on your street, Mr Collins. Just a street urchin—a crossing sweeper named Gooseberry—although you needn't hunt for him, sir. He has been directed to watch for you. If you tap the lamp post at the corner with your stick or an umbrella, the lad will make himself known to you. Day or night, sir. He will wait as long as needs be. The local constable has agreed not to 'move him along,' as we men on the beat tend to say. Send any message you might have for me, verbal or written, along with Gooseberry and I will be in touch with you immediately. I will consider such information a huge favour, Mr Collins. Ask anyone in London if Inspector Charles Frederick Field ever forgets a favour and you will hear that he does not. Is all that clear, sir?"

"Yes."

When I looked up, Inspector Field was gone. I could hear Caroline closing the door behind him downstairs and I could hear her footsteps on the main stairs.

Nothing of the inspector remained behind except for the pall of blue smoke near the ceiling in my study.

CHAPTER EIGHT

*G*ad's Hill Place gave the strong impression of a gay, relaxed family retreat when I arrived there in mid-afternoon on the crisp early-autumn day after Inspector Field's visit to my home. It was a Saturday, so the children and visitors were outside playing. I had to admit to myself that Gad's Hill was the very model of a happy family's beloved country home. Of course, Charles Dickens *wanted* Gad's Hill to be the very model of a happy family's beloved country home. In fact, Charles Dickens *insisted* that everyone within his circle do his or her part to maintain the image, fiction, and—I am certain that he hoped, despite the absence of the family's mother, now banished, and despite tensions from within and without the family—the *reality* of a happy family's beloved country home: nothing more complicated than a gay early-autumn retreat for the hardworking author and his worshipful, loving, and appreciative family and their friends.

At times, I confess, I felt like Candide to Charles Dickens's Dr Pangloss.

Dickens's daughter Kate was in the yard and approached me as I walked up the lane, sweating and mopping my neck and forehead with my handkerchief. It was, as I said, a crisp autumn day, but I had walked from the train station and was not used to the exercise. Also, in preparation for the meeting with Dickens, I had taken two glasses of my laudanum medicine much earlier in the day than I was used to doing, and while there were no negative effects from the medicine, I admit that the yard, the grass, the trees, the playing children, and Kate Macready Dickens Collins herself appeared to have a corona of golden glow around them.

"Hello, Wilkie," cried Kate as she came closer and took my hand. "We have seen too little of you in recent days."

"Hello, Katey. Is my brother here with you this weekend?"

"No, no. He was not feeling well and decided to stay at Clarence Terrace. I will rejoin him this evening."

I nodded. "The Inimitable?"

"In his chalet, finishing up a bit of work on this year's Christmas tale."

"I didn't know the chalet was ready for habitation," I said.

"It is. All furnished as of last month. Father has been working there every day since then. He should be stopping any minute so that he can get his afternoon walk in. I'm sure he won't mind if you interrupt him. It is a Saturday, after all. Shall I walk you through the tunnel?"

"That is a lovely idea," I said.

We strolled across the lawn towards the road.

The chalet to which Kate was referring had been a gift the previous Christmas from the actor Charles Fechter. According to my brother, who was one of the guests who stayed from Christmas Eve 1864 until the fifth of January, it wasn't the happiest of Christmases, not the least reason being that Dickens somehow had convinced himself that my brother, Charles, was dying rather than merely indisposed due to his frequent digestive problems. Of course, this may have been more wish than honest diagnosis on Dickens's part; Katey's marriage to Charles in 1860 had upset the author beyond the point of tears and quite to the point of distraction. Dickens felt that he had been abandoned in his time of need by an impatient daughter, and—indeed—that was precisely the case. Even my brother understood that Kate was not in love with him. She simply needed to escape Charles Dickens's household after the upset brought about by her father's banishment of their mother.

Kate—"Katey," as so many of us called her—was not a great beauty, but of all the Dickens children, she was the only one who had inherited her father's quickness, his wit, a more sardonic version of his sense of humour, his impatience with others, his speech patterns, and even many of his mannerisms. She had let my brother know, even as she was more or less proposing to him, that it would be a marriage of escape and convenience for her rather than one of love. Charles agreed.

So the cold, claustrophobically indoor Christmas of 1864 had been somewhat dour at the Dickens home at Gad's Hill, certainly compared to the great family-and-guest festivals of previous years at Tavistock House, at least until Christmas Day morning, when Charles Fechter presented to the Inimitable . . . an entire Swiss chalet.

Fechter, who was a strange man himself, brooding, sallow, given to explosions of temper towards his wife and others (but never towards Dickens), announced after breakfast that the mysterious crates and boxes he had brought with him were a disassembled "miniature chalet," although—as the group soon discovered—not so miniature after all. It was an actual full-sized chalet, quite large enough to live in should one choose to do so.

Energised, excited, Dickens immediately announced that all "strong and healthy bachelor guests"—by which he obviously meant to exclude my brother for more faults than not being a bachelor—should rush outside into the bitter cold to assemble his gift. But Dickens and his guests Marcus Stone (who was indeed a large and powerful man) and Henry Chorley and various male servants and gardeners and local handymen all summoned from their Christmas Days by the hearth found the fifty-eight boxes (there were ninety-four large, numbered pieces in all) more than they could manage. Fechter called for his French carpenter at the Lyceum to finish the job.

The chalet—which turned out to be so much more than the oversized dollhouse Dickens had anticipated when looking at the packing crates—now stood on the author's extra property on the other side of the Rochester High Road. Shaded by tall cedars, it was a lovely gingerbread chalet of two storeys with a large, single ground-floor room and a first-floor room with a fretted balcony which one reached by an outside staircase.

Dickens took a great and boyish delight in his chalet, and when the ground thawed that spring, he had workmen dig a pedestrian tunnel under the road so that the author would be able to pass all the way from his house to the chalet without being observed, disturbed, or run down by some runaway pony cart. Kate had told me how Dickens had applauded like a child when the workmen broke through at the centre in their tunnel, and then brought everyone—guests, children, workmen, gawking neighbours, and idlers from the Sir John Falstaff Inn across the road—into the house for grog.

As we reached the tunnel and began the cool stroll through it, Kate asked, "What are you and Father doing on all these long, secretive nights, Wilkie? Even Charles does not seem to know."

"What in heaven's name are you talking about, Katey?"

She looked at me in the dim light. She had taken my arm and now she squeezed it. "You *know* what I mean, Wilkie. Please don't be coy. Even with the press of finishing *Our Mutual Friend* and his other work, even with his current terror of rail travel, Father has been disappearing at least one night a week, sometimes twice a week, since that first secret adventure you and he shared in July. Georgina confirms this. He leaves in the evening, taking the slow train into London, and returns very, very late—as late as mid-morning the next day—and won't tell Georgina or any of us a word about the reasons for these nocturnal prowls. And now this most recent trip to France and him returning after a sunstroke. We've all assumed, even Charles, that you have introduced Father to some new form of debauchery in London and that he may have tried it on his own in Paris and found it too much for his constitution."

Beneath Kate's bantering tone, I could hear the real concern.

Patting her arm, I said, "Well, you know that we gentlemen are honour bound to protect each other's secrets, Katey…such as they are. And you, of all women, know that male writers are a mysterious species— we're always out doing some odd research about the world here or there, day or night."

She looked at me in the gloom of the tunnel and her eyes seemed luminous and dissatisfied.

"And you also know," I continued, my voice so soft that it was almost absorbed by the bricks overhead and under our feet, "that your father would never do anything to dishonour himself or your family. You must know that, Katey."

"Hmmm," said Kate. Dishonouring himself and his family was precisely what Kate Macready Dickens Collins honestly believed her father had already done in the affair of the banishment of her mother and his pursuit of Ellen Ternan. "Here," she said, freeing her arm. "The light at the end of the tunnel, Wilkie. I shall leave you to it. And to him."

MY DEAR WILKIE! Come in, come in! I was just thinking about you. Welcome to my eyrie. Step in, dear friend."

Dickens had jumped up from his small writing table and heartily shaken my hand as I'd stopped at the open door of his upstairs room. I confess that I had not been sure how he would greet me after the relative silence and separation of the past two months. His warmth surprised me and made me feel all that much more the traitor and spy.

"I am just jotting down revisions to the last line or two of this year's Christmas story," he said with enthusiasm. "A thing called 'Cheap Jack' that I assure you, my dear Wilkie, will be a great hit with the readers. Very popular, is my prediction. Perhaps my best since 'The Bells.' The idea occurred to me in France. I shall finish in a minute and then I am yours for the afternoon and evening, my friend."

"By all means," I said and stepped back as Dickens returned to his table and quill, striking out with great flourishes and writing between the lines and in the margins. He reminded me of an energetic conductor in front of an attentive and obedient orchestra of words. I could almost hear the notes as his quill rose, swung, dipped, scratched, lifted, and swept down again.

I admired the view from Dickens's "eyrie" and had to admit that it was wonderful. The chalet, standing between two tall, shading cedars that stirred now in the wind, had many windows that looked out over fields of ripened corn, forests, and more fields, and even allowed glimpses of the Thames, with the white movement of sails there. From the roof of Gad's Hill Place across the road, I knew, one could easily see London in the distance, but from the chalet the view was more bucolic, with the distant river, a glimpse of the spire of Rochester Cathedral, and the yellowing and rustling fields of corn. Traffic was light today on the Rochester Road. Dickens had outfitted his eyrie with a bright brass telescope on a wooden tripod, and I could imagine him pondering the moon at night and the ladies in their yachts on the Thames on warm summer days. Where there were no windows, there were mirrors. I counted five mirrors. Dickens loved mirrors. Every bedroom in his Tavistock House and now at Gad's Hill Place had always sported multiple mirrors and there were mirrors in hallways and foyers and a large one in his study. The effect up here in his chalet was to make one feel rather as if he were standing on an open platform—a child's house in a tall tree, minus all walls—with sunlight and blue sky and foliage and yellow fields and far views reflected everywhere. The breezes that passed freely through the open windows carried the scent of foliage and flowers, of the fields beyond, of the smoke from someone burning leaves or weeds from a field nearby, and even the salt tang smell of the sea.

I could not help but think how totally opposite this world of Charles Dickens was from our night expedition to Opium Sal's den and then the unmitigated nightmare of Undertown. All of that darkness seemed to be fading like the bad dream it had been. The daylight and clean scent of *this* world were real—as glowing and pulsing as it seemed through the pulse of my medicinal laudanum. I could not see how that reeking darkness of the catacombs and sewers, nor even the slums above, could co-exist with this clean reality.

"There," cried Dickens. "Done. For now." He blotted his last page and set it with others in a leather portfolio. He rose and took his favourite blackthorn walking stick from its place in a corner. "I've not had my walk today. Shall we away, my dear Wilkie?"

"By all means," I said again, although with less conviction this time.

He surveyed me with eyes at once analytical, amused, and mocking. "I thought perhaps a quick trek past Cobham Wood and then to Chalk and Gravesend and home again."

"Ah," I said. That would be twelve hard miles. "Ah," I said again and nodded. "But what about your guests? And children? Is this not the hour you usually play with them, amuse them, show the guests the stables?"

Dickens's smile was mischievous. "Is there another invalid in the family today, my dear Wilkie?"

I knew that by "family" he meant the Collins family. It seemed he would never cease the harping on my younger brother's presumed illness.

"A minor disposition," I said brusquely. "The rheumatical gout which pursues me from time to time, as you know, my dear Dickens. It chooses to be a bit difficult today. A shorter romp would suit me." A slow walk next door to the Sir John Falstaff Inn would have suited me perfectly was the message I intended to send.

"But your gout is not in your legs, is this not true, my dear Wilkie?"

"That is largely true," I said, unwilling to tell him that this gout hurt every part of my person when it spread as it had threatened to that morning. Without the early double doses of laudanum, I would have been in bed. "It tends to afflict my eyes and head the most."

"Very well," sighed Dickens. "I had hoped for a walking partner today—the Forsters are my guests this weekend and John has given up all exertion since coming into his wife's fortune, as I am sure you know—but we shall make a short outing of it, you and I, just over to Chatham and Fort Pitt, through Cooling Marsh and home. I shall make up the difference this evening, alone."

I nodded, although still without enthusiasm. That would be six miles and more with Dickens's unrelenting pace of four miles per hour exactly. My head and joints throbbed in anticipation.

IT WAS NOT as bad as I had feared. The afternoon was so pleasant, the air so cool, the scents so invigorating, that I kept up with Dickens as he led the way down the road to a lane, from lane to path, from path to grassy ruts along a canal, from the canal tow path through autumn fields of grain—taking care never to tread on a farmer's crop—and from the field to shady forest trail, then back to the roadside again and onward.

During the first half hour of silent walking—or rather, *my* silent walking, since Dickens chatted amiably the whole way, discussing Forster's increased Podsnapperies, the problems within the Guild, details of his son Alfred's business ineptitude and his daughter Mary's diminishing prospects for marriage, grousings about the Negro uprising in Jamaica that still rankled him, observations on his youngest son Plorn's apparent laziness and lack of intellectual depth—I spent my time nodding and thinking of how to trick the information desired by Inspector Field out of Charles Dickens.

Finally I surrendered that approach and said, "Inspector Field came to visit me yesterday."

"Oh, yes," Dickens said casually, his blackthorn rising and falling with his stride. "I assumed that to be the case."

"You're not surprised?"

"Hardly, my dear Wilkie. The wretched man was here at Gad's Hill on Thursday. I assumed that you would be his next victim. Did he threaten you?"

"Yes," I said.

"With what, may I ask? He was quite clumsy and heavy-handed with his minor attempts to blackmail me."

"He threatened me with public exposure of…my domestic situation." The only thing I was secure about at the moment was that Dickens did not know—could not have known—about the existence of Miss Martha R——. Inspector Field obviously knew, but it would not have been in his interest to tell the Inimitable.

Dickens laughed easily. "Threatened to tell the world about your Landlord and Butler, eh? Much as I had guessed, Wilkie. Much as I had guessed. Mr Field is a bully but—as is true of so many bully boys—not the ripest grape on the vine. How little he knows of your free spirit and disregard for society's opinions if he thinks that such a revelation would cause you to turn traitor. All of your friends know that you have skeletons in your closet—two delightful and witty female skeletons, to be precise—and none of your friends gives a fig for the fact."

"Yes," I said. "But why is he so eager to have this information on Drood? He acts as if his life depends upon it."

We passed from the road to a path that wound its way through and around Cooling Marsh.

"In a very real sense, our Mr Field's life *does* depend on discovering whether Mr Drood is real and where to find him if he is," said Dickens. "And you notice that I refer to our blackmailing friend as *Mr* Field, not *Inspector* Field."

"Yes," I said as we stepped gingerly from stone to stone in an especially swampy part of the path. "Field mentioned to me that his title was honourary now that he does his detective work in private life."

"A self-appointed honour that the Detective Bureau of Scotland Yard and of the Metropolitan Police do not appreciate, my dear Wilkie. I've kept some tabs on our *Mr* Field since I—if you forgive the immodesty—immortalised him as Inspector Bucket in *Bleak House* or even earlier, in my admiring little essay about him, "On Duty With Inspector Field," in our *Household Words* in 1851. He left his official capacity shortly after that, you know…1853, I do believe."

"But you admired him then," I said. "At least enough to create a fascinating character out of him."

Dickens laughed again as we turned back around the marsh towards distant Gad's Hill. "Oh, I admire *many* people for their potential as characters, my dear Wilkie, yourself not excluded. How else could I have suffered the Podsnapperies of Forster all these years? But there has always been the pungent scent of the schoolhouse bully hovering about our dear Mr Field, and bullies always tend to overreach and be called to task."

"You're saying that he is out of favour with Scotland Yard and the Metropolitan Police," I said.

"Quite so, Wilkie. Did you happen to follow the notorious Palmer poisoning case some time ago…my, a decade ago now. How time, to coin a phrase, does fly. At any rate, did you follow that in the papers or at the Club?"

"No. I can't say that I did."

"No matter," said Dickens. "Let us just say that our retired Inspector Field was involved with the sensational murder case, was quite popular with the press, and insisted on using the title *Inspector* Field. In truth, Wilkie, I believe our corpulently digited friend actively encouraged the press and populace to believe that he was still affiliated with the Metropolitan Police. And his successors there, the real police detectives and inspectors, did not appreciate it, Wilkie. Not one small smattering did they appreciate it. So they stopped his pension."

I stopped in my tracks. "His *pension?*" I cried. "His bloody *pension?* The man interrogates you and tries to blackmail me, all for a . . . bloody . . . *pension?*"

Dickens obviously was irked to be thrown off his walking rhythm, but he stopped, hacked at some weeds with his blackthorn, and actually smiled. "Yes, for his pension. Our *faux*-inspector acquaintance has his Private Enquiry Bureau and makes some money through it—indeed, I paid a pretty penny for our hulking friend Hatchery's one night of effort on our behalf—but you may remember me once telling you, Wilkie, how . . . avaricious is not too strong a word, I think . . . avaricious this former policeman named Field was, is, and ever shall be. He cannot abide not receiving his pension. I do believe he would murder to get it back."

I blinked at that. "But why Drood?" I asked at last. "What will it gain him if he finds this phantom Drood?"

"It may gain him his pension," said Dickens as we resumed our walk. "Or so he thinks. At this very moment, Home Secretary Sir George Grey is reviewing Field's suspension of payments, after the long growling from Field's solicitor—not a cheap undertaking that, I can assure you!—and I am quite sure that Mr Field, in his aged delusions . . ."

I did not interrupt here to remind him that Charles Frederick Field was only some seven years older than Dickens himself.

" . . . has concocted a *deus ex machina* plot in his own mind in which, when he tracks down and captures this criminal mastermind Drood . . . a spectral figure who evaded *Chief* Inspector Field some twenty years ago . . . the Home Secretary and Scotland Yard Detective Bureau and all of his former friends and indifferent successors at the Metropolitan Police shall not only forgive him, and reinstate his pension, but be forced to crown him with laurel leaves and carry him to Waterloo Station on their burly shoulders."

"And is he a criminal mastermind?" I asked softly. "This Drood? Field told me last night that Drood murdered some three hundred persons over the years…"

Dickens glanced at me again. I noticed that the wrinkles and furrows in his face had grown deeper over the summer. "Do you believe that figure to be reliable, my dear Wilkie?"

"I…have no idea," I said. "It does sound preposterous, I admit. I do not remember hearing of any three hundred unsolved murders, in Whitechapel or anywhere else. But that was an uncanny place we went to, Dickens. Uncanny. And you never told me what occurred after you left me in that absurd boat."

"No, I have not," said Dickens. "And I promised you that night that I would tell you someday soon, my friend. And two months have passed. I am sorry for that delay."

"The delay is no matter," I said. The headache was returning even as the laudanum glow around everything faded. "But I would like to know what occurred that night. I would like to know what you have learned about this Drood we spent the night chasing."

Dickens glanced at me again. "And I would have no concern about our mutual friend Field blackmailing this information out of you?"

I stopped. "Dickens!"

He did not stop with me, but he walked backwards, twirling his blackthorn and smiling. "I am joking, my dear Wilkie. Joking. Come…catch up to me; don't falter our pace at this advanced point. Catch up to me and walk alongside and pray quiet your wheezing to a mere bellows roar and I shall tell you all about that night after I left you on the brick quay in the sewers beneath the catacombs in Undertown."

CHAPTER NINE

*A*fter I left you sitting there on the quay," said Dickens, "I attempted to pay some attention to that rather absurd little boat I was in.

"The craft rather reminded me of my character Hexam Gaffer's miserable little boat from which he tows corpses and other found things from the Thames, but in this case as if some demented carpenter had decided to turn it into a parody of a Venetian gondola. As I studied the two tall, silent figures, one at the tiller or sweep in the stern, the other poling from the raised bow, they became less and less attractive to me, Wilkie. Their gold-dust-bedangled domino masks and smoked glasses disguised little more than their eyes, so I could tell they were male, but only nominally so. You know how angels portrayed in frescoes in the great Papist cathedrals on the Continent are disturbingly androgynous, my dear Wilkie? Well, my companions in this tiny boat were decidedly more so, and that androgyny was emphasised rather than diminished by the absurd medieval tights and tunics they were wearing. I decided to think of the *castrato* in the bow as Venus and the eunuch at the stern as Mercury.

"We poled down the broad stream of sewage for some hundred yards or more. I glanced back, but I do not believe you ever looked my way before our gondola-scull went around a bend and we were lost to each other's view, you and I. The small lanterns dangling from iron rods near the bow and stern did little to illuminate the rushing waterway. My primary impression was of lantern light reflected from the moist and dripping arch of bricks above us.

"I dare say I do not have to remind you, Wilkie, of the terrible stench of that first tributary. I was not sure that I could tolerate it for long without becoming physically sick. But luckily, after a few hundred yards of that reeking Styx, the masked form at our tiller turned us into a side tunnel so narrow that I was sure it was nothing more than a sewer pipe. Both Mercury and Venus had to bow low—I did as well—as they moved us along by pressing their gloved palms to the bricks of the low ceiling and encroaching sides. Then the way opened into a wider stream—and I say 'stream' advisedly, Wilkie, since this was less a sewer than a bricked and contained underground river, as wide as any aboveground tributary to the Thames. Did you know that some rivers have been partially or completely covered over in London…the Fleet, for instance? Of course you did. But one never thinks of their subterranean sections.

"My androgynous escorts piloted our little craft downstream for a long while and here—I must warn you, my dear Wilkie—the narrative becomes fantastical.

"Our first escort that night, Detective Hatchery, had called this subterranean world 'Undertown,' as had the Chinese opium apparition King Lazaree, but now I saw that this connected labyrinth of cellars, sub-cellars, sewers, caverns, side caverns, buried ditches, abandoned mines from some age before our city existed, forgotten catacombs, and partially constructed tunnels *was* quite literally a city beneath the city, a sort of terrible London beneath London. A true Undertown.

"We rode the slow current for some time, and as

my eyes adapted to the darkness along the sides of this wider stream, I realised that I was seeing people. *People,* my dear Wilkie. Not merely more of the Wild Boys, who were like the feral dogs or real wolves that once circled the outskirts of some medieval village, but actual people. Families. Children. Cooking fires. Crude hovels and stretched canvases and mattresses and even some stoves and discarded, sagging furniture set in amongst the niches in the brick walls and in the side caverns and on wide, muddy banks along this part of the tunnel.

"Here and there blue flames rose from the mud and ooze itself, rather like the flames which flicker on a Christmas pudding, Wilkie, and some of these wretched human forms huddled near these gaseous eruptions for light and warmth.

"And then, just as I thought Venus and Mercury were going to keep poling us down these dark, watery avenues forever, the way widened, and we came to an actual landing... broad stone steps carved into the rock wall of the tunnel with bright torches blazing on either side. Mercury tied us up. Venus helped me step out of the bobbing boat. Both of them stayed aboard the boat, motionless and silent, as I climbed those steps towards a brass door.

"There were large Egyptian statues carved from the stone on both sides of this staircase, Wilkie, and more carvings above the door, the kinds of ancient forms one sees in the British Museum and perhaps feels uncomfortable about being amongst on a winter's evening shortly before closing time. There were black bronze bodies of men with jackal heads or the heads of birds. There were forms holding staffs, sceptres, and curved crooks. The stone lintel above the broad doorway was carved with the sorts of picture-writing— hieroglyphics, they are called—one sees in illustrations of obelisks in books about Napoleon's adventures along the Nile. It was like a child's version of writing featuring carved wavy lines and birds and eyeballs…many bird-shapes.

"Two large, silent, but living and breathing black men—the word 'Nubians' came to mind as I passed them—stood just outside these massive doors and opened them for me as I approached. They were dressed in black robes that left their huge arms and chests bare and they carried strange hooked staffs that looked to be made of iron.

"Based on the imposing entrance stairs from the subterranean river, making a guess based on the statuary and bas-reliefs outside, and judging from the men at the door, I expected that I was entering a temple, but although the echoing, lantern-lit interior did have something of the hushed air of a heathen temple about it, in truth it was more library than temple. Shelves in the first room I passed through and along the walls of rooms I glanced into held scrolls, tablets, and many much more mundane books. I glimpsed scholarly and reference titles such as one might find in any fine library. The rooms were sparsely furnished with a few tables illuminated by torches or hanging braziers and the occasional low, backless couch of the sort historians tell us were present in some patrician's home in ancient Rome or Greece or Egypt. I could see various figures moving, sitting, or standing in these rooms, and most looked to be Lascar or Magyar or Hindoo or Chinese. But there were no ancient opium sleepers—no beds or bunks or opium pipes nor sign nor smell of the wretched drug. I noticed that most of the men in the various rooms, for whatever reason, had shaved their heads.

"Drood was waiting for me in the second room, Wilkie. He sat at a small table near a hissing lantern. Various books and scrolls covered the table, but I noticed that he was drinking tea from Wedgwood china. He was dressed in a tan robe that made him look quite different than my impression of him as a poorly tailored undertaker at Staplehurst—much more dignified—but his deformities were even more apparent in the lantern light: his scarred head almost devoid of hair, the missing eyelids, a nose that looked to have been mostly amputated in some terrible surgery, the slight harelip, and ears that were little more than stubs. He rose and offered his hand as I approached.

"'Welcome, Mr Dickensss,' he said with that hint of lisp and slide of sibilants which I have so unsuccesfully tried to reproduce for you. 'I knew you would come,' he said as he arranged the tea set.

"'How did you know that I would come, Mr Drood?' I asked, accepting his handshake and forcing myself not to flinch at the touch of his cold, white flesh.

"He smiled, Wilkie, and I was reminded that his teeth were small, oddly spaced, and very sharp, while his pink tongue seemed extraordinarily quick and busy behind them. 'You are a man of great curiosity, Mr Dickensss,' Drood said to me. 'I know thiss from your many wonderful booksss and storiess. All of which I have admired very much indeed.'

"'Thank you, sir, you are very kind' was my reply. You can imagine the sense of oddness, my dear Wilkie, sitting in this underground Undertown temple-library with this odd man who already, since the Staplehurst terror, had become a fixture of my dreams, hearing him praise my books rather as if I had just completed a reading in Manchester.

"Before I could think of anything else to say, Drood poured tea into the lovely cup set before me and said, 'I am sure that you have questionsss for me.'

"'I do, indeed, Mr Drood,' I said to him. 'And I

hope you will not consider them impertinent or overly personal. There is in me, I confess, a great curiosity as to your background, how you came to be here in this... place, why you were on the tidal train from Folkestone that terrible day at Staplehurst...everything.'

"'Then I shall tell you everything, Mr Dickensss,' said my strange interlocutor.

"I spent the next half hour or so drinking tea and listening to his story, my dear Wilkie. Would you care to hear a summary of Drood's biography now, or shall we save it for another day?"

I LOOKED AROUND. We were within a mile of Gad's Hill Place. I realised I was panting from the speed and distance of our walk, but my headache had been all but forgotten while I was listening to this fantastical tale. I said, "By all means, Dickens. Let us hear the end of this story."

"It is not the end, my dear Wilkie," said Dickens, his blackthorn stick rising and falling with his every second stride. "More the beginning, if truth be told. But I shall tell you what Drood told me that night, albeit in summarised form, since I see our destination in sight."

THE MAN WE CALL DROOD is the son of an English father and an Egyptian mother. His father, a certain John Frederick Forsyte, was born in the last century, graduated from Cambridge, and trained as a civil engineer, although the man's real passion was exploration, adventure, and literature. I have checked this out, Wilkie. Forsyte himself was a writer of both fiction and non-fiction, but is remembered today as a teller of traveller's tales. Part of his training was in Paris—this was after the end of the Napoleonic Wars, when Englishmen felt free to return to France, of course—and there Forsyte met numerous scientists who had gone to Egypt with Napoleon's expedition to that country. The tales he heard made him eager to see such exotic sights—the Sphinx that the French artillery had taken potshots at, successfully shooting off its nose, the Pyramids, the people, the cities, and, yes, the women. Forsyte was young and single, and some of the Frenchmen's tales of alluring Mohammadan women with their veils and kohl-enhanced eyes inflamed his desire for something more than travel.

"Within the year, Forsyte had arranged to travel to Egypt with an English engineering company that had been contracted by a French company owned by someone John Frederick Forsyte had met socially in Paris, hired by Egypt's young ruler, Mehemet Ali. It was Ali who first attempted to introduce Western knowledge and improvements into Egypt.

"As an engineer, Forsyte was staggered by the knowledge of the Egyptian ancients as evidenced in their Pyramids, colossal ruins, and networks of canals along the Nile. As an adventurer, the young man was exhilarated by Cairo and the other Egyptian cities, and even more so by his expeditions out of these cities to more remote ruins and sites up the Nile. As a man, Forsyte found the Egyptian women just as alluring as the Frenchmen's tales had promised.

"It was during his first year in Cairo that Forsyte met the young Egyptian widow who would become Drood's mother. She lived near the quarter where the English and French engineers and other contractors were essentially quarantined away from proper society—Forsyte's lodgings were in a converted carpet warehouse—and the woman spoke English, came from a wealthy and ancient Alexandrian family (her late husband had been a merchant in Cairo), and attended various dinners and gatherings arranged by the English engineering company. Her name was Amisi, meaning 'flower,' and many Englishmen and Frenchmen and Egyptian men told Forsyte that her quiet beauty earned her the right to the name.

"Despite the Mohammadan prejudice against Franks and Christians, the courtship with the young widow was simple—several times Amisi had 'accidentally' allowed Forsyte to see her face without a veil near the bathing place where the local women gathered, which was any Egyptian woman's tacit acceptance of engagement—and they were married under Mohammadan law without elaborate ceremony. In truth, it took only a single sentence muttered by Drood's future mother to seal the marriage.

"The boy whom we now call Drood was born ten months later. His father named the boy Jasper, which meant nothing to the mother, neighbours, or the poor lad's future playmates, who tended to beat the half-breed lad like a rented mule. For almost four years, Forsyte raised the boy as a future English gentleman, demanded that only English be spoken in the home, tutored his son in his spare time, and announced that the boy's future education would be at fine schools in England. Amisi had no say in the matter. But—luckily for young Jasper John Forsyte-Drood's future survival—his father was gone more often than he was home, working on engineering projects that took him great distances from Cairo and his wife and child. On the street, young Jasper John Forsyte travelled in rags by his mother's side—it was important, Amisi knew, that the other adults and children not know how well-off young Jasper truly was. His playmates, or even Egyptian adults, might have murdered the light-skinned boy had they known the extent of his infidel father's wealth.

"Then, as suddenly as whim had brought him to Egypt, John Frederick Forsyte's Egyptian engineering work ended and he followed whim back to England and a new life. He left his Mohammadan wife and mixed-breed child behind without so much as a letter of regret. They never heard from him again.

"Drood's mother was now twice disgraced—firstly for marrying a Christian and secondly for being abandoned by him. Her friends, neighbours, and relatives blamed her for both tragedies. One day while with the other women bathing, Amisi was dragged away by several men whose faces were hidden behind scarves, made to stand trial before a court of other faceless men, sentenced to be paraded through the streets on a high-saddled ass surrounded by the local police and by howling mobs of men, and then stoned to death by yet another crowd of men while ululating women in their black robes and veils looked on with satisfaction from rooftops and doorways.

"But when the police arrived to seize the dead woman's child at Forsyte's former home in the Old Quarter near the river warehouses, the boy was gone. Servants, neighbours, and relatives denied sheltering him. Homes were searched, but no trace of the child was found. Even his clothes and toys had been left behind, as if the boy had simply stepped out into the courtyard and been carried into the sky or dragged into the river by animals. It was assumed that upon hearing of Amisi's execution for the crime of immorality, some well-meaning neighbour or servant had told four-year-old Jasper to run and he had simply found his way to the desert and perished.

"But this was obviously not the case.

"You see, Wilkie, a wealthy and important uncle of Amisi's, a rug merchant named Amun who lived in Alexandria—a man who had always doted on his niece and had been sad when her first marriage had taken her away to Cairo and even sadder when he had heard she had married an infidel—also had heard of the Englishman's abandoning her and had made the trip to Cairo to urge Amisi to bring her child and to return to Alexandria with him. Amun, whose name meant "the hidden one," was almost an old man, but he had young wives. Besides being a rug merchant by day, Amun was by night a priest from one of the secret temples celebrating the old religion—the ancient, pagan, pharaonic, pre-Mohammadan religion of Egyptians before they had all been converted under the scimitar to Mohammadanism—and had been determined to convince Amisi to join him.

"He was only an hour late. Arriving in the neighbourhood just in time to see the execution of his niece but with no chance to stop it, he rushed to Amisi's house—the servants were sleeping in the heat of the day; the neighbours were off enjoying the stoning—and he stole young Jasper John Forsyte out of his bed and left Cairo immediately with the tiny boy clinging frantically around his waist on horseback. Young Jasper would not have known that Amun was his great-uncle or that his mother was dead, imagining in his four-year-old child's mind that he was being kidnapped by a desert bandit. Together, old man and young boy, they galloped Uncle Amun's white stallion out through the gates of Cairo and down the desert road to Alexandria.

"There in his home city, within the walls of his fortress of a compound guarded by his clan's well-armed circle of guards, fellow priests, and loyal Alexandrian assassins, Uncle Amun took Jasper in as one of his own without ever revealing the boy's identity to anyone. The morning after young Jasper John Forsyte awoke in his strange new surroundings, Uncle Amun took him out to a pen and told him to choose a goat. Young

Drood took his time the way only a four-year-old boy can, Wilkie, and finally chose the largest and silkiest white goat, one with the Devil's own vertically slitted eyes. Uncle Amun nodded and smiled, told the boy to take the goat from the pen, and led the bleating animal and the boy to a private courtyard deep within the sprawling compound. There Uncle Amun, no longer smiling, pulled a long, curved dagger from his belt, handed it to the boy, and said, 'This goat is all that there remains of the boy once known as Jasper John Forsyte, son of the English infidel John Forsyte and the shamed woman called Amisi. Jasper John Forsyte dies here, now, this morning, and none of these names shall ever be mentioned again—not by you, upon pain of your death, not by anyone else, upon pain of death.'

"And then Uncle Amun put his powerful hand over little Jasper John's hand on the hilt of the dagger and quickly slashed the goat's throat. The still-thrashing animal bled to death in seconds. Droplets of blood spattered the four-year-old's white trousers and shirt.

" 'From this moment forward, your name is Drood,' said Uncle Amun.

"Drood was not Amun's family name, Wilkie. It was not even a common Egyptian name. Its meaning was, in fact, lost in the mists of time and secret religious rites.

"In the years that followed, Uncle Amun introduced the boy to the secret world Amun and some of his acolytes inhabited. Mohammadans by day—little Drood learned to recite the Koran and say his prayers five times a day as any worthy believer in Islam must do—Amun and the other Alexandrians in Amun's secret circle followed the Old Ways, the ancient religious ways and rites, at night. Drood followed his uncle and these other priests into Pyramids by torchlight, and into hidden rooms deep beneath other such sacred sites as the

Sphinx. Before he reached his adolescent years, young Drood had travelled with his uncle and other secret priests to Cairo, to the isle called Philae and to ancient ruins of necropoli far up the Nile, including a valley where the long-dead Egyptian kings—pharaohs, I am sure you remember they were called, Wilkie—lay buried in elaborate tombs carved into cliffsides and hidden beneath the stone of the valley floors.

"In these hidden places the ancient Egyptian religion and its thousands of years of arcane knowledge flourished. There the boy Drood was initiated into the mysteries of that religion and taught the same secret rituals that Moses had mastered.

"Uncle Amun's speciality turned out to be in sacred healing sciences. He was—and Drood was trained to be—a high priest in the Temples of Sleep dedicated to Isis, Osiris, and Serapis. This so-called healing sleep, my dear Wilkie, went back in Egyptian lore and practise for more than ten thousand years. The priests who had the power to induce such healing sleep also gained power and control over their patients. Today, of course, we call this practise by its scientific name of mesmerism and know its magical effects as the induction of magnetic sleep.

"You are aware that I have an ability of my own— some say a rare talent—in this art, Wilkie. I have told you of my training with Professor John Elliotson at the University College Hospital in London, of my own private investigations into the power, and of my own use of Magnetic power to help poor, phantom-afflicted Madame de la Rue—at her husband's insistence—over a period of many months in Italy and Switzerland some years ago. I would have completely cured her, I am certain of this, if Catherine had not intervened because of her insane and baseless jealousy.

"Drood told me that he sensed my control of such

Magnetic mesmeric power the moment he saw me on the hillside above the accident carnage at Staplehurst. Drood said that he recognised the gods-given ability in me instantly, the same way Uncle Amun had recognised the latent abilities in him when he was a boy of four so many decades earlier.

"But I digress.

"For the rest of his boyhood and young manhood in Egypt, Drood pursued mastery of his powers through the rituals and knowledge of the ancients. Did you know, for instance, my dear Wilkie, that no less an historian than Herodotus tells us that the great king Rameses, Pharaoh of all Egypt, once became so seriously ill that there was no hope for him and he, in Herodotus' words but also the words of Drood's uncle and teachers, 'descended into the mansion of death'? But Rameses then returned to the light, cured. This pharaoh's return has been celebrated for thousands of years, and continues to be celebrated in Islam-dominated Egypt today. And Wilkie, do you know the mechanism for Rameses' miraculous return from the dark mansion of death?"

Here Dickens paused for dramatic effect until I was finally forced to ask, "What was it?"

"That magical power was mesmeric magnetism," he said. "Rameses had been mesmerised, according to ritual and method, at the Temple of Seag, was allowed to die as a man, but was brought back—cured of his fatal disease—as something more than a man.

"Tacitus tells us of the celebrated Temple of Sleep in Alexandria. This is where young Drood did most of his midnight studies and where he emerged as a practitioner of this ancient art of Magnetic Influence.

"That night in his temple-library in Undertown, Drood explained to me—actually showed me the parchments and books—that Plutarch reported that both the prophetic and curative sleep induced in the temples of Isis and Osiris utilised a mesmeric incense called Kyphi, which is used even today—Drood let me smell it from a vial, Wilkie—as well as the music of the lyre to bring on such mesmeric sleep. The Pythagoreans also used this Kyphi incense and the lyre in their secret cave and temple ceremonies, since they believed as the ancient Egyptians did that such Magnetic Influence, properly directed, can free the soul from its body and create a full rapport with the spiritual world.

"Don't look at me that way, my dear Wilkie. You know I am no believer in mere ghosts and spirit-rappings. How many have I exposed in my talks and essays? But I *am* an expert in Magnetic Influence, and I hope to become a greater expert in the science very soon.

"According to Herodotus and Clemens Alexandrinus, this prayer and mesmeric control of a dying man have been used for ten thousand years at all important Egyptian funerals—

"'Deign, ye gods, who give life to men, to give a favourable judgement of the soul of the deceased, that it may pass to the eternal gods.'

"But you see that *some* souls they do not release, Wilkie. *Some* souls they hold under their Magnetic Influence and bring back. Such it was with the Pharaoh Rameses. Such it was with the man you and I know as Drood."

DICKENS STOPPED WALKING and I stopped next to him. We were less than half a mile from Gad's Hill now, although we had been walking at something less than Dickens's usual frenzied pace. I confess that I had been half-mesmerised by the sound and tone and drone of Charles Dickens's voice for the past twenty minutes or so and had noticed almost nothing of our surroundings.

"Have you found this boring, Wilkie?" he asked, his dark eyes sharp and challenging.

"Don't be absurd," I said. "It's fascinating. And fantastic. It's not everyone who is permitted to, or every day that one is allowed to, hear an *Arabian Nights* tale from Charles Dickens."

"Fantastic," repeated Dickens, smiling thinly. "Do you find it too fantastic to be true?"

"Charles, are you asking me whether I think Drood was telling *you* the truth with this story or whether you are telling *me* the truth?"

"Either," said Dickens. "Both." His intense gaze never left my face.

"I have no idea whether this Drood spoke a word of truth," I said. "But I trust that you are telling me the truth in your narration of what he said."

I was lying, Dear Reader. The story was too absurd either for me to accept it or to believe that Dickens had accepted it. I remembered that Dickens had once told me that *1001 Arabian Nights* had been his favourite book when he was a child. I wondered now if the accident at Staplehurst had released some childhood strain in his character.

Dickens nodded as if I had answered the schoolmaster correctly. "I don't need to remind you, my dear old friend, that all of this information is told in confidence."

"Of course not."

He smiled almost boyishly. "Even if our Inspector Field friend threatens to tell the world about the Landlady and the Butler?"

I waved that away. "You did not tell the heart of Drood's story," I said.

"I did not?"

"No," I said flatly. "You did not. Why was he there at Staplehurst? Where had he come from? What was he doing with the injured and dying? . . . I believe that you once said it looked as if the Drood creature were stealing the souls of the dying there. And what on earth is he doing in a cave beneath the catacombs beyond a river in a tunnel?"

"Rather than continue the narration…" said Dickens even as he began walking again, "…since we are rather close to home, I shall just answer your questions, my dear Wilkie. But first of all, Hatchery was correct in his detective work and assumptions about Drood's presence at Staplehurst. The man was in a coffin in the baggage car."

"Good God!" I said. "Why?"

"For precisely the reasons we surmised, Wilkie. Drood has enemies in London and England who attempt to locate and harm him. Our Inspector Field is one of those enemies. Nor is Drood either a citizen of our nation or a welcome foreign visitor. In fact, in the eyes and files of all official sources, he has been dead for more than twenty years. So he *was* returning in a coffin from a trip to France…a trip in which he met others of his religion and expertise in the Magnetic Arts."

"Extraordinary," I said. "But what about his odd behaviour at the accident site, lurking and leaning over victims who were dead when you visited them next? 'Stealing souls,' you said."

Dickens smiled and beheaded a weed, swinging his blackthorn stick like a broadsword. "It shows how mistaken even the trained and intelligent observer can be when deprived of all context, my dear Wilkie. Drood was not stealing the souls of those poor dying wretches. On the contrary, he was mesmerising them to ease the pain of their passage and saying the words of the ancient Egyptian funeral ceremony to help them on their journey, using some of the very words I quoted to you a few minutes ago. Rather as if he were a Catholic giving the Last Rites to the dying. Only with mesmeric Sleep Temple rites, he was certain he really *was* sending their souls on to their judgement by whatever gods they worshipped."

"Extraordinary," I said again.

"And as for his history here in England and the reasons for his presence in Undertown," continued Dickens, "Drood's arrival in England and his altercation with a sailor, knife and all, are almost exactly as old Opium Sal related it. Except *in reverse*. Drood was sent to England more than twenty years ago to look up two cousins of his from Egypt—twins, a young man and young woman who had mastered another ancient Egyptian skill, the ability to read each other's minds—and Drood arrived with thousands of pounds in English cash and more wealth in the form of gold in his luggage.

"He was robbed the second night he was here. Robbed on the docks by British sailors and slashed viciously with a blade—it is there that he lost his eyelids, ears, nose, and part of his tongue and fingers—and thrown into the Thames like the corpse he almost was. It was some of the residents of Undertown who found him floating in the river and brought him below to die. But Drood did not die, Wilkie. Or if he did, he resurrected himself. Even as he was being robbed and slashed and beaten and stabbed by the unnamed English thugs in the night, Drood had deeply mesmerised himself, balancing his soul—or at least his mental being—between life and death. The scavengers from Undertown did find a lifeless body, but his Magnetic-induced slumber was broken by the sound of concerned human voices, just as he had commanded himself under mesmeric self-control. Drood lived again. To repay those wretched souls who had saved him, Drood built his library–cum–Temple of Sleep in their underground warren. There, to this day, he heals those he can heal, helps those he can help through his ancient rites, and eases the pain and passing of those he cannot save."

"You make him sound like a saint," I said.

"In some ways, I believe he is."

"Why did he not just go home to Egypt?" I asked.

"Oh, he does, Wilkie. He does. From time to time. To visit his students and colleagues there. To help with certain ancient ceremonies."

"But he continues to return to England? After all these years?"

"He still has not found his cousins," said Dickens. "And yes, he feels England is as much his home now as Egypt ever was. After all, he *is* half English."

"Even after killing the goat that bore his English name?" I said.

Dickens did not answer.

I said, "Inspector Field tells me that your Mr Drood—healer, master of Magnetic science, Christ figure, and secret mystic—has killed more than three hundred people in the past twenty years."

I waited for the laughter.

Dickens did not change expression. He was still studying me. He said, "Do *you* believe that the man I spoke to has killed three hundred people, Wilkie?"

I held his gaze and returned its noncommital blankness. "Perhaps he mesmerises his minions and sends *them* out to do the dirty work, Charles."

Now he did smile. "I am certain that you are aware, my dear friend, through the teachings of Professor John Elliotson if not through my own occasional writings on the topic, that a subject under the influence of mesmeric slumber or mesmeric trance can do *nothing* that would violate his or her morals or principles if that subject were fully conscious."

"Then perhaps Drood mesmerised killers and cutthroats to go out and do the killings that Inspector Field described," I said.

"If they were already killers and cutthroats, my dear

Wilkie," Dickens said softly, "he would not have had to mesmerise them, would he? He simply could have paid them in gold."

"Perhaps he did," I said. The absurdity of our conversation had reached some point where it was now unsustainable. I looked around at the grassy field shimmering in the afternoon autumn light. I could actually see Dickens's chalet and the mansard roof of his Gad's Hill Place home through the trees.

I put my hand on the Inimitable's shoulder before he could begin walking again. "Is increasing your knowledge and skill in mesmerism the reason you disappear into London at least one night a week?" I asked.

"Ah, so there *is* a spy in my family circle. One with frequent digestion problems, might I guess?"

"No, it is *not* my brother, Charles," I said a trifle sharply. "Charles Collins is a man who keeps confidences and is fiercely loyal to you, Dickens. And he will someday be the father of your grandchildren. You should hold him in higher esteem."

Something flickered across the writer's face then. It was not quite a shadow—perhaps an instant of revulsion, although whether it was at the thought of my brother married to his daughter (a union of which he never approved) or another reminder of Dickens himself being old enough to be a grandfather, I will never know.

"You are correct, Wilkie. I apologise for my jesting, although the jests have been made with familial affection. But some quiet voice tells me that there will be no grandchildren issued from the union of Katey Dickens and Charles Collins."

Now what the deuce did he mean by *that?* Before we came to blows or resumed walking in silence again, I said, "It was Katey who told me about your weekly trips to the city. She and Georgina and your son Charles are worried about you. They know that the accident still haunts and afflicts you. Now they fear that I have introduced you to some foul abomination in the fleshpots of London to which you are, if you will pardon the expression, magnetically drawn at least one full night a week."

Dickens threw his head back and laughed.

"Come, Wilkie. If you cannot stay for the delectable dinner Georgina has planned, at least you must stay long enough to enjoy a cigar with me as we look in on the stables and watch the children and John Forster at play on the lawn. Then I'll have little Plorn take you by cart to the station for the early-evening express."

THE DOGS RUSHED us as we came up the drive.

Dickens almost always kept dogs chained near the gate, since too many surly vagabonds and unkempt vagrants exercised the habit of wandering off Dover Road to ask for unmerited handouts at the back or front door of Gad's Hill Place. First to welcome us this afternoon was Mrs Bouncer, Mary's tiny little Pomeranian, for whom Dickens adopted a special, childish, almost squeaky voice for all his communications. A second later bounded up Linda, the ambling, bouncing, rolling Saint Bernard who always seemed to be in a perpetual tumbling match with the great mastiff named Turk. Now these three entered into an absolute ecstasy of leaping and licking and tail-wagging at the greeting of their master, who—I freely admit—did have an extraordinary way with animals. As with so many people, dogs and horses seemed to understand that Charles Dickens *was* the Inimitable and needed to be revered as such.

As I was trying to pat the Saint Bernard and pet the frolicking mastiff and avoid the leaping little Pomeranian, all of whom kept abandoning me to return to

Dickens in their transports of delight, a new dog—one unknown to me, a large Irish bloodhound—came broiling around the curve of the hedge and ran at me, growling and snarling as if it were going to rip my throat out. I confess that I raised my stick and took several steps backwards down the drive.

"Stop, Sultan!" shouted Dickens, and the attacking dog first froze a mere six paces from me and then crouched in pure canine guilt and submission as his master chided him in his equally pure dog-chiding voice. Then Dickens scratched behind the miscreant's ears.

I stepped closer, and the bloodhound growled and showed his fangs again. Dickens ceased scratching. Sultan showed guilt, shrank lower into the drive's gravel, and set his muzzle against Dickens's boots.

"I don't know this dog," I said.

Dickens shook his head. "Percy Fitzgerald made a gift of Sultan to me only a few weeks ago. I confess that at times the dog reminds me of you, Wilkie."

"How is that?"

"First of all, he is absolutely fearless," said Dickens. "Secondly, he is absolutely loyal . . . he obeys only me but he obeys me completely. Thirdly, he is contemptuous of all public opinion as regards his behaviour; he hates soldiers and attacks them on sight; he hates policemen and has been known to chase them down the highway; and he hates all others of his kind."

"I do not hate all others of my kind," I said softly. "And I have never attacked a soldier or chased a policeman."

Dickens did not appear to be listening as he knelt to pat Sultan's neck, the other three dogs leaping and roiling around him in spasms of jealousy. "Sultan has swallowed Mary's Mrs Bouncer Pomeranian only once and did have the good grace to spit her out when commanded to, but all of the kittens in the neighbourhood—especially the new batch born to the pussy who lives in the shed behind the Falstaff Inn—have mysteriously gone missing since Sultan arrived."

Sultan eyed me with an eager gaze clearly showing his willingness to eat me if the opportunity presented itself.

"And despite his loyalty, companionship, courage, and amusing traits," concluded Dickens, "I fear that our friend Sultan may have to be put down someday and that I shall be the one who has to do it."

I TOOK THE TRAIN back to London, but rather than walk home to Melcombe Place, I took a cab to 33 Bolsover Street. There Miss Martha R——, who was registered with the landlord there as Mrs Martha Dawson, met me at the rear and separate door to her small apartment that consisted of a tiny sleeping room and a slightly larger sitting room with rudimentary cooking facilities. I was arriving hours later than I had promised, but she had been listening for my step on the stairs.

"I made chops and kept the supper warm," she said as she closed the door behind me. "If you *want* to eat now. Or I could re-warm them later."

"Yes," I said. "Re-warm them later."

Now, Dear Reader from my distant future, I can almost—not quite, but almost—imagine a time such as yours when memoirists or even novelists do not draw a discreet curtain over the personal events that might follow here, the, let us say, intimate moments between a man and a woman. I hope your age is not so debauched that you speak and write without restraint about such totally private moments, but if you search for such shameless exposures here, you shall be disappointed.

I can say that if you were to somehow see a photo-

graph of Miss Martha R——, you might not be kind
enough to see the beauty I find in her every time I am
near her. To the mere eye, or camera lens (and Martha
told me that she had a photograph taken of her, paid for
by her parents, when she turned nineteen more than a
year ago), Martha R—— is a short, somewhat stern-
looking woman with a narrow face, almost Negroid
lips, severely parted straight hair (to the point she seems
bald along the crown of her head), deep-set eyes, and a
nose and complexion that might have had her in the
fields picking cotton in the American South.

There is nothing in a photograph of Martha R——
that could show her energy and eagerness and sensuality and physical generosity and adventurousness. Many
women—I live with one most of the time—can simulate and broadcast physical sensuality to men in public,
can dress for it and paint themselves for it and bat their
eyelashes for it, even while they feel little or none of it. I
believe they do so out of sheer habit. A few women,
such as young Martha R——, sincerely embody such a
passionate nature. Finding a woman like that amidst
the herd of half-feeling, half-caring, half-responding
females in our society of 1860s England was not so
much like finding a diamond in the rough as it was like
finding a warm, responsive body amidst the cold, dead
forms on slabs in the Paris Morgue that Dickens had so
enjoyed taking me to.

SOME HOURS LATER, at the little table she cleared off
for our meals, by candlelight, we ate the dried chops—
Martha was not yet a good cook and would never
become one—and moved the cold and desiccated vegetables around with our forks. Martha had somehow
chosen and paid for a bottle of wine. It was quite as terrible as the food.

I took her hand.

"My dear," I said, "tomorrow you must pack your clothes in the early morning and take the eleven fifteen train to Yarmouth. There you must get your old job at the hotel back or, failing that, obtain a similar one. No later than tomorrow night you must visit your parents and brother in Winterton and tell them you are well and happy—that you used your savings for a little holiday in Brighton."

To her credit, Martha did not whimper or simper. But she bit at her lip as she said, "Mr Collins, my love, have I done something to offend you? Is it the dinner?"

I laughed despite my fatigue and pain from the rising rheumatical gout in my eyes and limbs. "No, no, my dear. It's simply that there's a detective sniffing around and we must not give him reason to blackmail me—or you or your family, my dear. We must part for a short time until he tires of this game."

"A policeman!" said Martha. She was imperturbable, but she was still a serving-class provincial. The police, especially London police, held terror for her kind.

I smiled again to allay her fears. "Not at all. No longer a policeman, Martha my dear. Merely a self-employed detective of the sordid sort hired by ageing lords to follow their young wives when they go out to do charity work. Nothing to worry about."

"But must we part?" She looked around the room and I could tell that she was consigning the drab furniture and dreary prints on the walls to memory as surely as would some member of a royal family about to be banished from her ancestral castle.

"Only for a short time," I said again, patting her hand. "I will deal with this detective and then we will make our plans anew. In fact, this very suite of rooms shall continue being let in the name of Mrs Dawson, in the certainty of your returning soon. Would you like that?"

"I should like that very much, Mr...Dawson. Can you spend the night tonight? This last night for a while?"

"Not tonight, my dearest. The gout is heavy on me tonight. I need to get home to take my medicine."

"Oh, I wish you would leave a bottle of your medicine here, my love, so that it could alleviate your pain while I alleviate your other tensions and anxieties!" She squeezed my hand hard enough to send pain up my aching arm. There were tears in her eyes now, and I knew that they were for me and not due to her exile. Martha R—— had a sympathetic soul.

"The eleven fifteen train," I said, setting bills and coins totalling six pounds on the top of the dresser as I rose and pulled on my coat. "Make sure that you leave nothing behind here, my dearest. Travel safely and I shall be in contact with you soon."

FOURTEEN-YEAR-OLD HARRIET was asleep in her room, but Caroline was still awake when I arrived home at 9 Melcombe Place.

"Are you hungry?" she asked. "We had veal and I kept some for you."

"No, only some wine, perhaps," I said. "I've had the worst time with the gout today." I went to the kitchen, unlocked my private cupboard with the key from my waistcoat, drank down three glasses of laudanum, and returned to Caroline in the dining room, where she had filled two glasses with a good Madeira. The taste of Martha's wretched wine was still on my mouth and I sought to banish it.

"How was your day with Dickens?" she asked. "I did not expect you to stay so late."

"You know how insistent he can be when he invites one to dinner," I said. "He will not take no as an answer."

"I do not really know that, actually," said Caroline. "All of my meals with Mr Dickens have been with you and either at our home or in a private room at a restaurant. He has never insisted to *me* that I stay late at his table."

I did not dispute the fact. I could feel the laudanum beginning to work on the pulsating pain of my terrible headache. The medicine gave me the odd feeling of bobbing up and down, as if the dining room table and chair were a small boat caught in the wake of a larger ship.

"Did you have a pleasant day of conversation with him?" pressed Caroline. She was wearing a red silk dressing gown a bit too flamboyant to be of the highest taste. The embroidered gold flowers on it seemed to throb and pulse in my vision.

I said, "I believe that Dickens threatened to kill me this afternoon if I did not follow his commands. To put me down like a disobedient dog."

"Wilkie!" Her horror was real and her face went white in the low lamplight.

I forced a laugh. "Never mind, my dearest. Nothing of the sort actually happened, of course. Just another example of Wilkie Collins's penchant for hyperbole. We had a delightful walk and chat this afternoon and more enjoyable conversation over the long dinner and brandy and cigars afterwards. John Forster and his new bride were there."

"Oh, that bore."

"Yes." I removed my glasses and rubbed my temples. "I should go to bed."

"Poor darling," said Caroline. "Would it help to have your muscles rubbed?"

"Yes," I said. "I believe it would."

I do not know where Caroline G—— learned the art of muscular massage. I have never asked. As is true of so much of her life before I met her ten years earlier, that remains a mystery.

But the pleasure and relaxation her hands gave me were no mystery.

Some half an hour later in my bedroom, when she was finished, she whispered, "Shall I stay tonight, my darling?"

"Not tonight, my love. The gout is still very much with me—as pleasure ebbs, the pain flows back in, as you know—and I have serious work to do early tomorrow."

Caroline nodded, kissed me on the cheek, took the candle lamp on the dresser, and went downstairs.

I considered writing then, working through the night as I had so often done on *The Woman in White* and earlier books, but a subtle noise from the first-floor landing beyond my bedroom door convinced me to stay where I was. The woman with green skin and tusk-teeth was growing more bold. For months after we moved here she had contained her prowlings to the steep and dark servants' stairway, but now I frequently heard her bare feet on the rug and wood of the landing after midnight.

Or the noise could have come from my study. That would be worse, to go in there in the dark and see *him* writing in my place in the moonlight.

I stayed in my bedroom and crossed to the window, quietly parting the drapes.

Near the lamp post on the corner loitered a boy in rags. He was sitting with his back against a dustbin, possibly sleeping. Or possibly looking up towards my window. His eyes were in shadow.

I closed the drapes and went back to bed. Sometimes

the laudanum keeps me awake all night; at other times, it carries me away to powerful dreams.

I was drifting off to sleep, banishing Charles Dickens and his phantom Drood from my thoughts, when my nostrils were filled with a cloying, almost sickening scent—rotting meat, perhaps—and images of scarlet geraniums, bundles and heaps and funeral-thick towers of scarlet geraniums, pulsed behind my eyelids like spurtings of blood.

"My God," I said aloud, sitting up in the dark, filled with a certainty so absolute as to be a form of clairvoyance. "Charles Dickens is going to murder Edmond Dickenson."

CHAPTER TEN

*A*fter making notes of my conversation with Dickens the next morning, I breakfasted late and alone at my club. I needed time to think.

Dickens had pressed me several times the preceding day on whether I believed him, but the truth is, I did not. At least not fully. I was not certain that he ever met with anyone named Drood down there in the sewers and labyrinths under London. I had seen the rowboat-gondola and its two odd men, Venus and Mercury, Dickens had called them, so that was something certain to begin with.

Or had I seen them? I *remembered* the boat arriving and Dickens boarding and disappearing around the bend with the masked figure poling near the bow and the other masked figure steering with the stern sweep . . . or did I? I had been exhausted and frightened and yet also sleepy. I had taken extra doses of my medicine before joining Dickens that night and then drunk more wine than I usually did at dinner. The entire experience of that evening, even *before* we went down through a crypt to find the Chinese Lazaree opium lord, all seemed dreamlike and unreal.

But what about Dickens's biographical tale of Mr Drood?

What about it? Charles Dickens's imagination could furnish a thousand such tales with only seconds of notice. In fact, the story of Drood's childhood, English father, murdered Mohammadan mother...it all sounded contrived to a level far below Charles Dickens's creative powers.

But, oddly enough, it was the part of the story concerning Drood's abilities with mesmerism and Magnetic Influence that made me want to believe the bulk of the Inimitable's tale. It also explained why Dickens, terrified now of riding in trains and even carriages, would come into London from Gad's Hill at least once a week.

He was a student...or perhaps "acolyte" was a better word...of the Master Mesmerist named Drood.

AS I HAD KNOWN even before he had tried (and failed) to mesmerise me shortly after Staplehurst, Dickens's fascination with mesmerism went back almost thirty years, to the time when the writer was known everywhere primarily by his early *nom de plume* of "Boz." All of England was interested in mesmerism at that time: the phenomenon had been imported from France, where a "magnetic boy" seemed to be able to tell time on people's watches and read cards in a mesmeric trance even while his head and eyes were heavily bandaged. I did not know Dickens then, of course, but he had described more than once how he had attended as many demonstrations of mesmerism as he could find in London. But it was the professor Dickens had mentioned, a certain John Elliotson from University College Hospital, who most impressed the young Boz.

In 1838, Elliotson used his Magnetic Influence to place his subjects—some of them patients at his hospital in London—into a much deeper trance than most mesmerists could achieve. From the depths of those trances, his men and women, boys and girls, not only made strides towards cures of chronic conditions, but also could be induced into prophetic and even clairvoyant states. The Okey sisters, both epileptics, not only left their wheeled chairs to sing and dance while mesmerised by Professor Elliotson, but also showed strong evidence of second sight under what young Dickens had been convinced had been a controlled condition. Dickens was, in other words, a convert.

For a man with no real religious convictions, Dickens became a true believer in animal magnetism and in the mesmeric powers that controlled this energy. You must remember, Dear Reader, the context of our times: science was making huge strides in understanding the underlying and interrelated energies and fluids such as magnetism and electricity. The flow and control of mesmeric fluid common to all living things, but especially to the human mind and body, seemed to Dickens to be as scientific and as demonstrable as breakthroughs shown by Faraday when he generated electricity with a magnet.

The next year, 1839, when Elliotson resigned his position of Professor of Principles and Practices of Medicine at University College—due to pressure, everyone understood, because of the sensational nature of his mesmeric demonstrations—Dickens supported the doctor in public, loaned him money in private, arranged for Elliotson to attend to Dickens's parents and other family members, and—some years later—attempted to help the distraught and despondent doctor when he became suicidal.

Dickens never allowed himself to be mesmerised, of course. Anyone who thought that Charles Dickens might surrender such control of himself to another person, even briefly, did not know Charles Dickens. It was the young Boz, soon to be the mature Inimitable, who invariably sought to control other people. Mesmerism became just one of the tools he used, but it was one he would be interested in for the rest of his life.

It was not long, of course, before Dickens began attempting his own mesmeric experiments and therapies. By the time he was visiting America in 1842, Dickens told his friends there that he was regularly mesmerising Catherine to cure her of her headaches and insomnia. (Years later, he told me that he had been using animal magnetism to alleviate a much wider range of what he called "hysterical symptoms" exhibited by his hapless wife. He also confessed to me that his first mesmerism of his wife had been an accident; while discussing Magnetic Influence with some American friends he had been "holding forth upon the subject rather luminously," making hand movements around his listeners' heads and brushing their eyebrows simply to exhibit the proper procedures he himself had witnessed in demonstrations by experts, when he suddenly magnetised Catherine into hysterics. He had made more hand passes to bring her out of it, but that only succeeded in sending his wife into a deep mesmeric trance. The next night he again used Catherine as his subject in front of friends and shortly after that began his attempt to cure her of her "hysterical symptoms.") From Catherine he moved on to applying his growing mesmeric abilities to a small circle of family and friends.

But it was with Madame de la Rue that Dickens's use of Magnetic Influence led to trouble.

Madame Augusta de la Rue was the English wife of Swiss-born banker Emile de la Rue, director of the Genoese branch of the banking firm started by his grandfather. For a brief period starting in October of 1844, the year Dickens had brought Catherine to Genoa so that he could write there through the autumn and winter, the Dickenses and the de la Rues were neighbours and saw each other frequently in the small expatriate circle of Genoese society.

Augusta de la Rue suffered from symptoms of overwhelming nervousness that included insomnia, nervous tics, facial spasms, and attacks of anxiety so severe that they literally tied the poor woman in knots. People of a less sophisticated age than ours might have thought the woman possessed by demons.

Dickens proposed that he use his growing mesmeric abilities to help Madame de la Rue, and Emile, the lady's husband, thought it a grand idea. *"Happy and ready to come to you,"* Dickens announced to her in one note, and for the next three months, through November and December of 1844 into January of 1845, the author was with her several times a day. Her husband was present for some of these sessions. (Emile valiantly attempted to learn the mesmeric arts from Dickens so that he could help his wife on his own, but, alas, Emile de la Rue had no talent for Magnetic Influence.)

Central to the mystery of Madame de la Rue's malady was the presence of a lurking Phantom who haunted her dreams and somehow was the source of her illness. "It is absolutely essential," Dickens instructed Emile de la Rue, "that this Phantom to which her incapacitating thoughts are directed and clustered around, should not *regain its power.*"

To keep this from happening, Dickens began responding to summonses from the de la Rues at any time of the day or night. Sometimes Dickens would leave Catherine alone in their cold Genoese bed and rush to Madame de la Rue's bedside at four AM in order to help his poor patient.

Slowly Madame de la Rue's spasms, tics, contortions, and sleepless nights began to ebb. Emile was delighted. Yet every day Dickens continued to magnetise her to ask more questions about the Phantom. To those who watched the mesmeric sessions in the parlour of the de la Rue mansion, it seemed very much like a séance, with Madame de la Rue—deep in her trance—reporting of dark and light spirit forms shifting around her in some distant location. And always with the Phantom trying to bring her under his or its control, while Charles Dickens valiantly attempted to free Madame de la Rue from the creature's dark influence.

When Dickens and Catherine left Genoa in late January to continue their travels to Rome and Naples, Emile kept sending the author daily updates and diary entries reporting on his wife's condition. Dickens wrote back that it was essential that the de la Rues join him in Rome no later than late February, and Emile de la Rue and his wife arranged to travel there early.

Catherine did not know that her husband was planning to reunite with Madame de la Rue. Nor did she know that Dickens had made a private arrangement with his "patient": he would concentrate for one full hour on mesmerising her in his imagination starting at eleven AM each day. Madame de la Rue, far away, concentrated on receiving the radiation of Dickens's Magnetic Influence as he turned his "Visual Ray" in her direction.

They were travelling by carriage—Catherine riding atop the vehicle for air, Dickens within—when eleven AM arrived and Dickens began concentrating on his distant patient. He had no sooner begun visualising his mesmeric hand passes and directing the magnetic fluid when he heard Catherine's muff fall from the box above. Catherine, having no idea that Dickens was sending magnetic influences into the air towards Genoa, nonetheless had gone into a violent mesmeric trance on the carriage box above him, her eyelids quivering in a convulsive manner.

By the time the Dickenses had settled in Rome, the separation of the patient from her Magnetic Doctor had led to serious setbacks. Emile wrote that the Phantom showed signs of reappearing and taking control of Augusta. *"I cannot beat it down, or keep it down, at a distance,"* Dickens wrote back. *"Pursuing that Magnetic power, and being near to her and with her, I believe that I can shiver it like Glass."*

The de la Rues appeared in Rome soon after this—to Catherine's great astonishment—and Dickens resumed the daily sessions, now magnetising her, he wrote, *"under olive trees, sometimes in vineyards, sometimes in the travelling carriage, sometimes at wayside inns during the midday halt."*

It was during this time that Dickens reported to Emile that Madame de la Rue was showing disturbing symptoms. *"She was rolled into an apparently impossible ball, by tic in the brain, and I only knew where her head was by following her long hair to its source."*

It was at this point that Catherine (who had become pregnant again in late January, about the time she joined Dickens in climbing Mount Vesuvius as it was in full eruption) announced to her husband that she was distressed by the apparent impropriety of Charles's relationship with Augusta.

Dickens, as he always did when accused of something, became furious and railed at Catherine that her accusations were absurd, even obscene, and that it was obvious to everyone else involved and uninvolved that his motives were absolutely the pure concern of a doctor of mesmeric magnetism towards one of his most troubled patients. Dickens shouted, berated Catherine, and threatened to leave Rome without her.

Nonetheless, a three-months-pregnant wife—especially one standing as firm in her position as the Great Wall of China—is hard to bully.

For the first time, Catherine had spoken out against one of Dickens's obsessions and flirtations, and for the first and only time, he had relented. He explained to the de la Rues that Catherine was upset at the amount of time he was spending with his patient, but he also apologised profusely for Catherine's attitude, calling her oversensitive to her own needs and insensitive to others'.

And Dickens never forgot or forgave this insult to his honour. Years later, shortly before he cast Catherine out of the house after the incident of the Ellen Ternan bracelet, he brought up what he called her irrational jealousy from fourteen years earlier and the effect such an insult had on him. "Whatever made you unhappy in that Genoa time had no other root, beginning, middle, or end, than whatever has made you proud and honoured in your married life, and given you station better than rank, and surrounded you with many enviable things," he flung at her.

She had seen his relationship with poor, bedevilled Madame de la Rue as something suspect. Dickens informed her years later that she should have *known*— had she been a good and true wife she *would* have known—that his helping the poor woman had been the purest expression of his own innate creativity and nobility. His ability to mesmerise others, much like his ability to write great novels, was part of the firmament of character that was his greatest gift.

But now Dickens the minor master of Magnetic Influence had met the ultimate Master.

As I finished my breakfast at the club and folded my newspapers and left my napkin on the chair and found my hat and cane and went to the door, I had no doubt whatsoever that Dickens had been travelling into London every week on the train that terrified him into sweats to learn more about mesmerism from *someone*.

And it seemed to make sense that this someone was named Drood.

WELL, MR COLLINS. What a pleasant coincidence," said a brusque voice behind me as I walked up Chancery Lane towards Lincoln's Inn Court.

"Mr Field," I said, half-turning and nodding but not stopping, omitting the "Inspector" before his name by choice.

He either did not notice the omission or pretended not to. "It is a lovely autumn day, is it not, Mr Collins?"

"It is."

"It was a pleasant day yesterday as well. Did you enjoy your outing to Chatham and Gad's Hill?"

I double-tapped my stick on cobblestones. "Am I being followed, *Mr* Field? I thought you had a boy waiting on Melcombe Place and Dorset Square for any message I might want to send you."

"Oh, I do, Mr Collins," said Field, responding only to my second question. "The lad Gooseberry is there now, waiting patiently. He can afford to be patient, since I pay him to wait. My own profession does not allow for such patience without severe penalties. Time, as they say, is money."

We passed through Lincoln's Inn Fields. John Forster had lived here during his many years as a bachelor, and I always wondered if it was mere coincidence that Dickens had given the villainous lawyer Tulkinghorn in *Bleak House* Forster's old address.

When we passed through the Fields and reached Oxford Street, we both paused on the kerb as some dray waggons rumbled by. Then we had to wait for a line of carriages. Field removed his watch from his waistcoat and checked it. "Eleven twenty-five," he said. "Miss R—— should be on the outskirts of London by now, on her way back to Yarmouth."

I gripped the cane as if it were a club. "So you have people following all of us," I said through gritted teeth. "If you're paying your operatives to do that, Inspector, then you are wasting both time *and* money."

"I agree," said Field. "This is why your information will liberate both of us from wasted time, Mr Collins."

"If you had me followed yesterday," I said, "then you know everything I know."

Field laughed. "I can tell you the route you and Mr Dickens took on your three-hour walk, Mr Collins. But I cannot report even the gist of your conversation, although I know that the two of you were talking—or rather, Mr *Dickens* was talking—for most of the way back from Cooling Marsh."

I admit that a flush of real anger crept up from my collar to my cheeks at hearing this. I did not remember seeing any other pedestrians during my walk with Dickens. Yet some blackguard had been hovering nearby the entire time. I felt guilty and exposed, even though Dickens and I had been doing nothing more sinister than taking an afternoon constitutional. And how did Field know that Martha had left on the 11:15 train, only ten minutes before the infernal inspector announced it to me? Had one of his operatives rushed pell-mell from Charing Cross Station to inform his meddling and blackmailing superior of this vital fact? Were his agents signalling to him even now from some alley in the direction of Gray's Inn or Seven Dials? The anger continued to rise until I felt my heart pounding beneath my starched shirt.

"Do you want to tell me where I am headed *now*, Inspector?" I demanded angrily as I turned left and began striding briskly towards the west on Oxford Street.

"I would imagine that you are headed to the British Museum, Mr Collins, there possibly spend time in the Reading Room, but more likely to peruse Layard's and Rich's Ninevite and the ethnographical collection from Egypt."

I stopped. The hairs on the back of my neck were standing.

"The museum is closed today," I said.

"Yes," said Inspector Field, "but your friend Mr Reed will be waiting to open the side door for you and to give you a Special Visitor's ticket."

Taking a step towards the husky sixty year old, I said very softly but very firmly, "You are making a mistake, sir."

"Yes?"

"Yes." I squeezed the head of my cane until I imagined that I could feel the brass bending. "Your blackmail will not work with me, Mr Field. I am not a man who has much to hide. Either from my friends and family or my reading public."

Field raised both hands as if shocked by the suggestion. "Of course not, Mr Collins! Of course not! And that word...blackmail...is far from anything that can pass between two gentlemen such as ourselves. We are simply exploring areas of mutual concern. When it comes to helping you avoid potential difficulties, I am your obedient servant, sir. Indeed, that is my profession. A detective uses information to help men of parts, never to harm them."

"I doubt if you could convince Charles Dickens of that," I said. "Especially if he were to discover that you are still having him followed."

Field shook his head almost sadly. "My aim is *precisely* to help and protect Mr Dickens. He has no idea of the danger he is in because of his intercourse with this fiend that calls himself Drood."

"From what Mr Dickens tells me," I said, "the Drood he has met is more a misunderstood figure than a fiend."

"Indeed," murmured Field. "Mr Collins, you are young. Relatively young, at least. Younger than Mr Dickens or myself. But do you remember the fate of Lord Lucan?"

I stopped by a lamp post and tapped the paving

stones with my stick. "Lord Lucan? The Radical M.P. who was found murdered years ago?"

"Horribly murdered," agreed Inspector Field. "His heart ripped out of his chest as he was staying alone at his estate—Wiseton, it was called—in Hertfordshire, near Stevenage. This was in 1846. Lord Lucan was a friend of your literary acquaintance and Mr Dickens's old friend Edward Bulwer-Lytton, Lord Lytton, and Lord Lucan's estate lay only three miles from Lord Lytton's own Knebworth Castle."

"I've been there several times," I said. "To Knebworth, I mean. But what can this ancient murder have to do with anything we are discussing, Inspector?"

Field set his corpulent forefinger alongside his nose. "Lord Lucan, before he assumed his title after his older brother's death, was a certain John Frederick Forsyte ... rather the black sheep of his noble family, even though he had received a degree in engineering and privately published several books based on his travels. There were rumours that, in his youth, Lord Lucan had married a Mohammadan woman during his extended stay in Egypt ... and perhaps even fathered a child or two while he was there. Lord Lucan's terrible murder occurred less than a year after the man calling himself Drood first arrived at our London docks in 1845."

I stared at the ageing detective.

"So you see, Mr Collins," Field said, "it is quite possible that you and I could be of great assistance to one another should we share all information we have. I believe your friend Mr Dickens is in great danger. Indeed, I *know* that Mr Dickens is in danger if he continues to meet with this fiend called Drood. I appeal to your responsibility as the great author's friend to help me be his protector."

I caressed my beard for a moment. Finally, I said, "Inspector Field, what do you want of me?"

"Only information that may better allow us to protect your friend and to apprehend the fiend," he said.

"In other words, you want me to continue to spy on Charles Dickens and to report to you on everything he tells me about this Drood."

The old detective continued staring at me with those penetrating eyes. If I had not been looking for his nod, I would not have noticed it, so imperceptible was it.

"Is there anything else?" I asked.

"If you could convince Mr Dickens that your company would be required on another nocturnal expedition into Undertown, all the way to Drood's lair this time, that would be of great help," said Field.

"So that I could personally show you the way when it comes time to apprehend the man," I said.

"Yes."

It was my turn to nod. "It is a very hard thing, Inspector, to become an informant on one's closest friend—especially when that friend is of the temperament and position of power of Mr Charles Dickens. He could destroy me, professionally and personally."

"But you are doing this in his own best interests..." began the inspector.

"So we have ascertained," I interrupted. "And perhaps someday Dickens might see it that way. But he is a man of strong emotions, Inspector. Even if my...spying...were to save his life, it is quite possible that he may never forgive me. Even try to ruin me."

The detective continued to watch me closely.

"I simply want you to understand the risk I take," I said. "And why such a risk requires me to request two things in return from you."

If there was a smile, it appeared and disappeared too quickly to be caught by the human eye. "Of course, Mr Collins," he said smoothly. "This is, as I said, a transaction between two gentlemen. May I know the nature of your two requests?"

I said, "Inspector, did you happen to read Dickens's novel *Bleak House*?"

The older man made a rough noise. For a second I thought he was going to spit on the sidewalk. "I... looked at it...Mr Collins. In a passing way."

"But you are aware, Inspector, that many people believe that you are the original for the character named Inspector Bucket in that novel?"

Field nodded grimly and said nothing.

"You are not pleased with the depiction?" I asked.

"I thought the character called Bucket was a caricature and a travesty of proper police behaviour, procedure, and decorum," growled the old detective.

"Nonetheless," I said, "Dickens's novel—which I thought rather dreary and stodgy to that point, especially in the person of the cloying and saccharine narratoress named Esther Summerson, did seem to come alive in the penultimate chapters as our Inspector Bucket took charge of the murder case regarding Lawyer Tulkinghorn, as well as in his fruitless but exciting pursuit of Lady Dedlock, Esther's true mother, who was to die outside the city burial ground."

"Your point, sir?" asked Field.

"My point, Inspector, is that as a professional novelist myself, I see the potential for real interest in a book which has, as its protagonist and central character, a Scotland Yard or private detective not so different from Inspector Bucket, except...of course...more intelligent, more insightful, more educated, more handsome, and more ethical. In other words, Inspector Field, a fictional character not so different from yourself."

The older man squinted at me. His corpulent forefinger was resting next to his ear as if he were again listening to its whispered advice. "You are too kind, Mr

Collins," he said at last. "Too kind altogether. And yet, perhaps, in some modest way, I could be of help for your research into such a character and such a novel? Offering advice, perhaps, on the proper investigatory methods and police procedures, so as to avoid the sort of travesty shown in Mr Dickens's novel?"

I smiled and adjusted my spectacles. "More than that, Inspector. I would benefit greatly from having access to your…what would you call them?…murder files. I presume you keep such things, as ghastly as they must be?"

"Indeed we do, sir," said Field. "And they would indeed be of inestimable benefit to a literary gentleman wishing to achieve, as they say, verisimilitude, in the writing of such a work. This is an honourable request and I agree to it without hesitation."

"Good," I said. "My second condition also should not cause you any problems, since I am sure you will be carrying out the surveillance I wish access to whether or not I should be the one making the request for it."

"What surveillance is that, sir?"

"I want to know everything that you and your operatives can learn about the actress Ellen Ternan. Her whereabouts. The location of her lodgings—hers and her mother's—and whether Dickens is paying for them. The way she makes her money and whether those funds are sufficient to support her in the circumstances which she currently enjoys. Her comings and goings. Her relationship to Charles Dickens. Everything."

Inspector Field continued to bathe me in the blank, flat, mildly accusatory gaze which—I was sure—he had levelled at a thousand felons. But I was not a felon—not yet—and I did not wilt under its power.

"An odd request, Mr Collins, if you do not mind me saying so, sir. Unless you were to have your own *personal* interest in Miss Ternan."

"None whatsoever, Inspector. I can assure you of

that. Rather, I am convinced that Miss Ternan connects to this...mystery...that you and I are attempting to unravel, even as I am convinced that the best interests of Charles Dickens may have been compromised by this woman. In order to protect my friend...and perhaps myself...I need to understand more about her life and their relationship."

Field rubbed his lower lip with that curved and corpulent finger. "You think, Mr Collins, that Miss Ternan might actually be a co-conspirator with the monster Drood? An agent of his?"

I laughed. "Inspector, I don't know enough about the woman even to speculate. Which is why further knowledge of her, her sisters, her mother, and her relationship with my friend Dickens is essential if we are to enter into this pact."

Field continued to pat and press his lip.

"Then we understand each other, Inspector?" I said.

"I believe we do, Mr Collins. I believe that we understand each other very well indeed. I agree to your conditions and hope to provide you with all of the information you need." Field extended his calloused hand.

I shook it.

A minute later, resuming my walk towards the British Museum, Field hurrying alongside me, I told him everything that Charles Dickens had told me the day before on our walk to Cooling Marsh and back.

CHAPTER ELEVEN

*W*inter came in hard, stripping the leaves from all the trees near Gad's Hill Place by November, sending Dickens from his summer chalet into his front-of-the-house study with its green porcelain fireplace and crackling fire, killing the scarlet geraniums in his garden, and sending low grey clouds scudding over the low grey stone of the buildings and streets of London where I resided.

With winter came deeper bouts of illness for both Dickens and myself. The more famous writer continued to wrestle with his terrors from the Staplehurst accident and with constant exhaustion, with kidney pain that had pursued him since childhood, and with the deadness in his left side from his "sunstroke" in France in September. Clearly there was something more seriously wrong than the author would admit. Dickens and I shared a doctor—our mutual friend Frank Beard—and though Beard would rarely discuss his other patient, I sensed a deep concern.

I had my own problems, which included the terrible rheumatical gout and its accompanying pain, fainting spells, aching joints, a growing obesity which left me disgusted with myself even as I failed to reduce the size of the meals I enjoyed, flatulence, cramps, an assortment of other digestive disorders, and terrible palpitations of the heart. No one seemed aware of Dickens's physical disorders, but all the world seemed to know of mine. A Frenchman wrote me through my publisher to say that "he had betted ten bottles of champagne that I am alive, against everyone's belief," and if I were still breathing, he begged me to inform him of the fact.

I wrote to my mother that autumn—

> *Here is "forty" come upon me* [I was, in truth, forty-one that previous January]—*grey hairs shrinking fast...rheumatism and gout familiar enemies for some time past, my own horrid corpulence making me fat and unwieldy—all the worst signs of middle age sprouting out on me.*

And yet, I confided to her, I didn't feel old. I had no regular habits, no respectable prejudices.

Dear Reader, I have not yet told you anything about the most important woman in my life.

My mother, Harriet Geddes Collins, had met my father, the artist William Collins, when they were both in their mid-twenties. My mother was also descended from a long line of artists; she and both her sisters drew constantly and one of my mother's sisters had entered the school of the Royal Academy in London. Harriet Geddes and my father had first crossed paths at a ball given by some artist acquaintances of my father's for their girlfriends, subsequently seen each other several times in the London of their day, confirmed in 1821 that neither had cultivated other attachments, and were married in Edinburgh in 1822. I was born a little less than eighteen months later, on 8 January, 1824. My brother, Charles, was born in January of 1828.

One of my father's friends was the poet Samuel Taylor Coleridge, and I clearly remember the day when I was a young boy and the poet came to our home, found my father gone, and stayed to weep to my mother about his increasing dependence upon opium. It was the first time I had seen or heard a fully grown man weep—Coleridge was sobbing so hard he could not catch his breath—and I shall never forget my mother's words to him that day: "Mr Coleridge, do not cry; if the opium really does you any good, and you *must* have it, why do you not go out and get it?"

Many has been the time in recent years, as I wept my own bitter tears because of my growing need for the drug, that I have called back my mother's voice on the subject.

My father had come home just after this advice was given to Coleridge, and I remember the poet's cracked voice as he said, "Collins, your wife is an exceedingly sensible woman!"

My mother was a sensible woman, but my father was a great artist and a great man. I was given my Christian middle name—Wilkie—due to his relationship with the honourable Sir David Wilkie, an old friend of my father's from their school days, who lifted me up shortly after my birth, looked into my eyes, and pronounced, "He sees." (This seemed to have laid the mantle of succession, in artistic terms, from my father's shoulders to mine, but—as we shall see—that was not to be. My younger brother, Charley, was to inherit the stronger artistic ability and to be chosen for that role.)

My father was a great man with great men as friends. When I was growing up—a wide-eyed, rather gentle, bulbous-foreheaded child—I took it for granted that the Wordsworths, Coleridge, Robert Southey, and Sir Walter Scott would be familiar acquaintances of our family and visitors to our home. My father had not only received commissions from, but had spent much time with, such estimables as Sir Francis Chantrey, the Duke of Newcastle, Sir Robert Peel, Sir Thomas Lawrence, Sir Thomas Heathcote, Sir Thomas Baring, Sir George Beaumont, and Lord Liverpool.

Of course, it is true that the vast majority of my father's time spent with greatness was spent out of the sight of our mother. I am sure that my father was not *ashamed* of my mother, nor certainly of Charles or me, but he did prefer to spend his time amongst great men far from our hearth. But he wrote home faithfully and, often after listing the exciting events and personal encounters of his days and weeks away, might add such a codicil as this I found when arranging my mother's papers recently—

> *I cannot help longing for home, although I am so pleasantly spending my time, as pleasantly as the kindest friends, sprightly young ladies, and all the gaieties of this life can make me. I flatter myself that the idle life I am leading will please you, and perhaps make me stronger and therefore, I am determined to make the most of it.*

He did make the most of it, I believe, although, despite the many commissions by such famous men, his income was rarely solid or consistent. But my mother lived frugally and made sure that Charley and I did as well, so money was set aside.

My father was an extremely religious man. He had long since vowed to banish inclinations to indolence or impiety from his own life and would brook none in the lives of his wife or children. Some called him censorious, even priggish, but this was unfair. In another letter to my mother, sent from some Scottish castle when Charley and I were in short pants, my father wrote—

> *Tell the dear children that the only way they can serve their parents is to obey them in all things; let Charley find out the passages in the Scripture where this duty is most strongly insisted on, and write them down for me.*

And in a separate letter to my brother and me, one still in my possession and reread frequently, William Collins showed the true spirit of his religious intensity—

> *Your mother's account, in her last letter about you both, pleased me very much. Go on praying to God, through Jesus Christ, to enable you, by his Holy Spirit, to be blessings to your parents; and then you must be happy.*

True to his beliefs, my father became known for his denunciations. His tolerance for tolerance was very low. Once when our close neighbour, the artist John Linnell (who had painted several of our portraits), was seen working on Sunday—nailing his peach and nectarine trees to his northern wall—my father not only upbraided Linnell but denounced him to a visiting Congregational preacher. Father also believed and spread the rumour that Linnell had cheated one of his gardeners out of his wages, and when Linnell challenged him on the fact, Father cried, "Of what consequence is it, whether you cheated a man out of his wages or not, when you are constantly doing things ten times worse?"

The things-ten-times-worse included working on Sunday and becoming a Dissenter.

I was with my father when we met the poet William Blake in the Strand, and when Blake—an acquaintance—hailed my father and offered his hand, my father deliberately ignored him, turning his back on the poet and leading me away before I could speak. Blake, you see, was carrying a pot of porter in the hand he was not offering in friendship.

Later, when I was in my early twenties and writing my father's memoirs after his death, I realised how jealous of him many of the so-called great artists of the period were. John Constable, for instance, an acquaintance of many years, was receiving only a few hundred pounds for his cloudy, obscure paintings during years that my father earned over £1,000 a year on commissions for what Constable sneered at as "pretty landscapes" and "flat, soulless, fashionable portraits." When Constable could find no patrons at all (due, largely, to his persisting in painting such unpopular works as his *Corn-Field* at the same time that my father had his finger on the pulse of patrons' and the Academy's desires for more decorative works), the frustrated landscape painter wrote the following in a letter that was made public, much to my father's fury—*"Turner exhibits a large picture of Dieppe . . . Calcotte nothing I hear . . . Collins, a coast scene with fish as usual and a landscape with a large cow turd at least as far as colour and shape is concerned."*

I mentioned earlier that my father decided when we were still quite young that Charley, not I, would be the real inheritor of his artistic talents and career, despite the crib-side assurances of Sir David Wilkie, my name-sake. Father enrolled Charley in a private art school, spent much extra time with my brother during our long trips to Europe—analysing paintings in cathedrals and museums (although my father loathed entering Papist churches)—and helped Charley gain acceptance into the prestigious Royal Academy.

Father never really spoke to me about my future or how I would fill it, other than one suggestion, when I was thirteen, that I might consider going to Oxford with a view to entering the Church.

It was when I was thirteen, in Rome during one of our long family stays in Europe, that I experienced my first full love adventure. I remember telling the details to Charles Dickens precisely seventeen years later, during my next visit to Rome and my first trip there with the famous author, and Dickens was so pleased with the amatory precociousness of the affair that he later told me he had informed his sister-in-law, Georgina Hogarth, sparing her, he said, only the details of "how the affair had proceeded to the utmost extremities." He chuckled when he described how Georgina had blushed when Dickens had summarised my first complete physical encounter by saying, "Our young Willy came out quite a pagan Jupiter in the business."

At any rate, even at age thirteen I had no intention of entering Oxford with an eye on going into the Church.

Artists are notoriously sensitive—at least to their own feelings—and young Charley was more sensitive than most. It is not an exaggeration to say that he was a doleful child, constantly brooding about this or that, and both of my parents—but especially my mother—took this incessant unhappiness (bordering on sullenness) as a sign of his artistic genius. He also disliked women and girls.

I interrupt here, Dear Reader, to beg your indulgence on this point. Were this not a memoir consigned to the distant future, I would not mention it at all, but—as perhaps you have already detected in this memoir—there was a deep and constant tension between Charles Dickens and his son-in-law, Charles Collins, and I fear that this small matter of Charley's aversion to women (if not outright misogyny) may have played a part in Dickens's prejudice. You see, however such things have played out in your distant time, it was not uncommon in our era for young men to go through long periods where they much preferred the company of boys and men to that of women. Given the limitations to education of women in our time, much less the obvious difficulties of the fairer sex in acquiring and mastering more difficult aspects of learning throughout history, it was logical that thoughtful, sensitive men should focus their energies and intercourse on other men.

I remember once when Charley was about fifteen and I came across some of his sketch diaries, left lying about in his room in an uncharacteristic manner (he was always secretive and neat), and I joked with him about the fact that all of the figure studies in his drawing book were of nude men.

Charley had blushed crimson but said with real emotion, "I hate drawing women, Willy. Don't you? I mean, they are all heavy and pendulous and baggy and bulbous where the human body should *not* be. How much more delight I take in firm, flat buttocks and muscular thighs and flat bellies and masculine chests, rather than those appalling feminine absences and fleshy protuberances and miserable saggings."

I was searching for some humourous comment worthy of a sophisticated nineteen-year-old gentleman such as myself when Charley went on, "I mean, Willy, *Michelangelo's* female nudes on the ceiling of the Sistine Chapel—even Eve—are actually all paintings of naked men. Even the great Michelangelo disdained nude women! What do you say to that, Brother?"

I was tempted to say that I had been there in Rome that hot, muggy day years before when our father taught *both* of us that salient fact. But I resisted the temptation. All I said that afternoon in my brother's room as he tidied up the sketch diaries and set them away in a locked drawer was—"Those are very good drawings, Charley. Very good indeed." I did not comment at all upon the fact that not only had my brother violated the unwritten rule that an artist was not to show male genitalia in one's figure drawings—leaving an absence of graphite if nothing else, drawing a modest loincloth the preferred method—but Charley had drawn some of the male organs in an obvious state of excitement.

It was not too many months after this encounter that some revelation of the sort—perhaps a similar indiscretion in Charles's drawings, or in his comments—became apparent to my father. I remember Charley being called in to my father's studio one morning and the door being closed and then repeated screams from my brother as my father whipped the sensitive lad with either a branch, cane, or T square.

After my father died, I believe that Charley and I both would have enjoyed living with my mother in her wonderful home at Hanover Terrace for the rest of our lives. My liaison with Caroline G—— took me away from that safe haven. And yet, for months and even years after I moved in with Caroline and her daughter, Harriet—how I loved the coincidence of that name!—I would return to my mother's home to write and address letters to our mutual friends (my mother's and mine) from there even as I wrote to other friends from my new home. Mother did not know of Caroline's existence, of course; or if she did know, she never let on that she did. It was true that I regaled her with many tales of my bachelor life apart from her, never mentioning any woman, much less the widowed Caroline, but it was also true that my mother never once suggested that she visit my various homes during all the years I shared them with Mrs G—— and Harriet.

I was still living with Mother when I met Dickens in 1851. As a reporter later wrote of Dickens and me during that early period—"Both were lively men, passionate about the theatre, keen on drinks and company and excursions, on being intensely gay, relaxing strenuously, responding vehemently." And after our excursions and strenuous relaxations and vehement responses, Dickens would return home to his increasingly bovine wife and I would return home to my mother.

Charley would have lived with our mother until her death and perhaps remained in her home until his own death, I am quite sure, if it had not been for his marriage to Kate Dickens.

None of us shall ever know all the reasons for Charley's sudden proposal to Kate in the late spring of 1860.

In truth, from what I can gather, it was *Kate* who proposed marriage to *Charley* that spring. It was certainly Kate who hurried their wedding along to mid-summer—despite her father's outspoken and vehement opposition, not only to the date of the wedding but to the fact of it.

Charley had not had a long history of courtship and wooing. In fact, up to his thirty-second year (which was to be the year of his marriage), he had continued to avoid women. Whispers abounded that spring and summer that Katey Dickens had fallen in love with and had been pursuing Edmund Yates, a younger friend of the Inimitable who had helped promote the falling-out between Dickens and Thackeray by writing a profoundly unflattering profile of the old writer. A contemporary had described Yates as "...very fascinating too. Superficially, mind you."

Superficially fascinating or not, Kate Dickens had fallen in love with him and when Yates refused to notice the infatuation, despite the young man's frequent visits to Tavistock House and then to Gad's Hill Place and despite Katey's obvious flirtations—obvious to everyone, including Charles Dickens and me—the headstrong young woman (she had just turned twenty) proposed to my Charley.

A few months before the wedding, after a visit to Gad's Hill, where Katey's redirected matrimonial attentions were again obvious to everyone, I wrote to my mother, "...*Charley is still trying hard to talk himself into believing he ought to be married.*"

Years later, after my younger brother's death from the constant stomach ulcers that had proved cancerous, I did ask Kate why she had pulled him into marriage. "I had to get away from that house," she replied. "I had to get away from my father."

Dickens did not hide his disapproval of the match.

Despite that, Katey was his favourite child and he could not deny her anything, even this folly of a marriage.

On 17 July, 1860, St Mary's Church in Higham—the church's steeple would be visible from the writing room in Dickens's chalet when the latter structure was assembled five years later—was almost buried in white flowers. The lower-class neighbours had created floral arches that showed the way to the church. The night before, the villagers had fired off guns in honour of the nuptials, but a cranky and concerned Charles Dickens had come out onto the lawn of Gad's Hill in his nightshirt, shotgun in his hands, and said only, "What the devil is all that about?"

A special train had been laid on to bring wedding guests down from London. I remember chatting with Thomas Beard, the understated gentleman who had served as Charles Dickens's best man two decades earlier. Beard had the odd distinction of being the only person at Kate's wedding who had also been at the wedding of the bride's father, although in one brief, ad hoc toast, Dickens himself spoke ironically—almost bitterly, I thought—of "a similar ceremony performed in a metropolitan edifice some four and twenty years ago."

Kate's mother, Catherine, was not in attendance, of course. Nor was Elizabeth Dickens, the Inimitable's elderly but still-surviving mother. Georgina Hogarth was the only member of the bride's mother's side of the family present. Few seemed to notice the absences.

After the wedding ceremony, the mob of guests returned to Gad's Hill for a huge wedding breakfast. Again, everything on and around the table was decorated with white flowers. The wedding breakfast, while sumptuous, took only an hour. The host had promised everyone that there would be no speeches and there were none. I noticed that the bride and groom sat down at the table for a moment, then disappeared while the guests played games on the lawn. My mother, who sanctioned the match no more than did Charles Dickens, needed constant attendance that morning. When Charley and Kate reappeared, dressed for travel, the bride wore black. Katey broke down and cried bitterly on her father's shoulder. Charley's face grew more and more pale until I was afraid he was going to faint.

Mother and I gathered with the other thirty or so guests on the gravel path to kiss the newlyweds, shake hands all around, and to throw old shoes. After the carriage had departed, Mother announced that she was not feeling well. I left her seated in the shade just long enough to go inform Dickens of our departure, but could find him nowhere on the lawn amidst the young people playing nor in the parlour downstairs nor in the billiards room or study.

I saw Mamie coming downstairs, went up to Katey's bedroom—what had been Katey's bedroom until that morning—and found Dickens on his knees on the floor, his face buried in his daughter's wedding gown. The Inimitable was sobbing like a child. He looked up at me, his face streaming with tears, perhaps seeing only my silhouette in the doorway and perhaps thinking me still to be his daughter Mamie, and he cried out in a broken voice—"But for me, Katey would not have left home!"

I said nothing. I turned, went downstairs and out onto the lawn, fetched my mother, and called for the carriage to take us back to the station and thence to London.

CHARLES AND KATEY were to have no children. The rumour spread—perhaps started by Dickens, but also perchance from Katey herself—that the marriage had never been consummated. It certainly was true that by the summer of Dickens's railway accident in 1865, Katey was an unhappy and flirtatious woman, obviously searching for a lover. There were many men around who would not have shown scruples at making love to a married woman, had it not been for the ferocity and constant vigilance of her father.

Charley's chronic illnesses and stomach aches also became a problem within the Dickens household. I was sure they were only ulcers, and when my brother, Charles, finally died of stomach cancer in 1873, it was only slight consolation that Charles Dickens had preceded him in death.

Dickens said sharply to me that odd autumn of 1865—"Your brother brings a death's head to my table every breakfast here, Wilkie." It was obvious to all that Dickens was certain that Charley was dying and that he—the Inimitable, never acknowledging his own illnesses nor allowing for even the possibility of his own death—thought that Charley should get it over with sooner rather than later.

AND SO WE RETURN, Dear Reader, to the dismal state of my own health that winter of 1865–66.

My father had suffered from rheumatism that had concentrated itself behind his left eye, making it all but impossible for him to paint in his final years. My rheumatical gout inevitably migrated to my right eye, all but blinding me and causing me to squint out of my left eye as I wrote. The pain moved into my arm and hand to the point that I had to shift the quill from my right hand to my left to get a dip of ink.

Eventually I would be unable to write at all and would dictate some of my future books from the couch where I lay, but only after training my young secretary—first Harriet but then someone infinitely more ominous—to ignore my screams of pain and to listen only for the dictated sentences between the cries of agony.

I have mentioned that laudanum was my one relief from the pain. I may also have mentioned that it was traditional to take three to five *drops* of the liquid opium in a glass of wine, but by this time—the winter of 1865—66—I required two to three *glasses* of the medicine to allow me to work or sleep.

There were the drawbacks I mentioned. The feelings of always being followed and persecuted. The hallucinations. (At first I had assumed the woman with the green skin and tusks for teeth was such an hallucination; but then, after she assaulted me on the stairs in the dark, I awoke several times with deep scratches on my neck.)

One night I was working in my study—writing my novel *Armadale*—when I realised that a man was sitting in a chair only inches to my left. He was also writing. The man was my *Doppelgänger*. Or rather, he was I—wearing the same clothes, holding the same pen, turning towards me with the same dull but shocked expression which I must have been presenting to him.

He reached for my blank page.

I could not let him write my book. I could not let that page, my page, become *his*.

We scuffled. Chairs were knocked over. A lamp was dashed out. In the darkness, I pushed him away and stumbled out into the hall and off to my bedroom.

In the morning I went into my study and found the wall, sections of the window and sill, one corner of the expensive Persian carpet, my chair, its cushion, and two shelves of books absolutely dalmatianed with spattered ink. Six more pages of my novel had been written in a hand that was almost, but not quite, my own.

I burned them in the fireplace.

CHAPTER TWELVE

*I*n December of 1865, Inspector Field reported to me, using hulking Detective Hatchery as his messenger, that Dickens's "patient," Ellen Ternan, felt well enough not only to attend a Christmas ball hosted by the brother of her sister's soon-to-be husband, Anthony Trollope, but was sufficiently recovered from her June injuries at Staplehurst to *dance* at this party.

With scarlet geraniums in her hair.

By Christmas of that year, Inspector Field was actively complaining to me that he was providing *me* far more information than I was giving *him*. It was true. Although Dickens had invited me out to Gad's Hill several times in the autumn and although he and I had dined in the city and attended various functions together all through that season of his slow recovery from the Staplehurst disaster, we never truly discussed the topic of Drood. It was as if Dickens were somehow aware that I had entered into a covenant of betrayal with the scheming Inspector Field. And yet, if that were true, why would the Inimitable continue to invite me to his home, write me newsy letters, and meet me for dinner at some of our favourite London haunts?

At any rate, Inspector Field had informed me only the week after I had repeated Dickens's tale of his meeting with Drood, almost word for word, that the writer had lied to me.

If this was true, I realised, then there was no tributary to the buried river of the sort Dickens had described to me. No tunnel leading to another river, no underground rookeries filled with hundreds of the poor driven underground, no Egyptian temple along the banks of this unfound subterranean Nile. Either Dickens had lied to me to protect the real route to Drood's lair or he had made up the entire encounter.

Inspector Field was not pleased. Obviously he and his men had spent hours or entire nights and days exploring the catacombs and caverns and sewers down there…all to no avail. At this rate, he let me know during our infrequent and sullen meetings, he would never apprehend Drood and would die of old age before pleasing his former superiors at the Metropolitan Police headquarters to the degree that they would reinstate his pension and rehabilitate his good name.

Nonetheless, Field continued to share information with me through the winter. During those autumn months after finishing work on *Our Mutual Friend* and presumably while having the pleasure of watching its final instalments appear in *All the Year Round,* Dickens had leased a house for himself in London at 6 Southwick Place, near Hyde Park. There was little mystery in this; he had rented a similar house just around the corner from this one two years before so as to have a convenient place in Tyburnia for his London social engagements, and this new place near Hyde Park was meant to allow his daughter Mamie to come into town whenever she wished for her own society needs (such as they were, since Society seemed to be shunning both Katey and Mamie to a great degree at that time).

So there was no mystery to the lease of a house near Hyde Park. But—as Inspector Field would indicate some weeks later with a wink and a touch of his nose with his corpulent finger—there was significantly more mystery involved in Dickens's lease of two small homes in the village of Slough: one called Elizabeth Cottage in the High Street, and another one on Church Street only a quarter of a mile away. Although this revelation still lay in the future as the Christmas holiday arrived, I would later learn through Inspector Field that Dickens leased both of these properties under the name of Tringham—Charles Tringham for the Elizabeth Cottage and John Tringham for the house on Church Street.

For a while, Inspector Field would later inform me, the Church Street home lay empty, but then it was occupied by a certain Mrs Ternan and her daughter Ellen.

"We don't know why Mr Dickens used the name of Tringham," Inspector Field would say after the New Year as we walked around Dorset Square near my home. "It doesn't seem important, on the surface, you see, but in our business it always helps if we understand why someone chooses certain aliases under which to do his dirty work."

Ignoring the "dirty work" allusion, I said, "There's a tobacconist's shop on Wellington Street near the offices where Dickens and I work on *All the Year Round*. The owner, well known to both Dickens and me, is a certain Mary Tringham."

"Ahh," said Inspector Field.

"But I do not believe that is the source of the name," I added.

"No?"

"No," I said. "Do you happen to know, Inspector, a certain story published in 1839 by Thomas Hood?"

"I don't believe I do," the inspector said sourly.

"It's about village gossip," I said. "And there's a bit of a poem in it..."

"...learning whatever there was to learn
In the prattling, tattling village of Tringham."

"Ahhh," said Inspector Field again, but with more conviction this time. "Well, Mr Dickens...or Mr Tringham, if he prefers...goes to great lengths to hide his presence in Slough."

"How is that?" I said.

"He dates his letters from Eton, telling his friends that he was merely walking in the Park there," said Inspector Field. "And he walks miles across back fields from Slough to the Eton railway station, as if he chose to be noticed—if he were noticed at all—waiting for the train to London there rather than in Slough."

I stopped on our walk and asked, "How do you know what Mr Dickens tells his friends in his private letters, Inspector? Have you been steaming open his mail or interrogating his friends?"

Inspector Field only smiled.

But all of these revelations, Dear Reader, would come about by the spring of 1866, and I must return us now to that bizarrely memorable Christmas of 1865.

WHEN DICKENS INVITED ME up to Gad's Hill Place for Christmas Day, suggesting in his note that I stay through New Year's, I accepted at once. "The Butler and the Butler's Mother shall understand," he wrote in the same note, referring to Harriet (whom we called Carrie ever more frequently as she matured) and her mother, Caroline, in his usual bantering way. I am not sure Caroline and Carrie *did* fully understand or appreciate my absence that week, but that was of little concern to me.

As I took the short train ride to Chatham, I held the Christmas Issue of *All the Year Round* in my hands—

the one I'd just contributed to and helped put out and the one that held Dickens's Christmas story "Cheap Jack" in it—and I thought about the warp and woof of the Inimitable's fiction these days.

Perhaps it takes a novelist (or some Future Literary Critic such as yourself, Dear Reader) to see what lies behind the words of another novelist's fiction.

I shall start with Dickens's most recent Christmas tale:

Cheap Jack, the eponymous hero of the Inimitable's little fable and a common name in our time for the travelling salesman who moved from village to village with his inexpensive wares, was written about a man whose wife was no longer with him, whose child was dead, and who—for professional reasons—must hide his feelings from the world. Dickens's character was "King of the Cheap Jacks" and happened to be taking a paternal interest in a young girl with "a pretty face and bright, dark hair." Was this a twisted self-portrait by the author? Was the young girl Ellen Ternan?

Dickens being Dickens, of course, the girl with the pretty face and bright, dark hair also happens to be deaf and dumb. What would a Dickens Christmas tale be without pathos and bathos?

"See us on the footboard," Cheap Jack tells us of his time in front of audiences, "and you'd give pretty well anything you possess to be us. See us off the footboard, and you'd add a trifle to be off your bargain."

Is Charles Dickens telling us here about the great abyss between his gay public life and persona and his private sadnesses and bone-deep loneliness away from the public eye?

And then there was his huge novel *Our Mutual Friend,* completed (as was "Cheap Jack") the previous September and which had just ended its full run of nineteen installments in our *All the Year Round*.

It might truly take another professional author to see just how complex and dangerous a book *Our Mutual Friend* actually was. I had read it in instalments in our magazine over the past year and a half; I had heard Dickens read parts of it aloud to small groups; I had read some of the book in manuscript form; and after the final instalment was published, I had read it all again. It was incredible. For the first time in my life, I believe I hated Charles Dickens out of sheer jealousy.

I cannot speak for your age, Dear Reader, but already in our nineteenth century just approaching the two-thirds mark, tragedy was replacing comedy in the eyes and hearts and analytical minds of "serious readers." Shakespeare's tragedies were to be found on the stage more frequently than his brilliant comedies and they received more serious reviews and discussions. The sustained and profound humour of, say, a Chaucer or Cervantes was being replaced in the short list of masterpieces by the more serious tragedies and histories of both the classics and our contemporaries. If this trend continues, Dear Reader, then by the time you read this manuscript a century and more hence, the art and appreciation of comedies will be all but lost.

But this was a matter of taste. For years—decades now—the fiction of Charles Dickens had grown darker and more serious, allowing themes to dictate the structure of his novels and causing his characters to fit neatly (too neatly) into the pigeonholes of the overall thematic structure much like library cards might be shuffled into the proper drawer. (This is not to say that even the most serious Dickens novels of recent years had been without humour; I do not believe that Dickens could *write* something totally devoid of humour, any more than he could be trusted to stay completely serious at a funeral. He was truly irrepressible in that regard. But his topics had been increasingly serious as he abandoned the largely unstructured Pickwickian celebrations of life that had *made* him the Inimitable Boz and as social critique and social satire—all-important to him personally—had moved more towards the centre of his work.

But in *Our Mutual Friend,* Dickens had created a sustained comedic novel of more than eight hundred cramped pages without striking—as far as I could tell— a single false note.

This was incredible. It made my joints ache and my eyes burn with pain.

In *Our Mutual Friend,* Dickens had abandoned the grand motifs of *Little Dorrit* and *Bleak House* and *Great Expectations* and almost completely subordinated his personal and social opinions into a masterful display of language and nuance that came very close to perfection. *Very* close. The complexity of his characters in this book far surpassed anything he had done before; indeed, Dickens seemed to have resurrected many of his earlier characters and reimagined them with the focus of a newly gained maturity and a newly found sense of forgiveness. Thus the evil lawyer Tulkinghorn from *Bleak House* reappears as the young lawyer Mortimer Lightwood, but redeems himself as Tulkinghorn never could have. The vile Ralphy Nickleby is reborn as the bounder Fledgeby, but does not escape punishment as had Nickleby. (Indeed, the severe caning of Fledgeby by the other bounder, Alfred Lammle, is one of the high points in all of Charles Dickens's long list of fictions.) Similarly, Noddy Boffin turns into a Scrooge who avoids becoming a miser; the old Jew Mr Riah atones for the sins of Dickens's sometimes-criticised (especially by Jews) Fagin by not being a heartless money-lender but only the conscience-stricken *employee* of a Christian heartless money-lender; and Podsnap is—besides being a devastating portrait of John Forster (devastating and so subtle that Forster never recognised himself in the character, although everyone else did)—Podsnap is...Podsnap. The quintessence of Podsnappery. Which may well be the quintessence of our age.

Yet even while the tone and structure of *Our Mutual Friend* is one of flawless satiric comedy that would have honoured Cervantes, the underlying chiaroscuric background of the novel is dark to the point of despair. London has become a barren and stony desert, "cheaper as it quadrupled in wealth; less imperial as its empire widened." It is "a hopeless city, with no rent in the leaden canopy of its sky." The tones are sombre to the point of funereal, with even the sky being darkened by the inescapable fog from yellow and brown to an underlying creeping blackness—"a heap of vapour charged with muffled sounds of wheels and enfolding a muffled catarrh." The city so beloved by Dickens is portrayed as either grey or dusty or dark or muddy or cold or windy or rain-swept or drowned in its own refuse and filth. Most commonly in *Our Mutual Friend*, it is revealed to be all these things at once.

But within this horror of a landscape—and within great surges of distrust, vicious scheming, incipient dishonesty, ubiquitous greed, and murderous jealousy—the characters manage to find love and support not within families, as had been the example so used by Dickens and other writers of our era before this, but within small circles of friends and beloved, trusted individuals that make up ad hoc families which shield those characters we care about from the storm of poverty and social injustice. And it is these same circles of love which punish those whom we despise.

Dickens had created a masterpiece.

The public did not recognise this. The first number in *All the Year Round* had sold very well (it was, after all, the first new Dickens novel in two and a half years), but sales quickly fell off and the last number sold only

19,000 copies. I knew that this was a bitter disappointment to Dickens, and although he had personally profited (I learned from Katey's comments to my brother, Charley) to the tune of about £7,000, the publishers Chapman and Hall actually lost money on the book.

The critics either loved or hated the book without reservation and laboured over either verdict with their usual cock-sure hyperbole, but the general critical trend was one of disappointment. Those in the intellectual sphere had expected another thematic novel with social criticism front and centre, again in the mould of *Bleak House, Little Dorrit,* and *Great Expectations,* but all they received was a . . . mere comedy.

But, as I say, it took another professional author such as myself to see that Dickens had achieved the nearly impossible in sustaining such a gentle satirical tone at such length, and with such perfection, to see that the satire never slipped into cynicism, that the comic vision did not slide into mere caricature, nor the relentless critique of society devolve into mere rant.

It took me, in other words, to see that *Our Mutual Friend* was a masterpiece.

I hated him. As a competing writer, I wished at that moment—as the train left London for his home in Gad's Hill—that Charles Dickens had died in the Staplehurst accident. *Why had he not?* So many others had. As he so insufferably wrote and bragged to me and to so many other of his friends, his was the only first-class carriage that had *not* been thrown to the riverbed below and smashed to flinders.

But all that aside, it was the personal revelation in *Our Mutual Friend* that I found most revealing and relevant to the current situation we all found ourselves in.

To my trained writer's eye and experienced reader's ear, signs and echoes of Dickens's disastrous culmination

of his long relationship with his wife and the com-
mencement of his dangerous liaison with Ellen Ternan
were to be found everywhere in this book.

Most novelists create the occasional character—often
a villain—who leads a double life, but Dickens's fiction
now seemed saturated with such dualities. In *Our
Mutual Friend* the hero, young John Harmon (heir to
the Harmon dust heap fortunes), who appears to be
drowned under suspicious circumstances while returning to London after many years at sea, immediately visits the decomposing body (dressed in his clothes and
thus presumed to be him) at the police station. Harmon then changes his identity to Julius Handford and
then later to John Rokesmith so that he can act as secretary to the Boffins, lowly servants who have, by
default, inherited the fortune and dust heaps that
should have been John Harmon's.

The villains in *Our Mutual Friend*—Gaffer Hexam,
Rogue Riderhood, Mr and Mrs Alfred Lammle (grifters
who have deceived each other into a loveless and money-
less marriage and who join hands now only in deceiving
and using others), peg-legged Silas Wegg, and especially
the murderous headmaster Bradley Headstone—may
pretend to be someone or something else, but are allowed
to remain their sincere selves at heart. Only the positive
protagonists in the novel suffer from dual or multiple
identities amounting to an actual confusion of self.

And that tragic confusion is inevitably brought
about by one form of energy—love. Misplaced, dis-
placed, lost, or concealed romantic love is the engine
that drives all the secrecy, machinations, and violence
in Dickens's single most energetic (and terrible) comedy. *Our Mutual Friend*, I realised to my own pain and
horror, was a title and tale worthy of Shakespeare.

John Rokesmith/Harmon hides his identity from
his beloved, Bella, until long after they are married and

even after they have a child, all the better to manipulate and test and educate her—away from love of money towards love for love's sake. Mr Boffin becomes an ill-tempered miser to all appearances, driving the Boffins' ward, Bella, out of the house and back to her impoverished roots, but it is all a charade—another means of testing the true mettle of Bella Wilfer. Even the wastrel lawyer Eugene Wrayburn—one of the strongest (if most confused) personalities in all of Dickens's fiction—reaches, because of his illogical love for low-born Lizzie Hexam, a point where he taps his head and breast in confusion, speaks his own name, and cries out—"...perhaps you can't tell me what this may be?—No, upon my life I can't. I give it up!"

John Harmon, lost amidst all his disguises and manipulative strategies, reaches a similar loss of identity and cries, "But it was not I. There was no such thing as I, within my knowledge."

The weak and jealous headmaster Bradley Headstone seems to confess to all of Charles Dickens's own hidden passions and jealousies when he tells the much-in-demand Lizzie Hexam—

> "You draw me to you. If I were shut up in a strong prison, you would draw me out. I should break through the wall to come to you. If I were lying on a sick bed, you would draw me up—to stagger to your feet and fall there." And later—"You are the ruin of me... Yes! You are the ruin—the ruin—the ruin—of me. I have no resources in myself, I have no confidence in myself, I have no government of myself when you are near me or in my thoughts. And you are always in my thoughts now. I have never been quit of you since I first saw you."

Compare this to what Charles Dickens had written in a private letter not so long after he had met Ellen Ternan for the first time—"I have never known a moment's peace or content, since the last night of *The Frozen Deep*. I do suppose that there never was a man so seized and rended by one Spirit." And—"Oh, that was a wretched day for me! That was a wretched, miserable day!"

Charles Dickens's passion for Ellen Ternan, much less the destruction to his sense of self, family, and sanity that this passion was causing, cried out to me from behind the mask of every character and violent event in *Our Mutual Friend*.

In the terrifying scene where Bradley Headstone confronts the cowering Lizzie Hexam with his passion—set, I thought, quite appropriately in a foggy burial ground, since the schoolmaster's love is doomed and one-sided and short-lived even before it dies from jealousy and resurrects itself as murder—the deranged schoolmaster seems to cry out in a voice echoing Charles Dickens's silent screams of agony that year—

> *No man knows until the time comes, what depths are within him. To some men it never comes; let them rest and be thankful! To me, you brought it; on me, you forced it; and the bottom of this raging sea has been heaved up ever since. . . . I love you. What other men may mean when they use that expression, I cannot tell; what I mean is, that I am under the influence of some tremendous attraction which I have resisted in vain, and which overmasters me. You could draw me to fire, you could draw me to water, you could draw me to the gallows, you could draw me to any death, you could draw me to anything I have most avoided, you could draw me to any exposure and disgrace. This, and the confusion of my thoughts, so that I am fit for nothing, is what I mean by your being the ruin of me.*

And all the time Bradley Headstone is shouting these things, he is wrenching at the stone of the graveyard wall until powdered mortar spills and dribbles onto pavement and until, finally, *"bringing his clenched hand down upon the stone with a force that laid the knuckles raw and bleeding."*

Charles Dickens had never before written so clearly and painfully and forcefully about the terrible twinned power of love and jealousy. He was never to do so again.

As with Bradley Headstone, could the confusion of identities and loss of control over his own life, casualties of erotic and romantic obsession, lead Charles Dickens to madness in daylight and murder in the night? It sounded absurd, but it sounded possible.

I set aside the magazine as the train rolled into the station and shifted in my seat to look out into the cold, grey, shadowless Christmas Day. This promised to be an interesting visit.

A YEAR EARLIER before Staplehurst—Dickens's comparatively desultory Christmas gathering for 1864 had been composed of my brother, Charley, and his wife, Katey, the artist Fechter and his wife (and Fechter's amazing gift of the Swiss chalet), Marcus Stone, and Henry Chorley. This year I was mildly surprised to find another bachelor, Percy Fitzgerald, a guest for several days, not surprised at all to see Charley and Katey back at the Dickens hearth, pleased to find the other Gad's Hill residents Mamie and Georgina in relatively good spirits, and totally surprised—despite the fact that the young Staplehurst survivor had mentioned Dickens's invitation to me the previous summer—to find young Edmond Dickenson installed at Gad's Hill for the week. That made three bachelors at the table, if one did not count Dickens himself as such.

And that morning, Dickens promised me another

gratifying surprise by dinnertime. "My dear Wilkie, you shall *love* our surprise guests tonight. I promise you that. They shall be a delight to us, as always."

If it had not been for the plural, I might have mockingly asked the Inimitable if Mr Drood were making an appearance at our Christmas table. Or perhaps I might not have; despite his enthusiasm about the mystery guests, Charles Dickens seemed very tired and haggard this Christmas Day. I enquired about his health and he admitted to having been plagued with pains and mysterious weaknesses during the late autumn and early winter. Evidently our mutual friend and physician, Frank Beard, had been consulted frequently, although Dickens rarely followed Beard's advice. It seems that Beard had diagnosed "a want of muscular powers in the heart," but Dickens seemed certain that the injured heart in question lay more in the realm of emotions than in his chest cavity.

"It's these accursed muggy days this winter which prey upon the mind, Wilkie," said Dickens. "Then, after three or four days of unusually warm humidity, these constant cold snaps batter one's morale like a mace. But—have you noticed?—it never snows. I would give anything for the simple, cold, snowy Christmases of my childhood."

It was true that there was no snow on the ground in London or at Gad's Hill this particular Christmas. But we were in one of the cold snaps he had described and our afternoon walk that Christmas Day—Percy Fitzgerald came along, as did young Dickenson and Dickens's real son Charley, but my brother Charles stayed in the house—resembled more a waddling procession of insensate and multiple-layered bundles of wool than it did a gentlemen's outing. Even Dickens, who usually seemed oblivious to the rain or heat or cold, had added a thicker topcoat than he usually wore on walks and a second wool muffler, red, wound about his collar and lower face.

Besides the five of us men, there were five dogs with us on that outing: Linda, the lumbering Saint Bernard; Mary's little Pomeranian, living up to her name of Mrs Bouncer; Don, the black Newfoundland; the great mastiff named Turk; and Sultan.

Dickens had to restrain Sultan on a thick leash. The dog also required a leather muzzle. Percy Fitzgerald, who'd given Dickens the Irish bloodhound as a puppy the previous September, was happy to see Sultan almost grown and obviously healthy, but when Percy approached to pet the hound, Sultan growled ferociously and snapped within the constraints of his muzzle as if he were determined to bite Fitzgerald's hand off at the wrist. Percy drew back, frightened and mortified. Dickens seemed strangely pleased.

"Sultan continues to be gentle and obedient with me," he told us. "But he is a monster with most other living creatures. He has chewed through five muzzles and often comes home with blood on his snout. We know for certain that he bolted a certain blue-eyed kitten whole, but Sultan did show agonies of remorse for that dastardly deed…or at least agonies of indigestion."

As young Edmond Dickenson laughed, Dickens added, "But notice that Sultan has growled and snarled at all of you…except for Wilkie here. While Sultan is loyal only to me, there is some strange affinity between that dog and Wilkie Collins, I tell you."

I frowned over the rim of my wool scarf. "Why do you say that, Dickens? Because we both come from Irish stock?"

"No, my dear Wilkie," said Dickens from behind his own red scarf. "Because you both can be dangerous unless properly restrained and treated with a strong hand."

The idiot Dickenson laughed again. Charley Dickens and Percy merely looked puzzled at the comment.

Because of the cold, or because of Dickens's pity on his guests, or perhaps because of Dickens's own health problems, the afternoon walk was more of a leisurely stroll around the property than the usual Dickensian marathon. We ambled to the barn and looked in on the horses, including Mary's riding horse, Boy; the older Trotty Veck; and the always serious-demeanoured Norwegian pony named Newman Noggs. As we were standing in the clouds of warm exhalations of the horses' breath, feeding carrots to them, I remembered my summer visit here to see Dickens right after the Staplehurst accident and how the Inimitable's nerves could not bear even the slow trot of Newman Noggs pulling the basket cart. That cart and Noggs's harness, which was hanging on the wall of the stable, were decked out today as they usually were with a lovely-sounding set of Norwegian musical bells, but it was too cold to go for a ride.

We left the stables, and Dickens—with Sultan straining at the leash ahead of him—led us through the tunnel to the chalet. The green summer cornfields beyond had died into jagged expanses of frozen brown stubble. The Dover Road was all but empty this grey Christmas Day—a single, tilted hayrick waggon could be seen moving slowly far down its frozen-mud expanse. Brittle grass crackled and split asunder under our boots.

After leaving the empty chalet, our procession followed Dickens to and through the field behind his house. Here the writer paused and looked at me and for a second I flattered myself that I knew exactly what he was thinking.

Here on this very spot, a mere five years earlier, on a lovely day in the first week of September, Charles Dickens had burned every bit of correspondence he had received in the past three decades. With his sons Henry and Plorn hauling basket after basket of letters and files out from his study, and with his daughter Mamie begging him not to destroy such priceless literary and personal artefacts, Dickens burned every letter he had ever received from me, from John Forster and Leigh Hunt, from Alfred Tennyson and William Makepeace Thackeray, from William Harrison Ainsworth and Thomas Carlyle, from his American friends Ralph Waldo Emerson and Henry Wadsworth Longfellow and Washington Irving and James T. and Annie Fields, and from his wife, Catherine. And from Ellen Ternan.

Later, Katey told me that she had argued with her father as she held the letters in her hands, argued as she recognised the handwriting and signatures of Thackeray and Tennyson and so many others, and had begged him to think of posterity. But Katey, for whatever reason, was lying to me when she told that story. Kate was actually on her honeymoon in France with my brother, Charles, on 3 September, the day Dickens suddenly decided to burn all of his correspondence. She had not even learned of it until many months later.

Her sister Mamie was there—here, on this very spot where I now stood in Dickens's back yard overlooking the frozen fields and bare, distant forests of Kent—and Mamie *did* implore her father not to destroy the letters. Dickens's response was—"Would to God every letter I had ever written was on that pile."

When the files and drawers of Dickens's study were empty that day, his sons Henry and Plorn had roasted onions on the ashes of the great bonfire until a sudden afternoon rainstorm drove everyone inside. Dickens later wrote me—*"It then rained very heavily...I suspect my correspondence of having overcast the face of the Heavens."*

Why had Dickens burned his legacy of correspondence?

Just the previous year, in 1864, Dickens had told me that he'd written to his old friend the actor William Charles Macready—

> *Daily seeing improper uses made of confidential letters in the addressing of them to a public audience that have no business with them, I made not long ago a great fire in my field at Gad's Hill, and burnt every letter I possessed. And now I always destroy every letter I receive not on absolute business, and my mind is so far at ease.*

What improper uses? Some friends whom Dickens and I had in common—of the few who had learned of the mass burning—speculated that the Inimitable's difficult and public separation from Catherine (made public mostly through his own poor judgement, we should remember) had terrified him into imagining would-be literary biographers and other literary ghouls in the days and months after his demise poring over his confidential correspondence of so many years. For decades, these mutual friends speculated, Charles Dickens's life and work had been public property. He would be damned, they believed, if reactions from friends to his most private thoughts should also be gawped and gaped at by the curious public.

I had a slightly different theory about why Dickens burned the letters.

I believe that I put the idea of burning the letters into Dickens's head.

In the Christmas 1854 edition of *Household Words*, in my story "The Fourth Poor Traveller," the narrator, a lawyer, says, "My experience in the law, Mr Frank, has convinced me that if everybody burnt everybody else's letters, half the Courts of Justice in this country might shut up shop." The Courts of Justice, such as they were, were very much on Charles Dickens's mind in those days as he wrote *Bleak House* and then again in 1858 when his wife's family threatened to drag him into court for various injustices to Catherine, including, one presumes, adultery.

And just a few months before Dickens had committed his letters to the bonfire, I had written of burning a letter in my novel *The Woman in White,* which was then being serialised in *Household Words,* carefully edited by Dickens. In my tale, Marian Halcombe has received a letter from a certain Walter Hartright. Marian's half-sister, Laura, is in love with Hartright but has agreed to fulfil her promise to her dying father to marry someone else. Hartright is ready to sail away to South America. Marian decides not to tell Laura about the contents of the letter.

> *I almost doubt whether I ought not to go a step farther, and burn the letter at once, for fear of it one day falling into wrong hands. It not only refers to Laura in terms which ought to remain a secret forever between the writer and me; but it reiterates his suspicion—so obstinate, so unaccountable, and so alarming—that he has been secretly watched. . . . But there is a danger in my keeping the letter. The merest accident might place it at the mercy of strangers. I may fall ill; I may die—better to burn it at once, and have one anxiety the less.*
>
> *It is burnt! The ashes of his farewell letter—the last he may ever write to me—lie in a few black fragments in the hearth.*

My theory, such as it is, is that this scene from *The Woman in White* made a profound impression upon Dickens at the time that he was working so very, very hard to create a second and secret life with Ellen Ternan, but also that—for whatever reason—it was his daughter Kate's marriage to my brother in July of 1860 that finally forced him to burn his correspondence and, I am almost certain, to convince Ellen Ternan to burn all letters he had sent her in the past three years. I *am* certain that Dickens saw Katey's marriage to Charles Collins as a form of betrayal from within his family, and it is not too much to speculate that he could then imagine his daughters and sons, but especially his daughter Kate, she who everyone agreed was so much like him, betraying him yet again by selling or publishing his correspondence when he was dead.

Dickens had aged terribly in the years between 1857 and 1860—some say that he went from being a youth to an old man with almost no pause for middle age along the way—and it could very well have been his brush with illness and the spectre of death at that time which reminded him of my letter-burning scene and prompted him to get on with destroying all evidence of his inner thoughts.

"I know what you're thinking, my dear Wilkie," Dickens said suddenly.

The other men looked startled. Swathed in their layers of wool, they had been watching the weak sun set beneath the layer of clouds to the west across the rolling, frozen Kentish fields.

"What am I thinking, my dear Dickens?" I said.

"You're thinking that a great bonfire here would warm us wonderfully," said Dickens.

I blinked at this, feeling the stiffness of my frozen lashes against my icy cheeks.

"A bonfire!" cried the young Dickenson. "What a capital idea!"

"It would be if we weren't needed inside to join the women and children in their Christmas Day games," said Dickens, clapping his heavy gloves together with a sound like a rifle shot. Sultan shied suddenly, leaping sideways against the leash and cowering as if a real rifle had been fired at him.

"Warm punch for everyone!" cried the Inimitable, and our procession of woollen spheroids with bright scarves waddled into the house behind him.

I ABSENTED MYSELF from the felicity of playing games with the children and women and sought the refuge of my room. I always stayed in the same guest room at Gad's Hill Place and I was quietly relieved to discover that it was still mine, that I had not been demoted in recent months. (Because of the crowding with family staying over the holidays and the Mysterious Guests still to arrive that evening, Percy Fitzgerald had been relegated to a room in the Falstaff Inn across the street. I found this odd, since Percy was an old friend and certainly deserved a room in Dickens's home much more than did the Dickenson orphan, who was staying in the house. But I had long ago given up trying to understand or predict Charles Dickens's whims.)

I should note here, Dear Reader, that I had never shared my late-night laudanum insight that Dickens was planning to kill young rich-orphan Edmond Dickenson (all having something to do with scarlet geraniums spilled about the landscape and hotel room like blood) with Inspector Field or with anyone else. The reason is obvious—it *was* a late-night laudanum revelation, and although some of those have proven priceless to me as a novelist, it would be hard to describe to the squinting Inspector Field the chain of hidden logic and drug-induced intuition that had led to the insight.

But back to my room at Gad's Hill Place. Although I told Caroline otherwise after long stays with Dickens, his home was a comfortable refuge for guests. Every guest room had a marvellously comfortable bed in which to sleep, several expensive and equally comfortable items of furniture, and—always, in every guest room and in some hallways and public rooms—a table covered with writing materials, including headed notepaper, envelopes, cut quill pens, wax, matches, and sealing-wax. All this was arranged in a room that was invariably clean, scrupulously neat, and impeccably comfortable.

Each guest at Gad's Hill would also find himself with a veritable library to choose from in his room, with several volumes set out on the bedside table. These books would have been chosen specifically by Dickens for that particular guest. On my bedside table were a copy of my own *The Woman in White*—not the inscribed one I had personally given to Dickens but a newly purchased one with the pages not yet cut—as well as *Spectator* essays, a copy of *1001 Arabian Nights,* and a volume of Herodotus with a leather bookmark set in a chapter on the ancient historian's Egyptian travels, which opened to a discussion of Sleep Temples.

Above a dressing room mirror in my room was a card which read—"Hans Andersen slept in this room for five weeks—which seemed to the family AGES!"

I knew something about that extended visit. One night over wine, Dickens had described the friendly Dane (who spoke very little English, which must have made his long stay with the Dickens family even more stressful) as "a cross between my character Pecksniff and the Ugly Duckling, Wilkie. A very heavy Scandinavian cross to bear for a week, much less for two fortnights and more."

But when I frequently told Caroline or Harriet, after several days or even weeks as a guest at Gad's Hill, that the stay had been "a trial," I meant it in a more literal sense. Despite Dickens's very real good humour and very real efforts always to set his guests at ease, seeing to their every comfort, catering to them in conversation at all meals and gatherings, there was also a very real sense of *being judged* by the Inimitable when one was a guest in his home. At least I felt that. (My guess is that poor Hans Christian Andersen—who *had* commented, without complaining, on the brusqueness of Katey and Mamie and the boys during his long stay here—had not noticed the impatience and occasional censure from his host.)

In the quiet of my room—although I could hear squeals of delight from the children and Charles Dickens downstairs in the parlour as they played their games—I removed the jug of laudanum from its well-protected place in my valise and filled the clean glass that sat next to the constantly replenished jug of cool water by the hand basin. The evening, I was sure, would be a trial for me—physically as well as emotionally. I downed the first glass of medicine and filled the next.

You may be wondering, Dear Reader from my possibly judgemental future, why I had agreed to inform on Dickens to the inquisitive former policeman. I hope you have not thought less of me during the pages of memoir that have intervened here since I related consummating that conspiratorial deal.

The reasons I agreed to that Faustian bargain were threefold—

First, I believe that Dickens *wanted* me to tell former inspector Charles Frederick Field both everything that had happened that night we searched for Drood and everything the Inimitable had told me about Drood since that night. Why would Dickens want me to inform on him? you ask. I am not certain of all the reasons, but I am quite certain that the author wanted me to do so without actually requesting me to do so. Dickens knew that the private detective was querying me. He certainly knew that a man like Field would attempt to blackmail me beyond a mere threat to expose the very public nature of my relationship with Caroline. More to the point, Dickens would never have told me the story of Drood's background or admitted to the fact of his—the writer's—trips to London's Undertown *if Dickens had not anticipated, even wanted, me to forward the information to the bullying inspector.*

What Dickens's game was, I did not know. But the sense of silent collusion was thicker between the Inimitable and me than it was between the scheming Inspector Field and myself.

Second, I had my own strong reasons for using the inspector as my means to gather information about Charles Dickens and Ellen Ternan. There, I knew, in that aspect of his life, Dickens would never share information with me. His relationship with the actress, long before the expository intervention of the Staplehurst disaster, had changed every aspect of the Inimitable's life and every relationship—including his with me—in that life. Yet the details and extent of that secret relationship and busy Second Life would, if Dickens were to have his way (and when did he not?), remain a mystery until and after the end of his life. I had reasons, which I may reveal to you later, Dear Reader, for needing to know those details. Inspector Field, with his proclivity for prying and his complete lack of a gentleman's moral perspective and with the help of his far-flung group of busy detectives, was the perfect source of this information.

Third, I entered into the apparent conspiracy with Inspector Field out of my own need to rearrange elements of an intimate relationship with Charles Dickens that I had seen deteriorate over the past year, long before Staplehurst. In a real sense, I was transmitting the Drood information to the detective in order to help protect Charles Dickens at one of his most vulnerable times. I felt that a renewal of our endangered friendship—and the reassertion of my own eroded equality in it—was important if my friend Charles Dickens was to be helped and protected.

Twenty minutes had passed since I had drunk the laudanum, and I could feel the encroaching pain from rheumatical gout begin to release its vice around my aching head and bowels and extremities. A sense of deep equilibrium and mental alertness spread through my system.

Whatever the surprises Charles Dickens had for us at this Christmas Dinner, I now felt ready to face them with my usual and expected Wilkie Collins brand of poise and good humour.

CHAPTER THIRTEEN

*N*o—er—Dickens! I swear! Not this—er—
er—not this, this *Our Mutual Friend* nonsense! No! It is—er—it is—Copperfield, by God! I
swear to Heaven that, as a piece of passion and
playfulness—er, ah—indescribably mixed up together,
it does—No, really, Dickens!—Copperfield!—amaze
me as profoundly as it—er—as it moves me. But as a
piece of Art—and you know—er—that I—No, Dickens!
By God!—have seen the best Art in a great time—it is
incomprehensible to me. How it is got at—er—how it is
done—er—how one man can—well! It lays me on my—
er—back, and it is of no use talking about it."

This was our Surprise Guest speaking and mopping
at his huge, pale, perspiring forehead with his paisely
silk handkerchief. Then the old man began mopping
his rheumy eyes as they began leaking tears.

Our Mystery Guests were, of course, William Charles
Macready, the Eminent Tragedian, and his new wife,
Cecile.

I hope and pray that I do not sense a silence on your
distant end of this memoir through time, Dear Reader,
for if your era has forgotten William Charles Macready,
what hope do I have that the name or work of little
Wilkie Collins has survived?

William Charles Macready was the Eminent Tragedian of our age, inheriting Kean's mantle and—

according to many—surpassing that earlier giant of Shakespearean Theatre in both subtlety of interpretation and refinement of sensibility. Macready's most memorable roles in his many decades of dominating the English stage were as Macbeth in that unnameable production and as King Lear. Born in 1793, if my arithmetic is correct, Macready was already a mature and recognised star of the stage and famous public man when young Dickens—the Inimitable Boz, as he was known in his first flush of success after *The Pickwick Papers*—was just a stagestruck lad. Macready's unique mastery of pathos and remorse on stage, often at the expense of any sense of the nobility or greatness so often worn by Shakespearean actors, resonated strongly with the young writer's own abilities in those areas.

Macready also was, as was Dickens, a complex, sensitive, and paradoxical man. As outwardly certain of everything as the Inimitable himself, Macready was—according to those who knew him best—also privately in doubt much of the time. Proud of his profession in the same way that Dickens was of his, he also was insecure (just as Dickens sometimes was) that such a profession could allow him to be a true gentleman. But from the late 1830s on, the rising star Dickens and his friends Macready, Forster, Maclise, Ainsworth, Beard, and Mitton composed an inner circle of talent and ambition rarely equalled in our little island's history.

Of all these men, William Charles Macready was—until Dickens's ultimate ascendency—by far the most famous.

For many years (decades actually), the Inimitable Boz wrote admiring reviews from the sidelines, especially cheering on (along with his co-writer and editor John Forster) such theatrical innovations as Macready's production of *Lear*—which restored Shakespeare's true and tragic vision after more than a century and a half in which audiences had no choice but to suffer through Nahum Tate's abysmal "happy ending" adaptation. Macready had also reintroduced the Fool to the cast of *Lear*, an act of inspired salvage to which Charles Dickens's sensibilities had resonated as if he had been a bell struck by a hammer. I once looked up Dickens's writing on this particular matter, and beyond Dickens's referring to the renewed presence of the Fool as "singular and masterly relief" to the overwhelming presence of the Lear character, the ecstatic Boz had called Macready's production "magnificent" and had elaborated—

> The heart, soul, and brain of the ruined piece of nature, in all the stages of its ruining, were laid bare before us.... The tenderness, the rage, the madness, the remorse, and sorrow, all come of one another, and are linked together in one chain.

In 1849, the upstart American Shakespearean actor named Edwin Forrest—who had once been good friends with Macready and who had benefitted from his largesse—visited England and insulted Macready's interpretation of Hamlet, going so far as to say that our great English Tragedian minced his way across the stage and delivered his lines like an effeminate fop. Forrest was not treated well by the entirety of English audiences during the remainder of his tour here. Englishmen laughed at his Macbeth delivering the Bard's immortal lines in that atrocious American accent. Then, in May of that same year, Macready did his own tour of America—he had been there before and been welcomed warmly for the most part—and the gangs of Boston and New York, serious Shakespeare aficionados, theatregoers, and vicious hooligans all, had pelted Macready, *during his performances,* with rotten eggs, chairs, dead cats, and even more disgusting items. Many American theatre-goers attempted to defend our Eminent Tragedian. More of the hooligan gang members organised to strike a blow against Macready and the English ascendancy and hegemony in all things Shakespearean. The result, on 10 May, 1849, had been one of the bloodiest riots in the history of New York City. Before it was over, fifteen thousand people had turned into either a pro- or anti-Macready mob near the theatre called Astor Place, the mayor and governor panicked and called out a militia which the Americans called the National Guard, the crowd was fired into, and somewhere between twenty and thirty citizens lay dead on the street.

Through this all, Dickens had sent encouraging and congratulatory telegrams to Macready, as if he were the manager with the towel and smelling salts in a pugilist's corner.

Over the years, Dickens had quietly written and shyly submitted many short plays and theatre comedies to the great actor, but Macready had tactfully rejected all of them (although Dickens was involved in mounting such memorable performances for Macready as his 1838 presentation of *Henry V*). Somehow these rejections had not antagonised or alienated the Inimitable, who—in my experience—could tolerate no such rejection from anyone else, including the Queen.

So their friendship had endured and matured for three decades now. But as friends in common had fallen by the wayside—either falling out of Dickens's favour or dying—I had sensed from the Inimitable's comments in recent years that his prominent reaction to Macready was now one of sadness.

Life had not treated the Eminent Tragedian gently. The Astor Place riot had convinced the ageing actor to retire, but even as he hit the road for his farewell tour, his beloved oldest child, nineteen-year-old Nina, died.

Macready, always a soul-searching man of faith, literally locked himself away to confront his newly powerful doubts about both the universe and himself. His wife, Catherine, was in confinement at the time with their tenth child. (The parallels between the Dickenses and the Macreadys were more than superficial—the couples were so close that when Charles Dickens took his own Catherine on his first American tour in the early 1840s, it was the Macreadys to whom he entrusted their own children at the time—but William Charles Macready never fell out of love with *his* Catherine.)

Macready's last performance was at Drury Lane on 26 February, 1851. *Macbeth*—the role he had been most identified with and the play he had been booed and attacked during in New York two years before—was, of course, his choice for his farewell. There was the inevitable grand banquet as a footnote to this farewell, this one so large that it had to be held in the echoing old Hall of Commerce. Bulwer-Lytton lisped his way through a sincere speech. John Forster read an abysmally bad verse written for the occasion by Tennyson. Thackeray, whose only task was to toast the health of the ladies in attendance, almost passed out from nerves. Dickens, of course, who had organised the entire night and who was wearing a bright blue coat with astounding brass buttons and shiny black satin waistcoat, gave a moving and sad and humourous and heartfelt speech that was truly memorable.

Catherine Macready died in 1852. As had been the case with their daughter Nina, Macready's wife succumbed after a long, terrible battle with tuberculosis. Dickens had told me about his last visit to her bedside and how he had written a friend shortly after that—"*The tremendous sickle certainly does cut deep into the surrounding corn, when one's own small blade has ripened.*" The next year, both of Macready's sons, Walter and

Henry, also died, followed immediately after by their sister Lydia. None of his children had gotten out of their teens.

After eight years of mourning in seclusion in his gloomy Sherbourne retreat, in 1860, at the age of sixty-seven, Macready had remarried—the twenty-three-year-old Cecile Louise Frederica Spencer became the second Mrs Macready—and moved to a handsome new home in Cheltenham, only four or five hours from London. Soon after that they had a son.

Dickens was delighted. The Inimitable loathed, feared, and despised the idea of getting older (it was the reason that Mary Angela, his oldest grandchild, Charley and Bess's daughter, this very evening was calling Dickens "Venerables," as the writer had insisted—he would not allow the word "grandfather" to be used around him) and he did not wish to see or acknowledge signs of age or decay in those closest to him.

But the William Charles Macready at our table this Christmas Day night of 1865, at age seventy-two, showed every possible sign of age and decay.

The same features that so many had found interesting in an actor—the powerful chin, massive forehead, large nose, sunken eyes, pursed and budlike lips—now conveyed the sense of some once-proud bird of prey collapsed into itself.

As an actor, Macready had developed a technique, still taught at theatrical schools, called "the Macready pause." I had heard it on stage myself. Essentially it was nothing more than a hesitation, an odd pause or ellipsis put into a line of dialogue where no punctuation existed, and it's true that it could add impact or emphasis to a line, to the point of changing the meaning of the words on either side of the pause. Macready had incorporated this pause into his regular speech decades ago and his dictatorial ways as a director of plays had been parodied by many—"Stand—er—er—still, damn your eyes!" or "Keep your—er—er—eye on me, sir!"

But now the Macready pause had devoured most of the Macready meaning.

"I can't—er—er—can't *tell* you—er—er—Dickens, how...What *is* that preposterous and—er—er—horrible hubbub from the other...Children? *Your* children, Charley? What cat is that? Do—do—do—a—a—a—a—damn it! Cecile! What was I about to say before...Collins! No, *you,* the other one—with the spectacles! I read your—er—er—saw your—you—you—you—cannot possibly have meant that she...Do, fair Georgina, pray unburden us all of this—er—er—relieve us of this—a—a—banging of pewter pots from the kitchen, no? Yes! By God! Someone should tell the stage manager that these children should...Oh, *A Woman Is White* is what I meant to—er—er—capital turkey, my dear! Capital!"

THE TURKEY *WAS* good. Some people have written that no one in England had been more responsible in the past decades for turning English families gathering around their tables on Christmas away from the bony and greasy goose and towards the rich, plump turkey than had Charles Dickens. His ending to *A Christmas Carol* alone seems to have pushed thousands of our previously goosified countrymen over the poultry bodice brink onto the white breast of true turkey feasts.

At any rate, the turkey was good this day, as were all the steaming side dishes. Even the white wine was better than that which Dickens usually served.

This was a small Christmas gathering by Dickens's standards, but the long table was still more crowded than any Caroline had ever hosted for a Christmas dinner. At the far end was Charles Dickens, of course, the carved carcass of the larger of the two depleted turkeys still in front of him like a trophy of war. To his immediate right was Macready, and across the table from the Eminent Tragedian was his young wife, Cecile. (I am sure that there is some ironclad social rule against seating spouses across from one another—almost as bad as next to each other, I would think—but Charles Dickens was never one to pay much attention to Society's dictates. Mere Podsnappery, he would say.)

Next to Macready was his god-daughter and name-sake, Kate Macready Dickens Collins, but she did not look pleased to be seated next to her god-father—or pleased to be at the table with us, for that matter. After darting venomous glances at her father and wincing at Macready's endlessly elliptical and indecipherable pronouncements, she would look down the table towards her sister Mamie and roll her eyes. Mamie—Mary—who was seated on my left (since, for some unknown reason, Dickens had bestowed upon me the honour of sitting at the opposite end of the table from him), had put on even more weight in the few weeks since I had last seen her and was looking more and more like her matronly mother.

Across from Katey was my brother, Charles, who did indeed look ill this evening. As much as I hated to agree with Dickens on this particular matter, Charley's pale countenance did look like a death's head.

To Katey Dickens's right sat the Young Orphan, our very own Staplehurst survivor, Edmond Dickenson, who spent the evening grinning and gazing and beaming at everyone like the fool he was. Across from Dickenson was another young bachelor, twenty-six-year-old Percy Fitzgerald, who managed to be just as jovial and enthusiastic as Dickenson, *sans* the idiocy.

Sitting between Dickenson and Mamie Dickens was Charley Dickens. The Inimitable's oldest child seemed the happiest of any of us there that night, and the reason may have been sitting across the table from him. I confess that young Bessie Dickens, his wife, may have been the loveliest woman there that night—or at least a close second to Cecile Macready. Dickens had been furious at Charley for falling in love with Bessie Evans— her father, Frederick Evans, had been a long-time friend of the Inimitable's, but Dickens had never forgiven Evans for representing Catherine during the ugly separation negotiations—nor for being her trustee afterwards—*even though Dickens himself had asked Evans to take on those roles.*

Luckily for Charley Dickens's happiness and future, he had ignored his father's blusterings and ultimatums and married Bessie. She was quiet and contained this night—she rarely spoke in the presence of her father-in-law—but the candlelight on her lovely neck was statement enough. On Bessie's left sat Georgina Hogarth, who did her best to preside over the table and cluck about each dish and entrée in the author's wife's very palpable absence.

To Georgina's left and to my immediate right sat young Henry Fielding Dickens. As far as I could recall, this was the first time that the sixteen-year-old had eaten at the grown-ups' table on Christmas Day. The boy looked proud of that fact in his shiny new satin waistcoat with buttons far too visible. Less visible were the long side-whiskers the boy was attempting—none too successfully—to wish into existence along his downy cheeks. He kept touching, not consciously, I believe, his smooth cheeks and upper lip as if to see if the desired whiskers might have grown in during dinner.

To my immediate left, sitting between Mamie Dickens and me, was the true (for me) "Surprise Guest" of the evening—a very tall, very thickset, very ruddy-complexioned, very bald man with the kind of luxurious moustache and side-whiskers that poor young Henry D. could only dream of. The man's name was George Dolby and I had actually met him at the *Household Words* office once or twice, although my recollection was that his background was in theatrical or business management, not publishing. During the evening's introductions before dinner, it became obvious that Dickens had known Dolby slightly, had some business to discuss with him, and—since Dolby was at loose ends this Christmas—had invited him to Gad's Hill on the spur of the moment.

Dolby was an energetic and skilful talker, despite a stammer that disappeared only when he was imitating other people (which he did frequently). His stories centred on theatrical gossip and, except for the slight stammer when he was speaking as himself, were told with almost perfect theatrical emphasis and timing—but he also knew how to listen. And to laugh. Several times this evening he had given forth with a noisy, jolly, reverberating, unselfconscious laugh that may have made Katey Dickens and Mamie roll their eyes but which, I noticed, always brought a smile to the Inimitable's face. Dolby seemed especially amused by Macready's nearly impenetrable tales and waited patiently through the "—er—er—er" for the "by God!" final lines before erupting in mirth.

The communal part of the evening was almost over, the children and grandchildren had come in to wish "Venerables" and their parents good night, the conversation had reached a pause where even Dolby seemed thoughtful and a little sad, Katey and Mamie had quit rolling their eyes and looking displeased with us all, but obviously the women were ready to retire to wherever they retire when the men move to the library or billiards room for brandy and a cigar, when young Dickenson said, "Excuse me, Mr Dickens, but if I may be so forward, what are you writing now, sir? Have you embarked upon another novel?"

Instead of frowning at the upstart, Dickens smiled as if he had been looking forward to this question all evening.

"Actually," he said, "I have put aside my writing for the time being. I don't know when I shall pick it up again."

"Father!" cried Mamie in mock alarm. "You not writing? You not in your study writing every day? Shall the next announcement be that the sun no longer shall rise in the east?"

Dickens smiled again. "In truth, I have decided to embark upon a more rewarding endeavour over the coming months—perhaps years. A creative undertaking that shall be more rewarding to me in both artistic and financial terms."

Katey showed her own version of the Inimitable's smile. "You're becoming an artist, Father? An illustrator, perhaps?" She looked at her quiet husband, my brother, across the ruins of the turkey. "You had best watch out, Charles. You have yet another competitor."

"Nothing like that," said Dickens. Kate often irritated her father, but his response to her taunt tonight was filled with equanimity. "I have decided to create a new art form altogether. Something the world has never experienced—has never imagined!—before this."

"Another—eh—eh—a new—eh—eh, that is to say—by God, Dickens!" offered Macready.

The author leaned to his left and said softly to Cecile, "My dear, of all men at this table, your husband knows best the beauty and power of the new endeavour I shall be embarking upon in a very few weeks."

"You're going to become a full-time actor, Father?" chirped up Henry, who had seen his father on the amateur stage his entire life and who had been tossed around by him on that same stage during the early performances of my *The Frozen Deep*.

"Not at all, my boy," said Dickens, still smiling. "I daresay that our friend Wilkie at the other end of the table here might have a glimmer of what I have in mind."

"I have no clue whatsoever," I said truthfully.

Dickens set both hands on the table and spread his arms in a way that reminded me of da Vinci's *The Last Supper*. That thought had hardly entered my mind before another followed fast on its heels—*If this is the Last Supper, which amongst us here is Judas?*

"I have authorised Wills to negotiate on my behalf with Messrs Chappell of New Bond Street for an engagement consisting of at least thirty readings," continued Dickens. "While the negotiations have only yet begun, I am quite confident that this shall happen and that it shall herald a new era of my career and of public entertainment and education."

"But, Father," cried Mamie, obviously shocked, "you know what Dr Beard has said to you during your recent illnesses—degenerations of some functions of the heart, the need for more rest—your previous reading tours have so exhausted you..."

"Oh, nonsense," cried Dickens but with even a broader smile. "We are considering appointing Mr Dolby there..."

The huge man blushed and bowed his head.

"...as my business manager and companion on these trips. Chappell would organise all business and administrative arrangements, as well as pay for my own and Mr Dolby's and probably Mr Wills's personal and travelling expenses. All I shall have to do is to take my book and read at the appointed place and hour."

"But reading from your books is hardly...what did you call it, Father?...a new art form," said Katey. "You've done it many times."

"So I have, my dear," agreed Dickens. "But never the way I shall on this and future tours. As you know, I never simply...*read* from my books, although sometimes I feign to. All of my performances are done from memory and I reserve the right to edit, conflate, alter, and rewrite scenes to a great extent...even improvise completely upon occasion, just as the Eminent Tragedian here has done count-less times to the betterment even of Shakespeare." He patted Macready's arm.

"Ah—yes—I, of course—but, Bulwer-Lytton, yes, I would gag away at will," said Macready, reddening under his pale skin and wrinkles, "but the—er—er— the Bard. By God...never!"

Dickens laughed. "Well, my prose is not the Bard's. It is not inscribed in stone anywhere like Moses' Commandments."

"But still," said my brother, "a new art form? Can any reading be such?"

"Mine shall be from this tour forward," snapped Dickens. His smile had faded.

"Your readings are already unique in their tone and brilliance, sir," said young Dickenson.

"Thank you, Edmond. Your generous spirit is appreciated. But in my future readings, beginning on this tour and continuing...as I said...perhaps for many years, I plan to bring to the proceedings a totally unprecedented level of theatricality combined with a true understanding of the manipulation of animal magnetism."

"Magnetism, by Jove!" exploded Dolby. "Sir, do you propose to mesmerise the audience as well as to entertain them?"

Dickens smiled again and stroked his whiskers. "Mr Dolby, I shall assume that you read. Novels, I mean."

"Indeed I do, sir!" laughed Dolby. "I have enjoyed all of yours and also Mr Collins's here...Mr Collins at the end of the table to my right, I mean to say." He turned to me. "That book *Armadale* that Mr Dickens's press published for you, Mr Collins. Wonderful stuff, sir. That heroine—Lydia Gwilt, I believe her name was. What a woman! Wonderful!"

"We did not have the pleasure of publishing *that* book of Mr Collins's in serial form," Dickens said formally. "Nor shall we have the honour of publishing it in book form. It shall appear in May of the coming year from another publisher. Although I am delighted to be able to say that we are in the process of wooing our dear Wilkie back to publish his next novel in *All the Year Round.*"

"Ah, wonderful, wonderful!" said Dolby, all hearty good cheer. He had no idea of the *faux pas* he had committed with his praise.

Indeed, my most recent novel, *Armadale,* riding on the success of *The Woman in White* that had appeared in Dickens's *Household Words,* had been serialised—with a much higher payment for me—in *The Cornhill Magazine.* And it was to come out in full book form from Smith, Elder & Company, who also published *The Cornhill.*

But this was not the full *faux pas,* nor the reason that Dickens's face—beaming and relaxed and eager just a moment earlier—now looked pinched and old. The reason for his change of mood was, I am certain, precisely the heroine Lydia Gwilt whom Dolby had been so inopportune to mention.

At one point I had had Lydia, who was no stranger to pain, hers and that of those mortals close to her, say in the novel—

Who was the man who invented laudanum? I thank him from the bottom of my heart, whoever he was. If all the miserable wretches in pain of body and mind, whose comforter he has been, could meet together to sing his praises, what a chorus it would be! I have had six delicious hours of oblivion; I have woke up with my mind composed.

I had heard through numerous intermediaries, my brother and Katey included, that Dickens had not been pleased with those words...nor with the general tolerant tone towards laudanum and other opiates shown throughout the novel.

"But you were going to tell us how our act of reading novels relates to the new art form of your proposed readings," I said to Dickens down the length of the cluttered table.

"Yes," said the Inimitable, smiling towards Cecile Macready as if in apology for the interruption of his narration. "You know the incomparable and—I would dare say—*unique* feeling one has when reading. The focus of attention to the exclusion of all sensory input, other than the eyes taking in the words, one has when entering into a good book?"

"Oh, rather!" cried Dickenson. "The world just fades away. All other thoughts just fade away! All that remains are the sights and sounds and characters and world created for us by the author! One might as well be anaesthetised to the mundane world around us. All readers have had that experience."

"Precisely," said Dickens, his smile back in place and his eyes bright. "This happens to be precisely the receptive state a person must be in for a mesmeric therapist to be able to do his work. It is, through the judicious use of language, phrases, descriptions, and dialogue, a form of lowering the reader into the same sort of receptive state of mind that a patient under Magnetic Influence must feel."

"By God!" cried Macready. "The—er—the audience at the theatre enters into just such an—a—a—sort of receptive trance. I have always said that the—er—

er—audiences are the third point of the collaborative—ah—collaborative triangle with the playwright and the actor."

"*Exactly,*" said Dickens. "And this is the crux of my new performing art as opposed to mere readings. Building upon the receptive state of the audiences—so much more intense even than that of readers alone at home or in a railway carriage or even sitting in their gardens—I intend to use the incipient magnetism, combined with my voice and words, to put them into an even deeper receptive and appreciative and collaborative state than either literature or theatre alone could produce."

"Through mere words?" asked my brother.

"And the judicious and carefully honed gesture," said Dickens. "In the proper setting."

"That setting being the st...st...stage," said Dolby. "Yes, by Jove. That should be extraordinary!"

"Not merely the stage," said Dickens, nodding slightly as if he were already prepared to take his bows. "But the darkened room. The precise and scientific use of gas lighting to illuminate my face and hands above all else, the careful seating of the audience so that no one is out of direct line of sight with my eyes..."

"We shall be bringing our own gas and lighting experts on the tour," interrupted Dolby. "Wills has made it a central item to our negotiations."

Macready pounded the table and laughed. "Little do audiences know that the—er—er—the—er—er—gas-lights are a form of—er—intoxication. Intoxication, by God! They deprive the room, the theatre, the space, of oxygen!"

"Indeed they do," said Dickens with a mischievous smile. "And we shall be using that to our advantage in putting these—I should modestly hope—very large audiences at the readings into the properly receptive state."

"Into the properly receptive state for what?" I asked flatly.

Dickens pinned me upon the point of his mesmeric stare. His voice was soft. "That is what these readings— this new art form—shall determine."

AFTER DINNER, we men decamped with brandy and cigars to the billiards room behind Dickens's study. This was a pleasant space, well-lighted, with one wall half-tiled to prevent any damage from our flailing cue-sticks, and I had spent many a pleasant hour in it. Dickens took his game of billiards seriously—he liked to say that billiards "brings out the mettle in a man" and then, often, glancing at my brother, would add, "or the lack of." In either case I shall always remember the Inimitable leaning long over the green-baized table, his coat off and wearing those large double-glasses which gave him an odd, Pickwickian, earlier-era old-mannish look.

One of the reasons that Dickens enjoyed Percy Fitzgerald was that the younger man was serious about the game of billiards and quite good at it—at least good enough to give Dickens and me a game. I could more than hold my own at the game, as befits any serious bachelor, but I was surprised this night to find that our Resident Orphan, young Edmond Dickenson, played rather like someone who earned his living on the winnings. (And perhaps he did, for all I knew and for all of Dickens's talk of the boy's being independently wealthy.)

Macready played for a loud while before his wife trundled him off to bed after a glass of warm milk. But it was George Dolby—Dickens's future business manager and reading-tour companion—who brought that night's games to life: roaring with laughter, telling truly amusing stories with no hint of his earlier stammer, his great bald scalp and forehead gleaming with perspiration in the light from the overhead lamps, Dolby repeatedly dispatched Percy, then me, then Dickens, and finally the stubborn and oddly skilled young Dickenson, whose play showed both an appreciation of ballistics and a deviousness which one would never credit by looking at him.

Dickens, as was his usual habit, retired at midnight but urged us all to continue playing. Usually I did when there were interesting male guests still awake, often playing and enjoying our host's brandy until dawn, but when Dolby set down his cue and retired soon after Dickens said his goodnights—perhaps not yet certain of his prerogatives as a guest at Gad's Hill—the game broke up, Percy set off for the Falstaff Inn with a servant holding a lantern for him, and Dickenson and I went upstairs to our respective rooms.

Despite my earlier ministrations of my medicine, the rheumatical gout was racking me as I got ready for bed. Measuring the amount of laudanum remaining in my travel jug, I took two more glasses of the restorative and soporific.

I say "restorative and soporific" because laudanum, as you almost certainly know in your more medicinally enlightened future, Dear Reader, serves to quiet the nerves and allow sleep or to awaken the sensibilities and allow long bouts of hard work and provide a higher than usual level of attention. I did not know—perhaps no one knew—how the same drug served both opposing needs, but I knew beyond doubt that it did. This night I needed its ministrations as soporific.

My busy mind wanted to dwell on Dickens's bizarre plans for a reading tour to serve as "an entirely new art form" and to connect the strands of nonsense he'd spoken about mesmerism and magnetism to the visits he purported to have been making to see the cellar-dweller named Drood, but the blessed laudanum relieved me of those turgid questionings.

My last thoughts before going to sleep that night were about a piece of information that Inspector Field had given me some weeks earlier.

It seemed that Ellen Ternan had been followed to this area and even to Gad's Hill several times since autumn. Of course, reported Field, the former actress had relatives in Rochester which brought her to the area separate from any collusion with Dickens, but it was certain that she also came to visit at Gad's Hill repeatedly and appeared to have spent at least five nights here since September.

How, I wondered, did Mamie and Katey react to this usurpation of their mother's place? I could easily imagine Mamie following Georgina Hogarth's lead in welcoming the intruder into their home, knowing—as they must have—that Charles Dickens was a man racked by loneliness and a need for the illusions of youth that only romance can bring to the ageing male mind and soul. But Katey? Kate Macready Dickens, as lonely as she appeared to be in her own right—her father had mentioned to me in October that my brother's wife "was so discontented...so intensely eager to find other lovers, that she is burning away both character and health slowly but steadily, Wilkie"—still seemed to be loyal to the memory of her exiled mother. I could not imagine Katey, who was the same age as Ellen Ternan, opening her heart to her father's probable mistress.

It is a hard thing to tell the brother of your daughter's husband that she is so discontented with her husband that she is eagerly searching for other lovers, and I suspect that Dickens said those words so that I might repeat them to Charley. But, of course, I did not.

Yet Katey must not have vocally opposed Ellen's visits

or the former actress would not have kept returning to Gad's Hill.

With these thoughts still in mind, I fell into a deep and dreamless sleep.

SOMEONE WAS SHAKING me violently and whispering my name.

I rolled over groggily. The room was dark except for a strange light that seemed to be coming from the floor at the side of the bed. A fire? There was a dark form looming over me, shaking me.

"Get up, Wilkie."

I focused on that shape.

Charles Dickens in a nightshirt with a woollen coat thrown over his shoulders, carrying a two-barrelled shotgun in one hand and a crumpled shroud in the other.

The time has come, I thought.

"Get up, Wilkie," he whispered again. "Quickly. Just put your shoes on. I brought your coat."

The shape dropped the shroud on my legs and I realised it was my overcoat. "What..."

"Sshhh. You'll wake the others. Get up. Quickly. Before he gets away. We have no time to waste. Just the coat and shoes. That's a good man...."

We went down the back stairs, Dickens with his gun and lantern ahead of me, both of us trying to make as little noise as possible.

Sultan, the ferocious Irish bloodhound, was tied up in the back hall, muzzled and leashed but straining to get out the door.

"What is this?" I whispered to Dickens. "What's wrong?"

The Inimitable's wisps of hair atop his head and long whiskers were curled this way and that in the tangle of sleep, some standing straight up, all of which would have been very amusing under different circumstances. But not tonight. There was something like real fear in Charles Dickens's eyes—something I don't believe I had ever seen before.

"It was Drood," he whispered. "I could not sleep. I kept thinking of something I should have noted for Wills. So I rose from my bed, intending to go down to the study to make a note, and I saw it, Wilkie...."

"Saw what, man?"

"Drood's face. That pale, tortured face. Floating at the window. Pressed against the cold panes."

"Of your study?" I said.

"No," said Dickens, his eyes as wild as a runaway horse's, "at the windows of my bedroom."

"But, Dickens," I whispered back, "that is impossible. Your bedroom is up on the first floor, with the guest rooms. Drood would have to be standing on an eight- or ten-foot ladder to peer into those windows."

"I *saw* him, Wilkie," rasped Dickens.

He flung the door open and with the lantern and leash in one hand and his two-barrelled gun in the other, was pulled out into the night after his straining dog.

IT WAS VERY COLD and very dark in Dickens's back yard. There was no moon, no stars, no light from the house. The cold wind cut through my loosely donned coat in a second and I shivered under my fluttering nightshirt. My legs and ankles were bare between the coat and my shoes, and the night air was so frigid against my flesh there that I felt as if the frozen grass were slashing at me with tiny razors.

Sultan snarled and surged. Dickens let the dog lead us as if we were outraged villagers on the trail of a murderer in a second-rate sensationalist novel.

And perhaps we were.

We hurried around the side of the house in the dark and stood in the garden beneath Dickens's bedroom windows. Sultan pulled and snarled and tugged to continue, but Dickens paused long enough to unshutter the small lantern and focus its beam on the frozen soil in the flower bed. There were no incriminating footprints and no signs that a ladder had been set there. We both glanced up towards his dark bedroom window. A few stars appeared between rapidly moving clouds and were then erased.

If Drood had stared into that window without a tall ladder beneath him, he must have been floating ten feet off the ground.

Sultan growled and tugged and we followed.

We returned to the back of the house and paused in the small field where Dickens had burned all of his letters in 1860. The cold wind moved bare branches with skeletal clicks. I whispered to Dickens, "How could it be Drood? How could he be here? *Why* would he be here?"

"He followed me from London one morning," Dickens whispered back, slowly turning in a full circle, the long double-barrelled weapon in the crook of his right arm. "I am sure of it. I have seen a shadowy figure on the other side of the road, by the chalet, many nights now. The dogs bark. When I emerge, the form is gone."

More likely to be the agents of Inspector Field, I thought and was tempted to say aloud. Instead, I said again, "*Why* would Drood come out here to stare in your window on Christmas Day night?"

"Shhhh," said Dickens, waving me into silence and clamping his free hand around Sultan's jaws to silence the bloodhound's growling.

For a second I thought that a sleigh was approaching, even though there was not a hint of snow on the ground, but then I realised that the faint jingling of bells was coming from the dark stables. The pony Newman Noggs's Norwegian bells were hanging on the wall there.

"Come," said Dickens and hurried towards the barn.

The stable doors were open—a blacker rectangle in the near-black night.

"Did you..." I started to whisper.

"They are always closed," Dickens hissed back. "I checked them at sunset tonight." He handed me the suddenly silent dog's leash, set the lantern down, and lifted the shotgun.

From inside the stables there came a final faint jingle of bells then sudden silence, as if a hand were muffling the harness.

"Unclip Sultan's muzzle and then release his leash," Dickens whispered very softly, still aiming his weapon at the open doors.

"He'll tear whoever it is apart," I whispered back.

"Unclip the muzzle and release him," hissed Dickens.

I went to one knee, heart pounding, shivering in the cold, and fumbled with the clasps on the muzzle. I was half-certain that the straining, wild-eyed Irish bloodhound—he weighed almost as much as I—would rip *me* limb from limb the second I removed the muzzle.

He did not. Sultan ceased growling and straining as I dropped the muzzle to the ground and fumbled off the clip of the leash.

"Go!" Dickens said aloud to the dog.

Sultan went, exploding into a run as if he were made of metal springs rather than mere muscles. But he did not run into the darkness of the barn. Instead, the bloodhound veered to the left, leaped a hedge in a single bound, and disappeared out into the fields, heading towards the forest and distant sea.

"D——n that dog," said Dickens. I realised how few times I had heard the Inimitable curse. "Come, Wilkie," he said peremptorily, as if I were a second hound he had kept in reserve.

Handing me the shielded lantern, Dickens ran towards the open door of the stable. I hurried to keep up, almost slipping on the frozen grass even as Dickens reached the doorway and entered without waiting for light.

I came into the gloom feeling rather than seeing Dickens's presence a few feet to my left, knowing—perhaps clairvoyantly—that he stood there with his shotgun raised and aimed towards the long avenue within the barn, even as I sensed rather than saw the stir and breath of the horses and ponies standing here.

"Light!" cried Dickens.

I fumbled open the shutter on the lantern.

A vague blur in the stalls where the horses—all awake but silent—shifted uneasily, a glimpse of their breath like fog in the cold air, and then a blur of white motion at the far end of the dark space, beyond where the bells and harness and tack hung.

Dickens lifted the weapon higher and I could see his eyes white in the lantern light as he prepared to pull both triggers.

"Wait!" I shouted, the volume of my voice causing the horses to shy. "For God's sake, don't shoot!"

I ran towards the white blur. I believe Dickens would have fired despite my cries if I had not thrown my body between him and his target.

The white blur at the closed end of the darkness revealed itself in the circle of light from my lantern. Edmond Dickenson stood there, his eyes wide but staring blankly, not seeing us, not hearing us. He was in his nightshirt. His feet were bare and pale against the cold black cobbles of the livery stable floor. His hands hung like small white stars at the end of his limp arms.

Dickens came up and began laughing. The loud laughter further alarmed the horses but did not seem to register with Dickenson. "A somnambulist!" cried Dickens. "By God, a somnambulist. The orphan walks abroad at night."

I held the lantern closer to the young man's pale face. The flame reflected brightly in the boy's eyes, but he did not blink or acknowledge my presence. We were indeed in the presence of a sleepwalker.

"You must have seen him in the garden below your window," I said softly.

Dickens scowled at me so fiercely that I expected him to curse me just as he had cursed his failure of a dog, but his voice was soft when he spoke. "Not at all, my dear Wilkie. I did not see *anyone* in the garden. I arose from my bed, looked at my windows, and clearly saw *Drood's* face there—his foreshortened nose against the glass, his lidless eyes staring at me. Pressed against the window, Wilkie. My high, first-storey window. *Not* in the garden below."

I nodded as if in agreement but knew that the Inimitable had to have been dreaming. Perhaps he had taken some laudanum to help him sleep—I knew that Frank Beard the physician had urged the drug on Dickens when the writer had been unable to sleep in the autumn. I could still feel the pulse and ebb of the medicine in my own system, despite the cold that caused my arm holding the lantern to shake as if I were palsied.

"What do we do with him?" I asked, nodding towards Dickenson this time.

"What one must do with all serious somnambulists, my dear Wilkie. We shall lead him tenderly back to the house and you shall take him into his room to his bed."

I looked in the direction of the slightly lighter rectangle that was the open stable door. "And Drood?" I asked.

Dickens shook his head. "Sultan often returns the day after his nighttime hunts with blood on his muzzle. We can only hope that he does so again in the morning."

I was tempted to ask Dickens what he meant by this. (Inspector Field would value the information.) Had he and his Egyptian mesmerism mentor had a falling-out? Did he wish the phantom dead? Killed by Dickens's own killer dog? Was he no longer a student of the underground mastermind who—according to the former head of the Scotland Yard Detective Bureau—had sent out his agents to kill more than three hundred men and women?

I said nothing. It was too cold to start a conversation. My gout was returning, sending tendrils of agony through my eyes and into my brain the way it was wont to do before a serious episode.

We took Mr Dickenson by his limp arms and led him slowly out of the stable and across the wide yard to the back door. I realised that I would have to towel off the sleepwalking idiot's feet before I tucked him beneath his bedcovers.

As we reached the door, I looked back over the dark yard, half-expecting Sultan to come running into the circle of lantern light with a pale arm or albino ankle or dismembered head in his mouth. But nothing moved other than the cold wind.

"And so ends another Christmas Day at Gad's Hill Place," I said softly. My glasses fogged slightly as we stepped into the relative warmth of the house. I let go of Mr Dickenson long enough to remove and polish them on my coat sleeve.

When I had tucked the ends of the metal frames behind my ears and could see again, I noted that

Dickens's mouth had turned up in that boyish smile with which he had favoured me so many times in the past fourteen years of our acquaintance.

"God bless us, every one," he said in a childish falsetto and we both laughed loud enough to wake the entire household.

CHAPTER FOURTEEN

There was the glowing sphere...no, not quite a sphere, an elongated glowing blue-white oval... and there was the black streak against the dark background.

The streak was on the ceiling and was the result of so many years of smoke rising. The glowing blue-white oval was in front of me, closer, a part of me, an extension of my thoughts.

It was also a moon, a pale satellite in thrall to me. I turned to my left, rolled slightly to my left, and beheld the sun—*a* sun, orange and white rather than blue and white, flickering out rays into the black cosmos. As the glowing blue-white oval was moon to me, so was I satellite to this burning sun in the darkness of space and time.

Something eclipsed my sun. I felt rather than saw the blue-white oval and long pipe connecting it to me snatched away.

"Here, Hatchery, pluck him out of there. Get him on his feet and support him."

"'Ere, 'ere, 'ere," shrieked an utterly alien and totally familiar voice. "The gen'lmum paid for 'is night and product, all undisturbed-like-to-be. Don't be presumin' to..."

"Shut up, Sal," bellowed another familiar voice. A lost giant's voice. "One more peep out of you and the inspector here will have you in the blackest hole in Newgate before the sun comes up."

There were no more peeps. I had been floating above the cloud tops of shifting colours even as I wheeled in space around the spitting, hissing star-sun, my blue-white satellite—now gone—wheeling about me in turn, but now I felt strong hands pulling me down from the cosmic aether to lumpy, muddy, straw-strewn earth.

"Keep him on his feet," rasped the voice I associated with imperious forefingers. "Lift him when you have to."

I was floating again, between dark cribs set into dark walls, the hissing sun receding behind me. A thin colossus rose before me.

"Sal, get Yahee out of the way or I'll snap his smoke-clotted bones clean out of his rotted old flesh and sell them as three'a-penny flutes to the Wild Boys."

"'Ere, 'ere," I heard again. Shadows merged. One was laid back in his coffin. "That's a good, Yahee. Rest easy. 'Ib, Your 'Ighness, this 'ere gen'lmum hasn't paid in full yet. You're pickin' my pocket if you 'aul 'im out o' 'ere."

"You lie, crone," said the dominant of the two men's voices. "You just said he'd paid for the night and drug in full. There was enough in his pipe to keep him addled 'til dawn. But give her another two coins, Detective Hatchery. Anything small."

Then we were out into the night. I noted on the coldness of the air—it smelt of snow not yet fallen—and I noted the absence of my topcoat and my missing top hat and cane and the small miracle of the fact that my feet did not touch the cobblestones as I floated above them towards a distant, rocking streetlamp. Then I realised that the larger of the two shapes still escorting me was carrying me under his arm as if I were a prize pig won at a country fair.

I was recovering from the pipe fumes sufficiently to protest, but the dark form leading the way—I never doubted for a second that it was my nemesis Inspector Field—said, "Hush, now, Mr Collins, there's a public house nearby that will open for us despite the hour and we'll order something for you that will set you right."

A public house that would be open at this hour? As foggy as my sight might have been (and, I realised, as foggy as the cold air itself was this night), no such place could be open in this terrible hour just before dawn on such a harsh, wintry, early-spring morning.

I heard and half-saw Field pounding on a door under a dangling sign: Six Jolly Fellowship-Porters. I knew now, however much my middle hurt from being carried like a country fair pig by Detective Hatchery, that I was not really out here in the cold and dark with these two men at all. I had to be back in my crib-bunk at Opium Sal's, enjoying the last of my blue-bottle smoke.

"Hold your horses!" came a female voice barely audible over the throwing open of various bolts and the creak of an ancient door. "Oh, it's you, Inspector! And you, Detective Hatchery. Both out on so terrible a night? And is that a drowned man you have there, Hib?"

"No, Miss Abbey," said the giant carrying me. "Just a gentleman in need of restoration."

I was carried into the red-curtained tavern and appreciated the warmth—there were still embers in the fire here in the public space—even as I knew this was all a dream. The Six Jolly Fellowship-Porters and its proprietress, Miss Abbey Potterson, were fictions from Dickens's d——ned *Our Mutual Friend*. No public house with that name existed down here near the docks, although there were many that Dickens could have used for reference.

"They burn sherry very well here," said Inspector Field as Miss Abbey lighted various lamps and had a sleepy-eyed boy add more fuel to the small fire. "Perhaps the gentleman might like a bottle?"

I was sure that this dialogue was also straight from *Our Mutual Friend*. Who had said it that my opiated mind might structure this fantasy so? The "Mr Inspector," I realised, was yet another Dickens interpretation of this very same Inspector Field who took his place in a cosy booth.

"The gentleman would like to be turned upright and put *down*," I said in the dream. The blood was rushing to my head now and it was not a totally pleasant sensation.

Hatchery lifted me, righted me, and placed me gently on a bench opposite the inspector. I looked around as if fully expecting to see Mr Eugene Wrayburn and his friend Mortimer Lightwood, but with the exception of the seated inspector, the standing Hatchery, the hustling boy, and the hovering Miss Abbey, the public house was empty.

"Yes, the special sherry, please," said Field. "For the three of us. To take away the chill and the fogs." Miss Abbey and the boy hurried into the back room.

"It won't do," I said to the inspector. "I know this is all a dream."

"Now, now, Mr Collins," said Field, pinching the back of my hand until I yelped, "Opium Sal's is no place for a gentleman such as yourself, sir. If Hatchery and I had not escalpated you when we did, they would've had your wallet and gold teeth in another ten minutes, sir."

"I have no gold teeth," I said, taking care to enunciate each word correctly.

"A figure of speech, sir."

"My topcoat," I said. "My hat. My cane."

Hatchery magically produced all three items and set them in the empty booth across from us.

"No, Mr Collins," continued Inspector Field, "a gentleman such as yourself should contain your opium usage to laudanum as what is sold legally by such upstanding corner apothecaries as Mr Cowper. And leave the opium dens down along the dark docks to the heathen Chinee and the dusky Lascar."

I was not surprised that he knew the name of my principal supplier. This was, after all, a dream.

"It has been some weeks since I have heard from you, sir," continued Field.

I leaned my aching head on my hands. "I've had nothing to say," I said.

"That *is* a problem, Mr Collins," sighed the inspector. "In that it violates both the spirit and specific wording of our agreement."

"Bugger our agreement," I muttered.

"Now, sir," said Field. "We'll get some burned sherry into you so you remember your duties and behaviour as a gentleman."

The boy, whose name, I was certain, was Bob, returned with a huge sweet-smelling jug. In his left hand, Bob carried an iron model of a sugar-loaf hat— Dickens had described this, I remember, and I had paid attention to the written description just as if he and I had not shared a thousand such specialities—into which he emptied the contents of the jug. He then thrust the pointed end of the brimming "hat" deep into the embers and renewed fire, leaving it there while he disappeared, only to reappear again with three clean drinking glasses and the proprietress.

"Thank you, Miss Darby," said Inspector Field as the boy set the glasses in place and plucked the iron vessel from the fire. He gave it a delicate twirl—the thing hissed and steamed—and then poured the heated contents into the original jug. The penultimate part of this small sacrament was when Bob held each of our bright glasses up over the steaming jug, opaquing them to some degree of foggy perfection known only to the boy, and then filled them all to the applause of the inspector and his detective-henchman.

"Thank you, William," said Field.

"William?" I said, confused, even as I put my face forward the better to inhale the warm effulgence emanating from my glass. "Miss Darby? Don't you mean Bob and Miss Abbey? Miss Abbey Potterson?"

"I certainly do not," said Field. "I mean William—as in the good boy Billy Lamper you saw before you just a second ago—and his mistress, Miss Elisabeth Darby, who has owned and run this establishment for twenty-eight years."

"Is this not the Six Jolly Fellowship-Porters?" I asked, taking a careful sip of my drink. My entire body seemed to be tingling as if it were a leg or an arm I had allowed to fall asleep. Except for my head, which was aching.

"I know of no such establishment by that name in London," laughed Inspector Field. "This is the Globe and Pigeon, and has been for years and years. Christopher Marlowe probably dipped his learned wick in a back room here, if not across the street in the riskier White Swann. But the White Swann is not a gentleman's inn, Mr Collins, not even for a gentleman so adventurous as yourself, sir. Nor would the proprietor have opened the door for us and heated our sherry as my lovely Liza has. Drink up, sir, but pray tell me why you've had aught to report as you do so."

The heated drink was slowly clearing my clouded mind. "I tell you again that there's nothing to tell you, Inspector," I said a trifle sharply. "Charles Dickens is preparing for his triumphant tour of the provinces and—the few times I've seen him—there's been no mention of your shared phantom Drood. Not since Christmas Day night."

Inspector Field leaned closer. "When you say Drood levitated outside Mr Dickens's first-floor window."

It was my turn to laugh. I regretted it at once. Stroking my aching forehead with one hand, I lifted the glass with the other. "No," I said, "when Mr *Dickens* said that he saw Drood's face levitating outside his window."

"You do not believe in levitation, Mr Collins?"

"I find it very...unlikely," I said sullenly.

"Yet it seems you express a quite different view on the subject in your papers," said Inspector Field. He made a move of his corpulent forefinger, and the lad Billy hurried to refill both of our still-steamed glasses.

"What papers?" I said.

"I believe they were gathered under the title 'Magnetic Evenings at Home' and were each clearly signed 'W.W.C.'—William Wilkie Collins."

"Dear God!" I cried too loudly. "Those things must have appeared...what?—fifteen years ago." The series of papers he was referring to had been written for the sceptic G. H. Lewes's *Leader* sometime in the early fifties. I had simply reported on various drawing-room experiments that had been much in vogue then: men and women being magnetised, inanimate objects such as glasses of water being magnetised by a mesmerist, "sensitives" reading minds and foretelling the future, attempts to communicate with the dead, and...yes, I remembered now through the opium and alcohol and headache...one woman who had levitated herself and the high-backed chair upon which she sat.

"Have you had reason to change your opinion since you observed these things, Mr Collins?" I found Field's soft but somehow peremptory and insinuating voice as irritating as I always did.

"They were not my opinions, Inspector. Simply my professional observations at the time."

"But you no longer believe that a man or woman—say, someone trained in ancient arts of a long-forgotten society—could levitate ten feet in the air to peer in Charles Dickens's window?"

Enough. I had had *enough* of this.

"I *never* believed in such a thing," I said harshly, my voice rising. "Fourteen or fifteen years ago, as a much younger man, I reported on the…events…of certain drawing-room mystics and on the *credulity* of those gathered to watch such things. I am a modern man, Inspector Field, which in my generation translates to 'a man of little belief.' For instance, I no longer believe that your mysterious Mr Drood even exists. Or, rather, to state it more positively and in the affirmative, I *believe* that both you and Charles Dickens have used the legend of such a figure for your own different and disparate purposes, even while you have each endeavoured to use *me* as some sort of pawn in your game…whatever that game may be."

It was too long a speech for a man in my condition, at this hour of the morning, and I buried my face in the glass of steaming sherry.

I looked up as Inspector Field touched my arm. His florid, veined face was set in a serious expression. "Oh, there's a game all right, Mr Collins, but it's not being played at *your* expense. And there are pawns—and more important pieces—being put into play, but you ain't a pawn, sir. Although it's almost certain that your Mr Dickens is."

I withdrew my sleeve from his grasp. "What are you talking about?"

"Have you wondered, Mr Collins, exactly *why* I have placed so much importance on finding this Drood?"

I could not resist a smirk. "You want your pension back," I said.

I thought this would anger the inspector and therefore was surprised by his quick, easy laugh. "Bless you, Mr Collins, that's true. I do. But that's the least of my goals in this particular chess match. Your Mr Drood and I are on the verge of becoming old men and we've each decided to put an end to this cat-and-mouse game what we've been playing these twenty years and more. Each of us has enough pieces left on the board to make our final move, it's true, but what I believe you do not appreciate, sir, is that the end of this game must... *must*...result in the death of one or t'other of us. Either Drood dead or Inspector Field dead. There's no other way for it, sir."

I blinked several times. Finally I said, "Why?"

Inspector Field leaned closer again and I could smell the warm sherry on his breath. "You may have thought I was exaggerating, sir, when I said that Drood has been responsible, personally and through those mesmerised minions he sends out, for the deaths of three hundred people since he come here from Egypt more than two decades ago. Well, I was not exaggerating, Mr Collins. The actual count is three hundred and twenty-eight. This has to *end*, sir. This Drood has to be put a stop to. So far, all these years, in my service to the Metropolitan Police and out of it, I've been skirmishing with the Devil—we've each sacrificed pawns and rooks and better in this long game—but this is the true End Game, Mr Collins. Either the Devil checkmates my king or I check his. There's no other way for it, sir."

I stared at the inspector. For some time I had been doubting Charles Dickens's sanity; now I knew for certain that there was another insane man affecting my life.

"I know that I've asked for your help with no other offer in recompense than my assistance in keeping the knowledge of Miss Martha R—— from your lady Caroline, sir," said Inspector Field. I thought that was a very polite way to describe his blackmailing of me. "But there are other things that I can offer in exchange for your help, sir. Substantial things."

"What?" I said.

"What is your biggest problem in life at the moment, Mr Collins?"

I was tempted to say "You" and have done with it, but I surprised myself by uttering another syllable. "Pain."

"Aye, sir... you've mentioned the rheumatical gout you're suffering from. And it's visible in your eyes, if I may be so bold as to mention it, Mr Collins. Constant pain is no trifling thing for any man, but especially for an artist such as yourself. Detectives depend on deduction, as you well know, sir, and my deduction is that you've come this awful March night to Opium Sal's and this filthy neighbourhood just in some hope of further assuaging your pain. Is that not so, Mr Collins?"

"Yes," I said. I did not bother telling Field that Frank Beard, my doctor, had recently suggested to me that the "rheumatical gout" I'd long suffered from might very well be a virulent form of a venereal disease.

"It bothers you even as we speak, Mr Collins?"

"My eyes feel like bags of blood," I said truthfully. "I feel that every time I open them, I run the risk of haemorrhaging pints of blood down my face and into my beard."

"Terrible, sir, terrible," said Inspector Field, shaking his head. "I don't blame you for a moment for seeking some relief from your laudanum or the opium pipe. But if you don't mind me telling you so, sir, the grade of product at Opium Sal's simply will not do the trick."

"What do you mean, Inspector?"

"I mean that she dilutes the opium far too much for someone who is in your level of discomfort, Mr Collins. And it is not a pure product to begin with. It is true that a judicious combination of your laudanum and the opium pipe might have salutary—perhaps even miraculous—effects on your affliction, but these Bluegate Fields and Cheapside opium dens simply don't have the quality of drug to help you, sir."

"Where, then?" I asked, but even as I spoke, I knew what he would say.

"King Lazaree," said Inspector Field. "The Chinaman's secret den down in Undertown."

"Down in the crypts and catacombs," I said dully.

"Yes, sir."

"You simply want me to go back to Undertown," I said, meeting the older man's gaze. There was a dim, cold light filtering through the red-curtained windows of the Globe and Pigeon. "You want me to try again to lead you to Drood."

Inspector Field shook his balding and grey-cheek-whiskered head. "No, we'll not find Drood that way, Mr Collins. Mr Dickens undoubtedly told you the truth last autumn when he said that he's been returning regular to Drood's lair, but he's not gone back through the nearby cemetery. We've had men posted there for months. Drood has told him of some other route to his underground world. Either that or the Egyptian Devil is living aboveground all this time and has revealed one of his locations to your Mr Dickens. So your writer friend don't need to enter Undertown by that route any longer, Mr Collins, but *you* can if you wish the relief of King Lazaree's pure opium."

My glass was empty. I looked up at the inspector through eyes suddenly grown watery. "I cannot," I said. "I've tried. I cannot move the heavy bier in the crypt in order to gain access to the stairs."

"I know, sir," said Inspector Field, his voice as professionally smooth and sad as an undertaker's. "But Hatchery will be most glad to help you whenever you wish to go down there, day or night. Won't you, Hib?"

"Most glad, sir," said Hatchery from where he stood

nearby. I confess that I had almost forgotten that the other man was present.

"How would I get word to him?" I asked.

"The boy is still waiting on your street, Mr Collins. Send word through my Gooseberry, and Detective Hatchery will be there within the hour to escort you through the dangerous neighbourhoods, open the way to the staircase for you, and wait upon your return." The infernal inspector smiled. "He will even loan you his revolver again, Mr Collins. But you should have nothing to fear from King Lazaree and his patrons. Unlike Opium Sal's shifty clientele, Lazaree and his living mummies down there know that they are allowed to exist only upon my sufferance."

I hesitated.

"Is there something else we can help you with in exchange for your help in finding Drood through your Mr Dickens?" asked Field. "Some problem at home, perhaps?"

I glanced askance at the old man. What would he know of my problems at home? How could he know that my daily and nightly fights with Caroline had sent me to Sal's as surely as my need to lessen the pain from my gout?

"I've been married for more than thirty years, Mr Collins," he said softly, as if having read my mind. "My speculation is that your lady is, even after all this time, demanding marriage . . . even as your other lady in Yarmouth is demanding to return to London to be near you."

"D——n you, Field," I cried, banging my fist down on the heavy, worn planks of the table. "None of this is any of your business."

"Of course not, sir. Of course not," said the inspector in his oiliest voice. "But such problems can be a distraction to your work as well as to our common goals. I am trying to see how I could be of help...as a friend would."

"There's no help for this," I growled. "And you are no friend."

Inspector Field nodded his understanding. "Still, sir, if you don't mind advice from an old married man, sometimes a change of place buys a period of peace and quiet in such domestic disagreements."

"Move, you mean? We've talked about it, Caroline and I."

"I believe, Mr Collins, that you and the lady have several times walked to look at a fine home on Gloucester Place."

I was no longer surprised or shocked to hear that Field's men had followed us. I would not be surprised to learn that he had secreted a dwarf into the walls of our home on Melcombe Place in order to take notes on our quarrels.

"It is a fine home," I said. "But the current resident, a Mrs Shernwold, does not wish to sell. And I'd be strapped to find the funds for it at this time anyway."

"Both of these impediments could be eliminated, Mr Collins," purred Inspector Field. "If we were working together again, I could all but guarantee that you and your lady and her daughter could be moved into that fine residence on Gloucester Place within a year or two, even while your Miss R—— could be reinstated on Bolsover Street, if you wish, with our help in meeting her travel and other immediate expenses."

I squinted at the old man. My head hurt. I wanted to go home to breakfast and then bed. I wanted to pull the bedcovers over my head and to sleep for a week. We had moved from blackmailing to bribery. On the whole, I believe I had been more comfortable with the blackmail.

"What do I have to do, Inspector?"

"Nothing more than we have already discussed, Mr Collins. Use your good offices with Charles Dickens to find out where Drood is and what he is up to."

I shook my head. "Dickens is completely absorbed in his preparations for his imminent reading tour. I am sure he's had no contact with Drood since Christmas. Besides being frightened by what he thought he saw outside his window that night, Dickens is buried now in details. You have no idea the amount of preparation such a tour involves."

"I am sure I do not, Mr Collins," said Inspector Field. "But I do know that your friend will begin his tour with an opening night reading in a week, on the twenty-third of March, at the Assembly Rooms in Cheltenham. Then, on the tenth of April, he will appear at St James's Hall here in London, followed immediately by readings in Liverpool, then Manchester, then Glasgow, then Edinburgh. . . ."

"Do you have the entire itinerary?" I interrupted.

"Of course."

"Then you would know how impossible it would be for me to get Charles Dickens's attention during the tour. All authors' public readings are exhausting for the author. A Dickens reading is exhausting for the author and for everyone around him. There is simply nothing in the world like a Charles Dickens reading, and he promises this tour to be even more intense."

"So I have heard," Inspector Field said softly. "Somehow, Drood is involved in this reading tour of your friend's."

I laughed. "How could he be? How could a man of such appearance travel with Dickens or be seen at his readings without comment?"

"Drood is a man of infinite guises," Field said. His voice was hushed, as if Hatchery or Miss Darby or the boy Billy could be the Egyptian criminal in disguise. "I *guarantee* that your friend Dickens is—consciously or unconsciously, deliberately or as an instrument of Drood—carrying out that Devil's purposes on this tour."

"How could he…" I began and stopped, remembering Dickens's odd insistence that he would be magnetising the entire audience during each reading. *Mesmerising* them. But to what dark purpose?

This was all absurd.

"Still," I said wearily, "you know Dickens's schedule. And you know he has only a small entourage travelling with him."

"Mr Dolby," said Inspector Field. "His agent Mr Wills." Field went on to name the gas man and lighting expert and even those agents sent in advance to inspect the theatres and arrange for ticketing prices, advertising, and such. "But surely, Mr Collins, Dickens would enjoy seeing his dear friend during such an exhausting tour. I know that he plans to see Macready at the Cheltenham opening. Could you not arrange to spend a few days of travel with your famous friend, attend one or two of his readings?"

"That's all you want of me?"

"Your help in these small things—a simple matter of observing and chatting and reporting—could be invaluable," purred Inspector Field.

"How on earth do you plan to make ninety Gloucester Place available to us, even by next year, if Mrs Shernwold is reserving it for her missionary son and absolutely refuses to sell?" I asked.

The inspector smiled. I half-expected to see canary feathers protruding from between those liver-coloured lips. "That will be my problem, sir, although I expect no problems at all. It is a privilege to help someone aiding us in the public service of ridding London of its least notorious but most successful serial murderer."

I sighed and nodded. If Inspector Field had extended his hand then to seal our dark deal, I'm not sure if I could have touched him. Perhaps he sensed as much, for he merely nodded—the deal was set—and looked around.

"Would you like Miss Darby and the boy to burn us some more sherry, sir? It's a wonderful preparation for sleep."

"No," I said, trying to get to my feet and suddenly feeling Hatchery's huge hand on my arm, effortlessly lifting me out of the booth. "I want to go home."

CHAPTER FIFTEEN

$\mathscr{I}$ chose to join Dickens for a few days well into his tour.

Inspector Field had been correct in saying that Dickens would welcome the idea of my joining him for a bit of time on the road. I sent a note to Wills, who—exhausted as he must have been from travelling every day with the Inimitable—flitted back to London every few days from the tour to carry on his own and Dickens's business affairs at the magazine with Forster (who disapproved of the entire idea of the reading tour), and within a day I received back that rarest of things for me—a telegram—which read,

> MY DEAR WILKIE—THE TOUR IS <u>SUCH</u> FUN! OUR DOLBY HAS TURNED OUT TO BE THE <u>PERFECT</u> TRAVEL COMPANION AND MANAGER. YOU WILL ENJOY HIS ANTICS. I CERTAINLY DO. JOIN US AT ANY TIME AND TRAVEL WITH US AS LONG AS YOU WISH. AT YOUR OWN EXPENSE, OF COURSE. LOOKING FORWARD TO YOUR COMPANY!—C. DICKENS

I had wondered how the Staplehurst accident was affecting the Inimitable's almost daily railway journeys, and I discovered this a few minutes after we had departed the station in Bristol on our way to Birmingham.

I was sitting directly across from Dickens in the compartment. He was sitting alone on his bench. George Dolby and Wills occupied the seat beside me but they were chatting, and perhaps I alone could see that the author was becoming more agitated as our carriage got up to speed. Dickens's hands fiercely gripped first the head of his walking stick and then the sill of the window. He would glance out the window as the vibrations increased, then look away quickly, then glance out again. His face, usually darker than most Englishmen's due to the effects of the sun during his daily walks, grew paler and was moist with perspiration. Then Dickens removed his travelling flask from his pocket, took a long pull of brandy, breathed more deeply, took a second pull, and put the flask away. Then he lit a cigar and turned to chat with Dolby, Wills, and me.

The Inimitable preferred an interesting—even eccentric, possibly even dashing—wardrobe for his travel: a pea jacket over which he tossed an expensive Count D'Orsay cloak; his grizzled and weary visage, his lined skin bronzed by sun (the pallor had faded with the brandy and was now almost gone), peeking out from beneath a felt hat worn rather jauntily to one side. I'd overheard the bearlike Dolby tell the scarecrow-thin Wills at the Bristol station that the hat "makes the chief look like a modernised gentlemanly pirate with eyes in which lurk the iron will of a demon and the tender pity of an angel."

I think Dolby had also been partaking of some brandy that morning.

The conversation was lively—we were the only passengers in this first-class compartment, the rest of the small entourage having gone on to Birmingham before us. I had heard from Dickens that during the first days of the tour, Wills had put Dolby through very thorough cross-examinations on how the business manager would handle his work. During those first city readings, Dolby had gone ahead with the gas and lighting men and only Wills had travelled each day with Dickens. Now, with Liverpool, Manchester, Glasgow, Edinburgh, and Bristol behind them—and no major problems in any of those cities, so thorough was Dolby's work—the big business manager was travelling with Dickens, much to the Inimitable's obvious delight. The rest of the tour consisted of Birmingham, Aberdeen, Portsmouth, and then home to the final performances in London.

Dolby, whom a later client—an American writer named Mark Twain—would describe as "a gladsome gorilla," reached into the large wicker basket he had brought aboard, set linen on the tiny folding table he had thought to provide for the centre of our compartment, and proceeded to present a buffet luncheon of hard-boiled-egg sandwiches with anchovy, salmon mayonnaise, cold fowl and tongue, and pressed beef, with Roquefort cheese and cherry tart for our dessert. He also set out a rather good red wine and kept a gin punch chilled by filling the compartment's washstand with ice. As the rest of us finished this repast, Dolby warmed coffee over a spirit lamp. Whatever else the huge, whiskered man with his infectious laugh and rather endearing stammer might be, he was certainly efficient.

After a second bottle of wine was opened and the chilled gin punch was finished, the group began to sing travelling songs—some of which I'd sung with Dickens when it had been just the two of us wandering around the country or in Europe the previous decade. This day, as we approached Birmingham, Dickens was moved to dance a sailor's hornpipe for us as we all whistled accompaniment. When he was finished and out of breath, Dolby gave him the last glass of punch and Dickens began teaching us the drinking song from *Der*

Freischütz. Suddenly an express roared past us going the opposite way on the adjoining track and Dickens's lovely felt hat was whisked right off his balding head by the vacuum. Wills, who seemed more the consumptive type than an athlete, launched his long arm out the window and caught the hat just before it disappeared forever into the countryside. We all applauded and Dickens pounded the frail man heartily on the back.

"I lost a sealskin cap earlier on this tour under almost exactly the same circumstances," Dickens said to me as he took the felt hat from Wills and tugged it back on. "I would have hated parting ways with this chapeau. Thank God Wills is famous for his defensive fielding. I can't remember whether he was famous for playing at Deep fine leg or Backward short leg, but his fielding abilities are legendary. His shelves groan with silver cups."

"I have never played the game of…" began Wills.

"Never mind, never mind," laughed Dickens, clapping his companion on the back again. George Dolby boomed out laughter that must have been heard from one end of our express to the other.

IN BIRMINGHAM, I got a taste of the texture and timing of the tour.

I had certainly stayed in my share of hotels, and while such travel was usually enjoyable, I was very aware of Dickens's ill health the previous winter and spring and also knew from personal experience that constant travel and the vagaries of hotel life do little to allow recovery from ill health. He had confided in me that his left eye continued to blur and ache fiercely, that his belly constantly felt distended, that flatulence was a problem all during the tour, and that the vibration of the trains gave him a sort of nausea and vertigo from which he never had time to recover during his short stays in the cities in which he performed. Balancing near-daily travel and exhausting nights of reading was obviously pushing Dickens to and beyond the limits of his endurance.

Upon arriving in Birmingham, before resting or unpacking his valise, Dickens hurried over to the theatre. Wills was preoccupied with other duties, but Dolby and I followed the Inimitable.

Touring the hall with the theatre owner, Dickens immediately ordered changes. As per his instructions, seats on either side of the stage and certain box seats had been either removed or roped off, but now he stood at his customised reading lectern and ordered even more seats on either side of the large theatre to be eliminated. *Everyone attending his reading had to be within direct and unoccluded line of sight.* Not only to see him clearly, I understood, but so that he could make eye contact with *them.*

His advance workers had already erected a large maroon screen that would be behind him as he spoke; the screen was seven feet high and fifteen feet wide and there was a carpet of the same colour between the screen and his lectern. The unique gas lighting was also in place. Here Dickens's gas man and lighting expert had set two upright pipes rising about twelve feet on either side of his reading lectern. Connecting the two pipes but hidden from the sight of the audience by a maroon board was a horizontal row of gaslights in tin reflectors. In addition to this bright lighting, there was a gaslight on each pipe that was protected by a green shade and which was aimed directly at the reader's face.

I stood in the glow of this clever lighting rig and the two targeted lamps for only a minute but the glare was intimidating. I would have found it very difficult, if not impossible, to read from any book with those lights shining in my face, but I knew that Dickens rarely if ever *read* from his prompt books doing these ostensible readings. He had memorised all the hundreds of pages of text he would be performing—read and memorised and altered and improved and rehearsed each story at least two hundred times—and would either close the book he had in his hand after beginning his performance or merely turn the pages, absentmindedly and symbolically, as he went along. Most of the time his eyes would be staring through the blazing rectangle of gas lighting towards the audience. Yet for all that ferocious gaslit glow, Dickens could still see the faces of all those in his audience. He deliberately left the house lighting high enough for that.

Before relinquishing my spot at Charles Dickens's reading desk, I studied the desk itself. Propped on four slender and elegant legs, the table rose to about the height of the Inimitable's inimitable navel. Flat-topped, the desk was covered by a crimson piece of cloth this afternoon. On either side of the table were small ledges, the one on the right designed to hold a carafe of water, the one on the left meant for Dickens's expensive kid gloves and a pocket handkerchief. Also on the left side of the desktop was a rectangular block of wood on which Dickens could—and frequently did—rest either his left or right elbow when he leaned forward. (He often read from just to the left of the desk itself and, I knew from seeing him at previous readings in London, might suddenly lean forward almost boyishly with his right elbow on that raised block and his expressive hands in motion. The effect was to make the audience feel an even more personal and intimate bond with him.)

Now Dickens cleared his throat and I moved away from the desk and down off the stage as the author stood at his reading desk and tested the acoustics of the hall with various snippets from the readings he would do that night. I joined George Dolby in the last row of the balcony.

"The Chief began the tour by reading from his Christmas story 'Doctor Marigold,'" whispered Dolby although we were far away from Dickens. "But it didn't quite work, at least not to the Chief's satisfaction—and I do not have to tell you that he is the ultimate perfectionist—so he improves it while leaning towards more of the old favourites: the death scene of Paul from *Dombey and Son,* the Mr, Mrs, and Miss Squeers scene from *Nicholas Nickleby,* the trial from *Pickwick,* the storm scene of *David Copperfield,* and, of course, *A Christmas Carol.* The audiences can never get enough of *A Christmas Carol.*"

"I am sure they cannot," I said drily. I was on record for noting my disdain for the "Cant and Christmas season." I also noticed that Dolby's stammer was not present when he whispered. How very strange such afflictions are. Having been reminded of afflictions, I removed the small travelling flask that now held my laudanum and took several swallows of it. "I am sorry I cannot offer you some of this," I said to Dolby in a conversational tone, unintimidated by Dickens's still reciting snippets of this and that from his distant stage. "Medicine."

"I understand perfectly," whispered Dolby.

"I am surprised that 'Doctor Marigold' did not please the masses," I said. "Our Christmas Issue with that story sold more than two hundred and fifty thousand copies."

Dolby shrugged. "The Chief got laughs and tears with it," he said softly. "But not *enough* laughs and tears, he said. And not at precisely the right times. So he set it aside."

"Pity," I said, feeling the careless warmth of the drug enter my system. "Dickens rehearsed it for more than three months."

"The Chief rehearses *everything*," whispered Dolby.

I did not know how I felt about this absurd appellation of "Chief" that Dolby had assigned to Dickens, but the Inimitable himself seemed to enjoy the title. From everything I could perceive, Dickens enjoyed almost everything about the big, burly, stammering bear of a manager. I had no doubt that this common theatrical tradesman was usurping the position of close friend and occasional confidant that I had held with Dickens for more than a decade now. Not for the first time—and not for the first time under the clarity of laudanum—I saw precisely how Forster, Wills, Macready, Dolby, Fitzgerald—all of us—were mere planets vying and contesting to see who could circle the closest revolutions around the grizzled, flatulent, lined, and greying Sun that was Charles Dickens.

Without another word I rose and left the theatre.

I HAD INTENDED to return to the hotel—Dickens would go there to rest the few hours before his performance, I knew, but would withdraw into himself, not engaging in conversation until after the long night of readings was over—but found myself wandering the dark and sooty streets of Birmingham, wondering why I was there.

Eight years earlier, in the autumn of 1858—after I had accompanied Dickens on that fool's errand of a trip north pursuing Ellen Ternan (being convinced by Dickens that we were travelling as research for our collaboration on *Lazy Tour of Two Idle Apprentices*) and after I had almost died on Carrick Fell—I returned to London with my eye firmly fixed on the theatre. Immediately after the success of *The Frozen Deep* the previous year, the famous actor Frederick "Frank" Robson had purchased my earlier melodrama *The Lighthouse*—which Dickens had starred in just as he had in *The Frozen Deep*—and on 10 August, 1857, my dream of becoming a professional dramatist came true. Dickens sat with me in the author's box and applauded as others did (I confess to standing and taking a bow during the ovation) but "ovation" may be too strong a word; the applause sounded rather more respectful than enthusiastic.

Reviews of *The Lighthouse* were equally respectful and tepid. Even gentle John Oxenford of the *Times* wrote—*"We cannot avoid the conclusion that* The Lighthouse, *with all its merits, is rather a dramatic anecdote than an actual drama."*

Despite this effluvium of tepidity, for months in 1858 I had—to use a phrase I shared with Dickens then—exhausted my brains in the service of more theatrical composition.

It was Dickens's son Charley, just back from Germany and sharing impressions of a grisly place there in Frankfurt called the Dead House, who gave me my inspiration. I immediately put pen to paper and dashed off a play called *The Red Vial*. My two lead characters were a lunatic and a lady poisoner (I have always had a fascination with poison and those who poison). I set the main scene of *The Red Vial* in the Dead House. I confess, Dear Reader, that I thought the set and setting wonderful—a room full of corpses all laid out on cold slabs under sheets, each with a finger wrapped in a string that led upward to a dangling alarm bell, should one of the "dead" not be dead at all. The entire macabre setting reached into the deepest areas of our fears of premature burial and the walking dead.

Dickens himself said little when I proposed the idea and later when I read him the actual sections of the play as I finished them, but he did visit London's asylum in quest of small details that would add more believability to my lead lunatic. Robson, who had done such a fine job in *The Lighthouse*, accepted the play for the Olympic Theatre and took the role of the lunatic. I enjoyed the rehearsals immensely, and all of the actors involved assured me that the play was wonderful. They agreed with my premise that although London theatre-goers had become a lumpen lot with dulled minds, a sufficiently strong stimulation might awaken them.

On 11 October, 1858, Dickens accompanied me to *The Red Vial*'s premiere performance and arranged an after-theatre supper party for me and my friends at his now wifeless home at Tavistock House. A group of at least twenty of us sat together during the performance.

It was a disaster. While my friends shuddered at the delightfully morbid and melodramatic parts, the rest of the audience snickered. The loudest snickers came at the climax of my Dead House scene where—too obviously, according to critics after the fact—one of the corpses rang the bell.

There was no second performance. Dickens tried to be upbeat during all the rest of that endless night, telling jokes at the expense of London audiences, but the supper at Tavistock House was very trying for me. As I later overheard that brat Percy Fitzgerald say—*it was a real case of funeral baked meats*.

But the disaster of *The Red Vial* did nothing to dissuade me from my decided course of simultaneously disturbing, fascinating, and repelling my fellow countrymen. Shortly after the wild success of *The Woman in White*, I was asked the secret of my success and I modestly told my interlocutor—

1. Find a central idea
2. Find the characters

3. Let the characters develop the incidents
4. Begin the story at the beginning

Compare, if you will, this almost scientific artistic principle with the haphazard way that Charles Dickens had thrown his novels together over the decades: pulling characters out of the air (often based willy-nilly on people in his own life) without a thought as to how they might serve the central purpose, mixing in a plethora of random ideas, having characters wander off into incidental occurrences and unimportant side-plots having nothing to do with the overriding idea, and often beginning his story in mid-flight, as it were, violating the important Collins principle of first-things-first.

It was a miracle that we had been able to collaborate the number of times we had. I prided myself not a small bit on bringing some coherence to the plays, stories, travel accounts, and longer works we had outlined or worked on together.

So why, I wondered on this unseasonably cool and rainy May evening in Birmingham, was I here watching Dickens as he was entering the last legs of what sounded to be an amazingly successful reading tour of England and Scotland? Critics incessantly criticised my flair for what they called "melodrama," but what on earth should one call this new and bizarre combination of literature and rampant theatricals that Dickens was pursuing on the stage this very night? No one in our profession had ever seen anything like it before. No one in the *world* had ever seen or heard anything like it before. It demeaned the role of author and turned literature into a half-shilling carnival. Dickens was pandering to the masses like an onstage clown with a dog.

These were the thoughts that were in my mind at the time I walked down a dismal, windowless street—more alley than lane if truth be told—as I turned back towards my hotel, only to find two men barring my path.

"Excuse me, please," I said brusquely, waving my gold-headed cane to get them out of the way.

They did not budge.

I walked to the right in the narrow lane, but they moved to their left. I stopped and began walking to my left, and they shifted to their right.

"What is this?" I demanded. Their only answer was to begin moving towards me. Both men put their hands in their tattered jacket pockets and when those calloused, filthy hands emerged, it was with short knives.

I turned quickly and began hurrying towards the main thoroughfare, only to see a third man step into the lane and block it, his bulky form a threatening silhouette against the brighter evening light beyond him. He also held something in his right hand. Something that glinted in that failing light.

I confess here, Dear Reader, that my heart began to pound wildly and I felt an urgent liquidity in the region of my bowels. I do not like to think of myself as a coward—what man does?—but I am a small man, and a peaceful one, and though I might write fiction from time to time about violence, fisticuffs, mayhem, and murder, these are not things that I had then personally experienced, nor wanted to.

At that moment I wanted to run. I had the absurd but real compulsion to call out for my mother, although Harriet was hundreds of miles away.

Even though none of the three men said a word, I reached into my jacket and removed my long wallet. Many of my friends and acquaintances—certainly Dickens—thought me a shade too reluctant to part with money. Actually, Dickens and his friends, all having been gifted with money for many years, ignored my need for pecuniary discipline and thought me cheap, a penny-pinching miser in the mode of pre-revelation Ebenezer Scrooge.

But at that moment I would have given up every pound and shilling I had on me—and even my not-gold but quite serviceable watch—if these ruffians would only let me pass.

As I said, they did not demand money. Perhaps that is what frightened me most. Or perhaps it was the terribly serious and inhuman looks on their bewhiskered faces—especially the alert deadness combined with something like anticipatory joy in the grey eyes of the largest man, who approached me now with knife raised.

"Wait!" I said weakly. And again, "Wait...wait..."

The big man in the shabby clothes raised the knife until it was almost touching my chest and neck.

"Wait!" shouted a much louder and much more commanding voice from behind the four of us, towards the thoroughfare, where there was still light and hope.

My assailants and I all turned to look.

A small man in a brown suit was standing there. Despite the commanding voice, the figure was no taller than I. He was hatless, and I could see short, curly grey hair plastered to his head by the light rain that was falling.

"Go away, friend," growled the man holding the knife to my throat. "You don't want no part of this."

"Oh, but I do," said the short man and ran towards us.

All three of my assailants turned in his direction, but my legs felt too unsteady to allow me to bolt. I was sure that within seconds both I and my would-be rescuer would be lying dead on the filthy paving stones in that unnamed, lightless lane.

The brown-suited man, whom I had first thought to be as portly as I but who I now saw to be compact but as muscled as a diminutive acrobat, reached into his tweedy suit jacket and quickly brought out a short, obviously weighted piece of wood that looked like a cross between a sailor's marlin spike and a policeman's club. This club had a dull, heavy head and appeared to be cored with lead or something as heavy.

Two of my assailants leaped at him. The brown-suited stranger broke the wrist and ribs of the first thug with two quick swings and then cracked the second one over the head with a sound such as I had never heard before. The burliest of my attackers—the whiskered and deadly-eyed man who had, only a second before, been holding the knife to my throat—extended the blade with his thumb atop it and feinted and whirled and lunged and swung at my rescuer from a poised, catlike crouch, all dance-like motions which, I am sure, had been honed in a thousand back-alley knife fights.

The brown-suited man jumped back as his attacker's blade swung first right and then back left in vicious arcs that would have disemboweled him if not for his agility. Then—much more quickly than one could ever imagine judging from his stolid appearance—my saviour leaped in, broke our mutual assailant's right forearm with a downward swing of his small cudgel, broke the thug's jaw with the backhand return of the same swing, and—as the big man fell—struck him a third time in the groin with such violence that I winced and cried out myself, and then hit him a final time in the back of the head as the thug went first to his knees and then to his face in the mud.

Only the first assailant, the one with the broken ribs and wrist, remained conscious. He was staggering towards the darkness deeper in the alley.

The brown-suited man ran him down, spun him, struck him twice in the face with the short but deadly weapon, kicked his legs out from under him, and then struck him a final savage blow to the head as he lay there moaning. Then there were no more moans.

The compact man in brown turned towards me.

I admit that I backed away with my hands up, palms open imploringly towards the short, deadly figure that approached. I had come very, very close to soiling my linen. Only the incredible—I would say *impossible*—speed of the violence I had just witnessed had prevented my full and total reaction of fear.

I had written about violent altercations many times, but the physical events were all recorded as if choreographed and carried out in slow, deliberate motions. All of the real violence I had just witnessed—certainly the worst I had ever witnessed, and the most savage—had happened in seven or eight seconds. There was, I realised, a very real chance that I might vomit if the brown-suited terror did not kill me first. I held my hands up and tried to speak.

"It's all right, Mr Collins," said the man, tucking his cudgel into his jacket pocket and firmly taking me by the arm and leading me back the way I had come, out into the thoroughfare light. Broughams and cabs passed as if nothing extraordinary had just happened.

"Who…who…are you?" I managed. His grip was as relentless as one imagines a smithy vice's steel grip might be.

"Mr Barris, sir. At your service. We need to get you back to the hotel, sir."

"Barris?" I was ashamed to hear the quaver and stammer in my voice. I have always prided myself on being cool in difficult situations, at sea or on the land (although in recent months and years, I admit, that equanimity had been in small part due to the laudanum).

"Yes, sir. Reginald Barris. *Detective* Reginald Barris. Reggie to my friends, Mr Collins."

"You're Birmingham police?" I said as we turned

east and began walking quickly, his hand still on my arm.

Barris laughed. "Oh, no, sir. I work for Inspector Field. Came up from London by way of Bristol, just as you did, sir."

One uses the word "wobbly" in relation to "legs" often enough in fiction; it is a cliché. To actually *feel* legs so unsteady and wobbly that it is difficult to walk is an absurd situation, especially to someone like me, who loves to sail and who has not the slightest problem per-ambulating on a pitching deck in the high seas of the Channel.

I managed to say, "Should we not go back? Those three men might be injured."

Barris, if that was his true name, chuckled. "Oh, I guarantee that they are injured, Mr Collins. One is dead, I believe. But we are not going back. Leave them lie."

"Dead?" I repeated stupidly. I could not believe that. I *would* not believe that. "We must inform the police."

"The police?" said Barris. "Oh, no, sir. I think not. Inspector Field would sack me if I got my name and our Private Enquiries firm's name in the Birmingham and London papers. And you might be delayed here for days, Mr Collins. And called back to testify in an endless series of inquests and hearings. And all for three street thugs who were ready to cut your throat to steal your purse? Please, sir, put such thoughts out of your mind."

"I don't understand," I said as we turned east on an even wider street. I recognised the way back to the hotel now. The lamps were being lit all along this busy boulevard. "Did Field send you to...watch over me? Protect me?"

"Yes, sir," said Barris, releasing my arm at last. I could feel the blood rush in where he had cut off circulation. "That is, sir, there are two of us...ah...accompanying you and Mr Dickens on this tour. In case Mr Drood should make an appearance, sir. Or his agents."

"Drood?" I said. "Agents? Do you believe that those three men were sent by Drood to kill me?" For some reason, this thought caused my bowels to go loose again. This Drood fantasy had all been a clever if somewhat tiring game up to this point.

"Them, sir? Oh, no, sir. I'm quite sure that those blackguards had nothing to do with this Drood the inspector is hunting for. Nothing at all, sir. You can be confident of that."

"How?" I said as the hotel came into sight. "Why?"

Barris smiled thinly. "They were white, sir. Drood almost never uses white men in his service, although the occasional German or Irishman has been known. No, he would've sent Chinamen or Lascars or Hindoos or even some black just off a ship if he'd wanted you dead here or in Bristol, sir. Well, here is your and Mr Dickens's hotel, Mr Collins. One of my colleagues is there and will look after your well-being once you've entered the lobby. I'll stand here and watch until you reach the doors, sir."

"Colleague?" I repeated. But Barris had stepped back into the shadows of an alley and now raised his hand to his forehead as if tipping an invisible bowler.

I turned and wobbled towards the lighted doorway of the hotel.

I HAD NO INTENTION of attending Dickens's performance after such a terrible experience, but after a warm bath and at least four cups of laudanum—I drained my flask and refilled it from the carefully wrapped bottle I'd brought in my luggage—I decided to dress appropriately for the evening and go to the reading. This was, after all, the reason I had come to Birmingham.

I knew from Wills and Dolby that Dickens was all but unapproachable in the last hour or two before his nightly performance. He and his manager walked to the theatre and I took a cab over a bit later. I had no intention of walking alone, in the dark, on Birmingham streets again. (If Detective Barris or his colleagues were out there watching me, I did not see them as the hansom cab dropped me at the side door of the theatre.)

It was quarter to eight and the audience was just arriving. I stood at the back of the hall and watched as Dickens's gas and lighting experts appeared, appraised the structure of dark pipes and unlit lamps from positions on both sides of the theatre, and then withdrew. A moment later the gas man appeared alone, made some adjustment to the overhead lamps hidden behind the maroon cloth–covered board, and withdrew again. Several minutes later the gas man appeared a third time and turned on the gas. The effect of the lighting against the dark background, dim at this point but clearly illuminating Dickens's reading table, was quite striking. There were hundreds of people in their seats by this time, and all became quiet and strained to watch with a focused interest that was almost palpable.

George Dolby ambled onto the stage and peered up at the low lighting, down at the table, and out at the congregating audience with an air of self-importance. Dolby slightly repositioned the carafe of water on Dickens's table, nodded as if satisfied by this important and essential adjustment, and slowly disappeared behind the high screen that extended from the curtained side of the stage to the central reading area. As I walked up the side of the platform to go backstage myself, Dolby coming in just behind me, I thought of Shakespeare's most famous of stage instructions, from *A Winter's Tale*—"Exit, pursued by a bear."

In his dressing room, Dickens was in formal evening clothes. I was glad that I had decided to wear mine, although everyone who knew me also knew how little I cared for formal clothing or the proper appearance. But this night the white tie and tails seemed appropriate... perhaps even necessary.

"Ah, my dear Wilkie," said the Inimitable as I entered. "It is so *kind* of you to attend the proceedings this night." He appeared completely calm, but it was as if he had forgotten that I had spent the day travelling to Birmingham with him.

There was a bouquet of scarlet geraniums on his dressing table, and he now cut one for his buttonhole, adjusted it, and then cut another and set it in my lapel.

"Come," he said as he adjusted his gold watch-chain and made a final check of buttons and beard and oiled curls in the mirror. "We shall peek out at the natives in the hope that they are becoming restless."

We went out onto the stage itself, behind the shielding screen where Dolby was still hovering. Dickens showed me a small chink in the screen where—once a flap of fabric had been moved aside—we could look out at the now completely assembled and mildly fidgeting audience. He allowed me a glimpse. *I* felt anxious at that moment and wondered, for all my theatrical experience as an actor, if I should ever be able to carry out a reading without succumbing to nervousness, but Dickens himself showed no anxiety whatsoever. The gas man came up to him, Dickens nodded, leaned closer to the hole in the screen, and—as the gas man calmly walked out onto the stage to make the final adjustment to the lamps—the Inimitable whispered to me, "This is my favourite part of the evening, Wilkie."

I leaned so close that I could smell the pomade on the author's side curls as we both watched through the chink. Suddenly the lights went up dramatically and some two thousand faces were illuminated in reflected light as an "Aaahhhhh..." of expectation rose from the audience.

"You'd best take your seat, my friend," whispered Dickens. "I wait another minute or so to whet their anticipation, then we shall begin."

I had started to leave when he waved me back. Putting his mouth close to my ear, he whispered, "Keep your eye out for Drood. He might be anywhere."

I could not tell if he was serious, so I nodded and moved away in the dark and then out, finding my way to the side stairs, then up against the flow of late arrivers to the rear of the hall, and then down towards the stage again to my reserved seat along the aisle about two-thirds of the way back. I had asked Wills to set aside this seat for me so that I might slip out to join Dickens in the dressing room more easily at the break about ninety minutes into the two-hour reading. The maroon carpet on the stage, simple table, and even the carafe of water—illuminated as they were by the bright lights—seemed pregnant with potential in that last minute before Dickens appeared.

Suddenly there erupted an explosion of applause as Dickens's slim figure walked to his reading desk. The applause rose and continued at a deafening level, but Dickens ignored it completely, pouring some water for himself from the carafe and waiting silently for the ovation to abate much as one might wait for carriages to pass before crossing a street. Then, when silence finally descended, Dickens...did nothing. He merely stood there looking out at the audience, occasionally turning his head slightly so as to see everyone. It was as if he were meeting the gaze of every single man and woman there that night...and there now must have been more than two thousand of us crowded into the hall.

A few stragglers were finding their seats near the rear

of the theatre and Dickens waited with that total and somehow unsettling calm until they did so. Then he seemed to fix *them* for a few seconds with his cool, serious, intense, yet mildly questioning gaze.

Then he began.

Several years after this night in Birmingham, Dolby was to say to me—"Watching the Chief read during those last years was not like attending a performance; it was more like being part of a *spectacle*. It was not at all a matter of being entertained; it was a case of being *haunted*."

Haunted. Yes, perhaps. Or possessed, as the spirit rappers so in vogue in my day, Dear Reader, were supposedly possessed by their spirit guides to the Other Side. But it was not only Charles Dickens who seemed possessed during these readings; the entire audience joined him. As you will see, it was hard *not* to join him.

It saddens me, Dear Reader, that no one in your future generation will have heard or seen Charles Dickens read. There are experiments in my time as I write this with recording voices on various cylinders almost as photographers capture images of a person on film plates. But all this has come after Charles Dickens's death. No one in your day will ever hear his thin, slightly lisping voice or—since to my knowledge none of his talks were ever captured on daguerreotype or other photographic devices (and since such forms of photography available in Dickens's day were too slow to record any person in even the slightest motion anyway, and Dickens was *always* in motion)—see the strange change that came over the Inimitable and his audiences during these performances. His readings were unique in our day and—I would venture the opinion—will never be equalled or adequately imitated in yours (if authors still write books at all in this future you inhabit).

Even in the glare of those brilliant gaslights, a strange, iridescent cloud seemed to hover around Charles Dickens as he read from his most recent Christmas tale. That cloud, I believe, was the ectoplasmic manifestation of the many characters whom Dickens had created and whom he now summoned—one at a time—to speak and act before us.

As these ghosts entered him, Dickens's posture would change. He would jerk alert or slump in despondency or laziness as the character's spirit dictated. The author's face would change immediately and totally—some facial muscles used so frequently by Charles Dickens going lax, others coming into play. Smiles, leers, frowns, and conspiratorial glances never used by the man who lived at Gad's Hill flitted across the face of this spirit-possessed receptacle in front of us. His voice changed from second to second, and even in rapid-fire exchanges of dialogue Dickens seemed to be inhabited by two or more possessing demons at once.

In other readings, I had heard his tone shift instantly from the hoarse, rasping, lisping, urgent, whispered croak of Fagin—"Aha! I like that thellow'th lookth. He'd be of use to uth; he knows how to train the girl already. Don't make ath much noise as a mouthe, my dear, and let me hear 'em talk—let me hear 'em"—to the sombre tenor of Mr Dombey to the silly, mincing tones of Miss Squeers, and then to a Cockney so perfect that no actor then on the English stage could rival his accent.

But it was more than voice and language that drew us all in that night. Everything about Dickens would change in the instant when he slipped from one character to the next (or in that instant when one character departed his body and another entered). When he became the Jew Fagin, Dickens's eternally upright, almost martial posture would melt into the rounded, hunched-shouldered stoop of that evil man. The author's brow seemed to rise and elongate, his eyebrows grew bushier, as his eyes receded into two dark wells and seemed to gleam of their own accord in the bright gaslight. Dickens's hands, so composed and assured when he was reading descriptive passages, would quiver, clutch one another, rub themselves fitfully, twitch with money hunger, and try to hide themselves in sleeves when they belonged to Fagin. While reading, Dickens would pace several steps to this side of his customised desk, then several steps the other way, and though the motion was smooth and confident when it was Dickens standing there, it became lithe, shifty, and almost snakelike when he was possessed by the spirit of Fagin.

"These characters and changes are as real for me as they are for the audience," Dickens had told me before this particular reading tour began. "So real are my fictions to myself that I do not recall them but see them done again before my very eyes, for it all happens before me. And the audience sees this reality."

I certainly did that night. Whether it was because of the consumption of oxygen by the gas flames or because of the literally mesmeric quality of Dickens's face and hands illuminated so starkly against the dark maroon background due to the unique lighting, I constantly felt the author's eyes on me—even when those eyes belonged to one of his characters—and, with that audience, I entered into a kind of trance.

When he was Dickens again, reading narration and description rather than character-inhabited dialogue, I could hear the unfaltering certainty in his voice, sense the enjoyment revealed in the gleam of his eye, and perceive a real hint of aggression—masked as confidence to the majority of the crowd, I was sure—coming from his own knowledge that he could mesmerise so many for so long.

Then the Christmas tale and bit of *Oliver Twist* were finished, the longer, ninety-minute segment of the evening finished, the interval in the evening's performance arrived at, and Dickens turned and left the platform, as seemingly oblivious of the crowd's wild applause as he had been when first coming on stage.

I shook my head as if awakening from a dream and went backstage.

Dickens was sprawled on a couch and appeared to be too exhausted to rise or move. Dolby bustled in and out, supervising a waiter who was setting out a glass of iced champagne and a plate with a dozen oysters. Dickens stirred himself to sip the champagne and suck down the oysters.

"It's the only thing the Chief can eat in the evening," Dolby whispered to me.

Hearing the whisper, Dickens looked up and said, "My dear Wilkie... how splendid of you to pop in during the interval. Did you enjoy the first part of the evening's fare?"

"I did," I said. "It was... extraordinary... as always."

"I believe I told you that we shall be replacing the 'Doctor Marigold' parts should I accept more such engagements in the autumn or winter," said Dickens.

"But the audience loved it," I said.

Dickens shrugged. "Not as much as they love Dombey or Scrooge or Nickleby, which I shall read in a few minutes."

I was sure that the programme had listed the Trial from *The Pickwick Papers* as the thirty-minute reading scheduled for after the interval—Dickens always preferred to end the evenings with sentiment and laughter—but I was not about to correct him.

The ten minutes were almost up. Dickens rose with some effort, cast his heat-wilted scarlet geranium into the trash, and set a new one in his buttonhole.

"I shall see you after the reading," I said and went back out to join the eager multitudes.

As the applause died, Dickens took up his book and pretended to read aloud, "Nicholas Nickleby at Mr Squeers's School...Chapter the First." So it was to be Nickleby.

None of the exhaustion I had glimpsed backstage was evident now. Dickens seemed even more energetic and animated than he had been during the first ninety minutes. The power of his reading once again reached out like a magnetic current to fix and align the audience's attention as if their eyes and minds were so many needles on a compass. Once again, the Inimitable's gaze seemed to settle on each and every one of us.

Despite that powerful magnetic attraction, my mind began to wander. I began to think of other things—the publication of my novel *Armadale* in two volumes would be a fact within the week—and it occurred to me that I had to settle on a plot and theme for my next book. Perhaps something shorter and even more sensationalist, although with a simpler plot than the labyrinthine *Armadale*...

Suddenly I snapped back to attention.

Everything had changed in the huge hall. The light seemed thicker, slower, darker, almost gelatinous.

It was silent. Not the attention-silence of more than two thousand people that had existed an instant earlier—with coughs being stifled, laughter punctuating the silence, the stirrings of so many after more than two hours of listening—but now it was an *absolute* silence. It was as if twenty-one hundred people had suddenly died. There was not the slightest hint of breathing or movement. I realised that I could not hear or feel my own breathing, nor sense my own heartbeat. The

Birmingham hall had turned into a giant crypt and was just that silent.

At the same moment, I realised that up through the darkness rose hundreds of slender, white, barely perceptible cords, their ends tied to the middle finger on the right hand of every member of the audience. The air was so dark that I could not make out the point at which these twenty-one hundred cords converged above us, but I knew that they must be connected to a massive bell up there. We were, all of us, in the Dead House. The cords—silken ropes, I realised—were tied to us in case one of us might still be alive. The bell, whose tone and toll, I knew instinctively, would be too terrible to hear, was there to alert—someone, something—if any one of us stirred.

Knowing that I and that I alone was still alive out of these twenty-one hundred dead, I tried not to stir, and focused all of my attention on not tugging at the cord tied to the middle finger of my right hand.

Looking up, I realised that it was no longer Charles Dickens whose face and hands and fingers glowed in the thick, slow light of the gas lamps in the darkness on the stage.

Drood looked out at us.

I recognised at once the pale white skin, the brittle tufts of hair over the ravaged ears, the lidless eyes, the nose that was little more than two nictitating membranes above a hole in the skull, the long, twitching fingers, and the pale, constantly turning pupils.

My hands shook. A hundred feet above the heads of all the corpses in the audience, the bell vibrated audibly.

Drood's head snapped around. His pale eyes locked with mine.

I began shaking all over. The bell rumbled, then rang. No other corpse there breathed or stirred.

Drood came out from behind Dickens's reading table

and then out from the rectangle of turgid light. He leaped down from the stage and began gliding up the aisle. My arms and legs shook now as if agued, but I could move no other part of my body—not even my head.

I could *smell* Drood as he approached. He smelled like the Thames near Tiger Bay where Opium Sal's opium den rotted away in the general effluvium when the tide was out and the sewage high.

There was something in Drood's hand. By the time he was twenty paces from me up the steep aisle, I could see that it was a knife, but unlike any knife I had ever held or used or seen. The blade was a dark steel crescent on which hieroglyphs were visible. The handle was mostly hidden behind the Egyptian's pale and bony knuckles; the thin handle of the razor-crescent disappeared between Drood's fingers so the curved blade, at least eight inches across in its thinly gleaming arc of edge, extended from his fist like a lady's fan.

Run! I ordered myself. *Escape! Scream!*

I could not move a muscle.

Drood paused above me, at the farthest limit of my peripheral vision, and when he opened his mouth, a miasma of Thames-mud stench enveloped me. I could see his pale pink tongue dancing behind those tiny teeth.

"You ssseee," he hissed at me, his right arm and the blade pulling back for the decapitation's swing, "how easssssy it issss?"

He swung the blade in a flat, vicious arc. The razor-sharp edge of the crescent-blade sliced through my beard and cut through my cravat, collar, skin, throat, trachea, gullet, and spinal cord as if they were made of butter.

The audience began applauding wildly. The gelatin-thick air had lightened to normal. The silken cords were gone.

Dickens turned to leave the stage without acknowledging the applause, but George Dolby was standing at the edge of the curtain. A moment later, with applause still echoing, Dickens stepped back into the glow of the gaslights.

"My dear friends," he said after his raised hands had silenced the huge hall, "it appears as if there has been an error. Actually, it appears that I have *made* an error. Our programme had called for the Trial from *Pickwick* to be read after the interval, but I mistakenly carried *Nickleby* out to the podium and went on to read it. You were most gracious in your acceptance of that error and more than generous in your applause. The hour is late—I see by my watch that it is just ten, the precise time scheduled for the conclusion of our evening together—but the Trial was promised and if the majority of you would like, and you can show by your hands or applause if you would so like, to hear the Trial read, I shall happily add it to the unscheduled reading you have just enjoyed."

The audience *did* like. They applauded and cheered and shouted encouragement. No one left.

"Call Sam Weller!" bellowed Dickens in his judicial voice, and the crowd roared louder in its applause and cheers. As each classic character appeared—Mrs Gamp, Miss Squeers, Boots—the audience roared even louder. I put my hand to my temple and found my brow cold and covered with perspiration. As Dickens read on, I staggered out.

I went alone to the hotel and drank another cup of laudanum while waiting for the Inimitable and his entourage to arrive. My heart was pounding wildly. I was ravenous and shaken and would have welcomed a large meal sent up to the privacy of my own room, but although Dickens would eat nothing more this evening, he invited Wills, Dolby, and me to dine in his suite as he unwound. There he paced back and forth and talked about the next few days of the tour and about the offer he had received for another tour beginning about Christmastime.

I ordered pheasant, fish, caviar, pâté, asparagus, eggs, and dry champagne, but just before the waiter came in bringing this and Wills's tiny meal and Dolby's beef and mutton, Dickens turned from the fireplace where he had been standing and said, "My dear Wilkie! What on earth is that on your collar?"

"What?" I confess that I blushed. I had hurriedly carried out my ablutions before drinking my laudanum and coming up to Dickens's suite. "What?" My hands rose beneath my bearded chin and touched something thick and crusted above the silk of my cravat.

"Here now, move your hands," said Wills. He held the lamp closer.

"Good God," said Dolby.

"Good heavens, Wilkie," said Dickens in a voice that sounded more amused than alarmed. "There is dried blood all over your collar and neck. You look like Nancy after Bill Sikes has done with her."

CHAPTER SIXTEEN

The summer of 1866 was tiring.

My novel *Armadale* was released on schedule in June and the reviews were much as I expected from the usual hide-bound and tiresome critics. In the *Athenaeum*, their ancient music-critic and reviewer H. F. Chorley opined—*"It is not pleasant to speak as we must of this powerful story; but in the interest of everything that is to be cherished in life, in poetry, in art, it is impossible to be over-explicit in the expression of judgement."*

His judgement was that the book was immoral.

The reviewer of *The Spectator* came to the same conclusion in terms that bypassed the mere strident in favour of the near-hysterical:

> *The fact that there are such characters as he has drawn, and actions such as he has described, does not warrant his over-stepping the limits of decency, and revolting every human sentiment. This is what* Armadale *does. It gives us for its heroine a woman fouler than the refuse of the streets, who has lived to the ripe age of 35, and through the horrors of forgery, murder, theft, bigamy, gaol and attempted suicide, without any trace being left on her beauty. . . . This is frankly told in a diary which, but for its unreality, would be simply loathesome, and which needs all the veneer of Mr Wilkie Collins's easy style and allusive sparkle to disguise its actual meaning.*

This kind of critical attack meant nothing to me. I knew that the book would sell well. And perhaps I have told you, Dear Reader, that the publisher had paid me five thousand pounds—a record at the time and for many years after that—and paid it before a single word of the story had been written. I had serialised it in America in their magazine called *Harper's Monthly* and not only had *Armadale* been wildly popular there, but the editor had written me that my tale had single-handedly saved their magazine from extinction. Its serialisation in England through *The Cornhill Magazine* had also been wildly popular, certainly causing some of the jealousy we had heard from Dickens the previous Christmas. I was certain that I could adapt *Armadale* to the stage and that this might well be a greater source of income than the book itself.

It is true that the great sum paid in advance by George Smith at Smith, Elder & Company had all but bankrupted the publisher despite the brisk sales of the two volumes, but that was little concern of mine. It did frustrate me somewhat, however, in the sense that for my next novel—whatever its contents—I would almost certainly have to return to Dickens's magazine, *All the Year Round,* just as the author-editor had predicted during our Christmas dinner. The frustration was not merely because the monies in advance of publication would be less—Dickens, John Forster, and Wills were miserly when it came to paying writers *other* than Dickens—but rather the fact that Dickens would again be my editor.

Yet I remained serenely confident that the hostile reviews of the day meant nothing. Critics and bourgeois reviewers simply were not ready for the heroine of *Armadale,* my *femme fatale* Lydia Gwilt. Not only did Lydia dominate the book in a way that no female literary protagonist in my era had done, but she stood out from the pages in a way that no woman in all of

Dickens's fiction ever had or ever would. The full, three-dimensional portrait of this woman, as scheming and vicious as Lydia Gwilt may have seemed to the careless reader or clueless reviewer, was a *tour de force*.

And yes, speaking of occasionally vicious women, Caroline G—— chose this hot summer to upbraid me on a wide front of issues.

"Why will you not consider marriage, Wilkie? You pre-sent me as a wife—almost—to your friends who visit here. I am your hostess and proofreader and housekeeper and lover. Everyone who knows you knows that we live as man and wife. It is past time that we make that perception reality."

I said, "If you know anything about me at all, my dear Caroline, you must know that I do not care a fig for perceptions or other people's opinions."

"But I *do*," cried the woman with whom I'd spent the past ten years. "And Harriet is now fifteen. She *needs* a father."

"She had a father," I replied placidly. "He died."

"When she was one year old!" cried Caroline. She appeared to be teetering on that thin ledge between anger and tears, reason and hysteria, upon which women so frequently find themselves. Or deliberately find themselves. "She is becoming a young woman. She will enter into society soon. She needs your name."

"Nonsense," I chuckled. "She has a perfectly good name and a perfectly good home. She shall always have my support and our love. What more could any intelligent young woman wish to have?"

"You promised that we would buy or lease the nicer home on Gloucester Place by this year or next," whined Caroline. I hate and despise it when women whine. *All* men, Dear Reader, hate and despise it when women whine. It has always been thus. The only difference in men's reactions to whining is that a very few, like me, refuse to give in to this auditory and emotional blackmail.

I looked over the top of my glasses at her. "I said that we should have the place sooner or later, my pet. And so we shall."

"How?" demanded Caroline. "I spoke to Mrs Shernwold while you were having fun with Dickens in Birmingham. She says that she would consider leasing or selling ninety Gloucester to us except for the fact that her unmarried son is returning from Africa in a year or so and she has promised it to him."

"Trust me on this, Caroline my dear," I said. "I have promised you this home someday and you and Harriet shall have it. Have I ever failed you, my sausage?"

She glared at me. Caroline G—— was a handsome woman—some would say beautiful—despite her advancing years (although she would never tell me her age, Inspector Field had told me that in all likelihood Caroline had been born thirty-six years earlier, in 1830)—but she was neither handsome nor beautiful when she glared. Despite the tons of romantic literary twaddle to the contrary, trust me, Dear Reader, when I assure you that no woman can be attractive when she whines and glares.

"You fail me by not marrying me and giving Harriet a proper father," she all but shrieked at me. "Do not think that I am not capable of finding and marrying another man, Wilkie Collins. Do not think that for a second!"

"I do *not* think that for a second, my sausage," I said and turned back to the newspaper.

CHARLES DICKENS, DESPITE his continuing illnesses and growing anxieties when travelling by rail, seemed to be having a relaxed summer. I overheard Wills telling Forster at the offices of *All the Year Round* that the total receipts for Dickens's spring tour had earned the writer £4,672. The Chappells—whom Dickens had once described to me as "speculators, Wilkie, pure speculators, though, of course, of the worthiest and most honourable kind"—were so delighted with their share of the profits that no sooner had Dickens completed his last London reading on 12 June and returned to Gad's Hill "... to rest and hear the birds sing," than they proposed to Dickens another tour for the next winter, consisting of fifty nights on the road. Wills told Forster that Dickens had considered asking for £70 a night—he was sure that the ticket sales would support that—but instead offered the Chappells forty-two readings for £2,500. They accepted at once.

The days at Gad's Hill through June and July were busy with guests, local fairs at which Dickens judged everything from pie contests to cricket matches, and—of course—more business. The Inimitable was not working on a novel at the moment, but he had begun work on a projected new edition of his works, the so-called Charles Dickens Edition, that would have each of his novels, freshly set, appearing once a month for 3/6. Naturally he could not leave such well-enough alone, so he offered in his prospectus to write a new preface for each volume.

As it turned out, this would be not only the most popular of all the many editions of Dickens's work, but would be—for him—his *last* edition.

I saw Dickens frequently that summer, both at Gad's Hill (where he never seemed to be entertaining fewer than half a dozen guests) and in London (he came up to his offices at *All the Year Round* at least twice a week, and we would often meet for lunch or dinner). Besides already planning his next Christmas story for our magazine, rehearsing new material for his winter tour, and writing the prefaces for his new editions, Dickens told me that he had some ideas for a new novel that he hoped to serialise in the spring of 1867. He asked me what I was working on.

"I have a few ideas," I said. "A thread or two and a few beads to string on them."

"Anything that we might serialise?"

"Quite possibly. I've been thinking of a tale involving a detective."

"One from Scotland Yard Detectives Bureau?"

"Or one working for a private detection bureau."

"Ah," said Dickens and smiled. "Something along the lines of the further adventures of Inspector Bucket."

I shook my head. "I was thinking that the name Cuff might work," I said. "Sergeant Cuff."

Dickens's smile widened. "Sergeant Cuff. Very good, my dear Wilkie. Very good indeed."

I TOLD THE BOY waiting on my corner to tell the inspector that we should meet. The time and place had long since been prearranged, and the next day at two PM, I saw his short, squat figure hurrying towards me at Waterloo Bridge.

"Mr Collins."

"Inspector." I nodded towards the shadows under the bridge. " 'Unfurnished lodging for a fortnight.' "

"I beg your pardon, sir?"

"Sam Weller to Pickwick."

"Ah, yes, sir. Of course. Mr Dickens has always been an admirer of this bridge. I helped him with his piece 'Down with the Tide' by introducing him to the night toll-taker here some years ago. The literary gentleman was quite interested in the suicides and bodies floating in on the tides, I was told."

"Thirteen," I said.

"Pardon me, sir?"

"Thirteen years ago," I said. "Dickens published 'Down with the Tide' in *Household Words* in February of 1853. I edited it."

"Ah, of course," said Inspector Field. He brushed his chin with his thumb. "Is there a reason you suggested we meet, Mr Collins? News of any kind?"

"Rather an absence of news," I said. "You never responded to my written report or query."

"I apologise," said the inspector, but there was no real tone of apology in his husky voice. "It has been very busy, Mr Collins. Very busy indeed. I very much appreciated your report on Mr Dickens's reading in Birmingham, even though our friend Drood did not appear. Was there a specific query I could answer?"

"You could tell me if any of those three men died," I said.

"Three men?" The inspector's flushed, chapped, and heavily veined visage was the picture of innocent ignorance.

"The three men in the alley, Inspector. The three men who assaulted me and whom your Detective Reginald Call-Me-Reggie Barris clubbed down. Barris said that one or more of them might be dead from the blow. I went back to that alley the next morning before leaving Birmingham, but there was no sign of them."

Inspector Field was smiling and nodding now, his forefinger along the side of his nose. "Yes, yes, of course. Barris did report to me about the incident in the alley. I'm sure that all of those ruffians suffered no more than a headache and an insult to their thieves' pride, Mr Collins. You have to forgive Barris. He has a penchant for melodrama. Sometimes I believe he would have preferred a career on the stage to the life of private investigative enquiries."

"Why did you have him follow me, Inspector? I thought that the idea was to observe Charles Dickens

in the hope that Drood might contact him...not follow me around."

Field's bushy eyebrows lifted towards what remained
of his hairline. "Surely Detective Barris must have
explained that to you, sir. We have concerns that this
Drood might make an attempt on your life."

"Barris said that the three men in the alley were
most likely simple thieves," I said.

"Aye," agreed Inspector Field, nodding again. "Them
being white men and all, that is almost certainly the
case. But you must admit that it was fortuitous that
Barris was there. You might have been severely injured,
Mr Collins, and you certainly would have been robbed."

We had walked across the Waterloo Bridge twice by
now and this time continued walking north towards
the Strand. Somewhere to the west along the river here
was the Warren's Blacking Factory, where Katey Dickens had once told me her father had been sent to labour
as a child. He had mentioned it to her in an almost joking manner, but Katey confided in me that she felt it
may have been the most upsetting and formative event
of his life.

"I know where your Drood is, Inspector," I said as
we turned right on the Strand towards Somerset House
and Drury Lane.

Field stopped. "You do, sir?"

"I do, sir." I let the silence between us fill the air
under the rumble and roar of passing traffic. "Dickens
is Drood," I said at last.

"I beg your pardon?" said the inspector.

"Dickens is Drood," I said again. "There is no
Drood."

"That seems highly unlikely, Mr Collins."

I smiled almost patronisingly. "I've said before that
Drood appears to be a figment of the writer's imagination, Inspector. Now I know that the phantom is no

more than that. Dickens has created Drood to suit his own purposes."

"And what might those purposes be, sir?"

"Power," I said. "A mischievous sense of power over others. For many years, as I've told you, Dickens has played with magnetic influence and mesmerism. Now he invents this Master of Mesmerism as his alter ego, as it were."

We had resumed walking east and now Inspector Field tapped the pavement with his heavy stick. "He could hardly have invented Drood, Mr Collins, seeing as I have been pursuing the blackguard for twenty years come this August."

"Have you ever *seen* him, Inspector?" I said. "Drood, I mean."

"Seen him?" repeated the older man. "Why no, sir. I believe I've told you that I have never personally laid eyes on the murderer. But I have apprehended some of his agents and I have certainly seen the results of his *work*. More than three hundred murders in those twenty years, not the least terrible of which was the grisly death of Lord Lucan in 1846. You yourself told me the story that Dickens reported Drood telling *him*—and the identity of Lord Lucan, who was long rumoured to have had a son in Egypt, fits perfectly."

"Too perfectly," I said smugly.

"Pardon me, sir?"

"You may be a detective, Inspector Field," I said, "but you have never plotted and written a story with detective work in it. I have."

Inspector Field continued striding and tapping, but he looked my way and listened.

"Certainly there has been a *legend* of a murderous Egyptian named Drood for these two decades or so," I explained. "The shadowy dockside murderer. The phantom Oriental mesmeriser, sending his agents out to rob and kill. The unreal occupant of the very real Under-town. But he is only a legend, with no more real history to him than there is actual physicality. Charles Dickens has walked these riverside and dockside slums for years and years. He certainly has heard of this Drood—perhaps before you did twenty years ago, Inspector—and for his own purposes, he has incorporated actual events such as the murder of Lord Lucan (with its delicious element of the man's heart being ripped from his chest) into his biography of the unreal personage."

"What would those purposes be, Mr Collins?" asked Inspector Field. We had just passed Somerset House. Once a royal residence, the newer structure had housed government offices for the past thirty years. I knew that Dickens's father and uncle had been employed there.

We crossed the Strand and took a narrow lane as a shortcut in the direction of Drury Lane, where the fictional David Copperfield had ordered beef in a restaurant and where a very real Wilkie Collins hoped to have a successful staging of *Armadale* before too much more time passed.

"To what purpose, sir?" repeated the inspector when we were alone in the lane. "To what purpose would Mr Dickens lie to you about the existence of Drood?"

I smiled and swung my own walking stick. "Let me tell you a little story from Dickens's reading tour, Inspector. I heard it last week from George Dolby."

"As you wish, sir."

"The travel part of the tour ended in Portsmouth at the end of May," I said. "Dickens had a little time that was his own so he led Wills and Dolby on one of his walking expeditions and they found themselves in Landport Terrace. 'By Jove!' exclaimed Dickens. 'Here is the place where I was born! One of these houses must be the one.' And so he led Wills and Dolby from house to house, explaining that one must be it because it 'looked so like my father.' Then, no, another must be the correct one 'because it looked like the birthplace of a man who had deserted it.' But no again, a third must be it because it was 'most definitely like the cradle of a puny, weak youngster...' and so on through the row of homes.

"Then, Inspector, in an open square in the town, all lined with redbrick houses dotted by white window frames, Dickens decided to imitate the clowning of Grimaldi."

"Grimaldi?" said Inspector Field.

"A pantomimist whom Dickens adored," I said. "So, with Wills and Dolby watching, the famous writer Charles Dickens mounted the steps to one of these houses, gave three raps to the brass-plated green door, and lay down on the top step. A moment later when a stout woman opened the door, Dickens leapt up and took off running, with Dolby and Wills beating a hasty retreat behind him. Dickens would point behind them at an imaginary policeman pursuing and all three distinguished gentlemen would pick up their pace. When the wind blew off Dickens's hat and scuttled it ahead of them, the pursuit became real enough as all three chased the hat in comic pantomime."

Inspector Field stoppped. I stopped. After a moment, he said, "Your point, Mr Collins?"

"My point, Inspector, is that Charles Dickens, although chronologically fifty-four years of age, is a child. A mischievous child. He manufactures and plays the games he enjoys and—through his fame and force of personality—bullies those around him to play the game as well. We are now involved, you and I, in Charles Dickens's Game of Drood."

Field stood there, scratching the side of his nose while seemingly lost in thought. He suddenly looked very old to me. And not at all well. Finally he said, "Where were you on nine June, Mr Collins?"

I blinked at this. Then I smiled and said, "Didn't your agents inform you, Inspector?"

"Yes, sir. In truth, they did. You went to your publisher's offices in the late morning. Your new book was released that day. Then you went to several bookshops from Pall Mall along the Strand to Fleet Street, where you signed several copies of the volumes for certain friends and admirers. That evening you dined…*there*…"

Field was pointing his cane at the Albion, opposite Drury Lane Theatre.

"…with several artists, including one older gentleman who was a friend of your father's," continued the inspector. "You returned home a little after midnight."

He had managed to wipe the smile off my face and it irked me that he had. "The point of this intrusive and unwarranted recitation, Inspector?" I asked coldly.

"The point is that both you and I know where *you* were on the ninth of June, Mr Collins. But neither of us knows where Mr Dickens was on that important anniversary."

"Important anniversary?" I said and then remembered. It was the first anniversary of Dickens's near thing in the railway accident at Staplehurst. How could I have forgotten?

"Mr Dickens was at Gad's Hill Place that day," said Inspector Field without looking at any notes, "but took the four thirty-six PM express to London. Once here he began one of his long walks, this one in the general vicinity of Bluegate Fields."

"Opium Sal's," I ventured. "The entrance to Undertown through the crypt in the cemetery he called Saint Ghastly Grim's."

"Not this time, sir," said Inspector Field. "I had seven of my best agents following Mr Dickens. We felt that the odds were great that the author would contact Drood on this first anniversary of their meeting. But your friend gave my men and myself—I was involved in the tailing that night—quite a merry chase. Just when we were sure that Dickens had gone to ground, he would pop out of some ruin or slum, hail a cab, and be off. Eventually he left Bluegate Fields and the dock areas there and came quite close to where we stand at this moment. . . . To Saint Enon Chapel north of the Strand near the eastern entrance to Clement's Inn, to be precise."

"Saint Enon Chapel," I repeated. The name rang a faint bell. Then I remembered. "The Modern Golgotha!"

"Exactly, sir. A charnel house. The vaults under Saint Enon had so filled with unclaimed corpses that in 1844, after I had begun work in the Police Bureau but before I became Chief of Detectives, the commissioner of sewers sealed it off while creating a drainage tunnel beneath the building. Still the bodies festered there for years, until the premises were purchased by a surgeon in 1847 with the purpose of removing the remains to—I believe he called it—'a more appropriate place.' The exhumation continued there for almost a year, Mr Collins, with two giant heaps accumulating in the alleys above those vaults—one heap a pile of human bones, the other a mountain of decaying coffin wood."

"I went to view that as a young man," I said, turning slightly to look off in the direction of St Enon. I remembered the stench then on that cool February day I had viewed the awful spectacle. I could not imagine what the smell would be like on a hot and humid summer day such as this one.

"You and some six thousand other Londoners came to stare," said Inspector Field.

"What does Saint Enon Chapel have to do with Dickens and June nine?"

"He managed to vanish from our view near there, Mr Collins," said Field, tapping angrily at the cobblestones with his heavy brass-headed stick. "Seven of my best agents and myself, perhaps the finest detective London has ever known, in pursuit, and your writer gave us the slip."

I had to smile again. "He is enjoying this, Inspector. As I said, Dickens is a child at heart. He loves mysteries and ghost stories. And upon occasion he has a cruel sense of humour."

"Indeed, sir. But more to the point, somehow your friend knew about a secret entrance to that very drainage tunnel dug in 1844 when all the thousands of leaking and rotting corpses were still there. We found the tunnel eventually—it opens into scores of leaking, stinking holes where hundreds of squatters are living beneath the streets of London—and that in turn opens to another labyrinth of tunnels, sewers, and caverns."

"But you couldn't find Dickens?"

"We did, sir. We saw his lantern in the maze ahead of us. But at that point, we came under attack—hand-thrown and slingshotted stones, many as big as your fist, sir."

"The Wild Boys," I said.

"Precisely, sir. Detective Hatchery actually had to fire his weapon before the attackers—mere shadows, emerging from side tunnels and flinging at us, then retreating into deeper shadows—fled and we could continue our pursuit of your friend. But by then it was too late. He gave us the slip in the flooded labyrinth."

"It sounds to be very frustrating, Inspector," I said. "And exciting. But what, exactly, is your point?"

"My point, Mr Collins, is that it seems rather doubtful that Charles Dickens—*the* Charles Dickens—should go to such absurd lengths to lose us while traipsing through the Undertown of London all night...unless there *is* a man named Drood waiting for him."

I was able to laugh. I was unable *not* to laugh. "I would suggest just the contrary, Inspector. It is the fun of the pursuit and the fiction of the mystery he has created that brings Dickens to waste so much time leading you on this wild goose chase through the tunnels under London. Had he not been aware that your men would be following him, I assure you that he would not have come to London that night. *There is no Drood.*"

Inspector Field shrugged. "Have it as you wish, sir, but we appreciate your continued cooperation in helping us track down the murderer and mastermind whom you do not believe exists. Those of us in police work who have come up against Drood and his agents *know* him to be a real and frightening force."

There was nothing to be said to that.

"Was your query about the brigands in Birmingham the only reason you asked for this meeting, Mr Collins?"

"No, actually," I said, shuffling unconsciously in my embarrassment. "I wished to take you up on an offer you made to me."

"Ninety Gloucester Square and Mrs Shernwold?" said Field. "I am working on that, sir. I remain confident that you and your...Mrs G——...shall have the place by this time next year."

"No," I said. "The other offer. When you said that I might borrow the good services of Detective Hatchery should I wish to go back to Saint Ghastly Grim's Cemetery, move the slab in the crypt, and find my own way down to King Lazaree and his opium den in the catacombs there. The rheumatical gout has been all but intolerable in recent weeks...the laudanum helps almost not at all anymore."

"Detective Hatchery will be at your service whenever you wish," the inspector replied crisply with no discernible tone of censure or victory in his voice. "When would you like him to report for duty, Mr Collins?"

"Tonight," I said. I could feel my pulse accelerate. "Tonight at midnight."

CHAPTER SEVENTEEN

*O*ctober of 1866 turned especially cool and rainy. I split my days and nights between my club, my home, and King Lazaree's underground den, with many weekends given over to being a guest at Gad's Hill Place.

One rainy Saturday afternoon there, while under the mellowing influence of my laudanum, I told Dickens about various ideas I had concerning my next book.

"I am thinking of something in the line of the supernatural," I said.

"Do you mean a ghost story?" asked Dickens. We were in his study, enjoying the warmth of the fire. The Inimitable had finished his day's work on his annual Christmas story and been persuaded by me that the rain was too cold for his usual afternoon walk. Wind whipped raindrops against the bow windows beyond his desk. "Something involving spirit rapping?" he continued, frowning slightly.

"Not in the least," I said. "I was thinking rather of some adroit mixture of the themes I mentioned to you some time ago—detection, theft, mystery—along with some item that has a curse on it. The reality of that curse would, of course, be decided by the reader."

"What kind of item?" asked Dickens. I could tell that I had piqued his interest.

"A gem, I believe. A ruby or sapphire. Or even a

diamond. I can see the plotting arising from the effects of the cursèd stone on each person who acquires it by fair means or foul."

"Interesting, my dear Wilkie. Very interesting. The gem or diamond would be carrying some ancient family curse?"

"Or a religious one," I said, warming under the influence of the mid-day laudanum and Dickens's interest. "Perhaps if the stone had been stolen from some ancient and superstitious culture…"

"India!" cried Dickens.

"I had been thinking Egypt," I said, "but India would serve. Might serve very nicely, I think. As for a title, I've jotted down *The Serpent's Eye* or *The Eye of the Serpent.*"

"A bit sensational," said Dickens, steepling his fingers and extending his legs towards the fire. "But intriguing as well. Would you work your idea of a 'Sergeant Cuff' into this tale?"

I blushed and only managed a shrug.

"And would opium figure in this book as well?" he asked.

"It might," I said defiantly, all warmth at his earlier interest now fled. I had heard through several mutual friends of Dickens's absolute disapproval of my Lydia Gwilt's praise of the drug in *Armadale.*

Dickens changed the subject. "I presume you are using as a model here the Koh-i-noor diamond that was exhibited in the Crystal Palace here at the Great Exhibition and presented to the Queen in June of 1850."

"I have made some rough notes about that artefact," I said stiffly.

"Well, my dear Wilkie, there were certainly rumours that the Koh-i-noor was indeed cursed after it was exacted as tribute to the crown by the 'Lion of the Punjab,' that heathen Maharaja Dhulip Singh. Just the true story of how that diamond was smuggled from Lahore to Bombay by Governer General Lord Dalhousie himself, even while the Mutiny was still active, should give enough material for two or three exciting novels. It's said that Lady Dalhousie herself sewed the diamond into a belt which Lord Dalhousie wore for weeks until he handed the Koh-i-noor over to the captain of a British warship in Bombay Harbour. They say that he chained two fierce guard-dogs to his camp bed each night to wake him if thieves or Thugees entered his tent."

"I'd not heard this," I confessed. My thought had been to write about a ruby or sapphire sacred to an ancient Egyptian cult, but Dickens's true tale of the Koh-i-noor made my hands twitch in anticipation of taking notes.

We were interrupted then by an urgent pounding on the door to Dickens's study.

It was Georgina, in tears and almost beside herself with agitation. When Dickens calmed her, she explained that the Irish bloodhound—Sultan—had attacked yet another innocent victim, this time a little girl who was the sister of one of the servants.

Dickens sent her out to soothe the victim. Then he sighed, opened a cupboard door, and removed the two-barrelled shotgun I had last seen ten months earlier on Christmas night. He then went to his desk and pulled several large shells from a lower-right-hand drawer. Outside, the rain had ceased pelting the window glass, but I could see dark, fast clouds moving low above black branches that were quickly losing their leaves.

"I'm afraid that I have shown too much tolerance with this dog," he said softly. "Sultan has a good heart—and he is totally loyal to me—but his aggressive spirit was forged in the fires of hell. He refuses to learn. I can tolerate anything—in dog or man—save for the refusal or inability to learn."

"No more warnings?" I asked, rising to follow him away from the fire and out of the room.

"No more warnings, my dear Wilkie," said Dickens. "This hound's inevitable death sentence was pronounced by a power much higher than ours when Sultan was only a pup at his mother's teat. Now there remains only the execution of that sentence."

THE EXECUTION PARTY was, fittingly, all male: besides Sultan, Dickens, and myself, the fourteen-year-old Plorn had been summoned from his room. My brother, Charles, and his wife, Katey, had just arrived for the weekend, and Charley was invited along but declined. A weather-faced old blacksmith from across the road had been reshoeing two horses in Dickens's stable and joined the procession. (It turned out that the blacksmith was an old friend of the condemned—he had enjoyed the killer's antics from the time Sultan was a puppy—and the old man was honking into his handkerchief even before the execution party set out.)

Finally there were Dickens's oldest son, Charley, just up for the day, and two male servants, one the husband of the female servant whose sister had been attacked. One servant trundled the empty wheelbarrow that would bear Sultan's carcass back from the killing grounds and the other gingerly carried a burlap bag that would be the condemned's shroud in a few minutes. The women of the household and other servants watched from the windows as we walked out through the backyard, past the stables, and into the field where Dickens had burned his correspondence six years earlier.

At first Sultan bounded around with enthusiasm and excitement, unbridled by the new muzzle he was wearing. He obviously thought that he was on a hunting expedition. *Something was going to die!* Sultan leaped around from one trudging, high-booted, waxed-cotton-coated man to the next, his paws sending out ripples in the puddles and kicking up mud. But when the humans would not meet his gaze, the dog stood at the end of his leash—held by Charley Dickens—and cast an observing eye on the open shotgun under his master's arm and upon the empty wheelbarrow that had never been a part of any other grouse-hunting trek.

As the group stopped a hundred yards or so from the stable, Sultan's gaze became meditative, even gloomy, and he fixed the gun bearer—his lord and master—with a questioning look that soon became an imploring one.

Charley slipped the leash and stepped back. We had all stepped back behind Dickens, who continued standing there and returning Sultan's gaze. The big Irish bloodhound cocked his head to add a question mark to the end of his unspoken query. Dickens set the two shells in place and clicked the heavy gun shut. Sultan cocked his head farther to the left, his gaze never leaving his master's eyes.

"John," Dickens said softly to the blacksmith, who stood at the far left of our crescent of execution-witnesses, "I want him turned. Would you please peg a stone behind him?"

John the blacksmith grunted, blew his nose a final time, tucked away the kerchief in the coat pocket of his rain jacket, leaned over, lifted the kind of flat stone one would choose to skip across a pond, and tossed it just behind Sultan's tail.

The dog's head turned. Before Sultan could look back at him, Dickens had smoothly raised the shotgun and fired both barrels. Even though we were all expecting it, the double explosion seemed especially loud in the damp, cold, thick air. Sultan's ribcage exploded in a blur of red-shredded hair and striated flesh and shattered bone. I am certain that his heart was pulverised so quickly that no message from nerve-endings had time to reach the animal's brain. He did not whimper or cry out as the impact knocked him several feet across the wet grass in the opposite direction from us, and I was all but certain that Sultan was dead before he hit the ground.

The servants had the heavy carcass in the bag and then in the wheelbarrow in an instant. They trundled the corpse back towards the house as the rest of us gathered around Dickens, who broke the smoking gun, removed the spent shells, and set the empty cartridges carefully in his overcoat pocket.

He looked up at me as he did this and our gazes seemed to lock much as his and Sultan's had only a moment earlier. I fully expected the Inimitable to say to me, perhaps in Latin, "And thus death to those who betray me"—but he remained silent.

A second later, young Plorn, seemingly excited by the smell of blood and gunpowder in the air—the very boy whom Dickens had recently described to me as "wanting application and continuity of purpose" due to some "impracticable torpor in his natural character"—cried out, "That was smashing, Father! Absolutely smashing!"

Dickens did not reply. None of the men said a word as we walked slowly back to the warm house. The rain and wind came up again before we reached the back door.

Once inside, I started to head up to my room to change into dry clothes and take an additional brace of laudanum, but Dickens called out to me and I stopped on the stairs.

"Be of good cheer, Wilkie. Even so will I comfort dear Percy Fitzgerald, who gave me the doomed dog in the first place. Two of Sultan's children are rolling in the straw of the barn even as we speak. Blood inheritance being the iron master that it is, one of those two will almost assuredly inherit Sultan's ferocity. He will also almost certainly inherit the gun."

I could think of nothing to say to this, so I nodded and went upstairs for my anodyne.

KING LAZAREE, the Chinaman King of the Opium Living Dead, seemed to have been expecting me when I had first returned to his kingdom almost two months before Sultan's execution, in' late August of that summer of 1866.

"Welcome, Mr Collins," the ancient Chinee had whispered when I parted the curtains to his hidden realm in the *loculus* beneath the catacombs beneath the cemetery. "Your bed and pipe are ready for you."

Detective Hatchery had led me safely to the cemetery late that August night, had unlocked gates and crypt doors and moved the heavy bier again, and had once again loaned me his absurdly heavy pistol. Handing me a bullseye lantern, he promised to stay in the crypt until I returned. I confess here that it was more difficult going down through the tombs and hidden passage to the lower level this second time than it had been when I followed Dickens.

King Lazaree's robe and headpiece were of different colours this visit, but the silk was as clean, bright, and perfectly pressed as the time I'd first come here with Dickens.

"You knew I would be back?" I asked as I followed the ancient figure to the farthest, darkest reaches of the long burial *loculus*.

King Lazaree only smiled and beckoned me farther into the burrow. The silent forms on the three-tiered wooden beds set against the cavern walls appeared to be the same Oriental mummies that we had glimpsed during that first visit. But each mummy held an ornate opium pipe, and the smoky exhalations which filled the narrow, lamp-lit passage were the only indication that they were breathing.

All the other beds were occupied, but this three-level wooden bunk at the back of the room, separated by its own dark red curtain, was empty.

"You shall be our honoured guest," Lazaree said softly in his oddly lilted Cambridge accent. "And as such, you shall have your privacy. Khan?" He gestured, and another figure in a dark robe handed me a long pipe with a beautiful glass-and-ceramic bowl at the end.

"The pipe has never been used," said King Lazaree. "It is for you and your use alone. This bed also is for your use and your use alone. No one else shall ever lie in it. And the drug you will experience tonight is of the quality reserved for kings, pharaohs, emperors, and those holy men wishing to become gods."

I tried to speak, found my mouth too dry, licked my lips, and tried again. "How much..." I began.

King Lazaree silenced me with a touch of his long yellowed fingers and longer yellow nails. "Gentlemen do not discuss price, Mr Collins. First, experience this night—then you can tell me if such quality and uniqueness is worth the coin these other gentlemen..." He moved those long, curving fingernails in a sweep that included the rows of silent cots. "...have decided to pay for it. If not, there will be, of course, no charge."

King Lazaree glided into the dark and the robed figure named Khan helped me up into my bunk, set a notched wooden block under my head—it was strangely comfortable—and lit the pipe for me. Then Khan was gone and I lay on my side, inhaling the fragrant smoke and allowing my anxieties and worries to flow out of me.

Do you wish, Dear Reader, to know the effects of this ultimate opium? Perhaps in your day everyone avails himself of this amazing drug. But even so, I doubt if the efficacy of your opium could equal or come close to the perfection of King Lazaree's secret recipe.

If it is the effect of mere opium that piques your curiosity, I can quote to you here from the first paragraph of the last book ever written by Charles Dickens—a book he would not live long enough to finish:

> *An ancient English Cathedral Tower? How can the ancient English Cathedral tower be here! The well-known massive grey square tower of its old Cathedral? How can that be here! There is no spike of rusty iron in the air, between the eye and it, from any point of the real prospect. What is the spike that intervenes, and who has set it up? Maybe it is set up by the Sultan's orders for the impaling of a horde of Turkish robbers, one by one. It is so, for cymbals clash, and the Sultan goes by to his palace in long procession. Ten thousand scimitars flash in the sunlight, and thrice ten thousand dancing-girls strew flowers. Then, follow white elephants caparisoned in countless gorgeous colours, and infinite in number and attendants. Still the Cathedral Tower rises in the background, where it cannot be, and still no writhing figure is on the grim spike. Stay! Is the spike so low a thing as the rusty spike on the top of a post of an old bedstead that has tumbled all awry? Some vague period of drowsy laughter must be devoted to the consideration of this possibility.*

There you have it. An opium addict struggling to consciousness in a run-down tumbled opium den at dawn. Ten thousand scimitars flashing in the sunlight. Thrice ten thousand dancing girls. White elephants caparisoned in countless gorgeous colours. What poetry! What insight!

What rubbish.

Charles Dickens had not the slightest idea of the power or effect of opium. He once bragged to me that during his second reading tour—still in our future that summer and autumn of 1866—when he was racked by pain and unable to sleep, he granted himself the "Morpheus of laudanum." But when I enquired further—of Dolby rather than of the Inimitable, since I wanted the truth—I found that the wings of Morpheus to which he had abandoned himself consisted of two tiny drops of opium in a very large glass of port. By this time, I was drinking several port-glasses full of pure laudanum with not even a chaser of wine.

Dickens had no idea of the effects of laudanum, much less of rich opium.

Let me tell you, Dear Reader of my posthumous future, just what the effect of King Lazaree's opium *was* like—

— it was a warmth that began in your belly and veins, a little like a good whiskey, but which, unlike whiskey, never stopped expanding and growing.

— it was an elixir that transformed small, cherubic, usually pleasant, rarely-taken-seriously William Wilkie Collins, he of the absurdly large forehead, poor eyesight, and comically voluminous beard, he who was "always good for a laugh" and usually good to serve as what Americans call a "sidekick"—into the self-confident colossus that he knew in his heart of hearts he always was and always had been.

— it was a transformative agent that eliminated the soul-sickening anxiety that had haunted and weakened me since I was a child, that deepened perception, and which bestowed an insight into people, one's self, and relationships that illuminated even the most mundane object or situation in a brilliant, golden light that must be something like the vision of a divinity.

This is an inadequate description, I fear, but I hesitate before penning a complete description of the unique and beneficial effects of this ancient Chinaman's opium. (Too many others, those without my innate resistance to the oft-cited negative aspects of the drug, might rush to try it—not realising that opium of King Lazaree's quality of essence may never again be found in London or anywhere else.) Suffice it to say that the drug was worth every shilling the ancient Chinaman asked for it—asked for it many hours later, when I was helped from my couch and escorted, by the shadow called Khan, all the way back to the steep staircase above which waited the faithful Hatchery—and it remained worth the thousands upon thousands of pounds I would continue paying for it in the months and years to come.

Thank God for my huge payment from *Cornhill*'s George Smith in advance of my writing *Armadale*. I would not say that every cent of that windfall went for opium—I remember spending some £300 for wine and investing at least £1,500 in Funds (and, of course, there were gifts to Caroline and Carrie, as we called her daughter, Harriet, at home, as well as money sent to Martha R——)—but the majority of the astounding £5,000 I received from Smith did end up in the long-nailed yellow hands of the subterranean Mandarin.

Hatchery—huge, hulking, derby-topped—was always waiting for me in the crypt far above, no matter how overdue into the morning (or even afternoon) my return was. Each time he would take back the huge pistol (I always set it next to me in my cot in King Lazaree's Den, even though I felt safer there than anywhere else in the world) and each time he would escort me out of the crypt, cemetery, and slums back to the world of the sad, shuffling, unseeing mortals who knew nothing of the glories of Lazaree's premium opium.

I wished almost as much as my constantly whining Caroline did that the house on Gloucester Place would open up for us. Our current home at 9 Melcombe Place, Dorset Square, had always been comfortable enough for me, but it seemed smaller now between Caroline's constant complaining and Carrie's coming into womanhood.

Mostly, though, it was the uninvited inhabitants that made the old place too small.

The woman with the green skin and tusk teeth still haunted the stairways when they were not well lighted, but it was the Other Wilkie who caused me the most consternation.

The Other Wilkie never spoke; he simply watched and waited. No matter how I was dressed when I encountered him, he was always in collar and shirtsleeves and waistcoat, cravat in place. I knew that if I were suddenly to shave off my full beard—which was so much a part of me now that I never really noticed it in the mirror except when trimming it—the Other Wilkie would retain his. If I were to remove my spectacles, he would retain his. He never ventured out of my study and was there only at night, but on those nights I encountered him there, his presence was increasingly irritating.

Sensing someone else in the room with me, I would look up and see the Other Wilkie sitting silently in the yellow-upholstered spiderweb-backed chair in the far corner. Sometimes the chair would be reversed (his doing, I am certain), and he would be sitting spraddle-legged with his shirtsleeved arms on the back, head down and gaze intense, the lamplight glinting off his tiny spectacles. I would go back to work, but when I looked up again, the Other Wilkie would have somehow silently advanced until he was sitting in the curved-back wooden chair I keep near my desk for guests. His small eyes would be fixed intently—hungrily, I thought—upon the manuscript I was working on, and he never blinked.

Eventually I would look up with a start to see and feel the Other Wilkie standing or sitting so close to me that our arms were almost touching. These moments of pure fright and terror were made worse when the Other Wilkie lunged for my pen. He wanted to continue and to finish the work on his own—I had no doubt of that—and I have related to you how violent and ink-spattering these tussles for possession of pen, inkwell, and manuscripts had become before I abandoned the study at night and began to work there only during the day, at times when he would not make an appearance.

But in that autumn of 1866, I could hear the Other Wilkie breathing and occasionally shuffling his feet outside my closed study doors even in daylight. I would tiptoe to those doors—hoping that it might be a servant, or Caroline or Carrie playing a prank on me—and throw open a door, only—and always—to see nothing in the hallway. But—always—I could hear the echo of shoes my own size thudding down the dark servants' stairway on which also waited the Woman with Green Skin.

I knew then that it would be just a matter of time before the Other Wilkie would appear in the study with me during the daytime. Thus I began carrying my notes and writing material to the Athenaeum Club, where I would find a comfortable leather chair and table near a tall window and work in peace.

The problem was, I had little to work on. For the first time in some years at least, since Charles Dickens had first hired me on the staff to write for *Household*

Words ten years earlier (some five years after I had met him), ideas were not coalescing into plots. I had jotted down notes after my rambling discussion with Dickens about the supernatural-adventure novel I was thinking of calling *The Serpent's Eye,* but except for copying out some relevant entries on jewels from India from my club's library edition of *Encyclopaedia Britannica*—the eighth edition, 1855—I had made no progress. I went back to my earlier idea of writing about a former police detective now given to private enquiries—Inspector Field in the form of my detective Sergeant Cuff—but my understandable reluctance to spend more time with Field than I had to, combined with an aversion to the entire insidious idea of a detective's intrusive investigations, retarded that research as well.

Part of me simply was in no mood to write. I much preferred Thursday nights, with the escorted trip to St Ghastly Grim's Cemetery and the hours upon hours of ecstasy and soaring insight that followed. The great frustration was that this godlike insight could never be put down on paper—by anyone, no matter how gifted the wordwright, not even, I was certain during my Thursday-night/Friday-morning flights, by Shakespeare or Keats, should either genius reincarnate in a London opium den without warning. Certainly not by so timid a man and unimaginative a writer as Charles Dickens. Each week I could see in King Lazaree's dark-eyed look his absolute knowledge of both my growing divinity and growing frustration at not being able to share my new knowledge via the dead bulk of inert letters being set down and pushed around on a white page like so many inky-carapaced and quill-prodded beetles. These clumsy written symbols were merely shorthand, I now understood, for the plaintive sounds that lonely apes make and have been making since the Earth and her sister Moon were young.

Everything else whirling around me that late autumn of 1866 seemed too absurd to be of consequence: the ongoing nonsense of Drood or not-Drood; the endless chess game for power between Inspector Field, the Inimitable, and me; the sweet allurings and caterwaulings of the women in my life; my inability to find an entrance into the cave under the paper for my next book; my unspoken and definitely unsettled competition with Charles Dickens...

But all that was to change when, one Friday morning in late November, after a long, sweet night in King Lazaree's tomb, I returned home with my suit still reeking of opium to find Dickens in the sitting room with Caroline. Her eyes were closed, her head was tilted back, and there was a look of something like uncommonly rare rapture on her face. Dickens was making mesmeric passes around and above her head, pausing only to touch her temples and to whisper to her.

Before I could speak, both heads turned in my direction, Caroline opened her eyes, and Dickens leapt to his feet and cried, "My dear Wilkie! Just the man I came to fetch. We must leave for the railway station this very minute. There is something astounding I have to show you in Rochester and someone there I want you to meet."

CHAPTER EIGHTEEN

I need to murder someone," said Dickens.

I nodded but said nothing. The train to Rochester had passed Gad's Hill already.

"I am quite sure I need to murder someone," said Dickens. "It is the one thing missing from the readings. Every other emotion is included in the greater list of excerpts I have prepared for this upcoming tour. All but…murder." He leaned on his stick and looked at me. "What do you think, my dear Wilkie? A modified and intensified version of Bill Sikes murdering Nancy perhaps?"

"Why not?" I said.

"Why not indeed," chuckled Dickens, patting his jacket. "It is only a human life."

He was garrulous in part because he had thrice imbibed of brandy during the ride. Each time the carriage shook or jolted, Dickens would either grasp the seat ahead of him with a death-grip or feel in the pocket of his coat for the small flask.

When I had confronted Dickens about the scene I had come upon of him mesmerising Caroline, he'd laughed and explained that my dearest had been upset and telling him of my pain from rheumatical gout, my increasing difficulty in getting to sleep, and what she saw as my growing dependency upon laudanum. Dickens had assured her that magnetic influence would whisk me off to slumber without any of the harmful side-effects of laudanum, and he had been in the process of teaching her the art when I'd entered.

"She was an adept pupil," he said now as the train rumbled and jolted on towards Rochester, passing the marshes around which Dickens and I had walked more than a few times. "You must allow her to attempt the mesmeric influence tonight. I guarantee it will allow you to sleep without opiate dreams or morning fatigue."

I made a noncommittal noise. In truth, I was close to falling asleep to the rocking of the railway carriage and the metronomic sound of its wheels on rails. It had been a long night in King Lazaree's den and I could not say that I had actually *slept*. Luckily, although the November day was unusually pleasant, there had been a brisk wind and most of the telltale scent of the pipe had been removed from my clothing during our fast walk to the station.

"You say we're meeting someone in Rochester?" I asked.

"Precisely," said Dickens, clasping both hands on the brass head of his cane. "Two ladies. An old friend for me and a lady companion for you, my dear Wilkie. We are having a luncheon there in a splendid place. I understand that the service is exemplary."

The splendid place with exemplary service, as it turned out, was the graveyard behind the huge old heap of grey stone that was Rochester Cathedral. The two ladies were Dickens's not-very-secret love, Ellen Ternan, and Miss Ternan's mother. Logic dictated that Mrs Ternan was to be my "lady companion" for this outing.

As I stood there amidst the headstones while nodding, bowing, and making small talk with the two women in the weak November afternoon sunlight, I seriously considered the possibility that Dickens had lost his mind.

But no, the answer to Charles Dickens's behaviour was never that simple. I realised as the four of us strolled into the graveyard—Mrs Ternan and Ellen had explained that they were visiting Ellen's uncle in Rochester and could only stay a short while—that this meeting made sense from Dickens's tortured, twisted, self-exculpating way of looking at the world. His liaison with Ellen Ternan was something he was hiding from almost everyone in the world—my brother, Charles, had told me that Dickens had brought his daughters and Georgina somewhat further into the conspiracy after Mamie had stumbled across her father walking with Miss Ternan in London one Sunday, and Inspector Field had informed me that Ellen had visited Gad's Hill Place on several occasions—but Dickens obviously felt that I was harmless to his intrigues. Whom would I tell? Not only did Dickens know from experience that I would keep the confidence, but he also knew that because of my own domestic arrangement (which had become even more complicated in the past week as Martha R—— had returned to London for an extended visit), I was such a social outcast that I could never publicly look down on Dickens's own arrangements, in print or through gossip.

Perhaps Mrs Ternan knew of my situation with Caroline G——, for the old lady seemed very cool during our picnic. The former actress (I understood that both she and Ellen were now giving elocution lessons from their new home in Slough that Dickens paid for) obviously had accumulated more pretensions of gentility since I had gotten to know the two women during and after the performances of *The Frozen Deep*. Mrs Ternan carried her acquired gentility with her like an ageing sloop with a hull heavy with barnacles.

The four of us walked slowly through the graveyard until Dickens had found a flat gravestone to his liking.

This long marble block was surrounded on either side by lower flat stones. Dickens disappeared behind a nearby stone wall—one that was about five feet high and beyond which stood the rented carriage (with a liveried servant on the box)—we could see only the Inimitable's head as he conferred with the driver and as both then repaired to the boot of the carriage. Then Dickens returned with four cushions, set them on the flat gravestones on either side of the longest one, and bade us to sit.

We did so. Ellen and Mrs Ternan were obviously disconcerted by this unusual—not to say ghoulish—introduction of cushioned comfort to such surroundings. A tall tree to the west of us drew the ink-scrabble shadows of its bare branches across us and our chosen gravestones. None of us could manage any small talk as Dickens hurried to the gate and trotted around behind the wall to confer with his servant again.

In a flash, Dickens was back, carrying one long chequered cloth—which he proceeded to drape across the longest gravestone, transforming it into a caricature of a domestic dinner table—and with another white napkin draped over his free arm in the manner of self-important waiters since Adam's day. A few seconds later he was out of sight and—with little help from his man—had laid a row of plates atop the wall. I must say that it all felt very familiar—rather as if we were at a Parisian sidewalk dining establishment. Then Dickens bustled back into sight, napkin still in place, the very image of a first-class headwaiter, and one by one he served each of us, beginning, of course, with the ladies.

Out of a large hamper set atop the wall, Dickens magically produced fried sole and whiting with shrimp sauce, crackers and pâté, a brace of well-grilled birds which I first thought were squab but which I soon realised were delightful little pheasants (to which Waiter Dickens applied the sauce with a flourish), then ladles

380 • DAN SIMMONS

full of roast haunch of mutton with stewed onions and browned potatoes, all followed by pound puddings. Along with the food came a chilled white wine—which Dickens, now turned sommelier, uncorked and poured with much ado while awaiting our judgement with batting eyes and pursed lips—and then a large bottle of champagne still in its bucket of ice.

Dickens was having such fun playing waiter and wine steward that he had little time to eat. By the time he had produced the pound puddings—offering a rich sauce, which the ladies declined but which I accepted at once—his face was flushed and he was perspiring despite the November afternoon's slow cooling into evening.

At rare times in one's life, Dear Reader, even the most gentle person is given a tool—a weapon, actually—without wishing it, sometimes having it thrust into his hand, by which he can bring down an entire edifice with a single sentence. Such was my situation during our strange repast in the Rochester graveyard, for I had recognised much of the luncheon's menu from a book popular some fifteen years earlier. The book was titled *What Shall We Have for Dinner?* and the recipes therein had been accumulated, according to the publishers, by a certain pseudonymous Lady Maria Clutterbuck.

Oh, how the Ternan ladies, miss and missus, now gay from the wine and champagne, would have sobered instantly to learn that their delightful (if ghoulish) graveyard luncheon menu had been planned by none other than Catherine Dickens, the rejected and exiled wife. Although Catherine had been completely abandoned (my brother, Charley, told me that she had written Dickens an imploring letter about their son only a month earlier, requesting a conversation in person about Plorn's problems, to which Dickens refused even to pen a reply, instructing Georgina to send a cold, curt note in his stead), but quite obviously her incarnation as Lady Clutterbuck (Catherine had not yet become so heavy when she'd collected and published the menus in 1851) was still very welcome at Gad's Hill. Or at least her recipes were.

During the meal and the inconsequential conversation, I studied Ellen Ternan even as she ignored me. It had been eight years since I had spent any time in her presence. The years had not enhanced her beauty. She had been youthfully attractive as an eighteen-year-old ingenue but now qualified only as "handsome." She was the kind of woman with sad, soulful eyes (which did little for me, since such sad eyes usually hinted at a poetic character given to melancholy and a rigidly defended virginity), descending brows, a long nose, and a wide, thin-lipped mouth. (I prefer just the opposite in my young women—tiny noses and full lips, the latter preferably curved upward in an inviting smile.) Ellen had a strong chin, but where that edifice had suggested a certain perky strength in her youth, it now implied only the prideful stubbornness of a woman beyond her mid-twenties who had not yet married. Her hair was attractive, not terribly long and receding in artfully sculpted waves from a high, clear forehead, but the hairdo exposed ears that were much too large for my taste. Her earrings, which hung down like three bullseye lanterns, hinted of the underlying vulgarity of her former profession. Her carefully elocuted but somehow terminally empty sentences suggested stilted conversation arising from a simple lack of education. Her lovely vowels and precise, theatrically honed cadences could not conceal an underlying ignorance that should have instantly disqualified this ageing ingenue from being the consort of England's most honoured writer. Nor did I perceive from her the slightest hint of a hidden passionate nature that could have made up for her obvious shortcomings…and my Wilkie-antennae were highly sensitive to any such subtle *sub-rosa* erotic transmissions from even the most proper and upstanding ladies.

Ellen Ternan was simply a bore. She was as dull as the proverbial ditch water and soon would be a matronly bore to boot.

We finished dining as the shadows of the afternoon were falling across us and as the chill from our gravestone chairs had begun to creep up through the cushions into our posterior regions. Tired of playing waiter, Dickens wolfed the last of his pudding, gulped the last of his champagne, and summoned his servant to tidy up. Plates, glasses, utensils, serving dishes, and finally the table cloth, napkins, and cushions all disappeared into hampers and then into the back of the carriage in a blur of liveried efficiency. Only crumbs remained as evidence of our graveyard feast.

We walked the Ternans to the carriage.

"Thank you for a lovely—if unusual—afternoon," said Ellen Ternan, taking Dickens's cold hand in her gloved one. "It was a great pleasure seeing you again, Mr Collins," she said to me, her cool tone and curt nod belying the warm words. Mrs Ternan clucked similar sentiments while exerting even less effort to make them sound convincing. Then the servant was up on the box again, the whip was out, and the carriage clattered away into Rochester, presumably towards Ellen Ternan's waiting uncle.

I could tell by the concupiscent gleam in Charles Dickens's eyes that he knew he would be seeing Ellen that very evening, most probably in the privacy of his or her secret house in Slough.

"Well, my dear Wilkie," he said in a tone of pure satisfaction, tugging his gloves back on, "what did you think of our luncheon?"

"I thought it delightful, in a terrifically morbid way," I said.

"Mere prelude, my friend," chuckled Dickens. "Mere prelude. Fortifying ourselves for the serious purpose of our day...or evening. Ah, here's our man!"

THE MAN APPROACHING US there in the gathering gloom with his shapeless hat in hand was ragged, short, dirty, and drunk. He was clothed head to foot in layers of grimy grey flannel that seemed to have been liberally dusted with flakes of stone and a frosting of lime. At his feet he had dropped a heavy bundle tied in a grimy canvas cloth. I could smell the rum fumes flowing from him—from his pores, from his clothes, most probably from his very bones. At the same time I was sniffing him, he seemed to be sniffing me; perhaps he could smell the opium on me through his own reek. We stood and stared and sniffed each other like two dogs in an alley.

"Wilkie," said Dickens, "I would like to introduce Mr Dradles, who goes by just Dradles, although I have heard folks in Rochester say that his first name is Granite, which I have to assume is a nickname. Dradles is a stonemason—chiefly in a gravestone, tomb, and monument way—but he is also hired by the Cathedral for rough repairs and thus is the holder of all the keys for the Cathedral tower, crypt, side doors, and other such obvious and forgotten entrances. Mr Dradles, it is my honour to introduce you in turn to Mr Wilkie Collins."

The stooped, bewhiskered figure in the rough flannel and chipped horn buttons grunted something that might have been a greeting. I bowed and offered a more polite salutation in return.

"Dradles," I then said brightly. "What a marvellous

name! Is it real or a by-product of your profession in some way?"

"Dradles is Dradles's name," growled the little man. "And Dradles wonders—is Collins your real name or made up some way? And Dradles don't remember Wilkie as being no Christian name."

I blinked and straightened, gripping my walking stick more tightly in pure manly reflex to this hint of an insult. "I am named after Sir David Wilkie, the famous Scottish painter," I said stiffly.

"If you say so, gov'ner," grunted Dradles. "Although I never heard of a Scotsman who could paint a stables right, much less a church or house."

"Wilkie's given first name is actually William," said Dickens. He was smiling as if amused.

"Billy Collins," grunted Dradles. "Dradles knew a Billy Collins when Dradles was a lad. A troublesome Irish boy with no more brains nor common sense than a sheep."

I gripped my stick harder and looked at Dickens, sending the clear message—*Must I stay here and suffer this from the local village drunkard?*

Before Dickens—who was still smiling—could answer, we were both distracted by a missile that flew between us, barely missing Dickens's shoulder and my ear, and which then bounced off the russet-coloured cap that Dradles was holding in his filthy right hand. A second small stone zipped by my left shoulder and hit the stonemason squarely in the chest.

Dradles grunted again but seemed neither surprised nor injured.

Dickens and I turned in time to see a young boy, no more than seven or eight and all unkempt hair, ragged clothes, and untied bootlaces, hide behind a headstone near the wall that separated this graveyard from the road.

"It ain't time! It ain't time!" shouted Dradles.

"Yer lie!" shouted the ragged youth and pitched another stone at the mason. Dickens and I took a step away from the boy's sturdy target.

"D——n your blasted eyes!" shouted Dradles. "If Dradles says it ain't time, it ain't time. No tea today! Get yourself off to the Thatched and Twopenny and leave off on the pitching or there'll be no 'apenny from Dradles to you today!"

"Yer lie!" returned the Young Devil and pitched another rock, a larger one this time, which caught the stonemason just above the knee. Dirt, tiny chips of stone, clumps of old mortar, and lime dust flew from the man's trousers as his tormentor screamed, "Widdy widdy wee! I—ket—ches—'im—out—ar—ter—tea!"

Dradles sighed and said, "Dradles sometimes pays the lad a 'apenny to pelt him homewards should Dradles forget to head home for tea or t' the house after ten. This is my usual tea time and I forgot to turn the reminding apparatus off, as it were."

Dickens howled and slapped his thigh with delight at this information. Another small stone flew by us and just missed the stonemason's cheek.

"Hold your hand!" bellowed Dradles to the tiny loose-laced phantom flitting from headstone to headstone. "Or there'll be no 'apenny for you this fortnight and more! Dradles has business with these here gentlemen and they don't 'preciate the pelting."

"Yer lie!" shouted the boy from the gloom behind some shrubbery between ancient headstones.

"He'll not bother us more 'til our business is done," said Dradles. He squinted at me and then squinted less malevolently at Dickens. "What is it you wanted Dradles to show you this evening, Mr D.?"

"Mr Wilkie Collins and I would like to see if there's anything new down in your place of business," said Dickens.

Dradles grunted rum fumes at us. "Anything old is more what you mean," he growled. "The crypts ain't much for novelty. Not in these days, at least."

"We shall be delighted to see what is old, then," said Dickens. "Lead the way, sir. Mr Collins and I shall offer our willing, if not broad, backs as a shield between you and your quick-armed tormentor."

"Bother the Deputy," Dradles grunted cryptically. "Stones is Dradles's work and life and only love, other 'n drink, and a few more pebbles won't bother him none."

And thus, with Dradles striding ahead and Dickens and me muddling along shoulder to shoulder behind him, we proceeded towards the great cathedral whose cold shadow had now enveloped the entire graveyard.

BEYOND THE EDGE of the graveyard there was a high-mounded pit with fumes rising from it. Dradles, clutching his heavy bundle to his chest, walked past it without comment, but Dickens paused and said, "This is lime, is it not?"

"Aye," said Dradles.

"What you call quick-lime?" I asked.

The old man squinted over his shoulder at me. "Aye, quick enough to eat your suit and buttons and boots without any help, Mr Billy Wilkie Collins. And with a little stirrin', quick enough to eat most of your spectacles, watch, teeth, an' bones as well."

Dickens pointed to the fuming pit and smiled enigmatically. I removed my spectacles, rubbed my watering eyes, and followed them.

I had assumed we were going up into the tower. Dickens often brought guests to Rochester—it was a short enough ride from Gad's Hill—and he almost always arranged to have them go up into the tower to take in the view of the old city, all grey blocks and shadowed streets, and of the sea beyond to one side and the forests and roads stretching back to Gad's Hill and beyond to the other horizon.

Not this day.

After much clanking of key rings (the old man seemed to have keys in every oversized pocket of his flannel trousers, jacket, and waistcoat), Dradles opened a heavy side door and we followed him down narrow stone stairs into the crypt.

I do not mind telling you, Dear Reader, that I was terribly weary of crypts. I do not blame you if you are as well. I had spent the previous night in an opium-scented space that resembled nothing so much as a crypt, and too much of my following Charles Dickens the past year and more had led into dank places like this.

Dradles had brought no lantern and we did not need one: the dying November light came down from above in dim shafts through groined windows that had long been devoid of glass. We walked between massive pillars that rose above us up into the cathedral proper like great roots or tree trunks of stone, and in their shadows the darkness was almost absolute, but we kept to the narrow lanes of fading light.

Dradles set his lumpy bundle on a stone ledge, untied laces at the top, and fumbled in the bag. I expected him to disinter a bottle—I could hear it sloshing—but instead he came out with a small hammer.

"Watch this, Wilkie!" whispered Dickens. "And listen! And learn."

I thought I had learned quite enough for one day, but I followed as Dradles re-lashed his bundle and led the way down an even narrower corridor between even thicker columns and darker pools of shadow. Suddenly he began tapping the inner walls.

"Hear that?" the old mason asked—absurdly, I

thought, since the taps echoed and rebounded everywhere in the crypt. "Tap and solid," he whispered. "Now I go on tapping...solid still. And more. Solid still. And more...halloa! Hollow! We keep going around the corner here—mind your step; there's some stairs there in the dark—we keep going and keep tapping and Dradles's ear keeps hearing what your ear and others' don't and can't hear and...ahah! Solid in hollow there! And inside solid, hollow again!"

We all stopped. It was very dark here around the corner, where more steps presumably led down to deeper vaults.

"What does it mean?" I asked. "Inside solid, hollow again?"

"Why, it means that there's an old 'un tumbled and crumbled in there, Mr Billy Wilkie Collins!" growled Dradles. "An old 'un in a stone coffin, and the stone coffin in a vault!"

I could feel Dickens's gaze upon me as if this Dradles-person's deduction were a significant feat, but I reserved the right to remain something less than overwhelmed. This was not a case of that French phenomenon in which I had some interest—*clairvoyance,* or "bright seeing." I mean, it was, after all, a church crypt. It did not take a rude, drunken man playing with a mason's hammer to tell us that there were bones behind the walls.

Dradles led us deeper into the crypt vault. We needed a lantern now and we did not have one. I used my walking stick to sound out the irregular stone stairs beneath my feet as they spiralled down around one of the great stone trusses that housed the crypts and held up the cathedral. I had dressed for the unusually warm and sunny afternoon, and this subterranean cold made me shiver and wish for home and a fire.

"Aye," said Dradles as if I had spoken aloud, "the

cold here is worse 'n cold. It's the damp. The rising damp. It's the cold breath of the dead old 'uns on either side of us and beneath us and, in a minute, above us. The dead 'uns' breath reaches to the cathedral up 'bove and stains the stone and discolours them pretty frescoes and rots the wood and causes the choir to shiver in their robes. Dradles can hear the rising damp seeping out of the chinks and crevices of these older coffins as surely as Dradles can hear the dead old 'uns echo back their answer to his taps."

I started to give a sarcastic retort, but before I could speak there came the startling TAP, TAP, TAP of his hammer again. This time I imagined that I could hear something of the complex echoes myself. Dradles's voice seemed extraordinarily loud in the winding stone chamber.

"There's two of them about seven feet in, both of them old 'uns with a crook—I fancy they must've crook-hitched one another good when they met promiscuous-like, the way it must've been in the dark when candles were the thing—and they're laid out in what was an underground chapel here long time ago, closed up back when all the heads was rolling and everyone was lifting toasts to Bonnie Prince Charlie and all that."

Dickens and I stood in the dark where we were while Dradles descended another dozen steps. The chill touch of rising damp moving past our ankles and necks made my hackles rise.

TAP, TAP, TAP...TAP, TAP...TAP, TAP, TAP, TAP.

"There!" cried Dradles, his voice echoing terribly. "Hear that?"

"What do we hear, Mr Dradles?" asked Dickens.

There came a scraping and slithering sound.

"Just my foot rule," said Dradles. "Dradles measuring

in the dark. Measuring in the dark is what Dradles is doing. Wall's thicker here...two foot of stone, then four of space beyond. Dradles hears the tap-back of some rubble and rubbish that the careless ones who interred this old 'un left between the stone coffin and the stone wall. Six feet in there an old 'un is waiting amidst the fall-down and left-behind—just lying and waiting, no top to his box. If I were to break through with my larger hammer and pick, this old 'un, bishop-hatted crook-type or no, would sit up and open his eyes and say, 'Why, Dradles, my man, I've been waiting for you a devil of a time!' And then he'd turn to powder sure as not."

"Let us get out of this place," I said. I meant to whisper it, but my voice sounded very loud in the winding dark and rising damp.

OUTSIDE IN THE LAST of the November evening light, Dickens paid the insolent man some coins and waved him off with thank-yous and what I heard as conspiratorial laughter. Dradles slumped away, still clutching his bundle. He'd not got twenty feet when there was a cry of "Widdy widdy wive! I—ket—ches—'im—out—ar—ter—five...Widdy widdy wy! Then—E—don't—go—then—I—shy!" and there came an absolute hailstorm of small stones pelting around and against the grey-flannelled figure.

"What a character!" cried Dickens when Dradles and the insane child finally disappeared from sight. "What a wonderful character! Do you know, my dear Wilkie, that when I first met Mr Dradles he was busy tap-tapping away at an inscription on some headstone soon to be set in place—it was for a recently deceased pastry-cook and muffin-maker, I believe—and when I introduced myself, he immediately said, 'Here in my world I'm a bit like you, Mr Dickens.' And then Dradles gestured to all the tombs and headstones and headstones in the making around him and added, 'Surrounded by my works and words like a popular author, I mean.'"

Dickens laughed again, but I remained uncharmed and unmoved. Inside the now-lighted cathedral, a choir was singing, "Tell me shep-herds, te-e-ell me...."

"You know, Wilkie," said Dickens, still in good humour despite the late hour and growing chill as a breeze came up around us, stirring the brittle leaves across the flat headstone we had dined on only hours earlier, "I believe I know the name of that choirmaster."

"Yes?" I said, allowing my tone to convey my total lack of interest in this fact.

"Yes. I do believe his name is Jasper. Jacob Jasper, I believe. *No*, John Jasper. That is it. Jack to his beloved and loving nephew."

It was not like Dickens to babble on like this, at least not with such banal content. "You don't say?" I said, using the tone I used with Caroline when she prattled at me while I was reading a newspaper.

"I do say," said Dickens. "And do you know Mr Jasper's secret, my dear Wilkie?"

"How could I?" I said with some small asperity. "I did not even know of the choirmaster's existence until a second ago."

"Indeed," said Dickens, rubbing his hands together. "Mr John Jasper's secret is that he is an opium addict."

The skin on my face prickled and I found myself standing very straight. I do not believe I breathed for half a minute or so.

"The worst kind of opium addict," continued the Inimitable. "No laudanum or tincture of opium for Mr John Jasper, the way a civilised white man uses the drug for medicinal purposes. Oh, no! Mr John Jasper takes himself to the worst parts of London, then to the worst slums in those worst parts, and seeks out the worst—that is, to him, the *best*—opium den."

"Does he?" I managed. I could feel the rising damp stealing up through my bones to my brain and tongue.

"And our choirmaster Jasper is also a murderer," said Dickens. "A cold-blooded, calculating murderer, who, even in his opium dreams, plans to take the life of someone who loves and trusts him."

"Dickens," I said at last, "what in the blazes are you talking about?"

He clapped me on the back as we began walking across the graveyard towards the road where his carriage had just returned. "A fiction, of course," he said with a laugh. "That ghost of a glimmer of a shade of an idea—a character, a hint of a story. You know how such things happen, my dear Wilkie."

I managed to swallow. "Of course. Is that what this afternoon and evening have been about then, my dear Dickens? Preparation for one of your books? Something for *All the Year Round,* perhaps?"

"Not preparation for *my* book!" cried Dickens. "For *your* book, my dear Wilkie! For your *Serpent's Tooth.*"

"*The Eye of the Serpent,*" I corrected. "Or perhaps, *The Serpent's Eye.*"

Dickens waved away the difference. It was becoming difficult to see him in the growing darkness. The lamps on the carriage were lit.

"No matter," he said. "The idea is the *tale,* my friend. You have your wonderful Sergeant Cuff. But even the best detective requires a mystery to solve if he is to be of any use or interest to your readers. *That* is what I hoped would come of our luncheon and Dradles outing today."

"A mystery?" I said stupidly. "What mystery was there today?"

Dickens opened his hands and arms to take in the dark cathedral, the darker graveyard, and the many tombs and headstones. "Imagine a villain so devilish and clever, my dear Wilkie, that he murders someone simply to have had the experience of murder. Not murder a family member, as was the way of it in the Road Case in which you and I were both so interested—no, but to murder a stranger, or near-stranger. A murder with no motive whatsoever."

"Why on earth would any human being do that?" I asked. Dickens was making no sense to me whatsoever.

"I just explained," he said with perhaps some small exasperation. "*To have the experience of having murdered someone.* Imagine what a boon that would be to an author such as yourself—or to me. To any writer of imaginative prose, much less the sensationalist imaginative prose for which you are known, my dear Wilkie."

"Are you talking about preparation for reading a Murder in your upcoming tour?" I asked.

"Good heavens, no. I have my poor Nancy waiting to be done in by that ultimate villain, Bill Sikes, someday. Not now. Already I have jotted down improvements on the method and description of that bloody massacre. I am talking about *your* tale, my friend."

"But my tale is about a diamond that brings bad luck to the family that…"

"Oh, bother the diamond!" cried Dickens. "That was just an early draft of an idea. The Koh-i-noor diamond was a disappointment to everyone who went out of their way to see it at the Great Exhibition. Its color was a sickly, urine yellow—no real diamond to the English eye. Toss away your worthless gem, Wilkie, and follow the path of this new tale!"

"What tale?"

Dickens sighed. He ticked off the elements on the fingers of his gloved hand. "Element the first—the idea of someone murdering a near-stranger simply for the experience of having murdered. Element the second— the perfect way to dispose of a body. Your Sergeant Cuff will have a devil of a time figuring that out!"

"What are we speaking of?" I said. "I encountered no sure-fire way of disposing of a body in our bizarre luncheon or more-bizarre tour with the drunken Dradles."

"But of course you did!" cried Dickens. "First there is the quick-lime. Certainly you have not forgotten that Pit!"

"My eyes and nose have not."

"Nor should they, my dear Wilkie! Imagine your readers in terror as they come to understand that your murderer—your casual, random murderer, like Iago, moved by a motiveless malignancy—has dissolved the body of some poor chap in a pit of quick-lime. Everything down to the last few bones and pearl buttons and perhaps a watch. Or a skull."

"There would still be those remaining last bones. And the watch and skull," I said sullenly. "And the pit would be right there in the open for Sergeant Cuff and the police to discover."

"Not for a minute!" cried Dickens. "Did you not understand the gift I gave you in Dradles? Your villain shall enlist—knowingly or unknowingly shall be up to your novelistic judgement, of course—just such a *character* as Dradles to help him inter the poor, pitiful remnants of his murder victim in just such a tomb or vault as we saw, or heard, rather, this evening. The last bits of the murdered man—or woman, if you truly want a sensational novel, my friend—shall be interred alongside the old 'uns, and that will be an end to him—until your clever Sergeant Cuff works it all out through a series of clues that only Wilkie Collins could provide."

We stood there for a moment in a silence broken only by the shifting of the two carriage horses and the more furtive shifting of the cold servant on the driver's box. Finally I said, "All very wonderful...very Dickens-like, I am sure...but I believe I prefer my original idea of a fabled gem sacred to the Hindoos or other heathens, bringing bad luck to some illustrious English family."

Dickens sighed. "Oh, very well. Have it the way you insist. Look a gift horse in the withers, if you must." But I heard him say much more softly, "Even though the gem and the Hindoos were my idea, which I have now seen to be too weak to bear the tale."

More loudly, he said, "May I drop you at the station?"

Dickens's uncharacteristic omission of an invitation to Gad's Hill for supper told me what I already knew—that he would be dining with Ellen Ternan and that he had no intention of returning to Gad's Hill Place that night.

"That would be fine," I said. "Caroline will be waiting for me."

As he held the carriage door for me, Dickens said softly, presumably so the coachman would not hear, "Before you dine with the lovely Landlady or the delightful Butler tonight, my dear Wilkie, I would advise a change of raiments and perhaps a warm bath."

I paused with one foot on the step, but before I could say something related to opium or to anything else, Dickens added innocently, "The crypts do leave an echo of the rising damp on one, you know...as our friend Dradles illustrated so wonderfully this evening."

CHAPTER NINETEEN

*C*harles Dickens is going to murder Edmond
Dickenson."

It was the second time in eighteen months that I had
sat straight up in bed out of a deep laudanum sleep and
shouted those words.

"No," I said into the dark, still half-claimed by
dream but also imbued with the complete deductive
certainty of my yet-to-be created Detective Sergeant
Cuff, "Charles Dickens has *already* murdered Edmond
Dickenson."

"Wilkie, darling," said Caroline, sitting up next to
me and seizing my arm, "what are you going on about?
You've been talking in your sleep, my dearest."

"Leave me alone," I said groggily, shaking off her
hand. I rose, pulled on my dressing gown, and went to
the window.

"Wilkie, my dear..."

"Silence!" My heart was pounding. I was trying not
to lose the clarity of my dream-revelation.

I found my watch on the bureau and looked at it. It
was a little before three in the morning. Outside, the
paving stones were slick with a light sleet falling. I
looked at the streetlamp and then searched the small
porch on the abandoned house on the corner opposite
that lamp until I saw the shadow huddled there. Inspector Field's messenger—a boy with strange eyes whom

the inspector called Gooseberry—was still there, more than a year after I had first spied him waiting.

I left the bedroom and started for my study but paused on the landing. It was night. The Other Wilkie would be in there, waiting, most probably sitting at my desk and watching the door with unblinking eyes. I went downstairs instead to the small secretary in the parlour, where Caroline and Carrie kept their writing materials. Setting my glasses firmly in place, I wrote—

> Inspector Field:
> I have good reason to believe that Charles Dickens has murdered a young man who survived the Staplehurst train wreck, a Mr Edmond Dickenson. Please meet me at ten AM at Waterloo Bridge so that we can discuss the evidence and prepare a way of trapping Dickens into admitting to the murder of young Dickenson.
> Yr. Obedient Servant,
> William Wilkie Collins

I looked at the missive for a long moment, nodded, folded it, set it in a thick envelope, used my father's stamp to seal it, and placed it in an inner pocket of my dressing gown. Then I took some coins from my purse, found my overcoat in the hall closet, pulled on rubbers over my slippers, and went out into the night.

I had just reached the streetlamp on my side of the street when a shadow on the porch opposite separated itself from the deeper shadow of the porch overhang. In an instant the boy had crossed the street to meet me. He had no coat on and was shivering violently in the rain and cold.

"You are Gooseberry?" I asked.

"Yessir."

I put my hand on the letter but for some reason did not draw it out. "Is Gooseberry your last name?" I asked.

"No, sir. Inspector Field calls me that, sir. Because of my eyes, you see."

I did see. The boy's eyes were distinguished not only by their absurd prominence but by the fact that they rolled to and fro like two bullets in an egg cup. My fingers tightened on the letter to his master, but still I hesitated.

"You're a crossing sweeper, Gooseberry?"

"I *was* a crossing sweeper, sir. No longer."

"What are you now, lad?"

"I'm in training with the great Inspector Field to be a detective, is what," said Gooseberry with pride, but with no hint of boasting. Between shivers he coughed. It was a deep cough—the kind that had given my mother the horrors whenever any similar sound emerged from Charles or me when we were young—but the urchin had the manners to cover his mouth when he coughed.

"What is your real name, boy?" I asked.

"Guy Septimus Cecil," said the boy through slightly chattering teeth.

I let go of the letter and brought five shillings out, dropping them into Guy Septimus Cecil's hurriedly raised palm. I am not sure that I have ever seen another person quite so surprised, with the probable exception of the thugs Mr Reginald Barris had clubbed down in the alley in Birmingham.

"There'll be no message from me to your master tonight or for the next three days and nights, Master Guy Septimus Cecil," I said softly. "Go get a hot breakfast. Rent a room—a *heated* room. And with whatever you have left over, buy a coat...something made of good English wool to go over those rags. You'll be no good to either Inspector Field or to me if you catch your death of cold out here."

The boy's gooseberry eyes wandered, although they never seemed to fix on me.

"Go on, now!" I said sternly. "Don't let me see you back here until Tuesday next!"

"Yessir," Gooseberry said dubiously. But he turned and trotted back across the street, hesitated by the porch, and ran on down the street towards the promise of warmth and food.

HAVING DECIDED TO DO the hard detective work related to the murder of Edmond Dickenson myself, I set about it with a will the next morning. Fortifying myself with two-and-a-half cups of laudanum (about two hundred minims, if one were applying the medicine drop-by-drop), I took the mid-day train to Chatham and hired a cart to whisk me—although "plod me" would be a better choice of verb given the age and indifference of both the horse and cart-driver—to Gad's Hill Place.

As I approached the important interview with Dickens, I began to see more clearly the to-this-point-amorphous idea of my fictional detective in *The Eye of the Serpent* (or perhaps *The Serpent's Eye*), Sergeant Cuff. Rather than the brusque, stolid, and gruff Inspector Bucket of Dickens's *Bleak House*—an unimaginative character in the most literal sense, I thought, since he was based so clearly on the younger version of the actual Inspector Field—my Sergeant Cuff would be tall, thin, older, ascetic, and rational. More than anything else, rational, as if addicted to ratiocination. I also imagined my ascetic, grey-haired, hatchet-faced, ratiocinated, pale-eyed and clear-eyed Sergeant Cuff as nearing retirement. He would be looking forward, I realised, to devoting his post-detective life to beekeeping. No, not beekeeping—too odd, too eccentric, and too difficult for me to research. Perhaps—growing roses. That was the ticket...roses. I knew something about roses and their care and breeding. Sergeant Cuff would know...everything about roses.

Most detectives begin with the murder and spend ages following roundabout clues to the murderer, but Sergeant Cuff and I would invert the process by starting with the murderer and then seeking out the corpse.

"My dear Wilkie, what a pleasant surprise! The pleasure of your company two days in a row!" cried Dickens as I approached the house and he came out, tugging on a wool cape-coat against the chill wind. "You're staying for the rest of the weekend, I trust."

"No, just stopping by for a quick word with you, Charles," I said. His welcoming smile was so obviously sincere in his childlike way—a little boy whose playmate has shown up unexpectedly—that I had to return the smile, even though inside I was holding fast to the cool, neutral expression of Sergeant Cuff.

"Wonderful! I've just finished my morning's work on the last of the introductions and my Christmas story and was about to set out on my walk. Join me, dear friend!"

The thought of a twelve- or twenty-mile hike at Charles Dickens's pace on this windy, snow-threatening November day caused a headache to start its throbbing behind my right eye. "I wish I could, my dear Dickens. But as you mentioned Christmas...well, that was one of the things that I wished to talk to you about."

"Really?" He paused. "*You*—the original 'Bah! Humbug!' Wilkie Collins—interested in *Christmas*?" he said and threw back his head for a true Dickens laugh. "Well, now I can say that I have lived long enough to see all improbabilities come to pass."

I forced another smile. "I was just wondering if you were having one of your usual galas this year. The day is not too far distant, you know."

"No, no, no, it isn't," said Dickens. Suddenly he was

calmly and coolly appraising me. "And no, no gala this year, I fear. The new round of readings begins in early December, you may recall."

"Ah, yes."

"I shall be home for a day or two for Christmas itself," said Dickens, "and of course you shall be invited. But it shall be a modest affair this year, I'm sorry to tell you, my dear Wilkie."

"No worry, no worry," I said hurriedly, improvising my little scene in a way that I felt would do justice to the yet-to-be-created Sergeant Cuff. "I was just curious...will you be inviting Macready this year?"

"Macready? No, I think not. I believe his wife is indisposed this season anyway. And Macready travels less and less these days, you remember, Wilkie."

"Of course. And Dickenson?"

"Who?"

Aha! I thought. Charles Dickens, the Inimitable, the novelist, the man with the iron memory, would not, could not, ever forget the name of the young man whom he'd saved at Staplehurst. This was a murderer's— or soon-to-be-murderer's—dissembling!

"Dickenson," I said. "Edmond. Surely you remember last Christmas, Charles! The somnambulist!"

"Oh, of course, of course," said Dickens even while he waved away the name and the memory. "No. We shan't be inviting young Edmond this Christmas. Just family this year. And the closest friends."

"Really?" I feigned surprise. "I thought that you and young Dickenson were rather close."

"Not at all," said Dickens while he pulled on his expensive and far-too-thin-for-such-a-day kid gloves. "I merely looked in on the young man from time to time during his first months of recovery. He was, you remember, Wilkie, an orphan."

"Ah, yes," I said, as if I could have forgotten this

essential clue as to why Dickens had chosen him as his murder victim. "Actually, I had rather looked forward to chatting with young Dickenson on a couple of topics we were discussing last Christmas. Do you remember his address by any chance, Charles?"

Now he was looking at me most queerly. "You wish to pick up a conversation you were having with Edmond Dickenson almost a year ago?"

"Yes," I said in what I hoped was my most authoritative Sergeant Cuff manner.

Dickens shrugged. "I'm quite sure I don't remember his address, if I ever knew it. Actually, I believe he moved around quite a bit...restless young bachelor, always changing quarters and so forth."

"Hmmm," I said. I was squinting against the cold wind out of the north that was rustling Dickens's winter-pruned hedges and driving the last of the sere leaves from the trees in his front yard, but I might as well have been squinting through the suspicion I felt.

"In fact," Dickens said brightly, "I believe I remember young Dickenson left England last summer or autumn. To go make his fortune in southern France. Or South Africa. Or Australia. Some promising place like that."

He's playing with me, I thought with an electric surge of Sergeant Cuff–ish certainty. *But he does not know that I am playing with him.*

"Too bad," I said. "I would have enjoyed seeing young Edmond again. But there's nothing for it."

"There isn't," agreed Dickens, his voice muffled by the thick red scarf he'd pulled up over his lower face. "Are you sure you won't join me for the walk? It's a perfect day for it."

"Another day," I said and shook his hand. "My cart and driver are waiting."

But I waited until the writer was out of sight and the tap of his stick out of earshot and then I rapped at the door, handed my hat and scarf to the servant who answered, and went quickly to the kitchen, where Georgina Hogarth was seated at the servants' table going over menus.

"Mr Wilkie, what a pleasant surprise!"

"Halloo, Georgina, halloo," I said affably. I wondered if I should have wore a disguise. Detectives often wore disguises. I'm sure that Sergeant Cuff did upon occasion, despite his uniquely tall and ascetic appearance. Sergeant Cuff was almost certainly a master of disguises. But then, that ageing Scotland Yard detective did not suffer the handicaps of my disguise-proof shortness, full beard, receding hairline, weak eyes that demanded spectacles, and oversized, bulbous forehead.

"Georgina," I said easily, "I just ran into Charles on his way off to his walk and popped in because my friends and I are planning a small dinner party—a few artists and literary people—and I thought that young Dickenson might enjoy such an evening. But we don't have his address."

"Young Dickenson?" Her expression was blank. Was she an accomplice? "Oh," she said, "you mean that boring young gentleman who sleepwalked here Christmas Day night last."

"Precisely."

"Oh, he was terribly boring," said Georgina. "Hardly worth inviting to your wonderful party."

"Possibly not," I agreed, "but we thought he might enjoy it."

"Well, I do remember sending out the Christmas invitations last year, so please follow me into the drawing room to the secretary where I keep my files...."

Ahah! cried the successful ghost of the unborn Sergeant Cuff.

· · ·

GEORGINA HOGARTH'S FEW NOTES from Dickens to Edmond Dickenson had all been mailed to (and presumably then fowarded by) a barrister by the name of Matthew B. Roffe of Gray's Inn Square. I knew this area well, of course, since I had also studied for the law—indeed, I once described myself as "a barrister of some fifteen years' standing, without ever having had a brief, or ever having even so much as donned a wig and gown." My own studies had taken place at the nearby Lincoln's Inn, although I confess that my "study" there consisted much more of attending to meals provided than to studying, although I do remember reading seriously for the Bar for six weeks or so. After that, my interest in law books waned even as my interest in the meals persisted. At that time, my friends were mostly painters and my own efforts mostly literary. But the Bar was more generous to gentlemen with vague legal aspirations then, and somehow, despite my lack of attendant effort, I became licensed as a barrister in 1851.

I had never heard of Mr Matthew B. Roffe and—based upon the dinginess of his small, cluttered, dusty, and remote third-storey office near Gray's Inn—neither had any clients. There was no clerk present in the low-ceilinged little closet of an outer office and no bell to announce me. I could see an old man wearing clothing twenty years out of date, eating a chop at his desk piled high with folders, testaments, volumes, and bric-a-brac, and I cleared my throat loudly to gain his attention.

He pressed a pair of pince-nez into place on his hook of a nose and stared out of that papered cavern with much blinking of his small and watery eyes. "Eh? What's that? Who's there? Enter, sir! Advance and be recognised!"

I advanced, but when I was not recognised, I gave my name. Mr Roffe had been smiling through the encounter so far, but his expression showed no further recognition upon hearing my name.

"I received your name and business address through my friend Charles Dickens," I said softly. It was not the full truth, but it certainly was not an outright lie. "Charles Dickens the novelist," I added.

The wizened marionette of a man was galvanised into a response consisting mostly of twitches and jerks. "Oh, my, good heavens, oh, yes, I mean…how wonderful, yes, of course…*The* Charles Dickens gave me your, I mean, gave *you my* name….Oh, where are my manners?…Do sit down, please, be seated please, Mr…ah?"

"Collins," I said. The chair he had waved me towards probably had not been unburdened of its stack of opened volumes and scrolled documents in years, if not decades. I leaned back against a high stool instead. "This is quite comfortable," I said, and, in a flourish perhaps not unworthy of Sergeant Cuff, added, "and better for my back."

"Oh, yes…well, yes…Would you like some tea, Mr…ah…Mr…oh, dear."

"Collins. And yes, I would love some tea."

"Smalley!" cried Mr Roffe towards the empty outer office. "Smalley, I say!"

"I believe your clerk is absent, Mr Roffe."

"Oh, yes…no, I mean…" The old man fumbled at his waistcoat, removed a watch, frowned at it, shook it next to his ear, and said, "Mr Collins, I trust it is not a little after nine in the morning or evening?"

"Indeed not," I said, referring to my own watch. "It is a bit after four in the afternoon, Mr Roffe."

"Ah, that explains Smalley's absence!" cried the old man as if we had solved a great mystery. "He always goes home for his tea at around three, not returning until after five."

"Your profession demands long hours of you," I said drily. I would have liked to have had that promised tea.

"Oh, yes, yes... to serve the law is more like a... like a... well, perhaps 'marriage' is the term I am looking for. Are you married, Mr Collins?"

"No, sir. That happy domestic state has eluded me, Mr Roffe."

"Myself as well, Mr Collins!" cried the old man, slapping the leather binding of a volume on his desk. "Myself as well. We are two fugitives from bliss, you and I, Mr Collins. But the law keeps me here from before the lamps are lighted in the morning—although, of course, that is Smalley's job, the lighting of the lamps—until they are extinguished late in the night."

I slowly withdrew from my jacket pocket a new leather-bound notebook which I had purchased precisely for this purpose—detective work. I then drew out a sharpened pencil and opened my notebook to the first blank page.

As if a gavel had been pounded, Mr Roffe sat more upright, clasped his hands together in front of him—thus quieting his long, twitching fingers for the first time—and generally looked as attentive as a man of his advanced years and character and obvious failing senses could look under the circumstances. "Yes, indeed," he said. "Now to our business, Mr Collins. What *is* our business, Mr Collins?"

"Master Edmond Dickenson," I said firmly, hearing the flinty yet sensitive Cuff overtones in the syllables as I spoke. I knew precisely how my creation would carry out such an interview.

"Ah, yes, of course... Do you bring word from Master Edmond, Mr Collins?"

"No, Mr Roffe, although I am acquainted with the young gentleman. I came to ask you about him, sir."

"Me? Well... yes, of course... delighted to be of

help, Mr Collins, and, through you, of course, of help to Mr Dickens, if Mr Dickens is desirous of my help."

"I am sure he would be, Mr Roffe, but it is I who am interested in the present whereabouts of Mr Dickenson. Could you give me his address, sir?"

The old man's face fell. "Alas, I cannot, Mr Collins."

"It is confidential?"

"No, no, nothing of the sort. Young Master Edmond has always been as open and transparent as a...a... well, a summer shower, sir, if you do not mind me trespassing in Mr Dickens's literary realm with the simile. Master Edmond would not mind my passing on to you his current address."

I licked the carefully sharpened tip of the pencil and waited.

"But, alas," said old Mr Roffe, "I cannot. I do not know where Master Edmond is living at present. He used to keep a suite of rooms here in London—a short walk only from Gray's Inn Square here, to be precise— but I know he gave those up during the past year. I have no idea where Master Edmond resides now."

"With his guardian, perhaps?" I prompted. Sergeant Cuff would never be stopped by an old man's faulty memory.

"His guardian?" repeated Roffe. The old gentleman seemed slightly startled. "Well, that is...could be, I mean...might be...a possibility."

I had searched my own memory and notes of my discussion with young Dickenson eighteen months earlier in his sick-room at the Charing Cross Hotel before beginning this investigation. "That would be a Mr Watson in Northamptonshire, Mr Roffe? A onetime liberal M.P., I believe?"

"Well, yes," said Roffe, obviously impressed with my knowledge. "But, alas, no! Dear Mr Roland Everett Watson passed away some fourteen years ago. Young

Master Edmond moved from place to place after that at the whim of the Court's appointments of guardianship…you understand…an aunt in Kent, a travelling uncle with a town home in London—Mr Spicehead was in India most of the time Master Edmond was in his titular care…his grandmother's failing cousin for a year or so after that. Edmond was raised mostly by servants, you understand."

I waited as patiently as I could given the painfully impatient promptings of my rheumatical gout.

"And then, when Master Edmond turned eighteen years of age," continued old Roffe, "I was appointed his guardian, although of course it was a purely financial formality. Master Edmond had long since taken rooms in the City by then and because the stipulations of the will were very generous and elastic, Master Edmond, from a very young age, could…and did… gain access to his funds almost without adult supervision.…But since I had administered those funds for the years before that…I handled the legal work of Master Edmond's grandfather, long ago, you see, and his late parents' will stipulated that I should keep the books for the inheritance and…"

"How did Mr Dickenson's parents die?" I asked. It was not so much of an interruption as it appears here on the page, since Mr Roffe had paused to wheeze for breath.

"Die? Why, in a railway accident, of course!" he said when he could.

Ahah! I heard Sergeant Cuff cry in my ear. Dickenson comes to Charles Dickens's attention in a serious railway accident, and the boy's own parents died in a similar circumstance. Surely the odds of such a coincidence must have been remote. But what did it *mean*?

"Where was that accident?" I asked, making careful notes in my little book. "Not at Staplehurst, I trust?"

"Staplehurst! Good heavens, no! That was where young Master Edmond himself sustained injuries and was saved by your very own employer, Mr Charles Dickens!"

"Charles Dickens is not my..." I began but stopped. It did not matter if this old fool laboured under the delusion that I worked for Dickens. It might even loosen his tongue, although that tongue certainly seemed loose enough as it was.

"Back to the issue of guardianship," I said, lifting my little notebook. "You are Edmond Dickenson's *current* guardian and financial advisor?"

"Oh, my, no," said Roffe. "Besides the fact that the role of guardian passed from me almost a year ago to another more suited to the task, Master Dickenson came into his majority this very year. His twenty-first birthday came on September the fourteenth. I had Smalley send him our cordial congratulations every year. Every year but this one."

"And why no note this year, Mr Roffe?"

"Neither Smalley nor I had any idea where to contact him, Mr Collins." The old man looked woeful at this last revelation. I realised with a strangely sad certainty that young Dickenson was almost certainly this old man's only client—the only client of this dedicated husband to the law who worked in this tiny room from the time the lamps were lit before sunrise until long after that unseen sun had set.

"Could you tell me who Mr Dickenson's final guardian was...until he came of age two months ago?" I asked.

Mr Roffe actually laughed. "You're jesting with me, Mr Collins."

I gave him Sergeant Cuff's flintiest stare. "I assure you that I am not, Mr Roffe."

Confusion passed across the old man's features like

cloud shadows across an eroded field in winter. "But surely you must be, Mr Collins. If you come on the behalf of Mr Charles Dickens, as you say you do, then you surely must know that—upon the request of Master Edmond himself—legal guardianship and all control of Master Edmond's financial affairs passed from me to Mr Charles Dickens in early January of the present year. It is, I assumed, why you are here and why I could speak so freely of a former client's... Mr Collins, why *are* you here?"

I HARDLY NOTICED the traffic or streets I was passing as I walked towards Dorset Square and home. Nor did I notice the squat, stolid presence that had fallen into step alongside me until he spoke. "Just what exactly do you think you are doing, Mr Collins?"

It was Field, of course—the accursed inspector!— with his face looking redder than ever, whether from the cold wind or from advancing age and drink, I neither knew nor cared. He had a small bundle tucked under his left arm, but because of the wind, his left hand still had a firm grip on the brim of his silk top hat.

I stopped amidst the flow of other men holding fixedly to their hats, but Inspector Field released his hat brim and gripped my arm to move me along as if I were one of the countless tramps he'd found on his nightwatch.

"What business is it of yours?" I demanded. My mind was still spinning from the revelation in the old barrister's office.

"Drood is my business," growled the inspector. "And he should be *yours.* What is the import of your seeing Dickens two days in a row and then running back to London to speak to an octogenarian lawyer?"

I wanted to blurt it all out—*Charles Dickens insinu-*

ated himself into the position of becoming Edmond Dick-
enson's legal guardian before he murdered the boy! He
had to murder him before September because...—but
managed to remain silent and glowering at this real
detective. Both of us had death-grips on our hats as the
winter wind howled up the Thames at us.

None of this made real sense to me. My certainty—
whether from laudanum or not—had been that Dickens had murdered young Dickenson for the sheer sake of
the experience of murder, not for any pecuniary motive.
Had Dickens been hurting for funds? He had earned
almost five thousand pounds during his spring reading
tour and certainly had received a healthy advance against
sales for the special Charles Dickens Edition for which
he was currently finishing his forewords.

But if he had not murdered young Dickenson for
money, why become the boy's guardian and draw suspicion to himself? It went against Dickens's own lecture
in the graveyard at Rochester Cathedral, which I now
understood to have been a form of bragging after the
fact, a lecture about murdering almost at random, of
one's never falling under suspicion because one would
have had no motive.

"Well?" demanded Inspector Field.

"Well what, Inspector?" I snapped back. The beneficial effects of the morning's laudanum had long since
worn off, and the rheumatical gout was hurting my
every joint and sinew. My eyes were watering from both
the rising pain and rising cold wind. I was in no mood
for criticism, but most especially not from some mere...
retired *policeman*.

"What are you playing at, Mr Collins? Why did you
send my boy off to a warm bed and overpriced breakfast this morning in the wee hours? What were you and
Dickens and the man named Dradles doing in the
crypts at Rochester Cathedral yesterday?"

I decided to let Sergeant Cuff answer. One old detective refusing another. "We all have our little secrets, Inspector. Even those of us under twenty-four-hour watch."

Field's already reddened face grew even more crimson, turning into an ancient vellum map of tiny burst veins. "Bugger your 'little secrets,' Mr Collins. There's no d——ned time for them!"

I stopped in the middle of the pavement. I would not, under any circumstances, allow myself to be spoken to this way. Our working relationship was at an end. I clenched my hand on my stick to allay its shaking and had opened my mouth to say this, when suddenly the inspector thrust an unsealed envelope at me. "Read it," he said gruffly.

"I don't care to..." I began.

"*Read it*, Mr Collins." It was more growled command than gentleman's request. It left absolutely no room for debate.

I removed the single sheet of thick paper from the envelope. The handwriting was bold, almost as if it had been produced with a brush rather than a pen, and the letters were more printed than written. It read, in its entirety—

MY DEAR INSPECTOR—
    TO THIS POINT, WE HAVE GAINED AND SACRIFICED ONLY PAWNS IN OUR ENJOYABLE LONG GAME. NOW BEGINS THE END GAME. PREPARE YOURSELF FOR THE IMMINENT LOSS OF MUCH MORE IMPORTANT AND PRECIOUS PIECES.
        YOUR FAITHFUL OPPONENT,
    D

"What on earth can it mean?" I asked.

"It means precisely what it says," Inspector Field said through gritted teeth.

"And you interpret the signature 'D' as 'Drood'?" I said.

"It can be no one else," hissed the inspector.

"It could stand for 'Dickens,'" I said lightly, even as I thought, *Or for "Dickenson" or "Dradles."*

"It stands for Drood," the older man said.

"How can one be sure? Has the phantom ever written you a direct note in this fashion?"

"Never," said Inspector Field.

"Then it could be from anyone or..."

The inspector had been carrying a rolled-up canvas-and-leather bundle, rather like a countryman's portmanteau, under his left arm, and now he unrolled it and removed what looked to be a torn and befouled dark cloth. He handed the cloth to me as he said, "The note came wrapped in this."

Holding the strips of cloth gingerly—the rags were not only begrimed, I realised, but absolutely soaked through with what appeared to be newly dried blood, and the already ragged material had been serrated into strips as with a razor—I began to ask him what the importance of a few foul rags might be, but stopped myself.

I suddenly recognised the bloody cloth.

The last time I had seen these rags, more than twelve hours earlier, they had been on the back of the boy named Gooseberry.

CHAPTER TWENTY

I went to stay at my mother's home near Tunbridge Wells for most of December of 1866. I decided to remain there with her until I celebrated my forty-third birthday on 8 January. It is fine to spend time with one's mistresses, but—please trust me on this fact, since almost all men feel this way but few are courageous or honest enough to admit it—at very difficult times or on one's birthday, there is no place more welcome and comforting than at one's mother's side.

I recognise that I have said little to you about my mother in this document, Dear Reader, and I must confess to you that this was a deliberate omission. In this winter of 1866–67 and through most of the coming year, my beloved mother was quite well—indeed, most of her contemporaries and most of mine found her more active, energetic, and engaged with the world than many women of half her age—but as my story must soon relate, her health was to deteriorate quickly before the end of 1867, and she would greet the end in March of 1868, my own *annus horribilus*. It is still difficult for me to think about that time, much less write about it. The death of one's mother must be the single most terrible day in the life of any man.

But, as I mentioned, her health was still good this winter of 1866–67, so I can write about this period with something less than full pain.

As I have also previously mentioned, my mother's Christian name was Harriet and she had long been a favourite among my father's circles of famous painters, poets, and up-and-coming artists. After my father's death in February of 1847, my mother had truly come into her own as one of the preeminent hostesses among the higher circles of artistic and poetic society in London. Indeed, our home at Hanover Terrace (looking out at Regents Park) during the years my mother was hostess there is acknowledged as one of the centres of what some are now calling the Pre-Raphaelite movement.

At the time of my extended visit with her beginning in December of 1866, Mother had realised her long ambition of moving to the countryside and was dividing her time among various cottages she leased in Kent: her Bentham Hill Cottage near Tunbridge Wells, Elm Lodge in the town itself, and her most recent cottage at Prospect Hill, Southborough. I went down to Tunbridge Wells to spend some weeks with her, returning to London each Thursday in order to keep my late-night appointment with King Lazaree and my pipe. Then I would take the train back to Tunbridge Wells on Friday evening, in time to play a game of cribbage with Mother and her friends.

Caroline was not happy with my decision to be gone during all of what some were now calling "the holiday season," but I reminded her that we never celebrated Christmas to any extent anyway—a man and his mistress obviously were not invited to his married male friends' homes at any time of the year, but at Christmastime these male friends accepted even fewer invitations to our home, so it was always the social low-point of our year—but, showing a woman's resistance to simple reason, Caroline remained vexed that I would be gone all during December and into January. Martha R——, on the other hand, accepting with perfectly good grace my explanation that I wished to get away from London to spend a month and more with my mother, temporarily gave up the room rented to "Mrs Dawson" and returned to Yarmouth and Winterton and her own family.

More and more, I was finding life with Caroline G—— tiresome and complicated and my time with Martha R—— simple and satisfying.

But my time with Mother that Christmas was the most satisfying of all.

Mother's cook, who travelled with her everywhere, knew all of my favourite foods from childhood, and often Mother would come into my room in the morning or evening when the tray was delivered and I would enjoy my repast in bed while we carried on our conversations.

When I had fled London I was filled with a terrible sense of guilt and foreboding concerning the presumed death of the boy named Gooseberry, but after a few days at Mother's cottage, that dark cloud had moved away. What had the child's unusual real name been? Guy Septimus Cecil. Well, what nonsense to think that young Guy Septimus Cecil had actually been *murdered* by the dark forces of Undertown as represented by the foreign sorcerer Drood!

This was an elaborate game, I reminded myself, with Charles Dickens playing one game on his side, the elderly Inspector Field playing his corresponding but not identical game on the other side, and poor William Wilkie Collins caught in the middle.

Gooseberry murdered, indeed! The Inspector shows me a few tattered cloths sprinkled with dried blood— dog's blood for all I knew, or the vital fluid from one of the thousands of feral cats that roamed the slums from whence Gooseberry sprang—and now I was expected to fly all to pieces and to do Inspector

Field's bidding even more assiduously than I had to date.

Drood had moved beyond being a phantasm and had become more of a shuttlecock in this insane game of badminton between a disturbed author with an obsession for play-acting and an evil old gnome of an ex-policeman with too many secret motives to count.

Well, let them play their game without me for a while. The hospitality of Tunbridge Wells and my mother's cottage served me well for December and early January. Along with recovering some of my health—my rheumatical gout was strangely better there in Kent, although I continued administering doses of the laudanum, albeit in lower quantities—my sleep came easier, my dreams grew less clouded, and I began to think more earnestly about the elegant plot and fascinating characters of *The Serpent's Eye* (or possibly *The Eye of the Serpent*). Although the serious research would have to wait until I returned full-time to London and the library at my club, I could—and did—jot down preliminary notes and a rough outline, often writing from my bed.

Occasionally I thought of my duties as detective in discerning whether young Edmond Dickenson had been murdered by Charles Dickens, but my interview with Dickenson's solicitor had been singularly unenlightening—except for the shock of learning that Charles Dickens himself had been appointed the youth's guardian-executor in the last months of the young man's need for such care—and even my keen novelist's mind could find no next step to take in the investigation. I decided that when I returned to London life, I should discreetly ask around my club if anyone had heard of the comings and goings of a certain squire named Dickenson, but other than that, I could see no obvious direction to take in the investigation.

By the second week of December, the only thing that was disturbing my peace of mind was the lack of an invitation to Gad's Hill Place for Christmas.

I was not sure that I would have accepted the invitation that year (there had been subtle but obvious tensions between the Inimitable and myself in the preceding months, my suspicion of the author's being a murderer among them), but I certainly expected to be *invited*. After all, Dickens had more or less said the last time I saw him that I would be receiving the usual invitation to be a houseguest.

But no invitation arrived at my mother's cottage. Each Thursday afternoon or Friday mid-day, before or after my visit to King Lazaree's den, I would drop in on Caroline to pick up my mail and to make sure that she and Carrie had enough money to meet all accounts, but still there arrived no invitation from Dickens. Then, on the sixteenth of December, my younger brother, Charles, came down to Southborough to spend the day and brought with him an envelope addressed to me in Georgina's distinctive hand.

"Has Dickens said anything to you about Christmas?" I asked my brother as I searched for my knife to open the invitation.

"He has said nothing to me," Charley said sourly. I could tell that his ulcers—or what I then thought were his ulcers—were hurting him. My talented brother was listless and downcast. "Dickens told Katey that there would be the usual houseful of guests....I know the Chappells are coming down to Gad's Hill for a few days, and Percy Fitzgerald for the New Year."

"Hmm, the Chappells," I said while unfolding the letter. These were Dickens's new business partners in the reading tours and, I thought, interminable boors. I decided that I would definitely not stay at Gad's Hill for the full week that I usually tarried if the Chappells were going to be there for any extended length of time.

Imagine my surprise when I read the letter, which I reproduce here in its entirety—

> My Dear Wilkie—
>
> This is a pretty state of things!—That I should be in Christmas Labour while you are cruising about the world, a compound of Hayward and Captain Cook! But I am so undoubtedly one of the sons of Toil—and fathers of children—that I expect to be presently presented with a smock frock, a pair of leather breeches, and a pewter watch, for having brought up the largest family ever known with the smallest disposition to do anything for themselves.
>
> But as some of us must labour while others adventure onward and outward, we still extend to you the heartiest of Christmas greetings—should these greetings catch up to you during your farflung peregrinations—and wish you the most prosperous of new years.
>
> > Yr. Most Obedient Servant and
> > Former Fellow Traveller,
> > Chls. Dickens

I fairly dropped the letter in my amazement. Thrusting it at Charley, who read it with a quick glance, I spluttered, "What does this mean? Does Dickens somehow believe I have gone sailing somewhere?"

"You were in Rome in the autumn," said my brother. "Perhaps Dickens believes you are still there."

"I returned quickly to try to save the doomed production of *The Frozen Deep* at the Olympic Theatre," I said with some asperity. "I *saw* Dickens after I got back. There is no possibility that he does not know I am in England."

"He may believe you returned to Rome or Paris,"

said Charley. "For there was some speculation about that in the clubs, after you had told acquaintances that you had some business to settle in Paris. Or perhaps Dickens is preoccupied, thinking mostly of his children. Katey, as you know, is despondent much of the time. Mamie has fallen out of favour in London society. And his youngest son has been a great disappointment. Dickens recently told Katey that he had decided that Plorn should be sent to Australia to become a farmer."

"What the deuce does that have to do with my invitation to Christmas?" I cried.

Charley only shook his head. It was obvious that I had deliberately been left off Dickens's Christmas guest-list this year.

"Wait here," I said to my brother, who needed to catch the early train back to London. I went into Mother's sewing room, found her stationery with the address of the Tunbridge Wells cottage on it, and began a quick missive—

> *My Dear Charles:*
> *I am neither touring the world like Captain Cook nor visiting Rome or Paris. As you must already know, I am visiting my mother near Tunbridge Wells and I would be available for. . .*

I stopped, crumpled the sheet, threw it in the fire, and found a blank sheet of stationery in my mother's secretary.

> *My Dear Dickens,*
> *I return your Christmas greetings—in my absence this Holiday, please give the ladies a bow from me, and the children sweets in my name—and regret that I shall not be able to see you until sometime in the New Year. Rather than cruising the world like Captain Cook or touring*

Scotland and Ireland like an itinerant juggler, I am—as you may know—deeply involved in an investigation into a Missing Person or Persons that may have the most profound consequences. I look forward to surprising you with the imminent results of this investigation.

All of my love and Christmas cheer to Georgina, Mamie, Katey, Plorn, the Family, and your Christmas guests.

Yr. Most Obedient Detective,
Wm. Wilkie Collins

I sealed and addressed the note and—when giving it to Charley, who was pulling on his travelling cloak—said with the utmost seriousness, "This must be delivered into Charles Dickens's hands and his alone."

CHRISTMAS AND MY BIRTHDAY were most happy occasions for me in Mother's presence—and in the snug warmth of the Tunbridge Wells cottage, with its constant cooking smells and undemanding female company—but because both of those holidays fell on a Tuesday, I did not see Caroline until the Thursday of each of those weeks. (It was on Thursday the tenth of January that I returned to London with all of my luggage, work, and research materials, but since that was my night for King Lazaree and my pipe, I did not actually move back to the house on Dorset Square until the afternoon of Friday, 11 January.)

Caroline was not pleased with me and found innumerable small ways to show me her displeasure, but in my time away at Tunbridge Wells I had learned how to place less stock in Mrs G——'s pleasure or displeasure.

During the weeks that followed in early 1867, I spent more and more of my time at my club, using the Athenaeum's wonderful library as my primary research centre, taking my meals there, frequently sleeping there, and generally spending less and less time at my Melcombe Place address, where Caroline and Carrie still resided full-time. (Martha R—— remained in Yarmouth during this period.)

Since my business often brought me to the offices of *All the Year Round* (where, indeed, I still had an office of my own, albeit shared with other staff members and regular contributors from time to time), I heard much from Wills and others about Dickens's new tour. Thick envelopes of galley proofs and other magazine materials were constantly being mailed out, chasing Dickens from Leicester to Manchester to Glasgow to Leeds to Dublin to Preston. Amazingly, Dickens managed to get back to London at least once a week to give a reading at St James's Hall in Piccadilly and to come to the offices to deliver his own manuscripts, to check up on the books, and to work at editing the writing of others. He rarely got back to Gad's Hill on these flying visits but would sleep in his rooms above the office here or, frequently, at his private address in Slough (near Ellen Ternan).

I did not happen to cross paths with Dickens during this time.

Various stories of woe, hardship, and Dickens's amazing courage (or good luck) filtered back to the office and were repeated to me by Wills or Percy Fitzgerald or others.

It seemed that Dickens was still recovering from the discovery—this had been in the autumn, while I was briefly in Rome—that his personal servant and valet of the past twenty-four years, a dour and dyspeptic (I thought) but discreet shade of a man named John Thompson, had been regularly stealing from his master. Eight sovereigns had disappeared from these very offices at Wellington Street North, and when the theft was discovered, the sovereigns had quickly reappeared. But too late for Thompson, whose years of petty thefts from his employer had now come to light. Dickens sacked the man, of course, but could not bear to give the thief a "bad recommendation." He sent Thompson off to future employment with a vague but not clearly negative letter. According to Percy Fitzgerald, Dickens had been almost distraught at this betrayal, although all the Inimitable had said to Percy about his emotions was "I have had to walk more than usual before I could walk myself into composure again."

That composure seemed more and more rare if recent reports from Dolby to Wills were to be believed. Dickens was suffering more than ever from "nervous exhaustion," brought on, no doubt, by the rail travel— his reaction to the Staplehurst accident seemed to grow more, rather than less, pronounced as the months went by—and early in the tour, on only his second night in Liverpool, Dickens became so faint by the end of the first part of his performance that he had to be physically helped to a sofa backstage, where he lay prostrate until it was time for him to put on a fresh *boutonnière* and go out for the final part of the strenuous reading.

During his reading in Wolverhampton (the first reports had this incident occurring in Birmingham proper rather than its smaller neighbour, so I had first pictured the old theatre there as I had seen it the night the illusion of Drood had threatened me), a wire holding one of the reflectors above Dickens's head began to burn red-hot. The heavy bulb of this reflector projected out over the stalls and was suspended by a single, strong copper wire, but a new gas man only recently having joined the tour had mistakenly placed an open gas-jet beneath this supporting wire.

Dolby had seen the wire turning first red and then white and, shifting from foot to foot in his anxiety, had stage-whispered out to the reading Dickens, "How long shall you be?" while gesturing wildly at the heated wire. Dickens must have appreciated the danger: when the wire burned through, the heavy reflector would come crashing down to the stage, but not before careering through the maroon-cloth stalls and screens erected around the Inimitable. The result would be instant conflagration. The flammable screens themselves ran almost to the ancient cloth curtains above. Once the overheated wire parted, there was little doubt that the stage—and almost certainly the theatre—would go up in flames within minutes, if not seconds.

Dickens, still reading without missing a word or gesture, calmly showed Dolby two fingers behind his back.

The distraught stage manager did not know what this meant. Was the Chief telling him that he would be finished in two minutes or that the wire would be parting in two seconds? Dolby and Barton, the gas man, could do nothing but shuttle back and forth offstage, bringing sand and buckets of water and preparing for the worst.

Dickens, it turned out, had seen the wire heating in the middle of his reading and had coolly calculated how long it would take for the copper to burn through. Working from those quick mental calculations, the Inimitable had improvised instant alterations to the rest of his reading—editing and conflating as he went—and reached the end only seconds before the wire would have melted and parted. (Dickens had figured when Dolby signalled him that he had two minutes left before the reflector would have come crashing down.) The curtain closed, Barton ran out and turned off the misplaced flame, and Dolby—according to his later testimony to Wills—came close to fainting as Dickens patted him on his wide back, whispered, "There was never any real danger," and calmly went out to take his curtain call.

All these breathless reports from Dickens's tour were of little interest to me. None mentioned Drood, and I had my own literary work to do (more important, in my humble opinion, than reading one's old work to audiences of bumpkins in the provinces).

As I've mentioned, I settled into doing my preliminary reading and researching at my club, the Athenaeum. The club was most helpful—moving my favourite wing chair to a place by the window where the weak winter and spring light would be at its best, providing a small table for my materials, and appointing several of the servants to seek out the volumes I needed from the club's expansive libraries. I also appropriated Athenaeum stationery for my notes and kept these in a series of large white letter envelopes.

My first job was to gather information, and here my years as a journalist served me well (even as that profession had equally served Dickens, although I might remind you, Dear Reader, that I had been a true *journalist* and Dickens had written primarily as a mere court reporter).

For weeks I copied out pertinent entries on India, on various Hindoo cults, and on gems from *Encyclopaedia Britannica*, the eighth edition, copyright 1855. I also found a new book by a certain C. W. King, *The Natural History of Gems*, published in 1865, very helpful. For my specific India backgrounds that I thought might open *The Serpent's Eye* (or possibly *The Eye of the Serpent*), I consulted J. Talboys Wheeler's newly published *The History of India from the Earliest Ages* and both 1832 volumes of Theodore Hook's *The Life of General Sir David Baird*. The diligent servants at the club also sought out and provided relevant articles in recent issues of *Notes and Queries*.

And thus the early outlines of my magnum opus began to take shape.

I had known for some time that the plot would revolve around the mysterious disappearance, in England, of a beautiful but cursed diamond brought from India—a diamond sacred to some Hindoo thuggee sort of cult—and that the mystery would unfold in a series of accounts from various viewpoints (rather as Dickens had done in *Bleak House,* but, more pertinently, as I had done to better effect in *The Woman in White*). Because of my preoccupation—"distraction" might be the better word—with the whole Drood issue at this time, the story would hinge upon such themes as Eastern mysticism, mesmerism, the power of mesmeric suggestion, and opium addiction. The solution to the theft (as I knew from an early point in my envisioning of the tale) would be so shocking, so unexpected, so clever, and so unprecedented in the nascent field of detection fiction that it would astonish all English and American readers, including such supposed practitioners of such sensationalist serial authorship as Charles Dickens himself.

As is true of all writers of Dickens's and my level of accomplishment, I was never free to pursue just one writing project. (Dickens, while he prepared for and then travelled on tour, had written his usual Christmas novella, was editing *All the Year Round,* was completing elaborate forewords for the special edition of his works, and was generating ideas for novels even while writing actual stories such as his strange "George Silverman's Explanations," kindled, he told me later, by Dolby's and his coming across the ruins of Hoghton Towers between Preston and Blackburn. That ruined old manse happened to crystallise all the disparate, floating fragments of ideas Dickens had been playing with for some time, but rather than support a novel—

which he needed in order to offer something for serialisation in *All the Year Round*—it provoked this strange
story of a neglected childhood so very similar to Dickens's own. [Or at least to what he *thought of* as his childhood of neglect and want.]

So it was with my own multiple and often overlap-
ping literary and dramatic efforts that spring of 1867.
My rewritten *The Frozen Deep* had failed the previous
autumn at the Olympic Theatre, this despite the fact
that my revised version was, I believe, much improved,
after I had rewritten the character and passions of Richard Wardour, the character Dickens had—I was about
to write "played" but "occupied" might be a more precise word—making the man both more adult and
believable, freeing the character from Dickens's pathos
and overly sentimental gestures.) But my hopes for a
theatrical breakthrough remained high, and that
spring—when my health and research commitments
allowed—I travelled back and forth to Paris to consult
with François-Joseph Régnier (whom I'd met through
Dickens more than a decade earlier) of the Comédie-
Française, who was eager to adapt *The Woman in White*
to the stage there. (It was already the rage in Berlin.)

My own goal was to sell Régnier and the French
theatre-goers (and thence English theatre-goers) on an
adaptation of *Armadale,* which I was certain would be
warmly and enthusiastically received, despite what Dickens had considered its controversial aspects.

Caroline, who loved Paris beyond her limited means
of expressing such emotion, all but begged to go with
me, but I was firm: it was a business trip and there
would be no time for shopping, explorations, or any
social engagements outside the strict regimen of theatre business.

That month I wrote to Mother from my hotel in
Paris—"*I have breakfasted this morning on eggs and*

black butter, and pig's feet à la Sainte Mènéhould! Diges-
tion perfect. St Mènéhould lived to extreme old age on
nothing but pig's trotters."

Régnier and I attended a new opera at which the
theatre was packed, the intensity was astounding, and
the experience was electrifying. Also electrifying were
those "very special little periwinkles"—as Dickens and
I used to call the attractive young actresses and demi-
mondaines so available in a culture where the night life
was as rich and varied as the food—and with a bit of
guidance from Régnier and his friends, I blush to say
that I did not have to spend an evening or night alone
(or even with the same periwinkle) the whole time I
was in Paris. Before returning to London I remembered
to pick up a handpainted card of the city for Martha—
she loved such trifles—and a lovely chiffon robe for
Carrie. I also purchased some spices and sauces for
Caroline's kitchen.

My second night back at Melcombe Place after my
return from Paris, I may have taken too much (or too
little) laudanum, for I found it difficult to sleep. I was
tempted to go to my study to work, but the inevitable
confrontation with the Other Wilkie (even though he
had shown no recent signs of violence in his attempts to
seize my papers or pens) dissuaded me. Instead, I was
standing at the window of my bedroom (Caroline had
found reasons to sleep in her own room) when I saw a
familiar shadow near the lamp post at the end of the
street near the square.

I immediately pulled on a long wool coat over my
dressing gown—it was a bitter night—and hurried to
the corner.

The boy extracted himself from the shadows and
came towards me in the dark without so much as a
summoning gesture on my part.

"Gooseberry?" I said. It pleased me that my speculations on Inspector Field's contrivances had proved correct.

"No, sir," said the boy.

As he came into the light, I saw my error. This lad was shorter, younger, a bit less ragged, and his eyes—although too small and too close together in his narrow face for good looks, even for someone poor—were not the bulging, wandering, nickname-earning disasters that Gooseberry's had been.

"You're from the Inspector?" I said gruffly.

"Yes, sir."

I sighed and rubbed my cheeks above my beard. "Can you remember a message well enough to deliver it verbally, boy?"

"Yes, sir."

"Very well. Tell the Inspector that Mr Collins wishes to meet him tomorrow at noon—no, make that two PM—at Waterloo Bridge. Can you remember that? Two PM, Waterloo Bridge."

"Yes, sir."

"Deliver the message tonight. Off with you, then."

As the boy ran away, the loose sole of one ill-fitting boot slapping against the cobblestones, I realised that I had not thought to—had not wished to—ask his name.

THE INSPECTOR WALKED briskly to the middle of Waterloo Bridge at precisely two in the afternoon. It was a raw, cold, windy day and neither one of us wanted to conduct the conversation out in the elements.

"I've not had time for my luncheon," rasped Inspector Field. "I know an inn nearby with excellent roast beef served all through the afternoon. Will you join me, Mr Collins?"

"An excellent idea, Inspector," I said. I had partaken

of brunch at my club two hours earlier, but I was still quite hungry.

Sitting across the table from the inspector in our booth, staring at him in the wan light as he sipped eagerly from his first mug of ale, I found him looking older and rougher than I remembered from our last visit. His eyes seemed weary. His dress was a trifle in disarray. His cheeks showed more tiny rosettes of burst veins, and there was a line of grey stubble along the wild profusion of his whiskers that suggested a man of lesser circumstances or less prominence than a former Chief of the Scotland Yard Bureau of Detectives.

"Is there any news?" I asked when our food had come and after an interval of intense attention to our beef and gravy and vegetables.

"News?" said the inspector, taking a bite from his bread and a sip from the wine we had ordered to follow the ale. "What news do you await, Mr Collins?"

"Why, of the boy called Gooseberry, of course. Has he got back in touch with you?"

Inspector Field only stared at me, and his grey eyes were cold within their nest of wrinkles. Finally he said softly, "We shall not hear again from or of our young friend Gooseberry. His flayed body is in the Thames or . . . worse."

I paused in my dining. "You seem very sure of this, Inspector."

"I am, Mr Collins."

I sighed—not believing for a second this fantasy of young Master Guy Septimus Cecil being murdered—and applied myself to the roast beef and vegetables.

Inspector Field seemed to sense my silent disbelief. Setting down his fork and still sipping his wine, he said in a hoarse whisper, "Mr Collins, you remember the connection I told you about concerning the relationship between our subterranean Egyptian friend Drood and the late Lord Lucan?"

"Of course, Inspector. You said that Lord Lucan was the absentee English father of the Mohammadan boy who later became our Drood."

Inspector Field held one fat finger up to his lips. "Not quite so loud, Mr Collins. Our 'subterranean friend,' as I so affectionately call him, has ears everywhere. Do you recall the manner of Forsyte's—that is, Lord Lucan's—murder?"

I admit that I shuddered. "How could I forget? Chest torn open. Heart missing..."

The inspector nodded, motioning me to quiet again. "In those days, Mr Collins—1846—even the new Chief of Detectives could, and regularly did, accept positions as 'confidential agent' for people of importance. Such was my situation late in 1845 and throughout much of 1846. I spent much time at Lord Lucan's Wiseton estate in Hertfordshire."

I struggled to understand. "You were called in by Lord Lucan's family to solve the murder. But you were already attending to the case in your role as Chief of..."

Inspector Field had been watching my face and nodded. "I see that you now understand the chronology, Mr Collins. Lord Lucan—John Frederick Forsyte, father of the bastard who became the occultic shaman Drood—had hired me nine months before his murder. His need was security. Using private agents of my hire at the time, I attempted to provide it. Since the Wiseton estate already had adequate walls, fences, dogs, doors, latches, servants, and experienced gamekeepers wise to the ways of poachers and would-be trespassers, I thought the security was adequate."

"But it was not," I said.

"Obviously," grunted Inspector Field. "Three of my

best men were *in* Wiseton Hall at the time of the...
atrocity. I had been there myself until nine o'clock that
night, at which time my duties brought me back to
London."

"Incredible," I said. I had no idea what point the old
inspector was attempting to make.

"I did not advertise the fact that I had been working
in a private, confidential capacity for Lord Lucan at the
time of his murder," whispered Inspector Field, "but
detection is a small professional field, and word leaked
back to both my superiors and the detectives who
served under me on the Force. It was an unpleasant
period for me...at a time that should have been the
apex of my professional career."

"I see," I said, although in truth I saw nothing but a
man admitting to his own incompetence.

"Not quite," whispered the Inspector. "It was a full
month after the murder of Lord Lucan, the official
investigation still under way, of course—Her Majesty
herself had expressed interest in the outcome—when I
received a small package at my office in the Metropolitan Police Detective Bureau at Scotland Yard."

I nodded and sliced off a large shred of beef. It was a
bit chewy, but otherwise quite good.

"In the package was Lord Lucan's heart," rasped
Inspector Field. "Treated somehow—by some lost Egyptian art—so as not to decay, but most assuredly a human
heart and, according to several forensic physicians with
whom I consulted, most assuredly that of John Frederick Forsyte, Lord Lucan."

I set my knife and fork down and stared. Eventually
I managed to swallow the suddenly tasteless wad of
beef.

The old inspector leaned closer across the table. His
breath was strong with ale and beef. "I did not tell you,
Mr Collins, what arrived with Gooseberry's bloody

shirt and the note from Drood. I sought to spare your sensibilities."

"His . . . eyes?" I whispered.

Inspector Field nodded and sat back in the booth.

THIS EXCHANGE KILLED both appetite and conversation, at least for me. Inspector Field lingered for coffee and dessert. I drank the last of my wine and waited, lost in my thoughts.

It was a relief when we stepped outside into the cold wind. I welcomed the fresh air. I was not certain that I had believed Inspector Field's horror story about either Lord Lucan's wandering heart or Gooseberry's packaged eyes—a writer of sensationalist fiction knows another possible piece of sensationalist fiction when he hears it—but the topic had upset me and brought on a rheumatical gout headache behind my eyes.

We did not part immediately upon leaving the inn but walked back towards Waterloo Bridge together.

"Mr Collins," said the inspector after honking into a handkerchief, "my guess is that you wanted to meet with me for some reason other than to enquire into the fate of my unlucky young associate. What is it, sir?"

I cleared my throat. "Inspector, you know that I am embarked upon a new novel that requires research of the most unusual kind. . . ."

"Of course," interrupted the private policeman. "That is why I pay one of my most useful operatives—the esteemed Detective Hatchery—to spend every Thursday night in a crypt awaiting your return sometime the next morning. You assured me that your trips to King Lazaree's opium den were for relief from pain, not research. And I must say, Mr Collins, that my paying Detective Hatchery's hourly wage for that service, not to mention his unavailability for a full night and day in terms of my own service (for even detectives have to sleep, sir), has not been...balanced, shall we say...in terms of your promise to report on the whereabouts and activities of Mr Charles Dickens."

I stopped and clutched my stick with both hands. "Inspector Field, you certainly cannot be suggesting that it is my fault that Dickens is on yet another reading tour in the provinces and thus is out of my effective radius of investigation!"

"I suggest nothing," said the inspector. "But the truth of the matter is that the esteemed author returns to London for at least one day and night a week."

"To read at Saint James's Hall!" I said in some heat. "And occasionally to do some work at his office at Wellington Street North!"

"And to visit his mistress in Slough," Inspector Field said drily, "although my operatives tell me that he is now looking for another house for Miss Ternan—and possibly her mother—in the suburb of Peckham."

"This has nothing to do with me," I said coldly. "I am neither a gossip nor keeper of my fellow gentleman's affairs." I regretted that last choice of word as soon as it was out of my mouth. Pedestrians were beginning to stare at us as they passed, so I began walking again and Inspector Field briskly joined me.

"Our arrangement was for you to see Dickens as frequently as possible, Mr Collins, and thus to accumulate—and to convey to us—any and all information you received on the murderer who calls himself Drood."

"And so I have done, Inspector."

"And so you have done, Mr Collins...*to a very meagre degree*. You did not even spend Christmas with Mr Dickens, although he was at home in Gad's Hill for the better part of two weeks and came into the city repeatedly."

"I was not invited," I said. I meant my tone to be chilly, but it emerged as almost plaintive.

"Which you cannot help," said Inspector Field in a tone of sympathy that made me want to break my cane over the crown of his balding old head. "But you also have not availed yourself of obvious opportunities to join Mr Dickens either on his tour or during his London sojourns. It may interest you to know, sir, that Dickens continues to elude my operatives at least once every two weeks and disappear into slum basements and old church crypts, not to reappear until he takes the train to Gad's Hill the next day."

"You need better operatives, Inspector," I said.

The old man chuckled at this and blew his prodigious nose again. "Perhaps," he said. "Perhaps. But in the meantime, I wish not to chastise you, Mr Collins, nor to complain of an…imbalance…in the performance of our contractual agreements, but merely to remind you that our common interests lie in running this monster Drood to ground—or to *above* ground—before more innocents have to die by the creature's hand."

We had reached the bridge. I stopped at the railing and looked at the line of wharves, hovels, derricks, and low-masted rivercraft running in both directions. Rain squalls whipped the surface of the Thames to rows of white crowns.

The inspector pulled the plush collar of his out-of-date jacket up over the back of his neck. "Now please tell me the reason for this meeting, Mr Collins, and I will do my utmost to accede to your requests for further… ah…research assistance."

"I admit that my purpose was not merely to pursue research," I said, "but to offer you a suggestion that may be of inestimable assistance in your efforts to find this Drood."

"Really?" said Inspector Field, the bushy eyebrows

rising under the brim of his top hat. "Please go on, Mr Collins."

"In the novel I have almost finished outlining," I said, "there is a section that shall require a detective—one of great intelligence and experience, I might add—who knows all the techniques employed to track down a missing person."

"Yes? These are common procedures in both my former and current aspects of police work, Mr Collins, and I will be pleased to offer professional insights."

"But I did not wish this assistance to benefit me alone," I said, looking at the grey waves rather than at the grey inspector. "It occurred to me that a London man who has gone missing might be your missing link in tracing the chain of contacts and circumstances back to Dickens and Drood's contacts since the Staplehurst accident...if such contact actually exists."

"Really? Who might this missing man be, Mr Collins?"

"Edmond Dickenson."

The old man scratched his cheeks, tugged at his side-whiskers, and, inevitably, set that plump forefinger alongside his ear as if awaiting further information from it. Finally he said, "That would be the young gentleman whom Mr Dickens helped save at Staplehurst. And the same young man whom you reported as having sleepwalked at Gad's Hill Place a year ago this past Christmas."

"Exactly the same man," I said.

"How has he disappeared?"

"That is precisely what I would like to know," I said. "And it might be precisely what you need to know in order to close the connection to Drood." I handed him a folder of notes I had taken on my conversation with the solicitor Mr Matthew B. Roffe of Gray's Inn Square, the address of Dickenson's last known London dwelling place, and the approximate date when the young man had ordered Mr Roffe to transfer the duties of guardian-executor, for the last few months such a role was required, to none other than Charles Dickens.

"Fascinating," Inspector Field said at last. "May I keep these, sir?"

"You may. They are copies."

"This may indeed be of some service to our common cause, Mr Collins, and I thank you for bringing this man—missing or not—to my attention. But why do *you* think that Mr Dickenson might be important in this investigation?"

I opened my gloved hands above the railing. "Is it not obvious, even to a non-detective such as myself? Young Dickenson was perhaps the only other living person who we *know*—through Dickens's own testimony—was in the immediate area with Drood at the Staplehurst site. Indeed, it was Drood, according to Dickens, who led my friend to the young man, who was trapped in the wreckage and who would have died had it not been for Dickens's—*and Drood's!*—intervention. There is also, I would suggest, the inexplicable interest that Dickens took in the orphan in the months after the accident."

Inspector Field rubbed his cheeks again. "Mr Dickens is widely known to be a public altruist."

I smiled at this. "Of course. But his interest in young Dickenson bordered on the...shall I say...obsessive?"

"Or self-interested?" asked Field. The wind had arrived from the west, and we were both now holding our hats with our free hands.

"How do you mean, sir?"

"How much money," asked the old man, "was under trust to whomever the guardian of Edmond Dickenson was until the young man reached his majority last year? Did your investigations, Mr Collins, happen to extend to visiting young Dickenson's bank and having a chat with the manager?"

"Of course not!" I said, voice cold again. Such an idea was totally outside the scope of a gentleman's behaviour. One might as well open another gentleman's mail.

"Well, that will be easy enough to find out," muttered Inspector Field as he tucked my papers away into his jacket. "What did you wish in return for this possible help in our search for Drood, Mr Collins?"

"Nothing in exchange," I said. "I am neither a tradesman nor peddler. After you look into the disappearance of this man who, despite his claims to the contrary, actually may have seen Drood at Staplehurst—indeed, his having seen Drood may be the *reason* for his disappearance, who knows?—all I wish to hear are the details of your investigation...so as to add verisimilitude to my own writings about the investigation into a missing person, you understand."

"I understand perfectly." The old inspector stepped back and extended his hand. "I am delighted that we are working on the same side again, Mr Collins."

I looked at the extended hand for several long seconds before finally shaking it. It made a difference that we were both wearing gloves.

CHAPTER TWENTY-ONE

*I*t was May and we were in Dickens's alpine chalet. It was a pleasant place to be.

After a wet, cold, slow-to-waken spring, late May had
suddenly erupted in sunlight, flowers, blossoms, green
lawns, warm days, long evenings, soft scents, and gentle
nights perfect for sleeping. My rheumatical gout had
improved to the point that I was using the least laudanum in two years. I had even considered discontinuing
my Thursday-night trips into King Lazaree's world.

It was a beautiful day and I was on the upper level of
the chalet enjoying the breeze through open windows
and telling the partial story of my book to Charles
Dickens.

I wrote "telling" advisedly because although I had
forty pages of my written outline and synopsis on my
lap, Dickens could not read my handwriting. That has
always been a problem with my manuscripts. I have
been told that printers scream aloud and threaten to
resign when confronted with the manuscripts of my
novels—especially the first half of the book, where I
admit that I have a tendency to rush, to scratch out, to
write in all available margins and open spaces, and to
substitute until the cramped words and letters become
a blur of ink and a riot of lines, arrows, indicating
marks, and violent scratches. The laudanum, I admit,
does not increase the legibility.

I also wrote "partial story of my book" advisedly, since Dickens wanted to hear my general outline of two-thirds of the novel even though I had not decided the particulars of the specific ending. That longer reading-aloud, we had decided, would happen in June, when Dickens would make the final decision on whether my *Eye of the Serpent* (or perhaps *The Serpent's Eye*) would appear in his magazine *All the Year Round*.

So on this beautiful late-May day in 1867, I spent an hour reading and telling the story of my novel to Charles Dickens, who—to his credit—was fully attentive, not even interrupting to ask questions. Other than my voice, the only sounds were the occasional waggon going by on the road below, the soft wind rustling leaves and branches in the trees on either side of the chalet, and the occasional humming of bees.

When I was finished I set the manuscript notes aside and took a long drink of water from the chilled carafe that Dickens kept in his writing space.

After a few seconds of silence, Dickens literally leaped out of his chair and cried, "My dear Wilkie! That is a *wonderful* tale! Wild and yet domestic! Filled with excellent characters and carrying a great mystery! And the surprise near the part where you leave off—well, it was an *absolute* surprise to me, my dear Wilkie, and it is hard to surprise an old writer warhorse such as myself!"

"Indeed," I murmured shyly. I always craved praise from Charles Dickens, and now the pleasure from his words spread through me rather like the warm glow from my daily medicine.

"We shall definitely want this book for the magazine!" continued Dickens. "My prediction is that it shall outshine anything we have serialised to date, including your marvellous *Woman in White*!"

"We can hope," I said modestly. "But would you not prefer to hear the outline of the last fourth of the book—when I decide how to tie up the obvious loose ends, such as the reenactment of the crime—rather than commit to purchasing it now?"

"Not in the least!" said Dickens. "However much I look forward to hearing you tell me the true ending in a week or two, I have heard enough to know what a splendid story it is. And that plot surprise! To have the very narrator not know of his own culpability! Wonderful, my dear Wilkie, absolutely wonderful. As I say, I have rarely been so taken by surprise by another writer's dexterous plotting!"

"Thank you, Charles," I said.

"May I pose a few questions or make a few minor suggestions?" asked Dickens as he paced back and forth in front of the open windows.

"Of course! Of course!" I said. "Besides being my editor at *All the Year Round,* you have been my collaborator and fellow-plotter for too many years for me to not benefit from the sagacity of your advice at this stage, Charles."

"Well then," he said, "about the crucial plot twist. Is it at all possible that having our hero, Franklin Blake, perform the robbery of the diamond under the influence *both* of laudanum—however surreptitiously administered—*and* the mesmeric control of the Hindoo jugglers, too much of a coincidence? What I mean is, the Hindoos he encountered on the lawn could not have known that our Mr...what was his name?"

"Who?" I asked. I had taken out my pencil and was hurrying to make notes on the back of my manuscript page.

"The medic who died with a scrambled memory."

"Mr Candy," I said.

"Of course!" said Dickens. "Well, my only point is that the Hindoos encountered randomly on the estate's grounds that night could hardly have known that Mr

Candy would have put opium in Franklin Blake's wine as a sort of prank. Could they?"

"No..." I said. "I suppose not. No, they could not have."

"So, in truth, the dual revelations of secretly administered laudanum *and* the mesmeric magnetism of the Hindoo mystics on the lawn may be redundant, no?"

"Redundant?"

"I mean, my dear Wilkie, it would only take the coincidence of one or the other to allow Franklin Blake to carry out his somnambulistic thievery, isn't that so?"

"I think...yes...it is," I said, making a few notes.

"And how richer it is for the reader's imagination that poor Mr Franklin Blake steals the diamond from his beloved's bureau drawer in an attempt to *protect* it, not under the evil influence of the Hindoos, don't you think?"

"Hmmm," I said. This reduced my Huge Surprise to a sort of odd coincidence. But it might work.

Before I could comment, Dickens had gone on. "And the odd, lame servant—I apologise; what was her name?"

"Rosanna Spearman."

"Yes, lovely name for that odd and disturbed character—Rosanna Spearman. You say, early on, that she is a product of—that is, that Lady Verinder had hired her from, I believe—a Reformatory?"

"Precisely," I said. "I rather imagined that Rosanna had come from some institution very similar to your Urania Cottage."

"Ahh, which I set up some twenty years ago with Miss Burdett-Coutts's help," said Dickens, still smiling and pacing. "So I thought, my dear Wilkie. But I've taken you to Urania Cottage. You're quite aware that all of the women there are Fallen Women, being given another chance."

"As was Rosanna Spearman," I said.

"Indeed. But it's simply unthinkable that Lady Verinder or anyone of her obvious calibre would hire Rosanna if the lady knew that she had been a...a woman of the streets."

"Hmmm," I said. Having Rosanna being a reformed woman of the streets had been, precisely, my goal. It explained both her doomed infatuation with Mr Franklin Blake and the erotic subtext to that infatuation. But it *was* difficult to argue that anyone so refined as my fictional—and equally as doomed as Rosanna Spearman—Lady Verinder would have hired a prostitute, however reformed. I made a note on my page.

"A thief," Dickens said with that ring of certainty that was so common to him. "You can make the poor Rosanna a former thief—then Sergeant Cuff shall still be able to recognise her, but as someone who came through his jail rather than a woman on the street."

"Is thievery so much less evil than being a woman of the street?" I asked.

"It is, Wilkie, it is indeed. Make her a woman of the streets, no matter how well reformed, and Lady Verinder's home has been contaminated. Make her a former thief, and the reader shall see the magnanimity of Lady Verinder's spirit in her attempt to help her through honest employment."

"A point," I said. "A palpable point. I shall make a note to review Rosanna's background."

"And then there is the problem of Reverend Godfrey Ablewhite," went on Dickens.

"I wasn't aware that there *was* a problem with Reverend Ablewhite, Charles. During the reading you laughed and interjected that you loved the exposure of such a hypocrite."

"And so I do, Wilkie! So I do! And so shall your readers. The problem is not with the character—whom you have admirably drawn as the hypocrite, social climber, and would-be pilferer of a lady's fortune—but with his title."

"Reverend?"

"Precisely. I am pleased that you see the problem, my dear Wilkie."

"I am not sure that I do, Charles. Certainly the accusations of hypocrite and liar are all the more meaningful if it's a man of the cloth who..."

"Of course you are right!" said Dickens. "We have all known such sanctimonious men of the clergy—men who wish all to see them as doing *good*, even while they are secretly striving mightily to be doing *well*—but the charge is no less effective if we soften the indictment to a *Mr* Godfrey Ablewhite."

I started jotting the note but then stopped and rubbed my head. "It seems so...lessened, diluted, pared down. How is it that Reverend Godfrey is the chairman of so many Ladies Charities if he is not clergy? And what would such a change do to the wonderful line I had already set in my outline—'He was a clergyman by profession; a ladies' man by temperament; and a good Samaritan by choice.' You yourself laughed aloud when I recited that to you not an hour ago."

"So I did, Wilkie. But it shall work just as well if you substitute...say...'barrister' for clergyman. And we shall have saved the sensibilities of many, perhaps many thousands, of our readers from offence when none need be given in service of your admirable plot."

"I am not sure..." I began.

"Make a note, Wilkie. And merely promise me that you will consider this change during the composition. It is, of course, the kind of thing that any diligent editor of any general magazine such as ours would be remiss not to bring up with the author. Indeed, if *you* were editing another's manuscript, I am sure you would have raised the issue of demoting Reverend Godfrey Ablewhite to *Mr* Godfrey Ablewhite..."

"I am not sure..." I began again.

"And finally, my dear Wilkie, there is the matter of the title...." continued Dickens.

"Ahh," I said, with some eagerness this time. "Which do you prefer, Charles? *The Eye of the Serpent* or *The Serpent's Eye*?"

"Neither, actually," said Dickens. "I have been giving the titles some thought, my dear friend, and I confess that I find both a bit diabolical and perhaps a trifle wanting from the commercial point of view."

"Diabolical?"

"Well, the eye of the *serpent*. It does have Biblical connotations, Wilkie."

"It has heathen *Hindoo* connotations as well, my dear Dickens. I have done a tremendous amount of research into various cults in India...."

"And do any of them worship a serpent?"

"Not that I have discovered to date, but Hindoos worship... *everything*. They have monkey gods, rat gods, cow gods...."

"And undoubtedly serpent gods as well, I agree," Dickens said soothingly. "But the title still hints of the Garden and the serpent therein... that is to say, the Devil. And the obvious connection with the Koh-i-noor diamond makes any such connection absolutely unacceptable."

I was totally at a loss. I had no idea what Dickens was talking about. Rather than splutter, however, I carefully poured myself more water, sipped it, and eventually said, "Unacceptable in what way, my dear Dickens?"

"Your gem, diamond, whatever you end up calling it, is so very obviously connected with the Koh-i-noor...."

"Yes?" I said. "Perhaps. So?"

"You remember certainly, my dear Wilkie, or I am certain that your research has reminded you, that the original Koh-i-noor came from the region of India called, I believe, the Mountains of Light, and there was a persistent rumour, even before the diamond arrived on these shores, that the Mountains of Light had bad luck attached to every artefact from that area."

"Yes?" I said again. "Such a deeply buried mental association will be perfect for *The Eye of the Serpent*... or perhaps *The Serpent's Eye*."

Dickens stopped pacing and slowly shook his head. "Not if our readers associate such bad luck with the Royal Family," he said softly.

"Ahhh," I said. I had meant the syllable to be mildly and noncommittally ruminative, but it sounded, even to me, as if there were a chicken bone stuck in my throat.

"And I am sure you remember, Wilkie, what happened two days after that stone arrived in England and six days before it was to be presented to Her Majesty."

"Not precisely."

"Well, you were young at the time," said Dickens. "A fellow named Robert Pate, a retired lieutenant in the hussars, physically attacked the Queen."

"Good heavens."

"Precisely. Her Majesty was not harmed, but the public immediately connected the near-tragedy to the gift of the stone to the Royal Family. The Governor General of India himself felt he had to write an open letter to the *Times* explaining that such superstitions were absurd."

"Yes," I said, still jotting notes, "I have been researching Lord Dalhousie quite a bit in the Athenaeum library."

"I am sure you have," said Dickens in what I might have interpreted as an especially dry tone if I had been more critical. "And then there was the other terrible event associated with the Koh-i-noor...the death of Prince Albert."

I quit writing notes. "What? That was just six years ago, more than eleven years after the stone arrived in England and was displayed at the Great Exhibition. The Koh-i-noor had been broken up into smaller stones in Amsterdam long before Albert died. What possible connection could there be between the two events?"

"You forget, my dear Wilkie, that the consort had been the designer and chief sponsor of the Great Exhibition. It was he who suggested putting the Koh-i-noor in the odd place of honour it held in the Great Hall. Her Majesty, of course, is still in mourning black, and some close to her say that at times, in the depths of her mourning, she blames the Indian stone for her beloved's death. So you see, we must be careful in any names we give the book and any subtle references that might connect the Koh-i-noor and its effect on the beloved Royal Family with our fictional tale."

I had not missed the use of "we" and "our tale." Keeping my own tone dry, I said, "If not *The Eye of the Serpent*...or *The Serpent's Eye*...what title do you imagine might apply to the tale of a diamond that had been set in the eye of a Hindoo statue to a serpent god?"

"Oh," Dickens said airily, perching on the edge of his writing desk and grinning his editor's grin, "I think we can dispense with the serpent god and the eye altogether. What about a title that avoids the sensational and invites the young female readers into the novel a bit more enthusiastically?"

"My books do wonderfully well with women readers," I said stiffly.

"And so they do, my dear Wilkie!" cried Dickens, clapping his hands. "No one knows that more than I after your absolute triumph with *The Woman in White*. Why, there were a hundred eager readers for each instalment of that for every one reader who looked forward to my much more modestly selling *Our Mutual Friend*."

"Oh, I would hardly say that..."

"What about...*The Moonstone*?" interrupted Dickens.

"Moonstone?" I said stupidly. "Do you suggest I have the stone brought back from the moon rather than from India?"

Dickens laughed easily in that loud, boyish laugh of his. "A marvellous jest, my dear Wilkie. But seriously... something like *The Moonstone* would interest the potential lady readers—or certainly not alienate them—and it has an aura of mystery and romance about it, without any hint of the profane or diabolical."

"*The Moonstone*," I muttered, just to hear the sound of it from my own lips. It sounded terribly flat and colourless after *The Serpent's Eye* (or possibly *The Eye of the Serpent*).

"Wonderful," cried Dickens, rising again. "We shall have Wills draw up a draft of the agreement with that as the proposed title. I tell you again that your outline was as exciting as reading the finished—or almost-finished—work itself will surely be. A marvellous tale filled with marvellous and delightful surprises. Your twist of the opium-induced sleepwalking where the hero himself steals the stone without remembering he did so is a stroke of genius, Wilkie, sheer genius."

"Thank you, Charles," I said again, rising and putting away my pencil. My tone held a tad less enthusiasm than it had earlier.

"It's time to walk, my dear Wilkie," cried Dickens, going to the corner to take up his stick and to pull down his hat from a peg. "I thought perhaps all the way to Rochester and back this beautiful May day. You are looking fit and ruddy these days, my friend. Are you game?"

"I am game for the first half to Rochester, where I shall catch the afternoon train back to London," I said. "Caroline and Carrie expect me home for dinner this night."

This last was a tiny fib; Carrie was visiting relatives in the country and Caroline thought I was spending the night at Gad's Hill. But someone expected me for dinner that night.

"A half walk with a full friend is better than none," said Dickens, setting his own manuscripts away in a valise and striding quickly to the door. "Let us away before the roads and pathways get dusty and the day gets a minute older."

It was the evening of Thursday the sixth of June, and I was indulging in a minor pleasure I had cultivated since the early spring—that is, taking the mountainous mass of Detective Inspector Hibbert Aloysius Hatchery out for a pint and a snack at a local public house before turning myself over to his guardianship and then descending into the dockside slums and the even darker world beneath Ghastly Grim's Cemetery in order to partake of what I had come to think of as King Lazaree's Emporium of Subterranean Delights.

As I'd gotten to know Detective Hatchery better during our Thursday-night public-house stops, I had been surprised by some of the revelations from this huge man whom I had considered from our first meeting to be little more than a comic figure. It seemed he lived in a decent Dorset Square neighbourhood near my own home at Melcombe Place, and although his wife had died some years earlier, he had three grown daughters whom he doted on and a son who had just entered Cambridge. Most surprising, Hatchery himself read widely, and some of his favourite books, it turned out, were of my creation. *The Woman in White* was foremost amongst these, although he had only been able to afford reading it during its serialisation in *All the Year Round* some years before. I had brought a copy of the bound book this very night and was in the process of autographing it for my sometimes guardian when someone stopped at our table.

I recognised the brown tweed suit first, then the compact but heavy body poured into it. The man had removed his hat, and I noticed that his curly grey hair seemed longer than it had in Birmingham—but it had been wet then.

"Mr Collins," he said, two fingers flicking towards his brow as if touching the brim of a hat that was no longer there, "Reginald Barris at your service, sir."

I grunted a reply. I did not wish to see Detective Reginald Barris. Not that night, not any night. The memory of those terrible few seconds of violence in that Birmingham alley was just beginning to fade.

But Barris greeted Hatchery, who nodded back even as he was accepting the gift of my autographed *The Woman in White*—a conjunction of events that I found, unreasonably perhaps, treacherous—and Barris joined us at the table without even asking permission, boldly pulling up a chair and seating himself backwards on it, straddling it, his powerful forearms set atop the chair's back. Aghast at his bad manners, I wondered for a moment if Barris—despite his Cambridge accent—was an American.

"A fortunate coincidence, Mr Collins, running into you like this," said Barris.

I did not honour that nonsense with a reply, but looked at Hatchery in a way that showed cool disapproval of his being so free with the details of our habits.

Then I remembered wryly that the huge man *worked* for Inspector Field—and almost certainly reported to this insufferable Barris as well, since the younger man seemed to be a lieutenant of the tiresome inspector—and reminded myself that there had been no real friendship between Hatchery and me, despite my generosity towards him in recent weeks.

Barris leaned forward over his forearms and lowered his voice. "Inspector Field was hoping for a report, sir. I volunteered that if I were to run into you, I would mention it. Time is getting short."

"I gave Inspector Field a report less than a fortnight ago," I said. "And time is getting short for what?"

Barris smiled but set a quick finger to his lips, his eyes darting left and right in a melodramatic reminder that we must be discreet. I always forgot that Field and his men presumed agents of the phantasm Drood to be lurking everywhere.

"Until the ninth of June," Barris whispered.

"Ah," I said and took a drink. "The ninth of June. The sacred anniversary of Staplehurst and..."

"Shhh," said Mr Reginald Barris.

I shrugged. "I've not forgotten."

"Your report was a little less than clear, Mr Collins, on..."

"Less than clear?" I interrupted, my voice loud enough to be heard throughout the public house if anyone had been interested in eavesdropping—which certainly none of the few inhabitants seemed to be. "Mr Barris, I am a *writer*. A journalist for several years, a novelist now by vocation. I hardly think that my report could have been *less than clear*."

"No, no, no," agreed the young detective, smiling in his embarrassment. "I mean, yes. That is, no—I chose the wrong words, Mr Collins. Never less than clear, but...perhaps...perfectly clear but a trifle sketchy?"

"Sketchy?" I repeated, giving the word the disdain it deserved.

"As in perfectly captured in a few strokes," purred the young detective, leaning even lower over his massive forearms, "but not fully filled in with details. For instance, you reported that Mr Dickens continues to say that he has no knowledge of Mr Edmond Dickenson's current whereabouts, but did you...as we liked to say in school and the regiment...*drop the bombshell on him?*"

I had to smile at this. "Mr...Detective...Barris," I said softly, noticing Hibbert Hatchery's apparent lack of concern with everything his superior and I were saying, "I not only dropped the bombshell, as you put it, on Mr Dickens—I dropped the entire mortar."

BARRIS WAS TALKING about Dickenson's money as a motive in the boy's disappearance.

I was feeling so well that beautiful May day that I actually had been enjoying the long walk to Rochester from Gad's Hill Place, despite having to keep up with Dickens's killing pace, and we were about two-thirds of the way to our urban destination when I dropped the shell, mortar, and caisson on the Inimitable.

"Oh, I say," I said as we followed the walking path along the north side of the highway towards the distant church spires, "I happened to run into a friend of young Edmond Dickenson the other day."

If I had expected shock or surprise from Dickens, I received only the mildest twitch of one magisterial eyebrow. "Really? I would have guessed that young Dickenson had no friends."

"Evidently he had," I lied. "An old school chum by the name of Barnaby or Benedict or Bertram or somesuch."

"Are those the friend's last name or Christian name?"

asked Dickens, clicking along with his walking stick touching the ground at its usual precise and rapid intervals.

"It doesn't matter," I said, wishing that I had taken greater care in constructing this part of the introductory fiction I'd set to trap Dickens. "Just someone I met at my club."

"It might matter in the sense that the chap you met may have been a liar," Dickens said lightly enough.

"A liar? How is this, Charles?"

"I am quite sure that young Dickenson informed me that he never went to university—even to drop out—nor had ever darkened the door of any school," said Dickens. "It seems the poor orphan had a succession of tutors, each less imposing than the last."

"Well..." I said and hurried to catch up to Dickens. "Perhaps they weren't school chums, but this Barnaby..."

"Or Bertram," offered Dickens.

"Yes, well, it seems that this chap..."

"Or Benedict," said Dickens.

"Yes. *May I tell this,* Charles?"

"By all means, my dear Wilkie," said Dickens, smiling and extending his open hand. Some small grey birds—doves or partridges—exploded from the hedges we were approaching and flew into the blue sky. Without breaking pace, Dickens raised his walking stick to his shoulder like a shotgun and pantomimed pulling a trigger.

"It seems that this chap, a former friend of young Dickenson from *somewhere*," I said, "was told by Dickenson himself last year that he—Dickenson—had legally changed guardians during the last months before he reached his majority."

"Oh?" was all that Dickens said in response. It was a polite syllable only.

"Yes," I said, waiting.

We walked a hundred yards or so in silence.

Finally I dropped my bombshell. "This same chap…"

"Mr Barnaby."

"This same chap," I persisted, "happened to be involved with some transactions at his friend Dickenson's bank and happened to overhear…"

"Which bank is that?" asked Dickens.

"Pardon?"

"To which bank are you referring, my dear Wilkie? Or rather, to which bank was your friend of young Dickenson referring?"

"Tillson's Bank," I said, feeling the power in the two words. It was as if I were moving a knight into place before pronouncing checkmate. I believe it was Sir Francis Bacon who said, "Knowledge is power"—and the power I now held over Charles Dickens's head had come through the knowledge obtained by Inspector Charles Frederick Field.

"Ah, yes," said Dickens. He hopped slightly to clear a branch that had fallen in the gravel path. "I know that bank, my dear Wilkie…an old-fashioned, boastful, small, dark, and ugly place with a musty odour."

By this point I had almost, but not quite, lost the thread of the interrogation by which I'd hoped to catch the conscience of this king.

"A sound enough bank, it seems, to have transferred some twenty thousand pounds to the account of Edmond Dickenson's new guardian," I said and wondered if my Sergeant Cuff would have added an "Ah-hah!"

"I should have added 'indiscreet' to old-fashioned, boastful, small, dark, and ugly with a musty odour," chuckled Dickens. "I shall do no more business with Tillson's."

I had to stop. Dickens took a few final steps and then—frowning slightly at the interruption of our pace—also stopped. My heart was pounding in my chest.

"You do not deny receiving such monies then, Charles?"

"Deny it? Why would I deny it, my dear Wilkie? What on earth are you going on about?"

"You do not deny having become Edmond Dickenson's guardian and having transferred some twenty thousand pounds—his entire inheritance—from Tillson's Bank to your own bank and chequing account?"

"Not for a second could I or would I deny it!" laughed Dickens. "Both statements of fact are statements of fact, and therefore true. Come now, let's walk."

"But…" I said, catching up to him and trying to match him stride for stride. "But…when I asked some short time ago whether you knew where young Dickenson was, you said you had heard he'd gone to South Africa or somesuch place but otherwise had no idea."

"Which is, of course, the absolute truth," said Dickens.

"But you were his *guardian!*"

"In name only," said Dickens. "And only for a few weeks before the poor boy came into his majority and his full inheritance. He thought he was doing me an honour by naming me such, and I allowed him to think so. It certainly was no one's business other than Dickenson and myself."

"But the money…" I began.

"Withdrawn, on Dickenson's request, the day *after* he turned twenty-one and could do anything he wished with it, my dear Wilkie. I had the pleasure of writing him a cheque for the full amount that same day."

"Yes, but…why through *your* account, Charles? It makes no sense."

"Of course it does not," agreed Dickens, chuckling again. "The boy—still thinking I had saved his life at

Staplehurst—wanted to see *my signature* on the draught that would start his life anew as an adult. All nonsense, of course, but it cost me nothing other than the energy of receiving the payment and writing my own cheque to the lad. His former barrister and advisor—a Mr Roffe, I believe—made all the arrangements with both banks."

"But you say that you have no idea where Dickenson went..."

"And so I do not," he said. "He talked of visiting France and then truly beginning his life anew...South Africa, perhaps, or even Australia. But I received no letters from him."

I started to speak again and realised that I had nothing to say. When I had rehearsed this confrontation in my mind, I had imagined Sergeant Cuff surprising the culprit into an admission of murder.

Dickens seemed to be inspecting my face as we walked. He was clearly amused. "When you heard all this from this amazingly ubiquitous Mr Barnaby or Benedict or Bertrand, my dear Wilkie, did you imagine that I had insinuated myself into the position of guardian for poor young Dickenson and then murdered him for his money?"

"What!? I...Of course I did not...Ridiculous... How could you..."

"Because that would be what I would have made from all these otherwise circumstantial clues," Dickens said brightly. "An ageing writer, perhaps suffering from money problems, happens to save this rich orphan's life and soon realises that the boy has *no* friends, *no* family, *no* close acquaintances to speak of—only a doddering old barrister who tends to forget whether he has had lunch that day or not—and the writer then arranges to have the trusting boy appoint him, the avaricious writer with money problems, to a position as guardian...."

"*Are* you having money problems, Charles?"

Dickens laughed so loudly and easily that I almost laughed with him.

"How would I have killed him, do you think, Wilkie? And where? Gad's Hill Place? Frightfully public with so many visitors coming and going all the hours of the day and night."

"Rochester Cathedral," I said dully.

Dickens glanced up over the green trees. "Yes, so it is. We are almost there. Oh-*hoh!* No, wait, you mean... I would have *killed* Dickenson at Rochester Cathedral. Yes, of course. It all fits in. You are a genius of deduction, my dear Wilkie."

"You like to show it to people at night, in the moonlight," I said, not believing that I was saying these words aloud.

"Indeed I do," laughed Dickens. "And Mr Dradles and the cathedral's cleric, whom I shall call Septimus Crisparkle in my novel, have given me keys to gain access to the tower at all hours when I bring guests there...."

"And the crypts," I muttered.

"What's that? Oh, *yes!* Very good. The same keys would give me access to the *crypts.* So all I would have to do would be to invite young Dickenson on a private outing with me—showing off Rochester from its cathedral tower in the moonlight; why, I took you and Longfellow's brother-in-law and his daughters up there in the moonlight just last year—and, at the appropriate second, as I urged the boy to lean over better to see the moonlight on the sea around the base of the tower... just give him the slightest *shove.*"

"Let us stop this, Charles," I said raggedly. I felt the rheumatical gout creeping behind my right eye like a geyser of pent-up blood and pain.

"No, no, it is too wonderful," cried Dickens, twirling

his walking stick as if he were leading a parade. "No pistol needed—nor hammer, nor shovel, nor any grimy, heavy instrument needed to do the deed and then to be cleaned or disposed of—only gravity. A brief cry in the night. And then . . . what then? Say the boy had impaled himself on one of the black iron spikes rising from the fence surrounding the sacristy, or dashed out what few brains he had on one of the ancient headstones . . . what then, Sergeant Cuff?"

"Then the lime pit," I said.

Dickens actually stopped and seized his forehead with his free hand. His eyes were wide, his smile broad and beatific.

"The lime pit!" he exclaimed. A rider trotting past on a bay mare looked over from the road. "Of course! How could I have forgotten the lime pit? And then, perhaps in a few days' time . . . the crypts?"

I shook my head, looked away, and bit my lip until I could taste blood. We resumed walking.

"Of course," said Dickens, swinging his stick absently at a weed, "I would then need old Dradles as an accomplice, to take down and put back up the crypt walls, I mean. This is how murder plots are found out, you know, Wilkie—taking an accomplice is too often a step towards the gallows."

"Not at all," I said, my voice still flat and lifeless. "You will have used your power of magnetic influence on poor Dradles. He will have no memory of his aiding and abetting of your disposal of Dickenson's corpse . . . skeleton . . . watch, glasses, and other metal effects."

"Mesmerism!" cried Dickens. "Wonderful! Shall we add laudanum to the mixture here, my dear friend?"

"I don't believe that is required, Charles. Mesmeric control alone will account for the accomplice's unwitting help."

"Poor old Dradles!" cried Dickens. He was almost

skipping in his delight. "Poor young *Dickenson!* Those few people in this world who even knew he had ever lived believe him—on the word of his murderer!—to be off to France or South Africa or Australia. No one to mourn him. No one to bring a single flower to his sealed and shared crypt. And the killer solves his... money problems... and goes on as if nothing has happened. This is too wonderful, my dear Wilkie."

My heart pounding wildly again, I decided to explode the bombshell I had dropped perhaps so prematurely. "Yes, Charles, but this is all predicated on the murderer in question *knowing* that he is the murderer... knowing that he has done murder."

"But how can he not know..." began Dickens, and then ran his hand furiously through his scraggly beard. "Of course! The murderer, the same man who has mesmerised his crypt-keeper accomplice into compliance, has been acting under the control of magnetic influence himself!"

I said nothing but watched Dickens's face as we walked.

He shook his head. "I fear it breaks down here, Wilkie."

"How so, Charles?"

"Professor John Elliotson, my first instructor in the magnetic arts—you quoted him yourself, Wilkie!—and all other experts I have read and conferred with, insist that someone under the magnetic influence of another, stronger will, still cannot commit any deed which he would not perform or agree to when *not* under mesmeric control."

"But you had old Dradles help you dispose of the body," I said.

"Yes, yes," said Dickens, walking more quickly even as he ran his hands through his hair and beard, lost in deep contemplation of the plot elements here. "But burying the newly dead in graves and the crypts—transporting them when necessary—then walling up the corpses, is Dradles's *job*. The controlling mesmeriser would simply construct a waking dream of a story around him. But to command *murder*...No, I think that will not work in our story, Wilkie. Not if the murderer is a sane man."

"Even sane men have dark thoughts," I said softly as we came into the very shadow of Rochester Cathedral. "Even sane men—eminently sane men, public men—have dark sides which they show to no one."

"True, true," said Dickens. "But to the point of being able to do murder?"

"But what if the real puppet master behind this crime were to be a Master Mesmeriser and mass killer himself?" I said. "He might have many covert ways of convincing the men and women under his control to do his bidding, no matter how horrible. Perhaps they are made to think that they are players in some theatrical experience and that their murdered victims will hop up and take a curtain call bow at the end."

Dickens looked at me very sharply. "You are more of a sensationalist than I gave you credit for, Wilkie Collins. This new book of yours—*The Moonstone*—will do very well indeed, given the public's literally insatiable appetite for slaughter, gore, and the unwholesome aspects that stir to life in the darkest folds of the human mind."

"One can only hope," I said softly.

We had come into the town and were less than a block from Rochester Cathedral. The great tower threw its shadow over us and over the whole cluster of low, grey houses on either side of the road.

"Would you care to go up and look around?" asked Dickens, gesturing towards the tall stone spire. "I happen to have the key with me."

"Not today," I said. "But thank you all the same, Charles."

"Some other time, then," said the Inimitable.

So HE SHOWED no visible guilt or remorse about the twenty thousand pounds," said Reginald Barris. "But what about the anniversary?"

"I beg your pardon?" I said. I had been thinking of other things.

"The anniversary of Staplehurst," whispered the young detective. "Inspector Field asked you to do your utmost to accompany Dickens when he comes into town on that date, and the ninth is only three days away. You said nothing in your report on whether he had accepted or rejected your offer of spending the day and night with him at Gad's Hill Place or during his inevitable return to the city and Undertown London on that night."

I finished my ale and smiled at Hibbert Hatchery as the huge man, in his attempt not to overhear us, was respectfully browsing through the copy of *The Woman in White* that I had just signed for him. "Does the book meet with your approval, Detective Hatchery?"

"It is a gift beyond measure, Mr Collins," rumbled the giant.

"The anniversary, Mr Collins?" prompted the insufferable Barris.

"Mr Dickens did not invite me to stay at Gad's Hill or to wander the city with him on Sunday night—the ninth—in search of his phantom Drood," I said, still not turning to look at Barris.

"Then, sir," said the detective, "it is imperative that we arrange a time for you to meet with Inspector Field. He has laid on twenty-three operatives for Sunday night's watch and . . ."

"Instead," I continued, smoothly interrupting the upstart, "Mr Dickens has agreed to come to dinner at my house at Melcombe Place on Sunday and..." I paused just an instant for full effect. "...to spend the night there in my home."

Barris blinked. "Dickens will be at your house on the night of the Staplehurst anniversary?"

I nodded, feeling some well-earned condescension in the slow motion of my head.

Barris jumped to his feet and turned the chair around with a clatter. "I must deliver this information to the inspector at once. Thank you, Mr Collins. This is an... extraordinary...development." He touched his invisible hat brim and, to Hatchery, said, "Stay safe there, Hibbert."

And then Barris was out of the public house, and Hatchery and I walked the mile and a half or so to St Ghastly Grim's Cemetery. There he set out his few things for his long vigil—a small lantern, a greasy sack with his three AM dinner inside it (packed, no doubt, by one of his daughters), a small flask of water, and his pristine copy of *The Woman in White*.

Descending the stairs into the ancient catacombs, I reflected—not for the first time—on the human creature's infinite ability to adapt to circumstances. Two years ago, this descent as I followed Dickens down to the catacombs had been strange and not a little terrifying for me. Now it was as nothing—as commonplace as walking to my corner chemist's to renew my weekly jug of laudanum.

King Lazaree the Chinee and his two bodyguards met me at the tattered curtain to their alcove. My pipe was filled and ready for me.

Eight hours later, when I ascended the stairs to a new day, Detective Hatchery had tidily tucked everything away except the novel, which he was reading in a thin strip of morning light coming in through the partially opened crypt door.

"Everything all right, sir?" he asked as he slipped the book into one of his many voluminous pockets.

"Everything is very much all right, Detective Hatchery. Very much so. It appears to be a beautiful day."

CHAPTER TWENTY-TWO

On Sunday, 9 June, 1867, I returned home later than I had planned. I had told Caroline that morning that I would be at my club working on my book until evening but that I would be home before Dickens arrived for dinner. As you may have guessed, Dear Reader, I actually spent most of the day with Martha R—— in her rooms on Bolsover Street, had lost track of the time, and hurried home feeling slightly dishevelled and a bit knackered.

I came into the downstairs parlour to find Charles Dickens again making mesmeric passes over an apparently somnolent Caroline G——.

Dickens was the first to notice me. "Ah, my dear Wilkie," he cried jovially. "Just in time!"

Caroline opened her eyes and said, "Mr Dickens was mesmerising me."

"So it appears," I said coolly.

"Showing me how to apply the procedure to you!" she said. "To help you get to sleep on those nights when . . . you know."

"I know that I've been sleeping quite well of recent," I lied.

Dickens smiled. "But if Caroline can use the magnetic influence to help you drift off of an evening," he said, "you could cut back or eliminate your dependence on laudanum at night."

"I need hardly use any as it is," I said.

"Oh, Wilkie, you know that's not true!" cried Caroline. "Just two nights ago you were..." She broke off when she saw my cold stare. "I shall go talk to Cook," she said, "and see if dinner is ready."

Dinner was ready soon and it was a success, not only in taste and quality (a surprise, since our "Cook," Besse, was also our parlourmaid and one of only three servants we kept, the others being her husband, George, and their daughter, Agnes, who was Carrie's age) but also in terms of conversation and merriment.

Carrie, who always seemed to delight something in Charles Dickens (even as his own daughters did so less and less frequently those days), was at her blushing, school-girl best—young Harriet, like her mother, was intelligent enough and had already learned the subtle arts of being beguiling with older men without being coquettish—and even Caroline carried her own in our conversations. Dickens himself was relaxed and affable.

I do not know if I've described it accurately or sufficiently in this poor memoir, Dear Reader from my posthumous future, but Charles Dickens, while quite possibly a villain and even a murderer, was almost always a most pleasant man to be around. His conversation was easy, agreeable, almost never self-centred, and totally free of any effort or humbug. He held the unique position of being, at least among my circle of famous English friends and acquaintances, never boring and a capable and sympathetic conversationalist....He never reached after aphorisms or heavy wit...and one aspect of his active *listening* was that he laughed a lot. And infectiously.

Dickens laughed much this ninth of June in the Year of Our Lord 1867. It seemed at that dinner that he had no concerns and nothing on his mind.

After dinner, we went up to my study for brandy and cigars. I admit to being a bit concerned about going into the study so close to dark—the evenings were long in this time in June, and though the weather had turned and it was cool and pouring rain outside, dim light still came in through the drapes—but I comforted myself with the knowledge that I rarely saw the Other Wilkie this early at night. Nor had I ever seen the Other Wilkie when anyone else was around, even though—and perhaps I should have told you before this, Dear Reader—I have been haunted, in one way or the other, by the sensed and then-visible presence of the Other Wilkie since I was a small boy.

But not this night.

Dickens excused himself to visit the water closet, and I took my brandy and went over to part the drapes and look out into the darkness.

The rain still poured down. I smiled slightly, thinking of Inspector Field and his twenty-three operatives—most of them hired on just for tonight, I'd learned this week, since, surprisingly, Field's own private investigations agency had only seven men working full-time—out there now somewhere, unseen but also certainly uncomfortable in the rain and unseasonable cold. Carrie and our girl Agnès had got a fire going strong in my study and it felt quite cosy.

It had amused me, only the day before, when I had been required to get Caroline, Carrie, and the three servants all out of the house on various ruses so that Field, Barris, and several of his men could go through our Melcombe Place home from cellar to attic.

Inspector Field had insisted on this and I could do nothing but walk behind him as they inspected all doors and windows—estimating aloud how impossible a jump would be from the nearby roofs to these upstairs windows and deciding upon various vantage points in the neighbourhood from which to watch the alley, back yard, and nearby sidestreets. Finally they had gone through the cellar with a sort of fanatical intensity, even going so far as to move half a ton or so of coal in my coal-cellar. There, where the coal was always piled several feet high near the back wall, they had discovered a hole in the stone wall . . . a hole not ten inches wide.

The detectives shined their bullseye lanterns down the hole, but the corrugated tunnel so revealed simply curved down out of sight into stone and soil.

"Where does that go?" demanded Inspector Field.

"How could I know?" I said. "I have never seen it before."

Field then called for Barris and his men, who—unbelievably!—had brought bricks, mortar, and the tools with which they could close up such an innocuous aperture. They did so in less than ten minutes, with Barris himself laying the bricks and applying the trowel. I noticed the easy expertise with which he worked and could imagine the reasons for those massive forearms. However much Mr Reginald Barris might sport an Oxford or Cambridge accent, his background was decidedly that of a lower-class craftsman.

"Are you protecting Dickens and me from rats?" I asked with a smile.

The inspector aimed that corpulent and strangely ominous finger at me. "Mark my words, Mr Collins. Either Mr Dickens will strive to see Drood tomorrow, this important anniversary of their meeting at Staplehurst, or Drood will find a way to see Dickens. Either way, sir, you are in danger if that meeting takes place here."

I'd laughed and pointed to the tiny hole, now fully and redundantly bricked over. "You expect Drood to somehow slide his way through *that*?" I showed with my hands how narrow the aperture had been; a child oiled with grease could not have slithered through.

Field did not smile in return. "The thing that you call Drood can enter in through smaller apertures than that, alas, Mr Collins. If once invited, that is."

"Well, there you have it, Inspector," I said, still laughing softly. "I have never invited Mr Drood into my home."

"No, but perhaps Mr Dickens has," said Inspector Field. Then the men went on to inspect every square inch of the rest of my cellar.

I AM GOING to America," said Dickens.

We were relaxing with the last of our brandy and cigars, the fire hissing and spitting at our feet and the rain pounding at the windows. Dickens was as quiet and sombre in my study now as he had been jovial and talkative at our dinner table an hour earlier.

"You can't be serious," I said.

"I am."

"But..." I began and had to pause. I was about to say, *But surely your health will not allow this,* but discretion caught me in time. I had heard the serious state of Dickens's health from several sources, including Frank Beard, my brother, Charley, and Dickens's daughter Kate (often through Charley), as well as through other mutual friends, but it would only infuriate Dickens if I brought up my awareness of his several serious infirmities: among which were an increasing fatigue that had caused him to collapse between performances during his spring tour of Scotland and England, increasing trouble with his left leg and left kidney, difficulties with digestion, flatulence, and accompanying headaches, and—perhaps most visible to all of us—his rapid ageing.

I said aloud, "But surely your dislike of America and the Americans would preclude you from returning there. You certainly made your disdain clear in *American Notes* and *Martin Chuzzlewit*."

"Pfah," said Dickens with a wave of his hand. "I visited America twenty-five years ago, my dear Wilkie. Even such a backward place has had to reform in twenty-five years. They certainly have in terms of respect of copyright and payment to English authors for serialised works—as you must know, to your great benefit."

This last was true. I had made an excellent deal with the Americans for *Armadale* and had almost completed negotiations for an even better arrangement for *The Moonstone*, which I had just begun writing.

"Besides," continued Dickens, "I have many friends there, some of whom are too old or timid to make the Crossing. I should like to see them a final time before they or I die."

Dickens's talk of death made me anxious. I sipped the last of my brandy and stared into the fire, again imagining foolish Inspector Field and his small legion of men huddling out there in the rain somewhere. If Dickens was going to do what Field had insisted he might—plead some forgotten meeting somewhere and slip out of my house rather than spend the night—he had better hurry. It was getting late.

"At any rate," said Dickens, settling deeper into the leather cushions of his wing chair, "I've decided to send Dolby over in early August to investigate the lay of the land, as the Americans like to say. He'll be carrying my two new stories, 'George Silverman's Explanation' and 'A Holiday Romance.' They were commissioned by American publishers, and I believe the latter is appearing there in a children's magazine called *Our Young Folks* or something similar."

"Yes," I said. "You showed me 'A Holiday Romance' at Gad's Hill a few weekends ago, you might remember… told me that the tales in it *were* written by children, as was their whimsical conceit. And I believed you."

"I was not sure whether to be flattered or insulted, my dear Wilkie."

"Neither, of course, Charles," I said. "A mere statement of fact. As always, when you set out to do a thing with words, it is done in its convincing entirety. But I do remember you telling me that your strength was almost broken twenty-five years ago under the travel and labour of your first American tour. And Forster says to this day that the Americans were unworthy of a man of genius such as yourself. Are you certain, Charles, that you wish to put yourself under such a strain once again?"

Dickens had accepted my invitation to smoke a cigar and now blew smoke towards my ceiling. "It is true that I was younger then, Wilkie, but I was also worn out from writing *Master Humphrey's Clock* and—only days before departing—I had undergone a rather serious surgical operation. Also, the speechmaking I was required to carry out once in America would have exhausted an M.P. with nothing else to do. I was also—I admit it— less patient and much more irritable then than I am now in the serenity of my middle life."

I thought about the so-called serenity of this author's middle life. Inspector Field had informed me that Ellen Ternan had been ill throughout much of April and May, requiring that Charles Dickens—perhaps our nation's most public man—disappear for long days on end so that he could be by his ailing mistress's bedside. Dickens's habit of secrecy did not extend just to his alleged meetings with the creature named Drood; dissembling had become second nature to the writer. On at least two recent occasions I knew of for certain, Dickens had sent me letters purportedly written from Gad's Hill Place when, in actuality, he was with Ellen Ternan or staying at his secret home nearby.

"There are other reasons why I must leave the country," Dickens said softly. "And it has come time to speak to you of them."

I raised my eyebrows slightly, smoked, and waited. I expected some new fabulation, so Dickens's actual words were a surprise.

"You remember the personage I have referred to as Drood," said Dickens.

"Of course," I said. "How could I forget either your telling of the creature's purported story or our expedition two summers ago into the tunnels under the city?"

"Indeed," Dickens said drily. "I think that you do not believe me when I speak of Drood, my dear Wilkie...." He waved away my hurried objections. "No, now listen a moment, my friend. Please.

"There are many things I have not told you, Wilkie... many things I could not tell you... many things you would not have believed if I *had* told you. But the existence of Drood is real enough, as you almost discovered in Birmingham."

Again I opened my mouth, but found I could not speak. What did he mean? I had long since convinced myself that my waking nightmare-vision during Dickens's reading more than a year earlier in Birmingham had been a laudanum-dream brought on by the terrible confrontation with the thugs in the alley in that same city. The blood I had later found on my shirt collar and cravat had, of course, come from a reopening of the slight wound inflicted when one of the thugs had laid his knife to my neck that very afternoon.

But how could Dickens know about my drug-induced dream? I had told no one, not even Caroline or Martha.

Before I could formulate a question, Dickens was speaking again.

"Instead of wondering about the reality or non-reality of Drood, my dear Wilkie, have you ever wondered about your friend Inspector Field's true motivations in his obsession with capturing or killing the man?"

I blushed at the "your friend Inspector Field." I always assumed that Dickens knew little or nothing about my continued contact with the ageing detective—how could he know?—but I was often surprised by what Dickens actually *seemed* to know or had somehow managed to surmise.

Then again, if Drood were real—which I was not for a second ready to concede—it was possible that Dickens came by his information through that phantom and his agents, much as I was now doing through Inspector Field and *his* agents.

Not for the first time in the past two years, I felt like a pawn in some terrible chess game being played in the dark of night.

"You've told me your thoughts about Inspector Field's so-called obsession," I said. "You said that he thought such a *coup* would result in his pension being reinstated."

"That hardly seems adequate motive for the inspector's recent draconian…one might say *desperate*… measures, does it?" asked Dickens.

I thought about that. Or at least I frowned, squinted, and projected an image of thinking. In truth, I was most aware at that moment of the rheumatical gout gathering in a sphere of spreading pain behind my right eye, creeping around behind my right ear, embedding tendrils of itself deeper into my skull with each passing moment. "No," I said at last. "I guess it does not."

"I know Field," said Dickens. The fire crackled and coal embers collapsed in upon themselves. The study suddenly felt appallingly warm. "I've known Field for almost two decades, Wilkie, and his ambition surpasseth all understanding."

You are speaking of yourself, I thought, but said nothing.

"Inspector Charles Frederick Field wants to be Chief of Detectives again," said Dickens. "He fully plans on being head of Scotland Yard Detective Bureau."

I laughed despite my growing pain. "Surely this cannot be the case, Charles. The man is ancient...in his mid-sixties."

Dickens scowled at me. "We have admirals in the Royal Navy in their eighties, Wilkie. No, it's not Field's age that is laughable, nor even his ambition. Merely his means of reaching his goal."

"But," I said quickly, realising that I had offended Dickens with talk of old age, "you yourself told me that Inspector Field was out of favour with all of the Metropolitan Police for irregularities he committed as a private enquiries man. They denied him his pension, for heaven's sake! Certainly he could never reclaim his former position in the newer, larger, more modern London police force!"

"He might, my dear Wilkie. He might...if he were to bring to justice the purported mastermind of a nest of murderers whose crimes ran to the hundreds of victims. Field learned years ago how to use the city newspapers and he would certainly do so now."

"So you agree with the inspector, Charles, that Drood is a murderer and a mastermind of other murderers?"

"I agree with nothing that Inspector Field has said or imagined," said Dickens. "I am trying to explain something to you. Tell me, my dear Wilkie, do you enjoy Plato's Socrates?"

I blinked through my growing headache at this dizzying change of subject. Charles Dickens was, as everyone knew, a self-educated man and somewhat sensitive about the fact, despite his rigorous attempts at self-education throughout his lifetime. I had never heard him bring up Plato or Socrates before and could not guess at any connection these philosophers might have to the topics of our conversation.

"Plato?" I said. "Socrates? Yes, of course. Marvellous."

"Then you will forgive me if I put to you a few Socratic

questions in our mutual quest of discovering and bringing out an innate—but perhaps not obvious—truth."

I nodded.

"Assuming that the man we are referring to as Drood is more than an hallucination or cynically created illusion," Dickens said softly, setting down his brandy glass and steepling his fingers, "have you wondered, my dear Wilkie, why I have continued seeing him over the past two years?"

"I had no idea you *had* continued seeing him, Charles," I lied.

Dickens smiled sceptically at me from behind the pyramid of his long fingers.

"But if you had continued his acquaintance...for argument's sake," I went on, "then I would assume your earlier explanation to me would be the reason."

"Learning the finer and higher arts of mesmerism," said Dickens.

"Yes," I said. "And details of his ancient religion."

"All worthy goals," said Dickens, "but do you think such minor curiosity would justify the very real risks one would have to take? The hounding by Inspector Field's zealous agents? The repeated descents into Undertown? The mere proximity to a madman who—according to our esteemed inspector—has killed hundreds?"

I had no idea what Dickens was asking me now. After a laudanum-fuzzy moment of what I hoped was taken as deep contemplation, I said, "No...no, I think not."

"Of course not," said Dickens. He was using his schoolmaster voice. "Have you ever considered, my dear Wilkie, that I might be *defending* London from the monster's wrath?"

"Defending?" I repeated. The rheumatical gout had now encircled my head and enveloped both eyes and my cranium with pain.

"You have read my books, my friend. You have heard

me speak. You have visited the homes for the poor and for the lost women that I have helped start and have funded. You know my views on social issues."

"Yes," I said. "Yes, of course, Charles."

"Then do you have any idea of the anger seething and fomenting there in Undertown?"

"Anger?" I said. "Drood's anger, you mean?"

"I mean the anger of the thousands, perhaps tens of thousands, of men, women, and children driven into those subterranean vaults, sewers, basements, and slums," said Dickens, his voice rising to the point that Caroline might have heard it from downstairs. "I mean, my dear Wilkie, the anger of those thousands in London who cannot eke out a daily living even in the worst slums of the surface and who are driven down into the darkness and stench like rats. Like *rats,* Wilkie."

"Rats," I repeated. "What are we speaking of, Charles? Surely you are not saying that this...Drood... represents the tens of thousands of London's poorest residents. I mean, you yourself said that the man is grotesque...a *foreigner.*"

Dickens chuckled and tapped the ends of his fingers together in a manic rhythm. "If Drood is an illusion, my dear Wilkie, he is an illusion in the form of upper London's worst nightmare. He is a darkness in the heart of the soul's deepest darkness. He is the personified wrath of those who have lost the last meagre rays of hope in our modern city and our modern world."

I had to shake my head. "You have lost *me,* Charles."

"Let me begin again. It is growing late. Why would such a creature as Drood seek me out and select me in the fields of death that were the Staplehurst accident, Wilkie?"

"I wasn't aware that he *had* sought you out, Charles."

Dickens flicked his right hand in a quick gesture of impatience and raised his cigar again. Through the blue smoke he said, "*Of course* he sought me out. You need to *listen,* my dear Wilkie. As both novelist and dear friend, it is the one area in which your sensitivities should seek improvement. You are the only person on earth to whom I have revealed the existence of Drood and my relationship to him. You must listen if you are to understand the dire importance of this…drama. This drama that Inspector Field insists on treating as if it were a game and a farce."

"I am listening," I said coolly. I did not care for Dickens—a mere author whom I had outsold in numbers of recent books published and a man who had never received an advanced payment from a publisher on the level I had—when he chose to criticise me.

"Why would Drood choose me? Of all the survivors at Staplehurst, why would the awakened-from-his-coffin Drood choose me?"

I thought about this while I covertly massaged my throbbing right temple. "I am not sure, Charles. You were certainly the most famous man on the train that day." *With your mistress and her mother,* I silently appended.

Dickens shook his head. "It is not my fame that drew Drood to me and which now holds him in check," he said softly between long exhalations of blue smoke. "It is my ability."

"Your ability."

"As a *writer,*" Dickens said almost impatiently. "As… you will pardon my immodesty due to the centrality of this point…as perhaps the most important writer in England."

"I see," I lied. Then, perhaps, I did finally see. At least a glimmer. "Drood wants you to write something for him."

Dickens laughed. It was not a cynical or derisive laugh—I might have taken my headache and gone off to bed at that moment if it had been—but rather Dickens's usual boyish, deep, head-back, sincere laugh.

"I would say, yes," he said, tapping ashes into the onyx ashtray at his chairside. "He *insists* that I write something. Nothing less than his biography, my dear Wilkie. Certainly an effort that would require five long volumes, perhaps more."

"His biography," I said. If Dickens was weary of my repeating his statements, he was not as weary of it as I was. The evening that had started with a fine meal and laughter had now risen—or descended—into the realm of pure insanity.

"It is the only reason that Drood has not unleashed the full extent of his wrath upon me, upon my family, upon the accursed Inspector Field, upon you, upon all of London," Dickens said wearily.

"Upon *me?*" I said.

It was as if Dickens had not heard me. "Almost every week I descend into the Hades that is London Undertown," he went on. "Every week I take out my notebook and I listen. And I write notes. And I nod. And I ask questions. Anything to draw out the interviews. Anything to postpone the inevitable."

"The inevitable?"

"The inevitable explosion of this monster's anger when he discovers that, in truth, I have written not a word of his execrable 'biography,' my dear Wilkie. But I have heard much...too much. I have heard of ancient rituals disgusting beyond all abilities of a sane Englishman to comprehend them. I have heard of mesmeric magnetic influence turned to outrageous and unspeakable ends—seduction, rape, sedition, the use of others in revenge, terror, murder. I have heard...too much."

"You must cease going down into that world," I said, thinking of King Lazaree's quiet and pleasurable alcove deep beneath St Ghastly Grim's Cemetery.

Dickens laughed again, but more raggedly this time. "If I do not go to him, he comes to me, Wilkie. On my reading tour. At railway stations. In hotels in Scotland and Wales and Birmingham. At Gad's Hill Place. In the night. It *was* Drood's face floating outside my first-storey window that night Dickenson went sleepwalking."

"And did Drood kill young Dickenson?" I asked, seeing my chance to pounce.

Dickens blinked at me several times before he said slowly, wearily, perhaps guiltily, "I have no idea, Wilkie. The boy asked me to be his guardian for a few weeks, in name only. He had his inheritance paid through my bank and my cheque. Then he...went away. That is all I can tell you."

"But certainly," I said, pressing my advantage, "Drood would have liked to have the boy's money as well as a biography written. Could he have used his evil mesmeric influence to have someone kill the lad and steal his gold to be used in his—Drood's—service?"

Dickens looked at me so steadily and so coldly that I flinched back in my chair.

"Yes," said the Inimitable. "With Drood, anything is possible. The monster could have had *me* kill young Dickenson and bring his money to the Undertown temple and I would not remember it. I would have thought it a dream, a half-memory of some stage drama from long ago."

My heart pounded and my breathing all but stopped at this confession.

"Or," continued Dickens, "he could have had *you* do that deed, my dear Wilkie. Drood knows of you, of course. Drood has plans for you."

I exhaled, coughed, and tried to slow the pounding of my heart. "Nonsense," I said. "I have never met the man, if man he is."

"Are you *sure?*" asked Dickens. The wicked smile was there again beneath his whiskers.

I thought of Dickens's earlier, inexplicable mention of my experience in Birmingham. This was the right time to ask him about it—the *only* time, perhaps—but the pounding of my headache was now as rapid and insistent as the pounding of my heart there in that small, overheated room. Instead, I said, "You say he comes to your home, Charles."

"Yesss." Dickens sighed back into his chair. He stubbed out the short remnant of his cigar. "It has worn on me, Wilkie. The secrecy. The constant sense of terror. The dissembling and playacting in his presence. The trips into London and the effect of the descents into Undertown and its horrors. The constant sense of threat to Georgina, Katey, the children...Ellen. It has worn on me."

"Of course," I murmured. I thought of Inspector Field and the others out in the rain. Waiting.

"So you see, I must go to America," whispered Dickens. "Drood will not follow me there. He cannot follow me there."

"Why not?"

Dickens sat bolt upright and stared at me with wide eyes and, for the first time in our long association, I saw pure terror on my friend's countenance. "He can*not!*" he cried.

"No, of course not," I said hurriedly.

"But while I am gone," whispered Dickens, "you will be in great danger, my friend."

"Danger? Me? Why on earth should I be in danger, Charles? I have nothing to do with Drood or this dreadful game you and Field are playing with him."

Dickens shook his head but for a moment did not bother to speak or even look at me. Finally he said, "You shall be in great danger, Wilkie. Drood has already passed the black wings of his control over you at least once—almost certainly more than once. He knows where you live. He knows your weaknesses. And—most terribly for you—he knows that you are a writer and that you are now widely read both here in England and in America."

"What does that have to do with anything…" I began. When I stopped in mid-sentence, Dickens nodded again.

"Yes," he whispered. "I am his biographer of choice, but he knows he can find another should I die…or should he discover the extent of my desperate game and decide to dispose of me. I shall not depart for America until November at the earliest—I have much to do and much convincing of Drood that I go to the United States only to prepare the way for the publication of his biography—and you and I shall talk again many times and of many things before I sail, Wilkie, but promise me now that you will be very careful."

"I promise," I said. I knew at that moment that my friend Charles Dickens had gone mad.

We spoke of other things, but I ached abominably and Dickens was obviously exhausted. It was not even eleven PM when we said our goodnights and Dickens went off to his guest room and I to my bedroom.

I let the girl douse all the lamps in the house.

CAROLINE WAS WAITING in my bed, sleeping, but I woke her and sent her downstairs to her own room. This was no night for her to be up on the first floor where Dickens and I slept.

I got into my night gown and drank down three tall glasses of laudanum. The usually competent medicine did little to allay either my pain or my anxiety this June night. After lying in bed in the dark for an undetermined period, feeling my heart pound in my chest like the pendulum of some thudding but silent clock, I rose and went to the window.

The rain had stopped, but a summer fog had risen and was now creeping through the hedges and shrubs in the small park across the way. The moon had not worked free of the low overcast, but the clouds hurrying above the rooftops were limned with an almost liquid grey-white light. Puddles threw back a multitude of yellowed reflections from the corner streetlamp. There was no one out this night, not even the boy who had replaced Gooseberry. I tried to imagine where Field and his many operatives had positioned themselves. In that empty house near the corner? In the darkness of the alley to the east?

A real clock—the one in our downstairs hallway—slowly struck twelve.

I went back to bed, closed my eyes, and tried to slow my mind.

From somewhere far below, borne up by the medium of the hollow walls and occasional grates, there came a subtle rustling. A scuttling. A door opening? No, I thought not. A window, then? No. A cellar-dark slow shifting of bricks, perhaps, or some slow but minded movement amidst heaps of black coal. But definitely a scuttling.

I sat up in bed and clutched my bedclothes to my chest.

My accursed novelist's imagination, perhaps aided by the laudanum, offered up clear visions of a rat the size of a small dog pressing its way through the renewed hole in the coal cellar wall. But this oversized rat had a human face. The face of Drood.

A door creaked. Floor boards moaned ever so softly.

Dickens sneaking out into the night, as Inspector Field had so confidently predicted?

I slipped out of bed, pulled on my dressing gown, and went to one knee, opening the lowest drawer of my dresser with exaggerated care so as not to make a sound. The huge pistol given to me by Detective Hatchery was there where I had left it under my folded summer linens. It felt absurdly heavy and bulky in my hand as I tip-toed to my door and opened it with a wince-producing protest of hinges.

The hallway was empty, but now I could hear voices. Whispering voices. Men's voices, I thought but could not be certain.

Glad that I had left my stockings on, I moved out into the hall and stood at the head of the dark staircase. Other than the pendulum thud and inner ticking of the hallway clock downstairs, there was no noise coming up from the ground floor.

The whispers rose again. They came from just down the hall.

Could Caroline—angry at me for sending her away—have come up to talk to Dickens? Or Carrie, who had always considered Charles Dickens her favourite visitor to our house?

No, the whispers were not coming from Dickens's guest room. I saw a vertical slice of soft light coming through the partially opened study door and moved carefully down the hall, the heavy pistol pointing towards the floor.

There was a single lighted candle in there. By pressing my face against the door, I could make out the three chairs and three figures sitting near the cold fireplace. Dickens in a red Moroccan robe was sitting in the wing chair he had occupied earlier. He leaned forward above the only candle, his expression lost to shadows, but his hands busy working the air as he whispered urgently. Listening from the desk chair was the Other Wilkie. His beard was slightly shorter than mine, as if he had trimmed it recently, and he wore my spare set of spectacles. The two circles of glass reflected the candle and made his eyes look demonic.

In the tall chair I had occupied an hour earlier, the back of the chair now towards me, I could make out only a black arm, long pale fingers, and a hint of bare scalp rising above the dark leather. I knew who it was, of course, even before the form leaned forward into the candlelight to hiss-whisper some response to Dickens.

Drood was in my house. I remembered the image of the rat in the coal cellar, then saw instead a curling tendril of smoke or fog creeping between the bricks down there, coalescing into this simulacrum of a man.

I felt very dizzy. I leaned back against the doorjamb to steady myself, realising as I did so that I could open the door, stride in, kill Drood with two shots, and then turn the pistol on the Other Wilkie. And then, per-haps...upon Dickens himself.

No...I could *shoot* Drood, but could I kill him? And as for shooting the Other Wilkie, would that not be tantamount to shooting myself? Would the Metro-politan Police come at Caroline's hysterical behest in the grey light of morning to find three dead bodies on the floor of Wilkie Collins's study, one of them being the cold corpse of Wilkie Collins?

I leaned forward to hear what they were saying, but the whispering stopped. First Dickens raised his head to look at me. Then the Other Wilkie, his round face bunched up like a rabbit's above his beard and below that endless forehead, turned his pale face to stare at me. Then Drood turned...slowly, terribly. His lidless eyes gleamed as red as embers from Hell.

Forgetting that I still held the pistol, I pushed the door shut with a hollow thud and went back to my bed-room. Behind me, just audible through the closed study doors, the talk began again, but not in whispers now.

Did I hear soft laughter before I closed and locked my bedroom door? I shall never be sure.

CHAPTER TWENTY-THREE

*T*hat same summer of 1867 came close to see-ing Caroline, Carrie, our three servants (George, Besse, and Agnes), and me without a home. We were almost turned out onto the street.

We had known that the lease on 9 Melcombe Place was expiring, of course, but I had been confident that the terms of the lease could be and would be renewed for another year or two, at the very least, despite my frequent quarrels with the landlord there. My confidence turned out to have been misplaced. So July was given to much rushing around London trying to find a place to live.

It hardly bears saying that I was so busy with *The Moonstone* up through June—I had the first three numbers written to show Dickens by then—and so busy after June with another project that Dickens had brought to me, that it was Caroline who had to do the rushing about.

While she rushed, I retired to the peace of my club to complete work on the first three numbers of *The Moonstone*.

On the last two days of June, I spent the weekend at Gad's Hill and read the completed chapters to Dickens, who was so delighted with what he heard that he agreed on the spot to pay about £750 so that *All the Year Round* would have the rights, with publication of the first number slated for 15 December. I immediately used this news to get the Harper brothers in the United States to match that amount for serial rights there.

When I returned to London on 1 July, Caroline was buzzing around my head like a hungry fly, asking me to go see various possible homes that she had found for lease or sale. I did so and all were obviously a waste of my time except for the possibility of one place on Cornwall Terrace. I chastised Caroline for looking at places outside of Marylebone, since I had grown fond of that neighbourhood. (Also, of course, I needed any new residence with Caroline and Carrie to remain within easy distance of Bolsover Street, where "Mrs Dawson" had all but taken up permanent residence.)

My quarrelsome landlord at Melcombe Place now insisted that we have the house there vacated by the first of August—a demand that I met with equanimity and was willing to ignore when the time came, but one which gave Caroline severe headaches and provoked days of even more frenzied searching and long evenings of voluble complaining.

In May, Dickens had invited me to collaborate with him on a long tale for the Christmas 1867 issue of *All the Year Round* and I had agreed, but only after long and sometimes almost comically bitter negotiations on payment with Wills at the magazine (Dickens, prudently, avoided all financial negotiations with me). I had demanded the very high rate of £400 for my half of the tale, although I confess to you, Dear Reader, that this sum had come to mind only because it was precisely ten times what I had been paid for my first successful submission to Dickens's magazine—a story called "Sister Rose"—in 1855. I finally agreed to £300 not out of weakness or failure of nerve, but because I wanted to associate myself publicly with Dickens again and, in private, bind up any minor wounds that might have been inflicted over the Drood affair that month.

Dickens was, throughout that summer, in the best of spirits. I was ready to return to work on *The Moonstone* for the rest of July, but during my weekend at Gad's Hill Dickens convinced me that we should begin the collaboration on the Christmas tale immediately. He had suggested a story based upon our journey across the Alps in 1853—happier times for both of us in many ways—and had contributed the title, *No Thoroughfare*.

Caroline was delighted to hear that I was putting *The Moonstone* on the shelf for a while; she was furious to hear that I would be spending much of the next several months at Gad's Hill.

That same Monday upon my return from Gad's Hill—with Caroline locked in her room crying and snivelling accusations about my abandoning her to find a home for us with no help from me—I received a note from Dickens, who had come into town to work at his offices at the magazine:

> *This is to certify that I, the undersigned, was (for the time being) a drivelling ass when I declared the Christmas Number to be composed of Thirty-two pages. And I do hereby declare that the said Christmas Number is composed of Forty-eight pages, and long and heavy pages too, as I have heretofore proved and demonstrated with the sweat of my brow.*

This then was the bantering mood that Charles Dickens was in that July of 1867.

Martha R—— was in a much better mood than Caroline G—— that summer, and most days, after I finished my work at the Athenaeum Club, I found myself heading to Bolsover Street to dinner and to spend the night. Since I did keep a room at my club from time to time and since I was also frequently taking the train out to Gad's Hill to confer with Dickens on *No Thoroughfare* and would sometimes spend the night there as well, Caroline asked no questions.

Then one evening, just as I was finishing an early dinner at my club, I looked up to see Inspector Charles Frederick Field striding across the dining room. Without asking permission, he pulled a chair up to my solitary table and sat down.

My first temptation was to say, "Only gentlemen are allowed in this club, I fear, Inspector," but seeing his visage creased by a very uncommon smile, I merely dabbed a napkin at my lips, raised an eyebrow in interrogation, and waited.

"Good news, my dear Mr Collins, and I wanted to be the first to tell you."

"You caught…" I looked around at the few other diners in the large room. "…the subterranean gentleman?"

"Not yet, sir. Not yet. But soon enough! No, this concerns your current problem of acquiring new lodgings."

I had not told Inspector Field about our losing our lease, but I was far beyond being surprised at any information the man might have in his possession. I continued waiting.

"You remember the obstacle that Mrs Shernwold was presenting," he said softly, glancing around as if we were two conspirators.

"Of course."

"Well, sir, the obstacle is no more."

I was truly surprised at this. "The lady has changed her mind?" I said.

"The lady," said Inspector Field, "is dead."

I blinked several times and leaned forward myself, whispering even more conspiratorially than had the inspector. "How?" Mrs Shernwold was one of those skinny, crotchety crones in her sixties who showed every sign of living into her skinnier, even more crotchety nineties.

"She had the good grace to fall down a flight of stairs and break her neck, Mr Collins."

"Shocking!" I said. "Where?"

"Well, in the house at Number Ninety Gloucester Place, it is true, but on the servants' stairway. No place you would have to be reminded of her misfortune should you move there."

"The servants' stairway," I repeated, thinking of my lady of the green skin and ivory tusks. "What on earth was Mrs Shernwold doing on the servants' stairs?"

"We shall never know," cackled the inspector. "But the timing could not be more fortuitous, could it, Mr Collins? Nothing stands in the way of you making an offer for the house now."

"The missionary son," I said. "Surely he will return from Africa or wherever he is and..."

Inspector Field waved this consideration away with one calloused hand. "It turns out that the mortgage on Number Ninety Gloucester Place was never paid off by poor Mrs Shernwold. The house was never hers to give away, sir."

"Who has the paper on it, then?"

"Lord Portman. It turns out that the house was *always* under the control of Lord Portman."

"I have met Lord Portman!" I cried, loudly enough that several of the diners turned to stare. In a much lower voice, I said, "I know him, Inspector. A reasonable man. I believe that he owns much of the property there around Portman Square...on Baker Street as well as Gloucester Place."

"I believe that you are correct, Mr Collins," said Field with that satisfied and strangely evil grin.

"Do you have any idea what he is asking for the place?" I said.

"I did take the liberty of enquiring," said Inspector Field. "Lord Portman says that he would agree to a twenty-year lease on the property for eight hundred pounds. That includes those lovely stables in the mews, of course. One could sublet those to offset the rent."

My mouth went dry and I sipped some port. £800 was a fortune—more than I had free at the time—but I also knew that upon the event of my mother's death, Charley and I would inherit, in equal shares, some £5,000 left to her by her aunt, even though—due to the terms of our father's will—the rest of the capital in his estate and hers would remain tied up. And the inspector was undoubtedly right about the prospect of subletting the rather handsome stables.

Inspector Field had removed two suspiciously dark cigars from his jacket pocket. "I presume your club's policies allow smoking in the dining hall," he said.

"Of course."

He clipped off the ends of both cigars, handed me one, lit his, puffed happily, and held the match out to light mine. I bent forward and allowed him to do so.

Inspector Field waved over Bartles, the oldest and most dignified of the club's waiters, and said, "My good man, be so kind as to bring me a glass of what Mr Collins is drinking. Thank you."

As Bartles hurried away—frowning slightly at this indifferently dressed stranger's peremptory tone—I marvelled, not for the first time, at how my destinies had become so intertwined with this strange, imperious policeman's.

"Good cigar, don't you think, Mr Collins?"

It tasted like something grown and harvested in a mouldering boot in a forgotten cellar. "First-rate," I said.

The inspector's wine arrived and the always-aware and always-conservative parsimonious part of my mind added it, reluctantly, to my already significant tab here at the club.

"To your very good turn of fortune, sir," said Inspector Field, lifting his glass.

I lifted mine and touched crystal to crystal, thinking as I did so that perhaps Caroline would now—finally—quit complaining and caterwauling. I confess that not once then or in the coming days did I think of poor Mrs Shernwold and her ironic fate, except when I lied to Caroline about where and how the old lady had met her demise.

I BELIEVE THAT THIS is time, Dear Reader from my posthumous future, for me to tell you a little bit about the Other Wilkie.

I have to presume that until now you have believed this Other Wilkie to be either a figment of my imagination or a function of the laudanum I am forced to take. He is neither.

All my life I have been haunted by a second self. As a very young child I was sure that I had a twin as a playmate and often told my mother about him. As a boy, I would hear my father speak of giving drawing lessons "to Wilkie" and know that I had not been in the house at the time. It was my *Doppelgänger* who had benefited from those lessons. As a very young man of fifteen, encountering my first experience of physical love with an older woman, I was not surprised to look over into the shadowed corner and see the Other Wilkie—as young and bright-eyed and unbearded as myself—watching with great interest. In my early adulthood, this second self seemed to recede into the grey realm from which he had come. For several years, I was sure that I had left him behind.

But a few years before the period I write of in this memoir, when the rheumatoid gout became too persistently painful to endure without the help of tincture of opium, the Other Wilkie returned. While my personality had become softer, more convivial, friendly to all, that of the Other Wilkie seemed to have grown harsher and more aggressive during our absence from one another. Years earlier, when I had first met Percy Fitzgerald (before Fitzgerald had become such a favourite of Dickens), I confided to the younger man how I *"was subject to a curious ghostly influence, having often the idea that 'someone is standing behind me.'"*

I was never dismissive of the effect that the laudanum had on summoning this Other Wilkie. As Thomas De Quincey, author of *Confessions of an English Opium Eater* and a friend to both my parents, once wrote—*"If a man 'whose talk is full of oxen,' should become an Opium-eater, the probability is, that (if he is not too dull to dream at all)—he will dream about oxen."* My obsession, in both my writing and my life, has been about double identity—of a *Doppelgänger* hovering just beyond the hazy boundaries of day-to-day reality—so there is little wonder that the opium I consumed daily, a drug so frequently and effectively used to open doors to other realities, should have summoned the Other Wilkie who had been my nursery-room playmate.

Should you know my writings, Dear Reader, you would be aware that this question of identity has permeated most of my stories and all of my novels, beginning with *Antonina*, which I began when I was only twenty-two years of age. Doubles, often representing good and evil, wander the pages of my tales. Frequently my characters (I think of Laura Fairlie in my *Woman in White* and Magdalen Vanstone in my more recent *No Name*) have their identities cruelly and violently taken from them so that they must go inhabit the hollow husks of other names, other minds, other skins.

Even when my characters are permitted to retain their own identities, more often than not in my novels they must conceal those identities, assume the identities of others, or face the loss of that identity through injury to their sight, hearing, speech, or because of loss of limbs. New personalities are constantly surfacing within my characters, a transformation brought about more and more frequently by the use of drugs.

Charles Dickens despised this aspect to my writing, but my readers apparently loved it. And I should mention that I was not the only writer to be obsessed with the questions of "the other self" and of dual, twin, or confused identities: a certain scribbler with the name of William Shakespeare had included such themes and conventions in his work far more frequently than I.

I often wondered—even before the nightmare period of Drood began—if I was a lesser man because of the traits missing in me but presumably present in the Other Wilkie. There is, for instance, the matter of my name. Or, rather, other people's use of my name.

I seemed to be "Wilkie" to everyone: not "Mr Collins" (although Inspector Field and his operatives had gone out of their way to use the honourific) nor even "Collins" (as in the way I might call Charles Dickens "my dear Dickens" to his face)…merely "Wilkie." It was as if I had always remained a child to others, even to children. Carrie grew up calling me Wilkie. Dickens's many children, during all the years of their growth, called me Wilkie unless ordered otherwise by Dickens or Catherine or Georgina. Men at my club, who would never address their peers with their Christian names, even though they may have known these others for decades, felt free to call me Wilkie almost immediately after our introductions.

It was a curious thing.

The morning after I peered in on Dickens speaking with Drood and the Other Wilkie in my study—and then hastily retreated—I confessed to the Inimitable over breakfast that I had had a strange dream about such a meeting.

"But it was real!" cried Dickens. "You were there, my dear Wilkie! We spoke for hours."

"I remember none of the content of the discussion," I said, feeling my skin prickle with icy needles.

"That is perhaps for the best," said Dickens. "Drood sometimes uses his magnetic influence to erase some or all memory of a meeting, should he think that such a memory would put him or his interlocutor in danger. Such mesmeric erasure does not work with me, of course, since I am a co-practitioner of the mesmeric arts."

Are you indeed? I thought sarcastically. Aloud, I said, "If my dream was real, if the meeting was real, how did Drood get into the house? I happen to know that the building was securely locked."

Dickens smiled as he applied marmalade to a second piece of toast. "He did not enlighten me on that topic, my dear Wilkie. My impression over the past two years has been that there are few places that Drood cannot go if he wishes to go there."

"You're saying that he is some kind of ghost."

"Not at all, my dear Wilkie. Not at all."

"Will you tell me, then," I said with some asperity, "the content of our 'hours' of discussion…a content that this phantom has ordered me to forget?"

Dickens hesitated. "I shall," he said at last. "But I believe it might be best if I wait to do so. There are imminent events that may not be in your interest to know about at the present time, my dear Wilkie. And other facts that it is in your interest not to be aware of in terms of your own honour…so, for instance, you can be truthful when you tell Inspector Charles Frederick Field that you did not meet with Drood and have no knowledge of the phantom's plans."

"Then why did he—or you—tell me about them last night?" I pressed. I had not taken my morning laudanum yet and my body and brain ached for it.

"To receive your permission," said Dickens.

"Permission for what?" I was close to becoming angry.

Dickens smiled again and patted my arm in an insufferable way. "You shall see soon enough, my friend. And when these things come to pass, I shall tell you all the details of our long conversation last night. You have my word on this."

I had to settle for this, even though I was far less than convinced that there had *been* any meeting of Drood, Dickens, and the Other Wilkie. It seemed far more likely that Dickens was taking advantage of my laudanum dream for his own inscrutable purposes.

Or that the Other Wilkie had his own secret purposes and plans. This possibility made my skin grow even colder.

WE MOVED TO Number 90 Gloucester Place in early September of 1867. I had been forced to raise a loan through my solicitors for the £800 purchase of the lease, but Inspector Field had been correct about the prospect of renting the stables on the mews behind the house; I sublet them to a woman with four horses for £40 a year, although I was to have a devil of a time getting her to pay on time.

The house on Gloucester Place was much larger and grander than the home we had leased at Melcombe Place. This house was set back from the street and terraced, five storeys high, with ample room for a family much larger than ours and for servants far more numerous and well-trained and better turned-out than our three poor waifs. We now had enough guest rooms to accommodate a small army of visitors. The dining room on the ground floor was thrice the size of that in Melcombe Place, and we used a comfortable room behind it as our family sitting room. I immediately took possession of the huge L-shaped double drawing room on the ground floor as my study, although it was directly in the path of visitors passing by in the hall, servants cleaning, Caroline working in the nearby sitting room, and all the other intrusion and traffic of daily life. But with its huge fireplace, high windows, central location in the home, and airy feeling, it had none of the closed-off darkness of my Melcombe Place study. I could only hope that the Other Wilkie would not make the move with us.

When remodelling work on the house was finally completed in the late autumn, it was much to my liking. I had books and pictures everywhere, of course, and the panelled walls of Gloucester Place lent themselves to displaying my art much better than had the dark, wallpapered walls at our previous residences.

I had a portrait of my mother as a young girl in a white dress—painted by Margaret Carpenter—that I hung in my study. My mother never saw it there (since it would have been inappropriate for her to visit the house with Caroline G—— in it), but I reported to her in a letter that it was "still like you after all these years." (This was not quite true, since my mother was now in her seventies and age had taken its toll.)

Also in my study were a portrait of my father and a painting of Sorrento by him, large paintings that flanked my massive writing table, which had also been my father's. On another panelled wall in that room hung a portrait of me as a young man done by my brother, Charley, and another portrait of me by Millais. The only work of my own in the house was my Academy painting *The Smuggler's Retreat*, which I hung in the dining room.

I did not trust the novelty of gas lighting—although Dickens and others doted on it—so my rooms, books, drapes, writing table, and paintings in Number 90 Gloucester Place continued to be lighted by wax candles and kerosene lamps just as in my previous homes. I loved the soft light that candles and fireplaces imparted to everything—not the least to people's faces when gathered around a hearth or dining table—and would never have supplanted it with the harsh, inhuman glare of gas lighting, even though working by candlelight or lantern glow often gave me severe headaches which required the administration of more laudanum. It was worth the price for the ambience.

The house, however grand-looking from the outside, had fallen into some disrepair under the regime of the late Mrs Shernwold, and it took a small army of workmen more than a month to paint, repair or install plumbing, knock down partitions, repanel, retile, and generally bring the house up to the standards one would expect of a famous author's home.

My first step in dealing with this chaos was to end all social visitations, either coming or going. My second was to absent myself from the potential felicity of Number 90 Gloucester Place—sleeping and working for weeks exclusively at my mother's cottage at Southborough or at Gad's Hill Place—and to leave the dusty, dirty supervision to Caroline. As I wrote to my friend Frederick Lehman on 10 September, the day after we moved in—*"I had an old house to leave—a new house to find—that new house to bargain for and take—lawyers and supervisors to consult—British workmen to employ—and through it all, to keep my literary business going without so much as a day's stoppage."*

That autumn was a warm one, and Dickens and I carried out our collaboration on *No Thoroughfare* primarily in his lovely little Swiss chalet. Dickens had turned his long writing table up on the first floor there into a sort of partners desk—with two leg wells—and we put in long hours of scribbling together with only the hum of bees and the corresponding hum of the occasional comment or question passing between us to disturb the comfortable autumn silence.

Back near the end of August, Dickens had sent me a note that typified the easy give-and-take of ideas and narrative that would mark our work on this project:

> *I have a general idea which I hope will supply the kind of interest we want. Let us arrange to culminate in a wintry flight and pursuit across the Alps, under lonely circumstances, and against warnings. Let us get into all the horrors and dangers of such an adventure under the most terrific circumstances, either escaping from or trying to overtake (the latter I think) some one, on escaping from or overtaking whom the love, prosperity, and Nemesis of the story depend. There we can get ghostly interest, picturesque interest, breathless interest of time and circumstance, and force the design up to any powerful climax we please. If you will keep this in your mind, as I will in mine, urging the story towards it as we go along, we shall get a very Avalanche of power out of it, and thunder it down on the readers' heads.*

Even by late September we had no Avalanche yet and Dickens could only report that *"I am jogging at the pace of a wheelbarrow propelled by a Greenwich Pensioner"* and *"Like you I am working with a snail-like slowness…,"* but the work together at Gad's Hill accelerated both the pace of our separate and co-mingled narratives and raised our levels of enthusiasm.

By 5 October I was back at my mother's cottage, enjoying good meals and a feeling that the end of our joint endeavour was in sight, while Dickens was sending the following note:

I have brought on Marguerite to the rescue, and I have
so left it as that Vendale—to spare her—says it was an
accident in the storm, and nothing more. By the way,
Obenreizer has received a cut from Vendale, made with
his own dagger. This in case you want him with a scar. If
you don't, no matter. I have no doubt my Proof of the
Mountain adventure will be full of mistakes, as my MS. is
not very legible. But you will see what it means. The
Dénouement I see pretty much as you see it—without
further glimpses as yet. The Obenreizer question I will
consider (q'ry Suicide?). I have made Marguerite wholly
devoted to her lover. Whenever you may give me notice of
your being ready, we will appoint to meet here to wind up.

I wonder, Dear Reader, what importance these working notes between two such professional authors might
have a century and more hence? Very little, I would
suppose, but given Dickens's fame, even in my lifetime,
perhaps even these hastily scribbled and cryptic missives might be of some interest to some minor scholar
one day. Could we say the same of the notes I sent
Dickens? Alas, we shall never know, since Dickens still
regularly burned all correspondence sent to him,
continuing—as it were—the ongoing conflagration
that he first began in the autumn of 1860.

It was that same 5 October, the first Saturday of the
new month, that I returned home to Number 90
Gloucester Place—having not written or cabled Caroline ahead of time that I would be returning—only to
arrive late, to find most of the new home's rooms unlit,
and to discover Caroline having dinner with a strange
man in the kitchen.

I confess to being startled, if not angered. Caroline
smiled at me from her place at the table—the servants
were gone that night—although I saw the blush begin

at her neckline and work its way up behind her ears and then around to her cheeks.

"What is this?" I asked the man. "Who are you?"

He was a thin, sallow, short, unimpressive little weasel of a man, his jacket of the most common moleskin. Everything about him was common. He rose and began to answer me, but before he could speak, I said, "Wait, I know you....I *hired* you a month ago. Clow, isn't it? Or something like that. You're the plumber."

"Joseph Clow, sir," he said, his voice all whine and adenoids. "And yes you did, sir. We've just finished the last of the upstairs plumbing today, and your housekeeper, Mrs G——, graciously extended me an invitation to take dinner here, sir."

I gave my "housekeeper" a withering look, but she merely smiled back at me. Such insolence! I had just borrowed and spent a staggering £800 to buy this insolent baggage one of the finest mansions near Portman Square, and here she was arranging an assignation with a common workman behind my back in my own home!

"Very good," I said, giving a smile that communicated *I shall deal with you later* to Caroline. "I just dropped by to pick up some fresh linen. I shall be off to my club."

"Your housekeeper prepares an excellent spotted dick," said this person. Had I detected any insolence or sarcasm, I believe I would have struck him, but his comment seemed innocent.

"Mr Clow's father is a distiller and he has part-interest in the business," said Caroline, brazen to the end. "He brought a very fine sherry to help celebrate the completion."

I nodded and went upstairs. I did not lack for linen in my portmanteau. I had come back to renew the laudanum from my large jug. Filling my travel flask and drinking down two large glassfuls, I went to my dresser, felt around in the lower drawer beneath my linens, and found the loaded pistol that Hatchery had given me so long ago.

Who would blame me if I shot both Caroline and her skinny, moustached, grimy plumber of a lover? The man had probably been in my bed in my new home even before I had—or at least it was certain he had hoped to.

Then again, I realised, to the world at large, Caroline G—— was indeed my housekeeper, not my wife. I was certainly justified in shooting Joseph Clow as an intruder, but few juries or judges would see the justification of my shooting a gentleman caller who had agreed to have dinner in the servants' kitchen with my housekeeper. Even the accursed sherry might be put into evidence by an eager prosecutor.

Smiling grimly, I set the pistol away, gathered up a valise of clothing merely for the show of it, made sure my flask was topped off, and went out the front way to spend the night at my club. I did not go to the back of the house to look in again at Caroline—who had looked flushed and lovely in the candlelight, despite her advanced age of being in her thirties—or at her weasel-plumber of a prospective lover and husband.

By the time I reached my club, I was whistling and in a good mood. I could see even then how I could use Mr Joseph Clow to my own advantage.

DICKENS AND I completed *No Thoroughfare* in late October, weeks later than we had anticipated. I was in charge of reprint rights and dealt with Frederick Chapman in the negotiations, but in the end George Smith of Smith and Elder made a better offer and I immediately transferred the rights to him.

Dickens and I both saw the theatrical potential in *No Thoroughfare* and because, in those days, any thief with a stage and a few actors could steal literary material simply by adapting it first, we decided to steal a march on any potential thieves and adapt it ourselves. Dickens—in a hurry to wind up his affairs so that he could depart for America—rattled off a rough scenario to our actor-impresario mutual friend Fechter and gave me the responsibility of doing the hard work of adaptation after he, Dickens, had left the country.

At the end of October, the tall house at Number 90 Gloucester Place was finished to my satisfaction—even the plumbing—and Caroline and I gave a house-warming dinner that also served as a farewell party for Dickens, who was scheduled to sail for America on 9 November. I hired an excellent French cook for the affair—she was to work for us on a semi-permanent basis in the coming years, although she did not live in the house—and took an active part in preparing the menu and overseeing the preparation.

The party was a great success and the first of many at the Gloucester Place home.

A few days later, on 2 November, I was one of the stewards at a huge and much more formal farewell banquet for Dickens that we held at the Freemasons' Hall. There were 450 invited guests, the crème of London's art, literary, and dramatic universe—all male of course—crowding the main body of the hall, while some 100 women (including the duplicitous but lovely Caroline G—— as well as Dickens's sister-in-law Georgina and daughter Mary) sat sequestered up in the Ladies Gallery, though the women were allowed to join the men for coffee afterwards. Caroline's daughter, Carrie, now almost seventeen, was also there that night. In my nervousness, I had written the organisers twice to make sure that my request for tickets for the two ladies had been honoured.

The Grenadier Guards' band played from another balcony that night. One surprise guest was Dickens's son Sydney, a sailor whose ship had just docked in Portsmouth two nights before. British and American flags bedecked the main dining hall, and panels above twenty arches honoured with golden laurels each bore the title of one of Charles Dickens's works. Lord Lytton, now sixty-four years of age but looking twice that, was the chairman for the evening and hovered over the proceedings like a gimlet-eyed bird of prey in all-black formal dress.

When Dickens finally rose to speak after a series of increasingly hyperbolic speeches of praise, my collaborator at first faltered and then began to weep. When he finally could speak, his words were eloquent but not, many agreed afterwards, as eloquent as his tears.

I confess to sitting at the main table that night, my head spinning with wine and an extra fortifying round of laudanum, and wondering what all these famous guests—Lord Chief Justice Cockburn, Sir Charles Russell, Lord Houghton, a veritable gaggle of Royal Academicians, the Lord Mayor of London—might say if they could have seen Dickens descending into the sewers of Undertown as I had. Or if they had any suspicion of the probable fate of a lonely young man named Edmond Dickenson.

Perhaps it would not have mattered to them.

On 9 November, I went up to Liverpool with Caroline and Carrie to see Dickens off as he departed for America.

The author had been given the Second Officer's spacious cabin on the deck of the *Cuba*. (Carrie later asked me where the Second Officer might be sleeping during the crossing, and I had to admit that I had no idea.)

Unlike most accommodations on the ship, the cabin had both a door and a window that could be opened to take advantage of the fresh sea air.

Dickens was fretful and distracted during our short visit and only I knew why. And I knew why only because of my continued association with Inspector Field.

Despite his first-hand knowledge of the Puritanical conservative nature of Americans from a quarter of a century earlier, Dickens somehow had not yet surrendered his plan to bring Ellen Ternan to America so that she could share the tour with him, perhaps in the disguise of an assistant to Dolby. This would never come to pass, of course, but Dickens was truly a hopeless romantic when it came to such fantasies.

I was not supposed to know about it, but the Inimitable had arranged with Wills at the magazine office to forward a coded telegram to the young actress in which she would be instructed on what to do once Dickens arrived in the New World. A message of "All well" would have her speeding on the next ship to America, all expenses paid through an account Dickens had left under Wills's supervision. A reluctant code of "Safe and well" would mean that she would remain on the Continent, where she and her mother were currently vacationing while she waited word on her fate.

In his heart—or perhaps "in his rational mind" would be more appropriate—Dickens must have known that fair day of 9 November, as I had known when I first heard of the foolish scheme through Inspector Field, that the message "Safe and well," meaning "Lonely but very, very much in the scowling, prying, judging, public American eye," would be the one sent to Ellen via Wills.

Our own goodbyes were emotional. Dickens was aware of how much work he had left for me to finish— the proofings and revisions of *No Thoroughfare* as well as the scripting and staging with Fechter—but there was more to the emotion than that. After Carrie, Caroline, and I had descended the gangplank, I returned to the airy Second Officer's cabin under the pretext of having forgotten one of my gloves. Dickens was expecting me.

"I pray God that Drood will not follow me to America," he whispered as we again clasped hands in farewell.

"He will not," I said with a certainty I did not feel.

As I turned to leave, thinking that it was possible—even probable—that I would never see my friend Charles Dickens again, he stopped me.

"Wilkie…in the conversation with Drood in your study on nine June, the discussion you do not remember…I feel it necessary to warn you…"

I could not move. I felt as if my blood had turned to ice and that the ice had invaded my very cells.

"You agreed to be Drood's biographer if something happened to me," said Dickens. He looked seasick even though the *Cuba* was still firmly tied to the wharf in Liverpool Harbour and was not rocking in the least. "Drood threatened to kill you and all of your family if you reneged on this promise…just as he has threatened, repeatedly, to kill me and mine. If he finds out that I went to America to escape him rather than to speak to publishers there about his biography…"

After a minute I found that I could blink. In another minute I could speak. "Think nothing of it, Charles," I said. "Have a good reading tour in America. Return to us safe and healthy."

I went out of the cabin and down the gangplank to a waiting Carrie and a sulking, worried Caroline.

CHAPTER TWENTY-FOUR

*I*n the month after Dickens left for America I felt rather as if my father had died again. It was not an altogether unpleasant sensation.

I had never been busier. Dickens had not only left me the revisions and proofs of *No Thoroughfare*, but had also put me in charge of editing the entire Christmas Issue of *All the Year Round*. This nonplussed our friend William Henry Wills—the Inimitable's second-in-command at the magazine, who had been unalterably opposed to Dickens's going to America in the first place—but Wills, always the obedient soldier, soon settled into his position of second-in-command to *me*. I spent more and more time at the magazine's offices as November went on and—since Dickens had also requested that I check regularly on Georgina, Mary, and Katey at Gad's Hill (and since I found it easier to edit and work on *The Moonstone* there and since my brother, Charley, was also there much of the time), I was soon living more in Charles Dickens's life than in Wilkie Collins's.

Caroline tended to agree with that assessment, although not with the good grace and humour I had anticipated, and tended to begin arguments with me whenever I did spend a few days at Number 90 Gloucester Place. As we moved towards December, I spent fewer and fewer days at my new London house and more time at Gad's Hill or eating in Dickens's sparse rooms and sleeping in his comfortable bed above the magazine offices.

I happened to be there when the telegram "Safe and well" arrived for Wills and was duly sent on to Ellen Ternan in Florence, where she was staying with her mother and family. How Dickens had ever imagined that Ellen might travel alone from Italy across the Atlantic to America I cannot imagine. The fantasy was simply another sign of how lost in his romantic dreams Dickens was at this time. I did learn later from Wills, almost by accident, that Dickens had known before he set sail that Americans would not have countenanced the presence of this single woman in Dickens's small entourage. Dolby had sounded things out after his arrival and sent his verdict on the propriety of Ellen's presence in a single telegraphed syllable—"No."

Dickens and I had agreed that the stage adaptation of *No Thoroughfare* should be produced at the Adelphi Theatre as close to Christmas Day as possible and that our mutual friend Charles Fechter should play the villain, Obenreizer. I had first been impressed with Fechter's performances almost fifteen years earlier and had met him in 1860 when he was in London to play in Victor Hugo's *Ruy Blas.* By common impulse, immediately upon that meeting, Fechter and I had dispensed with the tentative formalities of acquaintance and had become fast friends.

Born in London of an English mother and a German father, raised in France but having now chosen London as his home again, Fechter was a man of incredible charm and loyalty—the gift of the complete Swiss chalet to Dickens two Christmases ago had been typical of his generosity and impetuousness—but he had no more business sense than a child.

Fechter's home in London may have been the only *salon* less formal than my own. Whereas I had the habit of leaving guests in Caroline's care at the table if I had to rush off for a theatre engagement or somesuch, Fechter had been known to greet guests in his dressing gown and slippers and to allow them to choose which bottle of wine they preferred and take it with them to their place at the table. He and I adored French cookery and twice we put the inexhaustible resources of gastronomic France to the test by dining on one article of food only, presented under many different forms. I remember that we once had a potato dinner in six courses and another time an egg dinner in eight courses.

Fechter's one flaw as an actor was terrible stage fright, and his dresser was known to follow him around with a basin backstage before the curtain went up.

This November into December I was hurriedly writing the script for the stage version of *No Thoroughfare* and sent proofs straight to Fechter, who reported that he had "fallen madly in love with the subject" and immediately collaborated on the dramatic scenario. I was not surprised that the actor loved the villainous lead character of Obenreizer, since Dickens and I had held Fechter in mind as we'd created him.

On the days when I rode the train out towards Rochester to Gad's Hill Place, it was easy to think that Charles Dickens was gone for good—I still felt it quite probable that he would be, given the sad (if hidden from most) state of his health and the rigours of the American reading tour—and that I not only could someday but already *was* filling his place in the world.

By early December *No Thoroughfare* would be out in *All the Year Round* and I had no doubt it would be a great success. Certainly Dickens's name had something to do with that—his Christmas stories had brought the public flocking to buy the Christmas Issue of his two different magazines for twenty years now—but it was also true that my *Woman in White* had sold better than some serialised Dickens tales and I was confident that

The Moonstone would do even better in 1868. Sitting at the dinner table at Gad's Hill Place with Georgina on my left, my brother, Charley, on my right, Kate down the table, and some of the other Dickens children there as well, it felt as if I had replaced the Inimitable as surely and easily and completely as Georgina Hogarth had replaced Catherine Dickens.

As for my ongoing research for *The Moonstone,* after contacting many people in my quest for first-hand knowledge about India (as well as in my search for details on Hindoo and Mohammadan religious practices), I was put in touch with a certain John Wyllie, who had served in the Indian province of Kathiawar during his time in the Indian Civil Service.

"There is no part of India...so fanatically Hindoo in religious and so startlingly barbarous in primitive ethics," Wyllie said to me between great drams of brandy. He directed me to "a collection of Wheeler's letters or articles in the *Englishman*...Eleusinian mysteries are a joke to the abominations there revealed."

When I explained that my small group of Hindoos in *The Moonstone* would indeed be villainous but would also have a certain noble martyrdom about them, since they would have to spend decades propitiating their gods for violating their caste rule of never travelling across the "Dark Water," Wyllie just scoffed and stated flatly that their reinstatement in caste would be more a question of bribes paid to the right Brahman parties rather than the lifelong quest for purification my tale required.

So I threw away most of the comments and advice from Mr John Wyllie, formerly of the Indian Civil Service, and went with the dictates of my Muse. For the English setting of my novel I simply reached into my memory of the Yorkshire coast. For the historical events—since the main part of the novel was to begin in 1848—I continued to rely upon the excellent library at the Athenaeum. The only thing I carried over from Mr Wyllie's recommendations was the wild Indian province of Kathiawar; so few white men had been there and lived to tell about it that I decided I could make up its geography, topography, and particular brands and cults of Hindoo belief.

I continued working on the novel every day, even amidst the unimaginable demands of preparing *No Thoroughfare* for the stage.

News of our play had somehow arrived in the United States before the co-author of the tale upon which it was based. I received a letter from Dickens in which he announced that he had been met by theatrical managers immediately upon his arrival in New York; the men seemed to be under the impression that the script for *No Thoroughfare* was in the novelist's pocket. Dickens asked me to send copies of each act as I finished it and added, *"I have little doubt, my dear Wilkie, of being able to make a good thing of the Drama."*

There followed a flurry of correspondence back and forth in which Dickens announced that he was hurrying to find an American citizen to whom we could consign the MS, thus assuring the right of playing it in America while equally assuring that we would gain some profit from such a production. By Christmas Eve, Dickens had received my final copy of the play, prompting this reply from Boston: *"The play is done* with great pains and skill, *but I fear it is too long. Its fate will have been decided before you get this letter, but I greatly doubt its success...."* The rest of the note was all about Dickens's fear of the inevitable American pirating of *some* version of our story, but, in truth, I had lost real interest after the words *"...but I greatly doubt its success."*

DESPITE ALL OF THE OBLIGATIONS upon my time and energy, I had honoured, in mid-December, a written request from Inspector Field to meet him at Waterloo Bridge. I anticipated the substance of what he had to say to me and I have to say that my prediction was not in error.

The old detective looked insufferably pleased with himself, which at first seemed odd, since after my telling him that nothing untowards had happened in my home the previous 9 of June, the trail of Drood had gone very cold indeed. But one of the first things that the inspector told me as we walked over Waterloo Bridge into a breeze carrying light snow, our collars turned high and Field's heavy wool cape flapping about his shoulders like the wings of a bat, was that the Metropolitan Police had captured a Malay suspected of murder. The Malay, it turned out, was one of Drood's lieutenants and was being interrogated "briskly" in a deep cell even as we walked. Early information from the interrogation suggested that Drood may have moved from Undertown and was hiding in the surface slums of London. It was only a matter of time, Inspector Field informed me confidently, before they would have the best lead on the Egyptian murderer that they had obtained in decades of ceaseless effort.

"So the police are sharing the information with you," I said.

Inspector Field showed his large, yellow teeth in a smile. "My own men and I are carrying out the interrogation, Mr Collins. I still have many close friends on the force, you see, even if the commissioner and those higher up continue to treat me with less than the respect I have earned."

"Does the current chief of detectives know that one of Drood's top lieutenants has been captured?" I asked.

"Not yet," said Field and set that corpulent forefinger of his alongside his nose. "Now, you may be wondering why I have called you for this meeting on such a bitter cold day, Mr Collins."

"Yes," I lied.

"Well, sir, it is with some regret that I have to declare that our long working relationship is at an end, Mr Collins. It grieves me to do so, but my resources are limited—as you might imagine, sir—and from this point on, I shall have to focus those resources on the End Game with the monster Drood."

"I am . . . surprised, Inspector," I said while wrapping my red scarf higher around my face in order to hide a smile. This was precisely what I had expected. "Does this mean that there will be no boy waiting near Number Ninety Gloucester Place to carry messages back and forth between us?"

"It does, alas, Mr Collins. Which makes me remember the sad fate of poor young Gooseberry." Here the old man amazed me by removing a huge handkerchief from his coat pocket and blowing his glowing red nose repeatedly.

"Well, if our working relationship *must* end . . ." I said as if filled with reluctant sadness.

"I am afraid it must, Mr Collins. And it is my opinion, sir, that Drood no longer has use for our mutual friend Mr Charles Dickens."

"Really?" I said. "How have you deduced that, Inspector?"

"Well, first of all, there is the fact of last June's anniversary of the Staplehurst meeting passing without Drood making any effort to contact Mr Dickens, or vice versa, sir."

"Certainly your cordon of trained operatives made such a rendezvous impossible for Drood," I said as we turned our backs to the wind and began our walk back over the bridge.

Inspector Field coughed a laugh. "No chance of that, sir. Where Drood wants to go, he *goes*. Five hundred of the Metropolitan force's finest would not have prevented him from meeting with Dickens that night—in your very house, sir, if necessary—if he had *wanted* to be there. Such is the diabolical nature of the foreign monster. But the final and absolutely convincing factor in deducing that Mr Dickens is no longer of service to Drood is the simple fact that the writer is in North America now."

"How is that a convincing factor, Inspector?"

"Drood would *never* have let Mr Dickens go so far if he still had use for him," said the old detective.

"Fascinating," I murmured.

"And do you know what that use *was,* Mr Collins? We have never spoken of it."

"I had never considered the matter, Inspector," I said, happy that the frigid air on my exposed cheeks would hide the blush of a liar.

"Drood was considering having Mr Dickens write something for him, sir," announced Inspector Field in a tone of revelation. "Under coercion, if necessary. I would not be surprised if Drood caused the entire tragedy of the train wreck at Staplehurst precisely to put England's most famous novelist under his thrall."

This was nonsense of course. How could even the "foreign monster" of the old detective's imagination have known that Dickens would not be killed in the terrible plummet of first-class carriages from the incomplete trestle? But all I said was "Fascinating."

"And can you guess, Mr Collins, *what* it is that Drood would have had Mr Dickens pen and publish for him?"

"His biography?" I ventured, if only to show the old man that I was not a complete dunce.

"No, sir," said Inspector Field. "Rather, a compilation of the ancient pagan Egyptian religion with all of its wicked rites and rituals and secrets of magick."

Now I was surprised. I stopped and Inspector Field

stopped next to me. Closed carriages passing had their side lamps lit, even though it was only mid-afternoon. The taller buildings along the river here were mere blue-black shadows with lamps burning in them as well.

"Why would Drood have a novelist write up the details of a dead religion?" I asked.

Inspector Field smiled broadly and tapped his nose again. "It ain't dead to Drood, Mr Collins. It ain't dead to Drood's legion of London Undertown followers, if you take my meaning, sir. You see that, sir?"

I looked towards where the inspector was pointing, northwest along the river's edge.

"The Adelphi Theatre?" I asked. "Or the site of the old Warren's Blacking Factory beyond? Or do you mean Scotland Yard itself?"

"I mean all of it, Mr Collins. And more—stretching down to Saint James Palace and back up Piccadilly to Trafalgar Square and beyond, including Charing Cross and Leicester Square back along the Strand to Covent Garden."

"What of it, Inspector?"

"Imagine a huge glass pyramid there, Mr Collins. Imagine all of London from Billingsgate to Bloomsbury to Regent's Park being huge glass pyramids and bronze sphinxes....Imagine it if you can, sir. For Drood certainly does."

"That's mad," I said.

"Aye, Mr Collins, it's as mad as a hatter's Sunday, sir," laughed Inspector Field. "But that's what Drood and his crypt-crawling worshippers of the old Egyptian gods want, sir. And it's what they mean to get, if not in this century then the next. Imagine those glass pyramids—and the temples, sir, and the secret rites in those temples, with mesmeric magic and slaves to their mental influence—rising everywhere you look in that direction come the twentieth century."

"Madness," I said.

"Yes, sir," said Inspector Field. "But Drood's madness makes him no less dangerous. More so, I would say."

"Well then," I said as we reached the end of the bridge again, "I am well out of it. Thank you for all your care and protection, Inspector Field."

The old man nodded but coughed into his hand. "There is one last detail, sir. One unfortunate by-product of the end of our working relationship, as it were."

"What is that, Inspector?"

"Your...ah...research, sir."

"I don't quite understand," I said, although I understood perfectly well.

"Your research into the Undertown opium dens, sir. Your Thursday trips to King Lazaree's den, to be precise. I am sorry to tell you that I can no longer offer Detective Hatchery as your personal guide and bodyguard."

"Ahhh," I said. "I see. Well, Inspector, think nothing of that. I was ready to terminate that aspect of my research at any rate. You see, what with the play I am putting on and the novel I am more than half done with, I simply do not have time or further need for that research."

"Really, sir? Well...I admit that I am relieved to hear it. I was worried that Detective Hatchery's reassignment would be an inconvenience for you."

"Not at all," I said. In truth, my weekly public house meetings with Hatchery before my descent to King Lazaree had long since turned into weekly dinings out. At one of these in November, Hatchery—my spy now—had warned me that Inspector Field soon would be relieving him of his duty of being my bodyguard during my weekly outings.

I had been prepared for this and had asked him—quite diplomatically—if he, Hatchery, were free to do detective duties outside Inspector Field's investigative agency.

He was, he said. Indeed he was. And, in fact, he had made sure that his renewed duties with Inspector Field would not include Thursday nights. "For my daughters, I told him," said Hatchery to me over our cigars and coffee.

I had offered him a generous sum for continuing his protective duties without telling his superiors. Hatchery had accepted at once and our handshake had sealed the deal, his gigantic hand enveloping mine.

So it was on this mid-December day in 1867 that Inspector Field and I also shook hands and walked in opposite directions on Waterloo Bridge, assuming—at least on my part—that we should never see each other again.

THAT SAME WEEK that I swept Inspector Field out of my life, I honoured another appointment, this time one that I had set, by going to the Cock and Cheshire Cheese in Fleet Street to dine. Deliberately arriving late, I found Joseph Clow already seated and, though dressed in an ill-fitting serge suit, looking decidedly ill at ease in the surroundings that must have been far more refined—and expensive—than those he was used to as a plumber and distiller's son.

I called the wine steward over and ordered, but before I could say anything to Clow, the thin, furtive little man said, "Sir...Mr Collins...if this is about my staying for dinner that evening in October, I apologise, sir, and can only say that your housekeeper, Mrs G——, had invited me as a reward for my finishing the upstairs plumbing ahead of schedule, sir. If it wasn't proper for me to do so, and I see now it mightn't have been, I just want to say that I am very sorry and..."

"No apologies, no apologies," I interrupted. Setting my hand on his rough-weave sleeve, I set the tone immediately. "I invited you here, Mr Clow...may I call you Joseph?...to apologise to *you*. I am sure that my look of surprise that night two months ago could have been...must have been...mistaken as one of disapproval, and I hope that my entertaining you to a fine meal here at the Cock and Cheshire Cheese will go some small distance towards making amends for that."

"No need, sir, no need..." Clow began again, but again I interrupted.

"You see, Mr Clow...Joseph...it is as Mrs G——'s employer of long standing that I speak to you now. Perhaps she told you that she has been in my employ for many years now."

"Yes," said Clow.

We were interrupted by the arrival of the waiter, who recognised me and greeted me effusively. Realising that Clow was at a loss to choose from the menu items, I ordered for both of us.

"Yes," I continued, "even though Mrs G—— is still quite young, she and her daughter have been in my employ for many years. In truth, ever since Harriet—that is her daughter—was a small child. How old are you, Mr Clow?"

"Twenty-six, sir."

"Please do me the honour of calling me Wilkie," I said expansively. "And you shall be Joseph."

The thin-faced young man blinked rapidly at this. He was obviously not accustomed to crossing class barriers.

"You realise, Joseph, that I have nothing but the highest regard for Mrs G——, and nothing but absolute respect for my obligation to look out for her and her delightful daughter."

"Yes, sir."

The wine arrived, was approved, and I made sure that Clow's glass was filled to the brim.

"When she told me of her affection for you, Joseph, I was surprised....I admit to being surprised, since Caroline...Mrs G——...has not spoken so highly of any gentleman during all the years she has been in my employ. But her feelings and ambitions are of the highest priority to me, Joseph. Of this you can be sure."

"Yes, sir," Clow said again. He looked like a man who had been struck on the head by one of his heavier plumber's instruments.

"Mrs G—— is a young woman, Joseph," I went on. "She was little more than a girl when she came into my service. Despite her many duties and responsibilities in my household, she is a young woman still, of an age very similar to your own."

In truth, Caroline would be thirty-eight on her next birthday on 3 February, less than two months away.

"Of course her father's dowry is considerable, and I would be more than pleased to add to it," I said. "This is in addition to her modest inheritance, of course." Her father had died in Bath in January of 1852 and there was no dowry, no inheritance, and I had no intention of adding a ha'penny to those cumulative zed sums.

"Well, sir...Wilkie, sir...it was only a late dinner because Mrs G—— said I'd worked so hard to get the plumbing done, sir," said Clow. Then the food began arriving, his eyes widened at the quality and quantity of it, and our conversation grew even more one-sided as I continued filling his glass and pressing my strange, subtle, seemingly selfless, and totally insincere point.

. . .

MY MOTHER WAS ALSO COMPLAINING and making demands on my time at this point. She had begun suffering, she said, from various indeterminate but excruciating pains. One resisted the urge to tell her that at age seventy-seven, indeterminate (and perhaps even occasionally excruciating) pains were part of the price of longevity.

My mother had always complained and my mother had always been healthy: healthier than her husband, who had died young; healthier than her son Charles, who was racked for years with stomach pains that would turn out to be cancer; healthier, certainly, than her poor son Wilkie, who suffered from a rheumatical gout that periodically blinded him with pain.

But Mother was complaining and asking—almost demanding—that I spend several days around Christmas with her down in Tunbridge Wells. This was impossible, of course, and not for the least reason that Caroline was also demanding that I spend Christmas or several days around Christmas at home with her and Carrie. This was also impossible.

The premiere of *No Thoroughfare* had been set for Boxing Day—the day after Christmas.

On 20 December I wrote to my mother:

> *My dear Mother,*
>
> *I scratch one line—in the midst of the turmoil of the play—to say that you may rely on my coming to you on Christmas Day—if not before.*
>
> *The delays and difficulties of this dramatic work have been dreadful. I have had to write a new 5th Act—which has been completed to-day—and the play must be performed on Thursday next, with a Sunday and Christmas Day between!*
>
> *If I can write again, I will. If not, let us leave it that I certainly will come on Christmas Day. And, if I am not*

wanted on the next Monday's or Tuesday's Rehearsal that
I come before. Your much-bothered son has hardly got a
minute he can call his own. But the writing of the play is
at last complete—so my principal worry is at an end.
How I shall enjoy a little quiet with you!

Send me a line between this and Christmas Day. I
have got your heart-burn lozenges—and some chocolate for
you which Charley brought from Paris. Can I bring
anything else which will go into my hand-bag?

Yours ever afftly WC
Charley proposes crossing to you from Gadshill on
Friday in Christmas week.

As it was, I spent part of Christmas Day afternoon
and evening with Mother in her cottage in Tunbridge
Wells—she spent most of our time together complaining of her nerves and her heartburn, and also of ominous strangers in the neighbourhood—and then I
returned to London on the earliest possible train the
next morning.

Fechter was his usual first-night ruin in the hours
before the curtain opened. His vomiting due to stage
fright was almost continuous in the last two hours, so
that his poor dresser was absolutely worn out from running to and fro with his basin.

Finally I suggested a few drops of laudanum to calm
the anxious actor. Unable to speak, Fechter answered
by putting out his tongue. The colour of it had turned,
under the nervous terror that possessed him, to the
metallic blackness of the tongue of a parrot.

Once the curtain went up, however, Fechter found his
voice and stride as the unspeakable villain Obenreizer.

I should report that I felt no anxiety whatsoever. I
knew that the play was to be a triumph, and it was.

On 27 December I wrote—from the offices of *All
the Year Round* at No. 26 Wellington Street:

My dear Mother,

I have a moment to tell you that the Play last night was an immense success. The audience were delighted—and the actors were excellent.

I have got the proofs which you sent me back quite safe.

Charley is, I suppose, with you today.

If you can write, tell me how you are, and what day next week I may come back to you? I sincerely hope and trust you are not suffering so much as when I was with you.

Love to Charley.

*Ever yours affly
WC*

The night of the play was the only Thursday of 1867 on which I had been forced to miss my weekly excursion to King Lazaree's subterranean den. But I had made prior arrangements to make up for it on that Friday, 27 December—which is one reason I wrote to Mother from Dickens's rooms at the magazine, since I had told Caroline and Martha both that I would be spending the night there—and Detective Hatchery had been kind enough to shift his night of work for me from Boxing Day to the Friday following.

CAROLINE G—— wanted marriage. This I would not consider. Martha R——, on the other hand, wanted only a baby. (Or babies, plural.) She made no demands for marriage, since the fiction of "Mr and Mrs Dawson"—her world-travelling merchant of a husband who rarely spent time at his home on Bolsover Street—was sufficient for her.

It was about this time, during the success of *No Thoroughfare* and near my completion of *The Moonstone,* and especially after a second secret meeting with

Mr Joseph Clow at a slightly less expensive London restaurant, that I began considering the possibility of agreeing to Martha's wishes.

The first two weeks of 1868 were quite frenetic for me and I suspect that I was happier then than at any time in my life. My letters to Mother (and scores of other friends and associates) were not exaggerations; *No Thoroughfare* was indeed—despite Charles Dickens's long-distance dismissal of it—a bona fide success. I continued making at least bi-weekly visits to Gad's Hill Place, enjoying the meals with Georgina, Charley and Katey (when Charley was there), Dickens's son Charley and his wife, Bessie (who were there often), Dickens's daughter Mamie (who was always there), as well as such occasional visitors as Percy Fitzgerald or William Macready and his lovely second wife.

I invited all of them to come to London to see *No Thoroughfare*. Through my many letters, I invited others such as William Holman Hunt, T. H. Hills, Nina Lehmann, Sir Edward Landseer, and John Forster.

I invited all of these people and more to dine with me at Number 90 Gloucester Place on Saturday, 18 January—*not* in evening costume, I emphasised—and to go from there to the theatre and to sit in the spacious author's box with me to enjoy the play. Caroline was delighted and began setting the three servants to with a metaphorical whip getting the huge house ready. She also spent hours conversing with the French cook.

Mother wrote—actually, she had dictated the letter to Charley, who had stopped in at Tunbridge Wells for the day—to say that she had been visited by a certain Dr Ramseys, a physician visiting a family in the village who had heard of Mother's problems and who, after a thorough examination, diagnosed her symptoms as heart congestion, gave her three medicines for the problem (which, she said, did seem to help), and recommended that she move out of the cottage in the village because of all the hammering going on there during renovations. When she told him about her beloved Bentham Hill Cottage nearby in the country outside the village, Dr Ramseys urged her to move there immediately. Charley added a note telling me that Mother had also invited her former housekeeper and cook and sometime neighbor, Mrs Wells, to join her at Bentham Hill Cottage, which was a relief to both Charley and me, since someone would then always be there to watch over her while she recovered from these minor problems.

Mother added that Dr Ramseys said that she required absolute rest and that—in both his medications and future ministrations—he would do everything in his power to provide it for her. In a postscript she added that poor Dr Ramseys himself had suffered terrible burns in a fire many years before, that the pains and scars were ever with him, and thus had dedicated his life to alleviating the pain of others.

OUR HOPES OF A GLORIOUS SALE of theatrical rights for *No Thoroughfare* to an American producer were dashed forever when a letter arrived from Dickens: *"Pirates are producing their own wretched versions in all directions."*

Dickens insisted that he had done everything in his power to place my script, or at least the rights to our collaboration, in honest hands—to the point that he registered *No Thoroughfare* as the property of Ticknor and Fields, his Boston publishers, but I had my doubts about the sincerity (or at least urgency) of his efforts. His earlier letters had, after all, condemned my final script as "far too long" and, even more irritating, as "perhaps crossing the line into mere melodrama," so I half-suspected Dickens of waiting until he himself could revise the play...or create a new adaptation from scratch. (This suspicion was borne out the following June when Dickens did precisely that, writing a new version of the play with Fechter's help for a premiere in Paris. It failed.)

At any rate, Dickens went on to say in his letter that the Museum Theatre in Boston had rushed a theatrical adaptation of our story onto the stage an astonishing ten days after the original tale arrived in the United States. This was pure piracy, of course—and Dickens insisted that he had prodded Ticknor and Fields into threatening an injunction—but the pirates, knowing that, given Americans' easy acceptance of such piracy, there would be an outcry against *Dickens* if he persisted, called the publisher's bluff and went on with their abominably bad version. *"Then,"* continued Dickens in his letter, *"the noble host of pirates rushed in, and it is being done, in some mangled form or other, everywhere."*

Ah, well. I paid little heed to this distant disaster. As I had written to Mother on 30 December—*"The play is bringing* money. *It is a real success—we shall all be rich."*

When I had visited her on the second of January, I brought legal papers for her to sign so that Charley and I might get our fair share of the £5,000 from Aunt Davis that was the source of her annual income—or be able to assign it to someone we chose—should Mother die before we did.

Everything proceeded at breakneck speed towards the gala dinner at Gloucester Place and theatre party immediately afterward. Caroline and Carrie had decorated the huge house as if there were to be a royal coronation there, and our food bill that week equalled six months of our regular purchases. No matter. It was a time to celebrate.

On a Thursday, I wrote:

90 Gloucester Place
Portman Square W.
Jan 17th, 1868
My dear Mother,

    It was a great relief to me and to Charley to hear that
you had made the move, and established yourself again
under Mrs Wells's care. I am not surprised to hear that
you are terribly fatigued by the exertion. But when you
have rested I hope and trust you will begin to feel the
benefit of this change. Let me hear——in two lines——how
you go on——and how soon you will let me come (or let
Charley come) and see you in the new place. Remember
that the quiet and the freedom from London interruptions
are sure to help me to get on with my work. Also——when
you can write without too much trouble——let me hear when
it will be convenient for me to send a small supply of
brandy and wine to Bentham Hill Cottage.

    The play goes on wonderfully. Every night the Theatre
is crammed. This speculation on the public taste is paying,
and promises long to pay me, from fifty to fifty-five pounds
a week. So make yourself easy about money matters.

    I am getting to nearly halfway through The
Moonstone.

    No more news at present. Goodbye.

              Yours ever afftly WC

LITTLE DID I KNOW that this would be the last letter I
should ever write to my dear mother.

That second week of the new year had been so con-
gested with work on *The Moonstone* and theatrical-
related labours that once again I had to move my night
at King Lazaree's from Thursday to Friday. Detective
Hatchery did not seem to mind—he said it was easier to

find the night away from his regular duties for Inspector Field on Friday than on Thursday—so once again I treated my huge bodyguard to an excellent dinner (this one at the Blue Posts tavern on Cork Street) before he led me into the darkness of the dockside slums and escorted me safely to that terrible place of cold granite and graves that Dickens had long since christened St Ghastly Grim's Cemetery.

Hatchery had a new book to read through that night of vigil—Thackeray's *The History of Henry Esmond,* I noticed. Dickens had once mentioned to me that he liked the way Thackeray had arbitrarily divided the large novel into three "Books" and had borrowed the idea for all of his own subsequent books. But I did not mention that small professional item to Hatchery, since I was in a hurry to get below.

King Lazaree greeted me as warmly as always. (I had mentioned to him the week before that I might be coming on Friday rather than Thursday, and he had assured me in his perfect English that I would be welcome and expected any time.) Lazaree and his large Chinese guard showed me to my cot and handed me my opium pipe, prepared and lighted, as always. Filled with good feeling about the day and my life—knowing that this pleasurable sense of satisfaction would be enlarged a hundredfold during my hours under the pipe—I closed my eyes and allowed myself, for the hundredth time in the safety of that deep-sheltered cot, to drift up and away on the rising, curling smoke of amplified sensation.

That moment was the end of my life as I had known it.

CHAPTER TWENTY-FIVE

*Y*ou may wake now," says Drood.

I open my eyes. No, that is not correct. My eyes were already open. Now, with *his* permission, I can see through them.

I cannot lift my head nor move it from side to side, but from where I lie supine on a cold surface, I can see enough to know that I am not in King Lazaree's opium den.

I am naked—that much I am able to see without moving my head and can tell from the press of cold marble on my back and buttocks that I am lying on what might be a block of stone or a low altar. I feel the movement of cold air across my belly and chest and genitals. Above me on the right, a giant black onyx statue, at least twelve feet tall, shows a man's body naked to the waist with a short gold skirt wrapped around his middle, and his powerful arms ending in huge, muscled hands hold a golden spear or pike. The man's body stops at the neck, and the head of a jackal completes the terrible black form. To my left, a similar lance-holding statue rises to the same height, but instead of a jackal's visage, this one sports the head of some great curved-beaked bird. Both heads stare down at me.

Drood steps into my field of vision and also looks down on me in silence.

The creature is as pale and loathsome as I had dreamt of him in Birmingham and as I had glimpsed him in my home in June of the previous year, but otherwise he looks very little the same.

He is naked from the waist up, except for a wide, heavy collar that appears to be made of hammered gold with inset rubies and strips of lapus. On his naked, grub-white chest hangs a heavy gold figure that at first I take to be a Christian cross, but then notice the elongated loop at the top. I have seen similar items behind glass in the London Museum and even know it is called an *ankh*, but I have no idea of its significance.

Drood's nose is still no more than two slits in a living skull's face, his eyelids are still missing, but around his deep-set eyes he has painted whorls of dark blue—so dark as to appear almost black—that come to points like cat's eyes at the sides of his temples. A stripe of blood-crimson rises from between where his eyebrows should be and then up over his forehead to bisect his bald, white, and seemingly skinless scalp.

He is carrying a jewel-encrusted dagger. Its tip has been freshly dipped into red paint or blood.

I try to speak but find I cannot. I am not able even to open my mouth or to move my tongue. I can feel my arms, legs, fingers, and toes, but cannot will them to move. Only my eyes and eyelids are mine to control.

He faces to my right, with the dagger in his hand.

"Un re-a an Ptah, uau netu, uau netu, aru re-a an neter nut-a.
I arefm Djewhty, meh aper em heka, uau netu, uau netu, en Suti sau re-a.
Khesef-tu Tem uten-nef senef sai set.

Un re-a, apu re-a an Shu em nut-ef tui ent baat en pet enti ap-nef re en neteru am-es.

Nuk Sekhet! Hems-a her kes amt urt aat ent pet.
Nuk Sakhu! Urt her-ab baiu Annu.

Ar heka neb t'etet neb t'etu er-a sut, aha neteru er-sen
paut neteru temtiu.

May Ptah give me voice, remove the wrappings! Remove
the wrappings which the lesser gods have placed over my
mouth.

Come unto me Djewhty, bearer of Heka, full of Heka,
remove the wrappings! Remove the wrappings of Suti
which fetter my mouth.

May Tem turn back those who would restrain me.

Give me voice! May my mouth be opened by Shu with
that divine instrument of iron with which the gods were
given voice.

I am Sekhet! I watch over the heaven of the west.

I am Sakhu! I watch over the souls of Annu.

May the gods and their children hear my voice, and resist
those who would silence me."

He takes the dagger and traces a vertical line in the air to my right, cutting downward in a smooth down deadly motion.

   "Qebhsennuf!"

What sound like a hundred other voices—all belonging to forms out of my line of sight—cry out in unison:

   "Qebhsennuf!"

He turns to the direction my feet are pointing and traces a vertical line in the air.

"*Amset!*"

The choir of bodiless voices answers him:

"*Amset!*"

Drood turns to my left and draws a vertical line in the air with the dagger.

"*Tuamutef!*"

"*Tuamutef!*" cries the choir.

Drood raises the dagger towards my face and traces another vertical line in air that I now realise is thick with smoke and incense.

"*Hapi!*

I am the flame which shines upon the Opener of Eternity!"

The invisible chorus cries out in a single, sustained note that sounds like the baying of jackals along the Nile at midnight.

"*Hapi!*"

Drood smiles at me and says very softly, "Misster Wilkie Collinss, you may move your head, but only your head."

Suddenly I am free to move. I cannot lift my shoulders but I throw my head from side to side. My glasses are gone. Everything more than ten feet away is cloaked in blur: marble columns rising into darkness, hissing braziers breathing smoke, robed figures by the score.

I do not like this opium dream.

I do not think that I've said this aloud, but Drood throws back his head and laughs. Candlelight glints on the gold and lapis collar around his thin neck.

I try to move my body until I weep from frustration, but only my head obeys my commands. I thrash my face back and forth, tears spilling onto the white altar.

"Misster Wilkie Collinss," purrs Drood. "Praise to the lord of truth, whose shrine is hidden, from whose eyesss mankind issued, and from whose mouth the godsss came into being. As high as isss the heaven, as broad as isss the earth, as deep as isss the sea."

I try to scream but my jaw and lips and tongue still will not obey me.

"You may speak, Misster Wilkie Collinsss," says the pale face. He has moved around to my right side now, the red-tipped dagger held in both hands against his chest. The circle of hooded forms has pressed closer.

"You filthy bugger!" I cry. "You wog bastard! You stinking foreign piece of dung! This is *my* opium dream, damn your eyes! You are not welcome in it!"

Drood smiles again.

"Misster Wilkie Collinsss," he whispers, the smoke from the braziers and incense burners swirling around his face, "above me stretchesss Nuit, the Lady of Heaven. Beneath me liesss Geb, the Lord of the Earth. At my right hand Ast, Lady of Life. At my left hand Asar, the Lord of Eternity. Before me—before you—risesss Heru, the beloved Child and the Hidden Light. Behind me and above us all shines Ra, whose namesss even the godsss do not know. You may be silent now."

I try to scream but once again I cannot.

"From this day forward, you shall be our scribe," says Drood. "In the yearsss remaining to your mortal life, you shall come to uss to learn of our faith's old day-sss, old waysss, and eternal truthsss. You shall write of them in your own language so that generationsss yet unborn shall know of usss."

I flail my head from side to side but cannot will my muscles or voice to work.

"You may speak if you wish," says Drood.

"Dickens is your scribe!" I cry. "Not I! Dickens is your scribe!"

"He isss one of many," says Drood. "But he…resist-sss. Misster Charlesss Dickensss believesss that he iss the equal of a priest or priestessss of the Temple of

Sleep. He believesss that his force of will isss equal to our own. He hasss taken instead the ancient challenge that would exempt him from being our full-time scribe."

"What is that exemption?" I cry out.

"To kill an innocent human being in full sight of otherssss," hisses Drood with a return of that small-toothed smile. "He hopesss that his imagination shall provide the equal service, that the gods will be fooled, but so far he...and hisss much-vaunted imagination... have failed."

"No!" I cry. "Dickens killed young Dickenson. Young Edmond Dickenson. I am sure of that!"

I understand the motive for the murder now. Some sort of ancient, pagan, spiritual escape clause that allowed Dickens to avoid complete control by this foul *magus*. He traded the life of that orphaned young man for his freedom from Drood's total domination.

Drood shakes his head and beckons a robed and hooded follower forward from the blurred circle of forms I sense all around me. The man pulls his dark hood back and down. It is young Dickenson. He has shaved his head and his eyes have that same heathenish blue shadow on them, but it is young Dickenson.

"Missster Dickensss was kind enough to suggest this soul for our small fold and our small fold to this soul," says Drood. "Both Brother Dickenson'sss money and hisss faith are welcome here. The offer of thisss convert to our Family has brought Missster Charlesss Dickensss a...small dispensation."

"Wake up!" I cry to myself. "For God's sake, wake up, Wilkie! Enough is enough! Wilkie, wake up!"

Dickenson and the circle of robed figures take several steps back into the gloom. Drood says, "You may be silent again, Missster Wilkie Collinsssss."

He reaches down at the side of the slab, below the

level I can turn my head to see, and when he straightens up, there is something black in his right hand. It is large and fills almost all of his pale palm with an even larger crescent on one end of the thing running almost the length of his absurdly long white fingers.

As I stare, the black thing stirs and moves.

"Yesss," says Drood. "It isss a beetle. My people call representationsss of thisss a scarab and venerate it in our religion and ritualssss...."

The huge black beetle flails six long legs and tries to crawl off Drood's hand. He cups his fingers and the huge bug falls back into his palm.

"Our usual scarab wasss modelled after several speciesss in the Family Scarabaeidae," says Drood, "but most were based upon the common dung beetle."

I try to writhe, kick out with my legs, stir my untied arms, but can move only my head. A great nausea fills me and I have to relax on the cold stone, focusing on not vomiting. If I were to vomit now, without the ability to open my mouth, I would surely asphyxiate.

"My ancestorsss thought that all beetless were malesss," hisses Drood, raising his palm so that he can study the loathsome insect more closely. "They thought that the little ball that the dung beetle ceaselessly rolls wasss the male beetle'sss seed substance—its sperm. They were wrong...."

I am blinking madly, since that is one of the few actions I can take. Perhaps if I blink rapidly enough, this dream will fade into another one or I will wake and find myself back on my familiar cot in the warm rear alcove of King Lazaree's den, not far from the small coal stove he keeps stoked there.

"In truth, as your British science hass shown us, it isss the female who, after dropping her fertilized eggsss on the ground, covers them in excrement on which the larvae feed and rolls thisss soft dung ball across the ground.

The ball of dung grows larger and larger as it accumulates more dust and sand, you see, Missster Wilkie Collinssss, which is why my great-great-grandfathers' great-great-great-grandfathers associated thiss beetle with the daily appearance and movement of the sun…and the rising of the great sun-god, the god of the rising sun rather than the setting sun, Khepri."

Wake up, Wilkie! Wake up, Wilkie! Wake! I scream silently to myself.

"Our Egyptian name for the common dung beetle was *hprr*," drones on Drood, "which means *'rising from, or coming into being itself.'* It issss very close to our word *'hpr,'* which means *'to become, to change.'* You can see how this made the small change to *'hpri,'* the divine name *'Khepri,'* standing for the young rising son—our god of Creation."

Shut up, God d——n you! I mentally scream at Drood.

As if he hears, he pauses and smiles.

"This scarab shall represent unalterable change for you, Misster Wilkie Collinsss," he says softly.

The hooded figures around us begin to chant again.

I strain and lift my head as Drood holds his palm over my bare belly.

"Thisss is not the common dung beetle," whispers Drood. "Thisss is your European-variety stag beetle—thusss the huge…what do you call them in English, Misster Collinsss? Mandibles? Pincers? They are the largest and most ferocious in all the beetle family. But this *hprr*—this holy scarab—has been consecrated to its purpose…."

He drops the palm-sized black insect onto my straining bare belly.

"Un re-a an Ptah, uau netu, uau netu, aru re-a an neter nut-a.

I arefm Djewhty, meh aper em heka, uau netu, uau netu, en Suti sau re-a.
Khesef-tu Tem uten-nef senef sai set," chants the invisible crowd.

The scarab's six barbed legs scrabble at my cringing skin and it begins to crawl upward towards my ribcage. I raise my head until my neck comes close to snapping, my eyes bulging as I watch the black object with pincers longer than my own fingers climbing towards my chest and head.

I have to scream—I *must* scream—but I cannot.

The chorus of voices rises in the incensed gloom:

"Un re-a, apu re-a an Shu em nut-ef tui ent baat en pet enti ap-nef re en neteru am-es.
Nuk Sekhet! Hems-a her kes amt urt aat ent pet.
Nuk Sakhu! Urt her-ab baiu Annu."

The stag beetle's gigantic pincers pierce my flesh just below the sternum. The pain is beyond anything I have ever experienced. The tendons of my neck audibly creak as I strain to lift my head further to watch.

The scarab's six legs flail at my flesh, the barbs finding purchase to push first the black crescent pincers and then the head of the beetle into the soft flesh of my upper belly. In five seconds the huge beetle is gone—completely submerged—and the flesh and skin close over its entry point like water sealing itself after being pierced by a black stone.

Jesus! God! No! Dear Christ! God! I scream in the silence of my mind.

"No, no, no," says Drood, reading my thoughts. "*For the stone shall cry out of the wall, and the beetle out of the timber shall answer it.*' But the scarab, not your man-god Christ, is the 'only begotten,' Misster Wilkie

Collinsss, sir, even though your people's pretender god once cried out, 'But I am a scarab, and no man,' in envy of the true Khepri."

I can feel the huge beetle *inside me.*

The choir of black-robed forms chants:

"Ar heka neb t'etet neb t'etu er-a sut, aha neteru er-sen paut neteru temtiu."

Drood turns his empty palms upward and closes his eyes as he recites: "Come, Ast! Life-truth comes to this stranger as it has come to our parents. Accept this soul as your own, O Opener of Eternity. Cleanse his former soul in the rising flame which is Nebt-Het. Sustain this instrument as you nourished and sustained Heru in the hidden place among the reeds, O Ast, You, whose breath is life, whose voice is death."

I can feel the thing move *inside me!* I cannot scream. My mouth will not open. My eyes shed tears of blood in my agony.

Drood lifts a long metal rod with a sort of bowl on the end.

"May this scribe's mouth be opened by Shu with that divine instrument of iron with which the godsss were first given voice," chants Drood.

My mouth opens—stretches wider, continues to open until my jaw cracks and groans—but still I cannot scream.

Inside my belly, the scarab's insect legs scrabble along my intestines. I can feel the barbs finding purchase. I can feel the chitinous hardness of its shell in my guts.

"We are Sekhet!" cries Drood. "We watch over the heaven of the west. We are Sakhu! We watch over the soulsss of Annu. May the godsss and the children hear our voice and hear our voice in the wordsss of this scribe, and death to all those who would silence usss."

Drood forces the ladle end of the long iron rod into my open, gaping mouth. There is something round and soft and covered with hair in the sharp bowl at the end. Drood tips the rod and the haired mass falls to the back of my throat.

"Qebhsennuf!" cries Drood.

"Qebhsennuf!" shouts the invisible chorus.

I cannot breathe. My throat is completely blocked by the furry glob filling it. I am dying.

I feel the beetle stop in my lower abdomen. The sharp legs scrabble against my intestines, rip at the outer walls of my stomach, climb higher under my ribs, towards my heart.

I will myself to vomit the hairy mass out of my throat but cannot do even that. My eyes have bulged until I am sure that they will explode out of my head. I think— *This is the way that famous novelist Wilkie Collins dies. No one will ever know.* Then all thought abandons me as my vision begins to narrow down black tunnels as the last breath in my lungs is trapped and useless.

I feel the scarab's legs flailing at my right lung. I feel the scarab's pincers dragging across the outside surface of my heart. I feel the scarab crawling up my throat, feel my neck bulging as it rises higher.

The insect seizes the hairy mass in my throat and drags it down deeper with it, back into my gullet and upper belly.

I can breathe! I cough, gasp, gasp more, try to retch, remember how to breathe.

Drood is passing a lighted candle over my chest and face in circular motions. Hot wax dribbles onto my bare flesh, but the pain of that is nothing compared to the pain of the scarab moving within me. It is climbing again.

"I fly up asss a bird and alight asss a beetle," chants Drood, deliberately dripping more hot wax across my chest and throat. "I fly up assss a bird and alight asss a beetle on the empty throne which isss on your bark, O Ra!"

The huge insect has filled my throat with its impossible, chitinous hardness and burrowed into my soft palate as easily as it would have burrowed into sand. I can feel it now filling the sinuses behind my nose, behind my eyes. Its barbed legs flail at the backs of my eyeballs as it forces itself higher. I can hear the huge pincers scraping bone as it burrows through the soft matter opening into my skull.

The pain is terrible—indescribable, unsupportable—but I can breathe!

Still unable to focus on anything beyond Drood—the jackal's-head and great-bird's-head statues mere blurs, the dark-robed figures melded together as blurs—I realise that I am looking out through a film of the blood I have wept.

I feel the huge stag beetle burrow into the soft surface of my brain—deeper, deeper. If this continues another second, I know I shall go mad.

The scarab stops moving near the centre of my brain. It begins to feed.

"You may shut your eyessss," says Drood.

I squeeze them shut, feeling the tears of blood and terror streaking my wax-spotted cheeks.

"You are our scribe now," says Drood. "You alwaysss will be. You will work when bidden. You will come when summoned. You belong to usss, Misster Wilkie Collinsss."

I can *hear* the scarab's pincers and jaws clicking and moving as it eats. I can visualise the insect rolling my half-digested brain matter into a grey and bloody ball and pushing it ahead of itself.

But it does not move forward again. Not yet. It has made a nest for itself in the lower-central base of my brain. When the scarab's six legs twitch, it tickles and I again have to fight the absolute need to vomit.

"All praise to the lord of truth," says Drood.

"Whose shrine is hidden," chants the chorus.

"From whose eyesss mankind issues," says Drood.

"And from whose mouth the gods came into being," chants the choir.

"We send forth this scribe now to do the bidding of the beloved Child and the Hidden Light," calls Drood.

"Behind him shines Ra, whose names the gods do not know," chants the crowd.

I try to open my eyes but cannot. Nor can I hear or feel.

The only sound or sensation in my universe now is the ticking and scrabbling as the scarab twists, turns, burrows slightly deeper, and eats again.

CHAPTER TWENTY-SIX

J awoke from my opium nightmare to find that I
had gone blind.

It was absolute darkness. King Lazaree always had
diffused lights in each room of his den, light from the
main room always filtered through the red curtain, and
the coal stove near the entrance to my niche of the
opium den always gave off a warm orange glow. Now
there was only absolute darkness. I raised my hands to
my eyes to make sure they were open and my fingertips
touched the surface of my eyeballs. Wincing away, I
could not see my fingers.

I cried out in the darkness and—unlike my dream—
I could hear my screams very well indeed. They echoed
off stone. I cried for help. I cried for King Lazaree and
his assistant. No one answered.

Only slowly did I realise that I was not lying on my
high cushioned bunk as I always did at King Lazaree's.
I was lying on a cold floor of stone or hard-packed dirt.
And I was naked.

Just as in my dream. Or just as in my real abduction
by Drood.

I was shivering violently. It was the cold that had
awakened me. But I could move, and within a minute I
was on all fours and feeling around in my blindness,
trying to touch the edge of one of the wooden bunks,
or even the stove or the edge of the doorway.

My fingers met rough stone and wood instead. I ran my hands over the shape, wondering if it was the wall and then the corner to one of the stacked bunks. It was not. The stone and wood were ancient—they *smelled* ancient—and the stone had partially fallen through in places. I could touch cold wood within. Everything smelled of age and corruption.

I am in one of the loculi—*one of the countless burial chambers in the multi-levelled catacombs. These are the stone or cement sarcophagi with the wood coffins within. And inside those wood coffins are lead liners. I am down with the dead.*

They had moved me.

Of course they moved me. They carried me down through the circular apse, through the rood screen, into Undertown proper. They carried me down the river to Drood's Temple. I may be miles from King Lazaree's den, a mile deep under the city. Without a lantern I shall never find my way to the surface.

I screamed again then and began flailing along the line of stacked coffins and biers, rising to my feet only to drop to all fours again and flail again with my out-thrust hands, seeking the bullseye lantern that I always brought down to King Lazaree's and always used to find my way back to the upper level and out.

There was no lantern.

Finally I quit flailing and simply crouched there in the dark, more panicked beast than man.

There were a dozen levels to these catacombs before one found a tunnel leading to a sewer or the under-ground river. There were hundreds of burial *loculi* run-ning off these countless straight and curved corridors on these dozen levels. The stairs from the highest level of burial chambers, the corridor just below St Ghastly Grim's Cemetery where Sergeant Hatchery presumably waited for me even now—*How long have I been down here!?*—was just ten yards to the left along the curving corridor from King Lazaree's den, then up those stairs, ducking one's head through the broken rear wall of a *loculus,* past the last stack of coffins, right then once in that last corridor, and up the ten steps to the crypt and—presumably, possibly—daylight. I had made that walk back a hundred times after my night of opium.

I reached for my waistcoat as if to pull my watch from its pocket and check the time. There was no watch, no waistcoat. No clothing at all.

I realised that I was freezing—my teeth were chattering violently, the sound echoing back from unseen stone walls. I was shivering so hard that my elbows and forearms were beating a tattoo on the not-quite-hollow stone sarcophagus that I had fallen against.

I had lost any sense of direction in my blind stumbling about; even if I were in the niche that once held King Lazaree's den, I no longer knew the way forward or back in it.

Still shaking wildly, my arms stretched straight out ahead of me and my fingers stiff and splayed, I began stumbling along the line of biers, sarcophagi, and coffins.

Even with my arms out ahead of me, I managed to run into something with my head that knocked me back on my arse. I felt blood running from the wound in my temple and immediately sent my fingers searching my forehead, uselessly holding my hands in front of my eyes as if I could suddenly see. I could not. I touched again. The cut was shallow; the bleeding was slight.

Rising carefully to my feet again, I waved my arms until I found the obstruction that had almost knocked me out.

Cold metal, so rusted that the empty-space triangles of the open grid were almost closed in.

The iron grille!! Each *loculus* along the catacomb corridors had been enclosed within an ancient iron grille. If

I had found the grille, I had found the corridor—or *a* corridor—there were scores on different levels down here, most of which I had never seen or explored.

What if the grille is closed and locked? I would never get to the corridor. Someone would find my skeleton in amongst the sarcophagi and coffins in twenty or fifty or a hundred years and merely think that I was another of what the crypt man at Rochester Cathedral, Dradles, had called "the old 'uns."

Panicked again, I pounded my palms and forearms and knees along the metal grille, feeling the rusted edges scrape skin away, but finally there was—an emptiness. An opening! At the very least, a fissure caused by a vertical segment of the grille rusting away.

It was only ten inches or so wide, and irregular, but I squeezed through, sharp edges of the grille scraping at my ribs and backside and shrunken genitals.

Then I was in a corridor. I was sure of it!

Unless you've passed through a grille behind *the coffins, in which case you're more lost than before on some unfathomable deep level of an endless labyrinth.*

I dropped to all fours and felt the stone under my palms and knees. No, this was one of the main corridors. All I had to do was follow it to one of the nearly hidden stairways to a higher level, then up the final steps to the crypt where Hatchery was waiting for me.

Which way?? How could I find the stairs in the absolute darkness? Which way??

I crawled to my left, found the grille I had just squeezed through, and rose carefully, not even sure how high the corridor ceiling might be down here. When I had followed Dickens to the river that night two years ago, some of the corridors had been ten feet high—others had been mere tunnels where one had to crouch to avoid bashing one's brains out. It had all been so simple with a lantern.

Which way???

I turned my face but could sense no movement of air. If I had a candle, perhaps I could sense the draft....

If I had a God-d——ned candle, I could easily find my way out without sniffing for drafts!! I screamed at myself.

I realised that I had screamed it aloud. Echoes died away in both directions. Dear God, any more of this and I would surely lose my mind.

I decided that I would follow my old instincts and walk just as if I were leaving King Lazaree's den. My body remembered that return walk I had made so many times, even if my brain—without vision to help—kept insisting that it did not.

Using my left hand as my guide, I began walking along the corridor. I came to other grates, other openings, although none of them had the tattered curtain that separated Lazaree's den from the corridor. At each opening that was not protected by a grille, I got down on my knees and felt for stairs or another corridor, but there were only collapsed grilles, more coffins, or empty niches in the walls.

I moved on, panting, shivering, my teeth still chattering audibly. My conscious mind told me that I would not freeze to death down here—did not caves stay at some constant temperature, in the fifties? It did not matter. My torn, gouged, shivering body was freezing.

Was the corridor curving slightly to the left? The way to Lazaree's den had curved slightly to the right as one approached it from the hidden stairs down from the first level of catacombs. If I was on that level and to the right of the stairs, the walls here would have to be curving slightly to my left.

I had no idea. It was impossible to tell. But I knew without doubt that I had gone at least twice as far as it took to walk from the entrance to the second and lower level to the curtained alcove that was King Lazaree's den.

I continued forward anyway. Twice there were cold draughts from my right. The touch of the colder air on my flesh caused my skin to ripple with revulsion—as if something dead and eyeless were caressing me with long, grub-white, boneless fingers.

I shivered and moved on.

There had been two corridors to the left—my right now—as Dickens and I had first found King Lazaree's den. I had walked past them without a glance or turn of my lantern so many times since. Down *one of them had been the corridor leading past even more* loculi *to the circular room with the altar and rood screen and hidden stairs down to the deeper levels of Undertown.*

Where Drood waited.

But I could already be *on one of those lower levels.*

Twice I had to stop to vomit. My stomach was already empty—I seemed to remember getting sick in the first *loculus,* where I had wakened—but still the retching bent me double and made me lean against cold stone until the spasms passed.

I passed another ungrilled opening—nothing but rubble within the niche—and staggered on another twenty paces or so before crashing into a solid wall.

The corridor ended. The wall was solid; behind me, the corridor stretched backward the way I had come.

I screamed then. And kept screaming. The echoes were all behind me.

They had bricked up the corridor they had left me in. Closed it so that no one would even find my bones.

I clawed at the wall, feeling ancient mortar, stones, and bricks fall away, feeling my fingernails tear off and the ends of my flailing fingers rip and shred.

It was no use. Behind the bricks were more bricks. Behind those bricks was heavier stone.

I dropped, gasping and retching, to my knees, then began crawling back the way I had come.

The last opening was on my right now—the rubble tumbled niche—but this time I crawled into it, lacerating my already-lacerated knees and palms on the jumble of stones.

They were not just stones. They were steps set into cold, loose dirt.

I scrambled up them, heedless of any obstacle that might be waiting to strike me in the face.

I crashed into a wall, almost fell back down the unseen stairs, but grasped at the edge of an opening. There *was* an opening. I could almost *see* the jagged masonry on either side.

I tumbled through and scraped my right cheek and temple against rough stone. Another bier. Getting to my feet, I realised there were more coffins stacked on the carved stone or shaped cement. I was in another *loculus*. Teeth chattering, I looked to my left and seemed to sense a lightening in my vision in that direction.

I crashed into another metal grate, smeared unseen blood on it from my torn fingers as I flailed until I found the opening to it, and staggered out into an emptiness that must have been another corridor.

There was definitely light—a thin, grey ghost of a glow—to my right, not twenty yards away.

My bare feet slapping on the stone or brick floor of this wider corridor, I fairly ran towards the light.

Yes. I could suddenly see my hands and arms in front of me. My fingers were crimson.

There was a stairway, huge stone steps rising up and curving out of sight.

I knew this stairway.

Weeping, crying out for Detective Hatchery's help, slipping, falling, rising, and clawing upward again, I went up the steps and squeezed through the familiar wedge of opening.

The light in the crypt, I would realise later, was only the dimmest of January predawn glows—certainly not enough to read by—but it blinded me with its brightness.

Staggering to the stone bier that overhung the secret entrance to Undertown—an entrance I swore then and there that I would never use again—I had to sag against the empty bier or collapse.

"Hatchery! For God's sake, help! Hatchery!"

My own voice startled me so badly that I almost urinated without volition. I did look down then, at my naked white body. I found that I was staring at my belly, just below the sternum.

There was a red wound or scrape there.

Where the scarab entered.

I shook my head to rid myself of the opium nightmare's image. I had scrapes and gouges all over my body. My feet and knees and fingers were by far the worse. My head ached abominably.

From the huge beetle moving…burrowing.

"Stop it!" I screamed aloud.

Why was Hatchery not here? Why had he abandoned me this one time I needed him most?

You may have been down there for days, Wilkie Collins.

I heard *Missster Wilkie Collinssss* echoing in my aching skull.

I laughed then. It did not matter. They had tried to kill me—whoever "they" were—certainly King Lazaree and his heathen, foreign-bastard friends and fellow opium addicts—but they had failed.

I was free. I was out. I was alive.

Looking up, I was startled to see that someone had decorated the interior high spaces of the small crypt with some sort of glistening garlands. The gleaming grey strips had not been there when Hatchery and I had entered hours—*days? weeks?*—ago, I was certain of that. Christmas was more than two weeks past. And why decorate an empty crypt in the first place?

It did not matter. Nothing mattered—not even my aching, shivering body, raging headache, terrible thirst, and surging hunger—except to get out of this place forever.

Avoiding the cold black hole-in-the-floor entrance to Undertown, I stepped around the bier—quickly, since my writer's imagination then gave me the vision of a long grey arm with long white boneless fingers suddenly sliding out of that hole like a snake and pulling me, screaming, back down into the darkness—but then I had to stop immediately.

I had no choice.

My way was blocked by the body on the floor of the crypt.

It was Detective Sergeant Hibbert Hatchery, his white face distorted into a huge, silent scream, his all-white eyes staring sightlessly towards the garland-festooned bas-relief carvings and tiny gargoyles set along the corners of the small crypt's ceiling. Scattered on the stone floor around his body were the remains of his three AM lunch, a small flask, his bowler hat, and the copy of Thackeray's novel. Rising from his gaping belly were the stretched and glistening grey garlands that were not garlands at all.

Unable even to scream, I leaped the body, ducked the taut grey strands, and ran naked into the predawn burial ground of St Ghastly Grim's Cemetery.

CHAPTER TWENTY-SEVEN

*T*wo hours later and I was back in another opium den. Waiting.

I was lucky to be alive. After all, I had been running, naked and screaming, through the worst slums of Bluegate Fields behind the docks, not even aware of which way I was running. Only the odd hour (even the thugs were inside and asleep at dawn on a cold, snowy January dawn) and the fact that even thugs might have been afraid of a screaming crazy man with bloody hands explained how the first person I encountered in my panicked flight was a police constable walking his patrol through the tenements.

The policeman himself had been frightened by my aspect and manner. He had removed a small weighted cosh from his belt, and I am sure that if I had babbled at him another minute without saying words that made sense, he would have clubbed me unconscious and dragged me by the hair to the nearest station.

As it was, he said, "What did you just say? Did you say—'Hatchery's body'? As in Hibbert Hatchery?"

"Former sergeant Hibbert Hatchery, now private detective Hibbert Hatchery, yes, Constable. They removed his insides and draped them around the crypt—oh, Christ! oh, God!—and he was working for *me*, privately, not for Inspector Field, for whom he worked privately publicly."

The policeman shook me. "What's that about Inspector Field? Do you know Inspector Field?"

"Oh, yes. Oh, yes," I said and laughed. And wept.

"Who are you?" demanded the heavily moustachioed police officer. Snow had coated his dark helmet-cap white.

"William Wilkie Collins," I said through chattering teeth. "Wilkie Collins to millions of my readers. Wilkie to my friends and almost everyone else." I giggled again.

"Never heard of you," said the constable.

"I am a personal friend of and collaborator with Mr Charles Dickens," I said. My jaw had been quivering so violently that I could only barely get out the word "collaborator."

The policeman allowed me to stand there naked in the snow and wind while he slapped his open palm with his heavy cosh and regarded me with a furrowed brow beneath the brim of his cap.

"All right, come along, then," he'd said, taking me by my pale, scratched upper arm and leading me deeper into the tenements.

"A coat," I said through chattering teeth. "A blanket. Anything."

"Soon enough," said the policeman. "Soon enough. Hurry on, now. Keep up."

I imagined the police station to which he was leading me as being dominated by a large stove so hot that it was glowing red. My upper arm shook in the policeman's grasp. I was weeping again.

But he did not lead me to a police station. I half-recognised the rotting stairway and darkened hallway up which he led and pushed me. Then we were inside and I recognised the wizened woman who was swooping around me, her beak of a nose extruding from her rotting black hood of a shawl.

"Sal," said the policeman, "put this...gentleman...

550 · DAN SIMMONS

somewhere warm and get him some clothes. The fewer lice the better, although it don't really matter that much. Make sure he don't leave. Use your *Malay* to make sure he don't leave."

Opium Sal had nodded and danced around me, prodding my naked flanks and aching belly with her long-nailed finger. "I seen 'ere this 'un before, Constable Joe. 'E used to be a cust'mer an' smoked 'is pipe right hup on that cot, 'e did. The Inspector Field tuk 'im away one night. Before that I first seen 'im with ol' Hib Hatchery and some gemmun they tol' me was tip-toff important. All 'igh 'n mighty this 'un was then; 'e was, scowlin' and looking down 'is plump l'il nose at me through them spectacles what he ha'n't got on now."

"Who was this someone important?" demanded the policeman.

"Dickens, the *Pickwick* man, was who," cried Sal triumphantly, as if it had taken all her resources to dredge the name up from the depths of her opium confusion.

"Watch him," growled the policeman. "Get him some clothes even if you have to send the idiot out to find some. Keep the Malay on watch so he don't go nowhere. And put him near that puny stove you keep one lump o' coal burning in so he don't die on us before I get back. You hear me, Sal?"

The old crone had grunted and then cackled. "I never seen a man wi' such a shrivelled li'l John Thomas an' company, 'ave you, Joe?"

"Do what I say," said the policeman and left with a blast of cold air roiling in over us like the breath of Death.

Do THOSE FIT ye, darlin'?" asked Opium Sal as I sat in an otherwise empty room at the back of her opium parlour. A huge Malay with ritual scars on his cheeks sat guard just outside the door. The window here was shuttered and nailed tight. The stench of the Thames came up through it with the freezing draught even on this January day.

"No," I said. The shirt was too small, too dirty, and stank. The heavy workingman's trousers and jacket smelled just as bad and itched much more. I was sure that I could feel small things moving in both. There were no underlinens, nor socks. The ancient, worn boots she had brought me were half again too large for my feet.

"Well, ye should be thankful for what's given ye," cackled the crazy woman. "Ye would'na had them weren't it for the fac' that Ol' Yahee died 'ere sudden-like two nights ago and no one's come to fetch away 'is things."

I sat there as the cold light of Saturday morning slipped through the shutters with the stink and...

Wait. *Was* it Saturday morning, the morning after I had descended into King Lazaree's world, or was it days later? It *felt* as if days, or weeks, had passed. I thought of calling out to Old Opium Sally, but realised that odds were great that the old crone would not know. I could have asked the scar-faced Malay outside my door, but he had shown no sign of understanding English or being able to speak.

I laughed softly, then stifled a sob. It didn't matter what day it was.

My head hurt so terribly that I feared I might faint from the pain. I could feel the locus of the pain deep, far behind my eyes, not at all like a mere rheumatical gout headache that I had once found so fierce.

The stag beetle scarab is excavating a wider hole for itself. Rolling a glistening grey globe ahead of it as it moves down its entrance tunnel towards...

I sat on the edge of a filthy cot and lowered my head to my knees, trying to hold in the nausea. I knew I had nothing more to vomit up, and the dry retching had turned my guts to bands of cramped pain.

The grey, glistening garlands rising to the ceiling.

I shook away the image, but the motion made my headache worse and brought on the nausea again. The air reeked of opium smoke—cheap, rotten, diluted, and polluted opium. I could not believe that for weeks I had come here for Opium Sal's terrible product—sleeping the sleep of the drugged in these same filthy cots, all crawling with lice and vermin. What had I been thinking?

What had I been thinking last night—or however many nights ago it was—when I had descended beneath the crypt to join the Chinese mummies in that other opium den?

It had been Inspector Field who came with Hatchery to take me out of here so many months ago. It had been Inspector Field who suggested I go to King Lazaree's den under Hatchery's protection. Could it have been a plot all along? Could Field *have murdered Hatchery—perhaps out of anger that the huge detective was working for me on the side?*

I shook my aching head again. None of that made any sense at all.

Deep inside my skull, I could feel something move with six sharp legs and stag beetle pincers. I could not help it—I screamed in terror as much as in pain.

Inspector Charles Frederick Field and Detective Reginald Barris burst in.

"Hatchery's dead," I said through teeth that were chattering again.

"I know," barked Inspector Field. He seized me by the upper arm in the same knowing grip that the other policeman had used that morning. "Come along. We're going back there now."

"*Nothing* can make me go back!"

I was wrong. Inspector Field's powerful hand found a nerve in my arm that I did not know I had. I cried out in pain, rose, and stumbled along between Barris and the heavier, older man as I clattered—half-pushed, half-supported—down the stairs into a group of other men waiting in the street.

Altogether, counting the inspector and Barris, there were seven of the quiet, tough men, and although none were dressed in police uniform, I knew immediately that all had been policemen for the better part of their lives. Three of the men carried shotguns of some sort. One openly held a huge cavalry pistol at his side. Having never had any interest in things or people military, I was shocked at the sight of all this weaponry on a London city street.

But it was not really London, of course. It was Bluegate Fields. As we left New Court and passed a litany of dingy streets I had seen in all seasons for at least two years now—George Street, Rosemary Lane, Cable Street, Knock Fergus, Black Lane, New Road, and Royal Mint Street included—I noticed that the rag-wrapped bundles of misery in the courts and tenement doors, both male and female, shrank back into shadows or disappeared into darker doorways as we passed. They also recognised the seven deadly-serious men with firearms as policemen when they saw the grim knot stride past their awful hollows.

"What happened?" demanded Inspector Field. His iron grip was still hard on my quaking arm. I had brought a blanket with me to act as a sort of shawl over the filthy workman's jacket, but the wool was cheap and the cold wind cut through it at once. It was snowing again.

"What happened?" prompted Field again, shaking me slightly. "Tell me everything."

At that second I made one of the most fateful decisions of my life.

"I remember nothing," I said.

"You're lying," snapped Inspector Field and shook me again. All pretext of his workingman detective status showing deference to my gentleman status was now gone. I might as well have been one of the Smithfield or Limehouse felons whom he had handled with such a similar iron grip over the decades.

"I remember nothing at all," I lied again. "Nothing after taking my pipe last night in King Lazaree's den at about midnight, as always. Then awakening in the dark some hours ago and finding my way out. And discovering...poor Hatchery."

"You're lying," the inspector said again.

"They drugged me," I said tonelessly as we entered the last of the alleys before reaching the cemetery. "Lazaree or someone put some drug in my opium pipe."

Detective Barris barked a laugh at this, but Inspector Field silenced him with a glance.

There was another tall man wearing a topcoat and carrying a shotgun standing guard at the entrance to Ghastly Grim's. He touched his cap as we approached. I pulled back as we came to the gate, but Inspector Field propelled me forward as if I were a child.

The snow had covered the headstones and statues and outlined the flat roofs and ledges on the crypts. The dead tree that brooded over the last crypt rose against the cloudy sky like a spill of black ink rimned with white chalk.

Three more men waited inside the crypt, their breath hovering over them like trapped souls in the cold. I looked away but not before seeing that they had covered Hatchery's eviscerated body with some sort of canvas tarpaulin. The grey, glistening garlands were gone, but I noticed a second, smaller tarpaulin in the corner covering something other than Hatchery's corpse. Even in the cold air, the small space smelled like an abattoir.

Most of the men who had accompanied us through

the streets peered in at the crypt door and waited just outside. The crypt was small and seemed absurdly crowded now with six of us in it, since everyone avoided standing too near to Hatchery's covered corpse.

I realised with a start that one of the three men waiting in the crypt was not a policeman or detective but was a giant Malay, his black hair hanging long, dirty, and lank down his neck, his arms behind his back and his wrists cruelly cuffed by iron manacles. For a confused second I thought him to be the Malay we had just left behind at Opium Sal's, but I saw this man was older and his cheeks were unscarred. He stared at me without curiosity or passion, his eyes dulled in the way I had seen in condemned men before or after their hangings.

Inspector Field moved me towards the narrow entrance in the floor, but I pulled back with all of my will and energy. "I cannot go down there," I gasped. "I *shall* not."

"You shall," said Inspector Field and shoved me forward.

One of the detectives guarding the tall Malay handed a bullseye lantern to the inspector; another was given to Barris. With the younger detective leading and Inspector Field holding me tight by the arm as he shoved me ahead of him, the three of us descended the narrow stairway. Only one other man—a detective who was a stranger to me and who carried a heavy shotgun—went down with us.

I CONFESS, Dear Reader, that many elements of the next half-hour or so are lost to me still. My terror, fatigue, and pain were such that my state of consciousness was rather like that which we experience when hovering near the threshold of sleep—now aware of our surroundings, now dropping off to dreams, now jerked back to reality by some sound, sensation, or other stimulus.

The stimulus I remember most was Inspector Field's insistent, incessant iron-grip on my arm pulling and pushing me this way and that in the lantern-lit darkness of the pit.

In the lantern light, the short descent and walk to King Lazaree's den was as familiar as a recurring dream, holding nothing of the nightmare of my panicked flight in the darkness.

"Is this the opium den?" asked Inspector Field.

"Yes," I said. "I mean, no. Yes. I don't know."

Instead of the red curtain hanging, there was a rusted grate just as on all the other *loculi*. The bullseye lanterns showed piles of coffins within rather than rows of three-tiered bunks and the bier with the ever-present Buddha figure of King Lazaree.

"This grate isn't set in the wall like the others," grunted Barris, grasping the rusty iron and shoving it in. It clanged like the bell of doom as it hit the stone floor. We entered the narrow space.

"No dust from the ceiling here," said Barris, moving the beam of his bullseye back and forth. "It's been swept clear."

The fourth man in our party remained in the corridor with his shotgun.

"Yes, this is King Lazaree's den," I said as the lanterns illuminated more of the familiar corridor and alcove. But nothing remained, not even marks on the stone where the heavy bunks and small iron stove had rested. The bier in the centre where King Lazaree had sat in his bright robes now held only an ancient and empty stone sarcophagus. My private alcove at the back was just another niche filled with more stacked coffins.

"But you did not wake in the dark here," said Inspector Field.

"No. Farther down the corridor, I think."

"We'll look there," said the inspector and waved Barris out ahead of him. The man with the shotgun lifted his own lantern and followed us.

I was thinking about Dickens. Where was he in his American tour now? The last letter I had received from him, written from New York just before the New Year, reported him sick with what he called "low action of the heart" and so unhappy where he was that he was staying in bed each day until three PM and only with great difficulty rousing himself for the inevitable evening performances.

Did Dickens have a scarab in him? Did it crawl from his brain to his heart and sink its huge pincers in when he did anything that would release him from Drood?

I knew from the original itinerary and from telegrams to Wills at the magazine office that in this January, Dickens was to have read in New York, Boston, Philadelphia, Baltimore, and Brooklyn—and that each hall was selling out to the tune of six- to eight-thousand tickets—but where was he now amidst that list of odd-sounding cities?

I knew Dickens well enough to know that he would have recovered from his illness and moral swoon and be capering around between readings, amusing children and onlookers on his trains connecting the cities, putting every ounce of energy and fibre of his being into the afternoon and nightly readings, but I also knew that he would be miserable at the same time, counting down the days until his ship sailed for England and home in April.

Would he live that long? Would the scarab allow him to live if it detected his betrayal?

"Is this the place where you woke?" demanded Inspector Field.

He had to shake me to bring me back from my revery.

I looked into a *loculus* identical to most of the others except that in the dust in this narrow niche there were footprints—of small, bare, naked, vulnerable feet—in the thick dust. There was also blood on the ragged grate where I had blindly squeezed through the break. I touched the clothing above the fresh wounds on my ribs and hips.

"Yes," I said dully. "I think so."

"It's a wonder you made it out of here in the dark," said Barris.

I had nothing to say to that. I was shaking as with the ague and wanted to leave this pit more than anything else in the world. But Inspector Field was not finished with me.

We walked back towards the entrance, light from the three bullseye lanterns dancing on the walls and *loculi* entrances in such a way as to make me feel faint. It was as if reality and fiction, life and death, light and its absolute absence, were whirling in a frenzied *danse macabre*.

"Is this the corridor leading to the rood screen and lower levels?" asked Inspector Field.

"Yes," I said, not having any idea at that moment of what he was talking about.

We followed the narrow corridor past black *loculi* to the circular subterranean room underneath the former Cathedral of St Ghastly Grim's apse. This was where Dickens had found the narrow stairway down to the real Undertown.

"I'm not going down there," I said, pulling myself free from Inspector Field's supporting grasp and almost falling. "I can*not* go down there."

"You do not have to," said Inspector Field, and the words made me almost weep. *"Today,"* he added. To the man with the shotgun, he said, "Bring the Malay down."

I stood there dully, outside of time, feeling movement deep in my head as the scarab stirred. I tried not to be sick again, but the air down there stank of rank soil and decay and the grave. When the detective with the shotgun returned, he had another detective with him—this man in a tan overcoat and carrying a rifle—and between them was the handcuffed Malay. The Oriental stared at me when he entered the subterranean apse; his narrow black eyes on either side of that flat blade of a nose were almost as dull with pain or despair as mine but more accusatory. He never looked at Field or Barris, only at me, as if I were his persecutor.

Inspector Field nodded, the two men with guns led the captive through the tattered rood screen and down the narrow passage, and Barris and the inspector brought me back into the corridor and then up into the light.

"I don't understand," I managed to gasp as we came out of the crypt into the freezing January air. The snow had stopped but the air was thick with winter fog. "Have you informed the police? Why are all these private detectives here? Certainly you must have informed the police. Where are the police?"

Inspector Field led me to the street where a black closed carriage waited. It reminded me of a hearse. The horses' exhalations added more fog to the air. "The police will be informed soon enough," he said. His tone seemed soft, but beneath that softness I could sense a fury and resolve as powerful as his grip on my arm. "These men knew Hibbert Hatchery. Many worked with him. Some loved him."

Barris and the inspector pushed me up into the carriage. Barris went around to get in the other side. Inspector Field, his hand still on my arm, stood in the open door. "Drood expects us to rush down into

Undertown today—a dozen of us perhaps, or twenty. He wants us to. But by tomorrow there will be a hundred private men here, all who knew Hatchery or who hate Drood. Tomorrow we will go down. Tomorrow we will find Drood and smoke him out of his hole."

He shut the door with a muffled slam. "Be available tomorrow, Mr Collins. You will be needed."

"I cannot..." I began but then saw the two men with guns emerge from the crypt. The Malay was no longer with them. I stared in horror at the right sleeve of the taller man. His expensive tan coat was crimson from the cuff upward, as if blood had wicked up the wool halfway to the elbow.

"The Malay..." I managed. "He must have been the one in police custody. The one the Metropolitan Detectives Bureau turned over to you for interrogation."

Inspector Field said nothing.

"Where is he?" I whispered.

"We sent the Malay down as a message," said Inspector Field.

"As a messenger, you mean."

"We sent the Malay down as a *message*," repeated Inspector Field tonelessly. He rapped on the side of the carriage and Barris and I rolled away through the narrow streets of Bluegate Fields.

BARRIS DROPPED ME off outside my home at 90 Gloucester Place without a word. Before I entered my own door, I stood shivering in the fog and watched the dark carriage roll out of sight around the corner. Another dark carriage came past, its side lamps lit. It also turned right at the corner. I could not hear if they both stopped—the fog and snow muffled even hoofbeats and axle rumbles—but my guess was that they had. Barris would be appointing lookouts, giving instructions. Inspector Field's men would be watching the front and back of the house, I felt sure, although not in the high numbers of the previous 9 June.

Somewhere out there in the fog were my new Gooseberries. But all I had to do to outsmart them was go down into my own coal cellar, knock down a few bricks, and crawl through the narrow hole into the upper levels of Undertown. The city would then be mine to travel in . . . or at least under.

I giggled at the thought but stopped when the hysterical giggle turned to nausea. The scarab shifted in my skull.

WHEN I STEPPED into the foyer of my home, I opened my mouth to scream in horror.

Detective Hatchery's intestines were strewn from cornice to chandelier, from chandelier to stairway, from stairway to candle sconces. They hung there just as in the crypt, grey and wet and glistening.

I did not scream. And after a moment in which I shook like a child, I realised that the "intestines" were simply garlands, grey and silver silk and ribboned garlands, left over from some inane party we had thrown at the old house ages ago.

The house smelled of cooking—pot roast and other beefs simmering, some sort of rich bouillabaisse getting started—and the urge to vomit rose in me again.

Caroline swept out of the dining room.

"Wilkie! Where on *earth* have you been? Do you think you can just disappear every night and not . . . Good Lord—where did you get those *atrocious* rags? Where are your real clothes? What is that *smell?*"

I ignored her and bellowed for our parlourmaid. When she rushed in, face flushed from the kitchen steams, I said brusquely, "Draw a hot bath for me—immediately. *Very* hot. Hurry on, now."

"Wilkie," huffed Caroline, "are you going to answer my questions and explain?"

"*You* explain," I growled, waving at the draped ribbons everywhere. "What is all this trash? What's going on?"

Caroline blinked as if slapped. "What is going *on*? In a few hours is your *very important* pre-theatre dinner party. Everyone is coming. We have to dine early, of course, as you specified, since we all must leave for the theatre by..." She paused and lowered her voice so the servants would not hear. What emerged was a steam kettle hiss. "Are you *drunk*, Wilkie? Are you addled by your laudanum?"

"Shut up," I said.

This time her head snapped back and colour rose to her cheeks as if she *had* been slapped.

"Call it off," I said. "Send the boy...send messengers...tell everyone the party is off."

She laughed almost hysterically. "That is *quite* impossible, as you well know. The cook has begun dinner. People have arranged transportation. The table is already set with the complimentary theatre tickets at each place. It would be quite impossible to..."

"Call it off," I said and brushed past her to go upstairs and take five glasses of laudanum, give the wretched clothes to our servant Agnes to burn, and bathe.

I SHOULD HAVE SLEPT in the steaming water had it not been for the crawling in my skull.

The pressure from the scarab was so great that three times I leapt from the bath to stand in front of the looking glass. Adjusting the candles for maximum light, I opened my mouth wider than I thought possible—my jaw muscles actually groaned in protest—and the third time I did it I was sure that I saw light gleam on a black carapace as the huge insect scuttled back out of sight, away from the light.

I turned and vomited into the basin, but there was nothing left in my stomach to bring up, and the beetle was back in my skull by then. I got back into the bath, but each time I approached sleep I relived the inside of the crypt, the grey gleaming, the abattoir stink of the place, and over that I smelled incense and heard the chanting and saw the huge black bug burrowing into my belly as if flesh were sand....

There came a rap on the door.

"Go away!"

"There is a telegram come for you," said Caroline through the door. "The boy said it was important."

Cursing, I rose dripping from the bath—which was growing cold at any rate—pulled on my robe, and opened the door long enough to grab the flimsy from Mrs G——'s thin white fingers.

I assumed the note was from Fechter or someone else at the theatre—they had the profligate habit of sending telegrams as if a simple messenger-borne note might not suffice. Or perhaps it was from Dickens. In a flash of revelation, I imagined him confessing to his own scarab and acknowledging that he somehow knew that I had gained mine.

I had to read the actual six words and signature four times over before the meaning sank into my exhausted, inhabited brain.

**MOTHER IS DYING. COME AT ONCE.
CHARLEY**

CHAPTER TWENTY-EIGHT

*M*y mother's face made me think of a newly dead corpse from which the silent soul was still trying frantically to escape.

Her eyes, showing mostly whites with only a hint of dark iris under the heavy and reddened lids, strained and bulged as if from some terrible internal pressure. Her mouth was open wide but her lips, tongue, and palate looked as pale and dry as old leather. She could not speak. She made no sounds except for a strange rasping, hissing sound emanating from her chest. I do not think she could see us.

Charley and I embraced in horror in full view of her sightless gaze and I gasped, "Dear God, how did this come to be?"

My beloved brother could only shake his head. Mrs Wells hovered nearby, her arthritic hands flapping from the folds of her black lace shawl, and somewhere in the far corner of the room waited Mother's longtime elderly physician from Tunbridge Wells, Dr Eichenbach.

"Mrs Wells said that she was well—no, not well, hurting, coughing some, but well enough to eat with an appetite and enjoy her tea of an afternoon and to be read to and to chat with Mrs Wells—yesterday evening," managed Charley. "And this morning... I came from London to surprise her... and discovered *this*."

"This is oft the case with the old waiting and willing and wanting to depart this world," muttered Dr Eichenbach. "No warning. No warning."

As Eichenbach, who was more deaf than not, was chatting in the corner with Mrs Wells, I whispered urgently to Charley, "I want my doctor to see her. Frank Beard will come at once."

"I have been trying to get in touch with her most recent physician, Dr Ramseys," Charley said softly.

"What was that?" called Dr Eichenbach from his corner near the fire. "You're calling Dr...who?"

"Ramseys," said Charley with a sigh. "Evidently a new local physician who took it upon himself to call on Mother in the past few weeks. I am quite sure that Mother had no reason to go to him...that is, to go outside your circle of excellent advice and care."

Eichenbach was frowning. "Dr Ramsey?"

"Ram*seys*," said Charley with the loud over-articulation so preferred by the frustrated speaking to the near-deaf.

Eichenbach shook his head. "No Ramsey or Ramseys practising around Tunbridge Wells," he said. "Nor in London, as far as I know, except for old Charles Bierbont Ramsey, and his practice now is restricted to Lord Leighton's family. Besides, his speciality is venereal diseases—it's all he's interested in—and I hardly doubt that Mrs Collins called him out here for *that* sort of consultation. And what kind of name is Ram*seys*? He sounds like a committee."

Charley sighed again. "I believe that Dr Ramseys was visiting family in Tunbridge Wells when he heard of Mother's illness. Isn't that right, Mrs Wells?"

The old woman looked flustered and her gnarled hands flapped again from her shawl. "Truly, I do not know, Master Charles. I only heard about Dr Ramseys from your dear, dear mother. I never spoke to him."

"But you *saw* him?" I asked. The scarab stirred in my skull at the same instant a cold hand closed around my heart.

"Only once," said the sincere old woman. "And from a distance. He was leaving one afternoon last week while I came down the path across the meadow."

"What did he look like?" I asked.

"Oh...I certainly could not say, Master Wilkie. I just glimpsed a tall, thin man walking away from me down the lane. He dressed very formally but rather—I should be one to speak!—rather in an old-fashioned manner, as the young people would say. He wore a black cut-away and had a top hat on of the older sort, if you understand what I mean."

"I am not certain I follow your meaning, Mrs Wells," I said in what I hoped was a steady voice. "How was the top hat old-fashioned?"

"Oh, you know what I mean, Master Wilkie. The sort with a slightly wider brim, a lower crown—more of the kind of riding hat one saw on gentlemen when I was a girl. And quite obviously made of beaver, not silk."

"Thank you, Mrs Wells," said Charley.

"Oh...and his veil, of course," added Mrs Wells. "Even from a distance, I could see the veil. Your mother mentioned it later."

"Actually, she did not mention it to me," said Charles. "Why was Dr Ramseys wearing a veil?"

"Because of the burns, of course. Terrible burns, said Harriet...that is, Mrs Collins. Your dear mother. Dr Ramseys did not want to frighten people on the street."

I turned my head and closed my eyes for a minute. When I opened them, I could see only Mother's straining face and the gaping, moistureless mouth in which her dry tongue lolled like a misplaced bit of rope. Her bulging white eyes looked like two eggs pressed beneath human eyelids by some terrible exertion of force.

"Mrs Wells," Charley said softly, "would you be so kind as to go fetch the neighbour boy who sometimes runs errands for Mother? We need to send a telegram to Dr Frank Beard in London. Wilkie shall write it out here and the boy will carrry it."

"This late, Master Charles? The telegraph office will close in less than an hour."

"Then we need to hurry, don't we, Mrs Wells? Thank you for your help. Mother would thank you if she could."

CAROLINE AND I had parted with harsh words.

Inexplicably, *unbelievably,* she had asked questions, demanded answers, and created obstacles to my going out the door even *after* I had shown her the telegram from my brother.

"Where were you last night?" she persisted. "Where did you get those terrible clothes that Agnes burned? What was that awful smell on them? When will you be back from Tunbridge Wells? What shall we do about the dinner party this evening? The theatre tickets? Everyone was counting on..."

"First, take down and throw away these damned garlands," I snarled. "And have your dinner party. Go to the theatre with all my male friends. It certainly won't be the first time you've entertained and been entertained at my expense when I could not be a part of it."

"What does *that* mean, Wilkie? Do you not *want* me to honour our dinner obligations with your friends? Do you not *want* me to use those tickets to *your* play, after you have promised a dozen people that they would see it tonight from the author's box? What would you have me do?"

"I would *have* you," I growled, "go to the Devil."

Caroline froze in place.

"My mother is dying," I said flatly and harshly and finally. "And as far as the question of with whom you choose to dine and go to the theatre, you can go *with* the Devil as far as I am concerned." I turned the full rage of my countenance on her. "Or with your plumber."

Still frozen, Caroline G—— blushed from her hairline to her bodice. "What…do you mean, Wilkie?"

I threw open the door to the fog and cold and laughed in her face. "You know d——ned well what I mean, my dearest. I mean Mr Joseph Charles Clow, son of the distiller on Avenue Road, one plumber by trade, seducer—or seducee—by avocation. The same *Mr Clow* whom you secretly fed at my table and with whom you've clandestinely met five times since Christmas Day."

And I went out and slammed the door in her flushed and terrified face.

TUNBRIDGE WELLS HAD BEEN EERILY SILENT and snow covered and filled with disturbingly white, thick fog when Charley arrived in a sleigh to pick me up at the station that afternoon, and it was even more oppressively silent and foggy at ten o'clock that night when a heavily bundled Frank Beard materialised out of the freezing mist from the same sleigh, handled yet again by the always-ill but seemingly indefatigable Charley. I had stayed with Mother and the sleeping Mrs Wells as my brother went to pick up our friend and physician. Dr Eichenbach had long since gone home.

Frank Beard clasped my hand a moment in silent commiseration and proceeded to examine Mother while Charley and I waited in the other room. The fireplace had burned low and we decided not to light other candles or lamps. Mrs Wells slept on the divan in the far corner. Charley and I spoke in whispers.

"She wasn't like this last week when you saw her last?" I asked.

Charley shook his head. "She complained of aches and pains and her breathing problems.... You know how she goes on, Wilkie...went on...but no, there was no hint of this terrible...whatever it is."

Beard came out after a while and we woke Mrs Wells for what he had to say.

"Harriet appears to have had a very serious brain haemorrhage," he said softly. "As you can see, she has lost her ability to speak, her control of voluntary muscles, and—quite possibly—her reason. Her heart also sounds compromised. Physically, she otherwise seems..."

Frank Beard paused and turned towards Mrs Wells. "Has Mrs Collins fallen recently? Injured herself with scissors or a kitchen knife or perhaps even a knitting needle?"

"Absolutely not!" cried the old woman. "Mrs Collins was not so active that any of those things could have happened, Doctor. Nor would I have *allowed* them to happen. And she would have told me if...No, no, no such injury could have occurred."

Beard nodded.

"Why do you ask, Frank?" said Charley.

"Your mother has a recent cut here...." said Beard, touching his diaphragm just beneath the sternum. "It is about two inches wide. Not serious and it is healing, but unusual for a person who has not been..." He shook his head. "But it does not matter. I am certain it has nothing to do with the brain haemorrhage and internal neuralgia that must have afflicted her sometime last night."

I had been standing, but now my legs went so weak that I had to sit.

"The...prognosis?" asked Charley.

"There is no hope," Beard said flatly. "The internal neuralgia and obstruction to the brain are too severe.

She may regain consciousness—she may even become more clear in her mind before the end—but I am certain that there is no hope. It is just a matter of days or weeks now."

Mrs Wells made as if to faint, and Charley and Frank helped her back to the divan.

I sat and stared at the fire. It was early afternoon in America. Somewhere comfortable and bright and clean, Charles Dickens was being treated like a king and was preparing for another evening of public adoration. In a recent note that Wills had shared with me, Dickens had written—*"People will turn back, turn again and face me, and have a look at me...or will say to one another, 'Look here! Dickens is coming!'"* and talked about being recognised every time he rode in a carriage—*"...in the railway cars, if I see anybody who clearly wants to speak to me, I usually anticipate the wish by speaking myself."*

What noblesse oblige! How unspeakably generous of my erstwhile collaborator and eternal competitor! There he was, condescending to speak to tens of thousands of adoring (if wilfully ignorant and terminally illiterate) Americans who worshipped the very ground he walked on, while I sat here in pain and misery and hopelessness, my mother dying horribly, a...scaraby thing...scrabbling in my skull like a...

"I'll be leaving now. I'll stay with friends in the village here and check on Harriet before taking the train back to London in the morning." Frank Beard had been speaking. Some time had passed. Evidently Charley had shown the weeping Mrs Wells to her room and was now in his topcoat and heavy artist's cap and waiting by the door to take Beard away. I jumped to my feet and shook my physician's hand with both of mine and thanked him profusely.

"I will stay with Mother," I told Charley.

"I shall sit up with her through the night when I

return," said my brother. "You look exhausted, Wilkie. Build up the fire so you can sleep on the long couch when I get back."

I shook my head then, although whether to say that I would stay up with Mother through the night or that I was not exhausted or that I did not need a fire, I do not know. Then Charley and Frank Beard were gone, and I could hear the treacherously false happy winter sounds of the bells on the horses' harnesses as they drove back into the village.

I went into Mother's room and sat on the hard chair pulled up next to her bed. Her eyes were still open but apparently sightless, the lids fluttering from time to time. Her arms and wrists were bent like a small bird's broken wings.

"Mother," I said softly to her, "I am sorry that..."

I had to stop. I was sorry that...what? That I had killed her through my association with Drood. *Had* I killed her?

"Mother..." I began again and stopped again.

For months I had written and spoken to her of little save for my own success. I had been too busy in writing of the play and rehearsals for the play and attending early presentations of the play to spend any time with her—even Christmas had been a grudging few hours before I'd rushed for the train back to the city. It seemed that every note I had written to her since last summer had been either about myself (although she dearly loved hearing about my successes) or about adjusting the terms of the inheritance that would come to Charley and me if she should die before us.

"Mother..."

Her eyelids fluttered wildly again. Was she trying to communicate? My mother always had been a busy, articulate, confident, capable, and socially secure person. For years, even after my father's death, she had presided over a *salon* of artists and intellectuals. I had always associated her with competence, dignity, an almost regal self-possession.

And now *this*...

I do not, Dear Reader, know how long I sat there by Mother's bedside. I do know that at some point I began sobbing.

Then, finally, I had to know. I set the candle closer. I bent over her insensate form and drew the bedclothes down.

Mother was in her nightgown, but there were only a few buttons at the neck—not enough for my purpose. Still weeping, wiping my streaming nose on my sleeve, I pulled the top sheet down to Mother's pale, blue-veined, and swollen ankles, and—sobbing more loudly while holding the candle in one hand—slowly pulled up her flannel sleeping gown.

I covered my eyes with my left forearm, the candle singeing my brow and hair, so that I—her loving son—would not see her ultimate nakedness. But I confess that I had rolled the sweat-clammy nightgown too high before looking, still shielding my range of vision, so that her wrinkled and sagging breasts were visible.

And below them, below the sharp chevrons of her ribs pressing against the pale flesh, there was the red mark beneath her sternum.

It seemed the same width, the same lividity, the same shape.

Half-mad with fatigue and terror, I ripped my shirt open, the buttons popping and rolling on the wooden floor out of sight beneath the bed. I had to bend almost double to see the red mark there on my upper belly and was moving the candle quickly back and forth to compare my scarab wound to the mark beneath Mother's chest.

They were the same.

There was a creak of boards and then a gasp behind

me and I wheeled—my shirttails out and buttons open, Mother's nightgown still pulled up to her collar—to find Mrs Wells staring at me with an expression of absolute wide-eyed horror.

I opened my mouth to explain but found no words. I pulled Mother's nightgown down, threw the covers over her, set the candle on her bedside table, and turned back to the elderly housekeeper, who shrank away from me.

Suddenly there came a terrible pounding at the door.

"Stay here," I said to Mrs Wells, but she only shrank back farther from me and bit her knuckles as I hurried past her.

I rushed to the door—in my confusion, I was thinking that Frank Beard had returned with some miraculously revised and hopeful prognosis—but as I reached it, I glanced back towards Mother's room. Mrs Wells was not visible.

The pounding continued, grew more violent.

I flung the door open.

Four large men, strangers all, dressed almost identically in thick black overcoats and workmen's caps, stood there in the post-midnight snow. A hearselike carriage waited, its lamps throwing wan light.

"Mr Wilkie Collins?" demanded the closest and largest of the men.

I nodded dumbly.

"It is time," said the man. "The inspector awaits. By the time we get back to London, all will be in readiness. Come at once."

CHAPTER TWENTY-NINE

*U*ndertown was burning.

Inspector Field had said that within twenty-four hours he would turn out a hundred men—ex-detectives, off-duty policemen, others—who would be eager to descend beneath the city to avenge the murdered Detective Hibbert Hatchery.

I had to think that he had understated the case. Even in the fragmentary glimpses I had over these ensuing hours, it was obvious that there were more than a hundred men involved.

There were more than a dozen men in the wide, flat-bottomed scow that Field had ordered me into. A bright lantern hung on a slanted pole rising over and beyond the long tiller at the stern. Near the bow, two men controlled a blinding carbide spotlight of the sort they used outside and within Welsh mines during emergencies such as cave-ins; that spotlight was on a pivot and now stabbed its bright white cone-circle of illumination ahead onto the broad, black waters of the Fleet Street Ditch subterranean river, now onto the arched brick ceiling, now against and across the curving walls and narrow walkways on either side.

Another scow followed us. I had heard that there were two working their way north from the Thames-end of this effluent. Ahead of us and behind us, a dozen small, narrow punts flitted along with our strange fleet, men at the bows and sterns with poles in their hands, men amidships with rifles and shotguns and pistols.

There were rifles and shotguns and pistols in hand here in the lead scow as well. I understood that many of the silent men in their dark workingmen's clothes were former sharpshooters from the Army or Metropolitan Police. Not being a fancier of things military, I had never seen so many firearms in one place before. I would not have guessed that London had so many private men with arms.

The long river-sewer tunnel was black and foetid, but at the moment it was filled with beams and spheres of light as men in the scows and on the punts added their shifting bullseye lantern shafts to the cyclopean glare of the massive carbide searchlights. Shouts echoed back and forth through the stench. Along with the dozens of men in the various boats, more dozens were striding along the narrow stone or brick walkways on each side of the curving waterway and they also carried lanterns and weapons.

We had not been required to return to St Ghastly Grim's Cemetery for our descent into this part of Undertown (and, in truth, Dear Reader, I do not believe I would have been capable of doing so). There were new corridors and stairways—part of a future underground railroad complex, I understood—that connected to the ancient catacombs that had been part of the Abney Park Cemetery in Stoke Newington and we simply had to clatter down well-lighted stairs, through less-lighted tunnels, down more stairs, through a brief but confusing labyrinth of still-reeking catacombs, then down ladders to the new sewers that were to connect the Main Drainage Works at Crossness to the still-incomplete Embankment Works, and then lower again down narrow shafts and ancient tunnels to true Undertown.

I have no idea how they got the scows and punts and searchlights down.

Our advance was anything but silent. Besides the echoing shouts and footfalls and occasional gunshot explosions as someone picked off an aggressive rat—the vermin swam and swarmed in front of our scow and the accompanying punts like a rippling river of brown backs—there were also frequent explosions from ahead of us that were so painfully loud I had to cover my ears.

Small sewer outlets, some no more than three feet across, some much larger—all tributaries to or from our primary Fleet Ditch river channel here—branched off at irregular intervals from both sides of the curving brick vault. Most were covered with corroded and slime-covered grates and grilles. Inspector Field brusquely ordered those grilles blown off with applications of gunpowder that had been brought down and sent along with the advance parties on foot and in punts.

The terrible booms—amplified beyond endurance by the vaulted brick sewer architecture—crashed every few minutes, making me think of some terrible Crimean battlefield with artillery to the left of us, artillery to the right of us, artillery straight ahead of us, and so forth.

It was intolerable, especially to nerve-ends that had been denied sleep for at least three days and nights, muscles and bones which had been drugged and left for dead in the dark, and senses which were even now screaming in pain and protest. I reached into my valise that I had brought along from Tunbridge Wells and drank four more doses of laudanum.

Suddenly the stench became worse. I set my handkerchief over my mouth and nose, but it did little to filter the eye-watering stink.

Inspector Field carried no visible weapon, but he was swathed in a black winter cape-coat, had a wide-brimmed countryman's hat pulled low, and showed a blood-red scarf wrapped several times around his neck.

The red scarf also covered the lower half of his face. Any weapon might have been hidden in a pocket beneath the folds of that cape.

He had not said a single word to me when the four black-coated wraiths and then Reggie Barris delivered me to Undertown and then to the scow, but now Inspector Field—between distant explosions—recited:

> *"How dare*
> *Your dainty nostrils (in so hot a season*
> *When every clerk eats artichokes and peason,*
> *Laxative lettuce, and such windy meat)*
> *'Tempt such a passage? When each privy's seat*
> *Is filled with buttock, and the walls do sweat*
> *Urine and plasters?"*

Barris and Field's other underlings stared at him as if he had gone mad, but I laughed. "You and Charles Dickens have something in common, Inspector."

"Yes?" The old man's dark, bushy eyebrow arched above the red slash of scarf.

"You both seem to know Ben Jonson's 'On the Famous Voyage' by heart," I said.

"What learnèd man would not?" said Inspector Field.

"Indeed," I said, feeling the magical laudanum somewhat reviving my all-but-extinguished spirits, "there seems to be an entire genre of sewer writing, sewer poetry."

"A synecdoche for the filth of the city squatting above us in all its cloacal corruption," said Inspector Field. The old man was showing me a rough alliterative eloquence that I never would have expected from our earlier encounters and conversations. Or, far more likely, he was very drunk.

"Would you care to hear some of Swift's 'Description of a City Shower'?" he continued. "I trust that you, a writer, Master Wilkie Collins, know that Swift did not mean a rain shower. Or, more appropriate to our reeking Fleet Ditch sewer odyssey, perchance you would care to hear a recitation of Book Two of Pope's scatological *Dunciad*?"

"Perhaps another time," I said.

THE FLEET DITCH widened until it became a true underground river, wide enough for eight or nine of our scows and punts to advance together. The brick roof of the sewer also disappeared as we entered a quarter mile or more of actual cavern—the ragged roof here rising high and unseen above layers of fog or steam or smoke. To the right of the river's course here a dozen grated sewer pipes, some ten or more feet in diameter, spilled their steaming effluent into the main current, but on the left side there came into sight low, broad shelves of mud and rubble—a sort of riverbank or shore. Rising above these rubbled dikes to a height of a hundred feet or more were ledges, openings, niches, and glimpses of tunnel-intersected crypts, ancient caverns, and deep cellars beneath cellars arrayed high on this cavern's pockmarked wall like multi-storeyed buildings on the Strand.

As we drifted closer to the rubbled shore, I looked up and saw movement—people in rags peering over low walls, campfires flickering, miserable rags hung out on washlines over the abyss, ladders and crude bridgings connecting the subterranean tenements.

Charles Dickens had always imagined that he had plumbed the depths of London's slums, learned the pathetic ways of the poorest of the poor in our capital, but here—far beneath the surface—was evidence that there were those poorer than the poorest of the poor in the rotting, typhus-lashed slums above.

I could see families in the hovels and on the high ledges now, what I took to be children dressed in a mere motley of filthy rags, all peering out at us or down at us in alarm, as if we were Vikings raiding some history-forgotten, God-forsaken Saxon settlement. The niches in the high wall, each holding hovels made of canvas and broken brick and mud bricks and old tin, reminded me of illustrations I had seen of abandoned Red Indian cliff dwellings in canyons somewhere in the American West or Southwest. Only *these* cliff dwellings were anything but abandoned; I estimated that hundreds of people were living in these high holes in the rock here far beneath the city.

More of Inspector Field's men arrived by foot from unseen caverns or stairways or along sewer-side paths from the south. The scows and punts ran up on the shore with a bone-mulch crunch, and our dark men with torches, lanterns, and rifles spilled out in all directions.

"Burn it all," said Inspector Field. Barris and other lieutenants turned the old man's soft command into a series of echoing cries.

The Fleet Ditch cavern echoed with shouts and screams. I could see Field's men climbing ladders and stone steps, running along the tunnelled terraces, and herding the rag-bundled figures away from the huts and hovels. There was no resistance that I could see. I wondered why anyone would come down here to this cavern beneath the old crypts, then realised that it was cave temperature here—mid-fifties at least—while it was below freezing on the hard-cobbled streets and in the sagging, unheated slums above.

When the first flames shot up from the warren of huts a great gasp went up, echoing through the space like a single breath exhaled by a hundred or two hundred separate forms. The dry rags and driftwood and old mattresses and occasional cast-off sofas burned like tinder, and in two minutes, despite the fact that most of the smoke was carried up and out the various shafts and stairways and corridors in the rock, there was a heavy black cloud under the ceiling of the cavern above us. New flames burned orange through that cloud and a series of explosions from Inspector Field's men blowing the grilles and grates off the sewer entrances on the opposite side of the river gave the whole scene an impression of a violent summer storm.

Suddenly a bundle of rags came flying from one of the higher terraces, flapped on the way down, and struck the underground river with a hiss before sinking.

I hoped to God it was only a bundle of rags. I hoped to God it was only rags flapping, not arms and legs kicking during the fall.

I went up to Inspector Field where he stood against the bow of the beached scow and I said, "Was it absolutely necessary to burn these people out?"

"Yes." He had not turned his head from the spectacle. Occasionally he would gesture, and Barris or one of his other favoured subalterns would send men to round up running forms or to set the torch to some hovel that had escaped the first flames.

"Why?" I persisted. "They're just poor beggars unable to compete even on the street. They do no harm down here."

Field turned towards me. "Down here," he said softly, "these miserable excuses for men and women and their offspring are not Her Royal Majesty's subjects. There are no Englishmen here, Mr Wilkie Collins. This is the kingdom of Drood and these are the minions of Drood. They give him their loyalty and—one way or the other—they offer up to him their service and succour."

I began laughing then and found it very difficult to stop.

Inspector Field raised a bushy eyebrow. "Did I say something humorous, sir?"

"The Kingdom of Drood," I managed at last. "The loyal minions of...Drood." I began laughing again.

Inspector Field turned away from me. Above us, the rag bundles of all sizes were being marched up out of the smoke-filled cliff dwellings and Fleet Ditch cavern to whatever or whoever waited above.

PLEASE BE SO KIND as to go with Mr Barris," the inspector said to me sometime later.

I was paying little attention to the proceedings. I remember that we had left the half mile or so of cavern and burning cliff dwellings behind and followed the river into a more contained Fleet Ditch tunnel once again. Ahead of us, the brick-arched way diverged into two major channels and on the left a sort of low dam or spillway required hoisting the chosen scow down with various bits of block and tackle; the punts had already gone ahead there. Inspector Field's scow had taken the right-hand channel, but there was a major sewer outlet ahead and evidently they wanted me to explore it in a punt with Reginald Barris.

"You've seen Drood's temple," explained the inspector. "We believe that access to it may be through a false wall or hidden channel."

"I haven't seen Drood's temple," I said wearily.

"You described it, sir. You said that there were steps leading up from the river, high bronze doors, and statues on either side—Egyptian reliquary, human forms with the heads of jackals or birds."

A chill ran up my spine as this brought back my beetle dream of less than thirty-six hours earlier—could that time span be correct? Could this actually be only the night after my awakening in the dark crypts above here?—but I said, "That was *Charles Dickens's description,* Inspector. I've never purported to have seen Drood's mythical temple...nor even Drood, for that matter."

"You were there yesterday, Mr Wilkie Collins, we both know that," said Inspector Field. "But we shan't argue it here. Please go with Detective Barris."

Before crawling to the punt, I asked, "Is your search down here almost finished, Inspector?"

The old man barked a laugh. "We've hardly begun, sir. Another eight hours, at least, until we meet up with my men coming from the Thames."

I felt dizzy and nauseated again at hearing this. How long had it been since I had truly slept—not lost consciousness due to King Lazaree's or Drood's drugs, but slept? Forty-eight hours? Seventy-two?

I clumsily climbed down to where Barris and two other men waited in the wobbling punt, and with one of those men poling gondolier-fashion at the front and the other steering with a sweep from the stern, we left the river and moved slowly up a brick side tunnel. I sat on a thwart near the centre of the sixteen-foot craft while Barris stood nearby, using a second pole to balance himself. The moss-covered brick roof was so low here that Barris could reach up and help push the punt along; I could see the green stain on his expensive tan gloves.

I was half-dozing when the narrow sewer channel opened to a stream twenty feet wide.

"Sir!" said the detective in the bow and aimed his bullseye lantern forward.

Four feral Wild Boys were in water up to their waists, wrestling with something heavy and soggy that looked to have just tumbled out of a smaller pipe high on this larger sewer's curved wall.

We slid closer and I realised that the "something soggy" was a man's corpse. The boys had been going through the green thing's disintegrating jacket and pockets. The four boys froze in our projected lantern light, their eyes reflecting back wide and white and inhuman.

An almost vertiginous sense of déjà vu rolled over me until I realised that I was seeing a scene straight out of the serialised sensationalist tale *The Wild Boys of London; or, The Children of the Night—A Story of the Present Day* that both Dickens and I had mentioned—each embarrassed that he had read it—when we had first come down here almost two years ago.

The dead man's face seemed to be moving, shimmering, as we approached, almost as if the grub-white and decaying features were covered with a very fine, translucent silken cloth. His eyes appeared to be blinking open, then closing; his mouth muscles seemed to be twitching as if he were attempting a smile, perhaps a rueful one at being part of a tableau out of such a poorly written and sensationalist tale.

Then I saw that it was not the facial muscles of the corpse moving. The man's face, hands, every exposed part, were totally covered with a thin film of constantly shifting maggots.

"Stop!" cried Barris as the Wild Boys dropped their soggy burden back into the thick sludge of the stream and turned to run.

Our man in the bow kept the bullseye's beam on the scattering pack while his compatriot gave our skiff or punt a powerful shove with his pole sunk deep into the sludge at the bottom of this pipe. Except for the distasteful addition of the maggots, I was enjoying the unreal, sensationalist absurdity of all this.

"Stop!" Barris cried again. Suddenly the detective had a small silver revolver in his hand. I had no idea then—nor to this day—why he would want to detain these feral creatures.

Two of the boys had pulled themselves up into a high drain that seemed too small to allow access even to these improbably thin and starving wraiths, but with a burst of wriggling, they disappeared. One almost expected the *pop* of a champagne cork as the second boy's pale, bare soles wriggled and thrashed out of sight. The third boy crouched low and slithered head-first into yet another pipe on the opposite side.

The fourth boy reached elbow-deep into the stream he stood in and hurled two handfuls of muck at our approaching boat. The detective with the bullseye ducked and shouted an oath. I heard filth splatter across the thwart where I sat and saw some strike Reginald Barris on the lapels of his heavy wool coat.

I laughed.

Barris fired the pistol twice. The report in the narrow brick tunnel was so loud and startling that I threw my hands over my ears.

The Wild Boy pitched face forward into the water.

The punt floated past the man's maggot-writhed corpse until we reached the boy. The detective with the pole reached down and turned the boy over, pulled him half into the boat. Filthy, reeking water dripped from the boy's rags and open mouth into our punt.

He was no older than ten or eleven. One of Barris's bullets had gone through his throat, severing the jugular. Blood still pumped from that wound, although very weakly. The other bullet had entered his cheek just below the boy's eye, which remained wide open and staring, as if in reproof. His eyes were blue.

Our man with the pole let the corpse slide back into the black water.

I got to my feet and grabbed Barris by his broad shoulders. "You've killed a child!"

"There are no children in Undertown," was Barris's cool, unconcerned reply. "Only vermin."

I remember attacking him then. Only profound exertions by the detective with the pole and by the one in the stern using the tiller as a balancing staff kept the wobbling punt from turning over, adding our four bodies to the stream holding the maggot-ridden man and the murdered boy.

I remember making sounds as I attacked Barris, but not forming words—mere grunts and half-stifled screams, garbled syllables without meaning. I did not attack the detective with my fists, as a man might, but with fingers raking like claws and fingernails clawing for his eyes, the way a madwoman might.

I half-remember Barris holding me off with one hand until it became apparent that I would not desist and was going to knock us all into the black water. I half-remember my screaming becoming more intense and my saliva spattering the young detective's handsome face and him saying something to the man in the stern behind me and then the silver pistol coming up, its barrel short but heavy and flashing in the bobbing bullseye lantern light.

And then—blessedly—I remember nothing but darkness with no dreams.

CHAPTER THIRTY

I awoke to find myself in my own bed in daylight, in my own nightshirt, in great pain and with Caroline hovering—and frowning—over me. My skull was pounding in a greater agony than I had hitherto experienced and every muscle, sinew, bone, and cell in my body was grinding against its neighbour in an off-key chorus of pain-filled physical despair. I felt as if days or weeks had passed since I had taken any of my medicinal laudanum.

"Who is Martha?" demanded Caroline.

"What?" I could barely speak. My lips were dried and cracked, my tongue swollen.

"Who is Martha?" repeated Caroline. Her voice was as flat and unsympathetic as a pistol shot.

Of all the various sorts of panic I had experienced during the past two years, including awakening blind in an underground crypt, none was as terrible as this. I felt like a man sitting fat and secure in his comfortable carriage only to feel it suddenly lurch off a cliff.

"Martha?" I managed to say. "Caroline…my dear… what are you talking about?"

"You've been saying…repeating…'Martha' in your sleep for two days and nights," said Caroline, neither her expression nor her tone softening. "*Who* is Martha?"

"Two days and nights! How long have I been unconscious? How did I get here? Why is this bandage on my head?"

"Who is Martha?" repeated Caroline.

"Martha...is Dickens's character from *David Copperfield*," I said, touching the thick bandage wrapped around my skull and feigning disinterest in the conversation. "You know...the girl of the streets who walks by the filthy, corrupted Thames. I think I was dreaming about the river."

Caroline crossed her arms over her chest and blinked.

Never underestimate, Dear Reader, the resourcefulness of a novelist in an untenable situation, even when he is in such a dire condition as I was that day.

"How long have I been sleeping?" I asked again.

"It's Wednesday afternoon," Caroline said at last. "We heard knocking at the door on Sunday mid-day and found you unconscious on the stoop. Where had you been, Wilkie? Charley—he and Kate have been here twice; he reports your mother is about the same—said Mrs Wells reported that you left your mother's without a word of explanation late on Saturday night. Where did you go? Why did your clothes—we had to burn them—stink of smoke and...of something worse? What happened to your head? Frank Beard has been here three times to look at you and was quite worried about the gash on your temple and the possible concussion to your brain. He was afraid you were in a coma. He was afraid that you might never awaken. Where have you *been*? Why in God's name are you dreaming about a Dickens character named *Martha*?"

"In a minute," I said, leaning over the side of the bed but deciding that I would not be able to stand, or, if I did manage to stand, be capable of walking. "I shall answer your questions in a minute, but first have the girl bring in a basin. Quickly. I am going to be sick."

Dear reader from my distant future, it seems quite possible—even probable—that in your Far Country a hundred years and more hence, all disease has been conquered, all pain banished, all the mortal afflictions so common to men of my time become no more than a distant hint of an echo of history's rumour. But in my century, Dear Reader, despite our inevitable *hubris* as we compared ourselves to more primitive cultures, in truth we had little knowledge with which to battle disease or injury and few effective chemists' potions to utilise in our pathetic attempts to ameliorate mankind's oldest enemy—pain.

My friend Frank Beard was better than most practitioners of his dubious trade. He did not bleed me. He did not apply leeches to my belly or bring out his arsenal of ugly steel instruments with which to trepan or trephine me (that nineteenth-century surgeon's habit of casually and obscenely boring a hole in the patient's aching skull as if coring an apple with a carpenter's bit-and-brace, popping the circle of white bone out as easy as popping the cork on a bottle of wine, all the while acting as though it were the most normal thing in the world to do). No, Frank Beard visited frequently, fretted and brooded honestly, checked the gash and bruise at my hairline, changed dressings, queried me anxiously about my ongoing and worsening pain, advised rest and a milk diet, gave quiet instructions to Caroline, tut-tutted to me about my laudanum intake but did not order me to stop it, and—in the end—honoured the true spirit of Hippocrates by first doing no harm. Just as with his more famous patient and friend—Charles Dickens—Frank Beard the physician worried about me without being able to help me.

So I remained in agony.

I had regained consciousness—such as it was—in my own bed on 22 January, five days after my final descent to King Lazaree's den. For the rest of that week I was too ill to get out of bed, even though my need to visit Mother was almost absolute. In all my years of pain from rheumatical gout, I had never experienced anything like this. Beyond the usual aches of muscles and joints and bowels, it was as if some great, throbbing, burning source of pain had embedded itself deep behind my right eye.

Or as if some huge insect had burrowed into my brain.

It was during this time that I remembered something odd that Dickens had said to me years earlier.

We had been discussing modern surgery in general terms, and Dickens mentioned in passing "a certain simple medical procedure I had undergone years ago, not long before my trip to America..."

Dickens did not elaborate, but I knew through Katey Dickens and others what that surgery—hardly a "simple procedure"—had been. Dickens, while then working on *Barnaby Rudge*, had begun experiencing ever more severe rectal pains. (How these would have compared to my present excruciating headache, I cannot say.) The doctors diagnosed a "fistula"—literally a gap in the rectal wall through which tissue was being forced.

Dickens had no choice but to undergo immediate surgery and chose Dr Frederick Salmon—the author thirteen years before of *A Practical Essay on the Structure of the Rectum*—to perform it. The procedure consisted of the rectum being widened by a blade, then opened up by a series of clamps, then held even wider apart by some vicious surgical appliance, while the intruding tissue was slowly and carefully cut away and then the loose ends pressed back out of the rectal cavity, and finally the rectal wall sewn together.

And Dickens had undergone this with no morphia, no opium, nor any sort of what some are now calling "anaesthetic." Katey reported (all this learned from her mother, of course) that her father had remained cheerful during the surgery and was active shortly afterwards. Within days he was writing *Barnaby Rudge* again, but, one must add, while lying on a sofa with extra cushions available. And his huge and exhausting First American Tour was looming.

But I digress from my point.

Dickens's comments about this "certain simple medical procedure" were about our fortunately fallible human memory in regards to pain.

"It's often struck me, my dear Wilkie," he said that day as we were riding somewhere through Kent in a brougham, "that in a real sense, we have no true memory of pain. Oh, yes—we can recall we had it and remember quite vividly how terrible it was and how we wish never to experience it again—but we cannot truly *recall* it, can we? We remember the *state*, but not the true *particulars* the way one might remember...say... a fine meal. I suspect that this is the reason that women agree to go through the agonies of childbirth more than once—they have simply forgotten the *specifics* of their earlier agonies. And that, my dear Wilkie, is my point."

"What is?" I had asked. "Childbirth?"

"Not at all," Dickens said. "Rather, the contrast between *pain* and *luxury*. Pain we remember in a general (yet terrible) way but cannot really recall; luxury we recall in every detail. Ask yourself if this is not true! Once one has tasted the finest of wines, smoked the best cigars, dined in the most wonderful restaurants... even ridden in such luxury as this brougham in which we ride today...much less gained an acquaintance of a truly beautiful woman, all lesser experiences in each category continue to pale for years, decades...a lifetime! Pain we cannot truly recall; *luxury*—in all its Sybaritic details—we can never forget."

Well, perhaps. But I assure you, Dear Reader, that

the terrible pain I was suffering in January, February, March, and April of 1868 was of a nature and horrible specificity that I shall never forget.

IF A FARMER IS ILL, others till the fields in his place. If a soldier falls ill, he reports to the infirmary and is replaced on the field of battle. If a tradesman falls ill, others—perhaps his wife—must perform daily duties in his shop. If a queen falls ill, millions pray for her and voices and footsteps are muffled in her bedroom wing of the palace. But in all these cases, the work of the farm, army, shop, or nation goes on.

If a writer falls terribly ill, everything stops. If he dies, his "business" ends forever. In this sense, a popular writer's career is most like that of a famous actor—but even the most famous actor has an understudy. A writer does not. No one can replace him. His distinctive voice is everything. This is especially true for a popular writer whose work is already in the process of being serialised in a major national magazine. *The Moonstone* had begun its serial run both in our English *All the Year Round* and the Americans' *Harper's Weekly* in January. Although I had several numbers written in advance of this initial publication, those were already being set in type; new instalments would be needed almost immediately. They existed only in rough note and outline form and were yet to be written.

This pressure brought on a terror on top of my terror, a pain of pressure on top of the pressure of pain crawling and digging its way through my screaming brain and body.

In that first week of my new misery, unable to sit up and hold a pen, racked in unspeakable pain and confined to bed, I attempted dictating the next chapter to Caroline and then to her daughter, Carrie. Neither could tolerate the screams and moans of agony that, unbidden, interrupted and punctuated my attempts at dictation. Both would rush to my side in an attempt to soothe me rather than sit and wait for dictation to resume.

By the weekend, Caroline had hired a male amanuensis to sit in a nearby chair and take my dictation. But this secretary, obviously of a sensitive nature, could also not bear my moans, expostulations, and involuntary writhings. He quit after the first hour. The second male amanuensis on Monday seemed to have little care or empathy for my pain, but he also seemed incapable of pulling the dictated sentences and punctuations out of the background of my cries and moans. He was fired after the second hour.

That Monday night, with the household asleep but the agony from hard-pincered scuttlings in my brain and then down along my spine keeping me from being able to sleep—or just to lie still—even after half a dozen self-ministrations of laudanum, I got out of bed and staggered to the window, pulling back the funereally heavy drapes and raising the blinds to look out at the slushy darkness towards Portman Square.

Somewhere out there, I was certain, however invisible to a layman's eye, one or more of Inspector Field's agents still stood watch. He would never abandon me now, not after what I had seen and learned of his operations.

For days I had begged Caroline for the newspaper and asked her for copies of the *Times* which I had missed while in my coma. But those newspapers had been thrown away and the few recent ones I was able to peruse made no mention of a former policeman's eviscerated body being found in a slum cemetery. There was no account of fires breaking out in areas near the Thames or in the Fleet Ditch sewer system, and Caroline only looked at me oddly when I asked if she had heard of such fires.

I queried Frank Beard when he came and my brother, Charles, in his turn, but neither had noticed mention of any detective's murder nor of any subterranean fires. Both Beard and Charley assumed that my queries were the result of nightmares I had been having—it was certainly true that my few scattered hours of sleep gained during this entire period were ruled by terrible nightmares—and I made no effort to disabuse them of that theory.

Obviously Inspector Field has used his influence to keep the police and newspapers quiet about Sergeant Hatchery's terrible murder... but why?

Perhaps Field—and his hundred or more men who had come to the punitive expedition beneath the city—simply had kept the fact of the murder from the police.

But, again... why?

I had neither strength of body nor adequate mental concentration that Monday night as I clung to the drapes and looked out at the cold, foggy London January midnight to answer my own questions, but I looked for Inspector Field's inevitable eavesdropping detectives as if peering into darkness in search of a Saviour.

Why? How can Inspector Field help me stop this pain?

The scarab moved an inch or two at the base of my brain and I screamed twice, muffling the second scream in a wad of velvet drapery stuffed into my mouth.

Field was the second chess player in this terrible game, matched in his ability to provide counterweight to the monster Drood perhaps only by the absent Charles Dickens (whose motives were even less understandable), and I realised that I had begun ascribing impossible, almost mystical, abilities to the old, fat, side-whiskered detective.

I needed someone to save me.

There was no one.

Sobbing, I staggered back to my bed, held on to the post as the moving pain blinded me for a moment, and then managed the few faltering steps to my dressing bureau. The key to the lowest drawer was there in my brush box, beneath the lining, where I kept it hidden.

The gun that Detective Hatchery had given me was still there beneath fresh linen.

I lifted it out—amazed again by its terrible weight— and staggered back to sit on the edge of the bed near the single burning candle. Tugging on my glasses, I realised that I must look as mad as I felt, my hair and beard in wild disarray, my face distorted in an almost constant open-mouthed moan, my eyes wild with pain and terror, and my nightshirt rucked up above pale, shivering shanks.

As best I could, given my total unfamiliarity with firearms, I ascertained that the bullets were still in their cylindered receptacles. I remember thinking, *This pain will never end. This scarab will never leave.* The Moonstone *will never be finished. In weeks, tens of thousands of people will line up to buy the next issue of* All the Year Round *and* Harper's Weekly *only to find empty white pages.*

The idea of emptiness, of void, appealed to me that night beyond all words to describe it.

I raised the pistol towards my face and inserted the heavy, broad barrel in my mouth. The small bead of what I assumed was a gun sight tapped my front tooth as the barrel slid in.

Someone long ago—it may have been the old actor Macready—had explained to several of us around a happy table that someone serious about blowing his brains out had to fire the bullet upward through the soft palate rather than against the hard outer bone of the skull that too frequently deflected the projectile and left the would-be suicide as a pain-riddled vegetable and object of derision rather than a corpse.

My arms shaking wildly—all of me shaking—I held the anvil-heavy weapon as steady as I could and raised one hand to pull the massive hammer back until it clicked into place. As I was finishing this operation, I realised that if my sweaty thumb had slipped, the gun would already have fired and the bullet would already have ricocheted around through the remaining pulp of my brain.

And the scarab would be dead—or at least would be left to eat and burrow in peace, since I would no longer be feeling this pain.

I began shaking harder, weeping as I shook, but I did not remove the obscene pistol's barrel from my mouth. The reflex to gag was very strong, and if I had not vomited half a dozen times already that afternoon and evening, I am sure I would have done so then. As it was, my stomach cramped, my throat spasmed, but I kept the barrel in place and angling upward in my mouth, feeling the steel circle touching the soft palate of which Macready had spoken.

I set my thumb on the trigger and began applying pressure. My chattering teeth closed on the long barrel. I realised that I had been holding my breath but could do so no longer and gasped in a final breath.

I could breathe through the pistol barrel.

How many people knew this was possible? I could taste the sour-sweet bite of gun oil—applied long ago by the dead Detective Hatchery, no doubt, but still strong to the tongue—and the cold, vaguely coppery taste of the steel itself. But I could breathe through the pistol even as I bit down on the barrel on all sides, and as I did so, taking long racking breaths, I could hear the whistle of my inhalations and exhalations around the cavitied cylinder and out the echoing chamber near where the hammer was pulled back and cocked.

How many men had ended their lives with this as the last, irrelevant thought passing through their brains so soon to be dead, scattered, cooling, and thoughtless?

The novelist-sensed irony of this was more painful than the scarab-pain and I began laughing. It was a strange, muffled, and oddly obscene sort of laughter, distorted as it was around a pistol barrel. After a moment I pulled the pistol from my mouth—the otherwise dull metal glistening in the candlelight due to the film of my saliva along its length—and, still idly holding the cocked weapon, I lifted the candle and staggered out of my room.

Downstairs, the doors to my new study were closed but not locked. I went in and pulled the broad double doors closed behind me.

The Other Wilkie sat sideways behind my desk, reading a book in the near total darkness. He looked up at me as I came in and adjusted spectacles that reflected my candle, hiding his eyes behind two vertical, flickering columns of yellow flame. I noticed that his beard was slightly shorter and slightly less grey than mine.

"You require my help," said the Other Wilkie.

Never, not in all the years since my first, vague childhood sense that my Other Self existed, had the Other Wilkie ever spoken to me or uttered any sound. I was surprised at how feminine his voice sounded.

"Yes," I whispered hoarsely. "I require your help."

I realised stupidly that the cocked and loaded pistol was still in my right hand. I could raise it now and fire five—six?—bullets into that too-solid-looking flesh sitting presumptuously behind my desk.

When the Other Wilkie dies, will I die? When I die, will the Other Wilkie die? The questions made me giggle, but the giggle came out as a sort of sob.

"Shall we start tonight?" asked the Other Wilkie, laying the book down open on my blotter. He removed his spectacles to wipe them on a kerchief (which he kept in the same jacket pocket in which I kept mine), and I noticed that even without the spectacle-glass in front of them to reflect, his eyes were still two flickering vertical cat's irises of flame.

"No, not tonight," I said.

"But soon?" He set the small spectacles back on his face.

"Yes," I said. "Soon."

"I will come to you," said the Other Wilkie.

I had just enough energy left to nod. Still in bare feet, still carrying the cocked pistol, I left my study, closed the heavy doors behind me, padded up the staircase, went into my room, collapsed onto my bed, and fell asleep atop the tumbled bedcovers with the gun still in my hand and my finger still taut on its curved, cold trigger.

CHAPTER THIRTY-ONE

*F*or years I had explained to Caroline that I was not free to marry her because my high-strung mother, who had always suffered from excitability and who was now dying from it (according to Dr Beard), simply would never understand—or agree to—such an arrangement with a formerly married woman who, it would be discovered after marriage, had shared my home for years. I explained that I had to spare the delicate old woman (who, in truth, was not that delicate at all except for her excitability) such a shock. Caroline never fully accepted the argument, but after some years she had ceased to challenge it.

Now Mother was dying.

On Thursday, 30 January—a week and a day after I'd awakened in my bed after the Undertown burnings and Barris's attack on me—Caroline helped dress me, and Charley all but carried me to a carriage that took us to the railway station. I had sedated the scarab into relative calm by doubling my usual high dosage of laudanum, sometimes drinking straight from a large decanter.

My plan was to continue this high dosage and to do my writing at Mother's cottage until she died. After that milestone was reached and passed, I would work out a way to deal with Caroline, the scarab in my brain, and my other problems.

. . .

Travelling by rail to Tunbridge Wells and South-borough, I was so sick and shaky that poor Charley with his aching stomach had to put his arm around me and sit sideways on the outside seat so as to shield me somewhat from public view. I tried to stifle my moans, but I am sure that some were audible to the other passengers over the sounds of the locomotive, rails, and our hurtling passage through the cold air of the countryside. God alone knows what noises the scarab and I might have made if I had not taken the massive doses of laudanum.

I had a sudden, terrible, total insight into what a hell it had been for Charles Dickens in the two and a half years since Staplehurst—especially on his exhausting and demanding reading tours, including the American one he was in the middle of at that moment—as he forced himself almost every day and night to ride the shaking, quaking, freezing or stifling, smoke-filled, rocking, coal-and-sweat-reeking carriages from city to city.

Did Dickens have his own scarab? Does Dickens have a scarab now?

This is all I could think about as the carriage rumbled on. If Dickens *had* a Drood-implanted scarab but some-how rid himself of it—*by the public murder of an innocent man?*—then Dickens was my only hope. If Dickens still carried the monster beetle but had learned to live and work and function with it, Dickens was still my best hope.

The carriage rocked and I moaned. Heads turned. I buried my face in the wet-wool scent of Charley's over-coat for solace and escape, then remembered doing pre-cisely the same thing in the dark cloakroom of the boarding school when I was a boy.

My letter to the Harper Brothers in America, I thought, opened with the perfect blend of masculine sadness and professionalism:

"The dangerous illness of my mother has called me to her cottage in the country and I am working at my story as best I can, in intervals of attendance at her bedside."

I went on—equally professionally—about my revisions and shipping of the twelfth and thirteenth weekly parts of the novel and spent some time first praising and then correcting some of the illustration proofs they had sent me. (My first of a series of epistolary narrators, head-servant Gabriel Betteredge, had been depicted in the artist's renderings as wearing *livery.* This would never do, as I explained to the Americans, since the head-servant in a fine house such as the one he served would wear plain black clothes and would look, with his white cravat and grey hair, like an old clergyman.) But I finished with what I considered to be a fine personal flourish—

> *You may rely on my sparing no effort to study your convenience, after the readiness that you have shown to consider mine. I am very glad to hear that you like the story so far. There are some effects to come, which—unless I am altogether mistaken—have never been tried in fiction before.*

I confess that this last sentence sounded a trifle bold, perhaps even a tad presumptuous, but my plan for the mystery of the stolen Moonstone depended upon a long and accurate description of a man walking and acting in the night totally under the influence of opium—performing complicated operations of which he would have absolutely no memory the next morning or any day thereafter until helped, by a more self-aware opium eater, to recover those memories—and I did believe that these scenes and themes were unprecedented in serious English fiction.

As for working during intervals of attendance at my mother's bedside, I did not feel it relevant or appropriate to explain that those intervals of attendance were very few and far apart, even though I was spending all my time in her cottage. The truth was, Mother could not abide my presence in her bedroom.

Charley had warned me that in the almost two weeks of my absence, Mother had regained the ability to speak, but "speech" certainly is not the accurate descriptor of the screams, moans, inchoate shouts, and animal-like noises she made when anyone—but especially I—was in attendance.

When Charley and I first stood in her presence that Thursday afternoon on the next-to-last day in January, I was shocked to the point of nausea by her appearance. Mother had seemed to lose all her living weight, so the figure in the bed, still distorted, was little more than mottled skin laid over bone and sinew. She reminded me—I could not help the association!—of a dead baby bird I had found in our garden once when I was very young. Like that young bird's corpse (with its terrible featherless and folded wings), Mother's dark and blotchy skin was translucent, showing the shape of things meant to be left unseen beneath.

Her irises—just barely discernible between half-lowered lids—still fluttered like trapped sparrows.

But she had indeed regained some vocal powers. When I stood next to her bed that afternoon she writhed, the folded bird wings flapped and vibrated, her twisted wrists fluttered her claw-hands back and forth wildly, and she screamed. It was, as I say, as much growl as scream—a calliope letting off terrible pressure—and the sound made what little hair I had left on the back of my head twist in terror.

As Mother twisted and moaned, I began to twist and moan. It must have been terrible for Charley, who had to grab my arms to hold me upright. (Mrs Wells had hurried away at my arrival and continued to avoid me for the three days I spent at Mother's. I had no way—and little reason—to explain to her what I had been doing the night she saw me raising Mother's nightdress to check for beetle entry; one does not explain oneself to servants.)

I could feel the scarab in my brain scuttling to and fro even as I writhed and moaned. I sensed—I *knew*—that an identical scarab in Mother was reacting to my (and my parasite's) presence.

There was nothing I could do but moan and collapse into Charley's arms. He half-dragged, half-carried me to the sofa in the other room. Mother's screams abated somewhat when we were out of her presence. My scarab quieted. I caught the shadow-glimpse out of the corner of my eye of Mrs Wells hurrying in as Charley tended to me near the fireplace in Mother's main living area.

And so it went for the three days I was with Mother—or that clawing, screaming, writhing, agony-filled thing which had *been* Mother—in her cottage at Southborough just beyond Tunbridge Wells.

Charley was there the whole time, which was good, since Mrs Wells certainly would have given up her duties caring for Mother if he had not been there as a buffer. If my brother ever wondered why Mrs Wells and I took pains never to be alone together in a room for a single moment, he never asked. On Friday, Frank Beard came—announced again that there was no hope—and injected her with morphia so that she could sleep. Before he left that night, he injected me with morphia as well. Those may have been the only few hours of silence in which poor, hurting Charley found a few hours' sleep while Mrs Wells watched over Mother.

I TRIED TO WORK while I was at Mother's. I had brought my japanned tin box of notes and research materials and sat as long as I could at Mother's tiny desk near the front windows, but my pen hand seemed to have no power in it. I would have to shift the pen to my left hand just to dip the nib in ink. And even then no words would flow. For three days I stared at a manuscript page unblemished by fiction save for three or four lame lines which I eventually scratched out.

After three such days, we all surrendered the pretence that my presence there was needed. Mother could not abide my proximity; every time I entered the room she would get worse, raving and writhing, and my pain would increase until I swooned or retreated.

Charley packed my things and brought me back to London on the afternoon express. He had wired ahead and arranged for Frank Beard and my servant George to meet us at the station—it took the three of them to lift me into the rented carriage. Once carried through my own front door and upstairs to my room, I did not fail to see the look that Caroline G—— gave me: there was alarm in that look, and perhaps affection, but there was also embarrassment and disdain, perhaps even disdain bordering on disgust.

Beard gave me an extra-large injection of morphia that evening and I fell into a deep sleep.

. . .

Awake in peace!
You yourself beautifully awaken in peace!
Heru of Edfu wakes himself to life!
The gods themselves raise to worship your spirit,
You who are the venerable winged disc that rises in the
sky!
For you are the one, the ball of the sun that pierces the sky,
That now floods the land rapidly in the east,
Then sinks as the setting sun each day, passing the night
in Inuet.

Heru of Edfu
Who wakes himself in peace,
The great master god of the sky,
The one whose plumage is multi-coloured,
Rising on the horizon,
The great winged disc that protects the sanctuaries!
You yourself awake in peace!
Ihy, who wakes himself in peace,
The Great, son of Hwt-Hwr,
Made noble by the Golden One of the Neteru!
You yourself awake in peace!
Awake in peace!
Ihy, son of Hwt-Hrw, awake in peace!
The beautiful lotus of the Golden One!
You yourself awake in peace!
Awake in peace Harsiesis, son of Osiris,
The inheritor without reproach originating from the
Powerful One,
Produced by Ounennefer, the Victorious!
You yourself awake in peace!
Awake in peace Osiris!
The Great God who takes his place in Iunet,
The elder son of Geb!
You yourself awake in peace!
Awake in peace the Neteru and the Neteretu that are in
Tarer,
The Ennead around His Majesty!
You yourself awake in peace!

I AWOKE IN DARKNESS and pain and confusion.

Never before had I dreamt only in words—in chants of words—and in a language I could not understand but which my mind—or scarab—somehow had been able to translate. The reek of incense and oily smoke from the braziers lingered in my nostrils. The echo of long-dead voices in stone barrows rang in my ears. Burned into my vision, as though a retinal red circle from staring into the sun for too long, were the faces and bodies of the Neteru, the Gods of the Black Lands: Nuit, Lady of the Stars; Ast, or Isis, Queen of Heaven; Asar, or Osiris, God of our Fathers; Nebt-Het, or Nepthys, Goddess of the Death Which Is Not Eternal; Suti, or Set, the Adversary; Heru, or Horus, Lord of Things to Come; Anpu, or Anubis, Guide to the Dead; Djewhty, or Thoth, Keeper of the Book of Life.

Filled with the pain of the scarab's stirrings, I cried out in the darkness.

No one came—it was sometime in the earliest morning hours, the door to the bedroom was closed, and Caroline and her daughter were downstairs behind their own closed doors—but as the echoes of my scream faded in my aching skull, I realised that there was someone or something else in the bedroom with me. I could hear its breathing. I could sense its presence, not as that slight, subliminal sensing of human warmth by which we sometimes become aware of the presence of other people near us in the dark, but by a perception of the thing's coldness. It was as if something were pulling the last warmth from the air.

I fumbled on the dresser, found matches, lighted the candle.

The Other Wilkie was sitting there on the small, hard chair just beyond the foot of my bed. He was wearing a black frock-like coat that I had cast away some years earlier and had a small writing board on his lap with some blank paper on it. There was a pencil in his left hand. The nails on his hand were bitten down closer than mine usually were.

"What do you want?" I whispered.

"I'm waiting for you to begin dictating," said the Other Wilkie.

I noted again that his voice was not as deep or as resonant as my own. But then...does one ever *really* hear the tone and timbre of one's own voice?

"Dictating what?" I managed to ask.

The Other Wilkie waited. After a hundred of my heartbeats he said, "Do you wish to dictate the content of your dreams or the next part of *The Moonstone*?"

I hesitated. This must be some sort of trap. If I did not offer to begin dictating the details and ceremonies of the Gods of the Black Lands, would the scarab begin tunnelling its way out through my skull or face? Would the last thing I ever saw or felt be the huge pincers cutting their way out of my cheek or eye?

"*The Moonstone*," I said. "But I will write it myself."

I was too weak to rise. A half-minute of struggling only got me propped awkwardly higher on my pillows. But the scarab did not assassinate me. Perhaps, I thought hopefully, it did not understand English.

"We should lock the door," I whispered. "I'll do it." But again I did not have the strength to rise.

The Other Wilkie got up, shot the bolt home, and resumed his seat, his pencil poised. I saw that he wrote with his left hand. I was right-handed.

He closed the bolt and locked the door, part of my aching brain was trying to tell me. *He...it...can affect things in the physical world.*

Of course he could. Hadn't the green-skinned wench with the tusk teeth left livid marks on my neck?

The Other Wilkie waited.

Between moans and the occasional cry of pain, I began—

"*FIRST NARRATIVE*—all capitals for that—*Contributed by MISS CLACK*—capitals on the name as well, mind you—colon after the name—*niece of the late Sir John Verinder*...triple spaces...*CHAPTER ONE*, in Roman numeral...double space...*I am indebted to my dear parents, who are now both dead*...no, change that...begin parenthesis, *both now in Heaven,* end parenthesis...*for having had habits of order and regularly instilled into me at a young*...no, Miss Clack was never young, make that...*at a very early age,* full stop, begin new paragraph."

I moaned and collapsed further back into the sweat-soaked pillow. The other Wilkie, pencil poised, waited patiently.

I HAD MANAGED ONLY two or three nightmare-riddled hours of sleep when there came a pounding on my bedroom door. I fumbled my watch off the nightstand and saw that it was almost eleven AM. The pounding resumed along with Caroline's stern but concerned voice, "Wilkie, let me in."

"Come in," I said.

"I cannot. The door is locked."

It took me a few minutes to gather the energy to throw back the covers and stagger over to throw the bolt.

"Why on earth was this locked?" asked Caroline as she bustled in and fluttered around me. I went back to bed and drew the bedclothes across my legs.

"I was working," I said. "Writing."

"Working?" She saw the small stack of pages still on the wooden chair and picked them up. "These are in pencil," she said. "When have you ever written in pencil?"

"I can hardly use a pen while lying here on my back."

"Wilkie..." said Caroline, looking at me strangely over the sheaf of papers "...this is not your hand." She gave me the pages.

It certainly was not my handwriting. The hastily pencilled words slanted the wrong way (as befitted a left-handed writer, I realised), the letters were formed differently—sharper, more spiked, almost aggressive in the indecorous bluntness—and even the spacing and use of margins were alien to my style. After a moment I said, "You saw that the door was locked. The pain kept me awake most of the night, so I wrote. Neither you nor Carrie nor any of the spineless amanuenses you brought here could take my dictation, so I have no choice but to write it myself. The new numbers will be due in both America and Wills's office *in a week*. What choice do I have but to work through the night, using my left hand to write with the pencil when my right hand fails me? It's a wonder that the hand is legible at all."

This was the longest speech I had given since I'd been discovered unconscious on our doorstep on 22 January, but Mrs G—— did not seem impressed.

"It's more legible than your usual manuscript," said Caroline. She looked around. "Where is the pencil you used?"

Absurdly, I blushed. The Other Wilkie must have carried it off with him when he left sometime after dawn. *Through the locked door and solid walls.* I said, "I must have dropped it. It may have rolled under the bed."

"Well...I have to say from the few paragraphs I've just read," said Caroline, "that neither this terrible new illness nor your mother's illness has dulled your writing ability. Just the opposite, from the short bits here. This narrative of Miss Clack is wildly funny. I had thought you were going to make her more pathetic and dour, a mere caricature—but on this first page or two she seems a truly comic character. I look forward to reading the rest soon."

When she left to direct the girl in the preparation of my breakfast tray, I looked through the surprisingly thick sheaf of pages. The first sentence was precisely as I had dictated it. Nothing else was.

Caroline had been correct in her hasty assessment: this "Miss Clack"—the insufferable old busybody religious pamphleteer—had been sketched in with great energy and dexterity. The paragraphs and descriptive passages, all seen from the old woman's distorted view of herself, of course, since she was the narrator, moved with a much greater authorial assurance and light comic hand than had the longer, more convoluted and heavy-handed passages I had dictated during the night.

D——n his eyes! The Other Wilkie was writing *The Moonstone* and there was nothing I could do about it.

And he was the better writer.

CHAPTER THIRTY-TWO

*M*other died on the nineteenth of March.

I was not there when she died. Since I was not able to attend the funeral, I asked my friend Holman Hunt, with whom I'd gone to the theatre just the week before to see my *No Thoroughfare* again, to go in my place, writing—*"I am sure it will be a comfort to him..."* by which I meant my brother, Charles, *"...to see the face of a dear old friend whom my mother loved, and whom we love."*

In truth, Dear Reader, I have no idea if Mother loved Holman Hunt or if he had any serious affection for her, but he had taken dinner with her a few times in my presence, so I saw no reason that he could not fill that missing presence at Harriet Collins's funeral.

You may think me cold or unfeeling for not going to my own mother's funeral, when my illness may have— *would* have—allowed me to, but you would not think this if you had known my heart and mind at this time. It was all too terribly logical. If I went to Mother's cottage with Charley to view the body, what reaction would her scarab and mine have to the other's proximity? The thought of that beetle lurching and digging and scrabbling in Mother's dead body was too much for me to bear.

And—before the funeral, when the casket was still in the parlour of her cottage and open so that friends could pay their respects—what would happen to me if I saw (especially if I were the only one who could see) those scarab pincers and that beetle head and carapace slowly creeping out from between Mother's dead white lips? Or what if it exited some other way—through her ear, or eye, or throat?

My sanity could not have borne it.

And for the funeral itself, as her coffin was lowered into the frozen hole next to our father's grave, I would have been the only one leaning forward and waiting, and listening, and waiting and listening more, even after the first clods of dirt struck the lid of the casket.

Who knew better than I that there were tunnels everywhere under London and terrible things moving in those tunnels? Who knew what awful impulses and manners and means of Droodish control the burrowing scarab, now almost certainly grown as large as Mother's brain had been after the chitinous creature had consumed all the dying and dead brain matter, was subject to?

So I stayed home, in bed, suffering.

By late february I had begun writing again, composing *The Moonstone* at my desk in my study when I was able, writing while propped up in bed more often than not. When I was working alone in my study or bedroom, the Other Wilkie often joined me, staring silently at me in an almost reproachful way. It had crossed my mind that he might have been planning to replace me (in writing this book and the next, in receiving plaudits for it, in Caroline's bed, in society at large) should I die. Who would ever know? Had I not recently planned to replace Charles Dickens in much the same way?

I realised that the suddenly revealed illness (and even

more sudden death) of one of my characters—the much-loved and much-respected Lady Verinder, never a central character but always a reassuring and noble off-stage presence—almost certainly came from the deeper parts of my creative mind and were a way of honouring Mother's death.

I should mention here that the scarab obviously could not read things through my eyes; each night that Frank Beard injected me with morphia, I continued to dream of the Neteru Gods of the Black Land and all their attendant and requisite ceremonies, but I never once became the scribe Drood had commanded me to become; I never once *wrote* about those dark and heathen gods.

The beetle in my brain seemed assuaged when I was writing, obviously fooled into thinking that I was recording my dreams of these ancient rituals. And all that time I was actually writing about curious old servant Gabriel Betteredge (and his obsession with *Robinson Crusoe,* a book I also venerated) and plucky (if stupidly headstrong) Rachel Verinder and heroic (if strangely duped) Franklin Blake and the misshapen and doomed-to-drown-in-quicksand servant Rosanna Spearman and the meddling, pious pamphleteer Miss Clack (whose hilarious malice was the Other Wilkie's contribution) and, of course, the clever (but never central to the solution of the mystery) Sergeant Cuff. The parasite within me thought all this frenzied scribbling through my illness was the obedient work of a scribe.

Stupid scarab.

The early numbers of my serialised novel were being met with continued and rising enthusiasm. Wills reported more and more people flocking to the magazine's offices on Wellington Street on the day each new issue was released. All the talk was of the Moonstone itself, the precious diamond, and who might have stolen it and how. No one knew, of course, the full extent of my ingenuity in providing that ending, but even before writing those chapters, I had full confidence that no one would guess the amazing revelation. Between this and the triumph of my play, I would have much to impress Charles Dickens with when he returned.

If he lived long enough to return.

More and more, Wills and I were receiving, through a variety of sources (but especially through candid notes from George Dolby to Dickens's daughters, as relayed to me by Charley), news that Dickens's health was failing alarmingly. Influenza caught during his almost daily travels through the American provinces required him to stay in bed until the afternoon and not eat anything until three o'clock or later. All of us were amazed to read that Dickens—who always insisted on staying in hotels during his tours and never at private homes—had been so ill in Boston that he had been forced to stay with his friends the Fieldses rather than at the Parker House as planned.

Besides the worsening influenza and catarrh, exhaustion and a return of swelling in his left foot seemed close to doing Dickens in. We were hearing that Dolby had to help "the Chief" onto the stage for each reading, although as soon as he was beyond the curtain, Dickens would stride to his reading stand with a perfect imitation of his old alertness and spryness. And during the intermission and after the reading, Dolby and others would have to catch the totally exhausted author to keep him from fainting. Mrs Fields wrote Dickens's daughter Mamie that during his last reading in Boston on 8 April, Dickens had boasted of a return of his old powers but still had not been able to change his clothes after the readings, but simply lay on the sofa for thirty minutes "in a state of the greatest exhaustion" even before allowing himself to be helped back to his room.

And—I took notice of this—Dolby had written in

an almost offhand manner that because of the Inimitable's inability to sleep, he had begun again to take laudanum—although only a few drops per glass of wine—each night.

Was there an insatiable scarab in America that also needed sedating?

At any rate, Dickens's daughters and son Charles were worried about their father, even though the Inimitable's own letters home were filled with optimism and bragging about crowds and adoration from his eager public at each American city in which he read. But as March and April passed and I slowly, slowly showed improvement and began to overcome some of the pain and debilitation (although setbacks would send me to bed again for days on end), I began to believe either that Charles Dickens would never return from America or that he would return a broken, dying man.

It WAS DIFFICULT communicating with Martha R——during my illness. I did manage to send one message to her via my servant George early in my crisis and during Mother's deathwatch, under the guise of enquiring about rental properties on Bolsover Street, but that was far too risky to continue.

Three times in February I did tell Caroline and Carrie that I was going to Tunbridge Wells with Charley to see Mother and turned back at the station, telling Charley I was simply not well enough to go on and would take a hansom cab home. Two of those three times I spent the night (or nights) with Martha—although I was too ill to enjoy the time properly—but that stratagem was also too risky, since Charles might, at any time, mention to Caroline or in Caroline's presence the occasions I was not able to travel all the way to Mother's.

Martha could have written me during this interval (using a false return address on the envelopes), but she preferred not to write letters. In point of fact, my Martha was close to being illiterate at this time, although later I would tutor her to the point she could read simple books and write basic letters.

Once I was ambulatory again by late March, I did work out ways to see her, explaining to Caroline and even to my doctor that I had to take solitary carriage rides (I was not up to *pretending* that I was walking for hours) to help me ruminate on my novel, or claiming that I must spend time at my club in its wonderful library, seeking out more books for my research. But these visits to "Mrs Dawkins" at Bolsover Street gave us, at most, a few stolen hours, and satisfied neither Martha nor me.

But Martha R——'s compassion for me during this most difficult time was sincere and palpable, in contrast to Caroline's grudging and often suspicious care.

MAAT GIVES MEANING to the world. Maat bestows order upon the chaos of creation in the First Times and maintains order and balance throughout all time. Maat controls the movement of the stars, oversees the rising and setting of the sun, governs the flooding and flow of the Nile, and lays her cosmic body and soul beneath all laws of nature.

Maat is the goddess of justice and truth.

When I die, my heart will be torn from my body and carried to the Judgement Hall of the Tuat, where it will be weighed against Maat's feather. If my heart is mostly free from the terrible weight of sin—sin against the Gods of the Black Land, sin against my duties as outlined by Drood and enforced by the sacred scarab—I will be allowed to travel on and perhaps join the company of the gods themselves. If my sinful heart outweighs Maat's feather, my soul will be devoured and destroyed by the demon-beasts of the Black Land.

Maat gave meaning to the world and still gives meaning to the world. My Day of Judgement in the Hall of the Tuat is coming, as is yours, Dear Reader. As is yours.

MORNINGS WERE VERY BAD for me. Now that I had quit dictating *The Moonstone* to the treacherous scribe of the Other Wilkie through the lowest-ebb hours of the night, I often awoke from my laudanum or laudanum-and-morphine dreams between two and three AM and simply had to moan and writhe my way through to the spring dawn.

I usually was able to get myself down to my large study on the ground floor by early afternoon, where I would write until four PM, when Caroline or Carrie or both would take me outside, at least to the garden, to get some air. As I wrote to one friend who wanted to come visit me that April—"If you are to come, it should be before four o'clock, because I am carried out to be aired *at* 4."

It was one such afternoon in mid-April, precisely two months to the day since Mother had died, that Caroline entered my study behind me.

I had paused in my writing and—pen still in my hand—was staring out the wide windows at the street. I confess that I was wondering how I might get in contact with Inspector Field. Though I remained certain that Field's operatives must be watching me, I had never seen one, despite my cleverest efforts to catch one out. I wanted to know what was happening with Drood. Had Field and his hundred-plus vigilantes burned the Egyptian murderer out, shot him down like a dog in the sewer the way Barris had shot the Wild Boy in front of me? And what of Barris? Had Inspector Field disciplined the blackguard for pistol-whipping me?

But it had occurred to me just the day before that I had no idea where Inspector Field's offices might be situated. I remembered that the first time he had visited me at 9 Melcombe Place, the inspector had sent up a card—certainly his business address would be on it—but after rummaging through my desk and finally finding it, the card read only:

**INSPECTOR
CHARLES FREDERICK FIELD
Private Enquiry Bureau**

Besides wanting to know what had happened in Undertown, I also wished to engage the inspector and his operatives on some work of my own: I wished to know when and where Caroline was meeting the plumber Joseph Charles Clow (for I had no doubt they *were* meeting secretly).

It was with these thoughts in my mind and my gaze turned to the street that I heard Caroline clearing her throat behind me. I did not turn.

"Wilkie, my dear, there is something I have been waiting to discuss with you. It has been a month now since your dear mother passed on."

This required no comment and I gave none. Outside, a junk waggon rumbled by. The old nag's flanks were covered with scabs, and even now the grizzled driver laid the whip on. Why, I wondered, would a rag-and-bone waggon have to hurry anywhere?

"Lizzie is reaching that age where she is ready to be

introduced to society," continued Caroline. "Ready to find a gentleman to be her husband."

I'd noted over the years that whenever Caroline wished to talk about her daughter—Elizabeth Harriet G—— as *her* daughter, she was "Lizzie." When she talked about her as our shared concern, she was "Carrie"—the name the girl actually preferred.

"It will be *so* much easier for Lizzie, in terms of matrimonial prospects and social acceptance, if she comes from an established and stable family," Caroline went on. I still had not turned towards her.

On the sidewalk across the street, a young man in a suit too light in colour and thinness of wool for the fickle spring season, paused, looked over at our house, checked his watch, and moved on. It was not Joseph Clow. Could it have been one of Inspector Field's agents? I doubted if any of the inspector's men would be so brazen, especially since I was quite visible sitting in the ground floor bow windows.

"She should bear the name of her father," said Caroline.

"She does bear the name of her father," I said tonelessly. "Your husband gave her that even if he granted neither of you anything else."

I've mentioned to you, Dear Reader, that Caroline was indeed my inspiration for *The Woman in White*. When, in the summer of 1854, my brother, Charley, and my friend John Millais came upon this apparition in white robes rushing from the garden of a North London villa in the moonlight—it was Caroline, of course, fleeing from her brute of a husband, who had, she told me at the time, been keeping her prisoner by mesmeric means—I, alone of the three of us men, had pursued her. And I had believed her about her drunken thug of a wealthy husband, a certain George Robert G——, and about how her life with one-year-old Carrie had been one of imprisonment and mental torture.

Some years later, Caroline had informed me that George Robert G—— had died. How she received this information I did not know nor ask (even while recognising how improbable it was that she had received it at all, since she had been living in my home all those years since the night she'd fled weeping across Charlton Street in the moonlight). But I accepted the news as fact and never asked her about it. For all these years, we had both pretended that she was Mrs Elizabeth G—— —I had given her the name Caroline when she had come under my care—who had been victimised by her husband with both mesmerism and a fireplace poker.

The probable truth, I had thought at the time—and had no reason to change my mind about the matter now fourteen years later—was that Caroline had been fleeing from a pimp or client turned violent that summer night in 1854.

"You see the advantages to Carrie over the next few years if our girl can say and show that she is from an established family," Caroline went on, speaking to my back. Her voice had a slight quaver to it now.

The "our girl" made me angry. I had always treated Carrie with the same love and generosity as if she had been my daughter. But she was not. She never would be. This was a sort of blackmail going on, a strategy I had reason to believe that Caroline had known well in the time before I rescued her, and I would have none of it.

"Wilkie, my dearest, you must admit that I have always been understanding when you have told me that your frail and aged mother was the absolute encumbrance to you marrying."

"Yes," I said.

"But with Harriet's passing, you are free now?"

"Yes."

"Free to marry if you like?"

"Yes." I kept my face turned to the window and the street.

She waited for me to say something else. I did not. After a long moment in which I could clearly hear every swing of the pendulum in the tall clock in the hallway beyond, Caroline turned and left my study.

But I knew this was not the end of the conversation. She had another and final card to play—one she thought foolproof. And I knew she would play it soon. What she did not know was that I had a full hand of cards to play myself. And more up my sleeve.

SCRABBLINGS. THERE ARE scrabblings."

"What?"

I had been wakened much earlier than usual—a check of my watch showed it to be not yet nine o'clock—and I was alarmed by the phalanx of faces hovering over me: Caroline, Carrie, my servant George, George's wife, Besse, who acted as our parlourmaid.

"What?" I said again, sitting up in bed. This invasion of my bedchamber before breakfast was intolerable.

"There are scrabbling sounds," repeated Caroline.

"What are you talking about? Where?"

"In h'our stairs, sir," said George, his face red with embarrassment at being brought into my bedroom. This was obviously Caroline's doing.

"The servants' staircase?" I said, rubbing my eyes. The previous night had not been a morphine-assisted one, but my head ached anyway. Abominably.

"They've been hearing it on every storey of the house," said Caroline. Her voice was as loud and grating as a Welsh calliope. "Now I've heard it as well. It's as if there's a great rat in there. Scrabbling up and down."

"Rat?" I said. "We had the exterminators here last autumn when we did all the work on the house and updated the *plumbing*." I put deliberate emphasis on the last word.

Caroline had the good grace to blush, but she did not desist. "There's something in the servants' staircase."

"George," I said, "haven't you looked into this?"

"Aye, sir, Mr Collins, I 'ave. I went in, sir, and oop and doon following the noise, sir. But each time I got close, it…I haven't found it, sir."

"Do you think it's rats?"

George was always a little slow, but he had rarely looked as completely half-witted as he did while wrestling with this question. "It sounds like one great 'un, sir," he said at last. "Not rats so much, sir, as…a single bloody great rat, beggin' your pardon, misses."

"This is absurd," I said. "Everyone get out. I will dress and be down in a minute and find and kill this 'single bloody great rat' of yours. And then perhaps you'll all be so kind as to let a sick man get his rest."

I chose to enter the stairway on the kitchen level so she could not get below me.

I was certain that I knew what had been making the noise. In truth, I wondered why I'd not seen the woman with green skin and tusks for teeth before this during the eight months we had been in the new house. The Other Wilkie had come along from Melcombe Place easily enough.

But why can the others now hear her?

In all the years the woman with the green skin had occupied my previous servants' staircases in the dark, no one but I had ever heard or seen her. I was certain of that.

Are the Gods of the Black Lands making her more real the way they have the Other Wilkie?

I set that disturbing thought aside and lifted the candle from the table. I'd ordered the others not to come into the kitchen with me and to stay away from all of the doorways to the servants' stairway on each storey of the tall house.

The woman with green skin and tusked teeth had drawn blood on my throat before this, long before Drood, the scarab, and the Gods of the Black Land had entered my life. I had no doubt that she could kill me now if I allowed her the proximity and opportunity. I had no intention of allowing her either.

Opening the door slightly, I removed Detective Hatchery's heavy pistol from my jacket pocket.

With the door closed behind me, the servants' staircase was almost absolutely dark. There were no windows along this side of the house, and the few candles in the wall sconces had not been lighted. The staircase was unusually—and disturbingly—steep and narrow, rising straight for three storeys before pausing on a short landing and continuing two storeys in the opposite direction to the attic.

I listened for a moment before starting up the stairs. Nothing. Candle in my left hand, pistol in my right, and stairway so narrow that my elbows on each arm brushed the walls, I moved quietly up the steps.

Halfway between the ground floor and first floor, I paused to light the first wall candle.

There was no candle there, although one of our parlourmaid's daughter's jobs was to replace them regularly. Leaning closer, I could see scratches and gouges on the firmly fixed old sconce, as if something had ripped the half-burned candle there out with claws. *Or with teeth.*

I paused to listen again. The softest of scuttling sounds came from somewhere above me.

The woman with green skin and tusked teeth had never made a loud sound before, I realised. She had always glided up and down stairs, towards or away from me, as if her bare feet barely touched the steps.

But that had been in my other houses. This servants' stairway may have had more resonance for such malign spirits.

How had Shernwold died? She had fallen down these very steps and broken her neck, but why had she been in the servants' staircase?

Investigating the sounds of rats?

And why had she fallen?

The candles missing from their sconces as if eaten?

I continued up to the first storey, paused in front of that doorway a moment—the doors were old and thick, and no sound came through, but there was a reassuring sliver of light at the bottom—and then I went on up the stairs.

The second candle was also missing from its sconce.

Something scuttled and scraped most audibly from not too far above me now.

"Hallo?" I called softly. I confess to feeling some sense of real power as I extended the pistol. If the woman with green skin had been corporeal enough to leave scratches on my neck—and she had—then she was corporeal enough to feel the effects of one of these bullets. Or several of them.

How many bullets were in the cylinder?

Nine, I remembered from that day Detective Hatchery had pressed the pistol into my hand, telling me as I went down to King Lazaree's den that I should have something to defend myself from the rats. I even remembered what he had said about the caliber....

"They're forty-two calibre, sir. Nine should be more

than sufficient for your average rat…four-legged or two-legged, as the case may be."

I stifled the giggle that rose in my throat now.

At the second-storey door, the staircase behind and beneath me, only dimly illuminated by my flickering candle, seemed so steep as to be vertical. It—and perhaps lack of breakfast and the after-effects of my three glasses of morning laudanum—gave me a sense of vertigo.

Something sounding far too much like claws on plaster or wood scrabbled above me.

"Show yourself!" I cried into the darkness. I confess that this was mere bravado, a hope that George, Caroline, Besse, and the girl, Agnes, might hear me. But they were, presumably, two storeys below me now. And the doors were *very* thick.

I began climbing even more slowly, the pistol directly in front of me and swinging from side to side like an absurdly heavy weather vane in variable winds.

The scrabbling was not only louder now, but it seemed to have a *direction*. I could not tell if it came from the third-storey landing, where the staircase turned back in the opposite direction, or from somewhere between me and that landing. I made a mental note to have at least one window set into the thick brick-and-masonry outer wall there at the landing if no place else.

I took three more steps.

I cannot tell you, Dear Reader, from where the apparition of my woman with green skin and yellow tusk-teeth had originally come from, only that she had been with me since my early childhood. I remember her entering our nursery when Charles was sleeping. I remember seeing her in the attic of my father's house when I had been so imprudent as to explore that dark and cobwebbed space when I was nine or ten years of age.

They say that familiarity breeds freedom from fear, but that is not quite the case. The green-skinned wench—her face was not of any living woman I had ever known, although I sometimes thought that she reminded me a bit of the first governess Charley and I had ever had—gave me the shudders every time I encountered her, but I knew from experience that I could fight her off when she lunged at me.

But no one else has ever heard her before. She's never made a sound before.

I took another three steps towards the third-storey landing and stopped.

The scraping and scurrying were much louder now. The sound seemed very close above me, although now the pale circumference of candlelight extended almost to the landing itself. But it was very loud and—I understood George's fear now—very ratlike indeed. Scrabble-scrape. Silence. Scrabble scrabble scrabble scrape. Silence. Scrabble scrabble.

"I have a surprise for you," I said, cocking the massive pistol one-handedly with some difficulty. I remembered Hatchery saying that the large bottom barrel was a sort of shotgun. I wished now that he'd given me shells for it.

Two more steps up and I could see the landing. It was empty.

The scrabbling came again. It seemed to be *above* and even *behind* me.

I raised the candle over my head and peered straight up.

The scrabbling had turned to wild screaming and I stood there, frozen, listening to the screaming for a full minute or more before realising that it was coming from me.

Turning to flee, I pounded down the stairs, reached the second-storey door, shook it while screaming, looked up over my shoulder, screamed again. I fired the pistol at least twice, knowing that it would do no good. It did not. Running and clattering down the stairs again—the first-storey door also locked from the other side—I screamed as something moist and foul dripped from... from above...and then I was hurtling down the stairway again, ricocheting from wall to wall. I dropped the candle and it went out. Something brushed my hair from above, curled along the back of my neck. Whirling in the absolute darkness, I fired the revolver twice more, tripped, fell headfirst down the last dozen steps.

I do not know to this day how I managed not to lose the pistol or shoot myself with it. Screaming more loudly now, I lay in a heap at the bottom of the steps and pounded at the ground-floor door.

Something strong and thin and very long wrapped itself around my right boot and ripped it off my foot. If I had buckled the boot properly before coming in, I would have been dragged back up the staircase with it.

Screaming again, I fired a final shot up into the darkness, tore open the door, and—blinded by the light—fell forward onto the long boards of the kitchen floor. Flailing wildly with both feet, I kicked the heavy door shut behind me.

George ran in despite my earlier commands for no one to be in the room. I could see Caroline's and the other two female faces staring white and round and open-mouthed from the doorway to the hall.

I almost pulled George down to the floor as I fiercely grabbed his lapel and whispered wildly to him, "Lock it! Lock the door! Lock it! Now!"

George did so, throwing the totally inadequate tiny bolt home. There was no sound from the other side. My panting and gasping seemed to fill the kitchen.

Getting to my knees and then to my feet, the pistol still raised and cocked, I pulled George back tight against me and hissed in his ear, "Get as much lumber as you need and as many men as you need. I want all the staircase doors nailed shut and then boarded over within the half hour. Do you understand? Do...you... *understand*?"

George nodded, pulled himself free from my grip, and ran out to get what he needed.

I backed out of the kitchen, never taking my eyes from the far-too-frail door to the stairway.

"Wilkie..." began Caroline, setting her hand on my shoulder but then jerking it away as I jumped.

"It was rats," I gasped, uncocking the pistol that was suddenly too heavy for me to hold. I tried to remember how many bullets I had fired but could not. I would count the remaining ones later. "It was only rats."

"Wilkie..." Caroline began again.

I shook her off and went up to my bedroom to vomit into the basin and find my flask.

CHAPTER THIRTY-THREE

*C*aroline played her trump card on Wednesday, the twenty-ninth of April, the day before the *Russia*, carrying Dickens and Dolby on the last leg of their long voyage, was scheduled to drop anchor in Queenstown Harbour.

Caroline knew that I was in a good mood, although she had no idea of all the reasons why. Those reasons were clear enough to me. When Charles Dickens had sailed for America the previous November, he had been the master and I the eager apprentice; now *The Moonstone* in serial form was the hit of the nation, crowds at the Wellington Street offices of *All the Year Round* were larger with each number released, and commoner and nobility both were hanging on each new instalment to see just who had stolen the diamond and how. And I was secure in the sure and certain knowledge that even the cleverest reader among them would never be able to guess.

When Charles Dickens had sailed for America the previous November, my play *No Thoroughfare*—and it was, indeed, *my play,* after all the rewrites, revisions, and fresh ideas I had poured into it since the previous autumn—had been just a dream in early rehearsal. Now it was a bona fide hit and had already run at the Adelphi Theatre for more than one hundred and thirty sold-out evening performances. There were eager negotiations under way for a Paris production.

Finally, Mother's death, while saddening me (and horrifying me with its insectoid aspects and uncertainty of cause) had also liberated me. Now, at the age of forty-four, I had finally and fully become a man unto myself.

So Caroline sensed that despite the incident of the servants' stairway (after two weeks I still would not go into the kitchen or any part of the upper hallways near the heavily nailed, boarded over, and fully sealed doors), and despite frequent relapses and the continuing pain that required larger doses of laudanum and morphine just to allow me to work a few hours each day, I was in the best mood I had enjoyed for years.

Dickens had left in November thinking of himself as the Master and me as protégé; he was returning (ill and disabled, from all accounts) to find me as the popular-selling novelist, successful playwright, and fully independent man I now was. We would meet this time as equals (at the very least).

And, I was increasingly convinced, we both carried Drood's scarabs in our skulls. That fact alone brought a grim new equality to our relationship.

CAROLINE CAME TO ME that Wednesday morning while I was in the bath. Perhaps she thought this was when I would be at my most mellow... or at least at my most pliable.

"Wilkie, my dear, I have been thinking about our earlier conversation."

"Which conversation is that?" I asked, even though I knew full well. My spectacles had steamed over and I reached for a nearby towel and squinted while I wiped the lenses clear. Caroline became a great white-and-pink lumpy blur.

"The one about Lizzie moving into society and

about the future of our own relationship under this roof," she said, sounding very nervous indeed.

I, on the other hand, was completely calm as I set the tiny spectacles back on my nose. "Yes?"

"I have decided, Wilkie, that for our Lizzie... Carrie...to have the proper advantages in life, her mother really must be married and she part of a stable family."

"I could not agree more," I said. The steam from my bath rose to the ceiling and curled to all sides. Caroline's face was flushed red with it.

"You do?" she said. "You agree?"

"Absolutely," I said. "Please hand me that towel, my dear."

Speechless, she handed me the towel and I proceeded to pat my rather pleasing rotundity dry.

"I did not know...all this time...I was not sure..." spluttered Caroline.

"Nonsense," I said. "Your well-being...and Carrie's, of course...have always been my primary concern. And you are correct. It is time for a marriage."

"Oh, Wilkie, I..." She could not go on. Tears ran down her steam-reddened cheeks.

"I presume you are still in touch with your plumber," I said, tossing aside the towel and pulling on my velour robe. "Mr Clow. Joseph Charles Clow?"

Caroline froze. The flush seeped out of her cheeks. "Yes?"

"And I assume that Mr Clow has proposed marriage to you by now, my dear. In fact, I presume that you were going to mention that fact to me in this very conversation."

"Yes, but, I did not...I have not..."

I patted her arm. "There is no need for further explanation between two such old friends," I said merrily. "It is time for marriage—for Carrie's sake, as well as your own—and our Mr Clow has proposed it. You must accept at once."

Caroline was pale down to her fingertips now. She took two blind steps backwards and bumped into the washbasin.

"I shall have Besse pack your clothes at once," I went on. "Your other belongings, books and so forth, we shall send along in due course. I shall have George go fetch a cab as soon as you're packed."

Caroline's mouth moved twice before a word came out. "Lizzie…"

"Carrie, of course, shall stay with me," I said. "This has already been arranged between Carrie and myself. It is her choice and it is final. However passionate and compliant your plumber…Mr Joseph Charles Clow… may be, and however well-regarded his distiller of a father might have been, your plumber's actual, hopeful, but sometimes struggling bourgeois existence is not appropriate for Carrie at this point in her life. As you have pointed out, Caroline, she shall soon be entering society. She has chosen to do this from this fine home, from Number Ninety Gloucester Place, secure in the company of writers, artists, composers, and great men. She shall visit you frequently, of course, but this shall remain her home. I've discussed this not only with Carrie but with your current mother-in-law, and they both agree."

Caroline had lowered both hands to the basin's counter behind her and seemed to be holding herself upright only by the force of those straight, stiffened, and quaking arms.

I did not reach out to touch her as I brushed past to step into the hall, and it seemed that Caroline could not then have lifted an arm under any circumstances.

"I believe your decision is wise, my dear," I said softly from the doorway. "You and I shall always be friends. Should you or Mr Joseph Charles Clow ever need assistance of any sort, I will endeavour to put both of you in touch with the kind of people who may be capable of helping, if they are inclined to do so."

Caroline continued to stare at the space where I had been standing next to the tub.

"I'll have Besse commence your packing," I said. "And I will send George down to the thoroughfare for a cab sooner rather than later. I don't mind paying the driver to wait a while if necessary. It's best to begin a journey like this in the morning, when one is fresh."

As I MENTIONED EARLIER, Dickens's and Dolby's ship, the *Russia*, arrived in Queenstown Harbour on the last day in April, but none of the Inimitable's friends rushed to Liverpool to welcome them. Telegrams from Dolby had made it clear that Dickens wished "a few days of solitary acclimatisation before resuming his duties and old habits."

I translated this as meaning that the exhausted author would not be going straight to Gad's Hill Place, nor would he stay in London (although he passed through there by train on May 2), but rather would continue on straight into the waiting arms of Ellen Ternan in Peckham. It turned out that I was perfectly correct in this assumption. I also knew through casual comments from Wills at the Wellington Street offices that the actress and her mother had returned from Italy only two days earlier.

How very convenient for the Inimitable.

It was another four days before Dickens made himself available for a welcoming from Wills, Frank Beard, and me. He took the train in from Peckham for an early dinner with Fechter and the rest of us, and then we all went to the Adelphi so that Dickens could finally see *No Thoroughfare*.

I had been more than prepared to express sympathetic concern and even shock at Dickens's aged, exhausted state after the American tour, but Beard spoke for both of us at the station when the physician cried out, "Good Lord, Charles! Seven years younger!"

It was true. There was no sign of the limp and swollen foot we had heard so much about through letters. He had lost some weight in America, but it made him look younger and healthier. The eight-day spring sea voyage had obviously given him some real rest away from all duties, and long hours on deck had turned the always quick-tanning Dickens's visage to bronze; somehow even his hair and beard seemed darker and fuller. Dickens's eyes were bright. His smile was quick and his laughter and resonant tale-telling voice filled the restaurant where we dined and the carriage the five of us later took to the Adelphi.

"Good God, Wilkie," Dickens said to me in private as we handed our hats, gloves, and sticks to the girl at the theatre, "I knew you'd been ill, but you look absolutely terrible, my dear boy. You're shaking and pale and shuffling along like Thackeray near the end. What on *earth* has gotten into you?"

Gotten into me. How very clever. How very... *droll*. I gave Dickens a wan smile and said nothing.

Later, during the play, I had the most extraordinary experience.

Our little group was in the authors' box—minus Fechter, of course, who had rushed backstage to put on his makeup and vomit in preparation for the show (even though everyone believed that this might be his last month of performing in England as the villain Obenreizer because of the actor's increasing health problems). Despite my own illness, I had been there in that box many times in the preceding five months, but this was the first time Dickens had been present for the play on which he had collaborated in the early stages. Naturally, Dickens received a standing ovation from the full house even before the curtain opened. But I had expected that and it did not hurt my feelings.

No, it was the play itself that was the extraordinary experience for me. Counting rehearsals, I had seen my *No Thoroughfare* from start to finish at least thirty times. I could recite every line and every rewrite of every line. I had every entrance and exit timed to the fraction of a second.

But this night it was as if I were watching the play for the first time.

In truth, Dear Reader, it was as if *one eye* were watching the play for the first time. The headache that was always with me had settled, as was its wont, behind my right eye with such intensity that I expected the back of my eyeball to hiss the way a pitcher of good grog does when the boy thrusts in a white-hot rod to heat it. I could also feel the pressure of the scarab there. Sometimes I believed that it burrowed forward precisely so that it could peer out through one of my eyes.

So it was that as I sat there holding my temple first with my right hand and then my left, covertly covering first my left eye and then my right, as if I were watching the play I had written and seen so many times for the first time.

The scene at the orphanage with the foundling children being switched, I saw at once, was pure nonsense rather than real pathos, despite the obvious emotional response from the gullible audience. That Dickens had been most active in his collaboration in this pathetic setup business was little solace to me as the play ground on.

The death of our Walter Wilding (from both a broken heart and sheer guilt at the thought that he had accidentally inherited another man's name and fortune) set the audience to boo-hooing as always, but it made me want to retch. Pure poppycock. Absolute drivel. How, I wondered, could any serious author have concocted such a scene?

And now Fechter was strutting to and fro in his guise as the villain Obenreizer. What an absurd character. What an absurd performance.

I remember showing one specific paragraph from the published story to Fechter, submitting it as the key to his character's secret motivations and internal psyche. Now I recalled the words with rue—

> But the great Obenreizer peculiarity was, that a certain nameless film would come over his eyes—apparently by the action of his own will—which would impenetrably veil, not only from those tellers of tales, but from his face at large, every expression save one of attention. It by no means followed that his attention should be wholly given to the person with whom he spoke, or even wholly bestowed on present sounds and objects. Rather, it was a comprehensive watchingfulness of everything he had in his own mind, and everything that he knew to be, or suspected to be, in the minds of other men.

I remembered writing that passage almost a year earlier and I also recalled having a distinct sense of satisfaction at my own abilities of expressing the complex mental and physical traits of a villain. I had thought, at the time, that I was conveying my own secret way of looking at a world that I knew was insincere and set on spoiling my own plans and ambitions.

But these words from the original Christmas tale—the so-called key to Obenreizer's character—were flat, I realised now. Flat and silly and empty. And Fechter had used my words to endow his Obenreizer with a constantly skulking, furtive walk and look, combined with a manic stare—all too frequently aimed at nothing at all—that now impressed me as not the traits of a clever villain, but rather those of a village idiot after a serious concussion to his skull.

The audience loved it.

They also loved our new hero, George Vendale (who took the heroic palm from Walter Wilding when the latter died of his guiltless shame). Tonight I saw that George Vendale was a worse idiot than the skulking, smirking, brainlessly goggling Obenreizer. A child of three could have seen Obenreizer's endless manipulations and falsehoods, yet Vendale—and several hundred people in that night's audience—accepted our silly premise that the hero was simply a sweet, trusting soul.

If our race had produced only a few sweet, trusting souls like George Vendale, the species would have died out from sheer stupidity millennia ago.

Even the setting in the Swiss Alps, I realised while watching with the scarab's clarity, was silly and unnecessary. The action leaping back and forth from London to Switzerland had no purpose except to bring in some of the spectacle that Dickens and I had seen in our journey across the Alps in 1853. The last scenes in the play, where Vendale's beloved, Margaret Obenreizer (the villain's beautiful and sinless niece), revealed that Vendale had *not* died from being hurled down the glacier a year earlier, but had been in her secret care all that time in a cosy little Swiss chalet presumably at the base of the aforementioned glacier, came close to making me bark with derisive laughter.

The scene where Obenreizer the Clever (who had lured Vendale all that way to that very ice-bridge above the abyss a year before) set forth across the treacherous slope for no other reason than the play's ending demanded a sacrifice of him, not only stretched my newly awakened scepticism to the breaking point, but snapped it entirely. I wished to God that Fechter had been flinging himself into an actual bottomless abyss that night rather than merely dropping eight feet to a pile of mattresses hidden from the audience's view behind a painted wooden spire of ice.

I had to close both eyes in the final scene where Obenreizer's body was being borne into the little Swiss village celebrating Vendale's and Margaret's marriage (why wouldn't they have married in London, for God's sake?), with the happy couple exiting in exultance on stage right and with Obenreizer's lifeless body being carried in a litter off stage left as the audience simultaneously hissed at the villain's funeral and wept and cheered the wedding. The juxtaposition, seemingly so clever when Dickens and I outlined it on the page, was puerile and absurd in the clarity of my scarab-vision. But the audience hissed and cheered on as Fechter's body was carried off stage left and our newly married couple rolled away in their marriage coach stage right.

The audience were idiots. The play was being performed by idiots. Its script was sheer melodrama idiocy penned by an idiot.

In the lobby after the play—and after five hundred people had pressed close to shake Dickens's hand or tell him how wonderful his play had been (I was all but forgotten, it seemed, as the true playwright, which—on this night of revelation—I did not mind a bit)—Dickens said to me, "Well, my dear Wilkie, the play is a triumph. There is no doubt of it. But, to use your Moonstone language, it remains a diamond in the rough. There are excellent things in it...excellent things!...but it still drags a tad."

I stared at him. *Had Dickens just seen the same play I had?*

"There are too many pieces of stagecraft missed as it is now being produced," continued Dickens. "Too many opportunities to heighten both the drama and Obenreizer's villainy have been missed in this version."

I had to use all my strength not to laugh in the Inimitable's face. More stagecraft, more drama, and more villainy were the last things on earth this giant, steaming pile of overacted, melodramatic heap of horse apples needed. What it needed, I thought, was a shovel and a deep hole in a distant place in which to bury it.

"You know, of course, that while Fechter soon may have to leave this performance for reasons of health," continued Dickens, "we fully intend to put on a new version of *No Thoroughfare* at the Café Vaudeville in Paris early next month with, one hopes, Fechter, sooner or later, reprising his success as Obenreizer."

Reprising this public pratfall onto our collective arse was my only thought.

"I shall personally oversee the revisions and perhaps act as stage manager at Vaudeville Théâtre until the play is on its feet," said Dickens. "I do hope you shall be coming along with us, Wilkie. It should be great fun."

"I am afraid that will not be possible, Charles," I said. "My health simply will not permit it."

"Ahh," said Dickens. "I am heartily sorry for that." I could detect no actual regret in his voice and almost certainly could hear an undertone of relief. "Well," he said, "Fechter will be too exhausted to go out with us afterwards, so I shall drop in on him backstage and convey our congratulations at the excellence of what may be his last performance as Obenreizer...in *this* version of the play at least!"

And with that, Dickens bustled away, still being congratulated by the last of the passing theatre-goers.

Beard, who was going out with us later, was chatting with others so I stepped out into the street. The air smelled of horse manure, as the air outside all theatres did after the carriages and cabs had taken away the well-dressed members of the night's audience. The stink seemed appropriate.

As it turned out, Dickens kept Beard and me waiting for more than half an hour. I later learned that he had loaned the weeping Fechter £2,000...a fact that was especially galling, since I had loaned the foolish actor £1,000 that I could scarce afford only two weeks earlier.

While I waited alone in the barnyard miasma, I drank deeply from my silver flask of laudanum and realised that for all of Dickens's talk of theatrical triumph in France, he would not be staying there past the first week of June.

Drood and the scarab would bring him back to London on or before 9 June. It would be the third anniversary of the Staplehurst accident. Charles Dickens had a date for that night, I was certain, and this year I vowed that I would spend it with him.

I swallowed the last of the laudanum and smiled a smile much colder and more villainous than anything Fechter as Obenreizer could ever have managed.

CHAPTER THIRTY-FOUR

By the end of May, I had learned (through Mrs G——, Caroline's elderly mother-in-law, who now came to stay with us from time to time at Number 90 Gloucester Place, since it would have been inappropriate for Carrie to live in a bachelor's home without at least an occasional chaperone for respectability's sake) that Caroline was now living with Joseph Charles Clow's mother, the widow of the distiller. They had set a wedding date for early October. The news did not discomfit me in the least; on the contrary, it seemed the proper step at the proper time for the proper people. And speaking of propriety, after I received a somewhat panicked letter from Caroline herself, I wrote to assure her that I would help her create and maintain to the death any fiction of her past or her family (much less of my own relationship with her) that she chose to present to the low-bourgeois and somewhat puritanical Clow clan.

In the meantime, I had found Carrie pleasant employment as a part-time governess with a good family I knew. She loved the work and enjoyed having some money of her own, but the best part was that the family often introduced her to society almost as if she were their daughter. Between her contact with the best people in the arts and literature at my table, and introductions to some of England's most notorious nobility and denizens of the political and business class at her adopted home's *salon*, young Carrie was doing an excellent job of preparing to come out.

Carrie was turning seventeen and Martha R—— was not quite twenty-three. Martha was much happier now that I felt well enough to drop by and see her from time to time—as her returning travelling husband, "Mr Dawson," of course—at her rooms on Bolsover Street. Martha had been aware of Caroline and probably aware that Caroline had been more than the housekeeper listed on my annual census forms, but Martha showed no emotion and offered no comments when I told her that "Mrs G——" had moved out and was planning to be married in the autumn.

Martha's passion, always very strong, seemed to blossom that late spring and summer. She did say that she wanted a child, but I laughed that away for the time being by joking that "poor Mr Dawson" had to be on the road so frequently to earn a living for his darling wife that it would hardly be fair for him to have a family at home when he could not be there to enjoy it.

. . .

Come, Isis, Queen of Heaven! Order that this child shall be conceived in the flames of Nebt-Het, holy Nepthys, Goddess of that death which is not eternal. Hide thyself with the child of Osiris, God of our Fathers. Nourish and sustain this child as you nourished and sustained Horus, Lord of Things to Come, in the hidden place among the reeds. This infant's limbs will grow strong, as will her body and mind, and she shall be placed upon the altar of her father and serve the Temple which carries the truth of the Two Lands. Hear us, O Osiris! You, whose breath is life! Hear us!

I awakened from my morphia dreams to find this and similar pages left on the table by my bedside. The hand was that of the Other Wilkie. I had no memory of dictating them. The words, without memory of the dreams, made little sense.

But my scarab seemed placated.

On the first day I found such pages, I made a fire in my bedroom fireplace and consigned the text to the flames. I was in bed screaming with pain for two days after that. From then on, each morning after the dreams from one of Frank Beard's evening morphia injections, I would gather up the tight-writ pages and set them in a locked box on a high shelf in my study closet. Then I would lock the closet. Someday they would all be consigned to the flames, but perhaps after my death. I had no illusions that the scarab could hurt me then.

IT OCCURRED TO ME sometime in May of that year, 1868, that being out of touch with Inspector Charles Frederick Field was working more to my disadvantage than to his.

As terrible as that final night on the Undertown river had been—I still had nightmares about the Wild Boy pitching face forward into filthy waters, and there was a scar near my hairline where Reginald Barris had clubbed me with the barrel of his pistol—there remained the fact that when I had been in touch with Inspector Field, I received much more information from him (about Dickens, about Drood, about Ellen Ternan, about what was going on around us) than the inspector had ever received from me. Now that I was approaching what I was certain would be the final confrontation between Dickens and me (after which there would be no doubt to anyone that I was his equal or superior), I realised that I needed precisely the sort of information that Inspector Field had provided until January.

So in May I began looking for him.

As an ex-newspaper reporter, I knew that the most certain approach would be to contact someone in authority from the Metropolitan Police or their Detective Bureau. Despite Field's being retired, there was no doubt that someone there would know both his personal address and the whereabouts of his Private Enquiry Bureau office. But there were compelling reasons not to ask the police. First of all, there was the fact of Field's ongoing feud with the Police Force over his pension, over his meddling in the Palmer poisoning case years earlier, and over other problems. Secondly, I was concerned that Inspector Field himself might be in trouble with the police after the January mob scenes and burnings and shootings I had witnessed in Undertown. I had no wish to associate myself with such illegal behaviour.

Finally, and most compelling, I knew that both Drood and Dickens had their contacts with the Metropolitan Police Force and I had no intention of letting them know that I was seeking Inspector Field.

I then considered going to the *Times* or other newspaper; if anyone knew where the old inspector's offices might be, I was sure that some enterprising street reporter would.

But here again, the negative points outweighed the positive aspects of such an approach. As little as I wanted the police to associate me with Inspector Charles Frederick Field, I wanted the newspapers to do so even less. I had been away from reporting so long that I no longer had any contact with the papers or magazines that I could trust.

So that left searching myself. Throughout May, I did this as best I could—walking the streets when I was well enough to do so, taking a cab through the downtown at other times, and sending my servant George into promising buildings and alleys to look for Field's office. Perhaps because of our walk up the Strand and through Lincoln's Inn Fields (or perhaps because young Edmond Dickenson's ancient barrister's office was there), or perhaps because of our repeated meetings on Waterloo Bridge, I had carried away the distinct impression that the old detective's offices had been between Charing Cross and Fleet Prison, quite probably within the warren of old buildings and legal offices between Drury and Chancery Lanes.

But weeks of searching there turned up not the slightest hint. I then dropped the word at my club that I was seeking (for literary research purposes) the former policeman whom Dickens had written about in the mid-1850s, but although many remembered that Field had been the template for Inspector Bucket (none had yet come to associate him with Sergeant Cuff, who was currently so popular in my still-serialised novel), no one at the club knew where he might be found. In truth, most of those to whom I spoke were under the impression that Inspector Field had died.

I still firmly believed that Field would be back in touch with me before the summer was out. As chagrined as he might have been about his subordinate's pistol-whipping of me in January—my guess was that Field was afraid that I might sue for damages—I was certain that he still wanted information from me. Sooner or later, one of his street urchins or an otherwise non-descript man in a brown suit (although I seriously doubted that he would used Reginald Barris as his agent for such a service) would approach me on the street and I would resume my relationship with the obsessed inspector.

Until then, I realised, I would have to use my own spies to prepare for my confrontation with Charles Dickens.

· · ·

By EARLY JUNE, Dickens was writing to me almost daily from the Hôtel du Helder, where he was staying in Paris. Fechter had joined him there to oversee rehearsals, but the true stage manager—as he had promised—was Dickens himself. The French were calling my play *L'Abîme* ("The Abyss"), and it was scheduled to premiere on 2 June. He also reported to me that the French version of *No Thoroughfare* (according to Fechter and Didier, Dickens's translator there, as well as his Parisian friends and actors) was an immense improvement over the London version and was bound to be a success. He also reported that he would, in all probability, stay in Paris until mid-June.

I accurately guessed his prediction of the play's wild success there to be wishful thinking and his stated plans to stay for two more weeks a simple lie. Scarab or no scarab, I knew that Drood would draw Dickens back to London for the 9 June anniversary of the Staplehurst accident. Of this I had no doubt whatsoever.

Accordingly, I activated my own modest network of spies. To Fechter in Paris I sent a confidential letter asking if he would telegraph me the instant Charles left the city to return home. Explaining that I was considering a small but pleasant surprise for the Inimitable that required me to know his return time, I requested that Fechter keep the telegram a secret between us. (Since the actor now owed me more than £1,500, I felt certain he would honour my request.) Next, I asked a similar confidential favour of my brother, Charley, who, with Katey, was spending several weeks at Gad's Hill recovering from a bout of moderately severe stomach pains. (Charley and Katey did employ one servant, but she was undependable and a poor cook. The amenities at Gad's Hill Place were infinitely more suitable to a convalescent than the younger couple's cramped and overheated home in London.) For Charley's place in my espionage net, I simply asked him to send me a private note letting me know when Dickens arrived home at Gad's Hill and another when he departed for London, which I was sure he would do soon after arrival.

And I also knew that London, per se, would not be the Inimitable's actual destination after touching briefly at Gad's Hill Place upon his return from France. Dickens would again be going to Peckham to see Ellen Ternan. It was from Peckham, I was sure, that Dickens would come back to the city to meet with Drood on the Anniversary.

I also did my own small bit of spying. An older female cousin of mine—more of my mother's generation than my own—lived in Peckham, and after years of being out of contact with the old maid, I visited her twice in May. The ostensible reason was to console her after Mother's passing, but in truth I spent time during each trip to Peckham walking or taking a cab past the Ternans' home—paid for by Dickens under the assumed name of "Charles Tringham," you may remember—at 16 Linden Grove. I also took time to stroll by the dark apartment Dickens kept—secretly—near the Five Bells Inn at New Cross, only about a twenty-minute walk (at Dickens's pace) from 16 Linden Grove.

The two-storey home that the author had provided for Ellen and her mother could have comfortably housed a well-to-do family of five with the appropriate number of attendant servants. The house—it was more small manor than cottage—was surrounded by a well-tended garden which, in turn, was surrounded by empty fields, giving the suburban home an almost resplendent country feel. It was evident that the reward for being an intimate but secret friend of the world's most famous author was substantial. It occurred to me that Martha R—— might not be so pleased with her small rooms on Bolsover Street should she ever see the home provided for Ellen Ternan and her mother.

Both times I visited my cousin in Peckham, I traced the shortest distance from the Ternans' house to Peckham's railway station.

My final guess was that Dickens would be leaving Paris a day or two after the premiere of his play.

I was wrong only on that final guess. As it turned out, both Dickens and Fechter were half-mad with tension on the evening of the June 2 premiere of *L'Abîme* and although Dickens attempted to enter the theatre, he found he could not do it. So rather than attend the performance, the writer and the actor clopped through the streets of Paris in an open cab all evening, returning frequently to a café near the theatre where Didier, the translator, would emerge between acts to inform the two nervous men that—so far—the play was a riotous success.

During the last act, Dickens tried to enter the theatre again—lost his nerve again—and ordered the cab to take him to the station so that he could catch the late train to Boulogne. At the station, Fechter and Dickens hugged farewell, congratulated each other on their success, and then the actor returned alone to his hotel, stopping only to send the telegram I had requested of him.

The next day, Wednesday, the third of June, Dickens was home at Gad's Hill Place and my brother sent me a note that the author would be leaving the following morning, "for London." I'd left my servant George at the Peckham station with instructions to follow Dickens (whom he knew from the writer's many visits to my home) at a discreet distance (I had to explain the meaning of "discreet" to George). Should the Inimitable notice George, I'd prepared a note to my cousin that my employee was delivering as an explanation for my none-too-bright man's presence on that street, but as it turned out, Dickens was oblivious to being followed the short distance. As per his instructions, George confirmed that Dickens entered the Ternans' home, waited two hours in the vicinity (discreetly, one hoped) to confirm that the author did not go on to his own lodgings near Five Bells Inn, and then George took the train into town and came straight home to report.

None of these machinations would have been possible, of course, if Caroline G—— had still lived with me at Number 90 Gloucester Place. But she did not. And her daughter, Carrie, was gone most days and many evenings in her employment as governess.

But if I were to intercept Dickens on his way to meet Drood—and this was one annual rendezvous with the Egyptian that I was *not* going to miss—then I had to do the final detective guesswork on my own. (Here was when I most wished that I once again had the aid of Inspector Field and his many agents.) Dickens had returned to Gad's Hill Place late on Wednesday, 3 June, had travelled to Peckham to visit Ellen on Thursday the fourth, and presumably would not be meeting with Drood until the following Tuesday, the ninth.

Or would he follow his usual summer schedule and come into town on Monday and stay in his Wellington Street flat above the magazine office through Thursday?

Dickens was a creature of habit, so that would suggest he would come to town on Monday morning, the eighth. But in this case he had written me earlier from France to tell me that he would, in all likelihood, be staying in Paris until at least the following week, so this made it much more likely that he planned to stay with Ellen Ternan until Tuesday, 9 June, while letting none of us—Wills, Dolby, anyone—know that he was back in the country or city.

Finding Dickens at Charing Cross Station would be difficult. Doing so in a way that made it look as though I had come across him by accident would be even more difficult. The crowds, even on a Tuesday evening, would be large, the confusion general. I needed to lure Dickens away to dinner for the conversation I envisioned. During that long conversation, I would talk him into taking me with him when he met with Drood later that night. To convince him to join me for dinner for that long conversation would require me to run into him earlier, either at Peckham Station or on the train itself.

But then again, Dickens might not be leaving from Peckham if he was not staying with the Ternans but was coming in from his place near Five Bells Inn. The closest station there was New Cross. I had to take a risk on this and choose Peckham or New Cross...or go to the safer alternative of Charing Cross.

I decided it would be Peckham Station.

But when on 9 June would Dickens be travelling into town?

For the first two anniversaries of Staplehurst, Dickens had escaped Field's agents and apparently met with Drood late at night. It had been after midnight that I saw him in my study, talking to Drood and the Other Wilkie.

If the Inimitable was staying with the Ternans—or at least with Ellen Ternan—up to the time of this third-anniversary rendezvous, my guess was that he would leave their home somewhere between late afternoon and late evening, taking the train to Charing Cross, having dinner at one of his usual haunts, and then disappearing down one of his secret entrances to Undertown somewhere after ten PM.

So the best course of action for me would be to stay on lookout at Peckham Station from sometime in the afternoon until whenever Dickens appeared.

This posed certain problems. The Peckham Station, as I may have mentioned, was never terribly crowded, and the sight of someone even so respectable-looking as myself might bring official attention, perhaps even of the Peckham constabulary, should I be standing around for seven or eight hours without boarding a train. There was also the problem of how I could wait for Dickens without being seen in return. The last thing I wanted was for the author to know that I had been stalking him.

Luckily, my previous reconnoitering had shown me a solution to these difficulties.

Behind Peckham Station, between the depot and the road that ran into the suburban village and to 16 Linden Grove, was a small public park consisting of little more than indifferently tended gardens, a central fountain, and a few gravel paths, including one that traced the perimeter of the park. To give privacy to the park and its occasional visitors (presumably travellers bored of waiting within the station or on the platform), the Peckham town fathers had planted a hedge that completely bordered the little space and was at its highest—about seven feet tall—between the park and the modest highway. The park itself, although opening onto the platform area via a path passing under a trellis, faced only the blind, largely windowless back of the station proper.

A traveller whiling away time in this pocket park would be far less noticeable than someone lounging on the platform for many hours. Especially if the traveller were a respectable, bespectacled gentleman sitting in the sunlight and working on a manuscript—in this case, the galley proof pages for the final number of *The Moonstone*.

Two of the stone benches were in the shade of young trees, but also—fortuitously—set close to the hedgerow bordering the road. Here even the fact that the garden was indifferently tended served my purpose:

there were narrow gaps in the hedge through which a waiting gentleman might watch the road from Peckham without revealing his own presence to those approaching on foot or via carriage.

So that became my final plan—to wait for Charles Dickens in the pocket park behind Peckham Station, to allow him to board before slipping aboard myself, and thence to run into him, quite by "accident," and then to convince him to join me for dinner in London.

By the morning of Tuesday, 9 June, I was sick with worry and convinced that my plan would lead to nothing and that it would be another year, at least, before Dickens might lead me to Drood. More than that, this dinner itself and its attendant conversation were overdue. This was the night that I planned to end forever the image of Wilkie Collins as an amenable and amiable but supplicating protégé to the Literary Master that was Charles Dickens. This was the night that Dickens would have to acknowledge my equality, if not my superiority.

But what if he did not come to town that night after all? But what if he were no longer staying with the Ternans and took the train from New Cross? Or what if he did indeed travel from Peckham but I somehow missed him at the station or…worse…he saw me watching him there and confronted me?

A hundred times I pondered these factors and a hundred times I changed my plans, only to revert to the Peckham Station plan each time. It was far from perfect but it seemed my best chance.

That afternoon of 9 June was pleasant. After days of rain, the sun shone, the flowers in my own garden gleamed, and the air was brisk, promising summer but not yet bringing the oppressive heat and humidity of a full London summer.

For my ride out to Peckham and my wait of unknown

length, I packed in my old leather portmanteau—which I carried with a shoulder strap—the proofs of my last number of *The Moonstone;* a portable pen-and-ink writing set; a copy of Thackeray's most recent novel (should I finish reading my own work); a light lunch and a late-afternoon snack consisting of cheese, biscuits, a few slices of meat, and a hard-boiled egg; a flask of water; another flask of my laudanum; and the deceased Detective Hatchery's pistol.

I had succeeded in checking the revolving cylinder. At first I was surprised to see all the cartridges in place, their round brass circles remaining in their cubicles, and wondered if I had only dreamt firing the weapon in the servants' stairwell. But then I realised that the bases of the brass cartridges remained in this sort of pistol after their lead bullets had been fired.

Five of the nine cartridges had been fired. Four remained.

I pondered whether to remove the spent cartridges or to leave them in place—I simply did not know the proper protocol—but in the end I chose to take the empty cartridges out of the weapon (disposing of them secretly) and remembered only later that I should make sure that the remaining cartridges be in place to fire when I next pulled the trigger. This was achieved simply by rotating the cylinder back to the position it had been in before I removed the empty cartridges.

I wondered if four workable bullets would be enough for my purposes that night. But the point tended to be academic, since I had no clue as to where I might find new bullets to purchase for this odd pistol.

So four would have to be enough. At least three for Drood. I remembered Detective Hatchery once telling me, after our Thursday-night visit to a public house and while on our way to St Ghastly Grim's Cemetery, that even for such a large-calibre pistol as the one he had given me (and I had no idea what "calibre" indicated), those very few detectives who carried pistols were taught to aim and fire at least two shots at the centre torso of their human target. Hatchery had added in a whisper, "And we boys on the street add one for the 'ead."

The words had made me shiver in revulsion on the night I heard them. Now I took them as advice from the grave.

At least three for Drood. Two for centre torso and one for that odd, balding, pale, repulsive, and reptilian head.

The fourth and final bullet...

I would decide later that night.

CHAPTER THIRTY-FIVE

*T*he early parts of my plan worked perfectly.

I spent my afternoon and early evening sitting in ever-more-slanting sunlight in the small park between Peckham Station and the rural thoroughfare. Carriages and pedestrians came and went. A single glance through the hedge from where I sat usually told me all I needed to know to certify the arrivals were not my quarry. The only sidewalk from the station driveway to the station platform ran directly past the trellised entrance to my little park, not thirty steps from my bench, and I found that I could keep pace along my side of the hedge and clearly hear the conversation between any pedestrians approaching the station along that walkway.

As I had hoped and planned, this hedge offered me both concealment and the ability to observe through thin gaps that were rather like vertical gun slits. In the parlance of our day, borrowed from English hunters of good Scottish goose on the wing or Bengal tiger in the jungle, Dear Reader, I was in a blind.

The pleasant afternoon passed into pleasant evening. I finished my lunch and my snack and two-thirds of the laudanum in my flask. I had also finished the proofing of the last instalment of *The Moonstone* and set the long galleys away in my valise with my apple core, cake crumbs, eggshell shards, and pistol. I should have been racked with anxiety as the hours slipped away, torn by the certainty that Dickens had used the New Cross Station or was not going to London at all that day.

But the longer I waited, the more calm I became. Not even the painful shifting of the scarab, which seemed to have burrowed down close to the base of my spine that day, disrupted the rising certainty that calmed my nerves more surely than any opiate. I had never been so sure of anything in my life than that Dickens would come this way this evening. Again, I thought of the experienced hunter of tigers on his raised and camouflaged shooting platform somewhere in India, his oiled, deadly weapon nested secure in the crook of his steady arm. He *knew* when his dangerous prey was approaching, even though he could not have told the non-white hunter *how* he knew.

And then, about eight PM, when the June evening shade was turning into cool twilight, I set down the Thackeray that was not holding my interest, peeked out through the hedge, and there he was.

SURPRISINGLY, Dickens was not alone. He and Ellen Ternan were walking slowly on the park side of the dusty thoroughfare. She was dressed as if for an afternoon outing and, despite the fact that the lane was in full shadow from trees and homes on the west side, carried a parasol. Behind the two of them and on the opposite side of the street, a carriage was creeping along—now stopping, now moving forward slowly—and I realised that it must be one that Dickens had hired to carry Ellen back to Linden Grove from the station. The lovebirds had decided to walk to the station together so that she could see Dickens off.

But there was something wrong. I could sense it in the halting, almost pained way that Dickens was walking and by the strained distance between the two of them. I could tell it by the way that Ellen Ternan would now lower the useless parasol, close it, grip it tightly with both hands, and then open it again. These were not two lovebirds. They were two injured birds.

The carriage stopped a final time and waited along the opposite kerb thirty yards from the entrance drive to the railway station.

As Dickens and Ellen came alongside the high hedge, I was suddenly frightened into immobility. The dying evening light and hedge-shadow should have worked in my favour, making the sometimes sparse hedge seem solid and dark to anyone walking beyond it, but for an instant I was certain that I was clearly visible to the two. In a few seconds Dickens and his mistress would see a familiar small man with a high forehead, tiny glasses, and a voluminous beard huddled on a bench less than two feet from the walkway they would be passing. My heart pounded so wildly that I was sure that *they* would be able to hear it. My hands were half-raised towards my face—as if I had been about to try to hide behind them—and set into the position in which they had frozen. I would appear to Dickens like a soft, pale, wide-eyed, and bearded rabbit caught in the beam of a hunter's lantern.

They did not look in my direction as they passed the hedge. Their voices were low, but I could hear them easily enough. The train had not arrived, the suburban thoroughfare was empty of traffic save for the parked carriage, and the only other sound was the soft coo of doves under the station's eaves.

"...we can put our *sad history* behind us," Dickens was saying.

The italics were obvious from his tone. So was an undertone of pleading that I had never...never...heard from Charles Dickens.

"Our *sad history* is buried in France, Charles," Ellen said very softly. Her broad sleeves brushed the hedge as they moved past me. "But it shall never be behind us."

Dickens sighed. It came out almost as a moan. The two stopped ten paces before the sidewalk reached the turn towards the station. They were not six paces past my blind. I did not stir.

"What is to be done, then?" he said. The words were so loaded with misery that they might have been extracted from a man being tortured.

"Only what we have discussed. It is the only honourable course remaining to us."

"But I cannot!" exploded Dickens. It sounded as if he was weeping. I could have leaned my face six inches closer to the hedge and seen him, but that was impossible. "I have not the will!" he added.

"Then have the courage," said Ellen Ternan.

There came a rustling, the small sound of her small shoes slightly scuffing pavement, the heavier sound of his. I pictured Dickens leaning towards her, she taking an involuntary step back, and Dickens resuming his strained distance from her.

"Yes," he said at last. "Courage. I can summon courage where will fails me. And summon will when courage flags. That has been my life."

"You are my dear good boy," she said softly. I imagined her touching his cheek with her gloved hand.

"Let us both be courageous," she went on, her voice lilting with a forced lightness that ill-befitted a mature woman in her late twenties. "Let us change to brother and sister from this day forth."

"Never to be...together...as we have?" said Dickens. His voice was the calm monotone of a man ordered to the guillotine repeating the judge's sentence.

"Never," said Ellen Ternan.

"Never to be man and wife?" said Dickens.

"Never!"

There was a silence then that stretched for such a length that I was again tempted to lean forward and peek through the hedge to see if Dickens and Ellen had somehow dematerialised. Then I heard the Inimitable sigh again. His voice was louder, stronger, but infinitely hollow when he spoke.

"So it shall be. Adieu, my love."

"Adieu, Charles."

I was sure they did not touch or kiss, although how I was sure, I could not tell you, Dear Reader. I sat motionless as I listened to Dickens's footsteps pass around the curve in the hedge. They paused once at that curve—I was certain he was looking back at her—and then resumed.

I did lean forward then and set my face to the branches of the hedge to watch Ellen Ternan cross the street. The carriage driver saw her and drove forward. Her parasol was folded once again and both her hands were lifted to her face. She did not look towards the station as she got into the carriage—the bewhiskered old driver helping her as she climbed up and took her seat and then softly closing the door behind her—and she did not look towards the station as the old man retook his seat and as the carriage made a slow, broad turn on the empty boulevard and headed back towards Peckham proper.

It was then that I turned my head to the left and looked through the open trellis.

Dickens had passed right in front of the opening, gone up the four steps to the platform level, and now he paused.

I knew what would happen next. He would turn to look out over the park and over the hedge to catch one final glimpse of Ellen Ternan's open carriage disappearing up the street. He *had* to turn. The imperative was written in the tense bunching of his shoulders under his summer linen suit and in the pain of his lowered head and in the half-step pause of his body itself on the platform.

And when he turned—in two seconds, perhaps less—he would see his former collaborator and presumed friend, Wilkie Collins, hunched over from staring through the hedge like the cowardly *voyeur* he was, his bloodless, guilty face staring back blindly at Dickens, his eyes mere blank ovals where the spectacles would be reflecting the paling sky.

But—incredibly, unbelievably, inevitably—Dickens did not turn. He strode around the curve of the station onto the platform proper without ever looking back at the single and greatest love of his sentiment-ridden and romance-driven life.

Seconds later the train to London arrived in the station with shocking exhalations of unseen steam and metallic grindings.

With wildly shaking hands, I pulled my watch from my waistcoat. The express was right on time. It would depart Peckham Station in four minutes and thirty seconds.

I stood, shakily, and retrieved my valise from the bench, but still waited a full four minutes for Dickens to board and take his seat.

Would he be sitting in a compartment on this side, staring out the window at the station as I went hurrying by?

So far this day, the gods had been kind to me. Knowing that they would continue to be for no reason that I could have explained then or now, I clutched the valise to my chest and ran to board before all my overly minded machinations were defeated by the departure of an unthinking but schedule-driven machine.

. . .

IT WAS NOT, of course, a long ride, this express suburban in from Peckham and New Cross to Charing Cross. And it took me most of the ride to work up my nerve to move forward from the rearward compartment of the carriage to which I had rushed. After so many trips with Dickens, I knew which carriage he would have boarded, of course, as well as which part of the almost-empty carriage he would have chosen for the ride.

And yet it was still a shock when, valise still clutched to my chest, I walked forward and found him alone in the compartment, staring at nothing but his own reflection in the window glass. He was a study in absolute sadness.

"Charles!" I cried, feigning pleasurable surprise. Without asking permission, I slipped in to sit opposite him "How uncanny but delightful to find you here! I thought you were in France!"

Dickens's head snapped around and up as if I had slapped him with my glove. In the next few seconds readable emotions flashed across the usually inscrutable Inimitable visage in rapid succession: first absolute shock, then anger bordering on rage, then a pained sense of violation, then a return to the sadness I had glimpsed in his reflection, and finally . . . nothing.

"What are you doing here?" he asked flatly. There was no pretence of greeting, nor the slightest simulation of *bonhomie*.

"Why, I was visiting my elderly cousin. You remember me telling you about her, I am sure, Charles. She lives between New Cross and Peckham, and since Mother died I have found that . . ."

"Did you board at Peckham?" he asked. His eyes, usually warm and animated, were cold and searching and set in a prosecutor's probing, basilisk stare.

"No," I said, feeling the risky lie catch in my throat like a fish bone. "Farther out towards Gad's Hill Place.

My cousin lives between Peckham and New Cross. I took a cab to the Five Bells and boarded there."

Dickens continued staring at me.

"My dear Charles," I managed after a moment of this silence. "You wrote me that you were staying on in France. I am astonished to find you here. When did you get back?"

His silence continued for a terrible, interminable ten more seconds, and then he turned his face back to the glass and said, "Some days ago. I needed a rest."

"Of course you did," I said. "Of course you did. After America…after the premiere of your play in Paris! But how splendid that I have stumbled upon you on this important night."

He slowly turned his face back in my direction. I realised that he looked ten years older than he had a month ago when I had greeted him upon his return from America. The right side of his face looked strangely dead, waxen, drawn down, and slumped. He said, "Important night?"

"The ninth of June," I said softly. I could feel my heart accelerate its pace again. "The third anniversary of…"

"Of…" prompted Dickens.

"Of the terrible event at Staplehurst," I finished. My mouth was very dry.

Dickens laughed then. It was a terrible sound.

"What better place to observe the anniversary of such carnage," he said, "than here in a rattling, swaying carriage set precisely in the same sequence of carriages as on that deadly, fated afternoon. I wonder…how many old bridges shall we cross this evening before reaching Charing Cross, my dear Wilkie?" He looked at me very carefully. "What do you *want*, sir?"

"I want to take you out to dinner," I said.

"No, impossible," said Dickens. "I have to…" He

paused then and looked at me again. "But then again, why not?"

We rode in silence the rest of the way into London.

WE DINED AT VÉREY'S, where we had enjoyed so many celebratory repasts in years gone by. This was not to be one of the more amiable times spent there.

In my planning for this confrontation I had intended to begin the meal and negotiations directly with *I need to see Drood again. I need to go with you tonight when you go into Undertown.*

If Dickens pressed me for a reason, I would describe to him the agony and terror I had suffered from the scarab. (I had reason to believe that he knew something about such agony and terror from that source.) If he did not ask for my reasons, I would simply go along with him that night.

I did not plan to tell him that I intended to put two bullets into the monster Drood's body and one into his ugly head. Dickens might have pointed out that Drood's subterranean minions—the Lascars and Magyars and Chinamen and Negroes and even young Edmond Dickenson with his head shaved—would tear us apart. *So be it* was my response, although I did not expect it to come to that.

But because of what I had overheard in Peckham between the Inimitable and the actress (former actress), I realised that a more subtle and roundabout approach might better serve my cause of going with him to see Drood. (Inspector Field and his agents had never been able to track Dickens into Undertown during the writer's various sojourns there, although they had witnessed him entering various cellars and crypts in central London. The actual secret doorways, passages, and access points remained a mystery known only to Dickens and Drood.)

We discussed the menu with Henry, the *maître d'hôtel,* and the conversation entered that foreign language (which I so loved) of sauces, gravies, and preparations. Then we took our time ordering wines and a cordial before the wines. Then we talked.

We did not have a fully private room—Vérey's now reserved those only for larger parties—but we might as well have: our table was a banquette set within flocked red walls, partitions, and heavy drapes in a raised area away from the main room. Even the noise of the other diners was shielded from us.

"Well," I said at last when Henry, other waiters, and the sommelier were gone and the red velvet drapes closed, "congratulations on the successful premiere of *L'Abîme!*"

We drank to that. Dickens, rousing himself from his thoughts, said, "Yes, it was a great success. Parisian audiences appreciated the revised tale in a way that London audiences did not."

As if you were here since January to see and hear the reaction of London audiences, I thought. I said, "The London production continues still, yet all honours to the new blood of the Parisian version."

"It is much improved," grunted Dickens.

I could put up with such arrogance because, thanks to secret letters from Fechter, I knew that for all of Dickens's illusion that the Parisian premiere had been a triumph, the French critics and enlightened audiences understood it to have been a mere *succès d'estime.* One Parisian critic had written—*"Only the sympathetic respect of the French prevented this* Abîme *from engulfing its authors."*

In other words, Dickens's and Fechter's beloved *Abyss* had been precisely that.

But I could not let Dickens know that I knew this. If he became aware that I was in secret communication with Fechter, he would also realise that I had known that he had left Paris the night of the premiere and had been hiding with his mistress this past week. It would have shown my feigned surprise at seeing him on the train as the lie it was.

"To more such successes," I said, and we touched glasses and drank again.

After a moment or two, I said, "*The Moonstone* is finished. I have completed the proofreading of the final number."

"Yes," said Dickens with no hint of interest. "Wills has sent me the galleys."

"Have you seen the commotion at Wellington Street?" I was referring to the crowds at the door each Friday as mobs pressed in to buy the newest instalment of *The Moonstone*.

"Indeed," Dickens said drily. "I had to use my stick as a sort of machete-knife to hack my way through the crush to get to my office towards the end of May before I left for France. Very inconvenient."

"I dare say," I said. "When I have brought corrections or business papers to Wills in person, I have seen the delivery boys and porters standing in various corners, their packs still on their backs, reading instalments."

"Hmmm," said Dickens.

"I understand that bets are being made on the street—and in some of the better clubs around town, including my Athenaeum—about when the diamond shall finally be found and who shall be revealed as the thief."

"Englishmen will bet on anything," said Dickens. "I have seen gentlemen on a hunt wager a thousand pounds on which direction the next flight of geese shall pass over."

Our sad history *is buried in France* was the phrase that kept going through my head in Ellen Ternan's voice. Had it been a boy infant or a girl? I wondered.

Weary of Dickens's endless condescension, I smiled and said, "Wills reports to me that sales of *The Moonstone* have put both *Our Mutual Friend* and *Great Expectations* in the shade."

Dickens raised his head and looked at me for the first time. Slowly—very slowly—a thin smile widened beneath his thinning moustache and greying beard. "Yes?" he said.

"Yes." I studied the amber of my cordial for a moment and said, "Are you working on anything now, Charles?"

"No. I've found it impossible to begin a new novel, or even a story, although ideas and images flit and buzz in my head as always."

"Of course."

"I have been . . . distracted," he said softly.

"Of course. The American reading tour alone would stop any writer from working."

I had offered the American reading tour as an opening for Dickens to change the subject, since he had much enjoyed discussing his various triumphs there with all of his friends, including me, during the weeks after he came back and before he decamped to Paris. But he chose not to accept my offered segue.

"I have read the galleys of your last numbers," he said.

"Oh?" I said. "Do you find them satisfactory?" It was a perfunctory question, for the first time in our relationship. He was not my editor—Wills had served that needless purpose during the months of Dickens's absence—and although Dickens was nominally my publisher through his magazine, I had already found a real publisher, William Tinsley, for the first book edition of 1,500 copies and had received a promise of £7,500.

"I find the finished book extremely tiresome," Dickens said mildly.

For a moment I could only hold my glass in both hands and stare at the older man. "I beg your pardon?" I said at last.

"You heard me, sir. I find *The Moonstone* tiresome in the extreme. Its construction is awkward beyond endurance; there is a vein of obstinate conceit that runs throughout the entire tale and makes enemies of readers."

I could not believe that my friend of long years was saying this to me. I was embarrassed to feel the blood rising to my cheeks, temples, and ears. Eventually I said, "I am heartily sorry, Charles, if the novel disappoints you. It certainly has not disappointed its many thousands of eager readers."

"So you have been telling me," said Dickens.

"What exactly about the construction do you find tiresome? It follows the structure of your very own *Bleak House*...only with improvements."

As I may have mentioned to you, Dear Reader, the construction of *The Moonstone* was nothing less than brilliant, consisting, as it did, of a series of epistles solicited by one of the offstage characters for most of the other central characters to tell their various stories in series via an assortment of diaries and notes and letters.

Dickens had the effrontery to laugh in my face.

"*Bleak House,*" he said softly, "was told from a limited series of third-person viewpoints, always with an authorial eye above, with the single first-person narration by the dear Miss Esther Summerson. It was constructed as a form of symphony. *The Moonstone* strikes any reader's ear as a contrived cacophony. The level of contrivance in the endless series of first-person written testaments is, as I say, unbelievable and tiresome beyond all words to convey it."

I blinked several times and set my glass down. Henry and two waiters bustled in with the first course. The wine steward bustled in with the first bottle—Dickens tested it and nodded—and the flurry of black tails and starched white collars bustled back out. When they were gone, I said, "I'll have you know that the testimony and character of Miss Clack are the talk of the town. Someone at my club said recently that he has not laughed so well since *The Pickwick Papers*."

Dickens winced. "To compare Miss Clack to Sam Weller or any of the other characters in *The Pickwick Papers,* my dear Wilkie, would be the equivalent of comparing a spavined, swaybacked mule to a thoroughbred racehorse. The characters in *Pickwick* were—as generations of readers and audiences might tell you, should you bother to ask—drawn with a loving eye and a steady hand. Miss Clack is a mean-spirited caricature of a poorly rendered cartoon. There are no Miss Clacks on this world or on any Earth generated by any sane Creator."

"Your Mrs Jellyby from *Bleak House*..." I began.

Dickens held up one hand. "Spare us comparisons with Mrs Jellyby. They simply won't do, dear boy. They simply won't do."

I looked at my food.

"And your character of Ezra Jennings, who springs from nowhere to solve all outstanding questions in the final chapters," continued Dickens, his voice as flat and steady and relentless as one of the tunnel-boring machines working along Fleet Street.

"What about Ezra Jennings? Readers believe him to be a most fascinating character."

"Fascinating..." said Dickens with that terrible smile. "And familiar."

"What do you mean?"

"Do you think I would not remember him?"

"I have no idea what you are talking about, Charles."

"I am talking about the physician's assistant we encountered during our northern walking tour in

September 1857—dear me, almost eleven years ago—when we climbed Carrick Fell and you slipped and sprained your ankle and I had to carry you down the mountain and then take you by cart to the nearest village, where that physician bandaged your ankle and leg. His assistant had precisely that incredible piebald hair and skin which graces your monster called 'Ezra Jennings.'"

"Do we not compose from real life?" I asked. My voice sounded plaintive in my own ears, and I hated that.

Dickens shook his head. "From real life, yes. But it cannot have escaped your attention that I had already created your Ezra Jennings in the form of Mr Lorn, the albino and piebald assistant to Dr Speddie in our collaborative *Lazy Tour of Two Idle Apprentices* in the Christmas Issue that same year."

"I fail to see the similarities," I said stiffly.

"Do you really? How odd. The tale of Mr Lorn—the dead man in the bed who came back to life in the young Dr Speddie's shared room in the overcrowded inn—took up the bulk of that rather forgettable short novel. The same tragic past. The same haunted expression and manner of speaking. The same albino complexion and piebald hair. I clearly remember writing those scenes."

"Ezra Jennings and Mr Lorn are two quite different characters," I said.

Dickens nodded. "They are certainly different in texture. Mr Lorn had a tragic past and character. Your Ezra Jennings, of all the diseased and unnatural characters you have created in your quest for the sensational, is the most repellent and disturbing."

"Disturbing in what way, may I ask?"

"You may ask and I will tell you, my dear Wilkie. Ezra Jennings, besides being the worst sort of opium addict—a trait shared by so *many* of your characters, my dear boy—shows every sign of inversion."

"Inversion?" I had lifted a forkful of something minutes earlier, but it had yet to reach my mouth.

"Not to mince words," Dickens said softly, "it is obvious to everyone reading *The Moonstone* that Ezra Jennings is a sodomite."

My fork stayed raised; my mouth remained open. "Nonsense!" I said at last. "I meant no such implication!"

Or had I? I realised that—as with the Miss Clack chapters—the Other Wilkie had written most of the Ezra Jennings numbers when I was attempting to dictate while in the deepest throes of my morphine and laudanum.

"And your so-called Quivering Sands…" began Dickens.

"Shivering Sands," I corrected.

"As you wish. They do not exist, you must know."

Here I had him. *Here* I had *him!* "They do indeed," I said, voice rising. "As any yachtsman such as myself would know. There's a shoal just like the Shivering Sands on the Thames Estuary, nine miles north of Herne Bay."

"Your Quivering Sands do not exist along the coast of Yorkshire," said Dickens. He was, I realised, calmly cutting and eating his meat. "Everyone who has ever visited Yorkshire knows that. Anyone who has ever *read* about Yorkshire knows that."

I opened my mouth to speak—to speak bitingly—and could think of nothing to say. It was at this point that I remembered the loaded revolver in my valise sitting next to me on the banquette.

"And many believe, as I do, as Wills does, that the scene with your Quivering Sands shivering is also indecent," said Dickens.

"For God's sake, Dickens, how could a shoal, a strand, a beach stretch, of quicksand be considered *indecent* by any sane person?"

"Perhaps," said Dickens, "through the author's choice

of language and insinuation. And I quote from memory—and from your poor, doomed Miss Spearman's observation—'*The brown face of it heaved slowly, and then dimpled and quivered all over.*' The brown face, my dear Wilkie, the brown *skin*, dimpling and quivering all over and then, and I believe I quote, *sucking one down*—which is precisely what it does to poor Miss Spearman. An overt and clumsy description of what some might imagine a woman's physical climax in the act of love to be like, no?"

Again, I could only stare with mouth agape.

"But it is the ending, your much-anticipated resolution to this much-admired mystery, that I find to be the apex and pinnacle of contrivance, my dear boy," went on Dickens.

I realised that he might never stop talking. I imagined the dozens of diners in the other alcoves and in the larger room of Vérey's all pausing in their meals, all listening, shocked but attentive.

"Do you *really* believe," bored on Dickens, "or expect *us*, the readers, to believe that a man, motivated by a few drops of opium in a small glass of wine, would walk in his sleep, enter his fiancée's sleeping room—a scene that was all but indecent for that impropriety alone—and go through her safe box and belongings, and then steal and secrete a diamond elsewhere, all *with no memory of the event afterwards?*"

"I am sure of it," I said coldly, stiffly.

"Oh? How can you be sure of such a ridiculous thing, dear boy?"

"Every reference to behaviour under the ministrations of laudanum, pure opium, or other drugs in *The Moonstone* was carefully researched and experienced by me before I put pen to paper," I said.

Dickens laughed then. It was a long, full, easy, and cruel laugh and it went on far too long.

I stood, threw down my linen napkin, lifted my valise, and opened it. The huge pistol was quite visible there beneath my curled galley sheets and the remnants of my lunch.

I closed the valise and stalked out, almost forgetting my hat and stick in my rush. I could hear Henry bustling into the alcove at the rear to enquire of "Mr Dickens" as to whether there was anything wanting with the food or service.

Three blocks from Vérey's I stopped, still breathing hard, still clutching my walking stick as if it were a hammer, not noticing the traffic or the busy streets on this lovely June evening or even the ladies of the night who were watching me from the shadows of an alley across the way.

"God d——n it!" I cried loudly, startling two ladies walking with an older, stooped gentleman. *"God d——n it!"*

I turned and ran back to the restaurant.

This time all conversation *did* stop as I ran through the main room and threw back the curtains to the alcove.

Dickens was gone, of course. And my last chance on the third anniversary of Staplehurst to follow him to Drood's lair was gone with him.

CHAPTER THIRTY-SIX

*I*n July, my brother was staying at Gad's Hill Place for an extended period because of his health. Charley had been very ill with terrible stomach cramps and had been vomiting for days on end. His wife, Katey, continued to find it easier to care for him at her father's house than at their home in London. (I also believe she found it more comfortable for herself to be waited on there.)

On this particular day, Charley was feeling somewhat better and was in the library at Gad's Hill, talking to the other Charley—Dickens's son—who was doing some work in the library there. (I don't believe I mentioned, Dear Reader, that in May, my editor and Charles Dickens's indefatigable sub-editor at *All the Year Round*, William Henry Wills, had somehow contrived to fall off his horse during a hunt and put a serious crease in his skull. Wills recovered somewhat but announced that he continued to hear doors slamming all the time. This reduced his effectiveness as an editor, also as Dickens's administrator, accountant, manager, marketing chief, and ever-faithful factotum, so Dickens—after asking me to come back to the magazine in May and receiving no positive reply—had put his rather ineffectual and disappointing son Charles in the position of filling at least some of Wills's many duties while he, the Inimitable, took care of the rest. What this amounted to was that his son was answering letters at the office and at home, but even this required at least 110 percent of Charles Dickens Junior's feeble capabilities.)

So on this July day at Gad's Hill, my brother, Charley, was in the library there with Charley Dickens when suddenly both young men heard two people, a man and a woman, shouting and arguing, the rising racket coming from somewhere on the lawn out of sight below and behind the house. It was the unmistakable sound of a quarrel escalating into violence. The woman's screams, my brother later told me, were terrifying.

Both Charleys rushed down and outside and around the house, Dickens's son arriving a full half-minute before my convalescing brother.

There, in the meadow behind the long yard and barn where Dickens and I had seen young Edmond Dickenson sleepwalking several Christmases earlier, Charles Dickens was now striding up and down, speaking and shouting in two different voices, one male, one female, all the while gesticulating wildly and finally rushing an unseen victim and attacking... attacking *her*... with a great, invisible club.

Dickens had become the bully-thug Bill Sikes from *Oliver Twist* and was lost in the bloody act of murdering Nancy.

She tried to escape, crying out for mercy. No mercy, bellowed Bill Sikes. She cried out for God to help her. God did not answer, but Bill Sikes did, shouting and cursing and striking her down with his heavy club.

She tried to rise, holding her arm and hand up to ward off the blow. Dickens/Sikes struck again, and again, breaking her delicate fingers, smashing the bones of her upraised forearm, then bringing the full weight of the club down on her bloodied head. And again. And again.

Charley Dickens and Charley Collins could *see* the blood and brain tissue flying. They could *see* the pool of blood growing beneath the now prone dying woman as Bill Sikes continued clubbing her. They could *see* the blood spattering Sikes's screaming, distorted face. The very paws and legs of Sikes's dog were bloody!

And still he kept clubbing her, even after she was dead.

Still crouched over the imaginary woman's corpse, the invisible club still held in two hands and poised above the battered and bloody form in the grass, Charles Dickens looked up at his son and my brother. His face was twisted and contorted in triumph. His eyes were wide, wild, and in no way sane. My brother, Charley, later said that he was sure he could see pure, murderous evil in the eyes of that twisted, gloating countenance.

The Inimitable had, at long last, found his Murder for his next round of public readings.

It was at about this time that I became certain that I had to kill Charles Dickens.

He would pretend to murder his imaginary Nancy on stage, in front of thousands. I would murder him in real life. We would see which ritual murder was more effective in driving the Drood-scarab out of a man's brain.

To prepare the way, I wrote him a letter of apology, even though I had nothing to apologise for and Dickens had everything for which to beg forgiveness. It made no difference.

90 Gloucester Place Saturday, 18 July, 1868
My Dear Charles:
  I write to offer my sincere and total apologies for the contretemps *I provoked last month at our favourite place of dining,* Vérey's. *My failure to consider that you were overtired from your many travels and exertions*

undoubtedly provoked the illusion of disagreement between us, and my not-unusual clumsiness in expression led to unfortunate consequences for which I again apologise and humbly ask your forgiveness. (Any accidental attempt on my part to compare my poor current literary efforts to your incomparable Bleak House were presumptuous and in error. No one shall ever confuse this humble protégé with Cher Maître.)

It is somewhat more difficult for me to entertain at home since Mrs Caroline G—— left my home and service, but I still hope that you will be my guest at No. 90 Gloucester Place before too much more of the year passes. Also, as I am sure you have noticed despite your business with All the Year Round in our poor friend Wills's absence, our wonderful success, No Thoroughfare, has finally closed at the Adelphi Theatre. I confess to have begun making rough notes about another play—I believe I shall call it Black and White, since it may be about a French nobleman who, for one reason or another, finds himself on the auction in Jamaica, being sold as a slave. Our dear mutual friend Fechter suggested the general idea some months ago—I plan to speak to him about it in detail in October or November—and Fechter would love to play the lead. In preparing this work I would be most grateful if I could avail myself of your advice and criticism so that I might avoid the more egregious errors so plentiful in my contributions to No Thoroughfare. In any case, I would consider it an honour if you and your entire family would be my guests at premiere night at the Adelphi should this modest effort ever succeed in being staged.

With final and abject apologies and most sincere wishes for a mending of this unforeseen and unwanted breach in the constant history of our cordial relationships, I remain . . .

Affectionately and Loyally Yours,
W. C. Collins

I looked this note over for some time, making small changes here and there, always in the direction of the contrite and servile. I had no fear whatsoever that this missive would someday come to light after Dickens's sudden and mysterious death and cause curiosity in the biographer who read it. Dickens was still in the habit of annually burning every letter he received. (He would have burned every letter he *sent* as well, if he could have, but most of us who corresponded with the famous man did not share his pyromaniacal tendencies when it came to communications.)

Then I had George send it off by post and I went out to buy a bottle of good brandy and a puppy.

THE NEXT AFTERNOON I carried the brandy, a copy of this week's *All the Year Round*, and the unnamed puppy with me as I took the train to Rochester and hired a carriage to take me to the cathedral.

I left the puppy in the carriage but took the brandy and paper as I walked through the graveyard to the back of the high, hulking cathedral. Rochester had always been a coastal city of narrow streets and redbrick buildings, which made this colossus of an ancient grey stone cathedral seem all the more impressive and oppressive.

This was the very landscape of Charles Dickens's childhood. It was the presence of this very cathedral that had caused him to say to me years ago that Rochester reflected, for him, "universal gravity, mystery, decay, and silence."

There was silence enough this hot, humid July day. And I could smell the stench of decay from the nearby tidal flats. Even with what Dickens had once called "the splash and flop of the tide" geographically nearby, there was no splashing audible this day, precious little flop, and absolutely no breeze. The full weight of the sun lay on the baking old headstones and browning grass like an incongruous gold blanket.

Even the shade of the cathedral tower gave little relief. I leaned back and stared up at that grey tower and remembered Dickens's comment about how it had affected him when he was a tiny boy—"...what a brief little practical joke I seemed to be, my dear Wilkie, in comparison with its solidity, stature, strength, and length of life."

Well, Dear Reader, if I had my way—and I fully intended to—the cathedral might go on for centuries or millennia more, but the length of life for that little-boy-turned-old-man-writer was all but at its end.

At the far end of the graveyard, beyond the head-stones, with only the slightest path leading to it, I found the quick-lime pit still open, still full, and as foul as ever. My eyes watered as I walked back through the graveyard, passing by the very stones and wall and flat headstone-table where Dickens, Ellen Ternan, Ellen's mother, and I had shared that macabre luncheon so long ago.

I followed the soft TIP-TAP-TIP-TAP around the cathedral, past the rectory, and into a courtyard on the far side. Between the stone wall and a low hovel of stones and thatch, Mr Dradles and an idiot-looking young assistant were working on a headstone taller than either of them. Only the name and the dates—GILES BRENDLE GYMBY, 1789–1866—had been chiselled out of the marble.

When Mr Dradles turned to me, I saw that his face, under a layer of stone dust riveted with tracks of his perspiration, was red to the point of bursting. He mopped his forehead as I came closer.

"You probably do not remember me, Mr Dradles," I began. "But I came here some time ago in the company of..."

"Dradles remembers 'ee, Mr Billy Wilkie Collins, named after a Sirred house painter or some'at," rasped the red-faced figure. "You was here with Mr Charles D., of all them books an' such, who was interested in the ol' 'uns in their dark beds."

"Exactly," I said. "But I felt that you and I got off on the wrong foot."

Dradles looked down at his worn, holed boots, which, I noted, were not "differentiated." That is, there was no left or right to them, as had been the custom decades ago. "Dradles's feet are the only 'uns Dradles has," he said. "The can't be no wrong 'un."

I smiled. "True, true. But I felt that I may have left the wrong impression. I brought you this…" I handed him the bottle of fine brandy.

Dradles looked at it, mopped his face and neck again, uncorked the bottle, sniffed it, swigged it, squinted at me, and said, "This 'ere is better drink 'an Dradles is used to at the Thatched an' Twopenny or anywheres else." He drank again. His assistant, whose face was as red from the heat and labour as Dradles's, stared stupidly but did not ask for a drink.

"Speaking of the Thatched and Twopenny," I said conversationally, "I do not see your rock-hurling young devil around. What did you call him? Deputy? Is it too early in the day for him to be pelting you homeward?"

"That d——ned boy is dead," said Dradles. He saw my expression and chuckled. "Oh, Dradles di'n't kill 'im, though Dradles thought to more 'an a time. No, the pox killed 'im and the pox be welcome to 'im." He took another deep drink and squinted at me. "No gen'lman, not even Mr D., come up from London to bring Dradles 'spensive drink for no reason, Mr Billy Wilkie Collins. Mr D. wanted me to open doors for 'im with me many keys and tap-tap out the where'bouts of the ol' 'uns in their hollers. What is that Mr Billy W. C. wants from old Dradles this hot day?"

"You may remember that I am an author also," I said. I handed the stonemason and crypt-cathedral caretaker the copy of *All the Year Round*. "This, as you see, was last Friday's number carrying the concluding chapters of my novel *The Moonstone*." I opened the periodical to the proper page.

Dradles stared at the mass of type but only grunted. I had no idea whether the man could read. My guess was that he could not.

"It has come to pass," I said, "that I also am doing some literary research involving a great cathedral such as this. A great cathedral and its attendant crypts."

"'E wants the keys, Dradles thinks," said Dradles. "'E wants the keys to the old 'uns' dark places." It would have seemed that he was addressing his idiot lop-eared assistant with the haircut that seemed to have been applied with sheep shears, but the boy appeared to be deaf and dumb.

"Not at all," I said with an easy laugh. "The keys are your responsibility and must remain such. I would merely like to visit from time to time and perhaps avail myself of your expertise in tapping out the hollow places. I certainly would never come empty-handed."

Dradles took another swig. The bottle was already more than half empty and the filthy mason's face, even under the Marley-was-dead coating of dust, was redder than ever (if such a thing was possible).

"Dradles does an 'onest day's work for 'is occasional tipple," he said thickly.

"As do I," I said with an easy laugh.

He nodded then and turned back to his carving—or, rather, to supervising the idiot boy in his carving. Evidently the interview was over and the contract had been consummated.

Mopping my own face from the heat, I walked slowly back to the carriage. The puppy—an ungainly but enthusiastic thing with long legs, a short tail, and spots—was leaping with joy on the cushioned seat at the sight of me.

"It will be just another minute, driver," I said. The old man, half-dozing, grunted and let his chin fall back to his liveried chest.

I carried the puppy back through the graveyard, past our picnic site. Remembering how Dickens had made us all laugh when he put a towel over his arm and perfectly mimicked the behaviour of an efficient but officious waiter, carrying our dishes from the wall to the table-headstone, expertly pouring wine for us all, I walked on with a smile. The puppy had settled in the crook of my arm, its tail still trying to wag from time to time, and its large eyes looking up adoringly at me. Caroline, Carrie, and I had owned several dogs in the past decade and more. Our last beloved pet had died only months earlier.

A gnarled old tree near the rear boundary of the cathedral yard had dropped a branch about four feet long. Still carrying the puppy in my left arm, rubbing the back of its head and neck absently with my thumb as I held it, I picked up the branch, kicked away its small protuberances, and used it as a sort of walking stick.

In the weeds beyond the cemetery, I paused and looked around. The carriage and road were out of sight. Nothing and no one moved in the churchyard proper. From far beyond the cathedral came the TIP-TAP-TIP-TAP of Dradles's—or, rather, Dradles's apprentice's—hot and careful work. The only other sound was the buzz and chitter of insects here in the weeds and high grass that led east to the tidal flats. Even the sea and its attending river were silent in this glare of sunlight.

With one smooth motion, I wrung the puppy's neck.

The snap was audible but not loud. The small body went limp in my arms.

I glanced around again and then dropped the puppy's carcass into the lime pit. There was no dramatic hiss or bubbling. The little black-and-white-spotted form just lay there, a bit more than half submerged in the thick grey gruel of quick-lime. Bending and using the branch, I carefully prodded the puppy's ribs and head and hindquarters until the tiny form was just beneath the surface. Then I tossed the branch into the high grass and marked the spot where it landed.

Twenty-four hours? Forty-eight? I decided to give it seventy-two hours—and a little more, since I planned to wait until dusk—before coming back to use the same branch to poke out and analyse the results.

Softly whistling a tune that had become popular in the music halls that summer, I strolled back through the graveyard to the waiting carriage.

hree days later I received a pleasant note from
Dickens thanking me for my letter, implicitly
accepting my apologies, and inviting me out to Gad's
Hill Place at my earliest convenience. He also graciously
suggested that I might want to visit my brother there,
as Charley remained too ill to return to London.

I accepted the invitation and left for Gad's Hill the
same day. It was excellent timing, since I wanted to go
to the Rochester graveyard lime pit that evening in any
event.

Katey Dickens met me on the front lawn as she had
some years earlier. The day was warm, but there was a
pleasant breeze that brought the healthy smell of the
surrounding fields. The carefully tended shrubs, trees,
and red geraniums all stirred to that breeze, as did
Kate's long, gauzy summer dress. Her hair, I noticed,
was pinned on the sides but down in the back: an
unusual and not-unpleasant look for her.

"Charles is sleeping," she said. "He had a terrible
night and although I know you wish to see him, I think
it better if he were not disturbed."

I knew she was talking about my brother, not her
father. I nodded. "I need to head back before supper,
but perhaps Charley will wake before then."

"Perhaps," said Katey, but her expression suggested
otherwise. She slipped her arm in mine. "Father is

working in the chalet. I'll walk you through the tunnel."

My eyebrows rose. "Working in the chalet? I was under the impression that he was not writing fiction at the present time."

"He's not, Wilkie. He's busy working on that terrible new murder-reading of his."

"Ahh." We strolled across the manicured lawn and down into the tunnel. As was almost always the case in summer, the cool air in the long, dark passageway was a relief from the humidity above.

"Wilkie, do you ever wonder about whether Father is right?"

No, I thought. *Never.* I said, "About what, my dear?"

"About your brother."

I felt some alarm course through me. "About the seriousness of his illness, you mean?"

"About everything."

I could not believe that she was asking *me* this. Rumours that Kate and Charley had never consummated their marriage continued, fueled by Charles Dickens's malicious comments. If her father's insinuations were to be believed, my brother was either a closet sodomite or impotent or both.

This line of questioning certainly would not do.

I patted her hand. "Your father hated losing you above all things, Katey. You have always been the closest to him. Any suitor or husband would have fallen under his wrath."

"Yes," agreed Katey. Modesty was never one of her more salient charms. "But Charley and I spend so much time here at Gad's Hill Place that it is almost as if I never left home."

I had nothing to say to that. Especially since everyone knew that it was *her* choice to live here when Charley was so ill—which was almost all of the time now.

"Do you ever wonder, Wilkie, what it would be like if *you and I* had married rather than your brother and me?"

I almost stopped walking. My heart, already accelerated by my mid-day liberal application of laudanum, began pounding against my ribs.

There was a time when I had considered courting the young Kate Dickens. During what everyone but the Dickenses thought of as "the divorce"—the terrible and permanent separation when Charles Dickens effectively sent his wife, Catherine, into permanent exile—young Kate, of all the children, seemed the most hurt and disoriented by the sudden dissolution of what most had thought of as the perfect English family. She was eighteen when all of the confusion and dislocation was going on—she became engaged to my brother when she was twenty—and I admitted to finding her attractive in some subtle way. Even then I sensed that she would not, as would her sister Mamie, put on the plumpness and matronly aspect of her mother.

But before I could even explore my interest in Katey, she had fallen in love—or at least become smitten— with Dickens's and my friend Percy Fitzgerald. When Fitzgerald rather coldly rejected her maidenly advances, Katey had suddenly turned to my brother, Dickens's illustrator and a frequent visitor to Gad's Hill at the time.

I may have mentioned previously, Dear Reader, that this romantic interest on Kate's part astounded all of us. Charley had only moved away from our mother's home some weeks earlier and had never shown any serious interest in girls or courting.

Now this. It did not escape my awareness there in that concealing tunnel that Katey must have known, if only via her father's love of gossip, that I had sent Caroline G—— away from my home and was now (to their knowledge) a prosperous and somewhat famous bachelor living alone with my servants and sometimes "niece" Carrie.

I smiled to show that I knew Kate was jesting and said, "It would have been a most interesting partnership, I am sure, my dear. Between your inimitable will and my unceasing intransigence, our quarrels would have been legendary."

Katey did not smile. The end of the tunnel was an arc of light when she stopped and looked at me. "I sometimes believe that we all end up with the wrong people in our lives—Father and Mother, Charles and me, you and...that woman—perhaps everyone but Percy Fitzgerald and that simpering lady of his."

"And William Charles Macready," I said in a pleasant, teasing tone. "We must not forget the ancient thespian's second wife. It truly seems a marriage made in heaven."

Katey laughed. "One woman who found happiness," she said and took my arm and led me out into the light and let me go.

My dear Wilkie! How wonderful of you to come!" cried Dickens as I came up into the chalet's airy first storey. He leaped to his feet, came around his simple desk, and clasped my hand in both of his. I half-recoiled in terrible anticipation of a hug. It was as if our night at Vérey's a month and some ago had never happened.

The Inimitable's chalet summer workroom was as pleasant as ever, especially with this breeze blowing in from the distant sea and rustling all of the two cedar trees' branches outside the open windows. Dickens had added a bent-back cane chair on the opposite side of his desk and now he waved me to it as he went back to his comfortable-looking heavy writing chair. He waved to boxes and a carafe on his desk. "Cigar? Some iced water?"

"No, thank you, Charles."

"I cannot tell you how glad I am that all is forgiven and forgotten," he said warmly. He did not specify who had had to do the forgiving and forgetting.

"I feel the same way."

I glanced at the stacks of pages on his desktop. Dickens saw my glance and handed me several of them. I had seen this method before. He had torn pages out of one of his books—in this case, *Oliver Twist*—mounted the pages on stiff pasteboard, and was busy scrawling changes, additions, deletions, and marginal comments. He would then send these to his printers and have a final version printed up—three lines of white space between the oversized text, wide margins in which to add more stage and reading comments, and notes in very large script. This would be his reading text for the coming tour.

The changes to the text were interesting enough, turning a novel meant to be read into a script meant to be heard, but it was the stage directions jotted in the margins that caught my eye:

"Beckon down...Point...Shudder...Look Round with Terror...Murder coming..."

And on the next pasteboard sheet:

> ...he beat it *twice* upon the upturned face *that almost touched his own...seized a heavy club,* and *struck her down!!...the pool of gore that quivered and danced in the sunlight on the ceiling...but such* flesh, *and so much blood!!!...The very feet of the dog were bloody!!!!...dashed out his brains!!!!*

I blinked at this. *His* brains. I had forgotten that Sikes killed both Nancy and the dog.

"Terror to the End!" was scrawled at least five times on the various page margins.

I set them back on the desk and smiled at Dickens. "Your Murder at last," I said.

"At last," agreed Dickens.

"And I thought that I was the novelist of sensation, Charles."

"This Murder shall serve more than sensation, my dear Wilkie. I wish to leave behind in those who attend my final, farewell round of readings a sense of something very passionate and dramatic, something done with simple means yet to a complex emotional end."

"I see," I said. What I actually saw was that Dickens intended to shock the everlasting sensibilities out of his audience. "Is it truly then to be a farewell round of readings?"

"Hmmm," grunted Dickens. "So our friend Beard tells me. So Dolby tells me. So the special physicians in London and even Paris tell me. So even does Wills tell me, although he never approved of the reading tours in the first place."

"Well, Charles, we can somewhat discount dear Wills. His opinions these days are filtered through the constant sound of doors slamming in his skull."

Dickens chuckled but then said, "Alas, poor Wills, I knew him, Horatio."

"On a hunt," I said, feigning sadness. As if on cue, a rider in fox-hunt red, white breeches, and gleaming high boots sitting astride a huge grey-dappled high-prancer straining at the bit passed on Gravesend Road below. A dray waggon filled with manure rumbled past immediately after that noble image. Dickens and I glanced at each other and laughed at the same instant. It was like the old days.

Except for the fact that I now wished him dead.

When our laughter died, Dickens said, "I have been thinking more about your *Moonstone,* Wilkie."

My entire body tensed. But I managed a wan smile.

Dickens held both his hands out and up, palms towards me. "No, no, my dear friend. I mean in totally admiring and professionally respectful ways."

I held the smile in place.

"You may not have been aware of it, my dear Wilkie, but it is possible that with that sensationalist novel you may have created an entirely new genre of fiction."

"Of course I am aware of it," I said stiffly. I had no idea what he was talking about.

Dickens did not seem to have heard me. "The idea of an entire novel revolving around a single mystery, with an interesting and three-dimensional detective character—perhaps a private enquiry detective rather than a formal police detective—in a central position, and with all character development and nuance of daily verisimilitude flowing from the side-effects and after-effects of whatever crime was the mainspring for the novel's central tale...why, it is revolutionary!"

I nodded humbly.

"I have decided to take a whack at it myself," said Dickens, using one of the more execrable American expressions he had picked up on his last tour there.

At that moment I hated the man without reservation. "Do you have a title for this theoretical work yet?" I heard myself ask in a normal-enough voice.

Dickens smiled. "I was thinking of something straightforward, my dear Wilkie...something like *The Mystery of Edmond Dickenson.*"

I confess that I started in my chair. "Have you heard from young Edmond, then?"

"Not at all. But your questions about him last year made me think that the idea of a young man simply disappearing, with no clue as to his whereabouts or reasons for leaving, might lead to some interesting complications if murder were involved."

I felt my heart pounding and wished that I could take a steadying drink of the laudanum from my flask in my jacket's chest pocket. "And do you think that young Edmond Dickenson was murdered?" I asked.

I remembered Dickenson with his shaved head and sharp teeth and fanatic's eyes, wearing a hooded robe and chanting at the ceremony in which Drood had loosed the scarab into my vitals. At the very memory of it, the scarab stirred and shifted in the back of my brain.

"Not a bit of it!" laughed Dickens. "I had every reason to believe young Edmond when he said that he was taking his money and travelling, perhaps relocating in Australia. And I certainly would change the character's name and the title. It was merely to give an idea of the overall story."

"Interesting," I lied.

"And mesmerism," said Dickens, steepling his fingers as he sat back and smiled at me.

"What about it, Charles?"

"I know you are interested in it, Wilkie. Your interest in it is almost as old as mine, although you have never practised it as I have. And you introduced it, subtly, into *The Moonstone*, although more as a metaphor than reality, but you failed to use it properly."

"How so?"

"The solution to your so-called mystery," said Dickens in that maddening, schoolmaster's tone he used with me so frequently. "You have Mr Franklin Blake stealing the diamond in his opium-dream sleep but not *knowing* that he has stolen it...."

"As I said before," I said coolly, "this is most feasible and totally possible. I have researched it myself and..."

Dickens waved that away. "But, my dear Wilkie, the

discerning reader—perhaps all readers—must ask, Why did Franklin Blake steal his beloved's diamond?"

"And the answer is obvious, Charles. Because he was *afraid* that someone might steal it and therefore, under the dream-influence of opium he did not know he had ingested, he walked in his sleep and...stole it." I heard the lameness in my own voice.

Dickens smiled. "Precisely. It strains credulity and endangers verisimilitude. But if you had one of your characters *mesmerise* Franklin Blake and *order* him to steal the diamond, and add to that the mischievous use of opium in his wine (although I would have had both the mesmerism and the opium a *deliberate* part of the plot, a conspiracy rather than mere accident)...well, everything falls into place, doesn't it, my dear Wilkie?"

I sat thinking about this for a moment. It was far too late to make changes. The last number of the serialised novel had already appeared in both *All the Year Round* and in the Harper brothers' magazine in America and the complimentary leather-bound three-decker copies of the Tinsley edition were already completed and ready to be sent by messenger to Dickens and others.

I said, "But I still maintain that it violates the rules of mesmerism, Charles. You and I both know that Professor Elliotson and others taught that someone cannot do under the influence of the magnetic powers anything he or she would not do—in moral terms—when fully conscious."

Dickens nodded. "Indeed, but Elliotson has shown—*I have shown*—that under the magnetic influence, the subject may alter his or her behaviour for extended periods of time because he or she has been told that something is true that is not."

I did not understand this and said so.

"A woman might never carry her baby outside at night," continued Dickens, "but if you were to mesmerise her and tell her that the house was on fire—or would *be* on fire, say, at nine PM—she would, either while in the mesmeric trance or much later under the influence of suggestion, seize up her baby and rush outside even when no flames were visible. In this way, your Hindoos in *The Moonstone* might have mesmerised Franklin Blake when he came upon them on the estate's grounds, and your meddling doctor . . . Mr Sweets?"

"Mr Candy," I supplied.

"Mr Candy then would have secretly administered the laudanum to poor Franklin Blake as part of a larger plot, not out of sheer random malice that should have seen him put in jail."

"You're saying that dear old Mr Candy was also under the mesmeric influence of the Hindoos?" I said. Suddenly I could see all these connections bringing together disparate and separate strands that I had left disparate and separate in my novel.

"That would have been elegant," said Dickens, still smiling. "Or perhaps the vile drug addict, Ezra Jennings, was in on the plot to steal the Koh-i-noor."

"The Moonstone," I corrected absently. "But *my* Ezra Jennings is a sort of hero. He is the one who explains the mystery and then re-creates it for Franklin Blake in Blake's aunt's house in Yorkshire. . . ."

"A re-creation of events that is very handy to resolving your tale," Dickens said quietly, "but which may strain the reader's credulity more than any other element."

"Why is that?"

"Because the conditions of the original night, the night the diamond was stolen, could *not be re-created*, my dear Wilkie. One essential element has been changed, and that would preclude all chance of the sleepwalking and theft occurring again."

"What element is that?" I asked.

"In the so-called experiment, Mr Franklin Blake *knows* that he was drugged; he *knows* that Jennings believes he stole the diamond; he *knows* the sequence of events that took place and should take place again. That in itself would absolutely eliminate any chance that the same amount of opium..."

"I had Jennings use more in the wine than Mr Candy originally used," I interrupted.

"Irrelevant," said Dickens with another infuriatingly dismissive wave of his fingers. "The point is that the re-creation of events itself is impossible. And your Mr Ezra Jennings—probable sodomite, addicted opium eater...his adoration of De Quincey's *Confessions of an English Opium Eater* comes close to being nauseating—is a poor hero-substitute for Franklin Blake. As it stands, Blake comes across as a sort of idiot. But if you had used the Hindoos properly to introduce *mesmerism* as part of the theft, included the administration of opium as a *means* to that conspiracy rather than as pure accident..."

Dickens broke off. I had nothing to say. A heavy waggon lumbered by out of sight on the highway below, pulled by four large horses by the sounds of it.

"But it is your use of the detective—Sergeant Cuff—that I find close to brilliant," Dickens said suddenly. "*That* is what makes me consider writing my own novel of mystery, preferably with such a keen mind at the centre of it. Cuff is wonderful...his lean build, his cold, penetrating gaze, and his almost mechanically perfect mind. A wonderful invention!"

"Thank you, Charles," I said softly.

"If only you had used him properly!"

"I beg your pardon?"

"You draw him brilliantly, introduce him brilliantly, and he behaves brilliantly...right up to the place where he wanders off the track, disappears from the narrative for an aeon's length, makes all the wrong assumptions despite so much evidence to the contrary, and then becomes unavailable, going off to Brighton to raise bees...."

"To Dorking to breed roses," I corrected with a strange surge of déjà vu.

"Of course. But the *character* of Sergeant Cuff—this idea, as I said, to have a private rather than public detective the centre of a novel of mystery—is wonderful. I believe that readers would resonate wonderfully to such a master of deduction, perhaps as lean and commanding as Cuff, eccentric, almost totally unemotional, if his background and character were fleshed out a bit more. I shall enjoy seeing whether I can create such a character for my *Mystery of Edmond Dickenson*, should I ever get around to writing such a thing."

"You can bring back your Inspector Bucket from *Bleak House*," I said morosely. "He was most popular. I believe we discussed the fact that there were images of Bucket on tobacco cards."

"We did. There were," chuckled Dickens. "He was perhaps the most popular character in the book, and I admit to enjoying his scenes very much. But Inspector Bucket was a man of the world and a man *in* the world...he lacked the mystery and appeal of your lean, cool, detached Sergeant Cuff. Besides, since the original for Bucket, Inspector Charles Frederick Field, is no longer among the living, I should, by all propriety, consign his copy to the grave as well."

For what seemed like a long time I could not speak. I had to concentrate on breathing and not showing through my expression the riot of thoughts and emotions that was surging through me. At long last I said, as calmly as I could, "Inspector Field is dead?"

"Oh, yes! Died last winter while I was on tour in America. Georgina noticed it in the *Times* and clipped the obituary for me, knowing that I should like it in my files."

"I've heard nothing of this," I said. "Do you happen to remember the date of his death?"

"I do," said Dickens. "It was nineteen January. Two of my sons—Frank and Henry—were born on fifteen January, you may recall, so I remembered the date for Field's death."

"Extraordinary," I said, although I have no idea whether I was commenting on Dickens's memory or Inspector Field's death. "Did the obituary in the *Times* say how he died?"

"In bed, at home, of ill health, I believe," said Dickens. The subject of the inspector obviously bored him.

January 19 would have been the day after—or perhaps the night of—our expedition into Undertown. I had been unconscious until 22 January and in no shape to read the newspapers carefully for some time after that. No wonder I had missed the notice. And no wonder I had never come into contact with Field's men in the months since. Undoubtedly the inspector's private investigations office had been closed, the agents disbanded and scattered to other work.

Unless Dickens was lying to me.

I remembered my insight the previous year that Dickens, Drood, and Inspector Field were all playing some complicated three-way game, with me caught as pawn in the middle. Could this be a lie as part of some ploy on Dickens's part?

I doubted it. It would be too easy for me to check with someone I knew at the *Times* to see if the obituary was real. And if there *had* been a death in January, there was a grave for poor old Charles Frederick Field somewhere. I could check on that as well. For a mad moment I wondered if this were another ploy by Inspector Field himself—faking his own death so as to be safe from

Drood's minions—but that was too far-fetched even for the events of the past three years. I shook that idea out of my head.

"Are you well, my dear Wilkie? You suddenly look terribly pale."

"Just this vicious gout," I said. We both stood.

"You will stay for supper? Your brother has not been well enough to attend regular meals, but perhaps tonight, if you are here..."

I looked at my watch. "Another time, Charles. I need to get back to the city. Caroline is preparing something special for us tonight and we are going to the theatre...."

"Caroline?" cried Dickens in surprise. "She has come back?"

I shook my head, smiled, and tapped my forehead with three fingers. "I meant *Carrie*," I said. I was lying there as well. Carrie was spending the entire week with the family for which she governessed.

"Ah, well, another time soon," said Dickens. He walked me outside and down the stairs and through the tunnel.

"I'll have one of the servants drive you to the railway station."

"Thank you, Charles."

"I am glad you came to Gad's Hill Place today, my dear Wilkie."

"As am I, Charles. It has been most edifying."

I DID NOT GO directly back to London. At the station, I waited until Dickens's man and his pony cart were out of sight and then I boarded the train to Rochester.

I had not brought any brandy so I waited until the cathedral graveyard seemed well and truly empty— the afternoon summer shadows creeping long from the headstones—and then I strolled briskly back to the lime pit. There was no sign of the puppy on the turgid grey surface. A moment's searching in the grass brought up the branch I had used before. Three or four minutes of stirring and poking brought up the remnants— mostly bone and teeth and spine and gristle, but also some hair and hide left. I found it difficult to bring what was left of the little carcass to the surface with the stick.

"Dradles thinks this mi' be the instroment Mr Billy Wilkie Collins needs," said a voice directly behind me.

I jumped so violently that I almost tumbled forward into the pit of quick-lime.

Dradles steadied me with a rock-hard hand on my forearm. In his other hand, he was carrying a barbed iron staff that looked to be about six feet long. It may have once been part of the cathedral's iron fence in front, or a decoration on a steeple, or a lightning rod from one of the spires.

Dradles handed it to me. "Stirs easier wi' this, sir."

"Thank you," I said. Indeed, with its length and barbs, it worked perfectly. I turned the puppy's carcass over, decided that five or six days in the lime pit would be required for a larger form, and used the iron staff to press what was left of the little shape back under the surface again. For a second I had an image of myself as some sort of grisly cook, stirring my broth, and I had to suppress the urge to giggle.

I handed the iron staff back to Dradles. "Thank you," I said again.

"Dradles urges the ge'mun to think nothing of it," said the filthy mason. His face seemed as red this cool evening as it had during the heat of the daytime labour some days before.

"I forgot brandy today," I said with a smile, "but I wanted to treat you to a few drinks at the Thatched and

Twopenny the next time you go." I handed him five shillings.

He clinked the coins in his begrimed and calloused palm and smiled broadly at me. I counted four teeth.

"Thank 'ee, Mr Billy Wilkie Collins, sir. Dradles'll be sure to drink your health when I go."

"Very good," I said with a smile and a nod. "I need to be going."

"Mr C. Dickens, the famous author, used that same iron instroment a year ago when 'e was 'ere," said Dradles.

I turned back. The fumes from the lime pit were causing tears to streak down my cheeks, but they did not seem to affect Dradles. "I beg your pardon?" I said.

Dradles smiled again. "'E used the same instroment I give 'im as I give you, to stir the stew, as it were, sir," he said. "But Mr C. Dickens, famous author, 'e brought a bigger dead dog, 'e did."

CHAPTER THIRTY-EIGHT

On 29 October of that year, 1868, I dressed in my finest formal clothes and took a hired carriage to St Marylebone Parish Church to see Caroline G—— be married to Joseph Charles Clow.

The bride looked every bit of her thirty-eight years, and more. The groom looked even younger than his twenty-seven years. Someone just dropping into the church and spying the wedding ceremony without knowing the Happy Couple might have been forgiven for thinking that Caroline was the mother of the bride or groom.

The mother of the groom was there—a fat, stupid little gnome of a woman in an absurd maroon dress ten seasons out of style. She wept through the entire ceremony and brief reception after and had to be helped to her carriage after the Happy Couple had ridden off, not to an elaborate honeymoon but back to the tiny home they would later share again with his mother.

There were few other guests on either side. Not surprisingly, Mrs G——, Caroline's mother-in-law, did not attend (although the old woman had been pining for her daughter-in-law to marry again). Another reason that Caroline's former mother-in-law chose not to attend (if the old woman was sufficiently aware of events in her current state of addlement to be able to choose) became clear when I glanced at the marriage book:

Caroline had invented a false name for her father—a certain "John Courtenay, gentleman." This was part of an entire reinvention of herself, her family, and her past, even her first marriage, which I had agreed to support in any particulars (as her "previous employer of record") if ever pressed to do so.

The temptation to reinvent oneself seemed contagious. I noticed that young Carrie, signing as a witness, had signed herself as "Elisabeth Harriette G——" on the marriage certificate, which was a reinvention of the spelling of her names. But perhaps the largest lie on the marriage certificate belonged to the groom, who signed his occupation simply as "gentleman."

Well, if a plumber with permanent ground-in filth behind his ears and eternal grime under his fingernails was now an English gentleman, England had reached that wonderful socialist state that so many medical reformers had agitated so diligently to bring about.

I have to admit that the only person to look happy at this wedding was Carrie, who, either through the obliviousness of youth or sheer dedication to her mother, not only looked beautiful but acted as if she and we were all attending a joyous occasion. But when I say "we," I mean just the tiny handful of people. There were two people on Joseph Clow's side of the aisle: the weeping, crepe-draped mother and an unintroduced, unshaven man who might have been Clow's brother or perhaps merely another plumber who had come hoping that there would be food after the service.

On Caroline's side, there was only Carrie and Frank Beard, and me. Our group was so small that Beard had to be the second person to sign alongside Carrie as one of the two required witnesses. (Beard suggested that I sign, but my taste for the ironic absurd was not quite that well developed.)

Joseph Clow looked paralysed with fear and tension

throughout the ceremony. Caroline's smile was so broad and her face so flushed that I felt certain she would burst into tears and hysterics any second. Even the rector seemed to sense something odd about the proceedings and glanced up frequently from his missal, peering myopically out at the tiny gathering as if waiting for some word that it had all been a joke.

Throughout the ceremony I felt an odd numbness spreading through my body and brain. It may have been the extra dose of laudanum I had ingested to help me through the day, but I believe it was more a sense of true detachment. As the bride and groom repeated their final vows, I admit to looking at Caroline, standing so tensely upright in her ill-fitted and rather cheap-looking bridal gown, and remembering the precise touch and texture of every soft—now too soft—curve and bulge under that fabric. I felt no emotion throughout the proceedings except for a strange, spreading emptiness that had first come over me the past weeks when I arrived at Number 90 Gloucester Place to find no Caroline, no Carrie, and even my three servants often missing (with permission) because of an illness in Besse's family. It was a large house to be so empty of human voices and sounds.

When the wedding was over, there was no food or reception to speak of—merely a brief and uncomfortable milling-about in the chilly courtyard of the parish church. Then the new bride and groom left in an open carriage—it was too cold a day for an open carriage and it had begun to rain, but the couple had obviously been unable to spend the extra amount for a closed carriage. The image of the happy couple headed off to bliss was spoiled a bit when Frank Beard offered to use his carriage to drop Carrie and Joseph Clow's mother at the same home for which the newlyweds had just left. (It had seemed important to Caroline that Carrie spend the first few weeks of her mother's married life in that crowded, spartan little house, although the girl would still be working as a governess from time to time and soon would move back to live with me at Gloucester Place.)

Finally, after the rector had retreated back inside his dark church in true confusion, there was only the other plumber (I had decided that he was no relation to Joseph) and me left standing in the chilly late-October wind in front of the church. I tipped my hat to the hungry man and walked all the way to my brother Charley's home in South Audley Street.

Charley's health had improved somewhat as the hot summer ended, and by mid-September he and Katey were spending most of their time at their London home rather than at Gad's Hill Place. Charles was also working on various illustration jobs when he could, although the stomach pains and general disability struck often.

Still, I was surprised to find him not at home on that Thursday, 29 October, when I knocked at their door. Katey was home and she greeted me in their small and rather dark parlour. She knew of Caroline's wedding and asked me to tell her "all the marvellous high points." She offered me some brandy—which I happily accepted; my nose, cheeks, and hands were red with the autumn cold—and I received the distinct impression that she had been drinking before I arrived.

At any rate, I told her "all the marvellous high points," but I expanded the definition of "high points" from the wedding ceremony to my entire history with Mrs Caroline G——. The tale is shocking, of course, to bourgeois sensibilities, but I had long known that Kate suffered from few of her father's middle-class illusions. If the many rumours and reports were to be believed, Katey had long since taken a lover—or several lovers— to make up for my brother's lack of ardour (or inability to express it). This was a woman of the world, sipping brandy so close to me in the dark and shuttered little parlour with its tiny coal fire offering most of the dim light we had, and I found myself telling her details of my history with Caroline that I had told almost no one, including her father.

And, as I spoke, I realised that there was another reason—beyond my need to unburden myself at long last—why I was telling Kate Dickens these things.

Reluctantly, secretly, painfully, I had come to agree with her insensitive father's prediction that my brother would not be so long for this world. It was true that Charley's affliction, while sometimes lessening, continued to grow worse in the overall scheme of things. It now felt probable, even to me (his loyal and loving brother), that Charles might be dead in a year or two, and this ageing (she was twenty-eight) but still-attractive woman would be a widow.

Katey showed her own indiscretion by saying, "You would be surprised what Father has had to say about Mrs G——'s marriage."

"Tell me," I said and leaned closer.

She poured us each another brandy but shook her head. "It might hurt your feelings."

"Nonsense. Nothing your father could say would hurt my feelings. He and I have been friends and confidants for far too long. Pray tell me. What did he say about today's ceremony?"

"Well, he did not say anything to *me*, of course. But I happened to overhear him say to Aunt Georgina… 'Wilkie's affairs defy all prediction. For anything one knows, the whole matrimonial pretence may be a lie of that woman's, intended to make him marry her, and— contrary to her expectations—breaking down at last.'"

I sat stunned. I *was* hurt. And amazed. Could it be true? Could even the *wedding* have been another of

Caroline's ploys to trap me into marriage? Was she hoping that I would feel such loss that I would come after her even into Joseph Clow's household, defying and denying all marriage bonds, and beg her to come back to me...to marry *me*? My skin rippled with something like revulsion.

Stricken, all I could choke out to Kate Dickens was "Your father is a very wise man."

Surprisingly—thrillingly—she reached out and squeezed my hand.

Over a third brandy, I heard myself whining to Katey some words that, much later and in a much different context, I would share almost verbatim with Charley himself.

"Kate...do not be too harsh on me. Between my illness and the death of my mother and my loneliness, it has been a terrible year. Seeing Caroline married today, while being strangely satisfying in one respect, was also oddly disturbing. She has, after all, been part of my life for more than fourteen years and part of my household for more than ten. I think, my dear Katey, that a man in my situation is to be pitied. I am not...I have not been for a long time...I am not *accustomed* to living alone. I've been accustomed to having a kind woman there to talk with me, as you are now, Kate...and to take care of me and perhaps to spoil me a bit from time to time. All men enjoy that, but perhaps I more than most. It is difficult for a woman, a wife, such as yourself, to know what it is like for a man to be used always to seeing a pretty creature in his home...someone always nicely dressed, someone always about the room or hovering nearby, bringing a form of light and warmth to an old bachelor's life...and then, suddenly, for no reason of one's own, to be left alone as I am now, to be left...out in the cold and the dark."

Katey was staring at me very intensely. She seemed

to have leaned closer to me as I was explaining all this. Her knee under her long green silken dress was only inches from my own. I had the sudden urge to kneel on the floor, throw my head into her lap, and to weep like a child. I was certain at that instant that she would have put her arms around me, would have patted me on my back and head, perhaps even raised my tear-streaked face to her breast.

Instead, I sat there but leaned even closer. "Charley is very ill," I whispered.

"Yes." The single syllable seemed to hold no special sadness, only agreement.

"I have also been ill, but my recuperation is assured. My illness is a transient thing. Even now it does not interfere with my faculties or my...needs."

She looked at me with what I thought was something like a thrilled expectancy.

I then said, softly but urgently, "Kate, I suppose you could not marry a man who had..."

"No, I could *not*," Kate said decisively. She stood.

Reeling in confusion, I stood as well.

Kate called for her maid-servant to bring my coat and stick and hat. I was out on the cold stoop before I could think of anything to say. Even then I could not speak. The door closed with a slam.

I was half a block away, leaning into the cold wind, rain blowing into my face, when I saw Charley on the sidewalk opposite. He hailed me, but I pretended that I had not seen or heard him and ran on quickly, my hand holding the brim of my hat and my forearm hiding my face.

Two blocks farther I hailed a hansom cab and had it take me to Bolsover Street.

Martha R——, with no servants there at that time, opened the door herself. Her unguarded expression showed her true pleasure at seeing me.

That night I impregnated her with our first child.

CHAPTER THIRTY-NINE

*I*n November, Dickens previewed his murder in front of an intimate audience of a hundred of his closest friends.

For more than a year now, the Inimitable had been negotiating with Chappell and Company for yet another reading tour—what he called his "farewell series of readings." Chappell had suggested seventy-five readings, but Dickens—whose illness, weakness, and list of other ailments were increasing almost daily—insisted on a hundred readings for a round sum of £8,000.

His oldest friend, Forster, who had always opposed reading tours for the very real reason that they kept Dickens from writing novels and always left him exhausted, weak, and ill, told the Inimitable flatly that if the author attempted one hundred readings now, in his current condition, it would kill him. Frank Beard and the other doctors whom Dickens had seen more frequently in the past year, fully agreed with Forster. Even Dolby, whose continued presence in Dickens's life depended totally upon these tours, felt it was a bad idea to enter into one now and a *terrible* idea to attempt one hundred separate readings.

And no one in Dickens's circle of family, old friends, physicians, and trusted advisors thought that he should include the Nancy Murder as part of his farewell tour. Some, like Wills and Dolby, simply thought it was far too sensationalist for such an honoured and revered author. Most others, like Beard, Percy Fitzgerald, Forster—and me—were all but certain it would kill him.

Dickens perversely saw the coming exhaustion of travel and performance, not to mention the mental anguish of travelling on railways every day, as (he told Dolby) "a relief to my mind."

No one understood Dickens's attitude in this except me. I knew that Charles Dickens was a sort of male *succubus*—he not only brought hundreds and thousands of people under his personal mesmeric, magnetic control at these readings, but he sucked the energy out of them as he did so. Without this need and ability, I was sure, Dickens would have died of his ailments years ago. He was a vampire and needed public occasions and audiences from which to drain the energy he needed to stagger on another day.

So he and Chappell agreed on his terms of one hundred readings in exchange for £8,000. The Inimitable's American Tour—which, he had confessed to me, had brought him to the verge of total prostration—had been scheduled for eighty readings but, in the end, reduced to seventy-six because of a few cancellations. It was Katey who had told me (long before our 29 October meeting) that Dickens's labours in America had brought in total receipts of $228,000 against expenses in that country—mostly travelling, rental of halls, hotels, and a 5 percent commission to the American agents of Ticknor and Fields—of not quite $39,000. Dickens's preliminary expenses in England had been £614, and, of course, there had been Dolby's commission of £3,000.

This suggests that Dickens's profits from the American readings in 1867–68 should have amounted to a small fortune—a serious fortune for any of us in the writing trade—but he had chosen to do his tour only three years after the Americans' Civil War had ended. That war had lowered the value of the dollar everywhere, and by early summer of 1868, the American currency had yet to go back to its earlier and more normal exchange value. Katey had explained to me that if her father had simply invested his American Tour earnings in securities in that country and waited for the dollar to regain its old level, his profits would have been almost £38,000. Instead, he had paid a 40 percent tariff for converting his dollars to gold at the time. "My profit," he had bragged to his daughter, "was within a hundred or so of twenty thousand pounds."

Impressive, but not reflective of the travel, labour, exhaustion, and diminishment of his authorial vigour that the tour had demanded.

So perhaps his current deal with Chappell was, after all, as much about simple greed as it was about his theoretical vampiric needs.

Or perhaps he was attempting suicide by reading tour.

I admit, Dear Reader, that this final possibility not only occurred to me and made sense to me, but confused me. At this point, I wanted to be the one to kill Charles Dickens. But perhaps it would be tidier if I merely helped him commit suicide this way.

DICKENS HAD BEGUN his tour in his favourite venue of St James's Hall in London back on 6 October, but without the Murder as part of it. He knew that there would be a necessary hiatus in his travels and readings—the national general election was to be held in November, and he would have to set aside his tour during that campaign if for no other reason than the fact that there would be no suitable public halls or theatres to rent while the politicians were on the rampage. (It was no secret that the Inimitable supported Gladstone and the

Liberal Party, but more—his closer friends knew—because he had always detested Disraeli than for any great hopes he had in the Liberals' carrying out the sort of reform that he, Dickens, had always advocated in his fiction, non-fiction, and public advocacy.)

But even the easier, Murder-less October readings—London, Liverpool, Manchester, London again, Brighton, London—took a great toll on him.

In early October, Dolby had told me of the Chief's high spirits and joy at renewing his readings, but two weeks into the actual tour and Dolby was admitting that his beloved boss was not sleeping on the road, suffered terrible bouts of melancholy, and was terrified every time he boarded a railway carriage. The slightest bump or swerve, according to Dolby, would cause the Chief to cry out in terror for his life.

More to Frank Beard's concern, Dickens's left foot was swelling again—always a sign of more serious troubles—and his old problems of kidney pain and bleeding bowels had returned more fiercely than ever.

Even more telling, perhaps, were the reports through Katey via my brother that Dickens was weeping frequently and was on occasion almost inconsolable during these early travels. It was true that Dickens had suffered enough personal losses during the summer and early autumn.

His son Plorn—now almost seventeen—had sailed in late September to join his brother Alfred in Australia. Dickens had broken down weeping at the station, which was totally unlike the coolness the Inimitable usually showed at family partings.

In late October, as his tour began wearing so heavily on him, Dickens learned that his brother Frederick, from whom he had been estranged for many years, had died. Forster told me that Dickens had written him— "It was a wasted life, but God forbid that one should be hard upon it, or upon anything in this world that is not deliberately and coldly wrong."

To me, during a rare dinner shared at Vérey's in London during a gap in his reading schedule, Dickens said simply, "Wilkie, my heart has become a cemetery."

By the first of November, with Nancy's Murder looming in two weeks, my brother reported Katey over-hearing the Inimitable telling Georgina, "I cannot get right internally and have begun to be as sleepless as sick."

And he had again written Forster, "I have not been well and have been heavily tired. However, I have little to complain of—nothing, nothing; though, like Mariana, I am weary."

Forster, who was weary himself in those days, had shared the note in confidence—the conceit was that there was a circle of us, Dickens's closest friends, who were monitoring his health with concern—but admitted to me that he could not immediately place the "Mariana" reference.

I could and did. And it was hard to suppress a smile as I recited to Forster Mariana's lines from Tennyson's poem to which I was certain Dickens was referring—

> "... I am aweary, aweary,
> Oh God, that I were dead!"

During one of his October London readings at St James's Hall to which I had gone without telling Dickens that I would be in attendance, I saw him begin the reading with his usual energy and with every appearance of personal delight at revisiting *The Pickwick Papers*—either a fact or an illusion that always delighted audiences—but within minutes he seemed to find it impossible to say "Pickwick."

"Picksnick," he called his character and then paused,

almost laughed, and tried again. "Peckwicks...I apologise, ladies and gentlemen, I meant to say, of course...Picnic! That is, Packrits...Pecksniff...Pickstick!"

After several more such embarrassing tries, he stopped and looked down at his friends in the front seats reserved for them (I was far back in the balcony on this night), and showed something like amusement in his expression. But it was also a look of some small desperation, I thought, as if he were asking them for help.

And—even far back in the laughing, loving mob—I could all but smell his sudden rush of panic.

Through all these weeks, Dickens had been honing his reading script for Nancy's Murder but had not used it. As he confided to me at Vérey's, "I simply am afraid to read it, my dear Wilkie. I have no doubt that I could perfectly petrify an audience with it...with reading one-eighth of it!...but whether the impression would be *so horrible,* so completely terrifying, as to keep them away from my readings another time, is what I cannot satisfy myself upon."

"You shall know when you have sounded them out through a few more readings, my dear Charles," I had said that night. "You shall know when the time is right. You always do."

Dickens had simply acknowledged the compliment with a nod of his head and a distracted sip of wine.

Then I heard, through Dolby, that I was to be a special guest—along with a hundred and fifteen or so other "special guests"—at a private reading (it was during the campaign hiatus) at St James's Hall on Saturday, 14 November.

Dickens was finally going to slaughter Nancy.

EARLY ON THE AFTERNOON of his reading, I went to Rochester. Mr Dradles met me in front of the cathedral and I went through my usual ritual of gift giving. The brandy that I was buying for this dusty old man was more expensive than that which I usually purchased for myself and special guests.

Dradles accepted it with a grunt and quickly tucked it away somewhere in his voluminous layers of thick canvas and flannel coats and moleskin and flannel waist-coats. He was so flannelly bulky and moleskin-and-canvas bulbous to begin with that I couldn't even make out the bulge where the bottle had gone.

"Dradles says, this way, Guv'ner," he said and led me back around the cathedral and tower to the crypt entrance. He was carrying a bullseye lantern with its cover down and set it down briefly as he patted himself for the proper key. The countless pockets on his person gave up countless keys and rings of keys before he found the right one.

"Watch yer 'ead, Mr Billy Wilkie Collins," was all he said when he lifted the blindered lantern as we entered the dark labyrinth. The November day was overcast enough that almost no light filtered down through the glassless trapezoids fitted into the groined ceiling. Tree roots, shrubs, and in some places actual sod had covered over the spaces that had been meant by the long-dead cathedral builders as skylights for this necropolis. I followed him mostly by sound, finding my way by sliding my hand across the slick-slate stone. *The rising damp.*

TIP-TAP-TAP-TAP-TAP-TIP-TIP-TAP. Dradles seemed to have found an echo he liked. He unshrouded the lantern and showed me a joining of masonry where the corridor curved and followed narrow steps lower into the crypt.

"Does Mr Billy W. C. see?" he asked. His breath filled the cold space between us with rum fumes.

"It's been taken down, newer stones set in place, and

remortared," I said. I had to work to keep my teeth from chattering. Caves are said to be warmer—with their constant temperature in the fifties or whatever—than the cold November wind outside this day. But not this crypt-cave.

"Aye, by Dradles 'imself not two year ago," he breathed at me. "No one there is, not the rector, not the choirmaster, nor even 'nother mason, would notice—after a day or three—if the new mortar were newer. Not if Dradles done it."

I nodded. "And this wall opens directly into a crypt?"

"Nay, nay," laughed the flannelled mason. "Be two more walls 'tween us an' the ol' 'un. This 'ere wall opens just to the first space 'tween it an' the older wall. Eighteen inches, at the most."

"Enough?" I asked. I could not finish the sentence properly with *"for a body?"*

Dradles's rheumy red eyes gleamed at me in the lantern light. He seemed very amused, but he also seemed to be reading my mind perfectly. "No' for no body, no," he said far too loudly. "But for mere bones, vertebrae, pelvis, 'tarsals, a watch or chain or gold teeth or two, an' for a nice, clean, smiling skull…more 'n 'nough room, sir. More 'n 'nough room. The ol' 'un farther in won't begrudge the new lodger 'is space, nosir, Mr Billy Wilkie Collins, sir."

I felt my gorge rising. If I didn't leave this place soon, I would be sick right across the headstone carver's filthy undifferentiated boots. But I stayed long enough to ask, "Is this the same spot you and Mr Dickens chose for any bones he's to bring?"

"Oh, no, sir. No, sir. Our Mr Charles Dickens, famous author, 'e chose a darker, deeper spot for the bones 'e'll bring Dradles, right down them stairs there, sir. Would the Wilkie gen'mun like to see?"

I shook my head and—without waiting for the little

lantern light to follow—fought my way up and out and into the air.

THAT EVENING, as I sat in St James's Hall with about a hundred of Charles Dickens's closest friends, I wondered how many times the Inimitable had stood on that stage and performed—either theatrically or as the first of a new breed of authors who read their works. Hundreds of times? At least. He *was*—or had been—that "new breed of authors." And no one seemed to be equalling or replacing him.

This public Murder of Nancy would be yet another unprecedented departure for a man of letters.

Forster had told me that it was he who had convinced Dickens to ask the Chappells their opinion on this—to Forster's mind—calamitous idea of including Nancy's Murder in the reading programme. And it had been the Chappells who had suggested this private audience to test the reaction to such a grim and grisly reading.

Just prior to the performance, I overheard a very famous London physician (not our dear friend Beard) say to the Inimitable—"My dear Dickens, you may rely upon it that if only one woman cries out when you murder the girl, there will be contagion of hysteria all over the place."

Dickens had only modestly lowered his head and given a smile that anyone who knew him would have classified as more wicked than mischievous.

Taking my place in the second row next to Percy Fitzgerald, I noticed that the stage was set a little differently than for Dickens's usual readings. Besides his regular personalised frame of directed gas lighting and the violet-maroon screen that set him off to such advantage on a darkened stage, Dickens had added two flanking screens of the same dark colour and even similarly hued curtains behind them, the effect of which was to narrow and focus the wide stage to the tiny, dramatically lighted space immediately surrounding him.

I admit that I had expected Dickens to open the reading with something less sensational—probably an abbreviated version of his perennial and always popular Trial Scene from *The Pickwick Papers* ("Calling Sam Weller!")—so as to lead up to the *Sturm und Drang* of Nancy's Murder and to give us all a sense of how the sensationalist finale would be somewhat ameliorated by the other readings in a full evening's presentation.

But he did not do this. He went straight to Nancy.

I know, Dear Reader, that I have described the Inimitable's own notes on an early summer draft of his reading script for this scene, but I cannot tell you how inadequate those notes—or my own poor powers of description, as honed by writing prose as they may be— are in describing the next forty-five minutes.

Perhaps, Dear Reader, in your incredibly distant future of the late twentieth or early twenty-first century (if you still even bother measuring time in terms of Years of Our Lord), you have, in your advanced scientific alchemy, created some looking glass that can peer back through time so that you can watch and listen to the Sermon on the Mount or Pericles' orations or Shakespeare's original performances of his plays. If so, I would suggest that you add to your list of Historical Orations Not to Be Missed a certain Charles Dickens's presentation of Bill Sikes murdering Nancy.

He did not leap immediately to the details of the Murder, of course.

You may remember my earlier descriptions of Dickens's readings—the calm demeanor, the open book held in one hand although never truly referred to, the element of theatricality coming primarily through the wide range of voices, dialects, and postures as Dickens recited. But never before had he fully *acted out the scene he was reading*.

With the Murder, Dickens began slowly but with much more theatricality than I had ever seen from him (or any author reading his work). Fagin, that evil Jew, came alive as never before—wringing his hands in a way that suggested both eager anticipation of money stolen and guilt, as if he were trying to wash away the blood of Christ even as he schemed. Noah Claypole came across even more cowardly and stupid than he had in the novel. Bill Sikes's entrance made the audience shudder in anticipation—rarely had male brutality been so conveyed through a few pages of dialogue and the dramatic portrayal of the drunkard thief and bully's demeanor.

Nancy's terror was palpable from the beginning, but by the time of her first of many shrieks, the audience was pale and totally absorbed.

As if showing us the boundary between all of his previous readings over the decades (not to mention the weak and inferior efforts by his imitators) and this new era of sensationalism for him, Dickens tossed aside his book of reading script, left his reading stand, and literally leaped into the scene he was depicting for us.

Nancy shrieked her entreaties.

Bill Sikes growled his relentless fury. There would be no mercy despite her cries—*"Bill! Dear Bill! For God's sake, Bill! For God's sake!"*

Dickens's voice filled St James's Hall so thoroughly that even Nancy's final, whispered, dying entreaties could be heard as if each of us in the audience were on stage. During the few (but terrible) silences, one could have heard a mouse stirring in the empty balcony behind us. We could actually hear Dickens panting from the exertion of bringing his invisible (all too visible!) club down on the dear girl's skull...again! Again! Again!

Dickens used the powerful lighting to amazing effect. Now he is on one knee as Nancy, the lighting showing only the bent-back head and two pale hands raised in useless imploring. Now he is rearing back as Bill—the club raised behind his shoulders and his body suddenly, impossibly, larger and burlier and taller than Dickens had ever been, the deep shadows filling his eye sockets except for the terrifying whites of Sikes's not-sane eyes.

Then the beating—and clubbing—and beating again—and worse clubbing. The dear girl's dying voice, growing duller and fainter as both life and hope departed, caused the breathless audience to gasp. One woman sobbed.

When Nancy's pleading ceased, there was an instant of relief—even hope—that her entreaties had been listened to by the brute, that some small bit of life would be left to the battered form, but even as many in the audience chose that second to open their eyes, *then* Dickens roared out Sikes's loudest and most insane bellows and began clubbing the dying girl again, then the dead girl, then the shapeless mass of battered and bleeding flesh and hair beneath him.

When he was finished, crouched over the body in the same terrible attitude that his son and my brother had first glimpsed in the meadow behind Gad's Hill Place, Dickens's laboured gasping for air filled the hall like the bellows of some deranged steam machine. I had no idea whether the panting was real or only part of his performance.

He finished.

Women in the audience were sobbing. At least one was hysterical. Men sat rigid, pale, with their fists clenched and jaw muscles working. I realised that Percy Fitzgerald next to me on one side and Dickens's old friend Charles Kent on the other were both struggling to take in a breath.

As for me, the stag beetle scarab behind my eyes had gone crazy during the reading, turning and burrowing and boring from one part of my brain to another. The pain had been beyond description, yet still I could not close my eyes or block my ears to shut out the Murder, so mesmerising had it been. As soon as Nancy was well and truly dead, I pulled out my silver flask and took four long drinks of laudanum. (I noticed that other men were drinking from similar flasks.)

The audience was silent for a long moment after Dickens finished, returned to his lectern, straightened his lapels and cravat, and bowed slightly.

For that moment, I thought there would be no applause and that the obscenity that was the Murder of Nancy would never be perpetrated on stage again. The Chappells would hear their verdict in the shocked silence. Forster, Wills, Fitzgerald, and all of Dickens's other friends who had advised against this will have been justified.

But then the applause began. And rose in volume. And continued to rise as people began to stand throughout the hall. And would not end.

Soaked with sweat but smiling now, Dickens bowed more deeply, stepped out from behind his high reading table, and gave a magician's gesture.

Members of his stage crew trotted out and the screens were whisked aside in an instant. The maroon-violet curtains pulled back.

On the stage was revealed a long, shining banquet table piled high with delicacies. Bottles of champagne lay cooling in countless silver buckets of ice. A small army of formally attired waiters stood ready to open oysters and send the champagne corks flying. Dickens gestured again and called his invitation (over a second round of enthusiastic applause) for everyone to come up on stage and partake of refreshments.

Even this part of the evening had been carefully staged. As the first men and women filed shakily onto the stage, the powerful gaslights illuminated their flushed faces and the men's gold studs and the women's colourful dresses in a wonderful manner. It was as if the performance were still under way but now all of us were to be included in it. With a terrible but darkly thrilling shock, we realised that we were all attending the wake of the murdered Nancy.

Finally on stage myself, I stood back from the banquet and eavesdropped on what people were saying to Dickens, who was all smiles behind a flurry of his handkerchief as he continued mopping his wet brow and cheeks and neck.

Actresses such as Mme Celeste and Mrs Keeley were among the first to reach him.

"You are my judge and jury," Dickens said happily to them. "Should I do it or not?"

"Oh, yes, yes, yes, *oui*, yes," breathed Mme Celeste. She looked to be close to fainting.

"Why, of course do it!" cried Mrs Keeley. "Having got at such an effect as that, it *must* be done. It must be. But I must say..." And here the actress rolled her large black eyes very slowly, very dramatically, and enunciated the rest of her line with elaborate slowness, "...the public have been looking for a sensation these last fifty years or so, and by heaven they have got it!"

And then Mrs Keeley took in a long, ragged breath, expelled it, and stood there as if speechless.

Dickens bowed low, took her hand, and kissed it.

Charley Dickens came up with an empty oyster shell in his hand.

"Well, Charley," said Dickens, "and what do you think of it now?" (Charley had been among those closest to Dickens who had advised against it.)

"It is even finer than I expected, Father,". said Charley. "But I still say, *don't do it*."

Dickens blinked in what looked to be real surprise.

Edmund Yates came up carrying his second glass of champagne.

"What do you think of this, Edmund?" said Dickens. "Here is Charley, my own son, saying it is the finest thing he has ever heard but who also persists in telling me, without giving any reason, not to do it!"

Yates glanced at Charley and—in serious, almost funereal tones—said, "I agree with Charley, sir. Do *not* do it."

"Dear heavens!" cried Dickens with a laugh. "I am surrounded by unbelievers. You…Charles!" he cried, pointing to Kent standing next to me. Neither of us had yet availed himself of refreshments. The crowd noise around us was growing louder and less restrained by the moment.

"And Wilkie," added Dickens. "What do my two old friends and professional accomplices think? Do you agree with Edmund and Charley that I should never repeat this performance?"

"Not a bit of it," said Kent. "My only objection is of a technical nature."

"Oh?" said Dickens. His voice was level enough, but I knew how little he cared for "objections of a technical nature" when it came to his readings or theatrical work. Dickens considered himself a master of stagecraft and technical effects.

"You end the reading…performance…with Sikes dragging the dog from the murder room and locking the door behind him," said Charles Kent. "I believe that the audience is ready for more…. Perhaps Sikes's flight? Almost certainly Sikes's fall from the rooftop on Jacob's Island. The audience wants…it *needs* to see Sikes punished."

Dickens frowned at this. I took his silence as an invitation.

"I agree with Kent," I said. "What you have given us is astounding. But the ending is…truncated? Premature? I cannot speak for the women in the audience, but we men are left lusting for Sikes's blood and death as much as he was lusting to kill poor Nancy. Adding ten minutes would move the ending from the current blank state of horror into a fierce and passionate rush for the end!"

Dickens clasped his arms across his chest and shook his head. I could see that his starched shirtfront had been soaked through with perspiration and that his hands were shaking.

"Trust me, Charles," he said, addressing Kent, "no audience on earth could be held for ten minutes—or five!—after the girl's death. Trust me to be right on this. I stand there…" He gestured to the lectern and low reading platform. "…and I *know*."

Kent shrugged. Dickens's tone of absolute certainty—the Master's voice, often used by him to settle discussions of things literary or theatrical—had spoken. But I knew then, and was not surprised later to see, that Dickens would brood over this suggestion and later lengthen the reading, adding at least three pages of narrative to the performance, to do precisely as Kent had suggested.

I went to get oysters and champagne and joined George Dolby, Edmund Yates, Forster, Charley Dickens, Percy Fitzgerald, Charles Kent, Frank Beard, and others standing farther back on the stage, just out of the rectangle of brilliant light. Dickens was now surrounded by ladies whom he'd invited to the event, and they seemed as emotionally overwrought and positively eager about his Murdering Nancy in the future as the actresses had been. (Dickens had told me to bring the Butler—meaning Carrie—but I had not passed on the invitation and was glad that she'd not been there.

Many of us, in crossing the stage with our drinks and oysters, unconsciously looked down to make sure that we were not placing our polished black pumps in the pools of Nancy's blood.

"This is madness," Forster was saying. "If he does this for any significant part of his remaining seventy-nine performances, he will kill himself."

"I agree," said Frank Beard. The usually jovial physician was glowering at the glass flute in his hand as if the champagne had gone bad. "This would be suicide for Dickens. He will not survive it."

"He invited reporters," said Kent. "I've heard them talking. They loved it. They will write it up wonderfully in the papers tomorrow. Every man, woman, and child in England, Ireland, and Scotland will be selling their teeth to get a ticket."

"Most of them have already sold whatever teeth they had left," I said. "They will have to find something else to bring to the Jews' pawnshops."

The men around me laughed politely, but most went back to frowns in the silence that followed.

"If the reporters praise it," rumbled Dolby, that bear of a man, "then the Chief will do it. At least four times a week until next summer."

"That will kill him," Frank Beard said again.

"Many of you have known Father for much longer than I have," said Charley Dickens. "Do *you* know of any way to dissuade him once he realises the sensation he has created and can create with this?"

"None, I fear," said Percy Fitzgerald.

"Never," said Forster. "He will not listen to sense. The next time we meet may be at Westminster Abbey for Dickens's state funeral."

I almost spilled my champagne at this.

For some months now, since Dickens had first declared his intention of performing Nancy's Murder in the majority of his proposed winter and spring readings, I had considered such suicide a mere means to an end for which I already devoutly wished. But Forster had made me realise something that was almost certainly true—however Dickens died, either through suicide-by-readings or by being run over by a dray waggon tomorrow on the Strand, there would be a huge public demand for a state funeral. The London *Times* or some other rag that had been Charles Dickens's political opponent and literary scold for so many years would lead the way in demanding that the Inimitable be interred in Westminster Abbey. The public—sentimental as always—would rally around the idea.

The crowds would be stupendous. Dickens would end up lying with the other most-loved bones of English literary genius.

The certainty of all this made me want to scream right there on the stage.

Dickens had to die, that was certain. But I realised now what my deeper, darker mind must already have known and begun advance planning for months earlier—*Dickens not only had to die, he had to* disappear.

There could be no state funeral, no burial in Westminster Abbey. That idea was simply intolerable to me.

"What do you think, Wilkie?" asked Yates.

Lost in the horror of my revelation, I had not been following their conversation closely, but I vaguely knew that they were still discussing ways and means of dissuading Dickens from murdering Nancy scores more times in public.

"I think that Charles will do what he believes he has to do," I said softly. "But it is up to us—his dearest friends and family—to keep him from being buried in Westminster Abbey."

"Soon, you mean," said Fitzgerald. "Buried there *soon*, you mean."

"Of course. That is precisely what I meant." I excused myself to get more champagne. The crowd was growing a little thinner now, but also more boisterous. The corks continued to pop and the waiters continued to pour.

A movement backstage, where the crew had been moving the lectern and equipment, caught my eye and made me stop.

It was not the crew moving now. A single figure stood there, all but cloaked in darkness, his silly opera cape catching the slightest gleam of reflected light from the stage. He was wearing an old-fashioned top hat. His face was absolutely white, as were his strangely long-fingered hands.

Drood.

My heart leapt to my throat and the scarab in my brain surged to its favourite viewing place behind my right eye.

But it was not Drood.

The figure bowed theatrically in my direction and swept off the top hat. I saw the blond, thinning hair that was growing back and recognised Edmond Dickenson.

Certainly Dickens did not invite Dickenson to this trial reading? How could he have found him? Why would he have…

The figure straightened up and smiled. It looked, even from this distance, that young Dickenson's eyelids were missing. And that his teeth had been filed to sharp points.

I wheeled to see if Dickens or the others had seen this apparition. No one else appeared to have noticed.

When I turned back, the form in the black opera cape was gone.

CHAPTER FORTY

J slept until noon on New Year's Day and awoke
    alone and in pain. The week before this first day
of 1869 had been strangely warm, with no snow, no
clouds, little sense of the season, and finally—for me—
far too little human companionship. But this day was
cold and dark.

My married servants, George and Besse, had asked
my permission to go to Besse's ancestral home in Wales
for at least a week. It seemed that both her senile father
and—until recently—healthy mother were choosing to
die at the same time. It was unheard-of (and ridiculous)
to release my entire staff at once for so long a time—I
assumed that their dull-witted and homely seventeen-
year-old daughter, Agnes, would be accompanying
them—but I let them go out of the kindness of my
heart (after informing them, of course, that they would
not be paid during their Welsh vacation). Because of a
party I had planned for Gloucester Place on New Year's
Eve, I made them delay their travels for a week; they
finally left on New Year's Day, two days after I returned
from my week at Gad's Hill Place.

Carrie had been staying with me for most of December (her time with her mother and new stepfather, who,
she whispered to me, drank heavily, had lasted less than
two weeks), but her employer family (who still treated
her more like a guest than a governess) were going to

the country on Christmas Eve for at least two weeks and I'd urged her to go along with them. There would be parties and masked balls and fireworks on New Year's midnight, there would be sleigh excursions, there would be ice skating in the moonlight, there would be young gentlemen....I could offer none of those things.

There was very little that I felt I could offer anyone that New Year's Day of 1869.

After Caroline's marriage, I had avoided the five-storey empty home at Number 90 Gloucester Place as much as I could, staying with the Lehmanns and the Beards in November as long as those kind people would have me. I had even spent time with Forster (who disliked me very much) at his ridiculous (but comfortable) mansion at Palace Gate. Forster had grown more pretentious and tiresome than ever after his marriage into wealth, and his dislike of me (or jealousy, I should say, since Forster had always competed angrily with anyone who was closer to Dickens than he) had grown apace with his wealth and girth, but he was still too much the presumed and assumed gentleman to turn me out or ask why I had chosen to come visit him at that time. (If he *had* asked, I could have answered honestly in three words—*your wine cellar.*)

But no one can visit friends forever, so for some of December it had been just Carrie and me in the large old place at Number 90 Gloucester Place, with George, Besse, and the shy Agnes all scuttling along busily in the background in an unsuccessful effort to avoid my surly moods.

When Dickens had sent word inviting me to come with Kate and Charley to spend yet another Christmas at Gad's Hill Place, I hesitated—it had felt almost dishonest to accept such hospitality from someone you fully planned to murder as soon as the time was right— but in the end I acquiesced. When the house at Gloucester Place was empty, it was just *too* empty.

Dickens was home for the week resting up in preparation for the remainder of his reading tour—he'd planned his first Murder of Nancy in front of the paying public for 5 January, again in St James's Hall—but was already exhausted and ailing from the limited readings he'd given in December. In a brief letter he'd written to me in December while travelling to Edinburgh on the "Flying Scotchman," he'd penned—

My dear Wilkie,

> *Dolby is sleeping stentoriously nearby as we have just jolted over what felt to be several disaster-inducing gaps in the rails, causing not so much as the slightest pause in our ursine friend's snores, so I have just taken a few minutes to calculate the amazing fact that travelling the distances required on a tour such as this involves more than thirty thousand distinct and separate shocks to the nerves. And my nerves, as you know, have not of recent been at their best. The memory of Staplehurst is never far from my mind, and when it does recede a bit, one of these shocks or jolts reminds me of it yet again. And even when I am stationary, there is no rest for the wicked. I said recently to our estimable American friend Mrs Fields that I spend most of the remaining and dwindling hours of my life travelling towards the tiring exposure to my special gas lamps on the platform and that the hour has almost come once more when I to sulphurous and tormenting gas must render up myself.*

Dickens had found ways other than his tour and this convoluted syntax by which to exhaust himself. Although he had finally abolished the accursed "Christmas Issue" of *All the Year Round* (years after it should have been discontinued, to my way of thinking), he was still spending many hours a week at the Wellington Street offices, fiddling with the look and layout of the magazine, testing typography sizes on anyone who wandered by, and writing enthusiastic "Editor's Notes" about the New Series he was launching, assuring any readers alarmed by the disappearance of the Christmas Issue that *"...my fellow labourers and I will be at our old posts, in company with those younger comrades whom I have had the pleasure of enrolling from time to time and whose number it is always one of my pleasantest editorial duties to enlarge..."*

I'm not sure who these "younger comrades" at the magazine were, since I had refused greater participation, his son Charley was allowed to do little but respond to letters and pursue the odd line of advertising, and, although Wills had returned to his post, he was capable of little more than sitting in his office and staring into middle space while doors kept slamming in his ruined skull. Wills would hardly have been counted as a "younger comrade" in any case.

All the Year Round was—as it had always been—an extension of the mind and personality of Charles Dickens.

As if all this office work and his readings in Scotland and continued rehearsals for the many Murders of Nancy yet to come were not enough, Dickens was spending many hours every day obeying the request in the will of his late friend Chauncey Hare Townshend, who'd asked in his dying delirium that the Inimitable collect his (Chauncey's) various and scattered writings on the subject of religion. Dickens did this doggedly and to the point of even deeper exhaustion, but on Christmas Eve, over an indifferent brandy, I heard Percy Fitzgerald ask him, "Are they worth anything as religious views?"

"Nothing whatever, I should say," said Dickens.

When Dickens was not in his study working during my week's stay at Gad's Hill Place, he was taking advantage of the clement weather to take walks of twenty miles and more per afternoon rather than his usual paltry twelve-mile winter outings. Percy and a few others attempted to keep up with him on these forced marches, but my rheumatical gout and Egyptian scarab would not allow me to take part. So I ate, drank brandy, wine, and whiskey, smoked the Inimitable's rather disappointing cigars, increased my laudanum intake to make up for melancholy, read the books that Dickens and Georgina always set especially for their guests in each guest room (De Quincey's *Confessions of an English Opium Eater* had been left un-subtly on my night table, but I had already read it and, indeed, had grown up knowing De Quincey), and generally lazed away the days before New Year's Eve, for which I had planned a dinner party at Gloucester Place for the Lehmanns and Charley and Kate and Frank Beard and a few others.

But my week at Gad's Hill was not totally wasted.

Charles Fechter did not have a complete Swiss chalet hidden in his pocket this particular Christmas, but he had brought a rough scenario for the play called *Black and White* that he had first proposed, in the most general outlines, some months earlier.

Fechter could be a tiring and tiresome friend; he was always in the middle of some sort of pecuniary disaster and his ability to handle (or retain) money approached that of a particularly careless four-year-old. Still, his story idea about an octoroon French nobleman who contrives to get himself on a Jamaican auction block to be sold as a slave seemed to me to have great potential. Perhaps more to the point, if I were to write the play based on his outline, Fechter promised to help me avoid the problems in theatrical pacing, economy of plot, conciseness in dialogue, et cetera from which—according to Dickens and my right-eye scarab—*No Thoroughfare* had suffered.

Fechter was as good as his word on this promise and

would be, for the next two months, quite literally at my elbow more often than not as I worked on *Black and White*—the actor excising, condensing, making dialogue more precise and "alive," fixing awkward entrances and exits, pointing out missed opportunities for exciting stage moments. We began our joint (and not unenjoyable) labours on *Black and White* over Dickens's brandy and cigars in our host's library on those days around Christmas 1868.

And then the visit ended and we all temporarily went back to our respective efforts—Dickens to killing Nancy, Fechter to scrounging for parts and plays worthy of what he considered his great talent, and me back to the great, empty pile that was Number 90 Gloucester Place.

My brother, Charley, came to my New Year's Eve dinner party despite his worsening stomach condition. To cheer everyone up, I treated Beard, the Lehmanns, and Charley and Kate (who had been chipper but formal in my company since my unfortunate visit to her on 29 October) to a pantomime at the newly reopened Gaiety Theatre just before the dinner party proper.

My New Year's Eve dinner party should have been a success: I had helped Nina Lehmann find a new cook, and this person had been on loan to prepare a fine French meal for us; I had supplied plenty of champagne and wine and gin; the pantomime had put us in a generally relaxed mood.

But the long night of forced amusement was a dismal failure. It was as if each of us had somehow suddenly become capable of peeking through the veil of time to see all the bad things that would happen to us in the year to come. And our obviously strained attempts at revelry were not aided by my servants George and Besse's equally obvious eagerness to finish their duties and be away in the morning to Besse's parents' respective Welsh deathbeds. (Their daughter, Agnes, was upstairs in bed with a vicious case of croup, so did not add her usual plodding clumsiness to the evening's service.)

So thus it was I awoke with a roaring headache on New Year's Day noon, rang for George to bring me tea and draw a hot bath for me, and then—when no one came—remembered with a curse that the three had already left for Wales. Why had I let them go when I needed their services?

Plodding around the cold house in my robe, I found all vestiges of last night's party tidied up, everything cleaned and put away, the teakettle ready to be put on to boil, and an assortment of breakfast choices ready for me on the kitchen counter. I moaned and made only the tea.

The fireplaces had all been set but not lighted, and I had to fumble with forgotten flues before I had flames going in the parlour, study, bedroom, and kitchen. The sunlight and unusually warm weather that had made the entire Christmas week seem so strange had fled as the new year came in—it was grey, windy, and sleeting outside when I finally parted the drapes to peer out.

After finishing my mid-day breakfast, I considered my options. I had told George and Besse that I would probably spend the week at my club, but a query at the Athenaeum two days earlier had informed me that there were no rooms to let to members until the sixth or seventh of the month.

I could always return to Gad's Hill Place, but Dickens was performing his murder before the unsuspecting public for the first time at St James's Hall on Tuesday, 5 January, and then resuming his tour to Ireland and beyond—this abominable New Year's Day I was suffering through was a Friday—and I knew his household would be in a buzz of preparation and rehearsal until then. I had *Black and White* to write,

Fechter was in London right then, and the distraction and isolation of Gad's Hill were the last things I needed.

But I needed servants, food prepared, and the company of women.

Still brooding about this, I wandered the empty house, finally looking into the study.

The Other Wilkie was there in one of the two leather chairs by the fire. Waiting for me. Just as I had expected him to be.

I left the study doors open, since there was no one else in the house that day, and took the other chair. The Other Wilkie rarely spoke to me anymore, but he did listen well and sometimes he nodded. Other times he might shake his head or give me a bland, noncommittal look that I knew from Caroline's comments about my own expressions meant disagreement.

Sighing, I began telling him about my plans to kill Charles Dickens.

I had been going on in a normal voice for ten minutes or so and had just gotten to the part about Mr Dradles finding the empty space between the walls of the crypt under Rochester Cathedral and the efficacy of the lime pit on the puppy's carcass when I saw the Other Wilkie's opiate gaze shift up and focus on something over my shoulder. I quickly turned in my chair.

Agnes, George and Besse's daughter, was standing there in her robe and nightgown and tattered slippers. Her round, flat, homely face was so pale that even her lips were white. Her gaze moved between the Other Wilkie and me, then back and forth again. Her small hands with their bitten nails were raised like a puppy's paws. I had no doubt whatsoever that she had been there for a while and had heard every word I'd said.

Before I could speak, she turned and ran to the stairs, and I heard the slap of her slippers on wood continue on towards her room on the third floor.

Panicked, I looked back at the Other Wilkie. He shook his head more in sadness than in alarm. His expression alone told me what I had to do.

EXCEPT FOR THE FIREPLACES, the house was now dark. Outside, the Christmas week that had been so warm was ending on a New Year's Day night ice storm. I kept rapping on Agnes's door.

"Agnes, please come out. I need to speak with you."

No response but sobbing. The door was locked. Candles were lit in her room, and from the shape of the shadows glimpsed in the crack under the door, she had pushed some heavy bureau or washstand up against that door.

"Come out, Agnes, please. I didn't know you were here, in the house. Come out and talk to me."

More sobbing. Then—"I'm sorry, Mr Collins...I ain't dressed. I ain't well. I didn't mean to do nothing wrong. I ain't well."

"Very well, then," I said calmly. "I'll speak to you in the morning."

I went back down to the dark parlour, lighted some candles, and found the note I'd missed earlier in the day. It was from George and had been left on the mantel:

> Mr Collins, Sir:
>
> Our daughter Agnes is sick. She was coming with Besse and me to Wales but we did think better of it early this Morning, as the Poor Child has Fever. It would Not Do, we think, to bring High Fever to two Death Beds.
>
> So with your permission, Sir, we leave Agnes behind under your Care and Protection until next Tuesday, when I (George) hope to Return to Your Service, no matter what the Disposition of Besse's parents' Fates be.

She can cook for you, Sir. (Agnes) After a fashion.
And though that will not be up to Your Standards, she
will keep the place Clean if you choose not to spend all the
time at Your Club. At the very least, Mr Collins, she will
let the Burglars, as she Recuperates and carries out her
Humble Duties, know that the House is not Empty in
your Absence.

Yours O'bdtly,
George

How had I not noticed the paper hours earlier when I had wrestled with the flue and lit the fire? I started to throw the note into the fire but then thought better of it. Careful not to wrinkle it, I set it back on the mantel where I had found it. What to do?

Too late for that now. I needed to deal with this first thing tomorrow. And for that I needed money.

I WOKE AT DAWN on Saturday, the next morning, and thought about the situation. As the grey light grew stronger in the room—I'd left the heavy drapes pulled back the night before for just that purpose—I noticed that there was a tidy stack of the Other Wilkie's notes on the straight-backed chair near the door. I hadn't noticed them the day before, but they had probably been written that night, since Frank Beard had been kind enough, in the early morning hours after our New Year's Eve dinner party, to inject my morphine before he'd left. Most of my Droodish dreaming and dictation occurred while under the influence of morphia.

There was no immediate urgency. I kept telling myself this. Whatever the dull-witted girl had overheard was safe within these walls until her parents returned— or at least until George came back.

It fascinated me, as I lay there in the big bed with

the light coming up, how little attention I had paid to Agnes's presence over the years. At first she had simply been the extra little mouth to feed (but not to pay)—a side condition to my hiring of George and Besse, who were themselves a compromise as servants: never terribly efficient, but always very cheap. With the money I had saved with George and Besse's wee salary over the years, I had always been able to hire a fine cook when necessary. Actually, the rent I received from the stables behind the big house there at Number 90 Gloucester Place paid for Agnes's parents' salaries with a good bit left over.

Agnes—with her chewed fingernails, flat, round face, constant clumsiness, and slight stammer—had been so familiar a part of the background here (and at Melcombe Place before this) that I simply thought of her as part of the furniture. For years she had also existed for me less as a servant than as a counterpoint to Carrie's intelligence and good looks, although the girls had played together when they were younger. (Agnes had been too dull and unimaginative a playmate to hold Carrie's interest once both girls were out of their nursery years.)

But what to do now that the girl had seen the Other Wilkie and overheard me describing my plans to murder Dickens?

I needed money, that was certain. The sum of £300 came to mind. Lying there visible and tangible in bills and gold coins, it would be a staggering fortune to the simple-minded girl, but not so much as to seem abstract to her; £300 seemed about right for what I was to propose.

But where to get it?

I'd spent the last of my cash and written too many personal cheques over the past few days, obtaining tickets for the pantomime, purchasing gin and champagne for the party, and paying Nina Lehmann's new cook for the feast. The banks were closed until Monday, and although I knew the manager of my bank, it simply would not do for me to show up at the door of his home on a weekend, asking to cash a personal cheque for £300.

Dickens would loan that amount to me, of course, but it would take half the day for me to get to Gad's Hill Place and back. I did not want to leave Agnes alone here for that length of time. She had no one with whom to speak with her parents and Carrie gone, but there was no guarantee that she would not write and post a letter in the time I was absent. That would be disastrous.

And I also did not want to raise Dickens's curiosity as to why I needed £300 that weekend.

The same applied to other people in London who might have loaned me that amount of cash on a moment's notice—Fred or Nina Lehmann, Percy Fitzgerald, Frank Beard, William Holman Hunt. None would let me down, but all would *wonder*. Fechter would never ask me *why* I needed that particular sum and would never worry about where it went or if he would ever get it back, but Fechter was—as always—broke himself. Indeed, I had made so many personal loans to him in the past year and poured so much of my own money into "theatrical expenses" (as yet unrecouped), first for *No Thoroughfare* and now, already, for *Black and White* (even though the writing for it had just begun), that I was in some financial difficulty myself as the new year began.

After I had bathed and dressed especially well, I heard bustling coming from the kitchen downstairs.

Agnes had also dressed to the apex of her poor ability—the thought that she was in her best clothes to travel caused a flurry of panic in me—and was in the process of fixing a full breakfast for me as I came into the kitchen.

736 • DAN SIMMONS

The girl actually flinched, pulling back into a corner.

I gave her my warmest and most avuncular smile, even as I held both hands up, palms towards her, and stopped in the doorway to show her that I held no aggressive intentions.

"Good morning, Agnes. You are looking especially lovely today."

"G-g-g-g-good morning, M-m-m-m . . . *Mr* Collins. Thank 'ee, sir. Your eggs 'n' beans 'n' bacon 'n' t-t-t-toast is almost r-r-ready, sir."

"Wonderful," I said. "May I sit here in the kitchen with you to eat it?"

The idea obviously horrified her.

"On second thought, I'll have it in the dining room as always. Has the *Times* arrived?"

"Y-y-y-yess—yesss—sir," she managed. "It's on the dining room table, as always." She omitted the second "sir" rather than get stuck on it again. Her face was a bright red. The bacon was burning. "D-do you want coffee this mornin' . . . Mr Collins . . . or tea?"

"Coffee, I think. Thank you, Agnes."

I went in and read the paper and waited. Everything on every plate she brought was either burned or raw or—somehow—both at once. Even the coffee tasted scorched, and the girl slopped it into my saucer when she poured it. I ate and drank it all with every sign of relish.

When she came in to refill my cup, I smiled again and said, "Can you sit down and talk to me for a minute, Agnes?"

She looked at the empty chairs at the table and gave me another look of horror. Sit at the master's table? Such things were not done.

"Or stand, if you're more comfortable with that," I added amiably. "But I think we should chat about . . ."

"I di'n't hear nothing las' noon," she said in a tumble of rushed syllables. The main word came out as *nothink*. "N-n-nothing at all, Mr Collins, sir. And I saw nothing as well. I di'n't see anyone else there with you in your study, Mr Collins, I swear I di'n't. And I heard nothing..." *Nothink*. "...about Mr Dickens or nobody and nothing else."

I forced a chuckle. "It's all right, Agnes. It's all right. My cousin was visiting..."

My cousin, yes. My identical-twin cousin. My Doppel-gänger *cousin. My perfectly identical cousin of whom I had never spoken, never mentioned to George or Besse. Identical down to the glasses and suit and waistcoat and belly and hint of grey beginning in the beard.*

"...and I would have introduced you to him if you'd not left in such a hurry," I finished. It was hard to hold such a wide and gentle smile in place for so long, especially while speaking.

The girl was shaking from head to foot. She had to set one hand on the back of a chair to help hold her upright. I noticed that the already-bitten nails were now bleeding.

"My...cousin...is also a literary gentleman," I said softly. "It's possible you heard the tag end of a fanciful story we were devising...about the murder of a writer somewhat like Mr Dickens, whom you know has visited here often and would have been amused by our tale. *Like* Mr Dickens—we used his name as a sort of shorthand—but not *really* Mr Dickens, of course. You are aware that I write sensationalist stories and plays, aren't you, Agnes?"

The girl's eyes were actually fluttering. What would I do if she fainted or screamed or ran out into the street in search of a constable?

"At any rate," I finished, "neither my cousin nor I wanted you to get the wrong idea."

"I'm sorry, Mr Collins. I di'n't see nor hear nothing." She repeated this four times.

I set down my paper and pushed back my chair. Little Agnes jumped half a foot into the air.

"I'm going out for a few minutes," I said briskly. There would be no more mentions of last night from me. Ever. "I shall be back shortly. Would you be so kind as to iron my eight best evening dress shirts?"

"They was ironed by Mum jus' before she left," managed Agnes, her voice constricted. At the words "Mum" and "left" her eyes grew moist and her hands shook more fiercely.

"Yes," I said almost harshly, "but they were not ironed to my satisfaction. I'm going to the theatre several times this week and will require those shirts to be perfect. Could you do that at once, please?"

"Yes, Mr Collins." She ducked her head and left with the coffeepot. As I went to the foyer closet to find my overcoat, I could hear the iron being heated in the kitchen.

I had to keep her busy the next hour. I had to be sure she would have no time to write and send a letter, nor time enough to think and then run away.

If I could keep her here the next hour, there would be nothing for me to fear.

Nothink.

MARTHA R—— WAS HAPPY to see me at her door. She was *always* happy to see me at her door. And her door was only a short distance from Gloucester Place, and I'd been lucky enough to find an empty cab leaving Portman Square near my home. With a little more such luck, I'd be back before Agnes had ironed the first shirt, much less before she had time to write and go post a letter.

At first blush, Martha—known to her landlady and other Bolsover Street residents as "Mrs Dawson"—

would be an unlikely place to find £300, despite the fact that I gave her a most generous allowance of £20 per month. But I knew Martha's habits. She purchased almost nothing for herself. She ate frugally, sewed her own dresses, and got by on very little. She always set aside some of the money I gave her monthly and had brought some savings with her from Yarmouth.

I told her what I needed.

"Of course," she said and went into the other room and came back with £300 in various bills and coins.

Perfect.

I had not taken off my overcoat and now I thrust the money into my coat pocket and opened the door. "Thank you, my dear. I will return the amount first thing Monday, after the banks open. Perhaps before then."

"Wilkie?"

Her voice stopped me. She rarely called me by name.

"Yes, my dear?" I had to work to keep the impatience out of my voice.

"I am with child."

I blinked rapidly behind my small round glasses. My neck was suddenly very warm and prickly.

"Did you hear me, Wilkie? I am with child."

"Yes, I heard you."

I opened the door to go but paused. She had no idea how precious were these seconds and minutes I was giving her. "How far along?" I asked softly.

"I believe our child will come in late June or early July."

A little over two months ago, then. It had been that night in October after all—the night of Caroline's wedding.

I smiled. I knew I should take three steps forward and put my arms around her—I knew that Martha expected this, even though she usually expected or asked for so little—but I could not. So I smiled instead.

"We shall have to raise your allowance when the time comes," I said. "Perhaps from twenty pounds to twenty-five pounds."

She nodded and looked down at the worn carpet.

"I shall return this three hundred pounds as soon as I can," I said. And then I left.

COME INTO THE PARLOUR, child," I said.

Agnes had been ironing my third shirt when I returned. I'd left the cab waiting outside. During the ride back from Bolsover Street, I'd given careful thought to where the girl and I should have our conversation. The kitchen was too informal…and I did not want her in that room yet. Normally, I would have asked a servant who needed a talking-to to come into my study, but that would have frightened Agnes now. So it was the parlour.

"Sit down, please," I said. I had taken the large leather chair near the fire and I waved her to a lower, less comfortable wooden chair I had pulled into place. This time my tone left no room for her not to comply.

She sat. Her eyes were down, focusing on nothing save for her red hands folded on her lap.

"Agnes, I have been giving much thought recently to your future…."

She did not look up. Her entire body was trembling slightly.

"You know that not too long ago I placed Carrie… Miss G——…in a wonderful position as governess to an excellent family?"

She said nothing.

"Speak up, please. You *are* aware of Miss Carrie's new position?"

"Yes, sir." The syllables were so soft that an ember crumbling in the fireplace could have muffled them.

"I have decided that it is time for you to have the same opportunities," I said.

She looked up then. Her eyes were as red-rimmed as her fingernails. Had she been crying while she ironed?

"Please read this," I said, handing her a letter I had written the night before on my best stationery.

The heavy cream paper vibrated in her hands as she read—slowly, her lips moving as she silently sounded out the words. Finally she finished and tried to hand it back to me. "That is...very kind of you...sir. Very kind."

At least the d——ned stutter was gone.

"No, you keep it, my child. That is your letter of reference and an excellently worded one, if I do say so myself. I have chosen the family you will work for. They have an estate near Edinburgh. I have sent word to them that you are coming and that you will begin your duties there tomorrow."

Her eyes widened and continued to widen. I thought she might faint.

"I don't know nothing about governessin', Mr Collins."

Nothink.

I smiled paternally. I was tempted to lean forward and pat her shaking hands, but was afraid she might bolt if I did so. "That doesn't matter at all, Agnes. Miss Carrie knew nothing about being a governess before she began her employment. And look how wonderfully that has worked out."

Agnes's eyes darted down to her folded hands. When I stood suddenly, she physically flinched. I began to understand at that moment why thuggish men beat their women; when someone acted as a puppy acted, the urge to beat them like a puppy was very strong. I was too aware of the heavy iron poker by the fireplace.

I parted the drapes. "Look out here, please," I commanded.

Her head came up, but her eyes were wide and wild.

"Stand up, Agnes. That's a good girl. Look out here. What do you see?"

"A closed carriage, sir."

"That's a cab, Agnes. It's waiting for you. The driver shall take you to the railway station."

"I ain't ever ridden in a cab, sir."

"I know," I sighed, allowing the heavy drapes to swing closed. "There are all sorts of new experiences waiting for you, my dear child. This will be the first of many wonderful new things."

I went to the nearby table and returned with a writing board, a page of stationery, and a pencil for her. In her current state, I did not trust her with pen and ink.

"Agnes, you are now going to write a short note to your parents, telling them that a wonderful employment opportunity has arisen and that you have left London to pursue it. You will give them no details... simply tell them that you will write them once you have begun employment there."

"Sir...I...I cannot...I do not..."

"Just write what I dictate to you, Agnes. Now take up the pencil. That's a good girl."

I made the note short—four sentences as simple as this dull child would write—and I looked it over when she had finished. The clumsy letters were formed in a spidery, nervous hand, the capitalisation was random, and several simple words were misspelled, but that would have been true in any case.

"Very good, Agnes. Now sign it. Add your love and sign it."

She did so.

I put the writing board and pencil back and folded the note, slipping it into my pocket.

I set the £300 on the ottoman between us.

"This is for you, my child. The family to whom I have recommended you will pay you, of course...pay you very well, in truth, even more than Miss Carrie is currently earning (old families in Scotland can be very generous)...but this amount, which you must admit is also very generous, will allow you to purchase new clothes, more fitting for your new employment and responsibilities, upon your arrival in Edinburgh. Even that shall leave adequate funds for your first year or two."

I had never noticed the girl's freckles. When she looked up at me now, her round face was so pale that those freckles stood out in bold relief. "Me mum..." she said. "Me dad...I can't...they..."

"They will be *delighted*," I said heartily. "I shall explain it all to them as soon as they return and they will almost certainly come to visit you as soon as they are able. Now go on upstairs and pack everything you want to bring to this new life. Do not forget your prettiest dresses. There will be parties and balls."

She continued sitting.

"Go!" I commanded. "No! Come back! Take the money with you. Now go!"

Agnes scurried up the stairway to pack her clothing and few pitiful personal items.

I followed her upstairs to check that she was complying. Then I went down to the basement to the workbench and toolbox that George kept in order there. Selecting the large hammer with its pry jaws and a heavy pry bar, I went back upstairs.

DEAR READER from another time, if at this point you are tempted to judge me, I would ask you not to. If you knew me in real life as opposed to through these mere words, you would know that I am a gentle man.

I have always been gentle in demeanour and actions. My fiction is—was—sensationalist, but my life is—was—a testimonial to quiet gentleness. Women always sensed this about me, which is why a short, bespectacled, slightly rotund gentleman such as myself was so popular with the ladies. Even our friend Charles Dickens used to joke about my gentleness, as if a lack of aggression were a reason to be made fun of.

During my ride home from Martha's, I'd realised again that I was incapable of harming a hair on young Agnes's head, no matter how devastating her inevitable indiscretion would be to my life and career. I had never raised my hand against anyone in anger.

But ah!, you say, Dear Reader, what of your plans to shoot Drood and Dickens?

May I remind you that Drood is not a human being as we estimate people as being human. He has murdered scores, if not hundreds, of innocents. He is a creature of and from the Black Lands I dream about every time Frank Beard injects me with morphia.

And Dickens... I have shown you what Dickens has done to me. You may be the jury there, Dear Reader. How many years of arrogance and condescension would *you* have tolerated from this man... this self-named *Inimitable*... before you finally raised a hand (or weapon) in righteous anger?

But you must understand that I would never raise a hand to a poor dull child like Agnes.

SHE CAME DOWNSTAIRS dressed in her best cheap outfit and wearing an overcoat that would not keep her warm for ten minutes out of doors in England, less than two minutes in Scotland. She was carrying two cheap valises. And she was weeping.

"Now, now, my dear young friend, none of that," I said

and patted her back. Again she flinched from me. I said, "Would you check to see that the cab is still waiting?"

She looked out through the blinds that covered the lights on either side of the front door. "It is, sir." She began weeping again. "I don't know how t-t-to pay the man who d-d-drives the cab. I d-d-don't know how to find my carriage at the st-station. I don't know how to d-do *anything*." The miserable child was working herself towards hysterics.

"There, there, Agnes. The driver has already been paid. And I have paid him extra to help you find your carriage and your seat. He will make sure you are on the right train, in the correct carriage, and comfortable in your seat before he leaves you. I asked him to watch and make sure you are safe until the coach actually departs. And I have telegraphed members of the fine family you will be serving.... They will meet you at the Edinburgh station."

"My mum 'n' dad..." she began again through her tears.

"Will be delighted that you were brave enough to rise to this singular and wonderful opportunity." I started to open the door and then stopped. "I had forgotten. There is one thing I would like you to help me with before you leave."

She stared at me with red, wide eyes, but I saw the sense of hope stirring there as well. Perhaps, she was thinking, this was a reprieve.

"This way," I said and led her back to the kitchen.

At first she did not notice that the boards and nails had been removed from the door to the servants' stairs, but when she did, she stopped in her tracks.

"I have decided to use this back staircase again, Agnes, and need the candles lit on all the landings going up. But my tired old eyes have trouble seeing in the dim light within...." I was smiling at her.

She shook her head. Her cheap valises dropped to the floor. Her mouth was open and her expression was—to speak frankly—very close to that of the kind of female idiot they lock away in asylums.

"No...sir," she said at last. "Dad said that I mustn't..."

"Oh, there are no rats or mice in there now!" I interrupted with a laugh. "Long gone! Your father knows that I am opening up the stairway. It shan't take more than a minute to light the candles in their sconces on each landing and then you're off on your adventure."

She only shook her head.

I had already lit a candle. Now I put it in her hand and stepped behind her. "Don't be stubborn, Agnes," I whispered in her ear. I wondered even at the time if my voice sounded a bit like Drood's hiss and lisp. "Be a good girl."

I moved forward and she had to move ahead of me to avoid my touch. She did not try to resist until the door was open and I had herded her into the black rectangle.

She balked then, and turned, her eyes as certain and sad and unbelieving as Dickens's Irish bloodhound Sultan's on that last walk he'd taken with us.

"I won't..." she began.

"Light every candle, Agnes dear, and knock when you want out," I said and pushed her in and locked the door.

Then I fetched the hammer and lumber and nails from where I had stored them on the counter and began pounding everything back the way it had been, making sure that the nails were driven into the same holes in the door frame so that everything would look undisturbed when George and Besse got home.

She screamed, of course. Very loudly, although the walls at Number 90 Gloucester Place were very thick and so were the doors. Her screams were just barely audible in the kitchen a few feet away and certainly could not be heard, I trusted, from the sidewalk or street outside.

She banged at the other side of the thick oak door, then clawed (from the sounds of it), then stopped about the time I had got the last board nailed into place at the bottom. This would have cut off any tiny bit of light that came from the kitchen under the door and into that dark stairwell.

I set my ear to the wood of the boards and thought I could hear ascending footsteps—slow and hesitant—as she started up the stairs. Part of her must have been certain even then that this was a cruel game on my part and that when she had lit the candles on each landing, I would let her out.

The final screams, when they came, were very loud. But they did not go on for long. They ceased—as I had known they would—suddenly and terribly and in mid-cry.

I went upstairs then and looked in her room. I looked carefully, not worrying about how late it was getting or about the coach driver I was paying to wait outside. When I was certain that the girl had not left a note in either her room or her parents' room or any-place else in the house, I made sure that all of her important clothes and belongings had been packed in her two cheap valises.

On her carefully made bed, under the coverlet, there was a shapeless and now eyeless little rag doll. *Would she have taken that to her new life in Edinburgh?* I decided that she might have and brought it downstairs and crammed it into the larger of her two bags.

There was no sound whatsoever from the sealed-up servants' staircase.

Taking the hammer and pry bar, I went back down

to the cellar. Once there, I put on the long rubber apron that George used when he did messy tasks down there. I also borrowed his heavy work gloves.

It took me only a few minutes to shovel coal clear of the back wall of the half-filled coal cellar. The blocked-up crack in that wall was still visible, but the mortar was loose between the bricks and stone blocks. Using the pry bar, I began to work the bricks loose.

It took longer than I had expected, but again, I did not rush. Eventually the gap that I had always known Drood had come through that ninth of June two years earlier was revealed. I extended a candle through the hole.

The flame flickered to distant and damp currents but did not quite go out. Everything beyond the circle of light was blackness and a long drop into more blackness.

I shoved both of Agnes's overpacked valises through and listened for the splash or crash of impact, but none came. It was as if there were no bottom to the pit beneath my house.

It took me even longer to wrestle the stones and bricks back into place and to trowel new mortar between them. The simple masonry was a skill my uncle had shown me and I had been proud of it when I was a boy. It certainly came in handy now.

Then I shovelled the coal back into place, stowed all tools and the apron and gloves, went upstairs, washed up carefully, packed a week or two worth of clothes—including two of my freshly ironed evening dress shirts—into a steamer trunk, went into my study and packed all of the writing materials and resources I would need (including the manuscript holding the beginnings of *Black and White*), went up to Agnes's tiny room and left her note where it would easily be found by her parents, made a final check of the house to be sure it was locked up with everything in its proper place—there still was no sound from the back stairway, of course, and, I trusted, never would be—and then I went outside with my large trunk and leather portfolio and locked the front door behind me.

The driver hurried off the cab to wrestle the trunk down the steps, over the kerb, and into place in the boot of the carriage.

"Thank you so much for waiting," I said, out of breath myself but in a good mood. "I had no idea packing would take me so long. I hope the cold and inconvenience haven't bothered you."

"Not a bit, sir," the driver said cheerily. "I had myself a bit o' a nap up on the box, sir." From the looks of his red cheeks and red nose, he'd availed himself of something more than a nap.

He held the door while I stepped up and into the carriage. Once in place above, he opened the trapdoor and called down, "And where to this afternoon, sir?"

"The Saint James Hotel," I said.

It was a bit of a luxury—Charles Dickens put up guests such as Longfellow and the Fieldses there when they visited London, and he sometimes stayed there himself, but it was more than I usually wished to pay for mere rooms. But this was a special occasion.

The little trapdoor closed with a thud. I raised my gold-headed stick, rapped sharply on the ceiling of the cab, and we rolled away.

It later dampened my spirits only a little when I remembered that I had forgotten to take back the £300 before closing the servants' staircase door forever.

CHAPTER FORTY-ONE

O n Tuesday evening, 5 January, Dickens murdered
Nancy in St James's Hall for the first time in front
of the paying public. Dozens of women screamed. At
least four fainted. One older man was seen staggering
out of the hall, gasping for air, helped out by two pale
friends. I left before the riotous applause began, but it
still chased me down the snow-covered street filled
with carriages and cabs waiting for the audience to
emerge. The breath of the muffled drivers huddled on
their high boxes mixed with the larger clouds of exhalations from the horses to rise like steam into the cold
glow of gas lamps.

THAT SAME AFTERNOON of 5 January, I had returned
home from the hotel for the first time since my departure. No terrible stench from the servants' stairway
greeted me in the foyer. I had not expected there to be
and not merely because I had been away for only three
days.

There would be no bad smell from the stairway. I
was sure of that. I had fired five bullets in that stairway,
but it had been a useless, hopeless thing to do so. The
target of those bullets cared nothing for bullets; it had
already devoured the woman with green skin and tusks
for teeth without leaving so much as a swatch of her

dress material or a chip of ivory. There would be nothing of Agnes in there.

I was in my bedroom, packing some fresh shirts into my valise (I was returning to the hotel, where Fechter had joined me for the past few days), when I heard footsteps in the hall and the soft clearing of a throat.

"George? You're back so soon? I'd forgotten when you were returning," I said happily, looking at the man. His face was clouded with some emotion to the point of being grey.

"Yes, sir. The missus is staying on two more days. Her mother passed first—we was expecting her father to, but it was her mother. He was goin' when I left, but we couldn't just leave you here without your loyal domestics, sir, so I come home."

"Well, I'm sorry to hear that, George, and..." I looked at the note he had in his hand. He was pointing it at me as if it were a pistol. "Why, what is that, George?"

"A note from our little Agnes, sir. You 'aven't seen it?"

"Why, no. I thought Agnes was in Wales with you."

"Aye, sir. I figured you 'adn't seen our note to you on the mantel in the parlour, since it was still where we'd left it. You probably never knew Agnes was in the house with you that night, sir. That is, if she *was* in the house that night...if she left that morning, before you woke and left, and not during the night."

"Left? Whatever on earth are you going on about, George?"

"'Ere, sir," he said, thrusting the note at me.

I read it and feigned surprise, all the while thinking, *Is this a trap? Has the stupid little girl managed to change her handwriting or do something in this note to alert her parents?* But the words were just as I had dictated to her. The misspellings seemed sincere.

"Another opportunity?" I said, lowering the note.

"Whatever does she mean, George? She's gone and taken employment elsewhere without talking to me? Or to you and Besse?"

"No, sir," George said solemnly. His dark-eyed stare seemed to bore into me. He did not blink. "That note isn't what it seems, sir."

"It's not?" I put the last of my clean linen in the valise and snapped it shut.

"No, sir. They ain't no t'other opportunity, Mr Collins. Who'd hire a lazy, clumsy child like our Agnes? That's not right, sir. Not right at all."

"Then what does this mean?" I asked, giving him back the note.

"The soldier, sir."

"Soldier?"

"The young rascal of a Scottish-regiment soldier who she met in market in December, Mr Collins. A corporal. Ten year older 'n Agnes he were, sir, with shifty little eyes and soft hands and a moustache like a greasy caterpillar what crawled up on his lip to die, sir. Besse, she seen our girl talking to 'im and got between 'em quick, you can imagine. But somehow she seen him again when she was out doin' chores. She admitted to such before Christmas, when we found 'er cryin' like a mooncalf in 'er room."

"You mean..."

"Aye, sir. The silly, stupid child's run away with that soldier as sure as Besse's mum's in the cold ground an' her papa now too, most likely. Our little family's all gone and scattered now."

Lifting the valise, I clasped George on his shoulder as I headed for the door. "Nonsense, my dear man. She'll be back. They always come back after their first love's disappointment! Trust me on this, George. And if she doesn't...well, we'll hire someone to track her down and talk sense into her. I happen to know several detectives in private consultation. There's nothing to worry about, George."

"Aye, sir," he said in a tone as grey as his complexion.

"I'll be at the Saint James Hotel for a few more days. Please be so kind as to bring my mail there each day and to have the house all aired and ready by Saturday, with a meal planned for that evening—Mr Fechter and others may come for a stay."

"Aye, sir."

We descended the stairs together.

"Be of good cheer," I said and patted him on the back a final time before stepping out to the waiting cab. "All shall turn out for the best in the end."

"Aye, sir."

ONE CAN ONLY IMAGINE how difficult it was for Dickens, with his Staplehurst-shattered nerves worsening rather than improving, as he again plunged into an exhausting tour which required travel by rail almost every day. Katey had informed me through my brother that the day after his St James's Hall readings on 5 January, Dickens had been too exhausted to get out of bed and take his usual cold shower-bath. Within a few days he had to do his final readings in Dublin and Belfast, and he decided to take Georgina and his daughter Mary with him to make it feel more like a festive occasion rather than a farewell. He was almost immediately confronted with a near-tragedy that took a terrible toll on his nerves.

Dickens, Dolby, Georgina, Mary, and the usual travelling entourage were returning from Belfast to catch the mail boat to Kingston when something went terribly wrong. They were riding in the first-class carriage immediately behind the engine when suddenly there was an incredible crash along the roof of their carriage and they looked outside just in time to see what appeared to be a huge, free-flying scythe of iron cutting through telegraph poles as if they were mere reeds.

"Down!" cried Dickens and everyone dived for the floor of the carriage. A fusillade of huge splinters, gravel, mud, stones, and water struck the windows on the side they had been riding. The carriage shuddered as if they had hit something solid and then there was a series of shocks so great that Dickens later admitted that he was sure they had once again derailed and were hurtling over an incomplete trestle.

The carriage came to a halt and the only sounds breaking the sudden silence were the steam-panting of the great engine and a few screams from the lower-class carriages. Dickens was the first to his feet and outside and immediately began talking quietly to the engineer as Dolby and other men with their wits about them gathered round.

The engineer, who (according to Dolby writing Forster) was far more agitated than Dickens, his hands shaking, explained that the metal tire on the huge driving-wheel had fractured—exploded—and sent its fragments flying into the air and scything through the telegraph poles. It had been the large section of that wheel that had crashed into the roof of Dickens's carriage. "If it'd been a little larger," said the engineer, "or travelling a little lower or faster, it would have cut down through the roof of your carriage for sure, doing to you poor passengers what its other parts did to those telegraph poles."

Dickens had calmed Mary and Georgina and the other passengers that day—even Dolby admitted to being deeply shaken, and it took much to shake George Dolby—but the next evening, after the Inimitable had Murdered Nancy yet again, Dolby had to help the Chief off stage at the end of the evening.

Dickens had arranged his schedule to read in Cheltenham just so that his dear and ageing friend Macready might hear the Murder. Afterwards, the failing seventy-five-year-old came backstage, shakily leaning on Dolby's arm, and was unable to speak until he had two glasses of champagne. The old man was so emotional after seeing the Murder that Dickens tried to make light of it, but Macready would have none of that. A hint of his old stage fury returning in that ruined voice, he bellowed out, "No, Dickens—er—er—I will NOT—er—er—have it—er—put aside. In my—er—best times—er—you remember them, my dear boy—er—gone, gone!—no!" And here the bellow became a roar. "It comes to this—er—TWO MACBETHS!"

This last was so loud and so emotional that Dickens and Dolby could do nothing but stare at the old actor who had made Macbeth his signature role and who was more proud of nothing else, not even his wife and lovely grown daughter. And he seemed to be saying that in terms of pure horror and emotion, Dickens's Murder of Nancy had been the equivalent—in acting as well as in effect—of the best of his best Macbeths.

Then the old giant stood there glaring at Dolby as if the manager (who had not said a word) had contradicted him. And then Macready simply . . . went away. His body was still there, the third glass of champagne still in his hand, the great jaw and profile both still jutting upwards and outwards in defiance, but Macready himself was gone, leaving behind, as Dickens later told Dolby and Forster, only a clever, pale optical illusion of himself.

In Clifton, the Murder brought about what Dickens gleefully called a contagion of fainting. *"I should think we had from a dozen to twenty ladies borne out, stiff and rigid, at various times. It became quite ridiculous."* The Inimitable loved it.

In Bath, it was Dickens who seemed close to fainting, as the place literally haunted him. "The place looks to me like a cemetery which the Dead have succeeded in rising and taking," he told Dolby. "Having built streets out of their old gravestones, they wander about scantily trying to 'look alive.' A dead failure."

Percy Fitzgerald let slip to me in February that after Georgina and Mary returned to Gad's Hill, Ellen Ternan was with Dickens again. Or so I surmised (Percy would never be so indiscreet as to say it outright). But Fitzgerald was getting married, at long last, and when he breathlessly told this to Dickens at the station, the writer said, "I must tell this to the one who is with me." *The one who is with me* . . . Dickens hardly would have used this circumlocution to describe Dolby or his lighting or gas man. Was Ellen staying in the same hotel as Dickens, but as a sister now, rather than a lover? One can only imagine the added torments this gave to the Inimitable.

I say "added torments" quite deliberately, since there was no doubt now that it was more than bad health that was tormenting Charles Dickens. Despite his gleeful reports about dozens of women fainting, the Murder of Nancy was obviously taking a terrible toll on his psyche as well as his body. Everyone I spoke to— Fitzgerald, Forster, Wills, everyone—agreed that the Inimitable's letters were filled with the Murder and nothing but the Murder. He was reading it at least four times a week, mixed in with his usual most popular readings, and he seemed obsessed not just with turning each hall in which he read into a Theatre of Terror, but in feeling Bill Sikes's guilt at the murders.

"I am murdering Nancy. . . ."

"My preparations for a certain murder . . ."

"I think often of my fellow criminals. . . ."

"I commit the murder again, and again, and again. . . ."

"I have a vague sensation of being 'wanted' as I walk about the streets. . . ."

"I imbue my hands once again with innocent blood...."
"I still have a great deal of murdering ahead of me and little time in which to do it...."

All these phrases and more poured out to those of us left behind in London. Dolby wrote Forster that Dickens could no longer abide staying in the town or city where he had done the reading, long-planned railway schedules had to be changed, tickets exchanged, new fees paid out, so that the exhausted Inimitable, barely capable of walking to the station, could flee the city that night, like a wanted man.

"People look at me differently after I have Murdered Nancy," Dickens told the vacant-headed Wills during one of his stops in London. "They fear me, I believe. They leave a distance in the room...not one of shyness towards someone famous, but rather the distance of fear and, perhaps, loathing or disgust."

Another time, Dolby told Forster that he came backstage after a performance to say that the carriage was waiting for departure to the station, only to find that Dickens had been washing his hands for fifteen minutes or more. "I cannot get the blood off, Dolby," said the exhausted writer, looking up with haunted eyes. "It stays beneath my nails and in the skin."

To London, to Bristol, to Torquay, to Bath—Dickens knew the hotels and stations and halls and even the faces in the audiences by heart by now—and then to London again in preparation to go on to Scotland. But now Dickens's left foot was so swollen that Frank Beard absolutely forbade the Scotland tour, which was postponed briefly. But five days later, Dickens was travelling again, despite urgent pleas not to from Georgina, his daughters, his son Charley, and friends such as Fitzgerald and Wills and Forster.

. . .

I DECIDED TO GO to Edinburgh to see Dickens Murder Nancy. And, possibly, to see the Murder murder Charles Dickens.

I felt almost certain now that Dickens was attempting suicide by reading tour, but my earlier anger at the idea had faded somewhat. Yes, this would leave Dickens with his fame and with his burial in Westminster Abbey, argued one part of my mind, but at least the man would be dead. But some suicides fail, I reminded myself with satisfaction. The ball rattles around in the skull, carving tunnels through the brain, but the would-be suicide does not die, merely remains a drooling idiot the rest of his life. Or the woman hangs herself, but the rope does not break her neck and someone cuts her down, but too late to prevent all that loss of circulation of blood to her brain. For the rest of her life she has a scar on her throat, an ugly twist to her neck, and a vacant stare.

Suicide by reading tour, I told myself, might misfire in the same delightful way.

I had arrived earlier and taken a room, so Dickens was surprised and pleased to see me waiting at the station.

"You look well, my dear Wilkie," he cried. "Healthy. Have you been out on one of your rented yachts in a late-February gale?"

"You look wonderful yourself, Charles," I said.

Dickens looked terrible—much older and greyer, the hair all but gone from the top of his head, the few greying strands combed over, and even his beard appeared sparse and ill-kempt. His eyes were red-rimmed and there were purple hollows beneath them. His cheeks were gaunt. His breath was rank. He limped like a Crimean war veteran with a wooden leg.

I knew that I looked little better. Frank Beard had been forced to increase the number of morphia injections—

always administered precisely at ten PM—from two or three a week to nightly. He had taught me how to fill the syringe and how to inject myself (not so difficult or onerous a project as it sounds) and had left a huge bottle of morphine for me. I doubled the nightly dose at the same time I was doubling the amount of laudanum I was taking during the day.

This led to increased productivity both day and night. When Dickens asked what I was working on, I told him truthfully that Fechter had all but moved in with me at Number 90 Gloucester Place and we were working long hours each day on our play, *Black and White*. I told him that I had an idea for another novel, one based on certain odd aspects of English marriage laws, that I would almost certainly commence work upon once the play premiered in late March.

Dickens clapped me on the back and promised to be at the premiere with his entire family. I wondered then if he would be alive a month from then, in late March.

What I did not tell Dickens was that each night now, after a brief morphine sleep, I awoke by one or two AM and dictated my dreams to the Other Wilkie. Our collaborative book on Ancient Egyptian Ritual of the Gods of the Black Lands now boasted more than a thousand handwritten pages.

That night in Edinburgh, Dickens performed the Murder brilliantly. I admit to having chills myself. The room was not overheated, as it may have been in Clifton, but still a dozen or so women fainted.

Afterwards, Dickens spent some time with members of the audience before staggering off to his dressing room, and once there he told Dolby and me again that he had noticed that people were strangely reluctant to come up and speak to him or stand in his presence after the performance. "They sense my murderous instincts," he said with a rueful laugh.

It was here that Dickens handed Dolby a list of the remaining readings and Dolby made the nearly fatal (in terms of employment) mistake of politely suggesting that the Murder might be left off the programme for the smaller towns, merely reserved for major cities.

"Look, Chief—look carefully through the towns you have given me and see if you note anything peculiar about them."

"No. What?"

"Well, out of four readings a week you have put down three Murders."

"What of it?" snapped Dickens. "What on earth is your point?" I believe he had forgotten that I was in the room. As the ancient Macready had, I stood straight and silent with a glass of warming champagne in my hand.

"Simply this, Chief," Dolby said softly. "The success of your farewell tour is certain, assured in every way, so far as human probability is concerned…no matter which selections you choose to read from. It therefore does not make a bit of difference which of the works you read from. This Sikes and Nancy reading is taking a terrible toll on you, Chief. I can see it. Others can see it. You yourself can see it and feel it. Why not save it for the big cities—or set it aside altogether for the rest of the tour?"

Dickens swivelled in his chair, away from the mirror in which he had been removing the modest amount of makeup he wore during readings. The only time I had ever seen his expression this furious was when he was play-acting at being Bill Sikes. "Have you *finished,* sir?"

"I have said all I felt on that matter," Dolby said flatly but firmly.

Dickens leapt up, taking the plate that had held a few oysters and slamming down the handle of his knife upon it. It shattered into half a dozen pieces. "Dolby! D——n you! Your d——ned infernal caution will be your ruin—and mine!—one of these days!"

"Perhaps so, Chief," said Dolby. The bear of a man was flushing bright red and I could swear I saw tears in his eyes. But his voice remained soft and firm. "In this case, though, I hope you will do me the justice to say that the infernal caution is being exercised in your own interest."

Stunned, still holding my glass of champagne, I realised that this was the only time in my long association with Charles Dickens that I had ever heard him raise his voice to another man (other than in playacting). Even when he had so hurt my feelings that night at Vérey's, his voice was always soft, almost gentle. The effect of Dickens visibly and audibly angry, in reality rather than performance, was more terrible than I could have imagined.

Dickens stood in silence. I remained frozen at the back of the room, forgotten by both principals in this unique dialogue. Dolby went to put the tour list on his writing case, turning away as if sparing his Chief his injured countenance. When he turned back, he saw what I had been seeing.

Dickens was weeping silently.

Dolby froze and before he could move a muscle, Dickens had—inevitably, characteristically—moved forward to embrace the bigger man with what appeared to be absolute affection. "Forgive me, Dolby," he choked out. "I did not mean it. I am tired. We are all tired. And I know you are right. We will discuss this calmly in the morning."

But in the morning—I was there at breakfast—Dickens left the Murder in all three readings and added one.

By the time I returned to London, I had observed or heard all of the following facts:

Dickens had been discharging blood, blaming his old problem of piles, but Dolby was less certain that this was the only reason for constant bloody diarrhoea.

The Inimitable's left foot and leg were swollen again to the point that he needed to be helped to the cab and then into the railway carriage. The only time he appeared to walk normally was when he was going onto or off the stage.

He was melancholy, he admitted, beyond all words to describe it.

In Chester, Dickens was dizzy and confessed that he was suffering a mild paralysis. When a doctor was summoned, he told the man that he was "giddy, with a tendency to go backwards and to turn around." Dolby later told me that when Dickens had tried to place a small object on a table, he had ended up awkwardly pushing the entire small table forward, almost toppling it.

Dickens told of a strangeness in his left hand and arm and explained that to use that hand—say, to set down an object or to pick it up—he had to look at it carefully and actively *will it* to do as he wished.

Dickens told me that last morning in Edinburgh— laughing as he said it—that he no longer felt secure lifting his own hands to his head, especially his rebellious left hand, and soon might have to hire someone to comb his few remaining hairs before he went out in public.

After Chester, however, he went on to read in Blackburn and then at Bolton, Murdering Nancy as he went.

By 22 April, Dickens had broken down. But I get ahead of myself, Dear Reader.

IT WAS SOMETIME AFTER I returned from Edinburgh that I received a letter. It was from Caroline. There was no pathos or bathos in her note—she wrote almost unemotionally, as if cataloguing the behaviour of sparrows in her garden—but she informed me that in the six months of their marriage, her husband, Joseph, was failing to earn a living for them, that they lived off crumbs from his mother (actually from his father's small estate, doled out grudgingly), and that he beat her.

I read this with mixed emotions, the primary one being—I admit—some small satisfaction.

There was no request from her for money or help of any sort, not even for a return letter, but she signed it, *"Yr Very Old and True Friend."*

I sat for a while in my study, contemplating what a false friend might be if Caroline G——, now Mrs Harriett Clow, were an example of a true friend.

That same day, a letter arrived for George and Besse, who had each been grieving in his or her own way—quietly, to be sure, but Besse had been hurt especially hard by Agnes's departure (more so than by the death of her parents, who left them no money at all)—and I had not seen the envelope when it arrived or the handwriting (laborious printing, actually) would have certainly caught my eye.

But the next day, George appeared at my study door, cleared his throat, and entered with an apologetic expression.

"Excuse me, sir, but since you showed such a kind interest in the fate of our daughter, dear Agnes, I thought ye'd want to see this, sir." He handed me a small piece of what turned out to be embossed hotel stationery.

> *DeaRe Mum an DaD—I Am welle and hop to*
> *Find you the Same in This Misiv. My Oportunyty has*
> *Turned out Very Well. Corpal MacdonalD, my Belovd,*
> *and I Plan to Marrye on Nin Jun. I Shall Write you*
> *agane After this Happye Event. W/ love and Afecton,*
> *yr. Dauter, AGNES*

For a moment after reading this, my face, lips, and muscles were as numb and frozen as they had been on the very few occasions when I dosed myself with too much morphia or laudanum. I looked up at George but found that I could not speak.

"Yes, sir," he said brightly. "It's grand news, ain't it?"

"This Corporal MacDonald is the chap she ran away with?" I eventually managed. My voice sounded, even to my shock-dulled ear, as if it had been poured through a strainer.

I had to have known that. George must have told me that. I was sure that he had. Hadn't he?

"Aye, sir. And I may amend my 'arsh judgement of the lad if 'e makes an honest woman out o' our sweet Agnes."

"I certainly hope this will prove to be the case, George. This is very happy news. I am overjoyed to hear that Agnes is safe and well and happy." I handed him back the note. The heading at the top of the cheap paper was from an Edinburgh hotel, but not the one I had stayed at while visiting Dickens.

Hadn't we walked over to another hotel to dine that evening after Dickens complained of the beef in the hotel in which we were staying being inferior? I was sure we had. Was it this one whose stationery I was still staring at as George tucked it into his moleskin waistcoat? I was almost certain it was. Had I picked up some of the stationery in the lobby while I was there—perhaps so. Quite possibly so.

"Just thought you'd be interested in 'earing our good news, sir. Thank ye, sir." George bowed awkwardly and backed out.

I looked down at the letter I had been writing to my brother, Charley. In my agitation, I had spilled a huge blob of ink across my last paragraph.

After the argument between Dickens and Dolby that night, I had used an unusually large amount of my laudanum. We went to dinner. I remembered little of the evening after our first drinks and glasses of wine. Did I return to my room and pen "Agnes's" letter? Certainly I knew her patterns of misspellings from the note she had copied from my dictation in January. Had I then gone down in the night and posted the letter to George and Besse at the front counter?

Possibly.

I must have.

That was the only explanation and it was a simple one.

I had done other things under the influence of opium and laudanum which I had forgotten about the next day and in days after. Thus the solution to The Moonstone.

But had I known the d——ned Scottish corporal's name?

Suddenly feeling dizzy, I walked quickly to the window and pulled up the sash. The early-spring air came in, carrying with it taints of coal and horse dung and the distant Thames and its tributaries already beginning to stink in the tentative spring sunlight. I gulped it in and leaned on the sill.

There was a man in an absurd opera cape on the sidewalk opposite the house. His skin was parchment white and his eyes seemed as sunken as a corpse's. Even from this distance I could see him smile at me and could make out the strange darkness between teeth preternaturally sharpened to points.

Edmond Dickenson.

Or the walking-dead servant of Drood who had once been young Edmond Dickenson.

The figure tipped his tall, shiny, out-of-style top hat and moved on down the sidewalk, looking and smiling back at me only once before making the turn at Portman Square.

CHAPTER FORTY-TWO

The premiere of my play *Black and White* was on a Sunday, 29 March, 1869. I hovered backstage in an advanced stage of nerves, too agitated even to gauge the audience response by the sound or absence of laughter and applause. All I could hear was the beating of my heart and the pounding of my pulse in my aching temples. My stomach revolted frequently in the carefully calculated ninety-one minutes that the play ran (not so long as to bore the audience, not so brief as to make them feel short-changed, all according to the accursed, hovering Fechter's calculations). Borrowing an idea from Fechter—who had called for the same boy earlier, before the curtain went up—I had the lad follow me around with a basin. I was forced to resort to it several times before the end of Act III.

Peeking out through the curtains, I could see my family and friends crowding the author's box—Carrie looking especially lovely in a new gown given to her by the Ward family (for whom she still worked); my brother, Charley, and his wife, Katey; Frank Beard and his wife; Fred and Nina Lehmann; Holman Hunt (who had attended Mother's funeral in my place); and others. In the lower omnibus-box closer to the stage was Charles Dickens and all of his family that was not scattered to Australia or India or to lonely exile (Catherine)—Georgina, his daughter Mamie, his son Charley and his wife, his son Henry, home for a break from Cambridge, and more.

I could not bear to watch their reaction. I went back to cowering backstage, the boy with the basin scrambling to stay close.

Finally the last curtain came down, the Adelphi Theatre exploded with wild applause, and Fechter and his leading lady, Carlotta Leclercq, went out to take their bows and then to summon out the rest of the cast. Everyone was smiling. The ovation continued unabated and I could hear the cries of "Author! Author!"

Fechter came back to lead me out, and I strode onto the stage with as much an appearance of modest aplomb as I could muster.

Dickens was standing and appeared to be leading the crowd's wild applause. He was wearing his spectacles and was so close to the stage that the limelights reflected in them turnd his eye sockets into circles of blue fire.

We had a hit. Everyone said so. The newspapers the next day congratulated me on having—at last—found the perfect formula for theatrical success by mastering, as they said, *"the essential business of neat, tight, dramatic construction."*

No Thoroughfare had run for six months. I fully expected *Black and White* to run (with a full house) for a year, perhaps eighteen months.

But after three weeks, empty seats began appearing like leprous lesions on a saint's face. After six weeks, Fechter and his troupe were emoting to a half-empty house. The play closed after a mere sixty days, less than half the run of the far clumsier and collaborative *No Thoroughfare.*

I blamed the bovine stupidity of London playgoers. We had laid a pure pearl at their feet and they had wondered where the rancid oyster meat had gone. I also blamed those elements in Fechter's original scenario for what I (and certain French newspapers) called the overly "Oncle Tommerie" aspects of the play. England in the early 1860s (just as America shortly before it) had gone ecstatically mad about *Uncle Tom's Cabin*— everyone in England with a threadbare suit of evening clothes had seen the thing twice—but interest in slavery and its cruelties had faded since then, especially after the American Civil War.

And in the meantime, Fechter's "Triumph" was coming close to driving me to Marshalsea debtors prison—although Marshalsea itself had been closed and partially torn down decades earlier. When he promised "copious backers" for *Black and White*, he essentially had me in mind. And I had complied—secretly pouring a fortune into expenses, actors' salaries, artists' fees for backdrops, musicians' fees, et cetera.

I had also been lending more and more money to the always-insolvent (yet always-living-well) Charles Albert Fechter, and it did not console me in the least to know that Dickens had also been subsidising the actor's extravagant style of living (to the combined tune, I knew now, of more than £20,000).

When *Black and White* closed after sixty days, Fechter shrugged and went off in search of new roles. I received the bills. When I finally cornered Fechter about what he owed me, he replied with his usual childish cunning—"My dear Wilkie, you know I love you. Do you think I should love you so if I were not firmly convinced you would do the same thing in my place?"

This response made me remember that I still owned poor Hatchery's pistol with its four remaining bullets.

So, to pay the bills and to begin digging myself out of the debt that had so soon followed and replaced true financial security (with Mother's inheritance and my earnings from *The Moonstone* and other projects now all but gone), I did what any writer would do in such an emergency: I drank more laudanum, took my nightly injections of morphine, drank much wine, bedded Martha more frequently, and began a new novel.

DICKENS MAY HAVE LEAPT to his feet applauding during the premiere of my *Black and White*, but a month later his reading tour had him flat on his back.

In Blackburn he was giddy and in Bolton he staggered and almost fell, although months later I overheard him telling his American friend James Fields, "...only Nelly observed that I had staggered and that my eye had failed and only she dared to tell me."

Nelly was Ellen Ternan, also still referred to by Dickens as "the Patient" because of the slight injuries she had suffered at Staplehurst four years earlier. Now *he* was the patient. And she was still travelling with him from time to time. This was interesting news. What a terrible and final turning-point it is in any ageing man's life when one's young lover becomes one's caretaker.

I knew from Frank Beard that Dickens had been compelled to write him describing these symptoms. Beard, in turn, had been sufficiently alarmed that he had departed by rail for Preston the very afternoon he received the letter.

Beard arrived, examined Dickens, and announced that there could be no more readings. The tour was over.

"Are you certain?" asked Dolby, who was in the room. "The house is sold out and it is too late to refund the tickets."

"If you insist on Dickens taking the platform tonight," said the physician, glowering at Dolby almost as fiercely as had Macready, "I will not guarantee but that he goes through life dragging a foot after him."

Beard brought Dickens back to London that very

night and the next morning had arranged a consultation with the famous physician Sir Thomas Watson. After a very thorough examination and interrogation of the Inimitable on his symptoms, Watson announced, "The state thus described shows plainly that C. D. has been on the brink of an attack of paralysis of his left side, and possibly of apoplexy."

Dickens rejected these dire predictions, saying in the following months that he had been suffering only from over-fatigue. Still, he called a pause in his tour. Dickens had finished seventy-four of his planned one hundred readings (this was only two fewer than the number that had driven him to near-collapse in America).

And yet, after a few weeks of relative rest at Gad's Hill Place and in London, the Inimitable began pressing Dr Watson to allow him to salvage his rescheduled tour. Sir Thomas shook his head, warned against the writer's over-optimism, prescribed extreme caution, and said, "Preventative measures are always invidious, for when the most successful, need for them is the least apparent."

Dickens won the argument, of course. He always won. But he agreed that his final readings—his *true* farewell readings—were to number no more than twelve, were to involve no railway travel whatsoever, and would necessarily have to be delayed until 1870, eight months away.

And so Dickens returned to London, living during the week—he was at Gad's Hill most weekends—in his rooms above the offices of *All the Year Round* at Wellington Street, and threw himself full-tilt into the editing, refurbishing, writing, and planning of the magazine. When he had nothing else to do (I saw this myself during a visit to pick up a cheque), he went into Wills's now frequently empty office and tidied and sorted and rearranged and dusted.

He also ordered his solicitor, Ouvry, to draw up and

finalise his will, which was done quickly and signed and executed on 12 May.

But little of the melancholy he showed during the most exhausted days of his reading tour was visible during these late-spring and early-summer months. Dickens was anticipating the long visit by his old American friends James Fields and his wife, Annie, in that feverish way that only a boy eager to share his toys and games could evince.

And, with his will signed, his doctors predicting imminent apoplexy and death, and the warmest and most humid summer in memory settling over London like a Thames-stinking wet horse blanket, Dickens was beginning to think about another novel.

By SUMMER I had already begun my new book and was researching and writing it with a will.

I had decided for certain the form and thrust of the book one weekend in late May, when I was visiting Martha R—— ("Martha Dawson" to her landlady) in the persona of William Dawson, travelling Barrister at Law. It was one of those rare times when, in order to please Martha, I stayed two nights. I had brought my flask of laudanum, of course, but decided to leave the morphia with its attendant syringe at home. This led to two sleepless nights (not even extra laudanum allowed me to sleep more than a few anxious minutes). So it was on the second of these nights that I found myself sitting in a chair, watching Martha R—— sleep. Because of the early-summer warmth I had opened a window and left the drapes wide, since this bedroom looked out only upon a private garden. Moonlight painted the floor, the bed, and Martha in a broad white stripe.

Now, some say that a woman with child becomes especially attractive. And it is true that there is—with all but the most sickly sort—a strange glow of joy and healthiness that tends to hover around a woman at least during part of her time in confinement. But many men, at least of my acquaintance, also subscribe to the odd theory that a woman with child is also *erotically* attractive (and I apologise for this candid and perhaps vulgar talk, Dear Reader of the Future—perhaps my time was a more direct and honest one), but I fail to see that.

In fact, Dear Reader, as I sat there in the deepest hours of the morning on that warm and sticky May night, turning the pillow over and over in my hands, I looked at Martha where she was sleeping and saw not the innocent young woman who had so enticed me just a few years earlier, but an ageing, ponderous, blue-veined, bosom-bloated, and bizarre figure that was, to my keen novelist's eye, not quite human.

Caroline had never looked this way. Of course, Caroline had had the good manners—at least in my presence—never to be pregnant. But more than that, Caroline had always looked like the lady she purported to be and worked so hard to become. This snoring form painted by the wide stripe of moonlight looked... bovine.

I turned the pillow over in my hands and thought about all this with the clarity that only the proper dosage of laudanum can bring to a mind already sharpened by education and logic.

Mrs Wells, Martha's landlady (not to be confused with the much cannier Mrs Wells who had been my mother's final caretaker), had not seen me arrive. She had been, Martha told me, shut up in her tower room with the croup for more than a week. A neighbour boy brought her soup in the evening and toast and tea in the morning, but I hadn't seen the boy when I'd arrived or during any of the time I was in Martha's private rooms. Mrs Wells was a foolish old woman who read nothing, almost never went out, and knew nothing of the modern world. She knew me only as "Mr Dawson" and we had spoken only a few times in passing. She believed me to be a barrister. I was sure that she had never heard of the writer named Wilkie Collins.

I held the pillow tight, compressing it and then stretching it in my soft-looking but (I believe) powerful hands.

There was, of course, the land agent with whom I had arranged to rent these rooms from Mrs Wells years before. But he also had known me only as Mr Dawson, and I had given a false address for myself.

Martha almost never wrote her parents, and not just because of an estrangement arising from her association with me. Despite my patient lessons with Martha, neither she nor her mother was really literate—they could form letters and sign their names, but neither could read with any assurance and neither took the time to write letters. Her father could but never chose to. Occasionally Martha went home to visit—she had no real friends in her former home town or in nearby Yarmouth, only family—but she always assured me that she'd given no details of her life here: not her address, never her true situation, and especially not the fiction of her marriage to "Mr Dawson." As far as her family knew, based on her last visit some time ago, Martha was single and working as a parlourmaid in some unspecified London hotel and living in a cheap tenement flat with three other good Christian working girls.

Could I trust that she had not told them the truth?

Yes, I was certain I could. Martha had never lied to me.

Had I ever seen anyone in the city—or, more important, had they seen us—when I went out in company with Martha R——?

I was all but certain that I had not. As small as

London seems at times, as frequently as friends and acquaintances in the upper crust of society cross paths, I had never taken Martha anywhere—especially in the daylight—where those in my true circle might have stumbled across us. On those few occasions when Martha and I had strolled together, I had always taken her to odd corners of the city—distant parks, poorly lighted inns, or back-alley restaurants. I was sure that she had seen through my explanation of wanting to explore, of seeking out new parts of the city like a child playing hide-and-catch, but she had never complained.

No, no one knew—or if they *had* seen us, they had no idea who the young woman had been and would have thought little of it. Just another young actress on that rogue Wilkie Collins's arm. I had spent time with so many. Just another young periwinkle. Even Caroline had known of the periwinkles.

I left my chair and went over to sit on the edge of the bed.

Martha stirred, half-rolled towards me, and ceased snoring for a moment, but she did not wake.

The pillow was still in my hands. Now the moonlight covered my long, sensitive fingers as if dabbing them with white paint. Each finger was whiter than the linen on the pillow and suddenly they all seemed to blend with that delicate linen, to sink into it, to melt and become one with the fabric. They became the hands of a corpse disappearing into chalk.

Or melting in a pit of lime.

I leaned forward and held the pillow over Martha's sleeping face. The scarab behind my right eye scuttled forward for a better view.

Frank Beard!

Two months earlier, I had told the physician about a married but abandoned female friend of an acquaintance of mine—the woman being alone and with child at the moment and with little money. Could he recommend a midwife?

Beard had given me a partially amused, partially scolding look and said, "Do you know when this female friend of an acquaintance is due?"

"Late June, I think," I said, feeling my ears burn. "Or perhaps early July."

"Then I shall look in on her myself in her ninth month...and most probably attend the birth as well. Some midwives are wonderful. Many are murderesses. Give me the lady's name and address."

"I do not know such information offhand," I'd replied. "But I shall ask my acquaintance and send her name and address to you in a letter."

And so I had. And then forgotten about it.

But Frank Beard might not forget if he read a newspaper this week and...

"D——n!" I cried and threw the pillow across the room.

Martha was awake in an instant, levering herself upright in bed like some Leviathan rising from the surface of a sheeted sea. "Wilkie! What is it?"

"Nothing, my dear. Just the rheumatical gout and a terrible headache. I apologise for wakening you."

The headache was real enough, as the scarab—furious for some reason—burrowed itself back into the deepest recesses of my brain.

"Oh, my darling boy," cried Martha R—— and hugged me to her bosom. Some time later, I fell asleep like that, with my head still on her swollen breast.

THE BOOK I WAS WRITING during this period was titled *Man and Wife*. The theme of it was how a man might be trapped into a terrible marriage.

I had recently read a report on marriage in our

kingdom published the year before by the Royal Commission; astoundingly, the Commission sanctioned the Scottish law which legalised marriage by consent and then *defended* these marriages by pointing out that they were "wronged-women's ways" of capturing men with dishonourable intentions towards them. I underlined and then wrote in the margins of the report—*"That they act, on certain occasions, in the capacity of a trap to catch a profligate man!!!!"*

The four exclamation marks may seem excessive to you, Dear Reader, but I assure you that they were a profound understatement of my emotion at this absurd and obscene twisting of the law to aid a man-hungry wench. The idea of being trapped into marriage—with the consent and help of the Crown!—was a Horror beyond imagining to me. It was a Horror beyond the Entity in the servants' stairway at Number 90 Gloucester Place.

But I knew that I could never write the book from the point of view of a victimised man. The Reading Public in 1869—nay, the General Public—simply would never see the pathos and tragedy of such a trap inflicted on a man they hypocritically would call a "cad" (even while the majority of those male readers and that male public had a similar "profligate" history).

So I cleverly turned my victimised male into a frail but very high-class and highbred lady trapped—by a mere moment's indiscretion—into a forced marriage to a brute.

I made the brute not only an Oxford man (oh, how I hated Oxford and everything it represented!!) but an Oxford athlete.

This last aspect of the brute's character was a stroke of genius, if I do say so myself. You must understand, Dear Reader from the impossibly distant future, that at this time in England, the idiocy of exercise and the absurdity of sports had melded with the hypocrisies of religion to create a monstrosity called "Muscular Christianity." The idea that good Christians should be "muscular" and throw themselves into any number of mindless, brutish sports was all the rage. More than the rage, Muscular Christianity was both an exercise in Mr Darwin's insights and an explanation of why England's Empire had the right to rule the world and all the weak little brown people in it. It was Superiority personified in barbells and track meets and fields of fools jumping and hopping and pushing themselves up and down. The proselytising for this Muscular Christianity belched out from the newspapers, the magazines, and the pulpits. And Oxford and Cambridge—those Grand Old English nurseries for pedantic dolts—embraced it with all their usual arrogant vigour.

So you see why I took such joy in tossing this fad right in the face of my unsuspecting readership. I might be the only one to know that my trapped and abused heroine was really the captured male, but my Oxford brute would create quite enough controversy.

Even in the early stages of writing *Man and Wife,* I made enemies through it. Frank Beard's children and Fred Lehmann's children—all of whom had loved me and whom I had entertained many a time by telling ripping yarns of classic prizefights and by describing the massive biceps of England's champion, Tom Sayers—heard about my Oxford brute and were furious with me. It was a betrayal to them.

This made me laugh all the more as I pressed Frank Beard into taking me out to various pugilistic and team sport training camps where he served as attending physician from time to time. There I would press the trainers and others for stories of how unhealthy this muscular life truly was—how it turned the athletes into brutes as surely as a return to Darwin's jungle would—and, through Beard, I hurled questions at the camp doctors about physical and mental breakdowns due to such training. Being out in the sunlight and taking such notes was difficult work for me, but I got through it by sipping from my laudanum flask at least hourly.

The secondary theme of *Man and Wife* (behind that of the injustice of marriage-by-capture) was that any morality is completely contingent upon a person's capacity for remorse: a capacity totally lacking in any animal's (or athlete's) life.

Beard, a huge sports fan himself, said nothing about my theories as he took me with him to one unhealthy den of sweat after another. On 4 July, 1869, it was Frank who delivered a girl child to Martha at her lodgings on Bolsover Street. It was also Frank who handled the somewhat tricky formalities of registering in the parish records the mother's name (Mrs Martha Dawson) and the infant's name (Marian, after my most popular female character) and the father's name (William Dawson, Esquire, travelling Barrister at Law).

Due to my heavy writing and research schedule, I was not present at the birth but looked in on the mother and squalling infant a week or two after the fact. As I had promised in January and on that October evening of my mistress's wedding when I had proposed marriage to my dying brother's wife, I now raised Martha R——'s monthly allowance from £20 to £25. The woman wept when she thanked me.

But I have galloped on too far in this tale and skipped a much more important detail, Dear Reader. For you to fully understand the ending of this story, you need to be with me on the night of Wednesday, 9 June, 1869— the fourth anniversary of Dickens's accident at Staplehurst and of his first meeting with Drood. It was the last such anniversary that Charles Dickens would live to see.

CHAPTER FORTY-THREE

$\mathscr{A}$s serious as Dickens's physical ailments were and as dire the predictions from his phalanx of doctors, he became a small boy again when good friends came from America to visit.

James and Annie Fields had been his friends since the time of the Inimitable's first triumphant American reading tour in 1842. James once mentioned to me that even before he and Dickens were socially introduced, he had joined a group of literary enthusiasts who had followed the "strangely dressed Englishman" around Boston during those heady days of Dickens's first trip there. The depths of Dickens's affection for these two was partially shown by the fact that when, during his second American tour, he finally was forced to break his usually steadfast rule of never staying in private homes, it was the Fieldses' lovely home in Boston that became his refuge.

With them on this visit to England came the Charles Eliot Nortons and Dickens's old friend James Russell Lowell's daughter Mabel. Also in the entourage was Dr Fordyce Barker and Sol Eytinge, who had illustrated the lovely "Diamond Back" American edition of Dickens's work.

Great adventures were planned for the period when this group visited Gad's Hill Place (with the bachelorly overflow staying in the best rooms of the Falstaff Inn across the road), but the Fieldses' first stop was London, and Dickens promptly took rooms at the St James Hotel in Piccadilly—the same hostelry where I had spent so much money on harbouring and feeding Fechter the previous January—just so that he could be close to the hotel on Hanover Square where the Fieldses were staying.

I had disguised myself in a broad-brimmed hat and dark summer cape-coat and followed them all from the hotels and then later from Gad's Hill Place. I had purchased a sailor's spyglass and hired my own cab (its driver and horse as nondescript as my disguise-clothing). All those days of detective work and the act of being in disguise and following someone invariably reminded me of poor, dead Inspector Field.

During the first days of their stay in London, the Fieldses & Co. were more or less launched into the pages of Dickens's novels; after brisk hikes alongside the Thames (as if to prove that he was as young and healthy as ever), the Inimitable showed them the rooms in Furnival Inn where he had started work on *The Pickwick Papers,* showed them the room at the Temple where Pip had lived in *Great Expectations,* and acted out Magwitch stumbling on the very darkened staircase where the scene had been set.

Travelling along behind them in the cab or on foot, I could see Dickens pointing out this old house or that narrow alley where his various characters had lived or died and I remembered a similar tour with him more than a decade earlier when *I* had been his friend.

I was not invited on their expedition during the day and night of 9 June, the Anniversary—although Dolby was invited to join Fields and Eytinge on the nighttime part of the adventure—but I was there waiting near the Fieldses' hotel when their carriages set out. Their first out-of-town stop that warm Wednesday afternoon was Cooling Churchyard.

This, of course, is the rural churchyard with its

lozenge-shaped graves that Dickens had described so well in the opening of *Great Expectations* (a disappointment of a book, if one were to ask me). And as I watched through my trusty spyglass from some hundred yards away, I was amazed to see Dickens re-creating the same macabre churchyard-pantomime dinner with which he had entertained Ellen Ternan and her mother and me so long ago in the churchyard at Rochester Cathedral.

There was the same type of flat gravestone selected and used as a dinner table; the same transformation of Charles Dickens, Writer, into Charlie Dickens, Waiter; the same use of a wall as a bar for the gentlemen's drinks; the same use of crystal and white linen and perfectly roasted squab lifted from hampers in the back of their carriages and delivered by the writer-waiter with the towel over one arm.

Even the nearby marshes and smell of the salt sea were the same, although this stretch of coastal marsh was more desolate and isolated than the Rochester graveyard.

Why was Dickens doing this again with his American friends? Even through the slightly shaky circle of the spyglass, I could tell that James Fields was a bit put off by this forced merrymaking in the midst of a boneyard. The ladies looked actively shocked and ate very little.

Only Eytinge, the illustrator, could be seen to be laughing and joining in the graveyard-theatre gaiety with Dickens, and that is most likely because he had enjoyed three glasses of wine even before the squab was served.

Was this some statement that Dickens, the mortal man, was making in the face of the imminent paralysis or death predicted by Beard and his other doctors?

Or was the scarab in his brain finally driving Dickens mad?

. . .

THAT NIGHT, the ladies and most of the other guests were left behind as Dickens took James Fields, a still-inebriated Sol Eytinge, and a very sober George Dolby into the Great Oven of London. (But he did not leave me behind, despite the lack of any invitation—when they left their cab, I followed stealthily on foot.) They paused briefly at a police station on Ratcliffe Highway to pick up a detective policeman who would be their bodyguard for the night's explorations. I needed no such bodyguard: Detective Hatchery's pistol was in the oversized pocket of my dark summer cape-coat.

What must have been so exotic, even terrifying, to Boston-born Fields was now, after more than two years of regularly traversing these streets with Hatchery, familiar almost to the point of comfort for me.

Almost.

Thunderstorms were brewing, lightning rippled all around the pitched, leaning roofs above the narrow lanes, thunder rumbled like constant cannon-fire around a besieged city, but it refused to rain. It only grew hotter and darker. Nerves were on edge everywhere in London, but down here in this suppurating pit of the hopeless poor, this nightmare-market of husbandless women, parentless children, Chinese and Lascar and Hindoo thugs and German and American sailor-murderers on the run from their ships, there was a madness in the air almost as visible as the electrical blue flames that played around the tilted weather vanes and leaped between the iron support cables that ran down like rusted mooring lines from buildings that had long since forgotten how to stand upright on their own.

The tour that Dickens and his police detective were giving the two Americans and Dolby was essentially the same as the ones that Inspector Field and Hatchery had shown the Inimitable and me so long ago: the poorest slums of Whitechapel, Shadwell, Wapping, and

New Court off Bluegate Fields; penny lodging houses outside of which drunken mothers insensibly held filthy infants (I watched from a dark distance as Dickens seized one of these children out of its drunken mother's arms and bore the babe into the lodging house himself); lock-ups filled with thugs and lost children; basement tenements where scores and hundreds of London's huddled outcasts slept in filth and straw within the constant miasmic stench from the river. The tidal mud this hot night seemed to be made up completely of horse dung, cattle guts, chickens' viscera, the carcasses of dead dogs, cats, and the occasional hog or horse, and acres upon acres of human excrement. The streets were filled with idle men carrying knives and even more dangerous idle women carrying disease.

Charles Dickens's beloved Babylon. His very own Great Oven.

In one of his lesser novels (I believe it was the plotting disaster he titled *Little Dorrit*), Dickens had compared the homeless children who skittered and scattered beneath the arches of Covent Garden to rats and warned that someday these rats, always gnawing at the foundations of the city and society that chose to ignore them, might "bring down the English Empire." His outrage was real, as was his compassion. This night of 9 June, as I watched through my little telescope from half-a-block distant, I saw Dickens take up a scabbed and filthy child who looked to be dressed in strips of rags. It appeared that James Fields and Dolby were dabbing their eyes while Eytinge watched with a drunken illustrator's disinterested gaze.

Because it was summer—or as hot as summer—the doors of tenements were open, the windows thrown up, and clusters and mobs of men and women were out in filthy courtyards and no less filthy streets. Even though it was the middle of the work week, most of the men (and not a few of the women) were drunk. Several times these groups would lurch towards Dickens's party only to back away when the police detective with them flashed his bright bullseye lantern at the thugs and showed his club and uniform.

For the first time, I began to be nervous about my own safety. Although my cheap cape and broad-brimmed hat hid my features and allowed me to mix with most of these mobs, some men took note of me and followed along, calling drunkenly for me to stand them to a drink. I hurried on behind the Dickens party. While they tended to keep to the centre of the street where it was lightest, I crept along in the darkest shadows under porches, tattered awnings, and the leaning buildings themselves.

For a while, I was certain that I was being followed.

There was a small bearded man in rags—it looked as if he had been dressed in filthy strips of seaweed—who lurched along behind me, turning when I turned to follow Dickens's group, pausing when I paused.

For a wild moment I was sure that it was the Other Wilkie following me and that he had escaped the confines of the house once and for all.

But while this figure (never seen distinctly) was as short as I (and the Other Wilkie), I realised that he was more burly and barrel-chested under those rags than stout in a Wilkie-ish way.

When we entered New Court proper in darkened Bluegate Fields, I no longer saw him following and put it down to coincidence and my nerves. I took several long sips from my flask, reassured myself by touching the pistol in my coat pocket, and hurried to get a bit closer to the strutting policeman, Dickens, Dolby, Fields, and Eytinge.

They stopped at Old Opium Sal's den, as I knew they would. Here I could have found my way around blindfolded, but because of the bright flashes of lightning—

the artillery barrage had grown louder, but still there came not a hint of refreshing rain—I waited until they had gone to the upper regions of the rotting building before I slipped up to the first-storey landing and edged around into the deeper darkness there. Because of open doors and raised voices, I could hear snatches of Dickens's and the policeman's explanations and the tourists' conversation as they toured the opium den.

There was just enough smell of burnt opium in the air to make my body and scarab-inhabited brain ache for the drug. To take the edge off the longing, I drank deeply from my flask.

"The Puffer Princess..." I heard Dickens's voice drift down in the thick air between thunder rumblings. It was not until months later that I understood this reference.

"Her pipe appears to be made from an old penny ink-bottle..." I heard Fields say.

Between all the understandable snippets, I could hear Opium Sal's familiar but unintelligible cackles, croaks, whines, and entreaties. The policeman shouted her into silence several times, but the cackles would rise in volume again and drift down to me as surely as the scent of opium smoke. I could tell from my hiding place on the floor below them (as well as from memory) that this opium was lesser stuff and none of the excellent variety burned in beautiful pipes down in King Lazaree's crypt-den. I sipped again from my flask.

Dickens and the policeman led the way down the sagging, rotted steps, and I had to shuffle back several paces into the deeper darkness of that empty first-storey landing.

Where were they going next? I wondered. Could he possibly take them all the way to St Ghastly Grim's Cemetery and the crypt-entrance to the upper reaches of Undertown?

No, I realised, Dickens would never do that. But this was the anniversary date on which he always met Drood. How was he to do this with Fields and the others in tow, much less with the policeman present?

The loud group had disappeared around the corner of the building and I'd taken a few steps to go down the stairway myself when suddenly a thick, powerful arm came around my throat and a hot breath whispered in my ear, "Don't move."

I did move—spastically, since I was filled with terror, but quickly—and fumbled Hatchery's pistol out of my pocket with my free hand even as the strong forearm was cutting off my air.

The bearded man swept the pistol out of my hand and deposited it in the pocket of his seaweed-rags jacket as easily as one would take a toy away from a small child.

A powerful hand shoved me up against the wall, and the filthy and bearded man struck a match. "It is I, Mr Collins," he rasped.

For a moment I could identify neither the voice nor the face, but then I saw the intensity of gaze as well as the filth and unkempt beard.

"Barris," I gasped. His hand still held me pinned to the splintered wall.

"Yes, sir," said the man whom I had last seen as he was clubbing me with a pistol after shooting a boy dead in an Undertown sewer river. "Come this way…"

"I cannot…"

"Come this way," ordered former detective Reginald Barris. He grabbed my cape sleeve and tugged me roughly along behind him. "Dickens has already met with Drood. There's nothing new for you to see tonight."

"Impossible…" I began as I stumbled along in his grip.

"Not impossible. The monster met with Dickens in his rooms at the Saint James Hotel just before dawn this morning. You were still home sleeping. Come along now and watch your step in this dark hall. I'm going to show you something quite remarkable."

BARRIS PULLED ME DOWN an absolutely black hall-way—not even the lightning flashes penetrated—then onto a side terrace to the building, one that I had never noticed when I was a regular patron upstairs at Opium Sal's. Here, fifteen feet above an alley not four feet wide, two planks had been laid in a gap in the rotted railing to cross to the next tenement's sagging terrace.

"I can't..." I began.

Barris shoved me onto the planks, and I tiptoed across the narrow, sagging bridge-way.

On this dark terrace, which wrapped around the old structure, we edged carefully (for there were gaps in the rotted floor) around to the river side. The stench was much stronger there, but the lightning flashes illuminated our way as Barris led me into another corridor and then up three full flights of stairs. None of the closed-off rooms here showed even a hint of light from under the doors. It was as if the entire building—in a stretch of slum where every foetid basement and former cowshed was crowded with poor families or entire legions of opium addicts—had been abandoned.

The stairs were as narrow and as steep as a thick-planked ladder, and by the time we got to the top level, the fourth storey five tall flights above the ground, I was panting and wheezing. The outside balcony-terrace there had fallen completely away, but through the raw opening to my right I could see the river, countless shingled roofs, and chimney pots all flickering into existence when the cannonade lightning flashed, then dropping immediately into darkness during the short intervals between flashes.

"This way," barked Barris. He forced open a warped and screeching door, then lit a match.

The room appeared to have been abandoned for years. Rats scurried along the baseboards and disappeared either into the adjoining room or into the rotting walls. The single window had been boarded over and not the slightest gleam of light entered there even when thunder roared and flashes of lightning slashed through the doorway behind us. There were no furnishings left behind, only something that looked like a broken ladder thrown into a far corner.

"Help me with this," ordered the former detective.

Together we carried the heavy lattice of thick boards to the centre of the room and Barris—who, despite his rag-clothing and filth and beard and wild, uncombed hair indicating a starving man, was still amazingly strong—forced the top of this ladder up against the cracked and sagging ceiling.

Prodded by the top of the ladder, a hidden panel in that ceiling flew upward and open, revealing a rectangle of blackness.

Barris propped the ladder against the inner lip of this opening and said, "Go up first."

"I will not," I said.

He lit another match and I could see white teeth flash in the center of that dark beard. Anyone who saw those healthy teeth would know that Reginald Barris with his Cambridge accent was no true resident of these New Court in Bluegate Fields sad streets. "Very well then," he said softly. "I shall go up first and light another match there. I have a small police bullseye in my pocket—next to your pistol. When you come up, I shall light that lantern. Trust me, sir, it is perfectly safe up there. But it shall not be safe for you if you try to flee back down those stairs and I have to descend to catch up with you."

"Still the ruffian, I see," I said contemptuously.

Barris laughed easily. "Oh, yes," he said. "More than you could imagine, Mr Collins."

He scrambled up the ladder and I could see the glow of a match flare in the darkness above. For a second I considered throwing down the ladder and then running for the hall and stairway. But I could feel Barris's terrible grip firm on the top of the ladder and I remembered the strength with which he had propelled me across that plank bridge and then up the stairs.

Awkwardly—for I had continued to put on weight through the preceding year—I made my way up the ladder and then onto my knees in the musty-smelling dark above and then, shaking off the detective's helping hands, to my feet. He lit the lantern.

Immediately in front of me loomed the ebony jackal-face of the god Anubis. I wheeled. Less than six feet away, a seven-foot-tall statue of Osiris stared down at me. The god was properly dressed in white with his tall white hat and carried his requisite crook and flail.

"This way," said Barris.

We made our way down the centre of what had once been a long attic. There were more tall statues set under the eaves on either side. To my left was Horus with the head of a hawk; to my right was Seth with his animal head and long, curved snout. We walked between ibis-headed Thoth and Bastet with her cat's face and ears. I could see where the sagging floor here had been reinforced by recent carpentry. Even the ceilings in the niches where the gods resided had been altered, built up like dormers so that the statues of the gods could stand upright.

"They're plaster of paris," said Barris, his lantern beam flashing back and forth as he led me farther down the length of the attic. "Even with the rebuilt floors here, stone effigies would crash through."

"Where are we going?" I asked. "What is all this?"

At the end of the attic there was a square door where Barris pulled aside a piece of canvas that kept the weather and pigeons out. The frame around this relatively new doorway was made of fresh wood. Lightning illuminated the opening and the thick night air flowed in and around us like some foul syrup. From the sill of this door, a single plank—not more than ten inches wide—ran a dozen feet or more to a dark opening on the opposite side of an alley fifty or sixty feet below. The wind had come up ahead of the approaching storm, and the door canvas flapped with the sound of a raptor's heavy wing.

"I'm not crossing that," I said.

"You have to," said Barris. He seized me under the arm and lifted me onto the sill and then shoved me out onto the board. With his other hand, he aimed the lantern to illuminate the impossibly narrow wooden plank. The wind threatened to topple me off before I took a single step.

"Go!" he ordered and shoved me out over the fatal drop. The beam disappeared for a moment and I realised that Barris was half-crouching on the plank and securing the canvas on nails behind us.

Holding my arms straight to either side, my heart racing, I set one foot in front of the other and shuffled forward like some circus clown preceding the real acrobats. Lightning flashed somewhere nearby and the following roll of thunder struck me like a giant open palm. The rising wind flipped my cape over my face when I was halfway across the impossible plank bridge.

Then somehow I found myself at the opposite window, but the canvas here was as taut as a drum's skin—I couldn't get in. I crouched fearfully and clung to the half-inch of wood frame around the opening, feeling the plank beneath us spring up and down and begin to slide—and slip off the sill—as Barris came up behind me.

His broad arm reached over my shoulder (if I had moved a muscle then, we would have both fallen to our deaths), his free hand fumbled with some opening in the canvas, and then the pitching lantern beam showed an opening. I threw myself forward into this second, larger attic.

Here waited Geb, the green-coloured god of Earth; Nut, with his crown of blue sky and golden stars; and Sekhmet, the god of destruction, his lion's jaws open wide in a roar. Holy Ra was nearby with his falcon's head, Hathor with the cow horns, Isis with a throne on her head, Amun crowned with feathers...they were all there.

I realised that my legs were so weak I could no longer stand. I sat on the path of fresh planks that ran down the centre of this larger attic. A new window, round, at least twelve feet in diameter, had been set into what I guessed was the Thames-facing southern rooftop, the circle of glass and wood placed directly above a wooden altar. The window was well constructed with thick, quality leaded glass not yet warped by gravity and there were metal circles within circles set into the glass much as I had always imagined some exotic gun sight on a naval ship.

"That points at the Dog Star, Sirius," said Barris, who had secured the canvas and turned off his lantern. The nearly constant lightning display was enough to illuminate this large attic space now empty except for us, the Gods of the Black Lands, and the black-linen-draped altar. "I don't know why Sirius is so important to their rituals—I dare say you may, Mr Collins—but one finds such a window aligned properly with that star in all their London attic nests."

"Nests?" My voice sounded as stunned as I felt. The scarab was so excited that it was tunnelling ragged circles through the riddled grey matter that passed for my brain in those days. The pain was excruciating. My eyeballs felt as if they were slowly filling with blood.

"Drood's followers have attic nests like this all over London," said Barris. "Dozens of them. And some of them connect half a dozen or more attics."

"So London has an Overtown as well as an Undertown," I said.

Barris ignored that. "This nest has been abandoned for some weeks," he said. "But they'll be back."

"Why have you brought me here? What do you want?"

Barris lit his lantern again and shined the bullseye beam on part of the wall and steep ceiling. I saw birds, eyeballs, wavy lines, more birds…what my clerk friend at the British Museum called "hieroglyphics."

"Can you read this?" asked Barris.

I started to answer and then realised, to my deep shock, that I *could* read the picture-words and phrases. *"And Djewhty came forth! Djewhty, whose words became Ma'at…"*

It was part of a ritual for naming and blessing a newborn child. And the words had been carved into the rotting wood of the ceiling, not painted on, just above a statue of Ma'at—the goddess of Justice—who stood there with a feather in her hair.

I said, "Of course I cannot read this gibberish. I am no museum docent. What are you asking?"

To this day, I believe this lie saved my life that night.

Barris expelled a breath and seemed to relax. "I thought not, but there are *so many* who have become slaves and servants of Drood…."

"What are you talking about?"

"Do you remember the last night we saw each other, Mr Collins?"

"How could I forget? You murdered an innocent child. When I turned to remonstrate, you brutally clubbed me on the head—you might have killed me! I was unconscious for days. For all I know, you were *trying* to kill me."

Barris was shaking his dirty, bearded head. His expression, what I could see of it through the grime and wild hair, seemed sad. "That was no innocent child, Mr Collins. That Wild Boy was an agent of Drood. He was no longer human. If he had escaped to tell of our presence there, Drood's hordes would have fallen on us there in that sewer within minutes."

"That's absurd," I said coldly.

I could see Barris smile so broadly that the image remained in my retina during the intervals between lightning crashes. "Is it, Mr Collins? Is it indeed? You do not know, then—for which I am particularly grateful—about the brain-beetles."

Suddenly my mouth was very dry. I forced myself not to wince as there came a stab of pincer-pain from behind my right eye. Fortunately, a solid wall of thunder ended conversation and gave me a moment to recover. "The what?" I managed to ask.

"Brain-beetles is what Inspector Field and I called them," said Barris. "Drood inserts these Egyptian insects—actually, English ones trained to his heathen Egyptian ways—into the bodies and brains of his slaves and converts. Or he makes them *think* he's done so. It's all actually a result of his mesmerising them, of course. They obey him for years in a sort of post-mesmeric trance, and he reinforces that control at every opportunity. The brain-beetles are the mesmerising symbol of that control to the victim."

"That's pure poppycock," I said loudly between

thunder crashes. "I happen to have researched mesmerism and the magnetic arts most extensively. It is *impossible* to control someone at a distance and over a long period of time as you suggest—much less enslave them to such a delusion as this...brain-beetle."

"Is it?" asked Barris. I could see in the flickering light that the blackguard was still smiling, but it was a terrible and ironic smile now. "You were not there, Mr Collins, to see the horror that occurred in Undertown an hour after I clubbed you down—for which I do apologise, sir, most sincerely, but I thought you were one of *them* at the moment, a beetle-controlled agent of Drood."

"What horror occurred after you clubbed me into insensibility, Detective Barris?"

"It isn't 'detective' for me any longer, Mr Collins. That title and occupation are lost forever to me. And what happened, sir, some few hours after you were carried up and out of Undertown, was an ambush and slaughter, sir."

"You exaggerate," I said.

"Is nine good men dead an exaggeration, sir? We were hunting for Drood's lair, Drood's Temple, and, of course, Drood...but all the time he was drawing us deeper and deeper into his trap."

"That is absurd," I said. "You must have had two hundred men there that night."

"One hundred and thirty-nine, Mr Collins. Almost all of them policemen away from duty at the time or former policemen, and almost all of them men who had known Hibbert Hatchery and who had come down with us to catch his killer. There were fewer than twenty of us who knew just what a monster Drood actually is—no normal killer, not a human being at all—and five of those men died at Drood's killer-slaves' hands that night. Those scores of thugs and Thuggees who *were* controlled by those magnetic-influence brain-beetles that you say don't exist. And the inspector was murdered the next day."

My jaw sagged at this statement. "Murdered? *Murdered*? Don't lie to me, Barris. I won't have it. I *know* better than this. The *Times* of London—I have spoken to the reporters who did the obituary, sir—reported that Inspector Field died a natural death. He died in his sleep."

"Oh? And were these *reporters* there that morning after he died to see the terror imprinted on the poor old man's dead face, Mr Collins? I was there. I was the first person Inspector Field's wife sent for when she found him dead. His open mouth and bulging eyes were not the expression of a man who died peacefully in his sleep from heart problems, Mr Collins. His eyes were filled with blood."

I said, "I understand that a stroke of the brain can cause just such symptoms."

The lightning flashed and there was no lag between the flash and thunder now. The storm was upon us. "And does a stroke of the brain leave a silken rope knotted twice, Mr Collins?"

"What are you talking about?"

"I am talking about the calling card of the Hindoo Thuggee who smothered poor Charles Frederick Field in his sleep, sir. Or in this case, three or four Thuggees. One to hold the pillow over my employer and friend's straining face and at least two—I would guess three, since Field was a powerful man despite his age—to hold him down as the noose was tightened. He died hard, Mr Collins. Very hard."

I could think of nothing to say.

"And the inspector had seven full-time operatives, including me, working for his agency," continued Barris. "These men—myself included—were some of the finest and most professional ex-policemen in all of England. Five have died under mysterious circumstances since January. The other has left his family and fled to Australia, the little good that will do him. Drood has agents in every port on Earth. I have survived only by going to ground here in Drood's own foul turf—and I have still had to kill three of his assassins who've come at me in the past six months. When I sleep at all, I sleep with one eye open, I assure you, sir."

As if remembering something, Barris reached into his pocket and handed Hatchery's pistol back to me.

Scarab-pain flared behind my throbbing right eye and the thought occurred to me that I could shoot Barris this moment and his corpse would lie here undiscovered for weeks or months until Drood's followers returned to this place. *Would that earn me some sympathy with them?*

Blinking with pain to the point of vertigo, I put the idiot weapon away in my cape-coat pocket.

"Why did you bring me here?" I rasped.

"To see, first of all, whether you had become…one of them," said Barris. "My estimate is that you have not."

"You did not have to drag me up to these filthy heathen attics to discover that," I shouted over the thunder.

"Actually, I did," said Reginald Barris. "But more importantly, I wanted to give you a warning."

"I need no more warnings," I said dismissively.

"This one is not for you, sir," said Barris. For half a moment there was silence—the first long lack of thunder since we had left Opium Sal's tenement—and the silence was somehow more terrifying than the preceding storm noises.

"It is for Charles Dickens," continued Barris.

I had to laugh. "You said that Dickens met with Drood this morning before dawn. If he's one of

Drood's…what did you call them?…beetle-slaves already, what could he have to fear?"

"I believe he is not a slave, Mr Collins. I believe that your friend has made some sort of Faustian deal with Drood—of what particular nature, I cannot guess."

I remembered Dickens once telling me that he had promised to write Drood's biography, but this was too silly even to consider, much less mention.

"At any rate," continued Barris, who suddenly looked exhausted under his scrim of dirt, "I learned from one of the assassins that Drood sent after me that Dickens will die in eighteen seventy."

"I thought you killed all the assassins Drood sent after you," I said.

"I did, Mr Collins. Indeed I did. But I urged two of them to talk to me before they shuffled off their mortal coils."

The thought of this made my skin grow clammy. I said, "Eighteen seventy is a year away."

"Actually just a little over six months away, sir. The assassin did not tell me *when* in the year they would move against Mr Dickens."

At that instant and as if on theatrical cue, the storm struck with full ferocity. We both flinched as rain suddenly pounded the old shingles just above us with incredible force. Barris's relit lantern beam danced wildly over the walls as he leaped back and then caught his balance. I saw a blur of the carved hieroglyphics and somehow my scarab or mind translated—"…*give soundness to our limbs, O Isis, and be the charm which shall ensure our justification in the Judgement soon to come.*"

I WAS DRENCHED by the time I got home. Carrie met me in the foyer, and I noticed that she was still fully dressed, not in her robe, at such a late hour and that she looked concerned.

"What is it, my dear girl?"

"There is a man here to see you. He arrived before nine PM and has insisted on waiting all this time. If George and Besse had not been home, I never would have let him in—his countenance is fearful—and he did not have a card. But he said it was urgent...."

Drood, I thought. I was too tired even to feel fear. "There is nothing to be alarmed about, Carrie," I said softly. "Probably some tradesman after a bill we forgot to pay. Where did you put him?"

"He asked if he could wait in your study. I said yes."

D——n, I thought. The last place I wanted Drood was in my study. But I patted her cheek and said, "You go on up to bed now, that's a good girl."

"May I hang up your coat for you?"

"No, I want to leave it on for a while," I said, not explaining to Carrie why I would want to keep on the thoroughly soaked-through cheap cape-coat.

"Won't you be wanting any dinner? I had cook make your favourite French beef before she went home...."

"I'll find it and warm it myself, Carrie. Now you go on up for the night. I'll call George if I need anything."

I waited until her footsteps had faded up the main stairway and then went down the hall and through the parlour and opened the doors to my study.

Mr Edmond Dickenson, Esquire, was sitting not in the leather guest's chair but behind my desk. He was insolently smoking one of my cigars and his feet were up on an opened lower drawer.

I went in and closed the doors tightly behind me.

CHAPTER FORTY-FOUR

*I*n early October, Dickens invited me to spend a
few days at Gad's Hill during the Fieldses' last
visit there before they returned to Boston. It had been
some time since I had been invited to spend the night
at Dickens's home. In truth, after Dickens's show of
support at my March premiere of *Black and White*,
intercourse between us had been somewhat rare and
decidedly formal (especially in comparison to our intimacy of earlier years). While we continued to sign our
letters "affectionately yours," there seemed to be little
affection left on either side.

As I travelled to Gad's Hill, I stared out the railway
carriage window and wondered both about the real
reasons for the Inimitable's invitation and also what I
might tell him that would surprise him. I rather enjoyed
surprising Dickens.

I could have described my Overtown excursion four
months earlier on 9 June while he and Fields and Dolby
and Eytinge went slum-hopping under the protection
of their policeman, but that would have been too much
of a revelation. (And I had no excuse for following them
through the first part of that night.)

I could certainly surprise Dickens and the Fieldses
and whoever the Inimitable's other guests were this
weekend by describing my new baby daughter Marian's
presumably cute facial antics and burbles and other

such ten-for-a-'apenny common baby anecdotes, but that would most definitely be too much of a revelation. (The less Charles Dickens and his entourage and sycophants knew of my private life, the better.)

What to amuse him with, then?

I would almost certainly inform everyone of how well my book *Man and Wife* was coming along. If Dickens was my only interlocutor, I might tell him about the letters that Mrs Harriette (Caroline) Clow was now sending me almost monthly—details of emotional estrangement and physical punishment from her plumber-lout of a husband. It made for wonderful research. All I had to do was substitute the Oxford-athlete lout for the almost illiterate plumber-lout—there was really very little difference in the two classes of men when one thought about it—and the beatings and occasions of being locked in the cellar that Caroline was suffering instantly became the plight of my highbred but poorly wed heroine.

What else?

I could, if we had an extended period alone and any renewal of our old sense of intimacy, tell Charles Dickens about my late-night visit on 9 June from the young man he had pulled from the wreckage at Staplehurst four years earlier to the day—our Mr Edmond Dickenson.

DICKENSON HAD NOT ONLY taken possession of my writing chair behind my desk and set his unclean boots on my extruded lower drawer, but the impertinent whelp had somehow got upstairs to my bedroom, unlocked the closet, and brought down the eight hundred pages of my dreams of the Gods of the Black Lands scrawled in the Other Wilkie's tight, slanting script.

"What is the meaning of this intrusion?" I snapped.

My attempt at masterly command may have been weakened somewhat by the fact that even with the cape-coat on I was as soaked through as a wet-slick alley cat and now dripping puddles onto my own study floor and Persian carpet.

Dickenson laughed and relinquished my chair (although not the manuscript). The two of us circled the desk as cautiously as knife-fighting adversaries in a New Court tavern.

I sat in my writing chair and slid the lower drawer shut, and Dickenson dropped into the guest's chair without asking permission. My coat made wet, squishy sounds beneath me.

"You look thoroughly miserable, if you don't mind my saying so," said Dickenson.

"Never mind that. Give me back my property."

Dickenson looked at the stack of papers in his hands and showed a caricature of surprise. "*Your* property, Mr Collins? You *know* that neither your dreams of the Black Land nor these notes are your property."

"They are. And I want them back." I brought Hatchery's pistol out of my coat pocket, set the base of the heavy stock or grip or handle or whatever it is called against the surface of my desk, and used both hands to pull back the resisting hammer until it clicked and cocked. The muzzle was aimed directly at Edmond Dickenson's chest.

The insufferable youth laughed. Once again I could see the strangeness of his teeth: they had been white and healthy when I had seen him during Christmas of 1865. Had they decayed or been filed down to these stumps and points since then?

"Is this *your* writing, Mr Collins?"

I hesitated. Drood had met with the Other Wilkie two years ago this very night. Drood's emissary here would certainly know about that.

"I want the pages back," I said. My finger was now on the trigger.

"And you intend to shoot me if I do not give them to you?"

"Yes."

"And why would you do that, Mr Collins?"

"Perhaps to ascertain that you are not the spectre you pretend to be," I said softly. I was very tired. It seemed like weeks, rather than a mere dozen hours or so, since I had watched Dickens take his guests out to luncheon at Cooling Cemetery.

"Oh, I will bleed if you shoot me," said Dickenson in that same maddeningly happy tone with which he'd infuriated me at Gad's Hill so long ago. "And die, if your aim is good enough."

"It will be," I said.

"But to what purpose, sir? You know that these documents are the property of the Master."

"By 'Master' you mean Drood."

"Who else? There is no doubt that I will leave with these pages—I would rather face your pistol at three paces than the Master's slightest displeasure at a thousandfold-greater distance—but, since you have me at this disadvantage, perhaps there is something you wish to know before I leave?"

"Where is Drood?" I said.

Dickenson merely laughed again. Perhaps it was the sight of those teeth that made me ask the next question.

"Do you eat human flesh at least once a month, Dickenson?"

The laugh and smile disappeared. "And where have you heard that, sir?"

"Perhaps I know more about your...Master...and his slaves than you give me credit for."

"Perhaps you do," said Dickenson. He had lowered his chin and now looked at me with eyes raised and brow lowered in a strangely disturbing way. "But you should know," he added, "that there are no slaves... only disciples and those who love and volunteer to serve the Master."

It was my turn to laugh. "You're speaking to someone with one of your accursed Master's scarabs in his brain, Dickenson. I can think of no worse form of slavery."

"Our mutual friend Mr Dickens can," said Dickenson. "That is why he has chosen to work with the Master towards their shared goal."

"What in the world are you gabbling about?" I snapped. "Dickens and Drood have no common goals."

The young man—formerly round faced to the point of being cherubic, now actively gaunt—shook his head. "You were in New Court and Bluegate Fields and the surrounding areas tonight, Mr Collins," he said softly.

How does he know I was there? I thought in some panic. *Have they caught and tortured poor mad Barris?*

"Mr Dickens understands that such social evil has to end," Dickenson continued.

"Social evil?"

"The poverty, sir," said Dickenson with some heat. "The social injustice. The children forced onto the streets with no parents. The mothers who have become... women of the street... out of sheer desperation. Those ill children and women who will never receive treatment, the men who will never find work in a system that..."

"Oh, spare me this communistic talk," I said. Water dripped from my beard onto my desk top, but the aim of the pistol did not waver. "Dickens has been a reformer for most of his life, but he is no revolutionary."

"You are wrong, sir," Dickenson said very softly. "He works with our Master precisely because of the revolution our Master will bring first to London and then to the rest of the world where children are left to starve. Mr Dickens will help our Master bring a New Order into being—one in which the colour of one's skin or the amount of money one has will never stand in the way of justice."

Again, I was forced to laugh and again my laughter was sincere. Four years earlier, in autumn of 1865, a mob of Jamaican blacks had attacked the Court House in Morant Bay. Our governor there, Eyre, had overseen 439 of those blacks being shot or hanged and another 600 flogged. Some of our more deluded liberals had opposed Governor Eyre's behaviour, but Dickens had told me that he'd wished the retaliation and punishment could have gone further. "I am totally opposed," he'd said at the time, "with that platform-sympathy with the black—or the Native or the Devil—and believe it is morally and totally wrong to deal with Hottentots as if they were identical with men in clean shirts at Camberwell...."

During the Mutiny in India long before I had met him, Dickens had cheered on the British general whose answer to the rebellion had been to tie captured mutinous Indians across the muzzles of cannon and to blast them "homeward" in pieces. Dickens's wrath and contempt, in *Bleak House* and a dozen other of his novels, had long been aimed more at the idiotic missionaries who were more concerned with the plight of native brown and black people abroad than with the problems of good Englishmen and Englishwomen and white children here at home.

"You're a fool," I said that night in June to young Edmond Dickenson. "Your Master is a fool if he thinks that Charles Dickens wants to plot against white men in favour of Lascars and Hindoos and Chinamen and Egyptian murderers."

Dickenson smiled tightly and rose. "I need to deliver

this instalment of the notes to my Master before dawn."

"Stay," I said and raised the pistol until it was aimed at the man's face. "Keep the d——ned papers, but tell me how to get this scarab out of my body. Out of my head."

"It will leave when the Master commands it to leave or when you die," said Dickenson with that hungry, happy cannibal's look again. "Not before."

"Not even if I were to kill an innocent person?" I said.

The young man's light-coloured eyebrows rose. "You've heard of that ritual exception, have you? Very well, Mr Collins. You might try that. One cannot guarantee that it will work, but you might try that. I shall show myself out. Oh, and be assured that the young lady who let me in tonight will *not* remember doing so tomorrow."

And without another word he had swung on his heel and left.

And it turned out that Dickenson was right about Carrie not remembering his visit; when I asked her the next morning about what aspect of our visitor's appearance had disturbed her, she looked at me oddly and said that she remembered no visitor, except for a bad dream about some stranger in the rain, beating at the door and demanding to be let in.

Yes, I thought as we pulled into the station where someone from Gad's Hill Place would be meeting me with a carriage or pony cart, telling my story of the end of that busy night in June might surprise the Inimitable.

But then, I thought, how terrible it would be if it did *not* surprise him.

ON THE SUNDAY of my pleasant weekend visit at Gad's Hill Place—and it is difficult for me, even now, to forget or overstate just *how* pleasant such convivial times at Dickens's home truly were—I was in James Fields's chambers talking with him about the literary life in Boston when there came a knock at the door. It was one of Dickens's older servants, who stepped into the room as formally as a courtier to Queen Victoria, clicked his heels, and handed Fields a note written in a fine calligraphic hand on a scroll of rich parchment. Fields showed it to me and then read it aloud:

> *Mr Charles Dickens presents his respectful compliments to the Hon. James T. Fields (of Boston, Mass., U.S.) and will be happy to receive a visit from the Hon. J.T.F. in the small library as above, at the Hon. J.T.F.'s leisure.*

Fields had chuckled, then coughed with embarrassment at having read it aloud, and said to me, "I am sure that Charles means for *both* of us to join him in the library."

I smiled and nodded but was sure that Dickens had *not* meant the joking invitation for me. He and I had not shared two private words in the four days I had been at Gad's Hill Place, and it was increasingly apparent that the Inimitable had no plans to alter that unhappy state of public politeness but private silence between us. Nonetheless, I followed Fields as the American hurried down to the small library.

Dickens could not quite conceal his frown when he saw me enter, even though the expression crossed his features for only a fraction of a second—only an old friend who had known him for many years would have noticed the flicker of surprised displeasure—but he then smiled and cried out, "My dear Wilkie—how fortuitous! You have saved me from labouriously writing out my invitation to you. Penmanship was never my strongest quality, and I feared it would take me another half hour to produce the document! Come in, both of you! Sit down, sit down."

Dickens was perched on the edge of a small reading table and there was a short stack of manuscript pages next to him. He had set out only two chairs where an audience might sit. For a slightly vertiginous moment I was sure that he was going to read notes from his own dreams of the Gods of the Black Land.

"Are we all the audience for...whatever this is?" asked the obviously delighted James T. Fields. The two men seemed to revel in each other's presence, almost literally shed years as they carried out their boyish adventures, and I'd sensed a sadness in Dickens the last few days. *Well, why not?* I thought at that moment. *When Fields and his wife leave England for America this week, it will be the last time the two men will ever see each other. Dickens will be long dead before Fields ever returns to England.*

"The two of you, dear friends, are indeed the only audience for this reading," said Dickens, who went to shut the door to the library himself and then returned to his easy perch on the edge of the thin-legged table.

"Chapter the First, The Dawn," read Dickens.

> *"An ancient English Cathedral Tower? How can the ancient English Cathedral tower be here! The well-known massive grey square tower of its old Cathedral? How can that be here! There is no spike of rusty iron in the air, between the eye and it, from any point of real prospect. What is the spike that intervenes, and who has set it up? Maybe it is set up by the Sultan's orders for the impaling of a horde of Turkish robbers, one by one. It is so, for cymbals clash, and the Sultan goes by to his palace in long procession. Ten thousand scimitars flash in the sunlight, and thrice ten thousand dancing-girls strew flowers. Then, follow white elephants caparisoned in countless gorgeous colours..."*

And so he read on for almost ninety minutes. James Fields was obviously enthralled. The longer I listened, the colder my skin and scalp and fingertips felt.

Chapter One was an impressionist (and sensationalist) description of an opium smoker coming up and out of his dreams in an opium den obviously based upon Opium Sal's. Sal herself is there—properly described as "a haggard woman" with a "rattling whisper"—alongside a comatose Chinaman and a Lascar. The viewpoint character, obviously a white man awakening from his own opium dream, keeps muttering, "Unintelligible" as he listens to (and struggles with) the incoherent Chinaman and unconscious but muttering Lascar. He leaves, returning to a "Cathedral town" that is obviously Rochester (under the clumsy pseudonym of "Cloisterham"), and there in the second chapter we meet a cluster of the usual Dickens-style characters, including the Minor Canon, the Reverend Septimus Crisparkle, who is one of those kindly and dim-witted but well-meaning "Muscular Christians" of precisely the sort I was parodying in my own novel-in-progress.

It also becomes clear in this second chapter that the rogue opium-eater whom we'd glimpsed in the first chapter is a certain John Jasper, the lay precentor of the Cathedral. Jasper, we understand at once, has a beautiful voice (strangely more beautiful at some times than at others) and a dark, convoluted soul.

Also in this second chapter, we meet Jasper's nephew, the shallow, callow, easygoing but obviously lazy and complacent Master Edwin Drood....I admit that I jumped when Dickens actually read that name aloud.

In the third chapter we hear some rather well-written but gloomy descriptions of Cloisterham and its ancient history and then are introduced to yet another of Dickens's near-infinite series of perfect, rosy-cheeked, virginal young heroine–romantic interests: this one with the cloyingly insipid name of Rosa Bud. Her few pages of presence did not make me want to strangle her immediately—as so many of his young, virginal, Dickens-perfect young characters such as "Little Dorrit" made me want to do—and by the time Edwin Drood and Rosa Bud take a walk together (we learn that they have been betrothed since childhood through the agencies of conveniently acquainted but deceased parents, but also that young Edwin is condescendingly complacent towards *Rosa* and the entire engagement, while Rosa simply wants *out*), I could *feel* the echoes of Dickens's estrangement from Ellen Ternan as I'd heard it discussed between them outside the Peckham rail station that evening.

And in these first chapters, Fields and I heard that Dickens had made *his* Drood—the boy-man Edwin Drood—a young engineer who is going off to change Egypt. And he will be, says some silly woman at the orphanage where Rosa lives (why, oh why must Dickens's young virgins always be orphans!), buried in the Pyramids.

"But *don't she hate Arabs, and Turks, and Fellahs, and people?*" asks Rosa, speaking of the fictional perfect mate for "Eddy" Drood.

> "'Certainly not.' Very firmly.
> 'At least she must hate the Pyramids? Come, Eddy.'
> 'Why should she be such a little—tall, I mean—goose as to hate the Pyramids, Rosa?'
> 'Ah! You should hear Miss Twinkleton,' often nodding her head and much enjoying the Lumps, 'bore about them, and then you wouldn't ask. Tiresome old burying-grounds! Isises and Ibises, and Cheopses, and Pharaohses; who cares about them? And then there was Belzoni, or somebody, dragged out by the legs, half-choked with bats and dust. All the girls say: Serve him right, and hope it hurt him, and wish he had been quite choked.'"

And I could see that Dickens was headed towards a continued and almost certainly elaborated comparison of the dust of the crypts and graves in Cloisterham—which is to say Rochester and its very real cathedral—with the real explorers of Egyptian tombs such as Belzoni, "half-choked with bats and dust."

His third chapter—which is as far as he read to us that day—ended with his coquettish (but still uninterested, in Edwin at least) Rosa saying to this "Drood"—

> "'Now say, what do you see?'
> 'See, Rosa?'
> 'Why, I thought you Egyptian boys could look into a hand and see all sorts of phantoms. Can't you see a happy Future?'
> For certain, neither of them sees a happy Present, as the gate opens and closes, and one goes in, and the other goes away."

It was as if Dickens were me writing about what I had seen of Ellen Ternan and him at Peckham Station.

When Dickens set down the last page of his short manuscript—his reading had been quiet, professional, cool, as opposed to the overheated acting of his recent reading tours and especially that of his Murder—James Fields burst into applause. The American looked to be close to weeping. I sat in silence and stared.

"Capital, Charles! Absolutely capital! A wonderful beginning! A *marvellous,* provocative, intriguing, and beguiling beginning! Your skills have never been more on display."

"Thank you, my dear James," Dickens said softly.

"But the title! You've not told us. What do you intend to call this wonderful new book?"

"Its title shall be *The Mystery of Edwin Drood,*" said Dickens, peering over his reading spectacles at me.

Fields applauded his approval and did not notice my sudden sharp intake of breath. But I am certain that Charles Dickens did.

FIELDS HAD GONE upstairs to change for dinner when I followed Dickens back to his study and said, "We need to talk."

"Do we?" said the Inimitable as he slipped the fifty or so manuscript pages into a leather portfolio and locked the portfolio into one of his desk drawers. "Very well, let us step outside away from the press and eager ears of family, friends, children, servants, and dogs."

It had been a warm October and it was a warm early evening as Dickens led me to his chalet. Usually by this time of the year the chalet was sealed for the coming wet winter, but not this year. Yellow and red leaves skittered across the lawn and were captured by bushes or the bloomless red geraniums planted along the drive as Dickens led me not down into the tunnel but straight across the highway. There was no traffic this Sunday afternoon, but I could see rows of high-spirited and well-bred horses tied or being tended outside the Falstaff Inn. A fox group had come by for refreshment after the hunt.

Upstairs on the first floor of his chalet, Dickens waved me to the spare Windsor chair and then sprawled in his own. I could see by the neatly arranged boxes of blue and cream paper, pens, ink pots, and his small statues of fencing frogs that Dickens had been writing out here recently.

"Well, my dear Wilkie, what do you feel we need to talk about?"

"You know very well, my dear Dickens."

He smiled, took his spectacles out of a case, and set them on his nose, as if he were going to read some more. "Let us assume I do *not* know and proceed from there. Is it that you did not like the beginnings of my new book? I have written more, you know. Perhaps another chapter or two and your interest would have been engaged."

"This is dangerous stuff, Charles."

"Oh?" His surprise did not appear fully feigned. "What is dangerous? Writing a tale of mystery? I told you some months ago that I was sufficiently intrigued by the elements of your *Moonstone*—the opium addiction, the mesmerism, the Oriental villains, the central mystery of theft—that I might try my own hand at such a novel. So now I am. Or at least I have made a start."

"You're using Drood's *name*," I said so softly that it came out as an urgent whisper. I could hear male voices rising in a drinking song from the inn nearby.

"My dear Wilkie," sighed Dickens. "Would you not agree that it's time that we—or you—got over this fear of all things Droodish?"

What could I say to that? For a moment I was speechless. I had never told Dickens about Hatchery's death—the grey glistening cords in the crypt. Or about my night at Drood's Temple. Or of Inspector Field's invasion of Undertown and what I now understood of its dire consequences to Field and his men. Or of Reginald Barris—filthy, bearded, living in rags and on scraps, hiding in fear—or of the Overtown temple-hideouts Barris had shown me just four months earlier...

"If I had time this evening," said Dickens, as if musing to himself, "I would cure you of that obsession. Release you from it."

I got to my feet and began pacing impatiently back and forth in the small room. "You'll release yourself from your life if you publish this book, Charles. You once told me that Drood had requested you write a biography of him...but this is a *parody*."

"Not in the least," laughed Dickens. "It shall be a

very serious novel which explores the layers and levels and contradictions of the criminal's mind—in this case, the mind of a murderer, but also an opium addict and both master and victim of mesmerism."

"How can one be *both* a master and victim of mesmerism, Charles?"

"Be so kind as to read my book when it is finished, my dear Wilkie, and you shall see. Much will be revealed...and not only of the mystery, but perhaps of some of your own dilemma."

I ignored that, since it made no sense. "Charles," I said earnestly, leaning on his table and looking down at him as he sat, "do you *really* believe that smoking opium causes one to dream of flashing scimitars, scores of dancing girls, and—what was it?—'countless elephants careering in various gorgeous colours'?"

"'...white elephants caparisoned in countless gorgeous colours, and infinite in numbers and attendants,'" corrected Dickens.

"Very well," I said and stepped back and removed my spectacles to clean them with my handkerchief. "But do you *really* believe that any number of caparisoned or careering elephants and flashing scimitars are the stuff of an actual opium dream?"

"I have taken opium, you know," Dickens said quietly. He seemed almost amused.

I confess to having rolled my eyes at this news. "So Frank Beard told me, Charles. A tiny bit of laudanum, and that just a few times, when you could not sleep on one of your last reading tours."

"Still, my dear Wilkie, laudanum is laudanum. Opium is opium."

"How many minims did you use?" I asked as I still paced back and forth, from open window to open window. Perhaps it was my own increased laudanum use that morning that kept me so excitable.

"Minims?" said Dickens.

"Drops of the opiate distillate in your wine," I said. "How many drops?"

"Oh, I have no idea. Dolby handled the ministrations the few evenings I tried that medicinal approach. I would say two."

"Two minims...two drops?" I repeated.

"Yes."

I said nothing for a minute. That very day, as a guest at Gad's Hill Place and having brought only a flask and a small refill jug in my baggage for the long weekend, I had drunk at least six hundred minims and possibly twice that. Then I said, "But you cannot convince me—or anyone who has actually researched the drug as I have, my dear Charles—that you dreamt of elephants and scimitars and golden domes."

Dickens laughed. "My dear Wilkie, just as you said you... 'tested,' I believe your word was...your *Moonstone* character Franklin Blake's ability to enter his fiancée's bedroom while she was sleeping..."

"Sitting room next to her bedroom," I corrected. "My editor insisted on it for propriety's sake."

"Ah, yes," said Dickens with a smile. He had been that editor, of course. "Enter into his fiancée's bedroom's sitting room to steal a diamond, all while he was asleep, merely under the influence of laudanum he hadn't known he'd taken..."

"You've expressed your doubts as to the realism of that more than once," I said sourly. "Even though I've told you that I did experiment with similar situations under the influence of the drug."

"Exactly my point, my dear Wilkie. You stretched the point to serve your plot. And so my caparisoned pachyderms and flashing scimitars—to serve the greater story."

"This is not the point, Charles."

"What is, then?" Dickens looked sincerely curious. He also looked sincerely exhausted. Those days, when the Inimitable wasn't reading to others or at play, he tended to look like the old man he had suddenly become.

"The point is that Drood will kill you if you publish this book," I said. "You told me yourself that he wants a biography, not a sensationalist novel filled with opium, mesmerism, all things Egyptian, and a weak character named Drood..."

"Weak but important to the story," interrupted Dickens.

I could only shake my head. "You won't heed my warning. Perhaps if you had seen the face of poor Inspector Field the morning after he was murdered..."

"Murdered?" said Dickens, suddenly sitting up straight. He removed his spectacles and blinked. "Who said that Charles Frederick Field was murdered? You know very well that the *Times* said he had died in his sleep. And what is this talk of having seen his face? *You* certainly could not have, my dear Wilkie. I remember you were in bed ill for weeks at the time and didn't even know that poor Field had died until I told you many months later."

I hesitated, considering whether to tell Dickens then about Reginald Barris's explanation of Inspector Field's true demise. But then I would have to explain Barris and why and where I saw him and all about the Overtown temples....

While I was hesitating, Dickens sighed and said, "Your belief in Drood is enjoyable in its own dark way, Wilkie, but perhaps it is time it drew to a close. Perhaps it was a mistake for it ever to have begun."

"Belief in Drood?" I snapped. "Must I remind you, my dear Dickens, that it was *your* story of your meeting with him at Staplehurst and *your* later stories of meeting with the monster in Undertown that got me involved in all this in the first place? It's a little late, I would say, for you to tell me to cease believing in him, as if he were the ghost of Marley or Christmas Yet to Come."

I thought Dickens would laugh at this last broadside, but he only looked sadder and more weary than before and said, as if to himself, "Perhaps it is too late, my dear Wilkie. Or perhaps not. But it is definitely too late this particular Sunday. I must go in and prepare to enjoy one of the last meals I may ever share with dear James and Annie...."

His voice had become so soft and sad by the end of that sentence that I had to strain to hear the words over the sound of the fox hunters riding away from the Falstaff Inn.

"We shall speak of this another time," said Dickens as he rose. I noticed that his left leg seemed unable to support his weight for a moment and that he steadied himself with his right hand on the table, getting his balance and teetering there a moment with his left hand and leg flailing uselessly, like a toddling infant taking his first steps, before he smiled again—ruefully this time, I thought—and hobbled out the door and down the stairs as we headed back to the main house.

"We shall speak of this another time," he said again.

And we did, Dear Reader. But too late, as you will see, to avoid the tragedies to come.

CHAPTER FORTY-FIVE

*T*hrough the final autumn, winter, and spring of Charles Dickens's life, he continued writing his novel and I continued writing mine.

Dickens—being Dickens—insisted, of course, on the suicidal folly of using Drood's name in the title of his new work, even though I heard through Wills, Forster, and that ponce-twit Percy Fitzgerald (who had all but taken my place in the offices of *All the Year Round* and in Dickens's confidences) that the Inimitable's earlier ideas for titles had included *The Loss of James Wakefield* and *Dead? Or Alive?* (He had obviously never seriously considered using Edmond Dickenson's name, as he'd mentioned to me the previous spring—that had been just to bait me.)

I had begun my book months before Dickens had started his, and thus had sold and was to start serialising *Man and Wife* in *Cassell's Magazine* in January of 1870 and had also sold serial rights to my old stalwart, *Harper's Magazine,* in New York and—to avoid piracy— had arranged for *Harper's* to publish their instalments a fortnight earlier than did *Cassell's.* Dickens's first instalment of *The Mystery of Edwin Drood*, serialised in green wrappers from Chapman and Hall, was not to see print until April. Meant for a dozen monthly instalments, it would end after six.

My brother, Charley, was hired to be the artist for

this ill-fated novel, and although it would turn out that he would be too ill to finish his labours, Dickens's impulse must have been to give his son-in-law (and thus his daughter) some income. I could also imagine Dickens making the commission simply to give Charley something to do other than lie around his home or Gad's Hill Place, unemployed and in pain. It had come to the point where even the sight of my brother seemed to incense Charles Dickens.

By continuing to work on the instalments, Dickens was breaking his previously inviolable rule—i.e., never to be working on a novel at the same time he was doing public readings or preparing for readings—since the time for the twelve "farewell readings" he had begged and bullied for was to begin in January.

For my own part, the instalments of *Man and Wife* were flowing easily, aided substantially by the now-monthly letters from Caroline in which she documented the torrent of abuse that her plumber was pouring down upon her. A jealous sort, Joseph Clow would lock her in the coal cellar when he was gone for any extended periods. A drunkard, he would kick and beat her after hours of drinking. A braggart, he would have his friends over for bouts of drinking and gambling and say crude and vulgar things about Caroline and laugh with the other louts as his bride blushed and attempted to flee to her room. (But Clow had taken the door off their tiny bedroom precisely so she could not hide in there.) A mother's-boy, he allowed Caroline's mother-in-law to insult her incessantly and would cuff my former lover if she cast so much as a defiant glance at the old woman.

To all these missives of misery, I replied with nothing more than a polite acknowledgement of receipt and the vaguest commiserations—sending the letters, as always, through Carrie (and assuming that Caroline would burn them after reading, since Clow might kill her if he discovered that she was receiving letters from me)—but the details and tone all went into my *Man and Wife*.

My seducer—Geoffrey Delamayn—was (and remains to my literary eye) a delightful character: a long-distance runner of superb physique and tiny brain, a player of many sports, an Oxford-educated ignoramus, a brute, a blackguard, a monster.

Critics of even the early instalments of *Man and Wife* would call my novel a bitter and angry book. And I acknowledge to you, Dear Reader, that it was that. It was also very sincere. I was pouring into *Man and Wife* not only my fury at the very *idea* of someone being trapped into marriage—trapped the way Caroline had attempted to trap me and the way that Martha R——, "Mrs Dawson," even at that moment was scheming to trap me—but also my righteous anger at the treatment that Caroline was receiving at the grimy hands and fists of the lower-class brute *she* had succeeded finally in trapping.

Charles Dickens's *The Mystery of Edwin Drood* was *not* an angry or bitter novel, but the truths and personal revelations that he was pouring into *it*, as I would understand only much later, were far more astounding than those I thought I was being so candid about in my own book.

When the last autumn of Dickens's life was over, he continued to work through his final winter and into spring. This is how all of us writers give away the days and years and decades of our lives in exchange for stacks of paper with scratches and squiggles on them. And when Death calls, how many of us would trade all those pages, all that squandered lifetime-worth of painfully achieved scratches and squiggles, for just one more day, one more fully *lived* and *experienced* day? And what price would we writers pay for that one extra day spent with those we ignored while we were locked away scratching and squiggling in our arrogant years of solipsistic isolation?

Would we trade all those pages for a single hour? Or all of our books for one real minute?

I WAS NOT INVITED to Gad's Hill Place for Christmas.

My brother went down with Kate, but Charley was in even worse favour than usual with the Inimitable, and they came back to London shortly after Christmas Day. Dickens had finished the second instalment of *The Mystery of Edwin Drood* by the end of November and was trying to hurry the artwork for the cover and early interior illustrations, but after sketching that cover based on Dickens's sometimes vague outline of the shape of the tale, Charley decided in December that he could not draw at such a rate without further harming his health. Showing his impatience—and perhaps even disgust—Dickens hurried up to London and conferred with his publisher Frederick Chapman, and they decided as a replacement on a young man new to illustration, a certain Luke Fildes.

Actually, as was almost always the case, it was Dickens who decided, this time based upon the advice of painter John Everett Millais, who had been staying at Gad's Hill Place and who showed the Inimitable a Fildes illustration in the first issue of a magazine called *The Graphic*. When Fildes interviewed with Dickens at the offices of Frederick Chapman, the young upstart actually had the audacity to say that he was "of a serious nature" and thus would be best at illustrating (unlike Charley and so many of Dickens's previous illustrators such as "Phiz," who best loved the comic scenes) the graver aspects of the Inimitable's novels. Dickens agreed—actually he loved both Fildes's more modern style and more serious approach—and thus my brother, after only a final cover sketch and two interior drawings, was finished forever as Charles Dickens's illustrator.

But Charley, who was in his own hell of battling his constant gastric problems, did not seem to mind (except for the loss of income, which was shattering to the couple's plans).

Nor did I mind Dickens's not inviting me to Gad's Hill for Christmas after so many years of a pleasantly contrary tradition.

Word came from my brother and others that Dickens's left foot had become so swollen that he spent much of Christmas Day in the library having it poulticed and sat at the dining table that evening with the swollen and bandaged limb propped on a chair. He was able—with help—to hobble into the drawing room after dinner for the usual Dickens-family games, although his contribution uncharacteristically (for Dickens did love his games) was to lie on the sofa and watch the others compete.

For New Year's Eve, Dickens accepted an invitation to spend that Friday and Saturday (for New Year's Eve fell on a Friday that year) at Forster's luxurious digs, but according to Percy Fitzgerald, who heard it from Wills, who heard it from Forster himself, Dickens's left foot (still poulticed) and left hand were still giving him much pain. However, he made fun of the discomfort and read the second instalment of *Edwin Drood* with such spirit and obvious good humour that the self-serious new illustrator, Fildes, would have almost certainly been at a loss to find a scene to illustrate if "grave" were his only criterion.

With his usual precision, Dickens timed the triumphant conclusion of his reading to the assembled party to finish exactly at the stroke of midnight. Thus 1870 began for Charles Dickens as it would continue until his end—with a mixture of extreme pain and loud applause.

I had considered giving another New Year's Eve dinner party at Number 90 Gloucester Place, but I remembered that it had not gone so swimmingly the year before. Also, because the Lehmanns and Beards were some of my favourite guests—and since their children were angry at me for telling the truth about sports athletes (and since I still felt a tad uncomfortable in purely social settings around Frank since he had delivered Martha R——'s baby the previous summer)—I decided to spend the evening with my brother and his wife.

THE EVENING WAS QUIET one could hear their two loudest clocks ticking—and Charley began feeling unwell and had to excuse himself halfway through dinner so that he could go upstairs and lie down. He promised to try to waken and join us by midnight, but judging from the lines of pain etched on his face, I doubted if that would happen.

I also stood and suggested that I go (since there were no other guests), but Kate all but ordered me to stay. Normally this would have seemed natural—when I lived with Caroline, as I believe I may have already mentioned, I would often go to the theatre or somewhere and leave her with our male guests and think nothing of it—but things had been strained between Kate and me since the day of Caroline's wedding more than a year earlier.

Also, Kate had been drinking much wine before dinner, during dinner, and now brought out brandy after dinner as we adjourned to the parlour, where the clock ticking was at its loudest. She was not slurring her words (Katey was a mistress of self-control), but I could tell from her rigid posture and the loss of plasticity in her expression that drink was affecting her. The girl I had known so long as Katey Dickens was—at almost thirty years of age—on the verge of becoming an old and bitter woman.

"Wilkie," she said suddenly, her voice almost shockingly loud in the draped dimness of the little room, "do you know why Father invited you to Gad's Hill last October?"

In truth, the question hurt my feelings. I had hitherto never required a *reason* to be invited to Gad's Hill Place. Sniffing my brandy to cover my discomfort, I smiled and said, "Perhaps because your father wanted me to hear the opening of his new book."

Kate waved her hand in a rather crudely dismissive manner. "Not at all, Wilkie. I happen to know that Father had reserved that honour for his dear friend Mr Fields, and that he—Father—was shocked when you came down to the library with him. But he could hardly tell you that it was a closed reading, as it was meant to be."

Now I *was* hurt. I tried to make allowances for the fact that Kate was clearly inebriated. Still trying to sound pleasant, even slightly amused, I said, "Well, why then did he invite me for that weekend, Katey?"

"Because Charles—your brother, my husband—has been deeply upset in the estrangement between you and Father," she said briskly. "Father believed that a weekend at Gad's Hill would quell some of the rumours of that estrangement and cheer Charles up a bit. Alas, it did neither."

"There has been no estrangement, Katey."

"Oh, posh!" she said, waving her fingers again. "Do you think *I* do not see the truth, Wilkie? Your friendship with Father has all but ended, and no one, in or out of the family, is quite sure why."

I did not know what to say to that, so I sipped my brandy and said nothing. The minute hand on the loudly ticking clock on the mantel crept far too slowly towards midnight.

I almost jumped when Katey suddenly said, "You have heard the rumours, I am sure, that I have taken lovers?"

"I certainly have *not!*" I said. But, of course, I had—in my club and elsewhere.

"The rumours are true," said Katey. "I have *tried* to take lovers...even Percy Fitzgerald before he married that simpering little charmer of his, all dimples and bosoms and no brains."

I stood and set down my glass. "Mrs Collins," I said formally, wondering at how strange it was that another woman now took my mother's name and title, "we have both, perhaps, celebrated with this wonderful wine and brandy a bit too much. As Charles's brother—and I love him very much—there are things I should not hear."

She laughed and waved her fingers again. "Oh, for heaven's sake, Wilkie, sit down. Sit down! That's a good boy. You look so silly when you play at being outraged. Charles knows that I have taken lovers and he knows *why*. Do *you*?"

I considered leaving without a word but instead sat down miserably. She had tried once before at Gad's Hill, you might remember, to bring up this rumour that my brother had never consummated their marriage. I had changed the subject then. Now all I could do was look away from her.

She patted my hands as they sat folded on my lap. "Poor dear," she said. I thought she was speaking of me, but she was not. "It is not Charley's fault. Not really. Charles is weak in many ways. My father...well, you know Father. Even while dying—and he *is* dying, Wilkie, of some affliction none of us can understand, not even Dr Beard—but even while dying, he remains strong. For himself. For everyone. It is why he cannot abide the sight of your brother at his breakfast or dining table. Father has always abhorred weakness. This is why I did not allow you to finish that pitiful proposal of marriage, to become effective only after Charles is dead, of course, which you made on the night of…that woman in your life's…marriage."

I stood again. "I really must go, Kate. And you should go up and look in on your husband before midnight. He may need your help. I wish both of you the best of new years."

She stood but did not move from the parlour as I went into the foyer and put on my coat and hat and muffler and found my stick. Their only servant had left after making dinner.

I went to the parlour doorway, touched the brim of my hat, and said, "Goodnight, Mrs Collins. I thank you for a lovely dinner and the excellent brandy."

Katey's eyes were closed and her long fingers were touching the arm of the sofa to keep her steady as she said, "You'll be back, Wilkie Collins. I know you. When Charley's in his grave, you'll be back before his corpse is cold. You'll be back like a hound—like Father's old Irish bloodhound, Sultan—baying after me as if I were a bitch in heat."

I touched my hat brim again and stumbled in my rush to escape out into the night.

It was very cold but there were no clouds. The stars were terribly bright. My polished boots sounded very loud as they crunched on the remainder of the week's snow on pavement and cobblestones. I decided to walk all the way home.

The bells at midnight surprised me. All over London, the church bells and city bells were ringing in the New Year. I heard a few distant voices crying out in drunken celebration and somewhere, far away towards the river, something that sounded like a musket being fired.

My face suddenly felt cold despite the muffler and when I raised my gloved hands to my cheek, I was astonished to find that I had been weeping.

DICKENS'S FIRST READING in his new and final series of London readings was at St James's Hall on the evening of 11 January. The plan for the rest of that month was for him to read twice a week—on Tuesdays and Fridays—and then once a week after that until the series was to be completed on 15 March.

Frank Beard and his other physicians were totally opposed to these readings, of course, and even more opposed to Dickens's making the frequent voyages into town by rail. To appease them, Dickens rented the Miller Gibson house at 5 Hyde Park Place (just opposite the Marble Arch) from January to the first of June, although he again told everyone he had done this so that his daughter Mary would have a local place to stay, as she became busier in society that winter and spring.

With Dickens in London most of the time, one would think that he and I would have crossed paths frequently as in the old days, but when he was not reading he was working on his book, and I continued working on mine.

Frank Beard had asked me if I might join Charley Dickens and him on nightly attendance at the Inimitable's readings, but I declined for reasons of both work and my own health. Beard was there every night in case of emergency and he admitted to me that he was actively worried that Dickens might die on stage. That night of the first performance, Frank had said to Charley, "I have had some steps put up at the side of the platform.

You must be there every night, and if you see your father falter in the least, you must run and catch him and bring him off to me, or, by Heaven, he'll die before them all."

Dickens did not die that first night.

He read from *David Copperfield* and the ever-popular Trial from *Pickwick*, and the evening, according to his own later accounts, "went with the greatest brilliancy." But afterwards, with the Inimitable collapsed on his sofa in his dressing room, Beard found that Dickens's pulse had gone from its normal 72 to 95.

And it continued to rise during and after each subsequent performance.

Dickens had scheduled two of his performances for afternoons and even one in the morning after a request for that hour from actors and actresses who wished to see him read but who could not come later in the day or evening. It was at this unusual morning reading on 21 January, with the seats filled with tittering and chattering young actresses, that Dickens first did the Murder reading again. Several of the periwinkles fainted, more had to be helped out, and even some of the actors in the audience cried out in alarm.

Dickens was too exhausted afterwards to show his usual delight at such a response. Beard later told me that the author's pulse that morning, in mere anticipation of Nancy's Murder, had risen to 90 and after the performance, with Dickens prostrated on the sofa and unable to get his breath back—"He was panting like a dying man" were Beard's precise words to me—the Inimitable's pulse was at 112 and even fifteen minutes later had dropped only to 100.

Within two days—he was meeting Carlyle for the last time—Dickens's arm was in a sling.

Still he went on, continuing the reading series as planned. His pulse rose to 114—then 118—then 124.

At each intermission, Beard had two strong men ready to half-carry Dickens to his dressing room, where the Inimitable would lie panting, too breathless to speak except for meaningless syllables or incoherent sounds, for at least a full ten minutes before the author of so many long books could speak a single coherent sentence. Then Beard or Dolby would help Dickens take a few swallows of weak brandy mixed with water and Dickens would rise, put a fresh flower in his lapel, and rush back onto the platform.

His pulse rate continued to rise at each performance.

On the first evening of March 1870, Dickens performed his final reading from his beloved *David Copperfield*.

On 8 March, he murdered Nancy for the last time. Some days after that, I happened to meet Charles Kent in Piccadilly, and over luncheon Kent told me that on his way to the stage for that final Murder, Dickens had whispered to him, "I shall tear myself to pieces."

According to Frank Beard, he had already torn himself to pieces. But he went on.

It was in the middle of March—right when the tour was taking its greatest toll on the man—that the Queen summoned Dickens to Buckingham Palace for an audience.

Dickens had not been able to walk the previous evening or that morning, but he managed to hobble into Her Majesty's presence. Court etiquette did not allow him to sit (although the previous year, receiving the same honour, old Carlyle, announcing that he was a feeble old man, had helped himself to a chair and etiquette be d——ned).

Dickens stood throughout the interview. (But so did Victoria, leaning slightly on the back of a sofa—an advantage denied to the author standing racked in pain in front of her.)

This interview had come about partially because Dickens had shown some American Civil War photographs to Mr Arthur Helps, Clerk of the Privy Council, and Helps had mentioned them to Her Majesty. Dickens had forwarded the photographs to her.

With his usual sense of mischief, Dickens had sent the hapless Helps a note in which he pretended to believe that he was being summoned to the palace in order to be made a baronet. *"We will have 'Of Gad's Hill Place' attached to the title of the Baronetcy, please,"* he wrote, *"—on account of the divine William and Falstaff. With this stipulation, my blessing and forgiveness are enclosed."*

Reports were that Mr Helps and other members of the court were quite beside themselves with embarrassment over the misunderstanding until someone explained the Inimitable's sense of humour to them.

During the interview with the Queen, Dickens quickly turned the subject to the prescient dream that President Abraham Lincoln was purported to have had—and told others about—the night before he was assassinated. Such portents of imminent death were obviously on the Inimitable's mind at that time, and he had brought up the Lincoln dream with many of his friends.

Her Majesty reminded him of the time she had attended the performance of *The Frozen Deep* some thirteen years earlier. The two discussed the evident fate of the Franklin Expedition for a few moments, then the current state of Arctic exploration, and then somehow got onto the perennial issue of the servant problem. From there the long royal audience's conversation shifted to national education and the appalling price of butcher's meat.

I can only imagine and envision, Dear Reader, much as you must so many decades beyond all this, how that audience must have looked and sounded, with Her

Majesty standing next to the sofa and behaving, as Dickens later told Georgina, "strangely shy...and like a girl in manner," and Dickens standing ramrod straight yet seemingly relaxed, perhaps with his hands clasped behind him, while his left leg and foot and left arm were throbbing and aching and threatening to betray him into collapse.

Before the audience ended, Her Majesty is reported to have said softly, "You know, it is one of our greatest regrets that we have never had the opportunity to hear one of your readings."

"I regret it as well, Ma'am," said Dickens. "I am sorry, but as of just two days ago, they are now finally over. After all these years, my readings are over."

"And a private reading would be out of the question?" said Victoria.

"I fear it would be, Your Majesty. And I would not care to give a private reading at any event. You see, Ma'am, a mixed audience is essential to the success of my readings. This may not be the case with other authors who read for the public, but it has always been the case for me."

"We understand," said Her Majesty. "And we also understand that it would be inconsistent for you to alter your decision. We happen to know, Mr Dickens, that you are the most consistent of men." She smiled then, and Dickens later confided to Forster that he was sure she was thinking of that time thirteen years before when he had flatly refused to appear before Her Majesty still in his costume and makeup after the comedic farce that had followed *The Frozen Deep*.

At the close of the interview, the Queen presented him with an autographed copy of her *Leaves from the Journal of Our Life in the Highlands* and asked for a set of his works. "We would prefer, if it is possible," she said, "that we receive them this afternoon."

Dickens had smiled and bowed slightly but said, "I ask once again for Your Majesty's kind indulgence and for a bit more time in which I shall have my books more suitably bound for Your Majesty."

He later sent her the complete set of his works bound in morocco leather and gold.

THE FINAL READING PERFORMANCE he had mentioned to the Queen occurred on 15 March.

On that last evening, he read from *A Christmas Carol* and from the Trial. They had always been the crowds' favourites. His granddaughter, tiny Mekitty, was present for the first time that night, and Kent later told me that she had trembled when her grandfather—"Wenerables" she called him—had spoken in strange voices. She wailed beyond consolation when she saw her Wenerables *crying*.

I was there in the audience that night—in the back, unheralded, in the shadows. I could not stay away.

For the last time on this Earth, I realised, English audiences were hearing Charles Dickens give voice to Sam Weller and Ebenezer Scrooge and Bob Cratchit and Tiny Tim.

The audience was huge and overflowing. Crowds had gathered outside the hall's two entrances on Regent Street and Piccadilly hours before the event. Later, Dickens's son Charley told my brother that "I thought I had never heard him read so well and with so little effort."

But I was there and I could see the effort that Dickens was using to keep himself composed. Then the trial scene from *The Pickwick Papers* was over and—as he always did—Dickens simply walked off stage.

The huge audience went berserk. The standing ovation verged on sheer hysteria. Several times Dickens returned to the platform and then left again and each time he was called back. Finally he calmed the crowd and gave the short speech that he obviously had been labouring on for some time and which he now had to overcome his visible emotions to give—tears were pouring down his cheeks in the gaslights while his grand-daughter wailed in the family's box.

"Ladies and gentlemen, it would be worse than idle—for it would be hypocritical and unfeeling—if I were to disguise that I close this episode in my life with feelings of very considerable pain."

He spoke briefly of those fifteen years during which he had been reading to the public—of how he had seen such readings as a duty to his readers and to the public—and he spoke of that readership's and public's sympathy in return. As if in recompense for his departure, he mentioned that *The Mystery of Edwin Drood* would soon appear (the audience was too rapt and silent and transfixed even to applaud this happy news).

"From these garish lights," he concluded, stepping slightly closer to the gaslights and to his silent (except for the soft weeping) audience, "I now vanish forever-more, with a heartfelt, grateful, respectful, affectionate farewell."

He limped from the stage then, but the relentless roars of applause brought him back one last time.

His cheeks wet with tears, Charles Dickens kissed his hand, waved, and then limped off the stage for the final time.

Walking back to Number 90 Gloucester Place through light showers that March night, a new unopened letter from Caroline Clow—more carefully detailed abuses, I was sure—in my pocket, I drank heavily from my silver flask.

Dickens's public—that mob of public which I had seen and heard roar that very night—would, whenever that d——ned beloved writer of theirs finally chose to die, insist on having him buried in Westminster Abbey next to the great poets. I was now certain of that. They would get him there if they had to carry his corpse on their rough-wooled shoulders and dig the grave themselves.

I resolved to take a day off from my writing the next day—a Wednesday—and go to Rochester and visit the cathedral and seek out Mr Dradles and there make my final arrangements for Charles Dickens's true demise and interment.

CHAPTER FORTY-SIX

*E*re is the block," whispered Dradles, patting the face of a stone in the wall that looked like all the others in the gloom. "And 'ere the tool to 'andle 'er with." In the weak lantern light, I saw him reach deep into his layers of flannel and moleskin and filthy canvas and bring out a pry bar as long as my forearm. "And 'ere on top, you see, the notch I chiselled in, Mr Billy Wilkie Collins, sir. Easy as the front door key to your very own 'ouse, you see."

I could not really see the niche at the top of the block where it met the mortar, but the flat end of the pry bar found it. Dradles grunted rum fumes at me as he leaned all his weight on the upper part of the bar. The stone screamed.

I write "screamed," Dear Reader, rather than "screeched" or "scraped" or "made a loud sound" because the noise this stone block made sliding back several inches out of its ancient place in the wall of the crypt was precisely that of a woman screaming.

I helped Dradles remove the surprisingly heavy block and set it on the dark, dank stones of the curving crypt stairs. The lantern showed a rectangular hole which I was sure was far too small for my purposes. When Dradles dropped the iron bar on the floor behind me, I confess I jumped several inches.

"Go on, lean 'n' peer in, make your acquaintance wi'

the old 'uns there," cackled the stonemason. He took another drink from his ever-present jug as I held the lantern to the aperture and attempted to peer inside.

From what I could see, it still looked too small for my purposes. Less than a foot of space separated this outer wall from the first inner wall of an old crypt, and although I could see that this narrow gap dropped a foot or two below the level of the outer walkway and floor where we crouched, much of this cavity stretching away on both sides of the hole we'd made was half-filled with broken stones, ancient bottles, and other rubbish.

I heard Dradles chuckle to my left. He must have seen my appalled expression in the lamplight.

"Y'er thinkin' it's too narrow, ain't you, Mr Billy Wilkie Collins? But it ain't. It's perfect. Shove aside 'ere."

I held the lantern as Dradles squat-walked forward. He patted his bulging pockets and suddenly there was an animal's long leg bone in his right hand.

"Where did that come from?" I whispered.

"One of yer bigger test dogs in the lime pit, 'course. It's me who does the rakin' out there, now, in't it? Now watch and learn."

Dradles pushed the long canine femur or whatever it was sideways through the small aperture and tossed it in with a flick of his fingers. I heard it clatter on the rubbish below and several feet to one side.

"You could get a kennel 'o dogs' skeletons in 'ere," he said too loudly. "But it ain't dogs we're thinkin' of to join the old 'uns with their crooks 'ere, is it?"

I said nothing.

Dradles patted at his layers of filthy, dusty garments again and suddenly he was holding a human skull missing only its jawbone.

"Who is...who was that?" I whispered. I hated it that my voice sounded like it was trembling in this narrow but echoing space.

"Oh, aye, names are important for the dead 'uns, though not for them, but for us quick 'uns, eh?" laughed Dradles. "Let us call 'im Yorick."

Once again, the old man must have seen my expression in the lantern light, for he laughed loudly—the echo of that drunken bark coming back from groined vaults on the level above us and from the walls of the curved and descending staircase-corridor we were in and from unimagined rooms and tunnels and pits in the absolute darkness far below.

"Mr Billy Wilkie Collins mustn't think that masons of stone don't know and can't recite the Bard," whispered the old man. "'Ere, let us see the last of Poor Yorick." And with that he fitted the skull carefully through the tight space, held it in one hand, and flicked it to the left and out of sight into the narrow cavity. The noise it made upon hitting the stone and bottles and rubbish below was memorable.

"Skulls is always the 'ardest part," Dradles said happily. "Spines, e'en wi' all the vertebrae intact, you can twist in like a petrified snake an' it don't matter if some o' the parts chip off. Where the skull can go though, there can go the whole man. Or ten whole men. Or a 'undred. Seen enough, Mr Billy Wilkie?"

"Yes."

"Be a good lad, then, and 'elp me lift this stone back in place. When you're done wi' your business down 'ere, you let old Dradles know and I'll touch up the grout 'ere so no one can ever tell that this wall ain't have been untouched since Noah's day."

Outside in the chilly March wind, I gave the old stonemason £300 in various-size bills. As I counted them out, Dradles's long, dry tongue kept flicking out like a Galapagos lizard's, licking his own dusty-stubbled cheeks and upper lip in startling pink-and-grey stabs.

"And there will be another hundred pounds each year," I whispered. "As long as you live."

He squinted at me. His voice, when he spoke, was much, much too loud. "Mr Billy Wilkie Collins ain't thinkin' that old Dradles's silence 'as to be bought, now, does he? Dradles can be as silent as the next good man. Or the next bad 'un, for that matter. If one who's done what you plan to do goes to thinkin' about payin' for silence, 'e might go to thinkin' about doin' more of what he done to *make sure o'* that silence. That'd be a mistake, Mr Billy Wilkie. It surely would. I've told me apprentice all about this 'ere business and sworn 'im to keep silence on pain of death by Dradles's wrath, but 'e knows, sir. 'E knows. An' 'e would let others know if something untowards-like were to 'appen to his good, stalwart old Dradles."

I thought a moment about his apprentice—an idiot deaf-mute, if I remembered correctly. But I said, "Nonsense. Think of it as an annuity. And annual payment in exchange for service and your investment in our common . . ."

"Dradles knows what an annuity is, sure as he knows ol' Yorick we left back there was a man of infinite jest, young 'Oratio. Just let Dradles know when you wants the stone, which looks perfectly fine and old now, grouted and mortared up for all of 'ternity." And with that he turned on his worn heel and walked away, touching his finger to what could have been a brim of what might have been a hat, without looking back.

MONTHLY SALES of the serialised *Man and Wife* were not as impressive as had been *The Moonstone*'s. No long lines waited for the monthly release of instalments. Critical reaction was tepid, even hostile. The English reading public was, as I had anticipated, angered by my careful and accurate description of the abuses and self-abuses of the Muscular Christian athlete. Word from the Harper brothers in New York indicated that the American reading public had limited interest in and even less outrage over the unfairness of our English marriage laws, which allowed—even encouraged—entrapment of one member of the couple into an unwanted matrimony.

None of these facts bothered me in the least.

If you have not read my *Man and Wife* there in the future, Dear Reader (although I sincerely hope it is still in print a century and more hence), let me give you a taste of it here. In this scene from Chapter the Fifty-fourth (page 226 in the first edition), I have my poor Hester Dethridge come upon a terrifying (to me, at least) encounter:

> *The Thing stole out, dark and shadowy in the pleasant sunlight. At first I saw only the dim figure of a woman. After a little it began to get plainer, brightening from within outwards—brightening, brightening, brightening, till it set before me the vision of MY OWN SELF—repeated as if I was standing before a glass: the double of myself, looking at me with my own eyes.....And it said to me, with my own voice, "Kill him."*

Cassell's Magazine had paid me an advance of £500 and a total payment of £750. I had made arrangements to publish *Man and Wife* in three volumes, with the initial release date being 27 January, with the firm F. S. Ellis. Despite the moderate sales in America, *Harper's* was so delighted with the quality of the early instalments that they sent me a totally unexpected cheque for £500. Also, I had written the novel *Man and Wife* with both eyes firmly set on its stage adaptation—in some ways, it and my ensuing novels would be theatrical scripts in shorthand—and I looked forward to further income from that very quick translation to both the London and American stage.

Compare all this to Charles Dickens's lack of literary production in the past year and more.

Thus it was all the more galling one day in May when I stepped into the Wellington Street offices of *All the Year Round* to discuss (demand) reversions of my copyrights with Wills or Charley Dickens—only to find both of them absent to lunch—and, wandering from office to office as was my old habit there, came across an open letter of accounting from Forster and Dolby.

It was a summary of earnings from Dickens's readings, and looking at it made the scarab scuttle behind my right eye and brought a band of excruciating headache pain tightening around my forehead. It was through just such rising agony that I read the following in Dolby's tight, ledger-columned script:

Charles Dickens's paid readings over the past years had totalled 423, including 111 given while Arthur Smith was the Inimitable's manager, 70 under Thomas Headland, and 242 under Dolby. It seemed that Dickens had never kept precise records of his profits under Smith and Headland, but this spring he estimated them at about £12,000. Under Dolby, those profits had reached almost £33,000. This gave a total of some £45,000—an average of more than £100 per reading—and, according to the note from Dickens appended, represented almost half of his entire current estate's value, estimated at about £93,000.

Ninety-three thousand pounds. All last year and this, because of my personal investment in the theatrical production of *Black and White*, my excessive loans to Fechter, the constant upkeep on the grand house on Gloucester Place (and the attendant salaries for the two servants and frequent cook there), my generous payments to Martha R——, and especially the constant need to purchase large quantities of both opium and morphia for personal medicinal reasons, I had been struggling financially. As I had written to Frederick Lehmann the year before (when that good friend had offered to lend me money)—*"I shall pay the Arts. Damn the Arts!"*

BECAUSE IT WAS BAD WEATHER, I was taking a cab home from Wellington Street that afternoon when I saw Dickens's daughter Mary walking along the Strand in the rain. I immediately had the driver stop the cab, ran to her side, and discovered that she was walking alone and unprotected in the rain (returning to the Milner Gibson house after a luncheon downtown) because she had been unable to hail a cab. Helping her into my coach, I rapped on the ceiling with my cane and called up to the driver, "Five Hyde Park Place, driver, across from the Marble Arch."

As Mamie dripped onto the upholstery—I had offered two clean handkerchiefs for her to dry her face and hands at the very least—and as I saw her reddened eyes, I realised that she had been crying. We talked as the cab moved slowly north through traffic and while she mopped at herself. The rain on the roof of the cab had a particularly insistent sound that afternoon.

"You are so kind," began the distraught young woman (although, at the advanced age of thirty-two, she was hardly still a young woman). "You have always been so kind to our family, Wilkie."

"As I shall always be," I muttered. "After having received unlimited kindness from the family over the years." The driver above us in the rain was shouting and cracking his whip not at his own poor horse but at some dray waggon driver who had crossed in front of him.

Mamie did not seem to be listening to me. Handing back my now-sodden handkerchiefs, she sighed and said, "I went to the Queen's Ball the other night, you know, and had ever so much fun! It was so gay! Father was to have been my escort, but at the last minute he was unable to go…"

"Not because of his health, I hope," I said.

"Yes, sadly, yes. He says that his foot—and these are his words, so you must forgive me—is a mere bag of pain. He can barely hobble to his desk to write each day."

"I am dismayed to hear that, Mamie."

"Yes, yes, we all are. The day before the Queen's Ball, Father had a visitor—a very young girl with literary aspirations, someone Lord Lytton had recommended visit Father and sent over—and while Father was explaining to her the enjoyment he was having in writing this *Drood* book for serialisation, this upstart of a girl had the temerity to ask, 'But suppose you died before all the book was written?'"

"Outrageous," I muttered.

"Yes, yes. Well, Father—you know sometimes in a conversation he smiles but how his gaze suddenly becomes focused on something very far away—he said, 'Ah-h! That has occurred to me at times.' And the girl became flustered…."

"As well she should have been," I said.

"Yes, yes… but when Father saw that he had embarrassed her, he spoke very softly in his kindest voice and said to her, 'One can only work on, you know—work while it is day.'"

"Very true," I said. "All of us writers feel the same on this issue."

Mamie began fussing with her bonnet, setting her wet hair and sagging curls to rights, and I had a moment to contemplate the rather sad future for both of Dickens's daughters. Katey was married to a very sick young man and was currently a social outcast both because of her father's separation from her mother and because of Kate's own flirtations and behaviour. Her tongue had always been too sharp for either Society's ear or that of most men who might have been marriage partners. Mamie was less intelligent than Kate, but her sometimes frenzied efforts towards social acceptance were always carried out at the fringes of society, usually within a maelstrom of malicious gossip, again because of her father's political attitudes, her sister's behaviour, and her own spinsterhood. Mamie's last serious marriage possibility had been Percy Fitzgerald, but—as Katey had said last New Year's Eve—Percy had settled on that "simpering charmer" and forgone his last opportunity of marrying into the Dickens fold.

"We shall be so glad to be back in Gad's Hill Place," Mamie said suddenly as she finished flouncing her wilted skirts and setting damp bodice lace to a semblance of propriety.

"Oh, you're leaving the Milner Gibson house so soon? I was under the impression that Charles had leased it for a longer period."

"Only until the first of June. Father is very impatient to get back to Gad's Hill for the summer. He wants us to be there with the house all opened up and happy and us all settled by the second or third of June. He shall have very little reason to come into town then, for the rest of the summer, you know. The rail travel is *so* hard on Father these days, Wilkie. Also, it will be easier for Ellen to visit there than it has been here in the city."

I blinked at this and then took off my spectacles to wipe them on one of the soggy handkerchiefs in order to hide my reaction.

"Miss Ternan still visits there?" I said offhandedly.

"Oh, yes, Ellen has been a regular visitor over the past few years—certainly your brother or Katey has told you that, Wilkie! Come to think of it, it's odd that you haven't been a guest there during the periods that Ellen has come to stay. But then—you are so busy!"

"Yes," I said.

So Ellen Ternan was still a frequent guest at Gad's Hill. This was a surprise. I was sure that Dickens had sworn his daughters into secrecy on this—another reason for Society to shun all of them—but that light-headed Mamie had forgotten. (Or assumed that I was still such a close friend of her father's that he would have told me.)

I realised at that moment that none of us—none of Dickens's friends or family or even his biographers in some future era such as yours, Dear Reader—would ever know the real story of his strange relationship with the actress Ellen Ternan. Had they actually buried a child in France, as I had surmised after overhearing that one snippet of conversation between them at Peckham Station? Were they now living merely as brother and sister, their passion—should they ever have acted on it in the first place—put behind them forever? Or had that passion resumed in a new form, edging towards being made public—perhaps a very scandalous divorce and second marriage for the ageing novelist? Would Charles Dickens *ever* find that happiness with a woman that had seemed to elude him throughout his passionate, naive, romance-haunted life?

The novelist in me was curious. The rest of me did not give a d——n for the answers. The old friend in me vaguely wished that Dickens had found that happiness in his lifetime. The rest of me recognised that Dickens's lifetime needed to be over and that he needed to be *gone*—missing, lost, expunged, eradicated, his corpse never found—so that the adulatory mobs could not bury him in Westminster Abbey or its churchyard. That was very important.

Mamie was babbling on about something—going on about someone she had danced and flirted with at the Queen's Ball—but suddenly the coach stopped and I peered out through the rain-streaked window and saw the Marble Arch.

"I shall walk you to your door," I said, stepping out and waiting to help the silly spinster down.

"Oh, Wilkie," she said, taking my hand, "you truly are the kindest of men."

I WAS WALKING HOME alone from the Adelphi Theatre several nights after this chance meeting when someone or something hissed at me from a darkened alley.

I stopped, turned, and lifted my bronze-headed walking stick as any gentleman would do when threatened by a ruffian in the night.

"Missster Collinsssss," hissed the figure in the narrow aperture.

Drood, I thought. My heartbeat raced and my pulse pounded in my temples. I felt frozen, unable to run. I grasped the stick in both hands.

The dark shape took two steps closer to the opening of the alley but did not emerge fully into the light. "Mister Collinsss...it's I, Reginald Barrisss." He gestured me closer.

I would not enter the alley, but from the opening to that stinking black crevice, I could see a trapezoid of light from the distant streetlamp falling on the dark form's face. There was the same dirt, the same wild beard, the same hooded eyes of a hunted man always flicking one way then another. I saw only a glimpse of his teeth in the dim light, but they appeared to have decayed. The once handsome and confident and burly Detective Reginald Barris had become this shadowy, fearful form whispering at me from an alley.

"I thought you dead," I whispered.

"I am not far from it," said the shadow-figure. "They hunt me everywhere. They do not give me time to ssleep or eat. I musst move consstantly."

"What news do you have?" I demanded. I still held my heavy stick at the ready.

"Drood and his minionss have set a date on which to take your friend Dickenss," he hissed at me. His breath was foul, even from three feet away. I realised that his missing teeth must be causing this Droodish hiss.

"When?"

"Nine June. Not quite three weeks from now."

The fifth anniversary, I thought. It made sense. I asked, "What do you mean they will *take* him? Kill him? Kidnap him? Take him down to Undertown?"

The filthy figure shrugged. He pulled his tattered hat brim lower so that his face went back to darkness.

I said, "What shall I do?"

"You can warn him," rasped Barris. "But there iss no place he can hide—no country where he would be ssafe. Once Drood decidesss a thing, it is done. But perhapsss you can tell Dickenssss to get his affairss in order."

My pulse still raced. "Can I do anything for *you?*"

"No," said Barris. "I am a dead man."

Before I could ask anything else, the dark figure backed away and then seemed to be melting down into the filthy stones of the alley. There must have been a basement stairway there that I could not see, but to my eye the shadowy figure simply melted vertically out of sight in the dark alley until it was gone.

Nine June. But how to arrange things with Dickens myself before that date? He would be back at Gad's Hill Place soon, and we were both working hard on our respective novels. How could I lure him away—especially to where I needed to take him—so that I could do what I had to? And before the ninth of June, that anniversary of Staplehurst that Dickens had always set aside in order to meet with Drood?

I had written a formal and rather cold letter to Wills demanding the reversion of copyrights for all of my stories and novels that had ever appeared in *All the Year Round,* and Dickens himself wrote me back in that last week of May 1870.

Even the business part of the letter was surprisingly friendly—he assured me that papers were being drawn up at that moment and that, even though we had not contractually arranged such returns of copyright, all such rights were to be returned to me at once. But it was his brief peroration that seemed wistful, almost lonely.

"My dear Wilkie," he wrote, *"I don't come to see you because I don't want to bother you. Perhaps you may be glad to see me by and by. Who knows?"*

This was perfect.

I immediately wrote Dickens a friendly note asking if we could meet "at your earliest convenience, but preferably before the anniversary you honour each year at this time." If Dickens did not burn this note, as was his habit, this wording might prove sufficiently cryptic to anyone who read it later.

When a warm and affirmative response came back from Dickens by the first of June, I completed the last of my preparations and set the Act III *finale* into motion.

CHAPTER FORTY-SEVEN

*W*here am I?

Gad's Hill. But not Gad's Hill Place, merely Gad's Hill, the site where Falstaff attempted to rob the coach but was set upon by "thirty ruffians"—actually just Prince Hal and a friend—and was all but robbed himself before he fled in panic.

My black coach is parked to one side of the Falstaff Inn. The hired coach looks rather like a hearse, which is fitting. It is almost invisible in the shadows under the tall trees as the last of the evening's twilight begins to fade. The driver up on the box is no driver, but a Hindoo sailor I have hired for this one night, paying him the equal of six months' salary for a real driver. He is a poor driver but he is also a foreigner. He speaks no English (I communicate with him through our mutual schoolboy bits of German and some sign language) and knows nothing of England or its famous people. He will be at sea again in ten days and may never return to English shores. He is curious about nothing. He is a terrible driver—the horses sense his lack of skill and show him no respect—but he is the perfect driver for this night.

When is it?

It is the gentle evening of 8 June, 1870, twenty minutes after the sun has set. Swallows and bats dart through the shadows and into the open, the wings of the bats and the forked tails of the swallows showing as flattened V's against the flat, clear pane of paling water-colours that is the twilight.

I see Dickens trotting across the road—or trying to trot, since he is hobbling slightly. He is wearing the dark clothing that I had suggested he don for this outing and has some sort of soft slouch hat on. Despite his obviously sore foot and leg, he carries no cane with him this evening. I open the door and he hops up into the coach to sit next to me.

"I told no one where I was going," he says breathlessly. "Just as you requested, my dear Wilkie."

"Thank you. Such secrecy will be necessary this one time only."

"This is all very mysterious," he says as I rap the ceiling of the coach with my heavy cane.

"It is meant to be," I say. "Tonight, my dear Charles, we shall each find the answer to a great mystery—yours being the greater."

He says nothing to this and only comments once as the coach careers and wobbles and jolts and lurches its way east along the highway. The sailor-driver is working the horses far too hard, and his crashing into holes and wild swerves from the slightest oncoming object threaten to spill the coach and us into the watery ditch from moment to moment.

"Your driver appears to be in an unholy hurry," says Dickens.

"He is foreign," I explain.

Some time later, Dickens leans across me and looks out the left window at the approaching tower-spire of Rochester Cathedral rising like a black spike against the dimming sky. "Ah," he says, but I believe I detect more confirmation than surprise in the syllable.

The coach grinds and squeals to a stop at the entrance to the churchyard and we climb out—me carrying a small unlighted lantern and both of us moving somewhat stiffly due to the jouncing and bouncing of the wild ride here—and then the driver applies his whip again and the black coach rumbles away into the deepening twilight.

"You don't wish the coach to wait for us?" Dickens enquires.

"The driver will come back for me when it is time," I say.

If he notices my use of "for me" rather than "for us," he does not comment on it. We move into the graveyard. The church and this old part of the city and the cemetery are empty and silent. The tide has gone out and we can smell the decaying reek of the mudflats, but from somewhere beyond that there comes the fresh salt scent of the sea and the sound of slow breakers. The only illumination is from a waning crescent moon.

Dickens says softly, "What now, Wilkie?"

I pull the pistol from my jacket—fumbling a moment to get the protruding hammer and sight free of the pocket lining—and aim it at him.

"Ah," he says again, and again there is no audible tone of surprise. To my ear, through the pounding of my pulse, the syllable sounds merely sad, perhaps even relieved.

We stand there like that for a moment, an odd and awkward tableau. The wind from the sea rustles the boughs of a pine tree close to where the graveyard wall hides us from the street. The hem and loose collars of Dickens's long summer jacket swirl around him like black pennants. He raises a hand to hold on to the brim of his soft cap.

"It's the lime pit, then?" asks Dickens.

"Yes." I have to try twice before the word comes out properly. My mouth is very dry. I am dying for a drink from my laudanum flask, but I do not want to divert attention from Dickens for an instant.

I gesture with the pistol and Dickens begins walking towards the blackness that is the rear of the graveyard where the open pit waits. I follow several feet behind, taking care not to get too close in case the Inimitable were to make some lunge for the gun.

Suddenly he stops and I do as well, taking another two paces away from him and raising and aiming the pistol.

"My dear Wilkie, may I make one request?" His voice is so soft that the words are all but lost to me under the hiss of the wind in the few trees and many marsh grasses.

"It hardly seems the time for requests, Charles."

"Perhaps," says Dickens, and I can see him smiling in the weak moonlight. I do not like him looking at me this way. I had hoped that he would keep his back turned until we reached the lime pit and the deed was done. "But I still have one," he continues softly. Maddeningly, I cannot detect fear in his voice, which is far steadier than mine has been. "But only one."

"What?"

"It may sound odd, Wilkie, but for some years now, I have had the strong premonition that I would die on the anniversary of the Staplehurst accident. May I reach in my waistcoat and look at my watch?"

To what purpose? I think dizzily. To prepare for the evening, I had drunk almost twice my usual allotment of laudanum and injected myself twice with the morphine, and now I feel the effects of these medicines not so much as reinforcment to my resolve but as a giddiness and odd light-headedness. "Yes, look, but quickly," I manage to say.

Dickens calmly takes out his watch, peers at it in the moonlight, and winds it slowly and maddeningly before setting it back. "It is some minutes after ten," he says. "The summer twilight lasts so late this time of year and we left late. It shan't be long until midnight. I cannot explain why—since your goal is obviously for no one to know the means or location of my death or interment— but it would mean something to *me* if I were allowed to fulfil my various premonitions and leave this world on nine June rather than eight June."

"You are hoping that someone comes along or that something arises to allow your escape," I say in my new and shaky voice.

Dickens merely shrugs. "Should someone enter the graveyard, you can still shoot me and make your escape through the sea grasses and back to your carriage waiting nearby."

"They would find your body," I say in flat tones. "And you would be buried in Westminster Abbey."

Dickens laughs then. It is that loud, unselfconscious, carefree, and infectious laugh that I have heard from him so many times before. "Is *that* what this is about, my dear Wilkie? Westminster Abbey? Does it calm your fears any that I have already stipulated in my will that I demand a simple, small funeral? No ceremonies at Westminster Abbey or anywhere else. I make clear that I want no more than three coaches in the final funeral procession and no more people at the burial than those three small coaches can carry."

My pounding pulse—and now pounding headache— seem to be trying to synchronise with the distant pounding of surf on a sandbar somewhere to the east, but the irregular rhythm of the wind denies the syncopation.

I say, "There will be no funeral procession."

"Obviously not," says Dickens and infuriates me with another small smile. "All the more reason to grant me this one, last kindness before we part company forever."

"To what purpose?" I ask at long last.

"You spoke of each of us solving a mystery tonight. Presumably my mystery to be solved is what—if anything—there might be after the instant of one's death. But what is yours, Wilkie? What mystery did you wish to have solved this beautiful evening?"

I say nothing.

"Let me venture a guess," says Dickens. "You would like to know how *The Mystery of Edwin Drood* was to have ended. And perhaps even learn how *my* Drood connects to *your* Drood."

"Yes."

He looks at his watch again. "It is only ninety minutes before midnight. I brought a flask of brandy—at your suggestion (although Frank Beard would be horrified to know this)—and I am sure you brought some refreshment for yourself. Why don't we find a comfortable seat somewhere in this place and have one last conversation before the bells in that tower toll my appointed day?"

"You think that I will change my mind," I say with a malicious smile.

"In truth, my dear Wilkie, I do not for a second believe that you will. Nor am I sure that I would want you to. I am very...weary. But I am not averse to a final conversation and taste of brandy in the night."

With that Dickens turns on his heel and looks amidst the surrounding stones for some place to sit. My choice is either to follow his lead or shoot him there and drag his corpse the many yards to the waiting lime pit. I had hoped to avoid this last indignity for both of us. And, in truth, I do not mind the idea of sitting for a few minutes until this temporary light-headedness passes.

THE TWO FLAT GRAVESTONES he chooses for our chairs, separated by almost four feet of a longer, wider headstone that might be a low table, remind me of the day in this very churchyard when Dickens played waiter to Ellen Ternan, her mother, and me.

After receiving permission, Dickens removes his brandy flask from his jacket pocket and sets it on the table-stone in front of him and I do the same with my silver flask. I realise that I should have patted the Inimitable's pockets when I first aimed my pistol at him. I know that Dickens keeps his own pistol in a drawer at Gad's Hill Place, as well as the shotgun with which he murdered Sultan. Dickens's apparent lack of surprise at the purpose of our "mystery outing" makes me think that he might have secreted a weapon on his person before coming out to the coach…and this might explain his otherwise inexplicable insouciance.

But it is too late now. I shall just keep a careful eye on him for the short time remaining.

We sit in silence for a while. Then the bells in the looming tower strike eleven, and my jagged nerves leap to the point that I almost accidentally pull the trigger on the pistol I am still aiming at Dickens's heart.

He notes my reaction but says nothing as I lay the gun along my upper leg and knee, keeping it aimed at him but removing my finger from the inside of what Hatchery called, I believe, the "trigger guard."

Dickens's voice after the long silence makes me jump in my skin again. "That is the weapon that Detective Hatchery showed us once, is it not?"

"Yes."

The wind rustles grasses for a moment. As if afraid of this silence, as if it is weakening my resolve, I force myself to say, "You know that Hatchery is dead?"

"Oh, yes."

"And do you know *how* he died?"

"Yes," says Dickens. "I do. Friends on the Metropolitan Police Force told me."

We have nothing else to say on this topic. But it leads me to the questioning that is the only reason Charles Dickens remains alive this final, extra hour. "I was surprised that you used a character—obviously a detective in disguise with his huge head of false hair—named Datchery in *Edwin Drood*," I say. "Such parody of poor Hatchery, especially given the...ah...lamentable details of his death, hardly seems sensitive."

Dickens looks at me. As my eyes have adapted to the churchyard darkness, so far from the nearest streetlamps or the windows of inhabited homes, the headstones around us—and especially the flat one of light marble lying between Dickens and me like a games table upon which we have laid our final hands in poker—seem to be reflecting the moonlight into Dickens's face like weak imitations of the focused gaslights he had rigged for his readings.

"Not a parody," he says. "An affectionate remembrance."

I sip from my flask and wave that away. It is not important. "But your *Drood* tale is less than half done—only the four monthly instalments have seen print and your entire manuscript to date is completed to only half the length of the full book—and yet you have already murdered young Edwin Drood. Asking as one professional to another—and as one with decidedly more experience and perhaps greater expertise in writing about mysteries—how can you possibly hope to sustain interest, Charles, when you have committed the murder so early in the tale yet have only one logical choice for the murderer...the very clear villain, John Jasper?"

"Well," says Dickens, "as one professional replying to another, we must remember that...wait!"

The pistol jerks up in my hand and I blink away distraction as I aim the muzzle at his heart some four feet away. Has someone entered the graveyard? Is he trying to distract me?

No. It appears that the Inimitable simply has been struck by a thought.

"How is it, my dear Wilkie," continues Dickens, "that you know of Datchery's appearance and even of poor Edwin's murder when these scenes, those numbers even, have not yet appeared and...ahh...Wills. Somehow you got a copy of the finished work from Wills. William Henry is a dear man, a trusted friend, but he has not been the same since that accident, what with all those doors creaking and slamming in his head."

I say nothing.

"Very well, then," says Dickens. "You know of the murder of young Drood on Christmas Eve. You know of Crisparkle's discovery of Edwin's watch and tie-pin in the river, although no body is found. You know of the suspicion falling on the fiery-tempered young foreigner from Ceylon, Neville Landless, brother to the beautiful Helena Landless, and of the blood found on Landless's stick. You know of Edwin's engagement to Rosa having been broken off and you know of Edwin's uncle, the opium-eater John Jasper, fainting after the murder when he first learns that there had been no engagement and that his obvious jealousy had been for naught. I currently have six of the contracted twelve instalments written. But what is your question?"

I feel the laudanum warmth in my arms and legs and I grow more impatient. The scarab in my brain is even more impatient than I. I can feel it scurry back and forth past the inside of the bridge of my nose, peering first from one eye, then from the other, as if jostling for a better view.

"John Jasper did the murder on Christmas Eve," I say, waving the pistol just a trifle as I speak. "I can even name the murder weapon...that long black scarf you have taken pains to mention at least three times so far for little reason. Your clues are hardly subtle, Charles!"

"It was to be an overly long cravat or neck tie," he says with another damning smile. "But I changed it to the scarf."

"I know," I say impatiently. "Charley told me that you emphasised that the cravat must be shown in the illustration and then told Fildes to change it to a scarf. Neck tie, scarf, it makes little difference. My question remains—how can you possibly hope to keep the readers engaged for the full second half of the book if we all know that John Jasper is to be revealed as the murderer?"

Dickens pauses before speaking as if struck by an important thought. He sets his brandy flask down carefully on the weathered stone. For some reason, he has put his spectacles on—as if discussing his never-to-be-finished book might require some reading aloud to me—and the moon's now twice-reflected glow turns the lenses of his spectacles to opaque silver-white disks.

"You want to finish the book," he whispers.

"What!"

"You heard me, Wilkie. You want to approach Chapman and tell him that you can finish the novel for me—William Wilkie Collins, the famous author of *The Moonstone*, stepping in to carry on the work of his fallen friend, his deceased onetime collaborator. William Wilkie Collins, you will tell dear mourning Chapman and Hall, is the only man in England—the only man in the English-speaking world—the only man in the entire world!—who knew Charles Dickens's mind sufficiently that he, William Wilkie Collins, can complete the mystery so tragically truncated when the aforesaid Mr Dickens disappeared suddenly, almost certainly taking his own life. You want to complete *The Mystery of Edwin Drood*, my dear Wilkie, and thus quite literally replace me in the hearts of readers as well as in the annals of great writers of our time."

"That's absolutely absurd," I shout so loudly that I cringe and look around in embarrassment. My voice has echoed back from the cathedral and its tower. "It's absurd," I whisper urgently. "I have no such thought or ambition. I have never *had* any such thought or ambition. I write my own immortal books—*The Moonstone* sold better than your *Bleak House* or this current tale!—and as a mystery tale *The Moonstone*—as I was pointing out to you tonight—was infinitely more carefully plotted and thought out than is this confused tale of the murder of Edwin Drood."

"Yes, of course," Dickens says softly. But he is smiling that mischievous Dickens smile again. If I had a shilling for every time I have seen that smile, I would never have to write again.

"Besides," I say, "I know your secret. I know the 'Great Surprise,' your clever plot hinge, upon which this rather transparent tale—by my professional standards—obviously hangs."

"Oh?" says Dickens affably enough. "Please be so kind as to enlighten me, my dear Wilkie. As a newcomer to this mystery business, I may have failed to see my own obvious Great Surprise."

Ignoring his sarcasm and idly pointing the pistol at his head, I say, "Edwin Drood is not dead."

"No?"

"No. Jasper *attempted* to murder him, that is clear. And Jasper may even think that he succeeded in his efforts. But Drood survived, is alive, and shall join forces with your oh-so-obvious 'heroes'—Rosa Bud; Neville and his sister, Helena Landless; your Muscular Christian, Minor Canon Crisparkle; and even that new sailor character you drag in so late . . ." I rack my memory for the character's name.

"Lieutenant Tartar," Dickens offers helpfully.

"Yes, yes. The heroic rope-climbing Lieutenant Tartar, so instantly and conveniently fallen in love with Rosa Bud, and all these other...benevolent angels... shall conspire with Edwin Drood to reveal the murderer...John Jasper!"

Dickens removes his spectacles, considers them with a smile for a moment, and then folds them carefully away in their case and sets the case back in his jacket pocket. I want to shout at him, *Throw them away! You will have no more use for spectacles! If you keep them now, I will simply have to fish them out of the lime pit later!*

He says softly, "And will Dick Datchery be one of these...benevolent angels...helping the resurrected Edwin to reveal the identity of the attempted murderer?"

"No," I say, unable to hide the triumph in my voice, "for the so-called 'Dick Datchery' is actually Edwin Drood himself...in disguise!"

Dickens sits on his headstone and thinks about this for a moment. I have seen this silent motionless statue of the always-in-motion Charles Dickens before, but only when I have put him in checkmate in one of my few victorious chess games against him.

"You are...this extrapolation is...*very* clever, my dear Wilkie," he says at last.

I have no need to speak. It must be almost midnight. I am both anxious and eager to get to the quick-lime pit and to finish the night's business and then to go home and take a very hot bath.

"But one question, please," he says softly, tapping at his flask with his manicured forefinger.

"What?"

"If Edwin Drood survived the murder attempt by his uncle, why does he have to go to all these labours... staying in hiding, enlisting allies, disguising himself as the almost comedic Dick Datchery? Why does he not just come forward and tell the authorities that his uncle attempted to murder him on Christmas Eve? Attempted, perhaps, even to the point of dumping Edwin's presumed-dead but in-truth-unconscious body into a pit of quick-lime (from which he must have awakened and crawled out as the acidic substance began to eat upon his skin and clothing...a delicious scene, I admit to you, as one professsional to another, but not, I also confess, one that I had cause to write)...but surely then we *have* no murderer, only a crazy uncle *attempting* murder, and no reason for Edwin Drood to remain in hiding. There is then no murder of Edwin Drood and precious little mystery."

"There are reasons for Drood to stay in hiding until the proper time comes," I say confidently. I have no idea what they might be. I take a long drink of lauda-num but make sure that I do not close my eyes for even an instant.

"Well, I wish you luck, my dear Wilkie," Dickens says with an easy laugh. "But you should know this before you attempt to complete the book according to the outline I never wrote... *young Edwin Drood is dead. John Jasper, under the influence of the same opium-laudanum you are drinking at this moment, murdered Edwin on Christmas Eve, just as the reader suspects at this point halfway through the book.*"

"That's absurd," I say again. "John Jasper is so jeal-ous of his nephew over Rosa Bud that he *murders* him? But what then...we have half the novel ahead to fill with nothing but...what? John Jasper's confession?"

"Yes," says Dickens with a truly evil smile. "That is precisely correct. The remainder of *The Mystery of Edwin Drood* is indeed—or at least the core of it shall be—the confessions of John Jasper and his alternate consciousness, Jasper Drood."

I shake my head but the dizziness only grows worse.

"And Jasper is not Drood's uncle, as we are given to believe," continues Dickens. "He is Drood's *brother*."

I mean to laugh at this but it emerges as a particularly loud snort. "Brother!"

"Oh, yes. Young Edwin, you must remember, is planning to go to Egypt as a member of a troupe of engineers. He plans to *change* Egypt forever, perhaps make it his home. But what Edwin does not know, my dear Wilkie, is that his half-brother (*not* his uncle), Jasper *Drood* (not John Jasper) was born there…in Egypt. And he learned his dark powers there."

"Dark powers?" I keep forgetting to aim the pistol but now bring the muzzle up again.

"Mesmerism," whispers Dickens. "Control of the minds and actions of others. And not merely our English parlour-game level of mesmerism, Wilkie, but the serious sort of mind-control which approaches true mind reading. Precisely the sort of mental contact we have seen in the book between young Neville Landless and his beautiful sister, Helen Lawless. They honed their mind abilities in Ceylon. Jasper Drood learned his in Egypt. When Helen Lawless and Jasper Drood finally meet on the field of mesmeric battle—and they shall—it will be a scene spoken of in awe by readers for centuries."

Helena Landless, not Lawless, I think, noting Dickens's confusion of his own characters. *Ellen Lawless Ternan. Even in this last unfinished fragment of a failed book, Dickens cannot restrain himself from connecting the most beautiful and mysterious woman in the novel with his own fantasy and obsession. Ellen Ternan.*

"Are you listening, my dear Wilkie?" asks Dickens. "You look as if you may be on the verge of dozing."

"Not at all," I say. "But even if John Jasper is actually Jasper Drood, the murder victim's older brother, what interest will that be to the reader who has to suffer through another several hundred pages of mere confession?"

"Never *mere* confession," chuckles Dickens. "In this novel, my dear Wilkie, we shall be in the mind and consciousness of a murderer in a way that no reader has ever before experienced in the history of literature. For John Jasper—Jasper Drood—is *two* men, you see—two complete and tragic personalities, both trapped in the opium-riddled brain of the lay precentor of the Cloisterham..."

He pauses, turns, gestures theatrically to the tower and great structure behind him.

"...of the *Rochester* Cathedral. And it is within those very crypts..."

He gestures again and my dizzied gaze follows his gesture.

"...those very crypts where John Jasper / Jasper Drood will hide the quick-lime-reduced bones and skull of his beloved nephew and brother, Edwin."

"This is sh——," I say dully.

Dickens brays a laugh. "Perhaps," he says, still laughing under his breath. "But with all the twists and turns ahead, the reader will be... *would have been*... delighted to learn of the many revelations that lie... *would have lain*... ahead in this tale. For instance, my dear Wilkie, our John Jasper Drood has committed his murder under the influence of both mesmerism and opium. The latter, the opium in greater and greater quantities, has been the trigger for the former—the mesmeric command to murder his brother."

"That makes no sense," I say. "You and I have repeatedly discussed the fact that no mesmerist can successfully command someone to commit murder... *to commit any crime*... against that person's conscious moral and ethical convictions."

"Yes," says Dickens. He drinks the last of his brandy and slides the flask away in his upper left inside pocket (and I make note of where it is for later). As always when discussing some plot device or other element of his art, Charles Dickens's voice is a mixture of the veteran professional and the excited boy eager to tell a story. "But you were not listening, my dear Wilkie, when I explained that a sufficiently powerful mesmerist—myself, for instance, but certainly John Jasper Drood or those other, as yet unmet, Egyptian figures beneath the surface of this story—*can mesmerise a person like the precentor of Cloisterham Cathedral to live in a fantasy world where he literally knows not what he is doing*. And it is the opium and perhaps—say—morphine in great quantities which fuel this ongoing fantasy that can lead him, without his comprehension, to murder and worse."

I lean forward. The pistol is in my hand but forgotten. "If Jasper kills his nephew...his brother...while under mesmeric control of this shadowy Other," I whisper, "who is the Other?"

"Ah," cries Charles Dickens, slapping his knee with delight. "That is the most marvellous and satisfying part of the mystery, my dear Wilkie! Not one reader in a thousand—no, not one reader in ten million—not even one fellow writer amongst the hundreds that I know and esteem—shall, until the full confession of John Jasper Drood is complete, be able to guess that the mesmerist and true murderer in the mystery of Edwin Drood is none other than..."

The bells in the tall tower behind Dickens begin tolling.

I blink at them. Dickens swivels on his headstone to watch, as if the tower is going to do something other than silently and coldly and blindly house the bells tolling his doom.

When the twelve strokes are sounded and the final

echoes die out over the low, dark streets of Rochester, Dickens turns back to me and smiles. "We have heard the chimes at midnight, Wilkie."

"You were saying?" I prompt. "The identity of the mesmerist? The real murderer?"

Dickens folds his arms across his chest. "I have told enough of this tale for tonight." He shakes his head, sighs, and gives the smallest of smiles. "And for this lifetime."

"Stand," I say. I feel so dizzy that I almost fall. It is difficult to get a proper grip on the pistol and the unlighted lantern, as if I have forgotten how to do two things at once. "Walk," I command, although whether to Dickens or to my own legs, I am not certain.

I REALISE LATER how infinitely easy it would have been for Dickens to flee in that brief moment or two as we walked to the rear of the graveyard and then into the rougher grasses at the edge of the marsh where the quick-lime pit waited.

If Dickens began running—if I missed with my first hurried shot—then it would have been child's play for him to run and crawl and hide amongst the high marsh grasses. It would be difficult to find him there in the daylight and nearly impossible at night, even with the small lantern I was carrying. Even the sound of his running or crawling would be disguised by the rising wind and crash of distant surf.

But he does not run. He leads the way. He seems to be humming a soft tune under his breath. I do not catch the melody.

When we stop, he is at the brink of the lime pit but facing me. "You must remember," he says, "that the metal objects in my pockets will not melt in the lime. My watch, given to me by Ellen...the flask...my pin and..."

"I remember," I rasp. I suddenly find it very difficult to breathe.

Dickens glances over his shoulder at the lime but remains facing me. "Yes, this is precisely where I would have had Jasper Drood confess that he brought the corpse of Edwin Drood...Jasper is younger than you and I, Wilkie, so even though the opium has reduced his physical abilities by half, carrying the dead boy a few hundred yards was no hardship..."

"Be silent," I say.

"Do you want me to turn around?" asks Dickens. "To look away? To face the pit?"

"Yes. No. Suit yourself."

"Then I shall continue looking at you, my dear Wilkie. My former friend and fellow traveller and once-eager collaborator."

I fire the pistol.

The incredible noise it makes and the unexpected recoil in my hand—I could not in all honesty say that I truly recall the experience of firing it in the servants' stairway two winters ago—causes me almost to drop the weapon.

"Good God," says Dickens. He is still standing there. He pats his chest, belly, groin, and upper legs almost comically. "I believe you missed," he says.

Still he does not run.

There are, I know, three bullets left in the gun.

My entire arm shaking, I take aim this time and fire again.

The tail of Dickens's jacket leaps up about level with his waist. Again he pats himself. This time he holds up the jacket and in the moonlight I can see his forefinger poking through the hole the bullet made. It must have missed his hip by less than an inch.

"Wilkie," Dickens says very softly, "perhaps it would be better for both of us if..."

I fire again.

This time the bullet strikes Dickens in the upper chest—there is no mistaking that sound, like a heavy hammer striking cold meat—and he spins around once and falls on his back.

But not into the lime pit. He lies at the edge of the pit.

And he is still alive. I can hear the loud, pained rasping of his breath. It seems to be burbling and gurgling somewhat, as if there is blood in his lungs. I walk closer until I am towering over him on the side away from the quick-lime. I wonder as he looks up if he sees me as a terrible silhouette against the stars.

In my writing, I have had—upon a few occasions—to use that ugly French term *coup de grâce*—and for some reason I always have trouble remembering how to spell it. But I have no trouble remembering of what it consists—the final shot must be to the brain, to be certain.

And there is only one bullet left in Hatchery's pistol.

Going to one knee, I set the lantern down and crouch next to the Inimitable, the creator of fools such as the Dedlocks and the Barnacles and the Dombeys and Grewgious, but also of such villains and parasites and dark souls as the Fagins and Artful Dodgers and Squeerses and Casbys and Slymes and Pecksniffs and Scrooges and Vholeses and Smallweeds and Weggs and Fledgebys and Bumbles and Lammles and Hawks and Fangs and Tiggs and . . .

I set the muzzle of Hatchery's heavy gun hard against the moaning Charles Dickens's temple. I realise that I am holding my empty left hand up as a sort of shield to protect my own face from the spatter of skull shards, blood, and brain matter that will erupt in a second or two.

Dickens is mumbling, trying to speak.

"Unintelligible..." I hear him moan. Then, "Wake up...awaken...Wilkie, wake..."

The poor deluded b——d is trying to wake himself from what he must think is a terrible nightmare. Perhaps this is how we are all dragged out of this life, moaning and grimacing and praying to an absent and unfeeling God that we might wake up.

"Awake..." he says, and I pull the trigger.

It is done. The brain that conceived of and brought to life David Copperfield and Pip and Esther Summerson and Uriah Heep and Barnaby Rudge and Martin Chuzzlewit and Bob Cratchit and Sam Weller and Pickwick and a hundred other living beings that live on in the minds of millions of readers is now spread across the edge of the lime pit in a grey-and-red line of slime that looks oily in the moonlight. Only the shattered bits of skull look white.

Even with his helpful warning, I almost forget to take his gold and other metal possessions before rolling the corpse into the pit.

I hate touching him and try to touch only fabric, which is possible in getting the watch, the flask, the coins in his pocket, and the pin, but for the rings and studs, I am forced to make contact with his cooling flesh.

I light the shielded bullseye lantern for this final operation and notice—with some small satisfaction—that my hand is steady as I strike the match and set it to the wick. I've brought a rolled-up burlap bag in my outside jacket pocket and now set all the metal objects in it, making sure not to drop anything into the high grass here near the pit.

Finally I am finished and set the sack away in my bulging pocket next to the pistol. I will have to remind myself to stop at the nearby river and throw all those things—pistol and sack—into the deep water there.

Dickens lies sprawled in the impossibly unselfconscious attitude known only to the dead. Standing with my booted foot on his bloodied chest, I consider saying some words but decide not to. There are times when words are superfluous, even to a writer.

It takes more effort than I have imagined, but after several strong shoves with my boot and a final kick, Dickens rolls once and slides into the quick-lime. Left to its own devices, the body would have half-floated and remained visible until daylight arrives, but I fetch the long iron pole that I have set away in the weeds for this night and push and poke and lean my weight into it—it feels rather like pressing a rod down into a large bag of soft suet—until the body goes under the surface and stays under the surface.

Then, holding the lamp close just long enough to check that I have no blood or other incriminating material on my person, I douse the light and walk back to the road to summon the waiting sailor-driver and coach. I whistle a soft tune as I walk through the glowing headstones. Perhaps, I think, it is the same tune that Dickens whistled under his breath just a few minutes earlier.

AWAKEN! WILKIE...wake up! Awake."

I moaned, rolled, thrust my forearm over my forehead, but managed to open one eye. My head pounded with a laudanum-morphia headache that sang of overdose. Thin moonlight painted random stripes across furniture in my bedroom. And across a face mere inches from mine.

The Other Wilkie was sitting on the edge of my bed. He had never come so close before...never.

He spoke.

His voice this time was not my voice, nor even an

altered imitation of my voice. It was the voice of an old, querulous woman, the voice of one of the Weird Sisters in the opening scene of *Macbeth*.

He or she touched my bare arm and it was not the touch of a living being.

"Wilkie..." he/she breathed at me, the bearded face almost touching mine. His breath—my breath—stank of carrion. "Kill him. Wake up. Listen to me. Finish your book...before June ninth. Finish *Man and Wife* quickly, next week. And on the day you finish it, kill him."

CHAPTER FORTY-EIGHT

*I*n response to my letter replying to his *"Perhaps you may be glad to see me by and by. Who knows?"* overture, Dickens invited me down to Gad's Hill Place on the fifth of June, a Sunday. I sent word that I would be there by three PM, after the Inimitable's usual Sunday writing time, but actually took an earlier train and walked the last mile or so.

The beauty of the June day was almost staggering. After the wet spring, everything that could turn green had outdone itself in greenness and everything that could even *dream* of blooming or blossoming *was* in bloom and blossom. The sunlight was a benediction. The breezes were so caressingly soft and intimate on the skin as to be embarrassing. A few white puffy clouds moved like aerial sheep above the green and rolling hills inland, but towards the water there was only more blue, more sunshine. The air was so clear that one could see the towers of London from twenty miles away. The farmlands beyond my carriage window and on either side of the dusty road as I walked the last mile or so were busy with playful little calves, running colts, and the occasional cluster of rural human children intent upon whatever games such a species pursues in early-summer fields and forests. It was almost enough to make a confirmed city-dweller such as myself want to buy a farm—but a jolt of laudanum followed by some brandy from a second, smaller flask cured that idiot's passing impulse.

No one greeted me at the drive of Gad's Hill Place this day, not even the pair of sentry dogs—sired by that assassinated Grendel-of-dogs, Sultan, I was sure—that Dickens usually kept chained there by the entrance pillars.

The red geraniums (still Dickens's favourite flower, the annuals faithfully planted by the author's gardeners every spring and left, at his command, as late into the autumn as possible) were everywhere—along the drive, in the sunny section near the bow windows outside Dickens's office in the main house, paralleling the hedges, out along the road—and, as always and for reasons I did not yet understand, I recoiled from their serried ejaculations of red blotches with a sense of real horror.

Guessing that Dickens might be in his chalet on such a perfect day, I went down through the cool tunnel—although there was almost no traffic on the highway above it—and emerged near the outside stairway that led up to the first-storey office.

"Halloa the bridge!" I called up.

"Halloa the approaching sloop," came down Dickens's strong voice.

"Permission to come aboard?"

"What is the name of your ship, sirrah? And where are you from and where are you bound?"

"My poor barque is called the *Mary Jane*," I called back up the staircase, putting on my best attempt at an American accent. "Set sail from Saint Looee and bound for Calcutta, by way of Samoa and Liverpool."

Dickens's laughter came down on the soft breeze. "Then by all means, Captain, you must come up!"

DICKENS HAD BEEN WRITING at his table and he was setting his manuscript pages into his oiled-leather portfolio as I came in. His left foot was propped up on a pillow which sat on a low stool, but he took his leg down as I entered. Although Dickens waved me to the only other chair in the room, I was too agitated to sit and contented myself with pacing from one window to the next and back.

"I am so delighted you chose to accept my invitation," Dickens was saying as he secured his writing utensils and buckled the portfolio closed.

"It was time," I said.

"You look a bit heavier, Wilkie."

"You look thinner, Charles. Except for your foot, which seems to have put on a few pounds."

Dickens laughed. "Our dear and mutual friend Frank Beard has warnings for both of us, does he not?"

"I see less of Frank Beard these days," I said, moving from the east-facing window to the south-facing one. "Frank's lovely children have declared war on me since I revealed the hypocrisies of Muscular Christianity."

"Oh, I hardly think it is the revelation of hypocrisy that has made the children angry at you, Wilkie. Rather the heresy of impugning their various sports heroes. I have not had the time to read it myself, but I hear that the instalments of *Man and Wife* have ruffled quite a few feathers."

"And sold more and more copies as it has done so," I said. "Before this month is out, I plan to publish it in book form, in three volumes, with the firm of F. S. Ellis."

"Ellis?" said Dickens, getting to his feet and reaching for a silver-headed cane. "I wasn't aware that the Ellis firm published books. I thought it dealt with cards, calendars, that sort of thing."

"This is their first venture," I said. "They will be selling on commission and I will be receiving ten percent on every copy sold."

"Marvellous!" said Dickens. "You seem somewhat restless—perhaps even agitated—today, my dear Wilkie. Would you care to join me in a walk?"

"*Can* you walk, Charles?" I was eyeing his new cane, which was indeed a *cane*, of the long-handled type one saw being carried by lame old men, rather than the sort of dashing walking stick preferred by young men such as myself. (As you may remember, Dear Reader, I was 46 in this summer of 1870, while Dickens was 58 and showed every year and month and more of that advanced age. But then, several people had recently commented on the grey in *my* beard, my ever-increasing girth, my problems catching my breath, and a certain hunched-over quality my tired body had assumed of late, and some had been so impertinent as to suggest that *I* was looking much older than my years.)

"Yes, I can walk," said Dickens, taking no offence at my comment. "And I try to every day. It is getting late, so I do not suggest a serious walk to Rochester or some other daunting destination, but we might manage a stroll through the fields."

I nodded and Dickens led the way down, leaving—one presumes—the portfolio with his unfinished manuscript of *The Mystery of Edwin Drood* there on his chalet worktable where anyone might come in off the highway and filch it.

WE CROSSED THE ROAD towards his house but then went around the side yard, past the stables, through the rear yard where he had once consigned his correspondence to a bonfire, and out into the field where Sultan had died some autumns earlier. The grasses here that had been dead and brown then were green and high and stirring in the breeze today. A well-worn path led off towards the rolling hills and a scrim of trees that marked the path of a broad stream that ran towards the river that ran to the sea.

Neither of us was running this day, but if Dickens's walking pace had been diminished, I could not discern it. I was huffing and puffing to keep up.

"Frank Beard tells me that you've had to add morphine to your pharmacopoeia in order to sleep," said Dickens, the cane in his left hand (he had always carried his stick in his right hand before) quickly rising and falling. "And that, although you've told him you discontinued the practice, a syringe he lent you some time ago has gone missing."

"Beard is a dear man," I said, "who often lacks discretion. He was keeping the world informed as to your pulse rate during your final reading tour, Charles."

My walking partner had nothing to say to that.

Finally I added, "The daughter of my servants, George and Besse—still servants of mine for the time-being at least—had been pilfering things. I had to send her away."

"Little Agnes?" cried Dickens. "Stealing? Incredible!"

We crossed the brow of the first low hill so that Gad's Hill Place, the highway, and its attending line of trees all fell behind. The path wound parallel to the tree line here for a way and then crossed a little bridge.

"Do you mind if we stop for a moment, Charles?"

"Not in the least, my dear Wilkie. Not in the least!"

I leaned on the little arched bridge's railing and took three sips from my silver flask. "An uncomfortably warm day, today, is it not?"

"You think so? I find it close to perfect."

We headed off again, but Dickens was either tiring or walking slowly for my benefit.

"How is your health, Charles? One hears so many things. As with our dear Frank Beard's ominous rumblings, one doesn't know what is true. Are you recovered from your tours?"

"I feel much better these days," said Dickens. "At least some days I do. Yesterday I told a friend that I was certain I should be living and working deep into my eighties. And I *felt* as if this were true. Other days... well, you know about the hard days, my friend. Other days, one does what one must to honour commitments and to honour the work itself."

"And how is *Edwin Drood* coming along?" I asked.

Dickens glanced at me before replying. With the terrible exception of Dickens's savaging of *The Moonstone,* we rarely, either one of us, offered to discuss work in progress with the other. The ferruled base of his cane swung with a sweet, summery *swish-swish* against the tall grass to either side of the path.

"*Drood* is coming along slowly but well, I think," he said at last. "It is a much more complicated book, in terms of plot and twists and revelations, than most I have attempted in the past, my dear Wilkie. But you know that! You are the master of the mystery form! I should have submitted all my novice's problems to you for a Virgil's guidance in the ways of mystery and suspense long before this! How goes your *Man and Wife?*"

"I look to finish it in the next two or three days."

"Marvellous!" cried Dickens once again. We were out of sight of the brook now, but its soft sounds followed us as we passed through more trees and then came out into another open field. The path continued winding towards the distant sea.

"When I do finish it, I wonder if you would do me a great favour, Charles."

"If it is within my poor and failing powers, I shall certainly attempt to do so."

"I believe it is within our powers to solve two mysteries on the same night...if, that is, you're willing to go on a secret outing with me on Wednesday or Thursday night."

"A *secret* outing?" laughed Dickens.

"The mysteries would have a greater chance of being solved if neither you nor I told anyone—no one at all—that we were going anywhere that evening."

"Now that *does* sound mysterious," said Dickens as we came to the brow of a hill. There were large barrow stones—Druid stones, the children and farmers called them, although they were nothing of the sort—scattered and heaped there. "How could keeping our outing a secret improve the chances at success of that outing?"

"I promise that if you join me when I come to fetch you a half hour or so after sunset on Wednesday or Thursday night, odds are great that you will discover the answer to that question, Charles."

"Very well, then," said Dickens. "Wednesday or Thursday night, you say? Thursday is the ninth of June. I may have a commitment for that evening. Would Wednesday suit you?"

"Perfectly," I said.

"Very good, then," said Dickens. "Now I have something that I have been waiting to discuss with *you,* my dear Wilkie. Shall we find a relatively comfortable perch on one of these great fallen stones? It should only take a few moments, but it is the reason I asked you here today and it truly is of some importance."

Charles Dickens stop and sit down during a walk? I thought. I never believed the day would come. But since I was soaked through with perspiration from our stroll and wheezing like a lung-shot warhorse, I welcomed it.

"I am your obedient servant, sir," I said and gestured for him to lead on and choose our fallen stone.

. . .

FIRST OF ALL, Wilkie, I owe you a deep and sincere apology. Several apologies, actually, but one above all for a certain treatment of you that is so unfair and so wrong that I truly do not know where to begin."

"Not at all, Charles. I cannot imagine anything that..."

Dickens stopped me with a raised palm. From where we sat on the high barrow stone, Kent stretched out and rolled away in all directions. I could see the haze of London in the pure light and the Channel to our left. The tower of Rochester Cathedral was like a grey tent spike in the distance.

"You may not be able to forgive me, my dear Wilkie," he continued. "*I* would not...could not...forgive you should the tables somehow be turned."

"What on earth are you going on about, Charles?"

Dickens gestured towards the distant treetops of the highway and his home as if that explained something. "For almost five years now—five years this week—you and I have jested back and forth about a creature named Drood...."

"Jested?" I said with some impatience. "Hardly 'jested,' I would say."

"That is precisely the point of my apology, my dear friend. There is, of course, no Drood...no Egyptian Temple in Undertown..."

What was he up to? What game was Dickens playing with me now? I said, "So all your tales of Drood, going back to the accident, were lies, Charles?"

"Precisely," said Dickens. "Lies for which I apologise abjectly and totally. And with a shame it is impossible even for me to express...and I have known shame."

"You would not be human if you had not," I said drily. Again I could but wonder what game he was at now. If I had been a simpleton depending upon Dickens's tales for my knowledge that Drood was real—as real as that white sail we both could see at that moment as we looked towards the sea—then perhaps the Inimitable would have something to apologise for.

"You don't believe me," said Dickens, looking warily at me.

"I don't understand you, Charles. You are not the only one who has seen Drood and suffered from his actions, you know. You forget that I have seen other living men and women who have become slaves of the Egyptian. What about the Undertown river gondola and the two masked men who piloted it that night we descended far below the crypts and catacombs? Are you trying to tell me that the gondola and those men who took you away were mere phantasms?"

"No," said Dickens. "They were my gardeners, Gowen and Smythe. And the 'gondola,' as you call it, was a mere Thames river barque with the roughest wooden adornments painted and hammered on fore and aft. It would not have passed muster in the crudest amateur theatrical—or any place that had lights. As it was, Gowen and Smythe had the Devil's own time carrying that leaking barque down endless flights of sewer-access stairs—they never did bring it back up, merely abandoned it there."

"You went off to Drood's Temple with them," I said.

"I sat there as we paddled around the bend of that stinking sewer until we were out of sight and then spent hours finding my way back through adjoining tunnels," said Dickens. "I almost became lost for good that night. It would have served me right if I had."

I laughed at this. "Listen to yourself, Charles. Someone would have to be out of his mind to plan and carry out such an elaborate charade. It would be not only cruel, but actively mad."

"Sometimes I agree with you on that point, Wilkie," sighed Dickens. "But you must remember that the descent into Undertown and the gondola were meant to be the last scene of the last act of this particular pretence, at least as far as I was concerned. How was I to know that your novelist's deeper consciousness and vast quantities of opium would keep the play going on in your head for years more?"

I shook my head. "Drood's men on the gondola were not the only others involved in this. What about Detective Hatchery? Did you even *know* that poor Hatchery was dead?"

"I did," said Dickens. "I heard about it upon my return from America and made it my business to enquire at the Metropolitan Police Force Detective Bureau to discover what had happened to him."

"And what did they tell you?"

"That former detective Hibbert Hatchery had been murdered in the same crypt in Saint Ghastly Grim's Cemetery where I had led you sometime earlier in our *faux* expedition into the underground world there."

"I fail to see what was *'faux'* about that descent into Hell," I said. "But that is irrelevant right now. Did they tell you *how* Hatchery died?"

"He was struck unconscious during an attempted robbery and then they disemboweled him," Dickens said softly. The words seemed to give him pain. "I guessed at the time that you were almost certainly there—down in Lazaree's den—and I know that coming upon his corpse when you emerged must have been horrible."

I had to smile. "And who is the *they* that the Detective Bureau thought responsible, Charles?"

"Four Hindoo sailors who had jumped ship. Thugs. Evidently they had followed you and Hatchery to the crypt—the police did not know it, of course, Wilkie, but I assumed that you were down in King Lazaree's den below and knew nothing of this—waited until the huge detective was sleeping in the crypt sometime before dawn, and attempted to rob him. Evidently they wanted his watch and the money he had in his pocket."

"That's absurd," I said.

"Given the size of our late detective friend, I agree," said Dickens. "And Hatchery did manage to break the neck of one of his four assailants. But this incensed the others, and after they knocked Hibbert unconscious with some sort of sap, they...did what they did to him."

How very tidy, I thought. *Scotland Yard would have an explanation for everything they did not understand.* "And how did the Detective Bureau know that it was four Hindoo sailors?" I asked.

"Because they caught the three living ones," said Dickens. "Caught them after the body of the fourth man was found floating in the Thames. Caught them and made them confess. They still had Hatchery's inscribed watch, purse, and some of the money with them. The police were not gentle with them...many of the officers had known Hatchery."

I had to blink at this. *They are* very *thorough in their lies.* "My dear Charles," I said softly but with some irritation, "none of this was in the newspapers."

"Of course it was not. As I said, the police did not deal gently with these Hindoo policeman-killers. None of the three survived to see trial. As far as the press was concerned, there had never been an arrest in the case of the murder of Hibbert Hatchery. Indeed, none of the details of the murder ever *reached* the press, Wilkie. The Metropolitan Police Force is, all in all, a good institution as government institutions go, but they have their dark side, as do we all."

I shook my head and sighed. "And this is what you wanted to apologise to me about, Charles? Lying to me about Drood? Staging such a farce with the crypts and gondola? Not telling me about how—you believe—Detective Hatchery died?" I thought of the many times I had seen Drood, talked to Inspector Field about Drood, listened to Detective Barris talk about Drood, seen Edmond Dickenson after his conversion to Drood, and seen Drood's minions in Undertown and his temples in Overtown. I had seen a note from Drood and seen Drood himself sitting and talking with Dickens in my own house. Dickens's simple lie on this beautiful Sunday was not going to make me believe that I was mad.

"No," he said, "that is not what I want to chiefly apologise for, although it is a subsidiary element of my larger apology. Wilkie, do you remember that first day you came to my home and office after the Staplehurst accident?"

"Of course. You told me all about your initial encounter with Drood."

"Before that. When you first came into the room. Do you remember what I was doing and what we talked about?"

I had to work to recall this, but eventually I said, "You were fiddling with your watch and we talked for a moment about mesmerism."

"I mesmerised you then, my dear Wilkie."

"No, Charles, you did *not*. Can you not recall that you said you would like to and began to swing your watch, but that I simply waved it all away? You yourself agreed that my will was too strong to submit to magnetic control of any sort. And then you put away the watch and told me about the Staplehurst accident."

"Yes, I said that your will was too strong to be mesmerised, Wilkie, but that was after ten minutes of having you in a mesmeric trance."

I laughed aloud at this. *What game is he playing here?* I adjusted my hat brim to keep the bright sun out of my eyes. "Charles, *now* you are lying...but to what purpose?"

"It was a sort of experiment, Wilkie," said Dickens. He was literally hanging his head in a way that reminded me of Sultan. If I'd had his shotgun right then, I would have dealt with Dickens precisely the way that Dickens had dealt with Sultan.

"Even then," continued Dickens, "even then, I had some vague notions of writing a novel in which a man carries out certain...actions...while under an incredibly extended period of mesmeric post-trance suggestion. I confess that I was especially interested in how such a suggestion of belief would affect a creative artist. That is, someone with a well-honed professional imagination to begin with and—I confess even more—such a creative person, a writer, who was, even then, using large quantities of opium, since opium was to be a *leit motif* in the mystery tale I had in mind."

Here I not only laughed but I slapped my leg. "Very good! Oh, very good, Charles! And you're telling me that you simply commanded me—via your mesmeric control—to believe in the Drood tale that you then told me when you awoke me from the trance?"

"I did not command such belief," Dickens said morosely. "I merely *suggested* it."

I patted both knees with both hands. "Oh, *very* good. And now you will tell me that you made up the entire idea of our friend Drood from whole cloth, using that incredible Charles Dickens imagination and love of the macabre!"

"Not at all," said Dickens. He looked towards the west and I could have sworn that there were tears in his eyes. "I had dreamt of Drood the night before—dreamt of the creature moving amongst the dead and dying at Staplehurst, just as I described to you, my dear Wilkie, mixing and interweaving the fantasy of Drood with the horror of the real experience."

I could not keep from smiling broadly. I removed

my spectacles, mopped my brow with a paisley hand-kerchief, and shook my head in admiration of the audacity of what he was telling me and of the game he was playing. "So now you say that you *dreamt* Drood into existence."

"No," said Dickens. "I had first heard the legend of Drood from Inspector Charles Frederick Field more than a decade before Staplehurst. Why I interwove the old inspector's obsessive fantasy into my nightmare about what happened at Staplehurst, I shall never know."

"*Field's* fantasy?" I cried. "Now it is Inspector Field who invented Drood!"

"Before you and I first met, my dear Wilkie. You remember that I did a series of essays on crime and the city that were published by my old magazine *Household Words* as far back as eighteen fifty-two. I was actually introduced to Inspector Field by other actors who had known Field when *he* had been an amateur actor at the old Catherine Street Theatre more than a decade earlier. But it was indeed Police Detective Charles Frederick Field, during our long walks through the night streets of the Great Oven back in the early eighteen fifties, who told me about the spectre in his mind whom he called Drood."

"Spectre," I repeated. "You are telling me that Inspector Field was insane."

"Not at first, I believe," said Dickens. "I later spoke to many of his colleagues and superiors in the Detective Bureau about this—as well as with the man who succeeded Field as Chief of Detectives when the inspector actually did break down."

"Broke down because of Drood," I said sarcastically. "Because of Field's *fantasy* about an Egyptian occultist killer named Drood."

"Yes. At first it was not a fantasy. There were a series of incredible murders about the time that Charles Frederick Field was becoming Chief of Detectives—all were unsolved. Some seemed to relate to cases that Inspector Field had been unable to solve in earlier years. Some of the Lascars and Malays and Chinamen and Hindoos that the police dragged in at the time tried to blame a spectral figure called Drood—the details were always hazy, but consistent at least on the basics that this monster was Egyptian, was a serial-murderer, could control other people by the powers of his mind and by the rituals of his ancient cult, and that he lived in some vast temple underground—or, according to some of the opium-eating villains, in a temple beneath the Thames itself."

"Shall we walk back?" I said.

"Not yet, Wilkie," said Dickens. He set his trembling hand upon my forearm for a moment but pulled it away when he saw my glare. "Do you see, though," he went on, "how this became first an obsession with Field, then a fantasy? According to the many policemen and detectives I later spoke to, including Hatchery, it was when Lord Lucan was murdered so foully while under Charles Frederick Field's personal protection, and the identity of the murderer never discovered that...what is funny, Wilkie?"

I simply could not stop laughing. This story, this plot, was so wonderfully baroque yet somehow so tidily logical. It was so, so...*Dickensian.*

"It was his fantasy about this make-believe master criminal, Drood, that eventually cost Field his job and then his pension," said Dickens. "Inspector Charles Frederick Field simply could not believe that the terrible crimes which he saw and had reported to him *every day* of his working life could be so random...so meaningless. In his increasingly confused mind, there had to be a single master criminal behind all the terror and misery he saw and experienced. A single villain. A master criminal *nemesis* worthy of him, of the great

Inspector Charles Frederick Field. And a nemesis who was not really human, but who—when caught (by Inspector Charles Frederick Field, of course)—would bring an end to the literally endless series of brutalities that he was spending his life observing."

"So you are saying," I said, "that the respected former Chief of Detectives whom we both knew, Charles Frederick Field, *was* insane by the end."

"As mad as a hatter," said Dickens. "For many years. His *idée fixe* had become an obsession, the obsession a fantasy, the fantasy a nightmare from which he could not awaken."

"It's all very neat, Charles," I said softly. This was such nonsense that it had not even caused my pulse to speed up. "But you forget the others who have seen Drood."

"Which others?" Dickens asked softly. "Besides those thugs from decades ago and your mesmeric hallucinations, my dear Wilkie, I can think of no other instances of persons who ever believed in the Drood phantom—with the possible exception of Field's son."

"His son?"

"He had a boy out of wedlock by a young West Indies woman he had been seeing for some years. She lived not far from Opium Sal's den that you and I got to know so well—you better than I, I believe. The inspector's wife never learned of the woman (who died, I learned, shortly after childbirth, probably from an opium overdose) nor of the boy, but Field did right by the lad, paying to have him raised by a good family far from the docks, then sending him to fine public schools, and finally to Cambridge, or so I hear."

"What was the boy's name?" I asked. My mouth was suddenly very dry. I wished that I had brought water rather than laudanum in my flask.

"Reginald, I believe," said Dickens. "I did enquire about him in the past year, but the young man seems to have disappeared after his father died. Perhaps he went to Australia."

"And how do you think Inspector Charles Frederick Field died, Charles?"

"A heart attack, my dear Wilkie. Just as the papers reported. We have discussed that."

I slid down from the stone and stood on legs that were tingling from lack of circulation. Not caring if Dickens watched, I drank deeply from my flask. "I need to get back," I said thickly.

"Surely you will stay for dinner. Your brother and Katey are down for the weekend. Percy Fitzgerald and his wife are coming by and..."

"No," I interrupted. "I have to get back to town. I need to work. I need to finish *Man and Wife*."

Dickens had to use his cane to get to his feet. I could tell that his left foot and leg were putting him through agony, although he refused to show it. He took his watch and chain from his waistcoat.

"Let me mesmerise you, Wilkie. Now. At this moment."

I took a step away from him. My laugh sounded frightened even to my own ears. "You have to be joking."

"I have never been more serious, my dear friend. I had no idea when I mesmerised you in June of eighteen sixty-five that the post-trance suggestions would—or could—go on for so long. I underestimated both the power of opium and the power of a novelist's imagination."

"I do not wish to be mesmerised," I said.

"I should have done it years ago," said Dickens. His voice was also thick, as if he were close to weeping. "If you remember, my dear Wilkie, I *tried* to mesmerise you again on more than one occasion—so that I could cancel the mesmeric suggestions and have you wake from this endlessly constructed dream you're in. I even tried to teach *Caroline* how to mesmerise you, giving her the single command code word I had implanted in your unconsciousness. Upon hearing that key word when you are in a mesmeric trance, you will awaken at long last from this extended dream."

"And what is the command…the code word?" I asked.

"'Unintelligible,'" said Dickens. "I chose a distinctive word you would not hear every day. But for it to work, you must be in mesmeric sleep."

"'Unintelligible,'" I repeated. "A word you said you used on the day of the Staplehurst accident."

"I did use it then," said Dickens. "It was my response to the horror."

"I believe it is you who is mad, Charles," I said.

He shook his head. He *was* weeping. The Inimitable, weeping in a grassy field in the sunlight. "I do not expect you to forgive me, Wilkie, but for God's sake—for your *own* sake—let me put you under magnetic influence now and release you from this accidental curse I put upon you. Before it is too late!"

He took a step towards me, both arms raised, the watch in his right hand glinting goldly in the sunlight, and I took two steps backwards. I could only guess what his real game was, and all those guesses were dark indeed. Inspector Field had once said that this was all a chess game between himself and Drood. I had once seen it as a three-way game with Dickens. Now I had taken the inspector's place as a player in this very real game of life or death.

"You really want to mesmerise me, Charles?" I said in a friendly and reasonable voice.

"I *must,* my dear Wilkie. It is the only way I can begin to make amends to you for what is the cruelest joke I have ever—however inadvertently—played on anyone. Just stand there and relax and I shall…"

"Not now," I said, taking another step back but holding both palms out towards him in a calm, placating manner. "I am too disturbed and agitated to be a successful subject now anyway. But Wednesday night…"

"Wednesday night?" said Dickens. He suddenly seemed confused, battered, like a prizefighter who has gone rounds beyond his stamina but who is still standing out of sheer reflex, yet unable to protect himself from further blows. I watched him hop, using the cane, unable to put any weight on his obviously swollen and throbbing left foot and leg. "What is Wednesday night, Wilkie?"

"The secret outing you agreed to accompany me on," I said softly. I stepped closer, took the watch from his hand—the metal was very hot—and tucked it into his waistcoat pocket for him. "You agreed to go with me on a short adventure during which I promised that we would solve at least two mysteries together. Remember the time we went to investigate that haunted house in Cheshunt?"

"Cheshunt," repeated Dickens. "You and Wills went ahead in a brougham. John Hollingshead and I walked to the village."

"Sixteen miles, if I remember correctly," I said, patting his shoulder. "It was long ago." Dickens was suddenly and irrevocably an old man.

"But we found no ghosts, Wilkie."

"No, but we had a wonderful time, did we not? Great fun! And so we shall on this coming Wednesday night, the eighth of June. But you must tell no one that you are going with me."

We had started walking back, Dickens hobbling painfully, but suddenly he stopped and looked at me. "I shall go on this…expedition…if you promise me, my dear Wilkie…if you promise me *now*, and give your word of honour…that you shall let me mesmerise you first thing that night. Mesmerise you and release you from this cruel delusion I foisted upon you through my sheer arrogance and lack of common sense."

"I promise, Charles," I said. And when he continued to stare, "Our first item of business shall be you mesmerising me and me helping you in that endeavour. You can say your magic word…'Unintelligible'…to your heart's content and we shall see what happens. You have my word of honour."

He grunted and we continued the slow hobble back towards Gad's Hill Place. I had left the Swiss chalet in the company of a middle-aged man filled with guilt, creative energy, and enthusiasm for life. I was returning in the company of a dying cripple.

"Wilkie," he muttered as we approached the shade of the trees. "Did I ever tell you about the cherries?"

"Cherries? No, Charles, I don't believe you did." I was listening to a confused old man gather wool, but I wanted to keep him moving, keep him hobbling forward. "Tell me about the cherries."

"When I was a difficult London youth long ago…it must have been *after* the awful Blacking Factory…yes, definitely *after* the Blacking Factory." He feebly touched my arm. "Remind me to tell you about the Blacking Factory someday, my dear Wilkie. I have never told anyone in my life the truth about the Blacking Factory in my childhood, although it was the most horrible thing that…" He seemed to drift off.

"I promise to ask you about that someday, Charles. You were saying about the cherries?"

The shade of the trees was welcome. I walked on. Dickens hobbled on.

"Cherries? Oh, yes…When I was a rather difficult London youth so long ago, I found myself walking down the Strand one day behind a workingman carrying a rather homely big-headed child on his shoulders. I presumed the boy was the workingman's son. I had used almost the last of my pence to purchase this rather large bag of ripe cherries, you see..."

"Ah," I said, wondering if Dickens might have had a sunstroke. Or a real stroke.

"Yes, cherries, my dear Wilkie. But the delightful thing was, you see, that the child looked back at me in a certain way...a certain, singular way...and I began popping cherries into the boy's mouth, one after the other, and the big-headed child would spit out the pits most silently. His father never heard nor turned. He never knew. I believe I fed that big-headed boy all of my cherries—every single last one. And then the workingman with the boy on his shoulders turned left at a corner and I continued on straight and the father was never the wiser, but I was the poorer—at least for cherries—and the big-headed boy was the fatter and happier."

"Fascinating, Charles," I said.

Dickens tried hobbling more quickly, but his foot could bear no weight at all now. He had to rest all of his weight on his cane at each painful step. He glanced at me. "Sometimes, my dear Wilkie, I feel that my entire career as a writer has been nothing more than an extension of those minutes popping cherries into the mouth of that big-headed boy on his father's shoulders. Does that make sense to you?"

"Of course, Charles."

"You promise that you will allow me to mesmerise you and release you from my cruelly inflicted magnetic suggestions?" he said suddenly, sharply. "On Wednesday night, eight June? I have your word on that?"

"My word of honour, Charles."

By the time we reached the stream with its small, arched bridge, I was whistling the tune I remembered from my dream.

CHAPTER FORTY-NINE

I finished my novel *Man and Wife* early in the afternoon of Wednesday, 8 June, 1870.

I told George and Besse—who would not, in any case, continue in my employ much longer—that I needed the house quiet so I could sleep and sent them away for a day to visit whomever they chose.

Carrie was gone for the week, travelling with the Wards.

I sent a note to my editor at *Cassell's Magazine* and another to my soon-to-be book publisher, F. S. Ellis, reporting that the manuscript was finished.

I sent a note to Dickens telling him that I had finished my book and reminding him of our appointment the next day, on the afternoon of 9 June. We did not have an appointment for 9 June, of course—our appointment was for that night of 8 June—but I was confident that the note would not arrive until the next morning, so it would serve as what those of us trained in the law call by its Latin name—an "alibi." I also sent friendly notes to the Lehmanns, the Beards, and others, crowing that I had finished *Man and Wife* and—after a long night of welcomed and well-earned sleep—planned to celebrate the completion by a visit to Gad's Hill Place the next afternoon, on the ninth.

Late that afternoon, dressed in black travelling clothes with a cape and broad hood thrown back, I took a rented carriage down to Gad's Hill and parked under the oldest trees next to the Falstaff Inn as the sun set and the darkness sent out fingers from the forest behind that establishment.

I had not succeeded in finding a Hindoo sailor ready to leave England (never to return) in ten days. Nor a German or American or even English sailor ready to be my coachman. Nor had I found the black coach of my opium- and morphia-assisted imaginings. So I drove myself that night—I had little experience in handling coaches or carriages and crept along to Gad's Hill far more slowly than my careering fantasy-Hindoo driver would have—and the rented vehicle I was driving was a tiny open carriage hardly larger than the pony cart in which Dickens used to fetch me.

But I set the small bullseye lantern under the single seat behind me and had Hatchery's pistol—all four cartridges unfired and nestled in place—in my jacket pocket next to the burlap sack for metal objects, just as I had planned. In truth, this arrangement wherein I drove myself made much more sense: no driver, Hindoo or otherwise, could ever be a blackmail threat this way.

The evening also was not the perfect June night I had envisioned.

It rained hard during the tiring drive out and between the showers and the splashes onto the absurdly low box this miniature carriage offered, all of me was soaked through by the time I arrived at the Falstaff Inn just after sunset. And the sunset itself was more of a grey, smudged, watery afterthought to the day than the beautiful scene I had painted in my mind.

I tucked the single (ancient) horse and wobbly carriage as far back under the trees to the side of the inn as I could, but the rain showers still soaked me when they blew in, and after they departed, the trees continued to drip on me. The footwell in the tiny carriage space was actually filling up with puddles.

And Dickens did not come.

We had set the rendezvous time for thirty minutes after sunset (and he could be forgiven for not noticing the exact time of that cloudy anticlimax of a sunset), but soon it was an hour after sunset and still no sign of Dickens.

Perhaps, I thought, he could not see my dark carriage and black, dripping horse and black, soaked self there in the darkness under the trees. I considered lighting one of the lamps on the side of the carriage.

There were no lamps on the side or back of this cheap carriage. I considered lighting the bullseye lantern and setting it on the box next to me. Dickens might be able to see me from the house or his front yard then, I realised, but so would everyone coming or going from the Falstaff Inn or even those just passing by on the highway.

I considered going into the inn, ordering a hot buttered rum, and sending a boy over to Gad's Hill Place to let Dickens know I was waiting.

Don't be an idiot, whispered the trained-lawyer as well as the mystery-book-writer parts of my brain. And there rose again the odd word but necessary concept—*alibi.*

Ninety minutes after sunset and still no sign of Charles Dickens, perhaps the most punctual fifty-eight-year-old man in all of England. It was approaching ten PM. If we did not start out soon for Rochester, the entire trip might be lost.

I secured the dozing horse to a branch, made sure the pitiful example of a carriage's brake was set, and I moved through the edge of the trees towards Dickens's Swiss chalet. Every time the chilly night wind came up, the fir and deciduous branches dumped more Niagaras of water on me.

I'd seen at least three carriages turn into Dickens's driveway in the past ninety minutes and two were still visible there. Was it possible that Dickens had forgotten—or simply decided to ignore—our mystery-trip appointment? (For a moment I had the chilled certainty that my false note reminding him of our appointment *tomorrow* had somehow arrived here at Gad's Hill this afternoon, but then I remembered that I had deliberately posted it late in the day. No mail courier in the history of England would have delivered the message so quickly; in truth, it would be a stroke of unusual competence if Gad's Hill Place saw the delivery of that reminder by late Friday—and this was Wednesday night).

I touched the pistol in my outer pocket and decided to approach the house through the tunnel.

What was I going to do if I peered through one of the windows of the new conservatory in back (just added this spring and Dickens's delight) and saw the Inimitable still sitting at his dining table? Or reading a book?

I would rap on the conservatory glass, beckon him out, and kidnap him at gunpoint. It was that simple. And it had come to that.

As long as Georgina and the others who depended upon Dickens's succour and income like sucking lampreys on a larger fish were not around. (And I had to include my brother, Charles, in that Pisces-metaphor group.)

The tunnel was *very* dark and smelled of the spoor of wild creatures who may have evacuated their bowels in there. I felt like one of them that night and, soaked as I was, could not stop shivering.

Emerging from the tunnel, I avoided the noisy gravel of the main drive and walked through the low hedge into the front yard. I could see now that there were three carriages crowding the inner turnaround—although it was too dark for me to identify any of them—and one of the horses suddenly raised its head and snorted as it caught my scent. I wondered if it smelled a predator.

Moving to my right, I stood on tip-toes to peer over the hedges and lower clipped cedars to see between white curtains. The bow windows of Dickens's study were dark, but that did seem to be the only unlighted room in the house. I saw a woman's head—Georgina? Mamie? Katey?—pass by one of the front windows. Was she moving with some haste, or was this observation merely a function of my taut nerves?

I took several steps back so that I could better see the upper lighted windows and removed the heavy pistol from my pocket.

An anonymous assassin's bullet crashing through the window glass, murdering the most famous author in all of…What idiocy was that? Dickens had not only to die; he had to *disappear*. Without a trace. And tonight. And as soon as he stepped out that door, belatedly remembering his meeting with me, he *would*. This I swore not only to God, but to all the Gods of the Black Lands.

Suddenly I was seized from behind by many hands and half-dragged, half-lifted as I was pulled backwards on my heels and away from the house.

This sentence does not do justice to the violence that was inflicted upon my person at that moment. There were several men's hands and they were *strong*. And the owners of those rough hands had no scruples whatsoever about my well-being as they dragged me through a hedge, through low branches of a tree, and threw me down onto the stones and sharp-twigged flower bed of closely packed geraniums.

The red geraniums! They filled my vision—along with flashing stars following my skull's impact with the ground—and the red of the blossoms struck me clearly, impossibly, even in the darkness.

Dickens's red geraniums. Blossoms of blood. A gunshot's flower blossoming on the white field of a formal shirt. The red geranium flower of Nancy's Murder as Bill Sikes bashed her brains out.

My nightmares had been premonitions, perhaps powered by the opium that also fueled my creativity when all else failed.

I tried to rise, but the strong hands forced me back down into the mud and loam. Three white faces floated above me as I caught a hint of crescent moon sliding between quickly moving black clouds.

As if to prove my prescience, Edmond Dickenson's face thrust itself into my field of vision just a foot from *my* face. His teeth had indeed been sharpened into tiny white daggers. "Easssy there, Mr Collinsss. Easy doesss it. No fireworksss tonight, sir. Not *thisss* night."

As if to explain that cryptic statement, other strong hands removed the pistol from my twitching hand. I had forgotten it was there.

Reginald Barris's face took the place of Dickenson's. The powerful man was smiling or grimacing horribly— I could not tell the difference—and I realised that it had not been dental decay that had shown dark places in his smile when I had seen him last in that narrow alley. Barris had filed his teeth down to sharp points as well. "Thisss iss *our* night, Mr Collinsss," the pale face hissed.

I struggled to no avail. When I looked up again, Drood's face was floating above me.

I use the word "floating" advisedly here. *All* of Drood seemed to be floating above me, his arms outstretched rather as would be those of one entering deep water, his face looking down at me, his black-cloaked body levitating on invisible supporting currents and hovering parallel to mine only five or six feet above the Earth.

The places where Drood's eyelids and nostrils should have been were so red-raw that they looked to have been cut away with a scalpel only minutes earlier. I had almost forgotten how the Drood-thing's long tongue flicked in and out like a lizard's.

"You can't kill Dickens!" I gasped. "*You* can't kill Dickens. It must be I who..."

"Hussssshhh," said the floating, hovering, expanding white skull-face. Drood's breath carried the stench of grave dirt and the sewer-sweetness of dead, bloated things floating in an Undertown river. His wide eyes were rimmed and riveted with blood. "Husssh, now," hissed Drood, as if soothing a demon-child. "It'sss Charlesss Dickens'sss sssoul we take tonight. You can have whatever isss left, Mr Billy Wilkie Collinssssss. Whatever isss left, isss yoursss."

I opened my mouth to scream, but at that second the floating Drood removed a redolent black silk handkerchief from his opera-cape pocket and pressed it down over my straining face.

CHAPTER FIFTY

I was wakened in late morning by Caroline's daughter, Carrie, even though—as I mentioned earlier—she was supposed to be travelling out of the city with the Wards, the family for whom she served as governess. She was weeping as she knocked repeatedly and then, when I did not answer, came into my bedroom.

Groggily, I sat up in bed and pulled the bedcovers up. All I could think of in my half-waking state was that somehow Carrie had come home early and gotten into the locked box in the locked lower dresser drawer where I kept her mother's letters. Caroline's most recent letter to me—received and read only three days earlier—reported that she had complained of one of her husband Joseph's late-night drinking parties with his sports-loving friends and she had come to consciousness the next day locked in the cellar with one of her eyes swollen shut and with a sure sense of having been violated by more than one man.

But this was not the reason for Carrie's weeping.

"Wilkie, Mr Dickens…Charles Dickens, your friend…he is dead!"

Through sobs, Carrie explained that her patrons, my friends Edward and Henrietta Ward, had been in transit to Bristol when they heard word of Dickens's death from a friend they met at the station, and they had immediately turned around and come back to the city so that Carrie could be with me.

"To...to think...of how many times Mr Dickens... was a guest at our ta...table...when Mother lived here..." Carrie was sobbing.

I rubbed my aching eyes. "Go on downstairs like a good girl," I said at last. "Have Besse put on coffee and prepare a late breakfast...."

"George and Besse are gone," she said. "I had to use the key we hide in the arbour to get in."

"Ah, yes," I said, still rubbing my face. "I gave them last night and today off...so that I could sleep. I finished my book last night, Carrie."

She did not seem properly impressed by this fact and made no comment. She was weeping again, although why she felt such a personal loss at the reported death of an old gentleman who hadn't visited the house in many months and who had called her "the Butler" for years, I had no idea. "Go around the block, then, and bring the cook back with you," I said. "But be a good girl and put the coffee and tea on first, please. Oh, and Carrie, go to the tobacco shop beyond the square and bring back every newspaper you can find. Go on, now!"

When she was gone, I threw off the covers and looked down. Carrie hadn't seemed to have noticed through her tears, but I was wearing a soiled white shirt and trousers rather than pyjamas. My boots were still laced, and the sheets were smeared with mud that looked—and smelled—far too much like excrement.

I rose and went off to bathe and change before Carrie returned.

As THE DAY WENT ON, more and more pieces of reliable information clicked into place.

After starting his day on the eighth of June by chatting over breakfast with Georgina, Dickens had violated his usual rules and work habits by working in the chalet all day, only returning to the house at about one PM for lunch before heading back to his eyrie to write again late into the day.

I later saw the final page for *The Mystery of Edwin Drood* that he'd written that day. The lines showed fewer corrections and crossings-out than the normal Charles Dickens first-draft page to which I was accustomed. It included this passage and obviously was describing a beautiful morning in Rochester very similar to the lovely morning he had just experienced at Gad's Hill. It began with *"A brilliant morning shines on the old city…"* and moved on to—

> *Changes of glorious light from moving boughs, songs of birds, scents from gardens, woods and fields—or, rather, from the one great garden of the whole cultivated island in its yielding time—penetrate the Cathedral, subdue its earthy odour, and preach of the Resurrection and the Life. The cold stone tombs of centuries ago grow warm; and flecks of brightness dart into the sternest marble corners of the building, fluttering there like wings.*

The last words he ever wrote of *The Mystery of Edwin Drood* that afternoon were—*"…and then falls to with an appetite."*

Dickens left the chalet late and went to his study before dinner. There he wrote two letters (according to Katey, who much later told my brother about them, who later informed me)—one to Charles Kent in which he, Dickens, said that he would be in London the following day (9 June) and would like to meet Charles at three o'clock that afternoon. Although, he added, *"If I can't be—why, then I shan't be."*

The other letter was to a clergyman, and it was in this letter that the Inimitable quoted Friar Laurence's warning to Romeo—*"These violent delights have violent ends."*

Then Dickens went in to dinner.

Georgina later told my brother that just as they sat down together to dine, she looked at him across the table and became very alarmed at the expression on the Inimitable's face.

"Are you ill, Charles?" she asked.

"Yes, very ill. I have been...ill...for the last hour."

Georgina wanted to send for a doctor at once, but Dickens waved her back to her seat and insisted that they go on with the meal. "We must dine," he said as if distracted, "for I must leave immediately after dinner. I must go...to London...at once. After dinner. I have... an...appointment tomorrow, today, tonight."

Suddenly he began to writhe as if in the midst of a violent fit. Georgina described it to Katey as if "there were some spirit trying to invade his body and poor Charles were trying to resist the possession."

Dickens was saying words that made no sense to Georgina. Suddenly he cried, "I must go to London *at once!*" and pushed back his crimson-damasked chair.

He rose but would have fallen if Georgina had not rushed forward and caught him. "Come into the parlour," she said, terrified by his ashen face and fixed expression. "Come and lie down."

She tried to help him to a sofa, but he could not walk and his body quickly grew heavier and heavier in her arms. Never before, she later told Katey, had she truly understood the term "dead weight."

Georgina gave up the attempt of getting him to a sofa and lowered him to the floor. There he placed both palms on the carpet, sank heavily on his left side, and murmured very faintly—"Yes. On the ground." Then he fell unconscious.

At this time, I had been leaving the last of London traffic on the highway to Gad's Hill and cursing the rain. But it was not raining there. Not yet.

Had I been there in the darkness under the trees where I would soon be waiting, I would have seen one of the young servants (perhaps Smythe or Gowen, the gardener-gondoliers according to Dickens) riding Newman Noggs, the pony who had so often trotted me from the station to the house, hell-bent for leather to summon the local doctor.

That physician, Mr Steele, arrived at 6.30 PM, still well before I had reached Gad's Hill, to find Dickens "lying on the floor of the dining-room in a fit."

Other servants carried a long sofa down to the dining room, and Mr Steele supervised placement of the unconscious but twitching author on it. Then Steele applied clysters and "other remedies" to the patient, but with no effect.

Georgina, meanwhile, had been firing off telegrams like a three-decker warship firing broadsides. One came to Frank Beard, who set off at once and arrived late that night, perhaps when I was being driven away—as unconscious as Dickens—in my own hired carriage.

I wondered then and wonder now who drove me into the city that night, rifled my pockets to find the key to my home, carried me to bed, and tucked me in. Not Drood, obviously. Dickenson? Reginald Barris-Field? Some other walking-dead lackey whom I had never even seen during the attack on me in the darkness?

Whoever it was had stolen nothing. I even found my pistol—Hatchery's pistol—still loaded with the final four cartridges and locked away in the drawer where I always kept it.

How had they known where I kept it?

And what, I wondered, had become of my hired carriage? Even my novelist's fecund imagination could not picture one of Drood's black-opera-cloaked assistant monsters returning it to the carriage-hire place in Cripplegate where I had rented it. Of course I had gone far from home in that hiring and used an assumed name for the transaction—Dickens's favourite assumed name, actually, "Charles Tringham"—but the loss of that damage deposit came at a hard time for me financially. And it had been a miserable little carriage in the first place.

And I never recovered the bullseye lantern either.

When Kate Dickens, my brother, Charles, and others summoned by Georgina's telegram barrage arrived very late that night, they found Dickens still unconscious on the sofa and unable to respond to their queries or touches. (The three carriages I had seen in the driveway had been only the beginning of the invasion.)

All through the long night—well, short night, to be more accurate, since it was so very close to the summer solstice—all through the short night, his family and Beard and my brother took turns holding the Inimitable's hand and setting heated bricks against his feet.

"Even by the early hour of midnight," my brother later told me, "Dickens's hands and feet had become the cold appendages of a corpse."

Early in the morning, Dickens's son telegraphed for a more famous London doctor, Russell Reynolds, who read the name "Dickens" and left London at once on the earliest express, arriving at Gad's Hill under the rising spring sun. But Dr Russell Reynolds's verdict was identical to that of Mr Steele and Frank Beard—the writer had suffered a massive "paralytic stroke" and there was nothing that could be done for him.

Katey was sent to London to break the news to her mother and to prepare her for worse news. No one I spoke to ever noticed or reported the reaction of Catherine Dickens, the Inimitable's banished wife of twenty-two years and the mother of his ten children. I know for a certainty that Dickens himself would not have cared or asked.

Ellen Ternan arrived early in the afternoon, about the time Katey returned.

Earlier that spring, on a visit during a brief layover between his readings, Dickens had shown me his newly constructed conservatory, which opened from the dining room. He showed me how it allowed sunlight and moonlight into what had been rather dark rooms and—seemingly most important to him when he was showing it off with all the delight of a boy sharing a new toy with a friend—how it now would fill the house with the mixed scent of his favourite flowers there. The ubiquitous scarlet geraniums (the same flower he had worn in his lapel during readings whenever he could) had no real scent from the flower, of course, but the leaves and stems gave off an earthy, musky scent, as did the stalks of the blue lobelias. This ninth day of June was lovely and mild, and all the windows in Gad's Hill Place were open wide, as if offering escape to the soul still caged in the failed body on the sofa, there where the dining room opened onto the green plants and crimson flowers of the conservatory.

But it was the scent of syringa that was heaviest in the air that day. Dickens would almost certainly have commented on the smell if he had been conscious and going about his business of killing Edwin Drood. As it was, his son Charley—who spent most of the day sitting with his sister Kate outside on the steps, where the syringa-scent was that much stronger—later could never bear having that flower anywhere near him.

As if he were deeply inhaling that scent which his son would hate for the rest of his life, Dickens's breathing grew louder and less regular as the afternoon faded into early evening. Across the highway—where traffic passed in ignorance of the drama playing out in the fine and quiet home—the shadows of the twin cedars fell across the Swiss chalet in which no pages had been written that day. (Nor ever would be again.)

Inside the main house, no one, it seems, was scandalised when Ellen Ternan took and held the unconscious man's hand. At about six PM, Dickens's breathing grew fainter. Embarrassingly—at least it would have been for me had I been there—the unconscious Inimitable began to make sobbing noises. His eyes remained closed and he returned no pressure to Ellen's hopeful, hopeless hand, but at about ten minutes after six, a single tear welled from his right eye and trickled down his cheek.

And then he was gone.

Charles Dickens was dead.

My friend and foe and competitor and collaborator, my mentor and my monster, had lived precisely four months and two days past his fifty-eighth birthday.

It was, of course, almost to the hour, the fifth anniversary of the railway accident at Staplehurst and his first meeting with Drood.

CHAPTER FIFTY-ONE

*T*hose who knew me at the time commented to one another later that I reacted rather coolly to Dickens's death.

For instance, in spite of the public knowledge of the estrangement between Dickens and myself, I had recently suggested to my publisher William Tindell that *Man and Wife* might be advertised by inserting a slip of coloured paper into the July number of *Edwin Drood* then being serialised. I had added in a postscript to Tindell—*"Dickens's circulation is large and influential.... If private influence is wanted here I can exert it."*

Tindell had replied on June 7, the day before Dickens collapsed, that he was not in favour of the idea.

On 9 June, I wrote him (and mailed it on 10 June)—

> *You are quite right. Besides, since you wrote, he is gone. I finished 'Man and Wife' yesterday—fell asleep from sheer fatigue—and was awakened to hear the news of Dickens's death.*
> *The advertising at the Stations is an excellent idea.*

On another occasion, my brother showed me a graphite sketch done by John Everett Millais on June tenth. As was the tradition in our era when Great Men passed (as I surmise it still may be in *your* era, Dear Reader), the family had rushed in an artist (Millais) and a sculptor (Thomas Woolner) to record Dickens's face as the corpse lay there. Both Millais's drawing that Charley was showing me and the death mask done by Woolner (according to my brother) showed a visage made younger by the slow fading of the deep lines and wrinkles that care and pain had brought. In Millais's drawing, the inevitable large bandage or towel is tied under Dickens's chin so that the jaw will not sag open.

"Does he not look calm and dignified?" said Charley. "Does he not look merely asleep—as during one of his short naps—and ready to wake and spring up with his characteristic bound and begin writing again?"

"He looks dead," I said. "As dead as a post."

As I had predicted, a national—nay, a near *global*—hue and cry for Dickens to be buried in Westminster Abbey began before *rigor mortis* had relaxed its grip.

The London *Times,* long an enemy of Dickens's and an opponent to every political and reform suggestion the Inimitable had ever made in public (not to mention a publication that had condescendingly dismissed almost all of his more recent novels), cried out in its bannered editorial—

> Statesmen, men of science, philanthropists, the acknowledged benefactors of their race, might pass away, and yet not leave the void which will be caused by the death of Dickens.... Indeed, such a position is attained by not even one man in an age. It needs an extraordinary combination of intellectual and moral qualities... before the world will consent to enthrone a man as their unassailable and enduring favourite. This is the position which Mr Dickens has occupied with the English and also with the American public for a third of a century... Westminster Abbey is the peculiar resting place of English literary genius; and among those

whose sacred dust lies there, or whose names are recorded on the walls, very few are more worthy than Charles Dickens of such a home. Fewer still, we believe, will be regarded with more honour as time passes, and his greatness grows upon us.

How I moaned at reading this! And how Charles Dickens would have roared with laughter if he could have read his old newspaper enemy grovelling so in its editorial hypocrisy.

The Dean of Westminster, far from being deaf to such outcries, sent word to the Dickens family that he, the Dean, was "prepared to receive any communication from the family respecting the burial."

But Georgina, Katey, Charley, and the rest of the family (Harry had rushed home from Cambridge too late to see his father alive) had already been informed that the little graveyard at the foot of Westminster Castle was overcrowded and thus closed to further burials. Dickens had, upon occasion, expressed the thought that he might like to be buried at the churches of Cobham or Shorne, but it turned out that these graveyards were also closed to future interments. So after the offer came from the Dean and Chapter of Rochester to lay Dickens's remains to rest inside the Cathedral itself—a grave had already been prepared in St Mary's Chapel there—the Inimitable's family had tentatively accepted when the note from Dean Stanley of Westminster arrived.

Oh, Dear Reader, how I adored the irony of the idea of Dickens's corpse being encrypted for all Eternity mere yards from where I had planned to slide his skull and bones into the rubble-strewn wall of the Rochester crypt. I still had the copy of the crypts' key that Dradles had made for me! I still had the short pry bar that Dradles had given to me (or sold to me for £300 and a lifetime annuity of £100 might be a more accurate way of thinking about it) with which I was to slide back the stone into the wall.

How wonderful! How totally delicious! I read all this in my morning letter from Charley and wept over my breakfast.

But, alas, it was not to be. It was too perfect to be true.

With Dickens's corpse in the house beginning to moulder in the June heat, Forster (how he must have loved this primacy, at long last!) and Charley Dickens came up to London to confer with the Dean of Westminster.

They informed the Dean that Dickens's will bound them, in no uncertain terms, to an absolutely private and unannounced funeral with no possibility whatsoever of any public homage. Dean Stanley agreed that the great man's wishes should be obeyed to the letter— but allowed that the "desire of the nation" should also be obeyed.

Thus they went ahead with burying Charles Dickens at Westminster Abbey.

To add insult to injury in all this—as was almost always the case in my two decades of dealings with Dickens, Dear Reader—I had my allocated role in this unceremonious ceremony. On 14 June, I went to Charing Cross to meet the special train from Gad's Hill and to "accept" the coffin bearing the mortal remains of Charles Dickens. The coffin was removed, as per the dead man's instructions, to a bare hearse devoid of funeral trappings (pulled by horses devoid of black feathers). It might have been a delivery waggon for all the fuss this vehicle and its team showed.

Again in keeping with Dickens's commands, only three coaches were permitted to follow this hearse to the Abbey.

In the first coach were the four Dickens children remaining in England—Charley, Harry, Mary, and Katey.

In the second coach were Georgina, Dickens's (mostly-ignored-in-life) sister Letitia, his son Charley's wife, and John Forster (who undoubtedly was wishing that he could be in the *first* coach, if not in the actual coffin alongside his master).

In the third coach rode Dickens's solicitor, Frederic Ouvry, his ever-loyal (if not always discreet) physician Frank Beard, my brother, Charles, and me.

The bell of St Stephen's was tolling half-past nine in the morning as our small procession reached the entry to the Dean's Yard. No word of this burial had got out—a small triumph there of the Inimitable's will over the habits of the press—and we saw almost no one lining the streets on the way. The public was banned from the Abbey that day.

As our carriages rolled into the courtyard, all the great bells began tolling. With help from younger men, we old friends carried the coffin through the western cloister door along the Nave and into the South Transept to the Poets' Corner.

Oh, Dear Reader, if my fellow pallbearers and mourners could have read my thoughts as we set that simple oak box down in the Poets' Corner. I have to wonder if such obscenities and imaginative curses had ever been thought in the Abbey of Westminster Cathedral, although some of the poets interred there certainly would have been up to the task had their brains been functioning rather than rotting to dust.

A few words were said. I do not recall who said them or what they were. There were no singers, no choir, but an unseen organist played the Dead March as the others turned away and filed out. I was the last to leave and I stood there alone for some time. The bass notes from the huge organ vibrated the very bones in my burly flesh, and it amused me to realise that Dickens's bones were similarly vibrating inside his box.

I know you would have preferred to have those bones dropped unmarked into the wall of Dradles's favourite old 'un's crypt in Rochester, I thought to my friend and enemy as I looked down at his simple coffin. The good English oak was adorned only with the words CHARLES DICKENS.

This is still too much, I thought when I finally turned to leave and join the others outside in the sunlight. *Far too much. And it is only the beginning.*

It was very cool and properly dim under the high stone vaultings of the Abbey. Outside, the bright sunlight seemed cruel in comparison.

Friends were allowed to visit the still-open grave, and later that day, after many medicinal applications of laudanum and some of morphia, I returned with Percy Fitzgerald. By this time there was a wreath of roses on the flagstones at the foot of Dickens's coffin and a huge bank of shockingly green ferns at his head.

In *Punch,* a few days later, the cloying elegy bellowed—

> *He sleeps as he should sleep—among the great*
> *In the old Abbey; sleeps amid the few*
> *Of England's famous thousands whose high state*
> *Is to lie with her monarchs—monarchs too.*

And, I thought again as Percy and I came out into the evening shadows and June garden scents, *it is only the beginning.*

Dean Stanley had given permission for the grave to be left open for a few days. Even that first day, the afternoon papers brayed the news. They were on the story the way dear old Sultan used to leap upon any man in uniform—worrying, tearing, chewing, and worrying it some more.

By the time Percy and I left when the Abbey closed at a few minutes after six o'clock—five days almost to the minute from when Dickens had sobbed and wept a single tear and finally condescended to quit breathing—there were a thousand people who had not yet received admittance, silently and solemnly queued up.

For two more days the grave remained open and for two more days the procession too long and endless for anyone to find its tail kept filing past. Tears and flowers were dropped into the grave by the thousands. Even after the grave was finally closed and a great block of stone bearing Dickens's name was slid into place above it—for months after this theoretical closure—the mourners kept coming, the flowers kept appearing, the tears kept falling. His headstone soon became invisible under a huge mound of fragrant, colourful blossoms and it would stay that way for years.

And it is only the beginning.

When Percy—who was blubbering as fiercely as had Dickens's tiny granddaughter Mekitty when she had seen her "Wenerables" cry and speak in strange voices on stage the previous spring—and I left that evening of 14 June, I excused myself, found an empty and private area behind high hedges in the surrounding gardens, and bit into my knuckles until blood flowed in order to stop the scream rising in me.

And that was only the beginning.

LATE THAT NIGHT of 14 June I paced back and forth in my empty house.

George and Besse had returned from their twenty-four-hour vacation on 9 June and I had promptly fired them, sending them packing that evening. I gave neither reason for terminating their employment nor any letters of recommendation. I had not yet gotten around to hiring their replacements. Carrie would be stopping by the next day—a Wednesday, one week from the day that Dickens and I had agreed to meet after dusk outside the Falstaff Inn—but that would be a brief interruption before she went off for her monthly visit to her mother in Joseph Clow's home.

In the meantime, I had the huge house to myself. The only sounds coming through the windows flung high for spring were the occasional rumbles of late-night traffic going by and the rustle of foliage as gentle breezes stirred the branches. Beneath that, there came the occasional scrape and scratch—like dry twigs or thorns brushing against thick wood—of whatever remained of poor little Agnes, clawing at the boarded-up doorway to the servants' stairs.

On the first two days after I'd heard of Dickens's death, the rheumatical gout pain had diminished astonishingly. Even more astonishing—and exciting to me—was the absence of any movement in my skull. I became certain that when Dickenson, Barris-Field, and Drood himself had somehow rendered me unconscious amidst the scarlet geraniums in Dickens's flower bed six days ago this night, Drood had removed the scarab from my brain.

But that day, during the carrying-in of the coffin to Poets' Corner and later with Percy, the old pressure and pain and skittering behind my eyes and even the *sound* of the beetle-burrowing in my brain had all come back.

I had self-administered three healthy injections of morphia on top of my usual nightly allocation of laudanum, but still I could not sleep. Despite the warmth and open windows, I built a large fire in my study fireplace.

Something to read . . . something to read!

I paced before my high bookcases, now pulling down a book I had promised to read or finish, standing by the fireplace or near the candles on the shelves or by the lamp on my desk as I read a page or two, then thrusting the volume back in its place.

That night, and every day and night since, seeing a book spine missing from its allotted space on my shelves reminded me of the stone that I should have removed from the wall of Dradles's crypt. How many bones and skulls and skeletons are thrust into the void of such missing or unwritten books?

Finally I took down the beautiful leather-bound copy of *Bleak House* that Dickens had inscribed and given to me two years after we had met.

I chose *Bleak House* without actively thinking about it because, I now believe, I both admired and hated that book as much as any writing in the dead man's *ouevre.*

I had been inhibited from telling any but a very few confidants of how absurd I found Dickens's much-lauded writing to be in that book. His occasional first-person narration by "Esther Summerson" was the height of this absurdity.

I mean, Dear Reader (if the unworthy book has survived until your time, which I very much doubt—although I truly believe that *The Moonstone* will and has), just look at Dickens's chosen primary metaphor that opens the book—that fog! It appears, it becomes the central metaphor, and it creeps off, never to be used as such again.

What amateur writing! What a failure of theme and intention!

And just look, Dear Reader—as I was madly doing that night of Dickens's funeral, flipping through the pages with the intensity of a lawyer seeking a precedent by which to save (or, in this case, condemn) his client—

at how ridiculous the totally unbelievable coincidences are in that book...and how unbelievably cruel the character of the always-a-child Harold Skimpole was, since we all knew at the time that he had based Skimpole on our common acquaintance Leigh Hunt or... there is the abject failure of his late-in-the-book mystery element, so inferior in every way to that in *The Moonstone* or...the shifting and contradictory impressions of Esther's looks after she has suffered the smallpox (I mean, was she disfigured or not!? Now yes! Now not at all! What a conspiracy of auctorial incompetence wrestling with narrative dishonesty) and then... but look here first!...look, if you will, at that entire narration by Esther Summerson! What do you say to that? What *can* you—or any honest reader sitting in judgement—say to that!

Esther begins her narration with the poorly educated and naive child's view we might expect for a poorly educated and unworldly child—she speaks in near-infant's sentences such as (I riffled and tore at the pages to find this)—*"My dear old doll! I was such a shy thing that I seldom dared to open my lips, and never dared open my heart, to anybody else.... O you dear faithful Dolly, I knew you would be expecting me!"*

You are pardoned, Dear Reader, if you suddenly were required—as I was—to rush to the water closet to vomit at that line.

But Dickens forgot that Esther thinks and speaks in such a manner! Before long, "Esther" is describing simple scenes with pure Dickensian alliteration and effortless assonance—"the clock ticked, the fire clicked"—and not long after that the poorly educated girl is narrating entire pages, complete chapters, with the devastating incantatory eloquence of Charles Dickens and Charles Dickens alone. What a failure! What a sheer travesty!

And then, on that night of Dickens's funeral—or

most likely it was the next day now, for had I not heard, unnoticed hours earlier, the ticking clock toll midnight above the clicking fire?—I was paging madly through the now-torn book to find more ammunition in my skirmish (if not war) to convince you, Dear Reader, (and perhaps my exhausted self) of the newly dead man's long-overlooked mediocrity, when I came upon the following passage. No, not a passage, actually, more of a fragment...no, a mere sliver of a fragment of a passage, the kind of thing that Dickens constantly dashed out without later revision or any serious conscious effort at the time.

Esther has travelled, you see, to the inn at the town near the harbour of Deal to see Richard, her dearest female friend's future husband and a young man with Fate and Unhappiness and Obsession and self-inflicted Tragedy expectantly hanging about him like a flock of crows (or what the Americans call buzzards) on the branches in a leafless November tree—expectantly hanging about him, waiting for their inexorable time to come, as surely as they always have and continue to do about me.

Over Esther's shoulder, Dickens allows us to catch a glimpse of the harbour. There are many boats there and more appear, as if by magic, as the fog begins to rise. Like Homer in the *Iliad,* Dickens briefly catalogues the ships becoming visible, including a great and noble Indiaman just back from India. And the author sees this—and makes *us* see this—just *"when the sun shone through the clouds, making silvery pools in the dark sea."*

Silvery pools in the dark sea.

Pools *in* the sea.

My one exercise and indulgence, Dear Reader, is hiring a crew to do the work and taking a yacht up along the coast. It was on just such an outing that I met

Martha R——. I have seen the sunlight on the sea thousands of times and have described it in my books and stories scores of times—perhaps hundreds of times. I have used words such as "azure" and "blue" and "sparkling" and "dancing" and "grey" and "white-topped" and "ominous" and "threatening" and even "ultramarine."

And I had seen that phenomenon of the sun "making silvery pools in the dark sea" scores or hundreds of times but had never thought to record it in my fiction, with or without that swift and certain and slightly blurred sound of the sibilants Dickens had chosen for its description.

Then, without pausing even for a breath (and possibly not even to dip his pen), Dickens had gone on having the fog in the harbour lift over Esther's shoulder by writing, *"these ships brightened, and shadowed, and changed…,"* and I knew in that instant, with my agitated, scarab-driven eyes merely passing over these few words in these short sentences, that I would never—not ever, should I live to be a hundred years of age and retain my faculties until the last moment of that life and career—that I would never be able to think and write like that.

The book was the style and the style was the man. And the man was—had been—Charles Dickens.

I threw the expensive, personally inscribed, moroccan-leather-bound and gold-leaf-edged copy of *Bleak House* into the ticking and clicking and crackling and cackling and f——ing fire.

Then I went upstairs to my room and tore my clothes off. They were sodden with sweat and I swear to this day that I could smell not just the overpoweringly sweet stench of the graveside flowers on them all, down to my clinging under-linens, but also the sweeter stink of the grave soil heaped nearby to make the hole—the final void—for the waiting (waiting for *all of us*) oak box.

Naked, laughing, and shouting loudly (although I forget what I shouted or why I laughed), I fumbled out the key and then fumbled open the requisite locks to get to Hatchery's pistol.

The metal thing was heavier than usual. The cartridges were, as I have endlessly described to you, still there in their nest.

I thumbed back the happy hammer and set the round ring of muzzle to my sweaty temple. Then I remembered. The palate. The softest way to the brain.

I started to put the long steel phallus in my mouth, but then could not. Without even lowering the hammer, I threw the useless thing into my linen drawer. It did not discharge.

Then, before bathing or getting into my pyjamas and robe, I sat down at the small secretary in my bedroom (near where the Other Wilkie usually sits when he takes dictation on the Gods of the Black Lands) and wrote a brief but very clear and concise letter. Setting it aside for personal delivery—not for posting—the next day, I finally went in for my bath and then to bed and then to sleep, skittering scarab or no scarab.

I left the front door unlocked and the windows open wide for burglars—if there were any who would dare burgle a home that the Master Drood had honoured with his visit—and the candles and kerosene lamps and the fire in the fireplace all burning downstairs. I had not even replaced the fireplace screen after burning *Bleak House*.

Whatever else I knew that night of 14 June, 1870, I knew beyond any doubt that my fate was not to burn to death in a house fire.

CHAPTER FIFTY-TWO

It was on the fourth day of July, 1870, my little daughter Marian's first birthday, that I finished work early (I was adapting *Man and Wife* to the stage) and took the early-evening train to Rochester. I carried with me a small embroidered sofa pillow that Martha had made for me before she first came down to London. Some children in the carriage noticed the pillow I carried along with my leather portfolio and pointed and laughed—an old man of forty-six years and almost seven months, with balding head and greying beard and weakening eyes, carrying his own pillow probably for physical reasons too absurd for Youth even to enquire into—and I smiled and waggled my fingers at them in return.

In Rochester I walked the mile or so from the station to the Cathedral. Dickens's most recent instalment of *The Mystery of Edwin Drood* was out, and this city and cathedral and adjoining churchyard—as poorly disguised as "Cloisterham" and "Cloisterham Cathedral" as Dick Datchery was within the same pages with the great wig he kept forgetting he was wearing—had already taken on literary and mystery resonances for the careful reader.

It was just after sunset and I waited with my pillow and my valise as the last visitors—two clergymen oddly holding hands (they had obviously come to trace headstone inscriptions with charcoal)—left through the open gate and disappeared towards the town centre and distant station.

I could hear two voices from the distant rear of the graveyard, but actual sight of the two people was obscured by the rise and fall of the cemetery fields, by the trees, by the thick hedges that shielded that poorer area near the marsh grasses, and even by the taller headstone monuments erected by such arrogant but insecure people as Mr Thomas Sapsea, still alive and walking and pontificating and enjoying his wife's long headstone-monument epitaph (written *by* him and *about* him, of course, and carved into stone by the colourful stonemason, chiefly in the monumental line, named Durdles). Still alive and walking and pontificating, I should point out, only in the pages of the serialised novel now hurtling towards its premature discontinuance as surely as the 2.39 tidal train from Folkestone had hurtled unstoppably towards the breach in trestle rails at Staplehurst some five years and a little less than a month before.

"This is an idiot's idea," bellowed a man's voice.

"I thought it might be gay," came a woman's voice. "A sort of evening picnic by the sea."

I stopped less than twenty feet away from the bickering couple but remained hidden behind a tall, thick marble monolith—a sort of Sapsea-esque obelisk to some local functionary whose name, never much remembered anyway, had been all but erased by the salt and rain and sea breezes.

"A d——ned picnic in a d——ned boneyard!" shouted the man. It was obvious to even the most disinterested (and distant) overhearing ear that this was a man who was never embarrassed by his own shouting.

"See how nicely this—piece of stone—serves as a table," came the weary woman's voice. "Just sit and relax a moment while I open your beer."

"My beer be d——ned!" bellowed the man. There came the sound of brittle china shattering after being thrown upon eternal—or at least monumental—stone. "Pack up these things. 'Ere, give me the glass and pail of beer first. You stupid cow. It'll be hours before I'm fed now. And you'll earn and pay back the railway fare or…Say, who are…what are *you* doing 'ere? What's that in your hands? A pillow?"

I kept smiling until I got within two feet of the man, who'd barely had time to struggle to his feet while trying not to spill his pail and goblet of beer.

Still smiling, I pressed the pillow tight against the man's sallow chest and pulled the trigger on the pistol I was holding behind that pillow. The gunshot was strangely muffled.

"What!?…" cried Joseph Clow. He staggered backwards a few steps. It appeared that he could not decide between looking at me, still holding the pillow—which was smoking slightly—or down at his own chest.

A single scarlet geranium flower had blossomed on his cheaply woven but immaculately white shirtfront. His grimy-nailed hands rose to his open waistcoat and he clawed weakly at that blossoming shirt, ripping buttons off.

I thrust the pillow against his now-bare and hairless flesh, just half a hand-span above his sternum, and fired twice more. Both cartridges fired true.

Clow stumbled backwards another few paces until his heels caught the edge of a low, horizontal stone similar to the one they had been prepared to dine at. He tumbled over backwards then, rolled once, and lay there on his back.

He opened his mouth to scream, but no sound emerged except for a sort of bubbling and gurgling which was coming—I realised—not from his throat but from his newly perforated lungs. His eyes rolled wide and white as he searched for help. His long legs were already twitching and spasming.

Caroline hurried over, crouched next to her husband, and took the small pillow from my steady hands. Kneeling, she used both hands to press the smoking pillow firmly down over Joseph Clow's open, straining mouth and bulging eyes.

"You have one bullet left," she said to me. "Use it. *Now*."

I pressed the pistol into the pillow with such ferocity that it felt as if I were using the barrel to cram the feathers and fabric down Clow's gaping maw as if to strangle him. His moans and attempts at a scream were completely muffled now. I squeezed the trigger and the faithful gun fired a final time. This time there came a familiar (to me at least, from my morphia dream) sound of the back of a skull splintering open like some huge walnut being cracked.

I stamped the smouldering pillow out.

Caroline was staring down at the white-and-red face with its shattered but now eternally frozen expression. Her own expression was absolutely unreadable, even by someone who had known her as long as I had.

Then we both looked around, waiting to hear shouts and running feet. I half-expected to see Minor Canon Crisparkle come loping manfully over the grassy hillocks separating us from the cathedral and street.

But there was no one. Not even a distant shout of enquiry. The wind blew out that evening, towards the sea rather than from it. The marsh grasses writhed in unison with one another.

"Get his feet," I said softly. I wrapped a towel around Clow's shattered head to prevent leaving a trail of blood and brain matter. I then donned the long yellow apron from my valise that Caroline had written to remind me to bring; she had even told me in which drawers in the

Gloucester Place kitchen to find the towel and apron. "We don't want to have his heels leave ruts in the sod," I said. "What on earth are you doing there?"

"I am picking up his shirt buttons," said Caroline from where she crouched. She spoke very calmly, her long fingers, educated by sewing and by playing card games, dancing nimbly in the grass as they retrieved the small horned circles. She did not rush.

Then we were carrying the body of Joseph Clow the sixty feet or so to the quick-lime pit. This was quite possibly our riskiest moment (I was carrying him under his arms and thankful for the apron that was absorbing the smeared contents of the back of his head, although how Caroline had known this would be a problem I had no idea; she carried his feet by the ankles), but although I kept swivelling my head, I could see no other person in the graveyard or beyond. I even glanced apprehensively at the sea, knowing that nautical types almost always carried small telescopes or other spyglasses. Suddenly she began laughing and I was so startled by the sound that I almost dropped our burden.

"What in heaven's name do you find amusing?" I gasped. I was not out of breath because of carrying Clow—the dead plumber seemed to be hollow he was so light—but simply due to the walking.

"Us," said Caroline. "Can you imagine how we appear—me all doubled over like a hunchback, you in your bright yellow apron, both of us turning our heads like mishandled marionettes...."

"I fail to see the humour," I said when we got Clow to his temporary destination and as I set his upper half down gently—far more gently than the circumstances warranted, I am sure—next to the pit.

"You will someday, Wilkie," said Caroline, brushing her hands together when she had released her share of the burden. "You take care of everything here. I will go pack the picnic things." Before walking back, she looked out towards the water and then back and up at the tower. "This actually could be a pleasant place to picnic. Oh—do not forget the bag in your portfolio and the rings, watch, coins, pistol...."

Despite my greater experience at all this (or what felt like it), I *would* have forgotten—and tumbled Clow into the pit with rings, a gold necklace and locket I would soon find (with a woman's picture in it, but *not* Caroline's), as well as his watch and many coins, all of which would have been very difficult or impossible to find in the quick-lime in a week or two when I returned—had it not been for her reminder. As it was, the metal objects, including Hatchery's now emptied and impotent pistol (for which I had no nostalgia whatsoever), were in the burlap bag in a minute and Clow was out of sight under the surface of the quick-lime two minutes after that.

I tossed the metal rod that I'd kept there in the weeds for so long into the marsh and walked back to the erstwhile picnic site. "What are you doing now?" I asked, my voice sounding odd. I could not catch my breath, as though we were climbing to some place high in the Alps rather than standing in a churchyard at sea level.

"Finding and fitting all the pieces of the plate he broke. That was a nice plate."

"Oh, for God's sa..." I stopped as I heard voices raised in the direction of the highway. It was an open carriage going by on the road. A man, a woman, and two children were laughing and pointing towards the pink clouds where the sun had set, in the opposite direction from the Cathedral and graveyard. Their heads and gazes did not turn back in our direction as I watched.

"You need to do something with *this*," said Caroline and handed me the stained, blackened, and still internally smouldering pillow.

It was my turn to laugh then, but I resisted the impulse, since I was not sure that I could stop once begun.

"And for heaven's sake, Wilkie," she said, "take off that bright apron!"

I did so, carrying the pillow and my leather lawyer's portmanteau holding the coins and other items back to the quick-lime pit. There was no sight of Clow in the pit itself. I had learned through my experiments with various dog carcasses that even with the bloating and putrefaction of decay adding to the dead body's buoyancy, once pressed far enough beneath the surface, anything deep in the thick lime tended to *stay* beneath the surface until raked out.

But what to do with the pillow? The quick-lime presumably would eat it away in a day or two, just as it had the various items of clothing I had tested here—buttons and belts (minus their brass buckles) and braces and laces and boot soles were the stubbornest of objects—but would the pillow stay submerged? And I had already tossed away the iron rod and had little wish to wade into the muck and reeds to retrieve it.

In the end I threw the brown embroidered thing as far out towards the sea as I could fling it. Were this in one of my sensationalist novels—or in Dickens's—I am sure that it would have been a major clue and the key to my (and Caroline's) undoing. Some more-clever version of Inspector Bucket or Sergeant Cuff or even of Dick Datchery, Detective, would find us out, and during Caroline's and my walk up the thirteen steps to the gallows, each of us would be thinking, *That d——ned pillow!* (Although I would never ascribe such language to a woman.)

But as it was, the miserable pillow—barely visible in the failing light, since the bright moon was yet to rise—merely arced far out over the reeds and cattails and then disappeared into the marsh and muck there.

Remembering who had given me the embroidered nightmare as a gift, I did finally smile as I thought, *This may be Martha R——'s greatest contribution to my future happiness.*

Caroline was ready, the shards of her broken plate all retrieved and packed away in her picnic hamper, and we left the graveyard together. We would catch the same 9.30 express to London but we would not sit together—or even in the same carriage. Not yet.

"Are all your things packed and shipped?" I asked softly as we walked through the narrow old streets of Rochester towards the lights of the station.

She nodded.

"No need to go back?"

"None."

"Three weeks," I said. "And I have Mrs G——'s address at the little hotel near Vauxhall Gardens where she will be staying."

"But no contact until the three weeks are up," whispered Caroline as we came out onto a busier street. "Do you really believe that I shall be able to move back in by the first of September?"

"I am absolutely certain of it, my dear," I said. And I was.

CHAPTER FIFTY-THREE

A short while ago as I write this, Dear Reader, a little after sunrise, just after I switched off the light next to the easy chair in which I rest, I wrote the following note to Frank Beard—*"I am dying—come if you can."*

I didn't believe I was actually dying when I wrote that, but I do feel worse now and may well begin that final dying any minute, and a good writer plans ahead. I may not have the energy to write the note later, you see, so I shall keep it on hand. I have not sent it yet, but since Caroline is elsewhere today, I may ask Marian or Harriet soon to send it along to Frank, who is as ancient and weary and worn-out as I. But he does not have far to come. I can see his home through my bedroom window here.

At this point you may well be asking—When *are you writing this?*

For the first time in our long voyage together, Dear Reader, I shall answer that question.

I am finishing this long manuscript to you in the third week of September of the year 1889. I was very ill this past summer—but still working towards finishing these memoirs—and then, as autumn approached, I was feeling much better. I wrote this note to Frederick Lehmann on September 3—

I have fallen asleep and the doctor forbids the waking of me. Sleep is my cure, he says, and he is really hopeful of me. Don't notice the blots, my dressing gown sleeve is too large, but my hand is still steady. Goodbye for the present, dear old friend; we may really hope for healthier days.

But the week after I wrote that, I came down with a respiratory infection on top of my other ailments and I can tell that dear old Frank Beard—although he has not said so to my face—has given up hope for me.

I trust you will notice but forgive the same blots in the last chapters of this manuscript I have set aside for you. My dressing gown sleeve truly is too large and, to be honest with you in a way I hesitate to be with Frederick or Frank or Caroline or Harriet or Marian or William Charles, my eyesight and coordination are not what they once were.

As recently as this past May of 1889, when an inquisitive and impudent young correspondent asked me directly about the rumour of my long use of stimulants, I responded thusly—

I have been writing novels for the last five and thirty years and I have been regularly in the habit of relieving the weariness which follows on work of the brain—declared by George Sand to be the most depressing of all forms of mortal fatigue—by champagne at one time and brandy (old cognac) at another. If I live until January next, I shall be sixty-six years old, and I am writing another work of fiction. There is my experience.

Well, I believe on this cool day of 23 September that I shall *not* live 'til January next, when my birthday would have sent the bells tolling sixty-six times. But already I have lived five years longer than my teetotalling father did and some twenty years longer than my dear brother, Charles, who never used a stimulant stronger than the rare sip of whisky as long as he lived.

Charley died on 9 April, 1873. He died of cancer of the bowel and stomach, which was precisely what Dickens had always insisted that Charley was suffering from, despite all our protests to the contrary. My only consolation is that Dickens had been dead almost three years by the time Charley finally succumbed and went under. I would definitely have had to murder Charles Dickens if I'd heard him gloating about the correctness of his diagnosis when it came to my dear brother.

Shall I summarize the nineteen years I have lived since the summer of the Inimitable's death? It hardly seems worth the effort for either of us, Dear Reader, and lies outside the purpose and purview of this memoir. And equally outside your range of interest, I am sure. This was about Dickens and Drood, and there your curiosity lies, not in your modest and unworthy narrator.

Suffice it to say that Caroline G—— returned to my home at Number 90 Gloucester Place in the early autumn of 1870, just weeks after...weeks after Dickens died and after her husband of the time disappeared. (Since Joseph Clow's mother had recently suffered a series of strokes, it was as if no one noticed that he had disappeared, and his wife with him. Enquiries were made by a few mildly interested parties, but all of Mr and Mrs Clow's bills had been paid, all debts met, the rent for their tiny house paid to the end of July, and the house itself sealed up tidily and emptied of all clothing and personal possessions before the couple were found to be missing—and then the house and its few pieces of cheap furniture were taken over again by the party who had rented it to them—and the few people who had known the Clows at all assumed that the hard-drinking workingman and his unhappy bride had moved away. Most of his ruffian friends believed that the unlucky plumber and his accident-prone wife had moved to Australia, since after a few drinks Clow had always threatened precisely such a sudden departure.)

By March of 1871, I was once again legally listing Mrs Caroline G—— on the parish records as my house-keeper. Carrie was delighted to have her mother home and never—to my knowledge—asked a single question as to how Caroline had extricated herself from the bad marriage.

On 14 May of 1871, my younger daughter, Harriet—named after my mother, of course—was born to "Mrs Martha Dawson." Martha and I had a third child—William Charles Collins Dawson—who was born on Christmas Day in 1874.

I hardly need tell you that Martha continued to get fatter during and after each pregnancy. After William was born, she made no pretense of trying to shed the weight that hung on her like great slabs of lard. It was as if she had given up caring about her appearance. I had once written about Martha R—— that she was a fine specimen of that type of girl I liked, *"the fine fleshy beef-fed English girl."* But all that fleshy beef-feeding had a predictable effect. If I had been asked to rewrite that sentence in 1874, it would have read—*"She is the perfect specimen of a vast, fleshy, girl-fed English beef."*

If Caroline G—— ever heard about Martha and the children, even after I moved them all to 10 Taunton Place to be more comfortable and closer to my own home, she never once mentioned it or let on that she knew. If Martha R—— ever heard or knew that Caroline G—— was living with me at Number 90 Gloucester Place (and then, in more recent years, on Wimpole Street) from 1870 onward, she never once mentioned it or let on that she knew.

IF YOU WANT TO KNOW about my literary career after Dickens's death, Dear Reader, I shall summarise it for you in a single cruel sentence: the World thought it and I were a success, while I knew all along that my career and I had conspired to become the most dismal of failures.

As Dickens had before me, I eventually took to giving public readings. My friends told me that they were delightful and a success. I knew—and the honest critics reported both here and in America—that they were mumbling, lifeless, incoherent failures.

As Dickens had before me, I continued to write books and turn them into plays whenever possible. Each book was weaker than the one before it and all were weaker than my masterpiece, *The Moonstone*, although I have seen for many years that *The Moonstone* was no masterpiece. (And it was the unfinished *Mystery of Edwin Drood* that made me see that.)

Perhaps my unpopularity with the public—for that is what it has been, Dear Reader from my future—began just days after Charles Dickens's death, for it is then that I privately approached Frederick Chapman of the publishers Chapman and Hall and suggested to him that I could complete *The Mystery of Edwin Drood* for them if they so chose. I let them know that while no notes for the remainder of the book were in existence—and it was true that none of Dickens's usual marginal notes and outlines on blue paper have ever come to light for the unfinished portions of *Drood*—Dickens had taken me (and me alone) into his confidence before the end. I—and I alone—could finish the writing of the entire second half of *The Mystery of Edwin Drood* for only a nominal fee and equal credit as author (just as the co-authorship of our earlier collaborations had been registered).

Chapman's response totally surprised me. The publisher was furious. He let me know that *no man in England*, no matter how gifted the writer might be or might *think he was*—and he implied that he did not think me all that gifted—could ever fill the shoes of Charles Dickens, even if I had a hundred completed outlines in my pocket. *"Better that the world never knows who killed Edwin Drood—or indeed, if Edwin Drood is dead,"* he wrote me, *"—than a lesser mind pick up the Master's fallen pen."*

I thought that last metaphor very garbled and grotesque indeed.

Chapman even swore that he would never let the slightest whisper of my offer to him slip out (and warned me never to tell anyone) for fear that *"You shall then inevitably and irretrievably become the most hated and assuredly assumed and presumed presumptuous man in all of England and the Empire and the World."*

How even a publisher and editor could write and express himself that poorly, in a sentence that spavined, I have no idea to this day.

But rumours and whispers against me did begin about that time and that is—as I say—when the active dislike of me by the public seems to have begun in earnest.

As DICKENS HAD BEFORE ME, I did a reading tour of the United States and Canada. Mine was in 1873 and 1874, and it could objectively be categorised as a total disaster. The travel by ship and by train and by coach exhausted me even before the tour was really under way. The American audiences seemed to agree with the English audiences that my readings lacked energy, even audibility. I was never well during the entire tour and reached a point where not even massive ministrations of my laudanum—which I found oddly hard to find and purchase in the States—could bring back any energy or pleasure. The American audiences were idiots. The entire nation was composed of prudes and bluestockings and boors. While the French had never had the least problem with Caroline travelling with me, the Americans would have been scandalised at the very idea of a woman not my wife in my entourage—so I had to suffer my travels and illnesses and nightly humiliations on stage without her help for those long months in America.

And I had no Dolby to organise my reading-tour life. The one manager I hired to oversee the production of one of my plays in New York and Boston—one of several theatrical premieres I had arranged for my tour there—tried to rob me blind.

In February of 1874, in Boston and in other urban pimples on that blank white canvas of a map they call New England, I spent time with the leading lights of American literature and intellectual life—Longfellow, Mark Twain, Whittier, and Oliver Wendell Holmes—and I have to say that if these men were the "leading lights," then the glow of literature and intellectual life in the United States was very dim indeed. (Although I did enjoy a verse tribute that Holmes wrote and performed in public for me.)

I realised then and still believe now that the majority of Americans in those crowds who jostled to see me or who paid to hear me read, did so just because *I had been a friend and collaborator of Charles Dickens.* Dickens was the ghost that I could not leave behind. Dickens was the Marley-face on the knocker who greeted me every time I approached a new door.

I saw Dickens's old friend James T. Fields and his wife in Boston—they took me out for a fine dinner and then to the opera—but I could tell that Annie Fields thought little of me, and I was not surprised when, sometime later, I read the following report she had made of me in private but which quickly found its way to public print—

A small man with an odd figure and forehead and shoulders much too large for the rest of him. His talk was rapid and pleasant but not at all inspiring....A man who has been fêted and petted in London society, who has over-eaten and overdrunk, has been ill, is gouty, and in short is no very wonderful specimen of a human being.

All in all, the only truly companionable and relaxed time I had during all those months in America was when I went down to stay with my old friend the French-English actor Fechter, he of Dickens's Christmas-gift Swiss chalet, at Fechter's farm near Quakertown, in the province of Pennsylvania.

Fechter had become a drunk and a raving paranoid. The once distinctive (if not overly handsome, since he specialised in villains) actor was now—all agreed—gross and bloated in both appearance and manner. Before leaving London forever, Fechter had quarrelled with his theatrical partners there—he owed them all money, of course—and then had quarrelled with and publicly insulted his leading lady, Carlotta Leclercq. When he went off to Pennsylvania in America to marry a girl named Lizzie Price—another actress but one with no discernible talent—no one even thought it pertinent to mention to Miss Price that Fechter already had a wife and two children in Europe.

Fechter died of cirrhosis of the liver in 1879 in a condition—one London obituary reported—of being "universally despised and isolated." His passing was a special blow to me, since even during my last visit to him in Quakertown six years before his death, he had once again borrowed money from me and never paid it back.

Last year as I write this (with blobs), or perhaps it was the year before—1887—at any rate, sometime shortly after I had moved from Number 90 Gloucester Place to where I currently am living (and dying) at 82 Wimpole

Street (Agnes was beginning to scream, you understand, and I do not believe that I was the only one who could hear her, since Mrs Webb and the other servants avoided being near the boarded-up staircase at all costs) and...

Where was I?

Oh, yes, last year or the year before, I was introduced to Hall Caine (I can only trust, Dear Reader, that you know who he is—was—as well as Rossetti, who introduced us), and Caine looked at me a long time and his impressions of me later found print:

> His eyes were large and protuberant, and had the vague and dreamy look sometimes seen in the eyes of the blind, or those of a man to whom chloroform has just been administered.

But I was not so blind then that I did not notice his horrified appraisal. I said to Caine that day, "I see that you can't keep your eyes off *my* eyes, and I ought to say that I've got gout in them, and that it is doing its best to blind me."

Only by then, of course, and for many years before that, I used the word "gout" to mean "beetle"—to mean "scarab"—to mean "Drood's insect burrowed into my brain behind my aching eyes." And it *was* doing its best to blind me. It always had been.

ALL RIGHT...Reader. I know that you could not care less for my history or pains or even the fact that I am dying as I labour to write this for you. All you want to hear about is Dickens and Drood, Drood and Dickens.

I have been wise to you from the start...Reader. You never cared about *my* part of this memoir. It was always Dickens and Drood, or Drood and Dickens, which kept you reading.

I started this memoir years ago with the hopeful dream that you knew me and—much more importantly—that you knew my work, had read my books, had seen my plays. But no, Reader there in the indifferent future, I know now that you have never read *The Woman in White* or even *The Moonstone,* much less my *Man and Wife* or *Poor Miss Finch* or *The New Magdalen* or *The Law and the Lady* or *The Two Destinies* or *The Haunted Hotel* or *A Rogue's Life* or *The Fallen Leaves* or *Jezebel's Daughter* or *The Black Robe* or *Heart and Science* or *"I Say No"* or *The Evil Genius* or *The Legacy of Cain*—or the book I am working so hard on now, when I can write at all, and which is being serialised in the *Illustrated London News,* my *Blind Love.*

You know none of these, do you . . . Reader?

And in your arrogant future, as you glide to the bookstore in your horseless carriage and come back to your underground home illuminated by garish electric lights, or perhaps even read in your carriage that may have electric lights *in it* (anything is possible) or glide to the theatre in the evening—I trust you still have theatre—I hardly think that you have read my novels or seen stage productions of my *The Frozen Deep* (it was never Dickens's, which was performed first in Manchester) or *Black and White* (which opened at the Adelphi) or *The Woman in White* (which opened at the Olympic) or *Man and Wife* (which opened at the Prince of Wales) or *The New Magdalen* (which opened at the Olympic and also premiered in New York while I was there) or *Miss Gwilt* (which opened at the Globe) or *The Dead Secret* (which opened at the Lyceum Theatre) or—at long last—*The Moonstone* (which opened at the Olympic) or . . .

Just writing the above has exhausted me, stolen the last of my strength.

All those thousands upon thousands of days and nights of writing—writing through unspeakable pain

and intolerable loneliness and in utter dread—and *you...
Reader...have not read or been in the audience for any
one of them.*

To hell with it. To hell with you.

It is Drood and Dickens you want. Dickens and
Drood. Very well, then—here, with my last drops of
mortal energy—it is after 9 AM—I shall give you Drood.
You can have Drood up your hairy arse, Reader. This
page is more blobs than words, but I do not apologise.
Nor do I apologise for the language. I am sick of apolo-
gising. My entire life has been one endless round of
apologies after another for no reason....

I once thought that I could see into the future—
"precognition" is the term that those on the far
edges of science use for this ability—but I was never
certain whether my second-sight was real or not.

Now I am sure. I can see every detail of the rest of
my life, and my ability to see clearly into the future—
even as my own eyes are failing—is no less impressive
for the fact that "the rest of my life" now consists of less
than two hours. So please forgive the future tense. It
shall be—as they say—short-lived. I shall write this
now, while I still can, because I see forward until then,
into later in this very morning, until the very end of my
life, peering forward into those final moments when I
shall no longer be able to write.

Drood has been with me, in one way or the other,
every day of the nineteen years and three months since
Charles Dickens died.

When I looked out into the rain on a cold autumn or
winter night, I would see one of Drood's minions—
Barris or Dickenson or even the dead boy with the
strange eyes, Gooseberry—across the street, staring
at me.

When I walked the streets of London, trying to lose some of this weight that now will never leave me except by rotting away, I could hear the footsteps behind me of Drood's men, Drood's watchers. And always there were the dark shapes and bright eyes in the alleys.

Imagine, Reader, if you *can*, what it is like to be in the arse-end village of, say, Albany, New York, where there are more cuspidors than people, and doing a reading in some great draughty freezing dark hall while a blizzard rages outside—I was helpfully told that more than 900 people had attended Charles Dickens's reading there sixteen years earlier—and I had perhaps twenty-five people. But among them, above them, sitting in the shaky old balcony that had been sealed off for that night's performance, sat Drood, his lidless eyes never blinking, his sharp-toothed smile never wavering.

And the provincial Americans wondered why my readings were so muted and stilted and lifeless.

Drood and his minions and his scarab have drained the life out of me, Reader, day by day and night by night.

Every time I open my mouth for one of Frank Beard's increasingly frequent examinations, I expect him to cry out—"Dear God! I see the black carapace of a huge beetle blocking your throat, Wilkie! Its pincers are eating you alive!"

Drood has been there at the premieres of my plays and at the failures of my novels.

Did you see the game of revelations I have been playing with my titles, Reader?

The Two Destinies. I had such once. But Dickens and Drood chose the more terrible for me.

The Dead Secret. This has been my heart. Towards the women who have shared my bed (but never my name) and the children who share my blood (but also never my name).

A Rogue's Life. I need not even comment.

Man and Wife. The only trap I have succeeded in avoiding, even while being caged in all others.

"I Say No." My entire life.

The Evil Genius. Drood, of course.

The Legacy of Cain. But have I been Cain, or Abel? I once thought of Charles Dickens as my brother. My only regret about my attempt at killing him was that I did not succeed, that Drood took that pleasure from me.

Do you see... Reader? Do you see how vile and terrible Charles Dickens's curse was upon me?

I did not and do not believe for a second that Drood was some mesmeric suggestion, made on a casual whim in June of 1865 and living on to curse every day of my life since then. But if Dickens *had* done that—if there were no Drood—what an abominable and vicious act that would have been. Dickens would have deserved to die and have his flesh burned away in the pit of quick-lime for that crime alone.

But if he had *not* suggested Drood to my unconscious and opium-laced writer's mind in a bout of forgotten (by me) mesmerism in 1865, how much more cruel and calculating and unforgivably terrible the fact that he *said he did*—that he had the cure for Drood in a few minutes' session with his swinging watch and the simple command "Unintelligible" to bring me out of the nightmare that has been my life.

Dickens deserved to die for that alone. Many times over.

And most of all... Reader... Dickens deserved to die and be damned because, despite all of his weaknesses and failings (both as a writer and as a man), Charles Dickens was the literary genius and I was not.

This curse—this constant knowledge, as painful and as irrevocable as Adam's awful awakening after being seduced into eating from the apple from the Tree of Knowledge—has been worse even than Drood. And nothing is worse than Drood.

BLIND LOVE. That is the book I have been writing and of which I have finished a first draft. I will not, I know this moment, live long enough to polish it.

But Blind Love for whom?

Not for Caroline G—— or Martha R——. My love for them has been provisional, rational and rationed, grudging at the best of times, and always—always—governed by lust.

Not for the grown and growing children—Marian, Harriet, and William Charles. I am glad they are alive. I can say little more than that.

Not for my books or the labours it took to produce them. I loved none of them. They were, like my children, mere products.

But, God help me, I loved Charles Dickens. I loved his sudden, infectious laugh and his boyish absurdities and the stories he would tell and the sense—when one was with him—that every moment was important. I *hated* his genius—that genius which eclipsed me and my work when he was alive, and has eclipsed me more every year that he has been dead, and which—I am certain of this, Faithless Reader—shall eclipse me even more in your unobtainable future.

I HAVE THOUGHT OFTEN, in the past nineteen years, of Dickens's last little story he told me. The one about him as a poor young man walking the streets of London while feeding cherries out of his bag to the big-headed boy riding on his father's shoulders. The boy ate all the cherries. His father never knew.

I think that Dickens told the story backwards. I think he was *stealing* cherries out of the boy's brown bag. And the father never knew. Nor did the world.

Or perhaps this has been *my* secret story. Or perhaps Dickens had been stealing the cherries from *me* as I rode on *his* shoulders.

An hour from now, I will have just sent Marian with the note for Frank Beard. *I am dying—come if you can.*

Of course he will come. Beard always has come.

And he will come quickly. His house is only just across the street. But he will not come in time.

I will be in my big armchair, just as I am now. There will be a pillow behind my head, just as there is now.

The fire will still be burning behind the grate.

I will not be able to feel its heat.

And I apologise for these blobs. The sleeve of my dressing gown truly is too large.

Sunlight will be coming in the high window, just as it is now, and only a little higher, just as the coal in the fireplace will be burned only a little lower. It will be sometime after 10 AM. And despite the sunlight, the room will be growing darker by the minute.

I will not be alone.

You always knew, Reader, that I would not be alone at the end.

Several figures will be in the room with me and gliding closer as—perhaps—I still strive to write, but my hand will be nerveless, my writing finished forever, and the pen will achieve only vague scratches and blobs.

Drood will be here of course. His tongue will flick in and out. He will ssso want to ssshare a ssecret with Mr Collinsssss.

Behind and to Drood's left, I think, I will see Barris, Inspector Field's son. Field will be there also, behind his son. They both will show cannibals' teeth. To Drood's right will stand Dickenson, not the adopted son of Dickens after all. He is and always will be Drood's creature. And behind these will be more shapes. All will be in black suits and capes. They will look silly here in the fading sunlight.

I will not be able to clearly make out their faces. The scarab will, at long last, have eaten through my eyes.

But there will be a huge, indistinct blur of a man near the back. It could be Detective Hatchery. I will just barely be able to make out a terrible concavity beneath the black waistcoat and funeral suit, like some sort of nightmare negative pregnancy.

But, Reader (I have spied you out—I know you care more about this than about me), Dickens will not be there among them. *Dickens is not there.*

But I believe that I will be. I am already.

Then I will hear dear Beard's footsteps on the stairs, but suddenly the figures in my bedroom will all begin crowding closer and speaking at once, hissing and slurring and rasping and spitting sounds as they press upon me, all speaking and gibbering at once. I would lift both hands over my ears, if I were able to. I would close what is left of my eyes, if I were able to. For the faces will be terrible. And the din will be intolerable. And it will be very painful in a way I have never known.

Forty-five minutes remain before all this comes to pass—before I send the note to Frank Beard and the Others arrive before he does—but already it is painful and terrible and intolerable and unintelligible.

Unintelligible.

ACKNOWLEDGMENTS

The author wishes to acknowledge the help and editing excellence of Reagan Arthur, executive editor at Little, Brown, as well as the truly extraordinary work of senior copyeditor Betsy Uhrig. I'm sure there still will be infelicities and errors in this novel, but in almost all cases, the fault will have been mine. (If stubbornness were a virtue, I'd have one foot in Heaven.)

Only a partial list of the biographical and other sources related to Charles Dickens and his era which I consulted is possible here, but the author would especially like to acknowledge the following—

Dickens by Peter Ackroyd, © 1990, pub. by Harper-Collins; *Charles Dickens: His Tragedy and Triumphs* by Edgar Johnson, © 1952, pub. by Simon and Schuster; *Dickens: A Biography* by Fred Kaplan, © 1988, pub. by The Johns Hopkins University Press; *Charles Dickens As I Knew Him: The Story of the Reading Tours in Great Britain and America (1866–1870)* by George Dolby, © 1887, pub. in Popular Edition by T. Fisher Unwin, London; *Charles Dickens* by Jane Smiley, © 2002, pub. by Penguin Putnam Inc.; *The Cambridge Companion to Charles Dickens* edited by John O. Jordan, © 2001, pub. by Cambridge University Press; *Life of Charles Dickens* by John Forster, © 1874; *The Mystery of Edwin Drood* by Charles Dickens, © 1870 by *Household Words*, Oxford University Press Edition © 1956.

Some other sources for Dickens and his era which the author would like to acknowledge include—

Dickens and His Family by W. H. Bowen, © 1956; *The Life of Charles Dickens as Revealed in His Writing* by Percy Fitzgerald, © 1905; *The Changing World of Charles Dickens* edited by R. Giddings, © 1983; *Victorian People and Ideas* by Richard D. Altick, © 1973; *The World of Charles Dickens (A Pitkin Guide)* by Michael St. John Parker, © 2005; *Subterranean Cities: The World Beneath Paris and London, 1800–1945* by David L. Pike, © 2005; *Dickens and Daughter* by Gladys Storey, © 1939; *Dickens, Reade, and Collins: Sensation Novelists* by W. C. Phillips, © 1919; *London 1808–1870: The Infernal Wen* by Francis Sheppard, © 1971; *Charles Dickens, Resurrectionist* by Andrew Sanders, © 1982; *The Speeches of Charles Dickens* edited by K. J. Fielding, © 1950; *The Actor in Dickens* by J. B. van Amerongen, © 1926; *Opium and the Romantic Imagination* by Alethea Hayter, © 1968; *Dickens and Mesmerism: The Hidden Springs of Fiction* by Fred Kaplan, © 1988; *The Shakespeare Riots: Revenge, Drama, and Death in Nineteenth-Century America* by Nigel Cliff, © 2007.

Internet sources relating to Dickens and his world are too numerous to list in full, but a few that the author especially wishes to acknowledge are—

"Inspector Charles Frederick Field" at www.ric.edu/rpotter/chasfield.html; "Victorian London—District—Streets—Bluegate Fields" at www.victorianlondon.org/districts/bluegate.html; "Dickens' London" at www.fidnest.com/~dap.1955/dickens/dickens_london_map.html; "Reprinted Pieces by Charles Dickens" at www.classicbookshelf.com/library/charles_dickens/reprinted_pieces/19/html; "Housing and Health (Deaths from cholera in Broad Street, Golden Square, London, and the neighbourhood, 19 August to 30

September, 1854)" at www.st-andrews.ac.uk/~city19/ viccity/househealth.html; "Beetles as Religious Symbols, Cultural Entomology, Digest 2" at www.insectos .org/ced2beetles_rel_sym.html; "Modern Egyptian Ritual Magick: Ceremony of Blessing and Naming a New Child" at www.idolhands.com/egypt/netra/naming .html.

For insight into Charles Dickens's *Bleak House*, the author wishes to acknowledge the amazing lecture on that novel given at Wellesley College by Vladimir Nabokov (even though Nabokov led the author astray on one central word in a powerful quotation, an error completely missed by the author—who'd just finished rereading *Bleak House*—but caught by the inimitable copyeditor Betsy Uhrig). That lecture is collected in *Lectures on Literature* edited by Fredson Bowers, © 1980, pub. by Harcourt, Inc.

The author wishes to acknowledge the following sources in his research on Wilkie Collins—

The Secret Life of Wilkie Collins by William Clarke, © 1988, pub. by Sutton Publishing Limited; *The Public Face of Wilkie Collins: The Collected Letters, Volumes I– IV* edited by William Baker, Andrew Gasson, Graham Law, Paul Lewis, © 2005, pub. by Pickering & Chatto; *The King of Inventors: A Life of Wilkie Collins* by Catherine Peters, © 1991, pub. by Martin Secker & Warburg; *Wilkie Collins: A Biography* by Kenneth Robinson, © 1952, pub. by the MacMillan Company; *Some Recollections of Yesterday* by Nathaniel Beard, © 1894, pub. in *Temple Bar, Vol. CII; Memories of Half a Century* by R. C. Lehmann, © 1908, pub. by Smith Elder; *The Moonstone* by Wilkie Collins, first published in *Temple Bar* © 1874, Hesperus Classics edition pub. by Hesperus Press Limited.

For those interested in Wilkie Collins, the author recommends one especially helpful Web site—"Wilkie

Collins Chronology" at www.wilkie-collins.info/wilkie_collins_chronology.html.

Finally, and always, my deepest thanks and dearest love to my first reader, primary proofreader, and ultimate source of inspiration—Karen Simmons.

Dan Simmons is the author of several bestselling novels, including, most recently, *Ilium*, *Olympos*, *The Terror*, and *Drood*. His new novel, *Black Hills*, will be published in February 2010.

He has been the recipient of a Rod Serling Memorial Award, the World Fantasy Award, the Bram Stoker Award from the Horror Writers of America, and the Hugo Award. He lives in Colorado.

For more information, visit www.dansimmons.com.

. . . AND HIS MOST RECENT NOVEL

In April 2011, Little, Brown and Company will publish Dan Simmons's *Flashback*. Following is an excerpt from the novel's opening pages.

"You're probably wondering why I asked you to come here today, Mr. Bottom," said Hiroshi Nakamura.

"No," said Nick. "I know why you brought me here."

Nakamura blinked. "You do?"

"Yeah," said Nick. He thought, *Fuck it. In for a penny, in for a pound. Nakamura wants to hire a detective. Show him you're a detective.* "You want me to find the person or persons who killed your son, Keigo."

Nakamura blinked again but said nothing. It was as if hearing his son's name spoken aloud had frozen him in place.

The old billionaire did glance to where his squat but massive security chief, Hideki Sato, was leaning against a step-*tansu* near the open *shoji* that looked out on the courtyard garden. If Sato gave his employer any response by movement, wink, blink, or facial expression, Nick sure as hell couldn't see it. Come to think of it, he didn't remember having seen Sato *blink* during the ride up to the main house in the golf cart or during the introductions here in Nakamura's office. The security chief's eyes were obsidian marbles.

Finally Nakamura said, "Your deduction is correct, Mr. Bottom. And, as Sherlock Holmes would say, an *elementary* deduction since you were the homicide detective in charge of my son's case when I was still in

Japan and you and I have never met nor had any other contact."

Nick waited.

After the glance in Sato's direction, Nakamura had returned his gaze to the single sheet of interactive e-vellum in his hand, but now his gray eyes looked up and bored into Nick.

"Do you think you *can* find my son's killer or killers, Mr. Bottom?"

"I'm certain I can," lied Nick. What the old billionaire was really asking him, he knew, was *Can you turn back the clock and keep my only son from being killed and make everything all right again?*

Nick would have said *I'm certain I can* to that question as well. He would have said anything he had to say to get the money this man could pay him. Enough money for Nick to return to Dara for years to come. Perhaps a lifetime to come.

Nakamura squinted slightly. Nick knew that one doesn't become a hundred-times-over billionaire in Japan or one of only nine regional Federal Advisors in America by being a fool.

"What makes you think that you can be successful *now*, Mr. Bottom, when you failed six years ago at a time you were a real homicide detective with the full resources of the Denver Police Department behind you?"

"There were four hundred homicide cases pending then, Mr. Nakamura. We had fifteen homicide detectives working them all, with new cases coming in every day. This time I'll have just this one case to concentrate on and to solve. No distractions."

Nakamura's gray gaze, as unblinking as Sato's darker stare and already chilly, grew noticably chillier. "Are you saying, former Detective Sergeant Bottom, that you did not give my son's murder the attention it deserved six years ago, despite the…ah…high profile of it and direction to give it priority from the governor of Colorado and from the president of the United States herself?"

Nick felt the flashback itch crawling in him like a centipede. He wanted to get out of this room and pull the warm wool cover of *then, not-now, her, not-this* over himself like a blanket.

"I'm saying that the DPD didn't give *any* of its murder cases the manpower or attention they deserved six years ago," said Nick. "Including your son's case. Hell, it could have been the president's kid murdered in Denver and the Major Crimes bureau couldn't have solved it then." He looked Nakamura straight in the eye, betting everything on this absurd tactic of honesty.

"Or solve it now," he added. "It's fifty times worse today."

The billionaire's office had not a single chair to sit in, not even one for Mr. Nakamura, and Nick Bottom and Hiroshi Nakamura stood facing each other across the narrow, chest-high expanse of the rich man's slim, perfectly bare expanse of gleaming mahogany stand-up .desk. Sato's casual posture over at the *tansu* didn't obscure the fact—at least to Nick Bottom's eye—that the security chief was fully alert, would have been dangerous even if he weren't armed, and that something about Sato gave off the indefinable lethality of an ex-soldier or cop or member of some other profession that had trained him to kill other men.

"It is, of course, your expertise after many years on the Denver Police Department and your invaluable insights into the investigation that are the prime reason we are considering you for this investigation," Mr. Nakamura said smoothly.

Nick took a breath. He'd had enough of playing by Nakamura's script.

"No, sir," he said. "Those aren't the reasons you're considering hiring me. If you hire me to investigate your son's murder, it's because I'm the only person still alive who—under flashback—can see every page of the files that were lost in the cyberattack that wiped out the D.P.D.'s entire archives five years ago."

Nick thought to himself—*And it's also because I'm the only person who can, under the flash, relive every conversation with the witnesses and suspects and other detectives involved. Under flashback, I can reread the Murder Book that was lost with the files.*

"If you hire me, Mr. Nakamura," Nick continued aloud, "it will be because I'm the only person in the world who can go back almost six years to see and hear and witness everything again in a murder case that's grown as cold as the bones of your son buried in your private family Catholic cemetery in Hiroshima."

Mr. Nakamura drew in a quick, shocked breath and then there was no sound at all in the room. Outside, the tiny waterfall tinkled softly into the tiny pond in the tiny gravel-raked courtyard.

Having played his only cards, Nick shifted his weight, folded his arms, and looked around while he waited.

Advisor Hiroshi Nakamura's office in his private home here in the Japanese Green Zone above Denver, although recently constructed, looked as if it might be a thousand years old. And still in Japan.

The sliding doors and windows were *shoji* and the heavier *fusuma* and all opened out into a small courtyard with its small but exquisitely formal Japanese garden. In the room, a single opaque *shoji* window allowed natural light into a tiny altar alcove where bamboo shadows moved over a vase holding cut plants and twigs of the autumn season, the vase itself perfectly positioned on the lacquered floor. The few pieces of furniture in the room were placed to show the Nipponese love of asymmetry and were of wood so dark that each ancient piece seemed to swallow light. The polished cedar floors and fresh *tatami* mats, in contrast, seemed to emanate their own warm light. A sensuous, fresh dried-grass smell rose from the *tatami*. Nick Bottom had had enough contact with the Japanese in his previous job as a Denver homicide detective to know that Mr. Nakamura's compound, his house, his garden, this office, and the *ikebana* and few modest but precious artifacts on display here were all perfect expressions of *wabi* (simple quietude) and *sabi* (elegant simplicity.)

And Nick didn't give the slightest shit.

He needed this job to get money. He needed the money to buy more flashback. He needed the flashback to get back to Dara.

Since he'd had to leave his shoes back in the entry *genkan* where Sato had left his, Nick Bottom's prevalent emotion at the moment was simple regret that he'd grabbed this particlar black sock this morning—the one on his left foot with a hole big enough to allow his big toe to poke through. He covertly scrunched his foot up, trying to worm the big toe back in the hole and out of sight, but that took two feet to do right and would be too obvious. Sato was paying attention to the squirming as it was. He scrunched the big toe up as much as he could.

"What kind of vehicle do you drive, Mr. Bottom?" asked Nakamura.

Nick almost laughed. He was ready to be dismissed and physically thrown out by Sato for his impertinent mention of all-hallowed son Keigo's cold bones, but he hadn't expected a question about his car. Besides, Nakamura had almost certainly watched him drive up on one of the fifty thousand or so surveillance cameras that had been tracking him as he approached the compound.

He cleared his throat and said, "Ah...I drive a twenty-year-old GoMotors gelding."

The billionaire turned his head only slightly and barked Japanese syllables at Sato. Without straightening and with the slightest of smiles, the security chief shot back an even deeper and faster cascade of guttural Japanese to his boss. Nakamura nodded, evidently satisfied.

"Is your…ah…gelding a reliable vehicle, Mr. Bottom?"

Nick resisted the temptation to grin and shook his head.

"The lithium-ion batteries are ancient, Mr. Nakamura, and with the way Bolivia feels about us these days, it doesn't look like they're going to be replaced any time soon. So, after a good twelve-hour charge, the piece of shi…the car…can go about forty miles at thirty-eight miles-per-hour or thirty-eight miles at forty miles per hour. We'll both just have to hope that there won't be any *Bullit*-style high-speed chases in this investigation."

Nick thought it'd been a pretty clever joke, but Mr. Nakamura showed no hint of a smile. Or of recognition. Didn't they watch great old movies in Hiroshima?

"We can supply you with a vehicle from the delegation for the duration of your investigation, Mr. Bottom. Perhaps a Lexus or Infiniti sedan."

This time Nick couldn't stop himself from laughing. "One of your hydrogen skateboards? No, sir. That won't work. First of all, it'd just be stripped down to the shell in any of the places I'll be parking in Denver. Secondly—as your director of security can explain to you—I need a car that blends in just in case I have to tail…follow…someone during the investigation. Low profile, we private investigators call it."

Mr. Nakamura made a deep, rumbling sound in his throat as if he were preparing to spit. Nick had heard this noise from Japanese men before when he'd been a cop. It seemed to express surprise and perhaps a little displeasure, although he'd heard it from the Nipponese men even when they were seeing something beautiful, like a garden view, for the first time. It was probably untranslatable.

"Very well then, Mr. Bottom," Nakamura said at last. "Should we choose you for this investigation, you will need a vehicle with a greater range when the investigation takes you to Santa Fe, Nuevo Mexico. But we can discuss the details later."

Santa Fe, thought Nick. *Aww, God damn it. Not Santa Fe. Anywhere but Santa Fe.* Just the name of the town made the deep scar tissue across and inside his belly muscles hurt. But he also heard another voice in his head, a movie voice, one of hundreds that lived there—*Forget it, Jake. It's Chinatown.*

"All right," Nick said aloud. "We'll discuss the car thing later. *If* you hire me."

Nakamura was again looking at the single sheet of e-vellum in his hand.

"And you're currently living in a former Baby Gap in the former Cherry Creek Mall, is that correct, Mr. Bottom?"

Jesus Christ, thought Nick Bottom. With his entire future probably depending upon the outcome of this interview, and with ten thousand questions Mr. Nakamura could have asked him that he could have answered while retaining at least a shred of the few tatters that still remained of his dignity, it had to be *You're currently living in a former Baby Gap in the former Cherry Creek Mall?*

Yes, sir, Mr. Nakamura, sir, Nick was tempted to say, *currently living in one-sixth of a former Baby Gap in the former Cherry Creek Mall in a shitty section of a shitty city in one-forty-second of the former United States of America, that's me, the former Nick Bottom. While you live up here with the other Japs on top of the mountain, surrounded by three rings of security that fucking Osama bin Laden's fucking ghost couldn't get through.*

Nick said, "The Cherry Creek Mall Condos it's called now. I guess the space my cubie's part of used to be a Baby Gap."

Of the three men, two were expensively dressed in the thin-lapeled, sleek-trousered, black-suited, crisp white-shirted, white-pocket-squared, skinny-black-tied 1960's JFK look retrieved from more than seventy-five years earlier. Even Mr. Nakamura, in his late sixties, wouldn't have been able to remember that historical era, so why, Nick wondered, had the style gurus in Japan brought this style back for the tenth time? The dead-Kennedys' style looked good on slim, elegant Mr. Nakamura and Sato was dressed almost as beautifully as his boss, although his black suit probably cost a thousand or two new bucks less than Nakamura's. But the security chief's suit would have required more tailoring. Nakamura was lean and fit despite his years, while Sato was built like the proverbial brick shithouse, if that phrase even applied to men. And if the Japanese had ever *had* brick shithouses.

Standing there, feeling the cool air of the breeze from the garden flowing across his curled-up bare big toe and realizing that he was by far the tallest man in the room but also the only one whose posture included his now-habitual slump, Nick wished that he'd at least taken the time to press his shirt. He'd meant to but had never found the time the past week since the call for this interview came. So now he stood there in a wrinkled shirt under a wrinkled, twelve-year-old suit jacket—no matching trousers, just the least-rumpled and least-stained of his chinos—all of it probably producing a combined effect that made him look as if he'd slept not only *in* the clothes but *on* them. Nick had discovered only that morning in his cubie that he'd put on too much weight the last year or two to allow him to button these old trousers or the suit jacket or his shirt collar. He hoped that his too-wide-for-style belt might be hiding the opened trouser tops and the knot of his tie might be hiding the unbuttonable shirt collar, but the damned tie itself was three times wider than the stylish ties on the two Japanese men. And it didn't help Nick's self-confidence when he considered that his tie, a gift from Dara, had probably cost one-hundredth of what Nakamura had spent on his.

To hell with it. It was Nick's only remaining tie.

Born in the next-to-last decade of the previous century, Nick Bottom was old enough to remember a tune from a child's educational program that had been on TV then and now the irritating sing-song lyrics returned from childhood to rattle through his aching, flashback-hungry head—*One of these things is not like the others, one of these things doesn't belong*...

Fuck it, thought Nick again and for a panicked second he was afraid he'd spoken aloud. It was becoming harder and harder for him to focus on anything in this miserable, increasingly unreal non-flashback world.

And then, because Mr. Nakamura seemed very comfortable with the stretching silence and Sato actively amused by it while Nick Bottom wasn't at all comfortable with it, he added—"Of course, it's been quite a few years since the Cherry Creek Mall was a mall or there were any stores there. BIAHTF."

Nick pronounced the old acronym "buy-ought-if" the way everyone did and always had, but Nakamura's expression remained blank or passively challenging or politely curious or perhaps a combination of all three. One thing was certain to Nick: the Nipponese executive wasn't going to make any part of this interview easy.

Sato, who would have spent time on the street here in the States, didn't bother to translate it to his boss.

"Before It All Hit The Fan," Nick explained. He didn't add that the more commonly used "die-ought-if" stood for "Day It All Hit The Fan." He was certain that Nakamura knew both expressions. The man had been in Colorado as a federally appointed four-state Advisor for five months now. And he had undoubtedly heard all the American colloquialisms, even if only from his murdered son, years before.

"Ah," said Mr. Nakamura and again looked down at the sheet of e-vellum in his hand. Images, videos, and columns of text flicked onto the single, paper-flexible page and scrolled or disappeared at the slightest shift of Nakamura's manicured fingertips. Nick noticed that the older man's fingers were blunt and strong, a working man's hands—although he doubted if Mr. Nakamura had ever used them for any physical labor that wasn't part of some recreation he'd chosen. Yachting perhaps. Or polo. Or mountain climbing. All three of which had been mentioned in Hiroshi Nakamura's gowiki-bio.

"And how long were you a member of the Denver Police Department, Mr. Bottom?" continued Mr. Nakamura. It seemed to Nick that the damned interview was running in reverse.

"I was a detective for nine years," said Nick. "I was on the force for a total of seventeen years." He was tempted to list some of his citations, but resisted. Nakamura had it all on his vellum database.

"A detective in both the Major Crimes Unit and then Robbery-Homicide division?" read Nakamura, adding the question mark only out of politeness.

"Yes," said Nick while thinking *Let's get to it, God damn it.*

"And you were dismissed from the detectives bureau

five years ago for reasons of...?" Nakamura had quit reading as if the reasons weren't right there on the page and already well-known to the billionaire. The question mark this time had come only from Nakamura's politely raised left eyebrow.

Asshole, thought Nick Bottom, secretly relieved that they'd finally reached the hard part of the interview. "My wife was killed in an automobile accident five years ago," said Nick with no emotion, knowing that Nakamura and his security chief knew more about his life than he did. "I had some trouble...coping."

Nakamura waited but it was Nick's turn not to make this part of the interview easy for the billionaire. *You know why you're going to hire me for this job, jerkwad. Let's get to it. Yes or no.*

Finally Mr. Nakamura said softly, "So your dismissal from the Denver Police Department, after a nine-month probationary period, was for flashback abuse."

"Yes." Nick realized that he was smiling at the two men for the first time.

"And this addiction, Mr. Bottom, was also the reason for the failure of your personal private-detective agency two years after you were...ah...after you left the police force?"

"No," lied Nick. "Not really. It's just a hard time for any small business. The country's in its twenty-seventh year of our Jobless Recovery, you know."

The old joke didn't seem to register on either of the Japanese men. Sato's easy, leaning stance somehow reminded Nick of Jack Palance as the gunfighter in *Shane,* despite the total difference in the two men's body form. Eyes never blinking. Waiting. Watching. Hoping that Nick will make his move so Sato-Palance can gun him down. As if Nick might still be armed after the multiple levels of security around this compound, after having his car CMRI'd and left half a mile down the hill, after having the 9mm Glock that he'd brought along—it would have seemed absurd, even to Sato, for him to have been traveling through the city without some weapon—confiscated.

Sato watched with the deadly, totally focused anticipation of a professional bodyguard. Or Jack-Palance-in-*Shane* killer

Instead of pursuing the flashback question, Mr. Nakamura suddenly said, "Bottom. This is an unusual last name in America, yes?"

"Yes, sir," said Nick, getting used to the almost random jump of questions now. "The funny part is that the original family name was English, 'Badham,' but some guy behind a desk at Ellis Island misheard it. Just like the scene where mute little Michael Corleone gets renamed in *Godfather, Part II*."

Mr. Nakamura, more and more obviusly not an old-movie fan, just gave Nick that perfectly blank and inscrutable Japanese stare again.

Nick sighed audibly. He was getting tired of trying to make conversation. He said flatly, "Bottom's an unusual name, but it's been our name the hundred and fifty years or so my family's been in the States." *Even if my son won't use it,* he thought.

As if reading Nick's mind, Nakamura said, "Your wife is deceased but I understand you have a sixteen-year-old son, named..." The billionaire hesitated, lowering his gaze to the vellum again so that Nick could see the perfection of the razor-cut salt-and-pepper hair. "Val. Is 'Val' short for something, Mr. Bottom?"

"No," said Nick. "It's just 'Val.' There was an old actor whom my wife and I liked and... anyway, it's just Val. I sent him away to L.A. a few years ago to live with his grandfather—my father-in-law—a retired UCLA professor. Better educational opportunities out there. But Val's fifteen-years-old, Mr. Nakamura, not..."

Nick stopped. Val's birthday had been on September second, eight days ago. He'd forgotten it. Nakamura was right; his son *was* sixteen now. God *damn* it. He cleared his suddenly constricted throat and continued, "Anyway, yes, correct, I have one child. A son named Val. He lives with his maternal grandfather in Los Angeles."

"And you are still a flashback addict, Mr. Bottom," said Hiroshi Nakamura. This time there was no question mark, either in the billionaire's flat voice or expression.

Here it is.

"No, Mr. Nakamura, I am not," Nick said firmly. "I *was*. The department had every right to fire me. In the year after Dara was killed, I was a total mess. And, yes, I was still using too much of the drug when my investigations agency went under a year or so after I left the... after I was fired from the force."

Sato lounged. Mr. Nakamura's posture was still rigid and his face remained expressionless as he waited for more.

"But I've beaten the serious addiction part," continued Nick. He raised his hands and spread his fingers. He was determined not to beg (he still had his ace in the hole, the reason they *had* to hire him) but for some stupid reason it was important to him that they trust him. "Look, Mr. Nakamura, you must *know* that it's estimated that about eighty-five percent of Americans use flashback these days, but not all of us are addicts the way I was... briefly. A lot of us use the stuff occasionally... recreationally... socially... the way people drink wine here or *saké* in Japan."

"Are you seriously suggesting, Mr. Bottom, that flashback can be used *socially*?"

Nick took a breath. The Japanese government had brought back the death penalty for anyone dealing, using, or even possessing flash, for God's sake. They feared it the way the Muslims did. Except that in the New Global Caliphate, conviction of using or possessing flashback by *sharia* tribunals meant immediate beheading broadcast around the world on one of the twenty-four-hour *al Jazeera* channels that televised only such stonings, beheadings, and other 'slamic punishments. The channel was busy—and watched—day and night throughout the Caliphate in what was left of the Mideast, Europe, and in American cities with clusters of *hajji* Caliphate-fans. Nick knew that a lot of non-Muslims in Denver watched it for the fun of it. Nick watched on especially bad nights.

"No," Nick said at last. "I'm not saying it's a social drug. I just mean that, used in moderation, flashback isn't more harmful than...say...television."

Nakamura's gray eyes continued to bore.

"So, Mr. Bottom, you are not addicted to flashback the way you were in the years immediately following your wife's tragic death? And if you were hired by me to investigate my son's death, you would not be distracted from the investigation by the need to use the drug recreationally?"

"That's correct, Mr. Nakamura."

"Have you used the drug recently, Mr. Bottom?"

Nick hesitated only a second. "No. Absolutely not. I've had no urge or need to."

Mr. Sato reached into his inside suit pocket and removed a cell phone that was a featureless chip of polished ebony smaller than Nick's National Identity and Credit Card. Sato set the phone on the polished surface of the top step of the *tansu*.

Instantly, five of the dark-wood surfaces in the austere room became display screens. In ultimate HD, but not full 3D, the view was clearer than that of looking out perfectly transparent windows.

Nick and the two Japanese men were looking at multiple hidden-camera views of a furtive flashback addict sitting in his car on a sidestreet not four miles from here, the images recorded less that forty-five minutes ago.

Oh, God damn it, thought Nick.

The multiple videos began to roll.